Streams of Water Duet

Part One

Written in the Waves

Dr. Michal Guter

ETERNUM
Publishing

Contents

Author's Note

Dear Reader,

Thank you for choosing to read my book, it truly means the world to me. By opening these pages, you've become part of a dream that's finally coming true.

This story has been almost a decade in the making, shaped by pauses, growth, and the time needed to give Logan and Adrian the epic love story they deserve.

But before you go any further, I feel I must tell you: this book is not for everyone. It is not a light read. It is a book for those who love words, who savor language, who long for stories that are as much poetry as they are prose. This is the book I always searched for but never found, so I wrote it myself.

And this is the first of many to come.

This is a love story that spans continents, defies differences, and treads the line between life and death. It is not just a story you read, it is one I want you to *feel*. Every word was chosen to bring you deeper into the emotions, into the world, into the love that binds these characters together.

I did not hold back. I did not aim for brevity. I wanted this book to be long, to be *worthy*, to be so deep that you don't just observe from the outside, you *live* within its pages. And in this book, I ask you, the readers, to linger. To sit in the gray, the pain, the beauty. To ask what love means when it's not convenient or easy.

If that is not what you're looking for, I completely understand. This is not a conventional romance. It is a drama, a lyrical and poetic journey, an experience meant to be *felt*.

If you are ready to take that journey, then welcome.

With all my heart,

Michal

BTW, if you would like to chat with me, throw a word or a question, you are more than welcome to reach out. I am always happy to hear from you.

AUTHORDRMICHALGUTER

Trigger Warnings

May contain spoilers

This novel contains emotionally complex themes. For readers who wish to know more before beginning, a detailed content note is provided on the next page.

If you prefer to experience the story without potential spoilers, feel free to skip ahead.

This is a story of love, loss, healing, and emotional depth. It explores themes of identity, intimacy, abandonment, and the long journey home to oneself.

Your mental health matters. I've included content notes to help you read safely and comfortably. Please take care of yourself and pause whenever you need to.

Content warnings include, but are not limited to:

- Mild depression

- Mild dissociation

- Mild isolation

- Cheating (not between main characters)

- Minimal intense emotional conflict

- Coming out

- Mild internalized homophobia

- Repression and living closeted

- Mild use of alcohol as an emotional escape

- Death of a parent (off-page, in childhood)

- Explicit sexual content

Soundtrack

1. *Everything* – Lifehouse

2. *Numb* – Linkin Park

3. *Anchor* – Skillet

4. *Never Let Me Go* – Florence + The Machine

5. *Dying in LA* – Panic! At the Disco

6. *Bottom of the Deep Blue Sea* – MISSIO

7. *Speeding Cars* – Walking on Cars

8. *Milim* – Harel Skaat

9. *Fai Rumore* – Diodato

10. *Lookalike* – Conan Gray

11. *Let Me In* – Skinny Living

12. *Oceans* – Jacob Lee

13. *Soldier's Eyes* – Jack Savoretti

14. *Sing to Me* – Darren Hayes

15. *A Drop in the Ocean* – Ron Pope

16. *Take Me to Church* – Hozier

17. *You Are the Reason* – Calum Scott

18. *If They Only Knew* – Alfie Arcuri

19. *Hold Me* – Savage Garden

20. *Letting Go* – Dotan

For every lost soul out there,
For everyone who had lost and survived,
For all of those who are still struggling,
Hold on,
Your lifesaver is on its way

Prologue

I pleaded with the sea, casting my words away to be carried by the streams into the depths of the water, to be taken by the waves.
I am the one who sat by the beach every night and every day, watched the stream, and memorized the riptide.
And then I pleaded with the ocean. I implored the waves to carry me back to you. In a way, I made a selfish request, but I made it, dropped to my knees, and carried a desperate plea to the sea to take me back to you. To let me raise my head over the waters, and breathe the fresh air as the waves took me on their shoulders, lovingly back to shore. To safety.
To you.
And my last request from the ocean was to take me.
It was either take me to you or take my life.
I've left that decision to be made by the waves.

June 28, 2020

THE STREAMS OF WATER moved at a rhythmic pace as though they drew breath, rising and falling in a quiet dance. A soft, gentle chorus of trickling notes, rippling, whispering as it brushed against stone and ended at the tip of his toes.

Beneath the steady pulse of the ocean's waves, he caught the faint crackle of the fire behind him—a soft crackling heartbeat woven into the night, whispering its warmth through the chill late-summer evening.

The streams of water moved up and down, dictating the future as the past pushed them farther and farther. Creating a wave that was destined to break on the shore with white foam and light splash that sounded like everything that was good in his world.

He watched as the sun dipped toward the edge of the horizon, slipping to the depth of the ocean, drawing her warmth and light away with her. He fixed his whisky-colored eyes on the sinking sun, his gaze on the final amber glow that was cast on the rippling waves, as the glow was sunk down. He lingered on this beach, as the beaming rays of the sun gave room to the white moon, rising in a quiet majesty, casting his cool, silvery glow across the deserted beach.

Beneath the pale gaze of the glowing moon, facing the ocean's endless breath, Adrian drew in a trembling breath of his own. The waves rose and fell in their unhurried rhythm, as though each pull of the tide was a quiet struggle, drawn reluctantly toward the shore, only to surrender in a soft, white foam. That steady, timeless pulse held him together, kept him breathing, kept him alive, even as his own breath slipped just beyond his grasp. His heart bled with a silent ache, and his soul smoldered, burning raw and fierce, as if flames licked at it from within, consuming him from the inside out.

The flames popped, licking the wood they were consuming, vanishing the memories it had once held.

He tucked his hands into the pockets of his worn jeans that had seen better days. His long hair, tied loosely at the nape of his neck, swayed gently with the breeze.

A single tear slipped from his eye, tracing a glistening mocking path down his cheek—the sole evidence for the turmoil that stirred beneath him.

The flames roared and pulsed with insatiable energy, their wild dance casting a flickering shadow that seemed to breathe with the rhythm of the ocean's tide. The wind whirled around him a restless spirit, playing with the grains of soft sand that cradled his feet. Everything around him thrummed with life, but within him lay a profound stillness, an echo of a soul that once lived. He felt as if he'd been dead for a while now, a ghost adrift in a world teeming with vitality, yet untouched by its warmth, by its life.

And then, he finally mustered the courage to meet the gaze of the flaming fire, watching the orange flames dancing underneath the moonlight glow, consuming his memories, reducing the fragments of his past to ashes as effortlessly as a feather caught in a gust of wind. At that moment, he realized that what once filled his dead heart with warmth was now becoming a pile of ashes that would soon be carried along with the wind. All of those cherished moments, the laughter, the joy, the melody, were nothing more than fuel for the ravenous flames, nothing more than fleeting whispers in the vastness of time.

Adrian cherished the warmth of the fire, a comforting embrace that felt so welcoming yet so misleading. In so many ways, the fire mirrored the ocean, though they both seemed so distinct. Both offered an inviting allure, nurturing life, and creating moments of beauty, yet, beneath their enchanting, alluring surface, fatality was concealed. The flames danced with a mesmerizing grace while the waves whispered secrets of the deep, both capable of consuming the unwary in an instant, turning their beauty into a dangerous tempest.

The most exquisite things were often the deadliest, a truth Adrian knew all too well.

He felt that deeply, resonating within him, an ache that pulsed through his very being.

The deadly flames rolled over the nearly consumed wood, devouring what he had once held so dearly. He could still make the shape of the guitar, half from his mind and half from the burning wood as it coaxed it into nothingness. The flame licked the surface; the fire mirrored in his whisky-colored irises. The engraved words on the guitar began to curl and smolder, dissolving into ashes before his eyes.

To my lifesaver. The words read.

As he closed his eyes against the wave of pain, he felt a warm palm gently brush against his own, a soft connection that sent a shiver of solace through him. The smoothness of the skin lingered on his fingertips, a tender reminder of comfort in his sorrow. At that moment, more tears slipped silently down his cheeks, mingling with the warmth of the memory, each drop a testament to his grief and longing.

He lowered his gaze to the small rectangular album nestled in the soft sand, untouched since he had placed it there. It had stood as a silent witness while he drenched the guitar in oil, preparing to surrender it to the hungry flames. The album's edges curled in the breeze, a stark reminder of the distant memories he was about to let go.

It was a daring move, yet Adrian felt compelled to glimpse the album one last time to see the memories reflected in his eyes—a solid, undeniable proof that he had not hallucinated it all. Somewhere, beyond his perception, those moments had existed, tangible in another universe. They were a testament to a happiness he had once known, a joy so profound it felt beyond recognition.

With a trembling hand, Adrian dared to flip through the pages, but the pain that accompanied this simple act surged like an unrelenting tide, threatening to overwhelm him. He found himself grappling with a hurt he knew he was too feeble to confront. In a moment of desperation, he hurled the small album into the fire, watching as the flames devour it, taking with it the remnants of a happiness he could no longer bear to face.

The flames flickered in his eyes, and though the pictures crumbled to ashes, he still saw the beautiful man with stormy gray eyes and sand-colored hair. He still heard the echoes of his laughter lingering in the air, accompanied by the warmth of his low voice calling Adrian's name. Wiping away the tears that blurred his vision, Adrian reached into his pocket and pulled out a small white envelope, rolling it between his fingers as he gazed into the fire. He had read the letter inside countless times, the words etched in his mind, each line a haunting reminder of the same news that had led to the same fate.

The guitar and the album were long gone.

The streams of water gave, and the fire took.

Adrian drew a ragged breath, the acrid scent of smoke mingling with the briny tang of salt in the air. At that moment, the cycle of beginning and end crystallized within him, clarity piercing through the haze of his grief.

With sudden resolve, he cast the envelope into the flames, watching as it surrendered to the fire's voracious appetite.

It had been far too long since life had offered him anything worth living for, and now he was ready to let death come and claim him. It didn't matter anymore; each breath felt like a lie, his heartbeat a mischievous trick. Every blink of his eyes served as a reminder of pain, each voice he heard failed to be the one he longed for, and every face passing by felt unfamiliar and hollow. No wonder he had surrendered the will to battle for his life, his very essence had faded long ago, leaving him a mere shadow of what he once was.

The moon emerged from behind the clouds, casting a silvery glow over the flickering flames. Shadows danced away from the fire, and Adrian could almost catch the faint sound of a playful giggle mingled with a throaty moan calling his name as the light wind caressed the flames, drawing nourishment from the wood.

His gaze drifted back to the ocean, shimmering ominously in the moonlight, but he didn't truly see it. Instead, his weeping heart and tear-stained eyes conjured an image of crystal-clear waters on a sun-soaked day. He felt the cool embrace of the water against his skin, even as he gasped for the night air. In his mind, he saw the man of his dreams, effortlessly surfing on his board, leaving behind a trail of glistening spray and white foam, as the ocean spoke to them, inviting them to ride its powerful barrels.

Hums surrounded him, voices weaving through the air, but there was only one that mattered. It belonged to a young, beautiful man, his smile radiant as he called Adrian's name, urging him to join him in the water. The voice echoed softly, a haunting melody that existed solely in Adrian's mind, pulling him into a distant, dreamlike realm. Yet the crackling of the fire cut through the reverie, anchoring him back to the present, where reality flickered like the flames before him. Adrian closed his eyes, surrendering to the tears that fell freely, the agony enveloping him as the salty wind tousled his hair and brushed against his face, like the ocean attempting to soothe his shattered spirit. As the pain intensified, becoming an all-consuming weight, he eventually stopped crying. There was nothing left within him but that relentless ache, a hurt so acute it had drained him of tears. He felt hollow, emptied of both sorrow and life, a mere shell adrift in the vastness of his despair.

He sank into silence, withdrawing into himself and abandoning all hope. The turbulence within urged his feet into the water, a silent plea for the ocean to embrace him, to soothe the heavy sorrow and pain he carried like an invisible weight. As he walked, his feet sank into the cool sand, each step toward the horizon pulling him deeper into the darkening blue.

With every move, his worn jeans soaked up the cold, briny water, an unwelcome reminder of the growing distance between him and the shore. A shiver coursed through him as the icy waves welcomed his toes, a sharp contrast to the ache in his heart. Perhaps, just perhaps, the water would summon Logan back to him, a flicker of hope amid the vast emptiness.

Chapter 1
An Ocean on Dry Land

Logan had left the ocean behind, but the ancient streams never stopped pulling at his veins.

November 13, 2018—Queensland, Australia—Two Years Earlier

LOGAN VAUGHN SAT AT the busy airport.

He gazed into the distance, his eyes fixed on a point that seemed to vanish into emptiness, surrounded by a world fading into a blur, blurred by the shimmering tears that hung perilously at the edges. Within him, a chaos of thoughts clamored for recognition, a symphony of mayhem that he strove to silence, yearning instead for the comforting embrace of serenity.

With one hand clutching his phone and the other grasping a bottle of Coke, its chilled, dark liquid remained unspoiled. Not a single sip had crossed his lips; the mere thought of it loomed large, an insurmountable challenge. He had purchased it simply to grip something tangible, a distraction to hold onto as he longed for his escape from this place. His nails pressed into the plastic while he quaked beneath the weight of his inner turmoil.

Logan sat in the bustling airport, surrounded by a whirlwind of travelers rushing to their destinations. To him, they felt like ghosts, fleeting and insubstantial, their faces a blur as they hurried past. He didn't see them; he could only sense the chaos they carried with them, a storm of urgency that swirled around him.

A wave of nausea rolled through him, threatening to overwhelm him. He fought the urge to be sick, trying to focus on the world on all sides. The burn of unshed tears filled his eyes, and he willed them to stay put. "Just a bit longer," he whispered to himself, clinging to the thought like a lifeline. He was returning to the Vaughn family, and he recalled the lesson he had learned long ago: *Be a man*. Men didn't cry; they faced their challenges head-on. And so, as he sat there, Logan steeled himself against the anguish within, determined to handle it all, no matter how heavy the weight felt.

The next flight to Seattle would depart in an hour, but Logan had already been waiting for two excruciating hours. Each minute stretched endlessly, and he could barely catch his breath. The thought of returning home was a mix of terror and angst, swirling in his chest like a tempest, taking his breath away. He felt the urge to scream, to unleash all the frustrations and agony that weighed him down, to let out a cry that would pierce the air and lighten his burden. Just then, his phone buzzed against his leg, the vibration low but enough to send a jolt through his entire body. He glanced at the screen.

Adrian.

The sight of that name conjured a heart-wrenching wave of emotion, making it nearly impossible to hold back the tears. With eyes tightly shut, he surrendered to the overwhelming pain bearing down on him. A fierce interplay of heat and cold surged through his body, while his hands trembled uncontrollably, betraying his attempts to maintain composure, showing the whirlwind of emotions that threatened to suffocate his soul.

Logan let the call slip into voicemail, caught in a fierce battle between the yearning for the phone to ring again and the desperate prayer for silence. He craved a savior to emerge from the shadows, to rescue him from this chaos that engulfed him. Yet, paradoxically, a part of him longed to escape on that flight, to flee. To go. To run.

Back to Adrian. His brain immediately completed as he thought of running.

Logan fixed his gaze into the void, the phone in his hand vibrating incessantly with calls and messages. Each buzz seemed to echo the unease lodged deep within him, a reminder of the chaos swirling and building in every fiber of his being. Memories flickered through his mind, and deep down, he silently called for Adrian, wishing he could conjure him up. Adrian had a way of grounding him, of bringing clarity to the storm that raged inside.

His heart felt like it was bleeding, aching for connection. It screamed at him to answer the call, to reach out and find solace in the familiar voice. He knew that with just the press of a button, everything could feel manageable again. But still, he hesitated, caught in the tension between his longing for comfort and the weight of his despair.

Logan Vaughn should have answered his phone. But he didn't.

He hated Adrian for caring so much. For calling non-stop.

7:04 AM

Where are you? Is everything okay?

Lo, answer your damn phone!

Please. Please just tell me you're okay.

I'm freaking out.

Please. Ahuv sheli, say something. Anything.

Logan. Please.

I'm sorry. If I did something, tell me. Just don't do this. Not like this.

Logan Vaughn, I swear to God. Talk to me!

What are you doing? Where are you going?

Lo. Please.

You can't just leave. You can't do this to me.

7:12 AM

This is us. You and me. Remember? It's me, Logan.

I'm begging you.

Please, answer the phone!

Please don't run. Please, not from me. Please pick up the phone!

I love you. Okay? There. I said it again. I LOVE YOU. So now what? You're gonna disappear on me?!

> Logan, please. Come back. Please pick up the phone!

> I'm not okay. I can't breathe.

> I don't know what to do. I don't know how to lose you.

7:25 AM

> Please answer. Please just… let me hear your voice. One word. Are you okay?

No.

Logan was the furthest from okay.

No.

Logan would not answer the phone.

The stream of messages kept strumming to his phone, and Logan lovingly let his fingers brush across the screen as if he could touch them, keep them inside of him where they would forever pump life into his veins.

In the midst of all this suffocating pain, a faint, worn-out smile stretched over Logan's face, as he could feel Adrian's worry and care embracing him; the genuine warmth of the man reached inside of him and softened the chill of the isolation, of the unspeakable thing he was about to do. Logan ached inside and let the tears stream freely down his cheeks. The quiet, steady loyalty was as unyielding as ever, and Logan knew that he wouldn't be let go so easily. And so, with his heart quietly bleeding and his breath trembling like a lone leaf in a chilled winter morning, he typed a message, pressing "send" the very moment his fingers released the last letter.

7:30 AM

I'm fine. At the airport, going back home. Goodbye.

The bitter words read. Every word was a lie, crafted to push Adrian further away, to sever the fraying connection, and to guide Logan back to where he believed he belonged. This was the moment Logan betrayed him, not to wound Adrian but to protect him.

Memories of the night before surrounded him, whispering around the brittle armor of his lonely heart.

His phone vibrated relentlessly, Adrian's name and the chosen picture flickering on the screen, hunting him with the most beautiful smile and soulful eyes he'd ever seen.

Again, and again.

Logan's gaze anchored to the display, a tumultuous ache unfurling within him, twisting his stomach in a vice grip, the nausea clawing at his throat like a rising tide. He craved nothing more than to answer that call, the temptation pulling at him with fierce urgency. But before succumbing to his foolish desires, Logan's trembling hand reached for his phone, blocking Adrian's number as tears streamed down his face, choking him with each sob.

Coward, he spat inwardly, shoving the phone back into his pocket.

He knew his own weakness, knew the pull of Adrian's voice and the unbearable ache of wanting to respond, the undeniable temptation to let himself be drawn back in. Blocking him was the only way.

Logan rose from the stiff airport chair, running a weary hand through his overgrown hair, letting the tousled sand-blond strands fall haphazardly over his face. He took one last breath—just one—to steady himself, to hold his cracking resolve in place. He mindlessly grabbed the small bag he carried with him, a bag he had hastily packed in the quiet, fragile hours of dawn. A few belongings thrown together with trembling hands as another man, the man he cared about more than he dared admit, slept soundly, unaware of Logan's silent departure.

With a heart as heavy as a stone sunk in a darkened sea, he moved toward the gate, barely aware as he handed over his passport and ticket to the steward, each motion distant and mechanical. He boarded the plane, found his seat, and slipped in his earbuds, hands moving almost by memory as he scrolled through his playlist. One song. There was only one he could bear to hear, a song that once held a quiet comfort but in recent months had swelled into something deeply necessary, its words clinging to him, grounding him, aching with him.

Lifehouse—Everything.

The soft strum of the guitar filled his ears, and with it came a surge of warmth and aching, a quiet comfort that cut deeper than any silence. The pain in his chest eased, then clenched all over again, unbearable yet oddly soothing, as if both the balm and the wound came from the same place. And then the chorus began. The raspy, soul-bare voice cut through him, loosening what little control he had left. The tears he'd managed to cage in the little time it had taken to board the flight slipped free, streaming down his face as if they'd waited just for this—one verse, one aching refrain to finally undo him. He closed his eyes, his chest heaving, and suddenly it wasn't the singer's voice he heard. It was a different voice entirely, one he knew intimately, one that filled him with memories he couldn't bear to revisit yet couldn't escape.

Adrian's voice roared in the silence of his thoughts, amidst the hum of people moving around.

Logan Vaughn was a broken man, hollowed by the loss he carried like a ghost within him, for he'd left his other half on an Australian beach. What remained of Logan was shadows, absences, hunting memories of sand, salty air, and cool waters, with the echo of Adrian's rolling laughter that he would never hear again.

"Hey, man, we're here," the cab driver called out, jolting Logan from a dreamless sleep.

"Sorry," Logan muttered, barely aware he'd nodded off. "Thanks." He fumbled for his wallet, pulling out a bill and passing it to the driver. "Keep the change," he added, grabbing his bag and stepping out of the cab.

"Thanks, man. Get some sleep, huh? You look like you need it," the driver called before pulling away.

"If you only knew..." Logan murmured to himself. He stood before the iron gates of his family home, the place where he'd grown up, a place he'd run from as soon as he could. The manicured lawns stretched out in perfect symmetry, leading up to the white mansion, as impeccable as ever, adorned to perfection. Everything was in its place, a polished scene of quiet wealth, and behind the lighted windows, he knew his parents would be home, waiting in their perfect world.

Logan steadied himself, lifted his bag, and punched the familiar code into the gate's keypad. As the iron gates swung open, he crossed the threshold, each step bringing him closer to the grand mahogany doors. He was actually grateful for the small walk across his family estate; it had given him the time to collect himself as he attempted to piece together the fragments of his soul on this quiet night. To compose himself. He practiced the smile he'd need to wear, rehearsing the easy expression that would assure everyone he was simply back from a pleasant vacation.

Before his hand even reached for the bell, the door swung open—no doubt one of the staff had already alerted his parents that their son was home.

"Logan!" His mother's voice rang out, and in an instant, she was wrapping him in a tight embrace, her smaller frame folding around him as he leaned down to return the hug. Over her shoulder, he met his father's eyes, cool and sharp, staring at him as though they could see everything he was trying to hide.

"Samantha, come on, you're suffocating the boy," his father said coolly, his sharp gaze unwavering as it flicked between them. Samantha took a step back, her eyes sparkling under the moonlight as she gazed adoringly at Logan.

"Welcome home, son," his father said, extending his hand for a handshake. Logan accepted it, the gesture formal yet familiar.

"Hey, dad, thanks," he replied, feeling the weight of expectation in that brief touch. As his father stepped back, allowing him to enter, Mrs. Donovon approached, her warm presence a comfort amid the tension of the moment. She had practically raised him, her nurturing spirit woven into the fabric of his childhood.

"Let me take your bag, dear," she offered, but Logan was quicker, pulling her into a hug.

"Hey, Mrs. Donovon!" he exclaimed, and she chuckled, wrapping her arms around him tightly.

"I missed you, boy," she said, her voice soft, filling him with a flicker of warmth that eased the chill settling in his heart.

"Go back to bed; I'm sorry for disturbing you. I'll handle the bag," he urged, trying to lighten the moment.

Mrs. Donovon smiled kindly at him, casting a wary glance at his father. Logan could only imagine the tension that had hung in the air during the last few months, the fury she must have witnessed in his dad's eyes as they navigated the storm that had brewed in their family.

"I will go to make your room, Logan," she added, taking in his appearance. "You look like you need a good night's sleep."

"Thank you."

Wordlessly, Mrs. Donovon retired, and he followed his parents to the main leaving room, the expensive carpets under his feet muffling their steps.

"I thought you'd be gone for a few more months," his mother said, gently urging him to take his bag off his shoulders and settle into the armchair. "We talked last week, and you never mentioned coming home. Why didn't you say something? We would have picked you up."

His father's gaze was steady, waiting for a response. Logan had skillfully dodged questions about his return for months now, and he felt the weight of their expectations hanging in the air.

"It was a last-minute decision, actually. I just felt like I'd seen everything I wanted to see..." Logan replied, his voice betraying a slight tremor, though he hoped it would go unnoticed. Robert sank into the opposite sofa, his blue eyes sharp, pinning Logan's soul beneath the scrutiny of his small glasses.

"I'm really glad you're home, Logan. I wasn't a fan of that trip of yours from the start," he admitted.

"Yeah, I know, Dad." Logan ran a hand through his sandy hair, feeling the awkward silence stretch between them.

After a moment, Robert broke the quiet. "Where's your board?"

Logan swallowed hard, knowing his father meant his surfboard. "Um, it broke the other day... I'll get a new one soon."

His father's expression faltered, skepticism creeping into his features. Logan could see him weighing whether to probe further, to ask how he had managed to surf without a new board. But Robert was pragmatic, a man who focused on the present and future, and he held his questions close to his chest.

"So, I think I can pull some strings to get you started in your position next week. What do you say?"

"Um, yeah. Sure," Logan murmured, though every word felt like an anchor dragging him down.

"Good. It'll give you a few days to rest before you start," his father continued, oblivious of the chaos hiding behind Logan's seemingly calm exterior.

The last thing Logan wanted was to join his father's company—a corporate empire so powerful it practically dictated the flow of trade along the entire West Coast and across the Pacific routes. Vaughn Global Lines, or more popularly known as VGL, commanded a staggering market share, its ships moving millions of tons of cargo across the globe each year, its name a synonym for generational wealth. Logan had grown up in its shadow, the heir everyone expected to follow the path laid out for him. But at twenty-four, he felt unmoored, unwilling to be chained to an empire he hadn't chosen, even if someday he would have no choice but to claim it.

He had completed a BA in Business Administration and Economics, then went straight on to earn his MBA, with the implicit expectation that he would step into his father's role one day. As the sole male in the Vaughn family, with his older sister, Jane, managing the legal department and his younger sister, Ann, choosing a completely different path by going to medical school, he felt the burden of obligation.

Another staff member entered, carrying a small tray with a steaming pot of tea and three mugs, setting it gently on the table.

"Thank you, Mr. Walker. You can go back to sleep; we'll handle everything. We're sorry to have disturbed you at this late hour," his father said sincerely, a reminder to Logan that while his dad was a hard man, he was not unkind.

Logan grabbed a steaming mug, feeling the warmth seep into his hands. He listened as his parents filled the air with updates about the family, their voices a comforting backdrop that felt both familiar and stifling. It was hard to breathe; the weight of the room pressed down on him like a heavy blanket.

As his mother animatedly shared the news that Jane was pregnant and due in five months, Logan forced a smile, his heart clenching. She went on about Ann, about her start in medical school. He laughed at the funny anecdotes his mother shared, but all the while, he battled the tears threatening to spill over.

He kept the truth locked away, the events that had led him back home buried deep beneath layers of practiced smiles.

When he finished his tea, he tucked his hands beneath his legs, desperate to hide the twitching and shaking that gnawed at him. "I really need to sleep," he finally said, his voice barely steady. "Let's call it a night?"

"It's almost morning, but yes, go get some rest," his father replied. "You look like hell."

"It's the flight." Logan offered weakly. Samantha reached over and brushed his hair back from his face.

"You need to sleep. Tomorrow, I want you to tell me everything about where you've been and what you saw. I want to see some photos!"

"No photos," Logan blurted out, the words escaping before he could contain them. "I... dropped my camera in the water."

"Oh. But your camera is waterproof, isn't it? How else did you film all those surfing videos?"

"It is, but I dropped it without the case... and... I lost it..." he replied, his voice trailing off.

"Oh... But you must have some on your phone—"

"I'm really tired," Logan interrupted, dismissing himself from the room. He grabbed his bag on the way out, focusing on one goal: getting to his own space.

Once inside his bedroom, he closed the door and locked it behind him, leaning against the sturdy wood for a moment before heading to the attached bathroom. Everything gleamed, clean and shiny, as if untouched by the chaos he carried. He opened one of the closets and found neatly folded towels, his soaps, and shampoos neatly stocked.

Logan stripped off his clothes and stepped into the shower, turning on the hot water. It cascaded over him like a comforting embrace, washing away the surface grime but failing to cleanse the hollow feeling lurking beneath. Soon enough, the heat of the water brought back memories of the night before—no, it hadn't been last night, the flight had taken about sixteen hours—but the moments rushed back nonetheless, everything he'd been running from.

As the water continued to flow, Logan felt his eyes burn with tears he could no longer hold back. He let them slide down his cheeks, releasing the dam he had built so carefully.

He closed his eyes and found himself once again on that beach with him, the waves crashing, the warmth of the sun blending with the ache of longing, the memories flooding in like the tide.

The next morning came all too soon as Logan dragged himself out of bed, refreshing his messages as he paced to the bathroom, knowing that he would not get any messages from the one he had longed to.

After brushing his teeth and washing his face, gazing at his lifeless eyes and the puffiness underneath, he paced to the walk-in closet, everything as if he had never left. He slipped into a light blue button-down shirt and black jeans, completing the look with polished black shoes. As he rummaged through the top drawer of his dresser for his car keys, he felt a flicker of relief that no one was home to witness his hurried departure.

Exiting his room, he inhaled deeply, a mix of anticipation and anxiety coursing through him as he stepped into the familiar confines of his black Mercedes. He braced himself, knowing he was about to leap back into a life he had tried so desperately to escape.

Sitting in the driver's seat, he reflected on what coming home truly meant. The thought had lingered in his mind during the long hours spent at the airport, where time stretched endlessly. His first stop would be the hairdresser's; getting a haircut was a necessity. He couldn't shake the memory of his father's disapproving glance at his long hair from the night before. Just because Robert hadn't voiced his thoughts then didn't mean he wouldn't today. Logan's hair didn't quite touch his shoulders, but it was still too long for a Vaughn.

Next on his list was the flower shop. He found himself spending an extravagant amount on a bouquet that was nearly cumbersome to fit into the car. It seemed fitting, a gesture that he hoped would smooth over the edges of his rocky relationship with Sandy.

Sandy.

Sandy had been his girlfriend for two years, a relationship that began during college. They met at a party through some shared friends, and from that moment on, they were inseparable. She was stunning, of course, but it was more than that; she came from a good family, was kind-hearted, and they simply clicked, later realizing they grew up near each other. There was never any drama between them; their relationship was easy, almost too easy.

Logan often found himself nodding along to her wishes, avoiding any conflict that might disrupt their tranquil existence. It was simpler that way. He accepted that there was no heat or longing in their bond, a reality he had grown accustomed to. He had never considered that anything more passionate might exist. Before Sandy, he had dabbled in a few other relationships, each mirroring the last. It had always seemed normal to him, the status quo of his life—until now.

Just before he left for his trip, he had kind of broken up with her, though he hadn't fully processed what that meant. It was an unsteady precipice he stood on, and as he drove through the familiar streets, he couldn't shake the feeling that something fundamental was about to shift.

Not long after, Logan found himself parked outside Sandy's parents' house, an ache he knew all too we twisting in his stomach. It was a Wednesday, which meant Sandy would be home, spending the day with her mom and grandmother.

As he approached the front door, it swung open, revealing Sandy leaning against the frame, her expression a blend of surprise and warmth. "Oh, Logan," she said coldly. "You're back. What are you doing here?"

"You're mad," he replied, forcing a smile as he handed her the bouquet of red and white roses.

"Roses," she murmured, taking them in her hands, her light brown hair falling over her shoulders. "You remembered," she said in delight.

He grinned, but the grin was a brittle gesture, a thin layer lacquered over years of practiced masks. This one had a new purpose: to hide the fracture lines beneath, to smother the restless churn inside, to pretend that he belonged here when every bone told him otherwise. His other half was an ocean and a continent away, yet here he stood, bouquet in hand, at the wrong door, wearing the wrong smile. "Have a date with me, let's talk about everything over dinner, I don't want to intrude on your time with your family."

Sandy hesitated, a flicker of doubt crossing her face. "I don't know if it's a good idea, Logan... You and I broke up. I'm seeing someone—"

"Yeah, but I'm sure I can beat him," he said, his voice barely above a whisper. "Just go out with me. It's just dinner. Doesn't mean anything. Just so we could talk a little."

"Logan—" she began, but he closed the space between them before she could finish. His mouth met hers in a kiss that felt like it belonged to someone else. It was clumsy, hollow, wrong. His lips moved against hers, but it was a body remembering the steps to a dance his soul no longer knew.

Because two nights ago, he had kissed Adrian.

Two nights ago, the world shattered beneath him as Adrian whispered his name like it was sacred, like it was something to be held, not spoken. Their lips had met like waves drawn by the same moon, inevitable and wild, as if the ocean itself had conspired to pull them together. In a bed that smelled of sun and sea, they lay tangled in breath and warmth, Adrian above him, kissing every inch of his skin as though memorizing the map of someone he'd waited his whole life to find.

Two nights ago, Logan was in the only place that truly felt like home, not a place, but a person. Adrian's hands had been reverent, trembling with quiet devotion. His voice, when he moaned Logan's name, carried a weight that shattered all the hollow spaces inside him. He tasted of salt and wind and something raw and unfiltered—truth, maybe. A dream, probably.

And in every kiss, Logan had been undone. Stripped of every layer of pretense, every story he'd told himself about who he was supposed to be. Adrian's kiss didn't just touch his lips—it sank into the marrow of him, rewrote the rhythm of his breath, made him remember what it meant to be alive.

That was the last time he had tasted something real.

Now, this—this kiss—was paper-thin and trembling. It was a lie dressed up as nostalgia.

When they pulled apart, Sandy looked dazed, lips parted, touched. But Logan... Logan felt like he had just betrayed something sacred. Not her. Himself.

Logan's lips were meant for someone else—one man who could ignite the world within him, whose kisses felt like they were made to hold everything he had ever desired. He stood there, a stranger in a familiar space, pretending that the ocean had not reshaped him, that the days spent with someone else hadn't etched new lines across his heart.

He wanted her to say no, to release him from this desperate plan he had concocted. But instead, she smiled softly, "Okay, Logan. I'll go on a date with you. But it doesn't mean anything."

He nodded, stepping back, the weight of his decision heavy on his chest. "I'll pick you up Saturday night. How does that sound?"

"Fine, I guess," she replied, the uncertainty clear in her soft voice.

"Great, because I've already made reservations," he said, winking, and turned to walk back to his car. Each step felt like a betrayal, his chest heaving with the empty words he had just spilled, the persona he was desperately trying to project.

As he reached his car, sorrow coiled tight in his chest, the reality of what he was about to do pressing down with the weight of a gathering storm.

He glanced at the clear blue sky, inhaling slowly, feeling sensations flood through him. At that moment, he thought of Adrian—the sun-soaked nights and the warmth of tanned skin pressed against him, the whisky eyes that held his gaze, the kisses that made him feel alive in a way he had never known.

Logan felt himself unraveling, caught between two lives, longing for the one he had left behind while facing the life he was returning to.

"Thanks for tonight, Logan," Sandy said, her voice low and soft.

He smiled, the same rehearsed and hollow grin that was nothing but a mask.

The evening had gone well. He had taken her to the most upscale restaurant he could find, knowing she relished places like that. She looked stunning in a beautiful dress and heels, her hair cascading in soft waves; he could tell she had spent the day at the salon for that night.

Being with Sandy was easy. She filled the air with stories of everything she had done while he was away, bubbling on about a job she had landed with a fashion company whose name slipped from his mind. He nodded and feigned interest, responding with the occasional "Really?" or "That's great!" But deep down, he was dying slowly, counting the words he had spoken on one hand.

Logan knew the next move. He leaned in and pressed his lips to hers, the kiss mechanical, a habit formed through years of routine. The kiss tasted like a greeting meant for someone else, addressed to Logan by mistake, warm in tone but foreign in intent.

As he pulled away, he was struck by the dreamy look in her eyes, while his chest throbbed with the truth he couldn't bear to voice.

"Maybe we can do this again sometime?" he suggested, his voice hoarse.

"I'd love to," she replied, a coy smile creeping onto her lips. She bit them and glanced at him with a flirtation he could not ignore. "Do you... want to come in?"

Logan swallowed hard, acutely aware of the invitation layered in her words. No, he didn't want to go in; he wanted to run, not from her, but from the life he had returned to. His heart ached for the world he had left behind, the one filled with sunlit beaches and an exhilarating freedom that now felt like a distant dream.

"No," he said finally, his voice barely above a whisper. "Tonight was just for catching up."

Sandy nodded, a blush creeping into her cheeks, and for a moment, he thought he had said the right thing.

"I'll call you," he promised as she stepped out of the car. He drove away, the weight of his decision pressing down on him, like water filling a sinking ship.

Five days home, and each had dragged him further beneath the surface, until he moved through the hours as though underwater, unable to break back into the air.

Pulling over to the side of the road, he reached for his phone, fighting against the urge that had haunted him since his return. He opened the Facebook app, scanning through posts that felt irrelevant, only searching for one name.

Typing it out, he hesitated, anger rising as he deleted the letters again and again. The frustration boiled over; he slammed his fist against the steering wheel, letting out a roar that echoed in the stillness of the car.

"Damn it!" he yelled, despair flooding his heart.

He closed his eyes for a moment, letting the memories wash over him. When he opened them again, he faced the man everyone expected him to be, but he knew it was a lie. He could never be the same.

He tossed the phone aside and shifted the car into gear, driving away from the memories that haunted him. The city blurred around him, lights and cars and people going about, unaware of the misery he felt.

As he pulled into his parents' driveway, Logan inhaled deeply, steeling himself for what lay ahead. The front door creaked open, and he was enveloped by the comforting aroma of baked goods wafting through the air. His mother's warm smile greeted him, a beacon of familiarity in the chaos of his thoughts.

Yet, despite the warmth of the moment, a sense of unease lingered in his chest. His current mood felt anything but hospitable. The relentless buzz of their concern gnawed at him, amplifying his need for space. He reminded himself that finding an apartment should be his priority now; solitude was a luxury he craved, far removed from the prying eyes of those who only wanted to help.

"Well?" she prompted; her eyes bright with anticipation, before backing away to the large kitchen.

"I think it went well," Logan replied, closing the door behind him as he approached her in the kitchen.

"That's good to hear. I like Sandy," she said, and he hugged her, planting a kiss on her cheek.

"Logan, is everything alright?" she asked, setting down a bowl of fruit she had been preparing for a cake.

"Yeah, why?"

"You seem a bit off... probably just jet lag," she reassured him or herself, brushing her hand gently across his cheek. "I like your haircut, it suits you."

"Yeah?"

"My boy, you're handsome no matter what," she said, returning to her task. "By the way, you have a surprise in your room."

"What?" His heart leaped.

"I'm not allowed to say—"

Before she could finish, he dashed up the stairs, a thrill pulsing through him with each hurried step. A small, reckless part of him dared to hope—foolishly, hopelessly hoping—that maybe, just maybe...

"Logan," he heard, but disappointment hit him like a wave.

Never mind that Adrian had no idea where he lived, or that they were worlds apart, or that he'd severed every last thread connecting them—still, somewhere deep down, he clung to the foolish, fragile hope that Adrian might be waiting there, against all reason.

"It's just you," he muttered, his voice deflated as he faced his older sister, Jane.

"Wow... you're not happy to see me," she pouted, feigning offense.

"No, no! Of course I'm happy to see you! It's just... Mom told me I had a surprise," he replied, forcing a smile. "Heard you're pregnant."

"Yeah," she beamed. "I wanted to surprise you, but Mom told me you went out with... what's her name? Sally?"

"Her name is Sandy," he corrected, "and you know it."

"Yeah, whatever. I don't like her," Jane declared, plopping onto his bed. "I wanted to hear how your trip was."

"That explains why Mom is making a cake in the middle of the night," he quipped, kicking off his shoes. "My trip was fine. Boy or girl?" he asked, glancing at her belly.

"Don't know yet," she replied, smiling. "I want to hear stories."

Logan rummaged through his closet, shedding his tie and shirt as he spoke. "Nothing to tell."

"I'm not buying it," she insisted, appearing at the entrance of his closet.

"Privacy, sis!"

"That's some good tanning you've got there," she teased, looking him over. "Oh, and someone's been working on their hot body."

"Shut up," he laughed, tossing his shirt at her.

Jane let out a laugh, flopping back onto his bed. "So, you didn't meet any nice girls out there... maybe someone who isn't slutty?"

"What's your problem with Sandy?" he sighed, now dressed down in sweatpants and a worn T-shirt.

Jane softened. "I'm sorry," she said, sounding more serious. "I shouldn't have called her that. It's just... I don't think she's with you for the right reasons."

The irony bit at him; Jane had it all wrong. *He* wasn't with Sandy for the right reasons. He was the one using her—a pawn in his carefully crafted image, just a role in the play he hated most. It was laughable that Sandy got pegged as the gold-digger when her family was plenty well off.

"She's just... not for you," Jane said, gentler this time, patting the spot beside her.

Logan joined her, heart heavy.

"Logan..." she said, her voice softening. He met her gaze, and she continued, "You look like shit."

"I'm just tired," he replied, shaking his head and looking away. How many times had he used this excuse already?

"Are you sure you're okay?" Jane asked, studying him with that big-sister gaze he could never quite dodge. "You graduated, packed a bag, and handed the rest of your stuff to Mom and Dad at graduation like it was nothing. Then you left without a word and disappeared off the map. And now... you're back just as suddenly. I'm just worried about you."

"I'm fine, Jane. Just tired. I cut my trip short because I felt like it. Nothing more." He lied, so easily now. He had studied this role his whole life after all.

"Okay. But please talk to me if you need to," she urged, hugging him tightly.

Logan nodded, biting his tongue to keep from spilling the truth.

"Now, let's go eat that cake," she teased, pulling him up with a grin. "I won't have you looking all hot while I'm over here, blowing up like a balloon." She linked her arm through his, leading him toward the door. "And you better eat at least three pieces, so you can tell me where you've been and keep up with me for once."

"Mostly Hawaii."

"I want more info... I'm spending the night here, and I will drive you crazy until you tell me," She said with a grin, and for the first time that evening, he felt a flicker of warmth amidst the confusion.

November 28, 2018—Seattle, Washington—10 Days Later

TWO WEEKS HAD FLOWED like a gentle stream since Logan returned home. He'd started his new job, settled into the role, learned faces, names, processes, and made all the right connections. The work hours stretched infinitely, devouring whole days and offering him a sturdy anchor, a comforting distraction from the deeper currents of his thoughts.

Outside the office, he fell back into things with Sandy, moving like clockwork. They went out, they met friends, she laughed and bragged to her circle about how he must have missed her, how he came to her first. He let her think what she liked. Whatever story she wanted to spin around them, he wouldn't stop her.

But today, sitting at his desk, Logan felt everything begin to slip. His hands curled tightly, knuckles pale, as he leaned into his own palms, elbows anchored to the desk. Breathing felt impossible, each breath shallow and choking. He tugged at his tie, fingers clumsy and desperate to loosen it, but the weight didn't lift.

Just breathe, count to ten, and it'll pass.

Damn it.

It wasn't passing.

A notification buzzed on his phone. He pulled it from his pocket and noticed Sandy's name lighting up the screen. Rather than opening the message, he quickly returned the phone to his jacket, focusing straight ahead as if he could force himself to remain in that moment. However, he felt all the things he believed he had buried creeping closer and pushing harder, determined not to let him be.

Logan rose from his chair and looked out the floor-to-ceiling window, gazing over the vast cityscape. The view was a perk, a privilege even, one he'd always appreciated. But today, the glittering high-rises and humming streets below felt hollow. He took a deep breath, but it felt shallow, insufficient.

He checked his phone and saw it was barely noon. *To hell with it.* He was the boss's son, and he'd been putting in the hours. He grabbed his things, shut the office door behind him, and headed for the parking garage, barely restraining himself from breaking into a run.

Once behind the wheel of his Mercedes, pulling out from the corporate tower and weaving his way into the stream of cars, he felt some of the tension begin to ease. He already knew where he was headed, the destination flashing clearly in his mind before he'd even reached the first intersection. He needed the water—the waves, the salt on his skin, the infinite blue that seemed to carry his worries away, even if just for a little while.

He drove for what felt like forever before he finally reached the beach, the stretch of shoreline he always returned to when he was home. The traffic crawled, and every stop-and-go only made the gnawing impatience worse. But at last, he parked. The ocean stretched before him, endless and wild, glittering beneath the early afternoon light. He longed for the water, to feel it crash around him, to let it pull him under, wrapping him in the power of its swell and pull.

But he sat there, unmoving, his hand resting on the door handle. He watched the waves curl and crash against the shore. He'd come all this way, and yet he couldn't bring himself to open the door, to step outside and let the ocean swallow him whole.

Finally, he reached for his phone. His fingers hovered over the screen, and without overthinking it, he unlocked it, opened Facebook, and typed in the name that had been haunting him since he'd returned. It was something he had wanted to do countless times before but had always stopped himself.

Adrian Leon.

Logan clicked on the profile, a wave of relief crashing into a storm of agony, nearly bringing him to tears as he took in Adrian's familiar face, frozen in a moment that felt achingly distant. He scrolled down, searching for any sign of life, but the emptiness was palpable—no updates, no posts, nothing since the day he'd left.

A question crept into his mind: Did Adrian think of him too? He shut his eyes tightly, squeezing out the thought, battling the emotions swirling within him. *I need to block him here too,* he told himself, a voice of reason amidst the chaos. Yet the idea felt like severing the last tether connecting him to Adrian, and he hesitated, hand trembling over the message option. He needed to reach out, to bridge the chasm that had formed between them.

As he shook his arm slightly, the sleeve of his shirt slipped back, unveiling a black and silver bracelet wrapped around his wrist—a delicate creation spun from strands of dark thread. At its center, held on either side by the black thread, lay a small lifesaver charm, a poignant token of their entwined past. His fingers found it instinctively, caressing the strings with his fingers, tracing the charm as if it were a lifeline, something solid to grasp amidst the turmoil of his emotions.

It was merely a bracelet, a simple adornment, yet it infused him with an unforeseen solace, even as it evoked the anguish that gnawed at his heart. The weight of yearning threatened to crush him, and in a moment of desperation, he slammed his hand against the steering wheel, frustration surging within him. Tears gathered at the corners of his eyes, and he hastily closed the app, shoving the phone back into his pocket, terrified of the chaos that might ensue if he relinquished control once more.

He wanted to scream, to let the anguish spill out in a cacophony of sound, but instead, he pulled away, driving back to his parents' home, the weight of his thoughts heavy in the silence. As he navigated the familiar streets, he felt like a ghost haunting his own life, the laughter of the past echoing in his mind while he sat in silence, pretending he could escape the darkness that loomed inside him.

As soon as he stepped through the door, a surge of determination propelled him up the stairs to his father's office. It didn't surprise him to find his father there, poring over work even in the evening light.

"Logan," his father acknowledged, looking up as Logan stormed in. "Can I help you?"

"Yes." Logan closed the door behind him, standing resolutely in front of his father's desk.

Logan had no idea what he was about to say until the words were out. He was somewhat convinced he would mention Adrian, but wasn't that ridiculous? He would never share anything about Adrian with his father. So why was he there? What had prompted his rush to come?

"I want to propose to Sandy," he blurted, the words escaping his mouth like a confession he hadn't meant to utter.

His father regarded him with a piercing gaze through his glasses, then pushed back his chair and rose to his feet, straightening his jacket as a proud smile spread across his face. "I think that's an amazing idea, Logan. One of the best you've ever had."

Logan inhaled deeply, a flicker of hope igniting in his chest, but it felt hollow. He was trying to fill a void with Sandy, to bury the darkness that was clawing at him. The corners of his mouth lifted in a tentative smile, but it didn't reach his eyes.

"You know," his father continued, "being a man is about making the right choices. Deciding to move on with your life is one of those choices. I have to admit, when you packed your bag and set off for God knows where, I had my doubts about your maturity. But lately, son, I see you growing into the man I always hoped you would become." His father's hand landed firmly on his shoulder. "Starting a family—that's what truly matters. I'm really proud of you, Logan."

Inside, Logan crumbled a little more. His father's pride rang in his ears like applause for a part he hadn't wanted to play, the sound chasing him deeper into a life that wasn't his. He forced himself to nod, to accept the praise, but all he could think about was how every choice he made was dragging him further away from the person he truly wanted to be.

His shaking fingers found the bracelet again, the cool metal carrying the echo of Adrian's touch or perhaps only the echo his longing had invented.

"Thanks, Dad," Logan managed, his voice barely above a whisper, a mix of gratitude and guilt tightening around his chest.

"I..." His father began, clearing his throat as if steeling himself for the words that were about to follow. "One question, Logan."

"Yeah?" Logan braced himself, sensing the weight of the inquiry.

"Do you love her?"

Logan swallowed hard, the question hanging in the air like a fragile glass ornament, cradling every secret that the fraying mask of his smile fought to hide. One small push, and it would fall and shatter as it hit the unforgiving ground, releasing a cascade of secrets like ghostly whispers spilling into the silence.

"I... I know her well, and we've been together for a long time..." he mumbled, the truth of his words feeling inadequate, as if they were merely a shield against the deeper reality.

His father nodded thoughtfully, a smile creeping onto his face. "Don't worry, son. You will love her with time. She's a good match for you. Your feelings will grow. You don't marry who you love; you marry who's right for you. Love will come with time. And if it doesn't, well, that's really not a big deal, because you'll be with someone good for you."

Logan felt as if the ground beneath him might crack open and swallow him whole. He wanted to scream, to tear apart the façade he was trying to uphold. He didn't love Sandy—not at all. She was lovely and kind, a warm presence in his chaotic life, but she didn't spark that exhilarating tingle in his chest or the electric thrill that surged through him when he thought of Adrian. There was no excitement, no rush of adrenaline; just a steady, comfortable rhythm that felt more like resignation than love.

"I'd love to come with you," his father said, breaking through Logan's turbulent thoughts. "What do you say? Take your old man with you to search for the perfect ring?"

"Sure... tomorrow?" Logan replied, his heart heavy as he forced a smile, the prospect of ring shopping feeling like a final nail in the coffin of his own desires.

Chapter 2
Where the Stream Rewrote the Storm

July 6, 2018—North Shore, Oahu, Hawaii—Five Months Earlier

LOGAN FELT A RUSH of exhilaration as he shut the shabby cabin door behind him. With a grunt, he tossed his oversized duffel bag to the floor, the thud echoing in the small room. In a flurry, he began shedding his clothes, eager to escape the confines of the musty space.

He had never been one to care much about where he slept or what he ate; all that mattered to him was the beach. The sound of the waves seemed to call out to him, their rhythmic crashing blending with the whispers of the wind urging him to come closer. Even his deep-seated aversion to flying faded into insignificance at the thought of the shimmering ocean waiting just beyond the horizon. The mere anticipation sent a thrill coursing through his body, igniting a longing for the freedom the sea promised.

He rummaged through his bag, finally finding his board shorts from within the mess he would never clear up. The sight of them filled him with uncontainable excitement. Hawaii—a paradise for surfers—was a dream he had long cherished. Born and raised in Seattle, he was an unlikely candidate for a surfer's life, yet the ocean had captivated him from a young age. Weekends were dedicated to the ritual of traveling back and forth to nearby beaches, chasing the perfect swell. Summers unfolded in endless drives to the sun-drenched shores of California, where he truly discovered the art of riding the waves. Those sun-soaked days and crashing surf solidified his passion for the sport, weaving it into the very fabric of his being.

With a burst of energy, he grabbed his surfboard, disregarding the need for shoes and leaving his duffel open on the floor of the too-small cabin. He had seen the beach from the cab, just a short distance away, and the urge to run—no, to sprint—was overwhelming.

As Logan stepped out of the cabin, he took a long, lingering look around him, allowing the intoxicating vacation vibes to seep deep into his very soul. It was uncanny how just a day ago he had been at his graduation ceremony, and now, liberated from all of that, he felt as if he were truly breathing in the crisp, clear air and soaking up the warmth of the sun on his skin. The serene atmosphere enveloped him, punctuated only by the gentle sound of waves lapping at the shore and the soothing hum of the wind dancing through the trees.

It was an addictive rush, like the first sip of a long-forgotten cocktail on a sweltering day. His body, almost instinctively, began to guide him toward the beach, drawn by the siren call of the coastline.

A wave of joy threatened to spill from his eyes as he stood on the shore, the warm sand cradling his feet and a gentle breeze brushing against his face, like a soft caress. The salty tang of the ocean filled his lungs, each breath a reminder of the freedom he had long yearned for. The tension that had wrapped itself around him like a vice began to dissolve with the rhythmic crash of monstrous waves meeting the shore.

He closed his eyes again for a moment, disbelief washing over him; he was here, he was free. A shiver of animation coursed through him, and he opened his eyes to feel the ocean's playful touch as it tickled his bare toes under the heat of the sun. He had never craved anything as intensely as he craved the embrace of the water at that very moment.

Logan's gaze hungrily sought out the ocean, where a lone surfer broke free from the undulating waves. The man emerged like a sea god, shaking his head to flick droplets of water from his long hair, each bead glistening like diamonds in the bright sunlight. His toned, sun-kissed body glimmered, every muscle defined and glistening with the remnants of the ocean's embrace. The black board shorts hung low on his hips, accentuating the powerful lines of his physique, a testament to hours spent riding the waves. Logan tore his eyes away, discarding the sensation is had stirred in him.

A little further down the shore, a small group of sun-drenched revelers laughed, their joy echoing in the crisp morning air.

The early hour that Friday morning kept the beach hushed, save for the slow whisper of waves meeting sand. Logan had read that this stretch of the North Shore could stay nearly empty in summer, and today proved it true. No crowds, no chaos, just a quiet swell rolling in with the grace of something half-asleep.

In winter, this coastline earned its infamy—thundering with double-overhead sets, spitting barrels, and reef breaks sharp enough to slice pride clean through. But July was different. The giants had long since retreated to deeper waters, leaving behind mellow, chest-high peelers that broke with a kind of kindness.

Logan didn't consider himself a pro, not by a long shot. And today, that was a blessing. He wasn't here to charge. He was here to breathe.

He craved the isolation, yearned for the challenge. Perhaps he sought to prove something—something impossibly futile—to someone who would never know, someone who would never see the struggle. Perhaps he was only trying to prove something to himself. Or perhaps he simply wanted to be free, to feel freedom in its wildest, most unbridled form. He wanted to dive headlong into the waves, into the vastness of the deepest swells he could find, to let the water lift him and carry him far away from the unbearable weight of a life that felt as if it had to be endured.

His eyes held a mischievous look, a glint of something untamed and restless, as a small smirk danced across his full lips as he surveyed the rolling waves, the thrill of anticipation igniting his spirit. He was determined to ride those beauties. Without a moment's hesitation, Logan snatched up his slender white board and sprinted toward the beckoning ocean, an uncontainable smile lighting up his face. As he plunged into the water, the cool embrace soaked through his shorts, invigorating his bare skin and washing away the remnants of his worries, while the salty spray dotted his cheeks like nature's confetti.

He began to paddle into the depths, each stroke slicing through the cool water, a soothing balm for his restless soul. The currents moved rhythmically beneath his board, urging him deeper into the embrace of the sea. As the waves swelled ahead, Logan prepared himself, gripping the rails of his board tightly. With a deep breath, he angled the nose downward, pressing his weight into it, and plunged beneath the cresting water. The wave rolled over him in a brief, muffled roar, the turbulence ruffling his hair and tugging at his body before releasing him into the calm on the other side.

He emerged, gasping lightly at the fresh air, and paddled forward, repeating the motion with precision each time another wave approached. Duck-diving became a rhythm, a partnership with the ocean's power. With every powerful stroke, and every deliberate dive beneath the waves, he fought against the ocean's gentle pull, proving to her that he could handle her wildness. He could ride her breath.

Even if he stumbled, he had nothing to lose. This moment was everything—he longed to become one with the water, to dive into its depths and let the waves cradle him like a protective blanket. In that fleeting moment, he felt like a child again, lulled to sleep by the very life force that created him, enveloped in the rhythmic lullaby of the ocean.

On the beach, Adrian Leon watched as a surfer sprinted into the embrace of the sea, the silhouette of the other surfer stark against the rolling waves. From his vantage point, Adrian felt an inexplicable tug at his heart—a resonance that stirred the broken fragments of his own soul, a soul that had witnessed the worst of humanity's depths. He had come to this secluded shore seeking solitude, so the presence of another person surprised him. This beach, which had become his sanctuary, was now shared, though there were moments when a kindred spirit would lace the fabric of his stillness.

The cool breeze tousled Adrian's hair, drying the remnants of seawater from his face like a soft caress. He laid his board on the warm sand, freeing his hair from its loose ponytail, only to gather it again into a messy bun. He rubbed his sore muscles and creaked his neck, feeling the tension ease but knowing all too well the power of the waves. They were fierce today, the currents relentless. He had learned to respect the ocean's whims, to recognize when her gifts were not to be trifled with. Now was not the time to test her limits.

He recalled the two hours he had spent battling the tumultuous surf, fighting against the capricious waves that seemed almost alive in their fury. The ocean was supposed to be tranquil today. All forecasts, charts, and whispers among the surfers spoke of perfect conditions for today. But as he paddled out, something felt off. The sea's surface betrayed no sign, yet its rhythm was dissonant, unsettled. Beneath the glittering sun, he felt the faintest tug of unease, as though the ocean herself was holding her breath.

He glanced at the reusable plastic water bottle he'd laid in the sand earlier and took a long swig of the liquid that had warmed during his time in the ocean.

Then he turned his gaze back to the water. When the other surfer, effortlessly riding a wave—a mere six meters, but small by the standards of this shore—moved with a grace that seemed almost poetic. Adrian watched as he flowed across the surface, a fluid motion that spoke of experience and confidence. The man emerged from the barrel just as it closed in around him, the wave crashing down in a spectacular display of power and foam before he plunged beneath the surface, a glimpse of sheer exhilaration on his face.

The wind whipped around Adrian, cold and biting, its strength suggesting an impending storm.

The sun was warm just moments ago, yet now the air felt off, felt charged. Adrian stood at the shoreline, the edge of the Pacific licking at his bare feet, when the first sliver of unease slid down his spine. The wind had shifted, subtle at first, just a whisper curling across the sand, then firmer, insistent, like unseen hands brushing past him.

He blinked and looked up.

The vibrant expanse of summer blue sky was fading quickly. Clouds gathered like ink poured into water, thickening over the horizon with unnatural speed. The light turned strange, metallic, as if the world had been pulled under a tinted lens. The ocean, which only moments ago had glimmered with lazy grace, began to stir with a different kind of energy, one that hummed beneath his skin.

Adrian felt it. In his *bones*.

The water was vibrating.

Not visibly, not yet—but beneath the surface, there was a tension, a readiness, like something was coiling itself up, ready to strike.

With a wistful glance at the sea, he noticed the lone surfer paddling further into the depths, preparing for the imposing waves that awaited just beyond the break. Adrian's eyes were fixated on the figure, which appeared to shrink against the expansive canvas of blue as he journeyed deeper into the ocean's embrace.

Minutes passed, each one thick with tension, until Adrian's instinct kicked in. He noticed the surface of the ocean beginning to rise ominously, a signal that the surfer must have sensed as well. The man turned, paddling with renewed urgency toward the shore, yet a knot twisted in Adrian's stomach. He couldn't shake the feeling that something was amiss, a residual fear that clung to him like a shadow.

The wind howled louder, and the surfer appeared as nothing more than a tiny speck against the swelling sea, where a massive wave began to loom, ominous and towering against the fragility of the human riding it.

This wave was not merely large; it was monstrous. Only a seasoned pro would dare to ride such a behemoth, and even then, it would be a perilous feat. Adrian felt his breath hitch in his throat as he watched the surfer rise to the crest, the water curving dramatically beneath him. The foam at its peak bubbled violently, and as the wave swelled higher, Adrian instinctively took a step forward, urgency coursing through him.

"*Kfotz!*" *Jump!* he muttered under his breath in his native language, his heart racing as he focused intently on the surfer, still poised atop his board. But time was running out. At least ten meters above the ocean's surface, the man finally grasped the edges of his board and shifted his weight, leaping with a light spring—but it was too late. The wave, too powerful and unforgiving, shattered his balance, sending him tumbling off his board in a breathtaking display of vulnerability.

Adrian's breath caught in his throat, and the water bottle slipped from his grasp, landing onto the sand with a gentle thud. He stood, entranced, as he beheld the surfer tumble into the shimmering depths, the board tethered to him by a leash following in a graceful arc. The impact of his body meeting the water echoed like a haunting melody, a visceral strike that sent ripples spiraling outward, breaking the surface with a sickening force.

Adrian ran a hand through his hair, eyes wide in disbelief, as the massive wave crashed back toward the sea, enveloping everything in its path and dragging a dangling body into its depths. The sound of the water splashing echoed in his ears, mingling with the roar of the wind, and he felt the chill bite on his skin as he stood there, a witness to the raw, untamed power of nature.

Adrian's heart raced, a loud sound in his ears, as he scanned the tumultuous water, his gaze piercing the surface like a heron searching for prey. He stood motionless, every muscle taut and alert, his body leaning forward with quiet intensity. His weight balanced on the balls of his feet, like a bullet in the chamber, ready to spring at the slightest trigger. His trained eyes scanned for any indication of the surfer. The ocean churned beneath a layer of foam and turmoil, yet there was nothing—just the unyielding assault of waves crashing brutally against the shore. He observed the water's surface, the currents preparing for another wave to arise, to rise ever higher.

"Shit! Shit! Come on!" he muttered in his native language under his breath, the urgency of the situation sharpening his senses. And then, like a beacon in the storm, he spotted it: the surfer's board bobbing perilously, its sharp edges gleaming in the sunlight. But it was not merely drifting; it was being tugged down, pulled into the depths below. Adrian's heart sank, and a wave of despair washed over him. The leash, still entwined around the man's ankle, served as a fragile connection between the world above and the soul battling the streams of water, yet it became painfully clear that time was slipping away with every passing moment.

Adrian didn't hesitate. The moment he saw the board drifting like a fragile leaf on the chaos of the sea, his body moved before his mind could catch up. He grabbed his board, his fingers trembling with urgency, and sprinted across the sand, the grains clinging to his damp skin. The roar of the ocean filled his ears, drowning out all other sounds, its ferocity a stark contrast to the serenity it had promised at dawn. He plunged into the waves, feeling the chaos of the roaring water surge through his adrenaline-fueled veins.

Mounting his board, he paddled with a desperation that burned in his shoulders and arms, his breaths sharp and shallow. The sea resisted him at every turn, each stroke feeling like a battle against the rising wrath of the waves. The horizon pitched and rolled as he duck-dived beneath the towering swells, the cold grip of the ocean swallowing him whole before spitting him back to the surface. The salt stung his eyes, and the crash of waves thundered in his ears, but he pressed on, cutting through the shifting walls of water.

The board he had seen moments ago was now a fleeting memory, vanished, swallowed by the surging waves. The ocean seemed alive, her rhythm chaotic, as though she were testing his resolve. The vast expanse stretched around him, the once inviting waters now a heaving, wild expanse. Adrian's muscles throbbed, yet his determination blazed even brighter. He ducked under another wave, the force crashing above like a hammer hitting water, then surfaced, gasping for air and searching the horizon for any hint of life, only to be struck again by a wall of water.

He broke the surface once more, panting and feeling the salt sting his eyes. His heart raced as he scanned the horizon, yearning for a sign, for the soul he sensed calling to him from beneath the tempest.

Then, a massive wave surged, a towering force of nature that obliterated the fragile boundary between sky and sea. It roared as it crested, the spray blinding him momentarily as it broke, its power enough to make him falter. His heart pounded like a drum, his instincts sharpening to a knife's edge. The ocean wasn't just testing him, it was leading him.

Images flashed through Adrian's mind as he fought against the persistent force of the ocean. Memories surged up unbidden, vivid and sharp: the tang of salt and diesel, the muffled crack of gunfire over open water, the rhythmic hum of an engine beneath his feet. The weight of soaked gear pressing against his body, the suffocating cold of long nights spent waiting in the dark, the silent tension before an assault—all of it came rushing back. War had its own kind of chaos, but this? This was something primal. He wasn't fighting an enemy now; he was fighting the sea itself. And this time, there was no margin for error.

Tisha'er regua, tisha'er regua. Stay calm, stay calm, he told himself, forcing his breath to steady even as it burned in his chest. *You have to stay calm.*

The seconds stretched, long and merciless, like time itself had cracked open and begun to bleed—*shtei dakot,* Adrian thought, *two minutes* since the surfer vanished beneath the waves, two minutes too long. The sea punished him with every stroke, crashing into him like a living thing: salt stinging his eyes, water flooding his mouth, the taste of desperation thick on his tongue.

Still, he held to his board with white-knuckled fists, duck-diving under each towering swell as though he could outpace the fury of the storm, his body aching, his lungs burning, his limbs trembling with exhaustion.

And through the roar of the ocean, a voice rose inside him, steady and unshakable—*lo mash'irim af echad meachora. We don't leave anyone behind.*

He repeated it like a prayer, like a command carved into bone, something deeper than fear, older than panic, something the army had engraved into him: every soul matters, every life, every mother's son, and you do not stop, you do not turn back, not when someone is still out there, not when you are the only thing between them and the dark. So he paddled, half-blind and breathless, with the weight of the waves pressing down on him like judgment, because he had made a vow long ago, and Adrian had never once broken a vow.

He flinched at the thought. But there was no time for that right now.

A life given, for a life taken.

Then, he saw it. Out of the corner of his eye, a flash of motion—the board leapt skyward, caught in the maw of a towering wave, its leash snapping like a thread. The ocean was swallowing everything.

Adrian's decision came without hesitation. There was no fear, no doubt—only action. His body had been trained for this, conditioned to move through chaos like it was home. He had spent years in the military navigating the violence of storms, the disorienting crush of darkness, the unforgiving force of nature. This ocean was no different. A battlefield of its own, ruled by currents instead of bullets, by waves instead of explosions. He understood it. Knew its rhythm. Knew how to move within its fury rather than fight against it.

He ripped the leash from his ankle, the sharp tear of Velcro cutting through the wind like a gunshot. The board was no longer his lifeline, he had become his own. This wasn't about staying afloat. It was about diving in.

Somewhere, far in the back of his mind, reason whispered of the danger, the recklessness, the thin line between bravery and tragedy, but clarity burned through him like fire. There was a man out there who might not make it back, and Adrian would not let the sea take him. Not when he was still breathing. Not when he could still swim. Not when his soul had already decided: *You go in, and you don't come out without him.* Failure was not an option; Adrian would not allow himself to be the reason another soul did not make it back.

The moment his body hit the water, he was gone. Submerged. The cold slammed into him, the salt stung his skin, but none of it mattered. His body reacted before his mind could catch up. Years of training, endless drills of breath control, pressure adaptation, navigating murky depths with nothing but instinct; this was what he was built for. His lungs expanded, then compressed as he dove deeper, his kicks powerful, efficient, cutting through the water with the precision of a predator.

Darkness swallowed him whole. The surface became a distant memory, lost above the turbulence. The world above was just a muted roar now, a blend of wind and crashing waves all insignificant. Here, in the silent depths, he was back in his element. His heartbeat steadied, his mind cleared. He searched, scanning through the shifting blue, the flickers of movement in the abyss.

He reached forward, hands outstretched, the seconds stretching long. The ocean was taking him too. Pulling him deeper, testing him, daring him to lose his way. But he never did. Because he had done this before—not here, not in those waters, but in war. In night raids through enemy territory, in the suffocating heat of tunnels, in the pitch-black unknown where every breath might be the last.

Then, like a ghost in the deep, a silhouette emerged—a fragile, sinking figure outlined in the dim light filtering from above. Adrian's heart lurched. Time slowed as he reached forward, his hand closing around a wrist that felt far too still, too cold.

Adrian pulled the man into his arms, locking his grip around his shoulders as though to shield him from the ocean's wrath.

A life given, for a life taken.

The thought cut through him, raw and unbidden, as he fought against the tide pulling them ever downward. His muscles strained, the burn of lactic acid a cruel reminder of his limits, but he refused to let go.

With a ferocious surge of energy, he kicked toward the surface, the weight of the unconscious man and the drag of the water battling him with every motion. The ocean seemed determined to keep them, its relentless currents clawing at their limbs. The seconds stretched into agonizing minutes, each heartbeat feeling like a final toll.

When they finally broke through the surface, Adrian's lungs screamed for air as he gasped in the sweet relief of oxygen. His vision blurred, his ears ringing from the exertion, but he held the man's face above the turbulent water, cradling him against his chest. Holding him as tightly as possible, he battled the relentless waves, a choice crystallizing in his mind: that man would either come to shore with him, or neither of them would see another sunrise. The ocean roared menacingly around them, waves crashing against their fragile bond, but Adrian remained resolute, his determination solidified. He would not lose him.

The shore seemed impossibly far, but Adrian didn't care. One stroke at a time, one battle at a time, he propelled them both forward. The taste of salt filled his mouth, the ache in his limbs grew unbearable, but still, he swam. Each wave that crashed over them felt like a test, but Adrian held the man tighter, his own breath becoming a whispered prayer against the roar of the sea.

As he strained against the crushing weight of the water, every stroke a battle against the unseen forces pulling him under, Adrian found himself pleading—not with words, but with his whole being, a silent cry flung into the chaos around him. *Please,* he begged the sea, the storm, the universe itself. *Tachziri li oto... bevakasha. Al tikchi oto. Give him back to me. Please. Don't take him.* The words echoed inside him in his native language, the language of his mother, of his childhood prayers, of soldiers muttering hopes beneath breathless skies. *Titen lo od hizdamnut... rak od pa'am. Give him another chance. Just one more time.* The ocean roared in response, vast and voiceless, but Adrian kept going, whispering into the deep with every aching stroke, a prayer of salt and breath and love, begging the sea to surrender the life it had tried to steal.

The water crashed around him, each wave a reminder of the precarious balance between life and death. He could feel the ocean's might, an ancient force that had taken countless lives before, and he prayed that today would not mark another.

His heart raced with a mix of desperation and hope, the weight of his own life hanging in the balance. Would the ocean's mercy come at a price? Would she demand his own life in exchange for another? The thought sent a chill coursing through him, but he refused to let fear dictate his actions. All that mattered was the man in his arms, and the promise of survival that he clung to.

A life given, for a life taken.

With one hand braced around the man, he kicked fiercely with his legs, every stroke a battle against the sea's insatiable hunger. He could feel the weight of the ocean pressing down on them, but he fought back with every ounce of strength he had left, every trick he had learned from his hard-earned experience with the sea and its inexorable force.

Just as he felt the water threatening to engulf them once more, he surged forward, finally managing to hoist both himself and the man above the water.

Air filled his lungs again, but before he could savor that breath, another powerful wave crashed down, threatening to sweep them away. Gritting his teeth, Adrian held onto the man with a tenacity borne from his Navy training, refusing to let the surging tides reclaim him. The currents battled against him, and Adrian was driven past the point of exhaustion, yet he was determined to bring them both back to shore.

Breaking through the surface once more, Adrian felt a surge of hope washing over him like the warm sun breaking through a stormy sky. They were closer to the sandy haven now, the distant roar of the beach calling to him like a lifeline, a beacon of safety in the chaos of the ocean's embrace. With one hand still tightly gripping the man, he swam with renewed vigor, each stroke a desperate prayer sent to the ocean for both their safety.

But as the shoreline loomed nearer, a sickening realization settled in his gut: the man wasn't breathing. Panic threatened to overtake him, but he fought it back, focusing on the task at hand.

Once he finally reached the shallows, he laid the man on the wet sand, collapsing to his knees beside him, breathless and trembling. His throat burned from swallowing saltwater, muscles screamed in protest, and anxiety clawed at the edges of his mind.

None of them should have made it out alive. None of them should have seen the light of day again, only the forever darkness at the bottom of the ocean. Smaller waves had claimed the lives of more experienced surfers. But perhaps, at this dawn, the ocean had shown mercy, a rare kindness that let them stumble out of her depths, battered but breathing. Still, as Adrian looked at the man's limp body lying on the wet sand, he wondered if life had truly been spared or if only the vessel had been returned, emptied, like a shell tossed ashore after a fierce tide.

"Okay, relax," he murmured to himself in his native language, shaking off the haze of panic. "You know how to perform CPR." He didn't waste precious seconds checking for responsiveness; three minutes submerged was far too long for hope.

Adrian pressed his ear to the man's chest, his heart racing as he listened for any sign of life. The silence was deafening. No heartbeat. No breath.

Adrian silently thanked every soul on Earth that he had been trained in CPR. On that deserted beach, it was clear no one had called for help, and with no phone and no time to lose, it was all on him. Drowning cases were his specialty. He knew oxygen was the real threat, and that every second without it could cost a life. With his heart racing wildly in his chest, he quickly positioned his hands: one under the man's chin, the other on his forehead, tilting it back to clear the airway. He opened the man's mouth, feeling a rush of urgency as he prepared for the next steps. Then, he leaned in, tilting the man's chin upward, ensuring his airway remained open. Pinching the man's nose, Adrian pressed his mouth against his, delivering a deep, forceful breath. Then another.

With steady determination, he rose, pressing one hand firmly in the center of the man's chest, layering his other hand on top. He began compressions, driving his weight into the lifeless form beneath him, strong and fast—each push a plea for life.

"*Echad, shtayim, shalosh...*" One, two, three, he counted silently, the rhythm guiding him through the haze of desperation. Thirty compressions later, he bent forward again, tilting the stilled man's chin upward, closing the man's nose, and delivering two deep breaths with tender urgency.

He returned to the compressions, but he felt his hands begin to shake with exertion and despair. The man remained unresponsive. The vastness of the empty shore enveloped him, a desolate silence where no one lingered, no voice to call for help. If Adrian faltered now, this man would slip away in his arms, and he feared his soul could not endure the weight of another loss.

"No," Adrian choked, refusing to let despair win. He pressed again, counting another thirty, his breaths coming quicker, more frantic.

With each attempt, Adrian's eyes began to well with tears, a painful swell of emotion threatening to overflow. Panic nipped at his heels, crawling up his spine as he whispered a silent prayer, fearing that he was failing—that the man beneath him had already slipped away, rendered a mere corpse. "*Bevakasha ten'shom! Kadima! Ten'shom!*" Please breathe! Come on! Breathe! He implored, his voice thick with urgency and emotion, the words tumbling out in his native tongue.

His body was exhausted, every muscle screaming, but he pressed on. He poured everything he had left into those compressions, refusing to yield to the despair that threatened to consume him. He couldn't bear the thought of losing another life, of allowing another soul to slip away.

In the sixth round, as Adrian leaned in to deliver his breath, he felt it—a tremor beneath his palms, a twitch like a thread snapping back to life. Then suddenly, violently, the man's body jolted sideways, convulsing as a guttural cough tore through him. Saltwater surged from his lips in choking bursts, his chest heaving as he turned, instinctively, onto his side. His whole frame shuddered, breath returning not as a whisper but a struggle, loud and raw and full of fight. *"Toda la'el..."* *Thank God*, Adrian breathed, the words breaking across his tongue like a wave, his voice low, trembling with relief, as he stayed bent over him, heart pounding in rhythm with the storm still echoing in his blood.

The man was still coughing, breathing heavily as he moved to a sitting position on the sand.

Then his eyes opened—wide, searching, and startlingly alive—and in that instant, they locked with Adrian's. A flood of relief surged through him, so profound it made his vision swim, as if the world had tilted under the weight of grace. Those silver-bright eyes, rimmed with the storm's residue, cut through the fog of panic like light breaking through a shattered sky. Clarity met chaos, and for a heartbeat, time forgot how to move. The man's chest heaved with effort, breaths dragging in as if the air itself was unfamiliar. Confusion painted his face in soft strokes—furrowed brows, parted lips—as he fought to understand where he was, what had just gripped him and let him go.

And now, truly seeing him for the first time, Adrian felt something shift. Awe bloomed quietly in his chest, unexpected and disarming. The man's skin, pale from the sea's hold, held the faintest echo of sun-warmed bronze, remnants of a summer long gone. His lips were full, tinged a soft red and kissed by hints of blue. Sandy-blond hair clung to his forehead in wet strands, framing features that seemed sculpted from some lost ideal: a straight nose, high cheekbones, a face both striking and impossibly serene—as though even drowning couldn't take away the beauty written into his bones.

"Ani me'olam lo ra'iti mishehu kol kach yafe", *I've never seen anyone so beautiful.* Adrian whispered in his language, his voice trembling with a mix of wonder and disbelief, his gaze locked onto the man's face.

In that moment, as he looked down at the stranger's face, Adrian felt something deep and unshakable take root within him. The ocean hadn't just tested him; it had delivered him here. Two lives colliding in the tempest, two fates tied by the force of something far greater than either of them.

"What?" The man's voice, marked by a strong American accent and a raw, hoarse quality, conveyed a trace of confusion as he tried to understand the language Adrian was speaking.

Adrian blinked, momentarily startled by the intensity of his own feelings. He sank back onto the sand, burying his face in his hands, a surge of self-awareness washing over him for how long he'd been staring. The man remained seated, gentle breaths escaping him, his eyes now fixed on Adrian, probing, curious, as if reading a hidden story in his soul.

"What did you say?" he asked, his voice softer now, despite the lingering rasp from his ordeal. A flush of color crept into his cheeks, adding warmth to his striking features.

"Um..." Adrian hesitated, grappling with the truth that bubbled on his tongue. "I asked if you were okay." The words tumbled out, English tinged with a soft foreign accent; his voice shaky but steady as his eyes remained glued to the stranger.

The man frowned for a moment, processing the situation before nodding slowly, the memories of what had just transpired flickering across his face. "Wait here," Adrian blurted out, still out of breath, urgency propelling him to his feet. He jogged back to where he had dropped his water bottle, racing against the tide of emotions that threatened to overwhelm him.

Returning to the man, Adrian crouched and handed him the bottle, the gesture infused with a desperate need to help. "Drink."

The man took the bottle and gulped down its contents in one swift motion, thirst overriding all else.

"Does your head hurt? You might have a concussion..." Adrian said, jumping to his feet and beginning to pace restlessly, the adrenaline was wavering down, and the restlessness was kicking in. "You felt pretty hard, so you should probably see a doctor or something."

"I'm good," the man managed to reply, though his voice was strained, confusion still flickering across his features as he scanned their surroundings.

"Good." Adrian breathed, his voice was shaky as the truth of it gripped him—this man had been lifeless for far too long, and the image of that still body haunted him, the weight of mortality pressing down like the heavy surf crashing behind them. His heart tightened as memories threatened to resurface, but he forced them down. "You almost died there," he added in a soft voice, turning his gaze toward the ruthless waves that churned in the distance.

I almost died there... the words echoed in his mind. Dying while rescuing someone—perhaps that would be the noble sacrifice that would atone for the sins he carried, a chance to escape the haunting shadows of his past.

The man hadn't replied. He sat motionless in the sand, his broad shoulders hunched as though carrying the weight of the entire ocean. His head hung low, eyes fixed on the waves, the rhythmic roar of the sea filling the silence between them. His chest rose and fell unevenly, his breath still catching, as if the air itself resisted him.

Adrian remained nearby, his own heartbeat slowly settling, but his gaze stayed on the man. The stillness wasn't just physical, it was deeper, a kind of quiet that came from the soul, like someone caught between drowning and resurfacing.

The ocean's fury had softened, but its echoes lingered in the spaces between them, a reminder of how close death had been. Adrian wanted to say something, anything to break through the fog that seemed to shroud the man, but he hesitated. Words felt too fragile, too small for the enormity of what had just happened. Adrian was still wrestling with his own demons, trying to make sense of the moment that had just unfolded.

Casting a glance at the beautiful stranger sitting on the beach, Adrian felt a chill running through him, the memory of the coolness of his own lips a stark contrast to the mellow fire of the sun overhead. The taste of salt lingered on his tongue, a reminder of the struggle that had just unfolded. He could still feel the stillness of the man's body beneath his hands, the moments stretching into eternity as he fought to bring him back to life. The eerie silence where a heartbeat should have been beating haunted him, echoing in the recesses of his mind.

Adrian crouched low, the sand cool and damp beneath his knees as the storm's fading winds brushed against his skin. Compelled by an instinct he couldn't quite name, his fingers worked quickly to untie the black and silver bracelet from his wrist. The threads, worn yet strong, slid free with practiced ease, the lifesaver charm nestled at its center. The charm gleamed faintly, a small beacon of resilience that had carried him through more battles, more losses, than he could count.

It wasn't just a bracelet—it was a talisman, a piece of himself that had borne witness to his survival through impossible odds. It had saved him, he believed that. And now, it felt as though it had done so again.

"Here," Adrian mumbled, his voice low and uneven as he placed the bracelet on the sand between the stranger's thighs. He didn't meet the man's eyes, focusing instead on the delicate motion of his hands as if the act required precision. "It seems you need it more than I do."

He would never understand the need, the fierce, indefatigable urge to leave a fragment of himself with this man whose name he didn't even know. A man who, with a careless flick of his hand, could cast away this priceless shard of Adrian's soul, letting it vanish into the endless rhythm of the ocean, to the never-ending waves, to be lost forever in the deepest blue. Yet, something deeper, something primal, screamed at Adrian to offer it—to place this talisman of survival, this guard against the chaos of the sea, into the hands of the life he had wrested back from the ocean's grasp. It wasn't logic that drove him, but the quiet, aching hope that a piece of him might anchor this stranger to the fragile thread of life.

The weight of his words hung in the air, carried by the rhythmic crash of waves behind them. Adrian lingered for a moment, his body still crouched close, his gaze flickering toward the stranger's hands as they hesitated before reaching for the bracelet. The man's fingers closed around the cool metal, tracing the life saver charm with a touch that was almost reverent. It was as though he understood, on some unspoken level, the significance of the gift.

Adrian's chest tightened as he watched, his heartbeat loud in his ears. There was something sincere in the way this stranger, so close to the edge of life and death mere moments ago, now held the piece of Adrian's history in his hands. The sight stirred a storm within him, a sense of protectiveness that felt entirely out of place for someone he had only just met. But there it was, undeniable and raw, pressing against the edges of his carefully built walls.

Adrian shook his head, as if trying to scatter the thoughts before they could take root. *Too much sun, too much adrenaline, too much of everything,* he told himself. But his chest felt heavy all the same.

As he stood up, he sensed the snugness of his damp shortboards against his thighs, the material serving as a reminder of recent events. He looked over the water, looking for his board, knowing—and mostly wishing—it had to be floating nearby. Spotting it floating near the edge of the surf, he felt a small rush of relief. He really could not afford to replace this one.

"What's this?" The man's voice was rough, edged with confusion, as he turned the worn bracelet between his fingers. This marked the second and third words he had directed at Adrian—soft, wavering, carrying the undeniable heaviness of disorientation. His robust American accent wrapped around the words, anchoring him and drawing Adrian deeper into the moment.

His gaze flickered from the simple woven threads to Adrian, stormy eyes searching, seeking something he couldn't quite name. "What happened?" he pressed again, his voice stronger this time.

Then he rose to his feet.

And *God help him*, Adrian was not ready for that.

When he had pulled the man from the water, when he had carried his lifeless weight onto the sand, he had known—*felt*—the size of him. The sheer heft of muscle, the stretch of long limbs. But now, standing, fully upright, dripping seawater and shivering under the glistening light of day, the man was *massive*.

At least 1.96 cm. Easily 6'6".

Adrian, standing at just 1.73 cm, about 5'8", had to tilt his head back just to meet his gaze. It was ridiculous, unfair, how broad he was, how easily he could dwarf Adrian without even trying. The sunlight carved sharp shadows across his chest, catching on every ridge of muscle, every line of strength.

Adrian found himself staring, just for a breath, caught somewhere between awe and disbelief.

Then he shook himself free, tearing his gaze away before his thoughts could wander too far.

"You fell," Adrian replied, his tone barely above a whisper as if voicing the harsh truth would make it all the more real. He deliberately ignored the first question the man asked. "I think you lost consciousness when you hit the water... you drowned." The words felt heavy on his tongue, a weight he was reluctant to share. He turned his head, trying to distance himself from the intensity of the moment, and focused on retrieving his board.

"I think..." Adrian began, his voice soft, laced with a hesitant finality, as though the words carried more meaning than he intended. "I think I should go."

The thought of leaving sat heavy in his chest, a quiet ache he couldn't name.

Had he overstepped? Had he lingered too long, pressed too much of himself into a moment that wasn't his to claim?

He had done what he vowed to do—he had saved this life. Pulled it from the arms of the ocean. Breathed it back into existence with lungs that had known the sting of goodbye too many times.

The man was standing now, alive, breathing, his broad chest rising and falling as he processed what had just happened. Adrian observed him intently, the realization striking him of their proximity, the weight of what was left unsaid, how deeply intertwined their fates had become.

Every detail, every heartbeat felt amplified in the stillness between them, painting an unscripted narrative of longing and uncertainty. His own presence felt like an echo overstaying its welcome, a shadow pressed too long against someone else's light. A thousand doubts surged louder than the sea had ever dared. Adrian was no longer certain of his place in the unfolding story. The man—alive, upright, whole again—was a stranger. And Adrian... Adrian had given him something far more than breath. Adrian suddenly felt like an intruder, crouched too heavily on the fragile edges of this stranger's life. He had pulled him from the water, had pressed breath into his lungs, had offered something—something raw, something unspoken. What if the gesture had been too much? What if the bracelet meant nothing to him? What if Adrian, with all his tenderness and ghosts, had misread the moment entirely? Had he given a piece of himself where none was asked for, none was earned?

Surely, now, this man—tall, strong, resilient in his own right—would want solitude. Space to reclaim himself, to rebuild whatever the ocean had tried to take.

The tide had given him back.

Adrian should leave before he would allow himself to wish he could stay.

"Wait a sec," the stranger called out, his voice softer now, like the gentle lull between waves. "I... uh, thank you."

Adrian paused, the words striking something deep within him. "You're welcome," he replied instinctively, though his voice felt distant, like it belonged to someone else. The weight of the moment pressed against his chest, heavy yet strangely grounding.

"I'm Logan, by the way. What's your name?"

"Adrian." The name fell from his lips with surprising ease, yet it felt heavier somehow. He shifted his weight, ready to walk away, to put distance between himself and the strange, uncharted current pulling at his heart.

"Well, Adrian," Logan said, his voice dipping into something warmer, richer. Adrian shivered, not from the cold, but from the way his name sounded as it danced from Logan's lips. "You saved my life. Can I at least buy you a beer?"

"Um... I..." Adrian hesitated, caught off guard by the offer, by the sudden lightness in Logan's tone that cut through the lingering gravity of the moment.

"Please," Logan added, his voice laced with a quiet urgency that made Adrian's pulse quicken. "I insist."

"Okay... sure. Yeah, okay," Adrian stammered, the words spilling out in a rush, clumsy and unguarded. Heat crept up his neck, and he turned his face away, embarrassed by his sudden lack of composure under Logan's steady gaze.

Logan chuckled softly, a sound that carried an unexpected warmth, like sunlight breaking through the storm clouds that still lingered in Adrian's chest. "Good," Logan said simply, his smile tugging at the corners of his lips.

Pointing down the beach, Adrian added, "Your, huh... board is over there," directing Logan's attention to where a second board floated nearby. Without waiting for a response, he hurried to retrieve it, moving as though he could force his actions to appear casual. Each step was an attempt to mask the chaos of emotions bubbling beneath the surface, a clumsy effort to regain a sense of control amid the strange connection that had formed between them.

As Adrian ran toward his own board, the sound of waves crashing against the shore faded into the background, leaving him grappling with a mix of anxiety and a flicker of something he couldn't yet name.

"You sure you're okay?" Adrian asked, genuine concern filled his tone as he returned, balancing the two surfboards under his arm.

"Yeah," Logan replied, reaching out to take hold of his board. There was a softness in the way he spoke, a hint of vulnerability that lingered in the air between them.

"Don't worry about it," Adrian assured him, his tone gentle as he held the boards steady. The heat of the sun wrapped around them like a comforting embrace, yet an undercurrent of tension still crackled in the atmosphere.

Logan glanced down at his wrist, where the black bracelet now rested, its dark surface catching the light. "What's the story behind this bracelet?" he asked, curiosity igniting his gaze.

Adrian's eyes flicked to Logan's wrist, and a wave of surprise washed over him as he saw the bracelet already adorning the man's wrist. He allowed his gaze to linger for a moment on the delicate jewelry, a thread of connection binding them together, offering a sense of comfort he hadn't realized he was missing. It felt as if a piece of himself had found a home in Logan's presence.

"A lifesaver," Adrian finally replied, his voice carrying the weight of memories. "I got it years ago." They began walking inland, toward town, the soft sound of their footsteps mingling with the distant crash of waves against the shore.

The bracelet was a gift from his mother, a token she believed would protect him. Maybe it had saved him, after all Adrian was still here, having survived bloody battles of war, explosions, and his fair share of near-drowning situations. Now, it felt crucial to pass that protection forward, to let the man whose life he had fought to save carry it with him. He needed the man whose breath Adrian had revived to carry this talisman with him, a constant reminder that he was not alone in this vast, unpredictable world. The bracelet would be more than mere adornment; it would be a shield against the unknown, a tangible connection to the life he had almost lost and the second chance they had both been granted.

"It's amazing. Thank you," Logan murmured, a note of sincerity threading through his words. "But... it looks important, you shouldn't give it to me." He wrapped his fingers around the bracelet, a gesture both reverent and uncertain, ready to take it off and give it back to its original owner.

"No, I want you to have it. Like I said, you need it more than I do." Adrian's heart raced as he spoke, a fierce desire to protect this man awakening within him. He made every effort to avoid meeting Logan's gaze, to resist the pull of those silver eyes—like storm clouds, swirling with mystery and unspoken stories. They sparkled under the soft rays of sunlight, a light that transformed their depths into a fascinating dance of color.

Logan's sandy blond hair glimmered in the sunlight, each strand a waterfall of liquid caramel that seemed to capture the essence of the perfect day. As they walked together, Adrian felt the weight of the moment settle heavily on his shoulders, a profound mix of gratitude and anxiety coursing through him. The world around them faded into a blur, leaving only the two of them entwined in a fragile connection, one that had been forged in the depths of the ocean and the uncertainty of life itself.

As they moved along the shore, Adrian found himself glancing up more than once, quietly taken by the way the man's shadow stretched longer than his own—broad, steady, quietly commanding, like something carved by wind and sea.

Adrian's height had always been a source of insecurity, making him self-conscious. While 5'8" isn't considered short, it also doesn't qualify as tall in his mind, especially for a man.

Wearing only board shorts, the sculpted lines of Logan's torso and the ripple of his abdominal muscles were there, entrancing Adrian's gaze. Every step Logan took seemed to exude strength and grace, his long legs pushing him forward with an effortless ease that captivated Adrian. Adrian found himself unabashedly staring, struck by the sheer beauty of the man beside him.

Logan's barely sun-kissed skin glimmered in the afternoon light, and his tousled sandy-blond hair framed a face that seemed sculpted by the gods themselves. It was a stunning sight, yet Adrian felt a flush of embarrassment creeping up his cheeks, realizing he was lost in admiration. And it was not even the first time in those mere moments that he had known Logan that he had been staring at him. Thankfully, Logan appeared still a bit dazed and fatigued from their earlier ordeal, oblivious to Adrian's lingering gaze.

They walked in companionable silence, the rhythmic sound of waves crashing against the shore accompanying their footsteps. Adrian's mind raced with thoughts, each one flitting through like a fleeting wave, as he sneaked furtive glances at the stranger who now held his full attention. Logan, once just an anonymous figure battling the ocean, had transformed into a focal point of intrigue and unspoken connection.

Just when Adrian thought the quiet would stretch indefinitely, Logan broke the stillness.

"That's me," he said, gesturing toward a quaint cabin just a few feet away, its wooden structure nestled among the vibrant greenery. "Where are you staying?"

"Not far, but in another resort," Adrian replied, extending his hand to pass Logan his board, their fingers briefly brushing against one another, sending a jolt of energy through him.

"Are you free tonight?" Logan asked, taking the board from Adrian with a slight hesitation. "For that beer, I mean..."

"Sure," Adrian answered, feeling a swell of anticipation bloom in his belly like the first stirrings of a long-forgotten excitement. Even if Adrian hadn't been available, he would have come. There was nothing in this whole island or world that could have stopped him from meeting Logan tonight.

"So, um..." Logan started, glancing around as if the very answer lay hidden in the landscape. He realized he didn't know any places around here.

"There's a bar down that road. It's nice," Adrian offered, tilting his head to his left, keenly aware of the slight tension radiating from Logan. "I'll meet you there tonight?"

"Great." Logan's face broke into a radiant smile that seemed to brighten the very air around him, causing Adrian's heart to race with a rhythm that was a little too fast, a little too intense. "See you tonight, Adrian. How does around eight-thirty work for you?"

Adrian nodded, a grin forming on his lips in response to Logan's infectious enthusiasm. As Logan took a measured step back, their eyes intertwined in a fleeting, tender gaze, a fragile connection sparking briefly in the air, before he turned away and slipped quietly into his small cabin.

Once inside, Logan peeled off his board shorts with a mix of relief and exhaustion, the cool air brushing against his skin as he headed for the shower. He grabbed his shower kit from the bag, feeling a wave of relief wash over him as the water ran down his body. The warmth enveloped him, soothing his aching muscles and washing away the remnants of panic that still clung to him.

His chest ached, and his heart raced like a frantic bird trapped in a cage. The remnants of that harrowing fall were still reverberating in his mind. As he worked the shampoo through his hair, his thoughts drifted back to the moment he had first taken a breath, feeling warm lips pressing against his own.

Closing his eyes, he relived the moment he had been on his board, the thrill of the wave, and then—darkness. The next thing he remembered was coughing up half the ocean, saltwater invading his lungs.

Pain throbbed at his temples, each beat a reminder of how close he had come to losing everything. His throat felt raw, still burning, but he hadn't yet got a chance to buy a bottle of water.

I wasn't breathing, he thought, standing in the middle of the shower, watching the high waves crash against the shore beyond the large window. He wondered why Adrian had jumped in after him. It felt like a suicide mission, a reckless gamble against the sea.

If he saw me falling and decided to help, it meant he'd been watching. The thought made Logan's insides warm, a strange mix of gratitude and exhilaration unfurling in his chest. *What the hell?*

Logan struggled to fathom the foreign language Adrian had spoken earlier, each syllable a tantalizing enigma that danced just beyond his grasp. The melodic cadence lingered in his mind, echoing with a sense of urgency and passion that seemed to weave into the very fabric of the moment they shared. He recalled the way Adrian had looked at him, his eyes reflecting a complex tapestry of emotions—concern, relief, and something deeper that sparked a flutter of curiosity in Logan's chest.

As he sat there, the warm water cascading over him, he couldn't shake the vivid memory of that gaze.

As the last droplets of water flowed down his back, Logan emerged from the shower, invigorated yet contemplative. He toweled dry and slipped into a simple T-shirt and a pair of shorts, the fabric clinging comfortably to his skin, then stepped outside into the humid air of late afternoon. The salty tang of the ocean air filled his lungs, awakening his senses as he ventured off in search of the bar and a much-needed supply of water.

An hour later, he returned to the modest cabin, arms carrying a few crinkling supermarket bags. Inside were bottles of water, chilled beers, an assortment of snacks, and a few sodas. He stocked the fridge with his finds, taking another bottle of water after he had already drunk two on the way. Snatching his phone from his bag, he felt an involuntary shiver of anxiety course through him, but he pushed it aside as he collapsed onto the bed.

"This cabin might be crappy," he murmured to himself, a wry smile ghosting across his lips as he sank into the mattress, "but the bed is good."

As he turned on his phone, a wave of noise erupted from the screen—predictable text messages, missed calls, and urgent emails flooding his notifications. Since he had packed his bag and left home, he had deliberately kept the device silent, avoiding the preachy voices of his parents and the anxious concern of his friends, all of whom believed he was making a grave mistake.

He had taken a cab to the airport and boarded the first available flight, surrendering himself to the whims of fate, trusting it would lead him somewhere new, somewhere different. But as he stared at the screen, a dark thought flickered through his mind: *Fate wants me dead...* The idea was unsettling, a shadow lurking at the edges of his consciousness.

He sighed deeply, feeling the weight of the world pressing down on him. With each predictable message that pinged incessantly, he resisted the urge to read or respond. Instead, he silenced the phone and set it gently on the nightstand, where it sat like a dormant bomb waiting to go off. Then, without ceremony, he fell into a deep sleep, the exhaustion of the day washing over him like a gentle tide.

Logan jolted awake, heart racing, and peered outside to find night's embrace already settled in.

Damn it! Adrian! He snatched his phone, inhaling sharply as he noted it was only seven-thirty. Relief washed over him, and he sank back into the pillows, a smile breaking through the anxiety; how humiliating it would be to stand up to the very man who had saved his life.

Finally, he rose and stepped into a quick shower, the warm water chasing away the remnants of sleep. After brushing his teeth, he grabbed his bag from the floor, tossing it onto the bed with a sense of purpose.

He hadn't packed anything fancy—just a handful of basics: fitted tees, lightweight shorts, boardshorts, linen-blend pants, a pair of jeans, a hoodie, and one button-down, tucked into his suitcase more out of habit than need. Tonight, he reached for a slate-blue T-shirt, soft and snug at the shoulders, paired with tailored sand-colored chino shorts that hit just above the knee. He slipped on his clean white low-tops, worn just enough to suggest he lived in them but still kept them looking sharp. But as he glanced at himself in the mirror, running a hand through his hair, he caught the question lingering beneath the surface—*why do I care how I look?*

At the last moment, he darted into the shower, spraying a hint of cologne on himself, an instinct he couldn't quite explain. His heart raced wildly, an unexpected thrill coursing through him, and he reasoned it was merely the aftermath of a long, stressful day.

Exiting his cabin, he made his way to the bar, fervently hoping he was heading to the right place, aware of other establishments nearby. He found a table for two and informed the pleasant waitress that he was awaiting another guest.

It was eight-fifteen.

He rested his hands on the table, leaning back in his chair as his gaze drifted to the black bracelet encircling his wrist. The small, round lifesaver charm caught his attention, its metal slightly worn and weathered, a soft gleam hinting at age. The thin black leather cords had frayed just enough to suggest they'd been through time's gentle wear. His fingers traced them, feeling an unexpected fondness for the charm's quiet resilience.

"You're early," Adrian's voice cut through his thoughts. Logan looked up, meeting Adrian's gaze and instinctively pushing himself to stand before he could fully process it. In a rush of awkwardness, he nearly sent the chair sprawling but managed to steady it just in time. A flush illuminated his cheeks as he returned his focus to Adrian, who regarded him with a spark of mischief in his kind eyes.

"So are you," Logan replied, a subtle smile gracing his lips alongside the delicate blush that now adorned his face. He half-extended his hand for a handshake but faltered, a nervous chuckle escaping him before he offered it anyway. Adrian blinked in surprise, then accepted his hand, smiling at Logan with awe, and was that a blush there? Logan wondered.

There was an awkward pause—just long enough for both of them to feel it.

"Hey," Logan said awkwardly, retracting his hand after a handshake that had lingered a bit too long. His palm began to sweat, and he felt uncomfortably aware of his heart racing in his chest, with Adrian's gaze fixed on him.

"Hey," Adrian responded, a soft chuckle dancing on his full lips as he settled into the chair across from him. "Have you waited long?"

"Not really, maybe ten minutes." Logan returned to his seat, observing Adrian do the same.

Just then, the smiling waitress approached to take their orders, but Logan's eyes kept returning to the man across from him. Adrian's long, elegantly flowing hair, a blend of straight and wavy strands, fell gracefully over one shoulder, secured with a thin rubber band. Sun-kissed and bleached blonde, it revealed an undertone of faint brown roots that whispered of its darker origins, transitioning from deep hues at the base to shimmering highlights under the sun's loving embrace. His skin radiated a warm, sun-kissed glow, bronzed by the sun's rays. Dark stubble adorned his cheeks and chin, contributing to his distinctive allure and enhancing his charm.

A small smile began to unfurl on Logan's lips as he observed the man before him.

"Something funny?" Adrian asked softly, his voice as gentle as the ocean at dusk, as the waitress slipped away with their order, and Logan knew that he just mumbled faintly, "a beer" and went back to glance at Adrian as he talked to the waitress.

"No, sorry," Logan said, quickly averting his gaze. "This place is... really nice."

And it was. A small, inviting space, cozy with music loud enough to muffle the surrounding chatter but quiet enough to allow conversation.

"I know, right?" Adrian said, settling in, his hands resting casually on the table. His sleeves were rolled up just past the elbow, the soft fabric of his button-down framing forearms shaped by quiet strength. The collar was open just enough to reveal the suggestion of muscle beneath.

Logan tried not to notice. But he did.

Something flickered—uninvited, visceral. A split-second memory from earlier that day surfaced: Adrian standing next to him on the edge of the water in nothing but board shorts, water gliding down his torso, every line of his chest and abs catching the light like a sculpture breathed into life. The easy way his biceps flexed as he carried his board, the way his skin held the sun. Logan blinked, hard, shaking the thought from his mind as if it hadn't happened. It meant nothing. Just a flicker. Just heat. It wasn't anything.

"Have you been here long?" Adrian asked, unaware—or pretending to be—of Logan's gaze on him.

Logan shifted, his eyes dropping to the table as he cleared his throat. "No, not really. I actually got in this morning."

Adrian's eyes widened, brows arched. "No way!" he exclaimed, his accent roaring as he pronounced the words. "First day here and you're already making a scene in the ocean?" The line could've landed sharp, but it didn't. There was warmth beneath it, humor tempered by something gentler, like concern wrapped in sunlight.

"Yup..." Logan replied, laughing nervously. "What can I say? I like to make an entrance."

Just then, the waitress returned with their drinks and a plate of nachos, a perfectly timed rescue.

"So, I've got to ask," Logan ventured after a sip of his beer, setting the glass down with a soft clink. "And don't take this the wrong way…"

"Go ahead," Adrian leaned back slightly, lifting his drink. "I can take it."

Logan hesitated, then smiled, half-embarrassed, half-curious. "I can't quite place your accent," he said, realizing a beat too late how blunt it sounded. "I mean, sorry, I meant, where are you from?"

"An accent, really? Do I have an accent?" Adrian's eyes widened, and he feigned a look of deep offense, raising a hand to his heart. "How could you suggest that?" he added, thickening his accent deliberately, his smirk breaking into a low laugh. "It's fine! I'm from Israel."

Logan raised his brows, pausing with a nacho halfway to his mouth. "No way."

Adrian tilted his head, a slow smile tugging at the corner of his mouth. "Why not?"

Logan hesitated, trying to find words that felt true. "I mean… I've just never met anyone from Israel. You hear about it on the news, but…"

Adrian's expression shifted, the humor still in his eyes, but something steadier settled in behind it. "They love to spin stories, stir up fears. At that point, it's more antisemitism than actual news. The truth is, it's a beautiful country." He paused, eyes glinting with curiosity. "But you, no mistake where you're from. American, right?"

Logan tried to feign surprise, a grin playing at the corners of his mouth. "What gave me away?" he teased. "Seattle, Washington."

"Seattle? Never been there. Always wanted to see a big city like that," he said, leaning in just a little, as if drawn closer by Logan's words.

"It's not all skyscrapers and glamour," Logan replied, sipping his beer thoughtfully, "but I could show you around. We have beaches, too, ones you wouldn't expect."

A subtle pause hung between them, stretching like the tide pulling back before the next wave.

Adrian had imagined this meeting in a hundred different ways. If he was being honest, he'd spent most of the day circling it in his mind—picturing how it might unfold, fearing how it might fall apart. He had feared it would be stiff, filled with obligatory gratitude and a beer that neither of them really wanted. He had overthought it, running through every possible scenario, trying to temper the excitement that had sparked in him the moment Logan had opened his eyes on the shore. That spark had caught him off guard. He'd told himself it was adrenaline. Relief. Nothing more. But here, now, in the soft noise of a bar that smelled of sea air and Logan's cologne that drove him crazy, it didn't feel like nothing.

It was nothing like he'd expected.

The conversation flowed like an easy current, carrying them forward without effort. Adrian hadn't anticipated how natural it would feel, how every sentence seemed to unravel something deeper, pulling him in like an undertow he didn't want to escape. Logan wasn't just a man he had pulled from the sea—he was a quiet storm of his own, a contradiction of sharp wit and soft laughter, of eyes that held both gratitude and something else, something Adrian wasn't ready to name.

For a moment, their conversation fell into a tender silence, like the hush between waves. They leaned in, words lingering on their lips, tasting the promise of all that might follow. At last, Adrian broke the quiet, his voice soft, colored by curiosity.

"When did you first start surfing?"

Logan smiled, the memory already pulling him inward. "I was about nine or ten. We were getting ready for a summer vacation in Costa Rica. My mom had just bought me a camera, one of those waterproof ones, because I was obsessed with taking pictures. I'd spend hours on the beach, just watching the waves and trying to capture the surfers through the lens."

He paused, the edges of the memory soft and sunlit.

"I kept going back. Every day. Just standing there with my camera, taking the same shots over and over. I guess one of the surfers noticed how long I stood there watching. One afternoon, he came over. He didn't say much, just offered me a board. Told me I should try it instead of only watching it." Logan's smile deepened, quieter now. "He taught me that summer. Nothing official, just here and there—little tips, bits of balance, how to read the water. And I don't know... it just stayed with me. Like the ocean gave me something that never really left."

Adrian studied him, his interest warm and unguarded. "And now here you are," he said, the words almost a thought being uttered aloud, an ocean of secrets and unsaid words behind the soft voice and gentle, inviting smile. "How old are you now?"

"Twenty-four. You?"

"Twenty-five." A slight smile softened Adrian's features.

Logan looked at him, intrigued. "So, how did you start?"

Adrian's gaze dropped, his words slower now, thoughtful, as if each one needed to be chosen with care. "I was six," he said, his accent curling gently around the memory. "My mother had just died. Everything felt... hollow after that."

His eyes flicked toward the bracelet on Logan's wrist, then back to the table.

"My father... he didn't really know how to live without her. He was there, but not really. Just a shadow of himself. He was not in a good place, mentally, after she died, and I didn't really understand it." He paused, turning slightly to glance at the ocean beyond the bar, as though the memory had drifted there and he was trying to catch it.

"Some of my mom and dad's friends were surfers," he continued. "They started taking me with them. Let me sit on the sand, then on the boards, then eventually... they pushed me into the waves." He let out a breath. "They gave me a board that year. Encouraged me. Taught me how to move with the water instead of against it."

Adrian's eyes met Logan's for a second—quiet, unguarded—before looking down again.

"It was an escape, at first. But it became something else. It made me feel... steady. Like I belonged somewhere, even if it wasn't with anyone." He let a small, breathy laugh slip out, almost self-conscious. "It saved me," he said, voice roughening at the edges. "Back then, I didn't understand grief. I just knew I missed my mother. And I missed my father, like... you know I missed how he was before she..." A beat passed. He smiled faintly, then shook his head. "I'm oversharing, sorry."

"No. That's okay." Logan's voice softened. "I'm sorry. I didn't mean to... bring up anything painful."

"It's alright." Adrian's gaze was open, reassuring, as if the waves of the past had long since softened their edges. "It's been a long time."

Logan caught the waitress's attention, and they ordered another round, a quiet camaraderie settling over them. "So, how long have you been in

Hawaii?" he asked, trying to hide the fact that he'd been observing every detail of Adrian's face—the strength in his jawline, the way his laugh flickered just behind his whiskey-brown eyes.

"A week, give or take," Adrian replied, his gaze steady, almost as if he knew Logan's thoughts.

"So, you're heading out again soon?"

"No deadlines," Adrian replied, his words barely above a whisper, carrying a quiet invitation. "I'm in no hurry to leave here." The phrase hung between them, its meaning like a hidden reef beneath the waves. Did he mean here, this table, this instant suspended in time—or Hawaii, the island of dreams? But before Logan could follow that thread too far, Adrian's voice drifted on, easy and unhurried, yet touched by something deeper.

"I go wherever the world calls me," he continued, his gaze drifting somewhere distant, beyond even the horizon. "Australia's next... at least, that's what I think."

Logan's face lit up. "No way. I've always wanted to see Australia. Sri Lanka too. Those are my dreams, you know? To drift, to feel places rather than just see them."

"You should," Adrian replied, his eyes meeting Logan's with an almost electric sincerity. "I started about six months ago."

"And you'll keep going?"

"Until the world has nothing left to show me," Adrian said, his lips curving into a smile that held both lightness and gravity, "or until my money runs out. Whichever comes first." They laughed, lifting their glasses in a silent toast, and as they drank, they could each feel it—the undercurrent of a story yet unwritten, hanging in the balance between the present and the unknown, like a wave waiting to break.

"And you..." Logan started, the question slipping out with a softness he hadn't expected. "Traveling the whole world... alone?" Logan did not expect the expectation burning in his chest as he held his breath, waiting for the answer.

Adrian's mouth tilted in a faint, knowing smile that made Logan's heart stir—a look that carried something implicit, something shared only between them. "Not sure I'll see the *whole* world," Adrian's tone was as light as the night air, "but mostly, yeah. Solo." His eyes held Logan's a moment longer, that smile turning almost playful. "Though some friends are out there too, wandering their own trails. We meet up when we can. Surf. Hike. Drift."

Logan leaned in, something wistful pressing at his words. "Must be nice, to have friends willing to do that with you." He said it casually, like a small truth he barely noticed—as if it weren't a lie. As if he, too, had a circle of friends ready to follow him into new worlds.

Adrian nodded, watching him, a gentle understanding in his gaze. "In Israel, it's tradition," he began, his voice taking on a reflective note. "Everyone travels after the army." Adrian paused, catching Logan's questioning look. "It's a way of finding yourself, after years of being... someone else. I guess."

Logan's eyebrows lifted. "The army? Did you serve?"

Adrian nodded, a shadow of a memory in his eyes. "It's no big deal. In Israel, every citizen must enlist at the age of 18; it's the law. It's just life there. A rite of passage, part of growing up." But his words carried a weight, as if the past lingered beneath them, an undertow pulling him briefly back.

Logan dropped his gaze, tracing the edge of his beer bottle, a smile curling at his lips. "Where'd they put you?"

"Navy," Adrian said, his gaze drifting as if following something across a distant horizon, a faint, quiet ache there.

Logan chuckled, his laugh barely louder than a breath, touched by a sudden lightness. "Of course," he muttered, half to himself, shaking his head with a slow smile. "Well, that explains how you pulled off the impossible mission of rescuing me."

Adrian's gaze snapped back to Logan's, his eyes darkening, as if shadows of unspoken memories had flickered to life. For a moment, something haunted passed over his face—a vision of Logan, motionless, adrift in the ocean's unfeeling pull. He could still hear the silence beneath Logan's chest, feel the weight of those towering waves crashing toward shore, indifferent to life or death.

Then, as if severing himself from the memory, Adrian's expression softened; the smirk returned, quieter now, a look that reached across the table, bridging the fragile, wordless space between them. Their laughter faded, slipping into silence, as both felt the presence of what had just been shared and the countless words left unsaid. In that stillness, past and present seemed to fold together, binding two lives for this single, breath-held moment.

Adrian's voice dropped a little, teasing but genuine. "How about you? Are you traveling with anyone? Someone waiting for you back home... or maybe joining you out here soon?"

Logan gave a short laugh, low and almost sheepish, shaking his head. "No," he said simply, and for a beat, something flickered through his expression; a brief, raw honesty he didn't bother hiding. "Just me."

Adrian nodded to him and took another sip of his drink.

"I can't believe I haven't asked you this yet," Adrian murmured, shaking his head in frustration at his own manners. He was drawn to Logan, utterly captivated, as if Logan were the ocean itself and he felt the overwhelming need to immerse himself in that depth. "How are you feeling?" Adrian asked, his gaze locking onto Logan's silver-gray eyes, searching for the truth hidden within their shimmering depths.

"Way better," Logan replied. "I slept, drank about a gallon of water. I feel like a human again." Even as the words left his mouth, the air around them began to shift. The previously quiet and lazy atmosphere of the bar transformed into a lively buzz. Tourists flooded in, their laughter and chatter rising over the soft music, filling every crack and corner with noise. The music grew louder, the bass thrumming against the floorboards like a restless heartbeat. Logan felt the crowd pressing closer, an invisible wall of energy that made the air heavier with every passing second.

He stiffened slightly, glancing around as the easy quiet he had enjoyed with Adrian dissolved into chaos. He was familiar with crowded places filled with people—having traveled through countless cities and encountered endless new faces through his life—yet tonight, he found himself longing, craving the stillness, not noise. He had wanted this moment to stay small, just the two of them, untouched by the piercing world outside.

A flicker of unease passed through him as he turned back to Adrian. What if Adrian thrived in this? What if he loved the pulsing crowd, the heady thrill of a summer night in Hawaii? Logan's chest tightened with a quiet, unfamiliar panic. If Adrian wanted to stay, to revel in it all, Logan would force himself to stay too—even if every fiber of him ached for the quiet they'd just lost. Because somehow, already, the idea of leaving this moment, leaving *him*, was worse than the noise.

Logan wasn't ready to part ways; he wasn't ready to end this night with Adrian. It had been so long since he had felt a genuine connection with another person, and their conversation flowed like a gentle breeze, effortless and inviting. He craved for this evening to stretch on, yet the encroaching crowd threatened to drown out their intimacy, the noise rising, pushing against the fragile sanctuary they had carved out for themselves.

"Do you want to leave?" Adrian asked, his voice low, almost casual, though Logan could feel the weight behind it. Adrian had noticed the way Logan's eyes kept drifting over the crowd, the way his shoulders had tightened, the quiet distress he hadn't managed to hide.

"Ummm... I huh..." Logan hesitated, caught off-guard. He didn't know what the right answer was. If he said yes, would Adrian simply wish him a good night and slip back into the sea of people without him? If he said no, would they stay here, surrounded by noise, with the fragile thread between them stretched thin until it snapped? Panic, swift and disorienting, curled in Logan's chest, and before he could think better of it, he blurted, "Are you hungry?" The words felt clumsy and too loud in his ears, but it was something—a tether he threw between them, desperate and a little breathless.

For a heartbeat, Adrian just looked at him, and Logan steeled himself for the sting of rejection. But then Adrian smiled, a single note struck in silence, vibrating through everything in him—a slow, effortless beam that brightened his eyes and brought forth a gentle nod. And just like that, the tight, anxious coil inside Logan began to loosen, the crowded room fading a little around them, as if they had built a small world of their own.

Logan spotted the waitress weaving through the mass and called her over for the check. Moments later, she set it on the table, and Logan noticed Adrian's hand reach for it. In a swift motion, he snatched it up, fishing for his wallet with the other hand.

"Forget it," Logan insisted, a warning in his voice. "It's on me. No arguments," he warned, his tone firm yet playful. His eyes flicked to the total, and he pulled out bills, adding a generous tip for the waitress. Logan waited, watching as Adrian rose, each movement captivating him, and he was drifting in their bubble. They moved toward the exit in unspoken harmony, their footsteps soft and measured, both trying to maintain a socially accepted distance while being pulled to the aura of one another.

Outside, the night unfolded like velvet, the air thick with the scent of salt and hibiscus, the cool bite of the breeze brushing against their skin. There was something electric woven into the darkness, a subtle promise of possibility, humming in the spaces between streetlights.

"Do you have a good restaurant in mind?" Adrian asked, his voice low and smooth, the words lingering in the night air like smoke.

Logan glanced over, catching the small, eager glint in Adrian's eyes, and felt a strange flutter in his chest he couldn't explain. "I'm not picky. You've been here longer, anything good I should try?" he replied, and as he spoke, his stomach gave a low rumble of agreement, reminding him just how long it had been since he'd eaten anything real.

Adrian smiled—not the casual grin he'd worn before, but something softer, almost shy, before slipping his gaze back to the road ahead. "Well... there's this place that's kind of known for its garlic butter shrimp and kalua pork, and Spam musubi," he said, laughing a little awkwardly. "But I'm Jewish," he added quickly, scratching the back of his neck in a gesture that made him look boyish for a moment. "I don't keep kosher strictly, but... I still avoid pork and shellfish. It's sort of wired into me, you know?" he glanced at Logan. "But I don't mind going with you, really."

There was a hesitant pause, like he was expecting Logan to be disappointed.

But Logan only gave him a dry, unimpressed look, the kind that carried a quiet sort of loyalty without needing to be spoken. "No, of course I don't want that. Take me to a good place *you* eat around here. I have no problem trying something new," he said easily, without a flicker of hesitation.

Adrian turned his head toward him, as if the words had caught him off guard, his smile widening into something warmer, something that touched the edges of his eyes. "Thanks," he murmured, almost sheepish. "And I'm sorry—" Adrian started to add, but Logan cut him off, nudging his shoulder with his own in a light, familiar way that sent a surprising jolt of happiness through Adrian's chest.

"Don't you dare," Logan said firmly, grinning. "Come on. I'm starving. Get me to a place that's got some good food before I waste away."

Adrian smiled, a glint of fondness in his gaze as he pointed down the dimly lit street. "It's this way," he said, stepping forward.

Logan matched his stride without a second thought, the two of them falling into rhythm as they paced side by side, their bodies cutting through the humid air like familiar shadows. Around them, the town drifted by in soft edges: the glow of porch lights, the murmur of late-night conversations, the distant crash of the ocean hidden beyond the trees.

Adrian led him through a maze of winding streets, past closed surf shops and darkened cafés, until they reached a small restaurant tucked beneath a cluster of swaying palms. Its porch was wrapped in strings of golden lights, spilling warm halos onto the worn wooden boards. The tables outside were half-empty now, the dinner rush long gone, leaving only a few locals lingering over their late plates, speaking in low, lazy tones that blended with the sigh of the sea.

It was perfect—quiet, unhurried, open to the stars—and simple in a way that still felt like a gift.

They chose a table near the railing, where the breeze slipped through unhindered, carrying with it the mouthwatering scent of grilled fish, roasted vegetables, and spices. Logan let out a breath, letting the night fold around him, the worries and noise of the bar falling away.

Across the table, Adrian leaned back in his chair, his fingers lightly drumming against the wood, his eyes catching the light and holding it there—not sparkling exactly, but alive with something bright and almost secretive. And somehow, even though they had just met, Logan felt as if they'd stepped into a different world entirely—one carved out of salt air and soft smiles and the slow, sweet ache of something beginning.

Two menus were set before them, but Adrian was hardly aware, lost in the pull of Logan's presence, a magnetic warmth that seemed to hold the room itself still. Adrian watched, captivated by the way Logan's silver-gray eyes glinted in the dim light, occasionally darting up to catch him looking, then dipping back to the menu. His gaze wandered, resting on Logan's mouth, which softened when he spoke, and on his grayish-blue shirt that accentuated the lovely gray tones of his eyes. The shirt clung to his wide frame, enhancing his intensity. A flash of humor danced through Adrian's mind: *who on earth had gray eyes?*

"What're you having?" Logan asked, setting his menu down with a satisfied thud. "I'm going for the fried fish plate," he continued, a grin curling at the edge of his mouth. "Fries on the side. Maybe the poke bowl, too, why not? And whatever beer they have on tap."

"Sounds good, I'll have the same," Adrian replied easily, setting his own menu aside, though he hadn't really looked at it. The truth was, he would have ordered anything Logan chose. His focus wasn't on the food, not really. It kept slipping back to Logan, to the way the ocean breeze lifted the collar of his shirt, to the way the dim candlelight carved soft gold into the strong lines of his face.

Logan, for his part, was now eyeing the small candle flickering between them, housed in a simple glass cup. Without warning, Logan reached across and pinched the flame dead between his fingers. Adrian's hand flew to his mouth, stifling a laugh that spilled over in bursts. He shook, barely breathing from laughter, the absurdity of the gesture catching him off guard. "What?" Logan asked, his brows drawing together in mock confusion, though a smile tugged insistently at his lips.

"You—" Adrian gasped between laughs, wiping at his eyes as if it would somehow stop the tidal wave of joy rolling through him. "You couldn't leave the candle alone, could you?"

Logan's half-smile finally broke into full laughter, deep and rough and entirely contagious. They leaned into it, the two of them caught in a shared, fleeting weightlessness, the kind of laughter that felt as if it had been waiting for them all night, tucked in the folds of the dark, waiting for the right moment to unfold.

"Fuck you," Logan smirked, pointing across the table at Adrian, who only laughed harder.

As their laughter faded, leaving a faint warm glow in its wake, Adrian's gaze settled on the man across from him, a stranger yet so oddly familiar. He knew almost nothing about him, yet the pull was undeniable.

"So, what do you do for a living?" Adrian asked, curiosity lacing his voice.

"Nothing." Logan shrugged, an easy roll of his eyes and a smirk playing at his lips. "Just graduated with my master's... what, two days ago? Lost track of time." He rubbed his neck absently. "Anyway, I graduated, packed a bag, and now... well, now I'm here."

Adrian leaned forward, intrigued. "Just like that? No plans, no deadlines?"

"Yup." Logan exhaled, eyes drifting past Adrian, as though seeing the open road. "I worked a bit through undergrad and grad school, but nothing serious. I had a job lined up... but I kind of ran away from it." A faint shadow crossed his face, like the brush of a cloud against the sun. "Guess it can wait."

"What did you study?"

"Business administration and economics."

Adrian's eyebrows lifted. "Wow, that sounds—"

"Boring?" Logan cut in, a sly smile tugging at his mouth.

"Actually, I was going to say challenging." Adrian chuckled. "Did you enjoy it?"

Logan shrugged, the easy grin slipping into something a little wryer. "Not really. College was alright, but business?" He rolled his eyes dramatically. "Econ was fine, I guess. But it was hard to care about supply and demand curves when all I really wanted was to be by the ocean." He grinned then, the boyish light returning to his eyes.

"I get that," Adrian replied, grinning back. "But somehow, I can picture you as the math type."

"Ugh, no way." Logan threw his head back, groaning with mock agony. "Three classes of math were all it took. I swear, I almost tried bribing my professors just to survive. But chemistry was the real nightmare. I stared at my professor so blankly that she thought I was having a stroke."

Adrian laughed, the sound rich, filling the air between them. He watched Logan talk, every gesture animated, his bright smile radiating. It sent a quiet thrill through Adrian's chest, one he couldn't explain. He felt it deep, the kind of stirring that crept in when least expected, the kind that lingered.

Logan's voice softened, and he looked at Adrian with a spark that felt like a secret shared. "But hey, at least marketing and trading, stocks... they made sense. Sort of."

Adrian nodded, though he hardly heard the words, his thoughts swirling, caught in the rare, perfect alchemy of this moment. The restaurant faded into a blur, leaving only the two of them at that little table, framed by the hum of the sea beyond.

The waitress arrived, setting their plates down with a clink and a flourish, the scents of char-fried fish and crispy fries enveloping them. They dug in, speaking here and there, casual exchanges drifting across the table like leaves caught in a gentle current.

When Logan excused himself to the restroom, Adrian watched him go, feeling a slight hollow where Logan's presence had been. He called the waitress over. "Excuse me," he murmured, a half-smile at his lips. "Do you happen to have a lighter?"

"Of course," she replied, reaching into her pocket and handing him a small silver lighter. Adrian flicked it, the tiny flame dancing to life. He leaned forward, lighting the candle that sat between them, feeling a flicker of his own satisfaction as the soft light settled over the table once more. He returned the lighter, exchanging a quick word of thanks as she cleared their empty plates.

Moments later, Logan returned, pausing ever so slightly when his gaze fell on the candle, its flame casting a golden halo that seemed to draw his attention. He shook his head, a faint smirk tugging at his lips as he rubbed the back of his neck.

"The waitress came over and saw that the candle was off," Adrian explained, the words smooth but laced with mischief. "So, she thought she'd light it again."

Logan narrowed his eyes, suspicion flashing behind the growing grin he couldn't quite suppress. He shook his head, laughter bubbling under his words. "You're full of shit," he muttered, the tenderness in his voice undeniable.

He leaned back in his chair, studying Adrian with a look that made the small flame between them feel somehow brighter, as if it fed on the gravity building quietly across the table.

"For dessert," Logan said, flashing an easy, mischievous smile, "what are we having?"

Adrian matched his grin, the playfulness lighting up his face. "I still haven't tried anything from the desserts, actually," he admitted.

"Well, then we have to," Logan said firmly, flipping the menu back open and scanning the options with theatrical seriousness. His eyes caught on something, and he looked up, triumphant. "Chocolate haupia pie. That's it," he declared.

Adrian laughed, the sound low and genuine, and gave a small nod of agreement. "Chocolate haupia pie, it is."

As they stepped out into the cool night air, Adrian sighed, a hand on his stomach. "I'm going to sleep for a week after that meal."

Logan chuckled, his voice rolling against the crisp breeze. "Oh, come on. I bet you'll burn it off by morning."

"Only if I can walk by morning," Adrian groaned, glancing at Logan with a grin. They ambled back toward Logan's resort, taking the longer way back, each step a little slower, savoring the night that lingered between them. His stomach still full, Adrian couldn't help but think back to their half-playful, half-serious argument when the check arrived—how Logan had stubbornly insisted on paying, his voice unwavering, saying it was only fair since he'd invited him. He remembered the look in Logan's eyes, unexpected and impossibly direct, a look Adrian had no defense against, not tonight, not when everything between them was still so new. It caught him off guard and left him unable to argue. Adrian sensed, maybe Logan did too, how quickly he could be pulled under that soft, intent gaze Logan seemed to slip into without even noticing.

"Thanks for tonight," Adrian said softly as they reached Logan's cabin. The air was still, weighted, as though something more should follow, something to keep the night from closing. "Oh, I almost forgot!" Adrian slipped a hand into the pocket of his shorts and pulled something free. "This is for you."

He pressed a new board leash into Logan's hands. He had meant to give it earlier, back at the bar, but the moment he sat across from him, his mind had emptied. The words he'd rehearsed scattered like sand, and all he could do was watch Logan speak, as though under some spell.

Logan's eyes moved from the leash to Adrian's face, dumbfounded, his breath caught somewhere between them.

"Yours... it broke? Or tore?" Adrian frowned, searching for the word. "I don't know the right word. But I got you this."

The leash felt heavier than it should have in Logan's palm.

"Thank you," Logan murmured. "You really didn't have to."

"It's nothing." Adrian shrugged, too quick, almost embarrassed. "There are many surf stores here, but not all good ones. Didn't want you buying something bad." His smile wavered, a shy, uncertain curve of the mouth.

Logan tightened his grip around the leash, as though holding onto something more than cord and rubber. He dragged a hand through his hair, restless, clumsy, trying to scrape together the courage that stalled in his throat.

"Thank you." He said again.

Silence settled between them, taut and uncertain, neither of them sure how to step into the next breath.

Logan's throat worked, a rough sound breaking free as he scraped against the edges of his own fear. His body leaned forward, then stilled, caught between retreat and confession. For a heartbeat, it seemed he would let the moment collapse, that he would simply nod, turn, and vanish into the night, just as the world had trained him to do.

But something in him—something small and scared and breaking open—made him stumble forward: "So, um... will I... see you around tomorrow? At the beach, maybe? Or whatever," he added quickly, tossing the words out like loose change, pretending he didn't care even as they scraped his throat on the way out.

He was aiming for casual, for breezy, for harmless. He missed by a mile.

Beneath the surface, he reached out, aimlessly and perhaps unwittingly, driven by a desperate hope that filled him with dread. What if, in the days ahead, their eyes met, and Adrian simply bestowed that courteous, detached smile commonly exchanged with strangers? What if tomorrow, their paths crossed, leading to nothing more than a nod, a casual, "Hey man," or a "How's the surf?" before they parted ways, the memory of tonight fading into just a whisper in the dark?

Would Adrian be enveloped in laughter among the other surfers, arms draping over sun-kissed shoulders, while Logan remained a silent observer, lost to the shadows? Would he catch a glimpse of Adrian sipping drinks beneath the soft glow of string lights, vibrant and full of life, while Logan lingered on the outside, feeling like nothing more than an afterthought, a fleeting presence without meaning?

That was fine.

It was fine.

They barely knew each other. They weren't friends. Barely acquaintances.

It wasn't supposed to matter.

It *shouldn't* matter.

Then why did it feel like the ground would fall out from under him if Adrian just... moved on?

The night itself seemed unwilling to let them part, weaving around their ankles, tugging at their sleeves, whispering, *stay, stay, stay.*

Logan swallowed hard against the tightness rising in his throat, so thick it almost choked him. He jammed his hands deep into his pockets, anchoring himself there, willing himself not to reach out, not to say something reckless, something stupid, like *don't go yet* or *show me around the area* or *do you want to come in?* Anything to keep that feeling alive, to keep Adrian there for a moment longer.

He wanted—*needed*—to say something, anything, to tether this moment to something real, to carve it into the world before it slipped away.

But the words stayed trapped behind his teeth, trembling and wild.

And so he stood there, silent and aching, hoping to God that Adrian would understand everything he couldn't say.

"Yeah," Adrian replied, his voice light, stepping back just a touch, careful, measured.

He could see it; the confusion flickering inside Logan, the way he started, almost imperceptibly, to raise his protective walls, as if bracing for something he didn't even understand yet. Adrian had spent the whole evening doing nothing but watching him, studying him, letting himself be quietly, hopelessly drawn in. So even the smallest shift in Logan's posture, the slightest flicker in his eyes, was obvious to him, was sharp and blinding and imperative.

There was nothing, absolutely nothing on this earth, that could have kept Adrian from showing up tomorrow if Logan only wanted him there. Did he not see? Did Logan not grasp that Adrian lingered, waiting for just a hint, a fleeting opportunity to gaze upon him again, to bask in his orbit for one more hour, one more breath? That every smile Logan had graced him with tonight, Adrian had consumed like a starving man, desperate, thankful, almost in awe, surprised by how much it mattered, how much it unnerved him? That Adrian, without fully understanding why, would have traversed any distance, faced any challenge, simply for the chance to stand before him once more?

Yet, he was unable to voice any of those thoughts. Instead, he chose to tease, yearning to elicit that smile once more. "Six a.m.? I'll teach you to swim," he teased, a glint in his eyes.

Logan's mouth twisted into a mock scowl, though a smile quickly overtook it. "Go to hell!" he snorted, unable to keep from laughing.

Adrian started to walk backward, a teasing grin tugging at his mouth. "Don't forget your floaties!" he called out goodheartedly, his whisky-colored eyes sparkling with mischief, his long hair flipping in the breeze as he moved. He stole one last glance—quick, almost coy—at the tall, beautiful man he'd been lucky enough to spend the evening with, imprinting the moment into his memory before he finally turned and let the night surround him.

Logan was smiling, and that was all Adrian had wanted—a small, quiet victory tucked safely into his chest.

The first thing Logan felt as he drifted awake was a peculiar, almost aching excitement. It settled in his chest like a weight, a pleasant pressure that spread outward, filling every corner of his body with an electric warmth, a strange rightness that he couldn't quite name. He lay there for a moment, savoring the way it tingled down to his stomach, sending small sparks that made him want to laugh for no reason at all.

Blinking to clear the last shreds of sleep, he gazed up at the ceiling, his eyes resting upon a knot in the wooden beam. Gradually, he allowed the sleep to evaporate from his mind. With a yawn, he reached for his phone.

It was 5:40 a.m.—the early rays of the sun emerging, the world outside soft and untouched. With a jolt, he swung his legs over the side and got up, his steps quick as he padded to the bathroom. The cool water felt sharp and refreshing against his face, the mirror catching his reflection, a face that felt both new and deeply familiar, softer somehow, less guarded. He hardly recognized the relaxed man staring back.

Grabbing his board shorts from the day before, now dry and smelling faintly of salt, he slipped into them, then rummaged through his bag until his fingers found the sole black hoodie he'd packed. He tugged it over his head, sparing his unpacked bag a glance but feeling no urge to tend to it just yet.

He stepped to the small kitchen table where the brand-new leash lay waiting, the one Adrian had pressed into his hands the night before. Logan picked it up, turning it over slowly between his palms. Adrian was still a stranger... or he should have been. How could it be that after a single night he felt the pull of him so sharply? How could it be that Adrian, not even knowing him, had thought ahead, had bought this for him?

The leash was only gear, yet in Logan's hands it carried more: a gesture, a promise, a reminder that someone had already chosen to care.

His fingers moved with unsteady urgency as he fastened it to his board. The rip of Velcro echoed in the quiet, clean and final, and something in him settled, as if the sound had tethered him not only to the board, but to Adrian too. He paused only to tuck a few bills into his pocket before grabbing his board and slipping out into the cool early morning air.

The coffee shop's glow was a welcome sight against the dimness, and he ducked inside, the smell of coffee thick and rich in the air, warming him even before he placed his order, as he watched the staff still preparing the place for the busy day ahead. He ordered two large cups, figuring Adrian might prefer his coffee black. Wasn't there some saying about military types taking it that way? Logan stuffed a few sugar packets into his pocket just in case, the rough paper crinkling softly. A tray of mini donuts on the counter glistened under the lights, so he grabbed a cardboard containing six and nodded gratefully when the clerk, noticing his juggling act, packed everything neatly: a paper bag for the donuts and a small cardboard carry-on for the cups so he could carry everything while still balancing his board under his arm.

As he reached the beach, he spotted Adrian already down by the water, lounging with the practiced ease of someone who lived close to the sand and sea. Wearing a pair of light blue board shorts, his sun-kissed hair flipped in the breeze, caressing his bronzed, broad shoulders. The morning light played across his skin, casting a warm glow against the pale dawn as waves broke rhythmically, their foam lapping at his toes. The scene sharpened every one of Logan's senses, the last traces of sleep lifting like mist in the rising sun.

Logan drifted closer to Adrian, unsure whether the pull guiding him was the ocean's eternal song or the quiet magnetism of the man stretched out on the cool, damp sand.

As he approached, Adrian's whiskey-colored eyes lifted to meet his, lighting with a smile that broke slowly across his face. His gaze was so unguarded, so utterly intent, that Logan felt seen to his very core, as if, for Adrian, he was the essence of something vital. The feeling was as disorienting as it was familiar, as if drawn from a place older than memory. Could this truly be only their second meeting? It felt instead like an ancient recognition, two souls long entwined, meeting anew.

"Hey," Adrian greeted kindly, just a simple word compared to what was going on in Logan's head.

"Hey," Logan replied, "morning," he added, flustered.

"For a moment there, I thought that you might have overslept," Adrian smirked timidly.

Logan sat down beside Adrian, the sand clammy and chilly beneath him, and he placed his board down carefully before handing Adrian one of the steaming cups. Adrian took it, and for a heartbeat, he gazed at Logan with a kind of surprised warmth. "No, just stopped for some coffee. You cannot start a morning without a coffee."

"Th... thanks," Adrian flustered, his voice quiet and genuine like it was a gift in itself. "I'm glad you came," he added, almost reverently.

"Yes, of course." *I would not have missed it for the world.* He found his mind uttering, almost sharing that too-intimate detail with the man beside him. Logan popped open the donut box and grabbed one for himself.

"You're eating six donuts at six in the morning?" Adrian inquired, a playful glint in his eyes and a smirk dancing on his lips as one eyebrow quirked up in curiosity.

Logan grinned around a mouthful, his lips sugar-dusted, the bitter taste of coffee still curling in his throat. "Nope," he said, smug, licking glaze from his thumb. "I'm eating three donuts at six in the morning." He nodded toward the open box between them with theatrical seriousness. "Come on, eat up."

"Is this your idea of pre-surf nutrition?"

"If you're a health nut, please say so now. That way, we can go our separate ways before things get too real." His smile cracked wider as he chewed. "Mmm. Tastes like happiness."

The joy in Adrian didn't just rise—it *bubbled*, fizzing through his chest like champagne, quick and effervescent. It startled him that Logan could make the world seem so light just by sitting beside him, barefoot in the sand, talking through a mouthful of sugar. Logan was... something. Alive in a way that seemed to crackle, captivating without effort, clever without arrogance, careless and charming and infuriatingly magnetic.

He didn't know how to contain it—Logan—so he didn't even try.

"You going to stare at me all morning," Logan murmured, voice lower now, teasing but edged with something warmer, "or are you going to eat something? We've got a lot of energy to burn today."

Adrian's face flushed, heat blooming across his cheeks and crawling down his neck. He dropped his gaze too fast, tried to disguise the movement with a casual sip of coffee, but his hands betrayed him with the slightest tremor.

His stomach twisted—hunger, maybe, or nerves—but either way, food was suddenly the last thing he could imagine keeping down.

"Hum..." he began, voice thinner than intended, catching himself mid-thought, mid-glance, as if realizing too late that he'd been watching Logan like he was a work of art—delicate, surreal, maybe too bright to look at directly. "I..."

Words failed. Not because he didn't have them, but because none of them felt true enough.

"Well," Logan said, breaking the silence with a slow, lazy drawl. He reached into the box, pulled out another donut, and turned to Adrian with a half-smile. He held it out, inches from Adrian's face, like it was a dare. "Here. Consider this a peace offering. Or a bribe."

Adrian stared at the donut. Then at Logan. "You always this pushy?"

"I'm not pushy," Logan said, his tone dropping just slightly, like he was letting Adrian in on a secret. "I'm... persuasive." Then, after a breath, "Besides, I'm really doing this for me. If I need rescuing again, I need you at your prime."

In an instant, a wave of dark thoughts engulfed Adrian. The casual tone with which Logan recounted his near-drowning experience was unsettling; it felt surreal. A vivid image rushed to Adrian's mind—Logan lying motionless on the sand. The heart-wrenching vision made Adrian's heart shatter in its confines, and a chill coursed through his veins.

Adrian tried to dispel those lingering thoughts, turning his attention to Logan sitting beside him, amidst the breathtaking beachscape on that glorious morning.

"You're impossible," Adrian muttered. His lips quirked just enough to reveal the fondness stitched into the words.

For a fleeting moment, Adrian contemplated leaning in and biting into the donut held out by Logan, sensing that perhaps this was Logan's intention. Yet it felt too soon, too overwhelming, a connection too intimate to share with someone he had only known for a day. It seemed like crossing an invisible boundary that could drive Logan away. Instead, Adrian reached out and took the donut, a spark of electricity igniting as his fingers brushed against Logan's. That small touch resonated within him, igniting every atom of his being.

A beat passed.

The ocean kept breathing beside them, steady and eternal, but something had changed between them. The air thickened with something neither of them could look directly at just yet. It was alive and present, yet it dwelled in the faint space between them, reflected in the way they exchanged shy glances.

Adrian sat back, chewed in silence. The sweetness danced on his tongue, while his heart raced as though he had been running for an hour, despite merely sitting comfortably beside Logan.

"That is good," he admitted after a moment.

Logan cast a dazzling side smile, a radiant curve that surely shattered thousands of hearts and sent countless souls into a swoon of infatuation.

They fell into a contemplative silence as they shared their breakfast and sipped their coffee—not one marked by a lack of words, but rather a silence thick with significance, rich and palpable between their bodies. It was a silence that conveyed emotions and thoughts far beyond what language could ever articulate.

Adrian pondered whether Logan felt the palpable air crackling between them on that serene morning; the sweet electricity of unspoken thoughts lingering in the atmosphere. Did he sense the tether that connected them, like Adrian did? Or perhaps it was merely Adrian's mind plaiting illusions. In that still, tranquil dawn, he couldn't help but wonder if he was the only one experiencing such deep emotions for the man beside him, and how he might navigate this tender territory.

Above them, the sky was beginning to melt into morning, not quite light, not quite dark, streaks of pink and gold seeping across the horizon like watercolor left too long in the rain. The ocean moved, waves folding over themselves with a rhythm that felt older than time, lulling the shore back into waking life.

Adrian tried to anchor his eyes to the horizon, to the line where sea met sky, but his gaze kept pulling back. To Logan's hands, still sticky with sugar. To the soft arch of his mouth, flushed from the cold and from laughter. To the way the rising light kissed the angles of his face, casting soft shadows beneath his cheekbones, turning his profile into something quietly devastating. Something that didn't make sense to feel this strongly about, not yet, and yet here it was.

Logan didn't meet his gaze again. But Adrian saw the way his cheek caught color beneath the golden light. The way his mouth pressed into a line, a twitch, maybe, or restraint.

Neither of them spoke. But the silence loomed.

Adrian swallowed the bite still in his mouth, slow and careful, like chewing sugar could steady his pulse. He glanced sideways, caught Logan watching him, or maybe watching the space between them, that charged, fragile air. Logan's smile had faded now, drawn into something quieter. There was a flicker behind his eyes, not fear exactly, but something adjacent, something brittle, barely masked. His fingers trembled slightly as he finished the last bite, his jaw working like the motion might distract him from whatever had just passed silently between them.

Then he looked away.

The sky shifted again, deepening from blush to flame, a sweep of tangerine spilling across the clouds like fire catching cotton. The waves kept their slow rhythm, unbothered, as if the whole world hadn't just tilted slightly off its axis.

Adrian sat perfectly still, both hands wrapped around his coffee cup, though he hadn't taken a sip in minutes. His fingers idly traced circles into the cardboard sleeve of the cup, small, absent movements that betrayed nerves he wouldn't voice.

Across from him, Logan finished the last of his coffee and set the empty cup into the sand with a soft thud. His eyes flicked toward Adrian and caught—for just a second—the way Adrian was looking at him. And when their eyes met, neither of them looked away.

Logan's body thrummed with an ineffable tension, a quiet storm with no name, lingering just beyond reach. It was there, elusive and intangible, yet he could feel it seep into his skin, down to his core. Suddenly, every inch of him became vivid—how the hoodie was conveniently draped over his lap, the rhythmic pulse in his neck, the subtle hum beneath his skin that persisted since that near-touch.

"Ready?" Logan asked suddenly, his tone airy, trying to deflect yet the atmosphere was still thick, as if an unseen force had changed things, and they were both acting as if nothing had happened. He took a few deep breaths, moving a bit on the sand, trying to discreetly arrange himself.

"Or..." he added, casting a sidelong glance at Adrian with a crooked grin as he took the hoodie off, "do you want to keep sitting here and watch how it's done?"

Adrian just blinked at him, stunned, mouth ajar, caught somewhere between amusement and speechlessness.

Then, without warning, Adrian scooped up a handful of sand and tossed it straight at Logan's shoulder. The grains were scattered across his bare chest and arms, some dancing along his neck, clinging to the sheen of sweat shimmering at his collarbone.

Logan gasped, eyes going wide in mock betrayal. "Oh, *no*. You did *not* just throw sand at me."

Adrian gave him a smug little shrug, barely suppressing a grin. "Oh, I definitely did."

Logan narrowed his eyes, dramatic. "I'm gonna remember this."

Before Adrian could answer, before he could even shift back into smug composure, Logan lunged.

They crashed into the sand with a soft thump, Logan's arms around Adrian's waist as they tumbled sideways. Adrian let out a breathless laugh that caught somewhere in his throat as they rolled, limbs tangled, sand spraying in arcs around them. The air between them was filled with salt and sunlight and something sharper.

They grappled playfully, half-hearted and full of intent, hands slipping on sand and skin, laughing so hard, their stomachs hurt. Adrian tried to twist out from under him, but Logan was faster, pinning him for a second before letting go, letting them roll again, still breathless.

Sand clung to their hair, their arms, the corners of their mouths. The tide whispered behind them, a steady hush like the world was holding its breath.

And for a moment—just a moment—they stopped moving. Logan hovered above Adrian, both of them panting, eyes locked. Adrian's chest rose and fell beneath him, and the heat between their bodies was unmistakable now.

Then, suddenly, the world stilled. In one swift, fluid motion, Adrian moved with the precision of a soldier, a man who had molded his body to discipline and instinct. In an instant, he was above Logan, his hands capturing Logan's wrists and pressing them into the cool sand, his knees expertly bracing his legs. Logan lay beneath him, breath caught, the weight of Adrian's strength and focus pinning him in place, grounding him against the earth. The sun cast a golden halo around them, the only sound now the faint murmur of the waves and the steady rhythm of their breathing, the distance between them charged, electric, yet still.

Their laughter faded into silence as their eyes locked. Logan felt himself pulled into the depths of Adrian's whiskey-colored gaze, the weight of him pressing down, solid and warm. Adrian's chest rose and fell in rhythm with his own, each breath a silent conversation neither dared break.

A soft shiver ran through Logan, though he couldn't tell if it was his own or Adrian's. Adrian's long hair, tossed by the wind, brushed across Logan's face, tickling his skin with a featherlight touch that made every nerve tingle. Slowly, Adrian's grip softened, his fingertips grazing Logan's wrists with a gentleness that stirred a mellow heat rippling beneath his skin. And then, just like that, the pressure of Adrian's hands faded, leaving Logan's skin tingling where they'd touched, as if the warmth lingered, echoing long after the contact had ended. They were skin to skin, Logan's every sense tuned to the solid warmth pressed against him. He could feel the taut muscles of Adrian's stomach, the hard curve of his chest, the rough skin of his legs brushing his own, grounding him in this fleeting moment. Logan's breath quickened, chest rising and falling as his heart drummed faster, echoing in his ears. All he wanted was to stay right here, feeling this impossible closeness, though he couldn't quite understand why. He only knew that something essential and hushed held him captive, rooted in the space between breath and heartbeat.

Time, suspended for one breathless moment, began to flow again. Logan swallowed hard, the spell breaking, and with a soft, unsteady laugh, he nudged Adrian off him and stood, brushing sand from his skin. He stole a glance at Adrian as he rose, catching a faint smile—somewhere between sheepish and amused—though neither said a word. Logan returned the smile, masking the wild beat of his heart as he bent to pick up his board.

"Shall we?" he asked, breath still catching.

"Yeah," Adrian replied, and without hesitation, he gathered their things into the paper bag to put in the recycling bin later. Board in hand, he sprinted after Logan, their laughter mingling with the roar of the waves as they raced together toward the sea, the water cool and endless before them.

By the time they drifted back to shore, the sun hung low, spilling gold across the restless waves, gilding the sea in light as if blessing their return. They had spent the day immersed in the ocean's rhythm, weaving through its rise and fall, their laughter carried on the salty breeze. It was a language only they seemed to understand; a conversation spoken in the spray of waves and the silence of shared glances.

They had paused here and there, lazily basking in the sun's embrace, their bodies warmed by the soft sand beneath. Lying side by side, their faces kissed by sunlight, the ocean's gentle roar became a lullaby as they drifted into a light nap beneath the endless sky. They had shared stolen hours of idle talk, quick bites of lunch between breathless stories, their words flowing seamlessly, effortlessly. Between rides, they chased each other in the water, playful and unguarded, the kind of joy Adrian had almost forgotten existed.

He couldn't deny it; this was the best day he'd had in years. If he was honest, perhaps in his whole life.

And Logan... Logan was remarkable. He moved through the waves like he belonged to them, each leap and turn effortless, each glide a testament to his soul-deep bond with the sea. He didn't fight the water but became a part of it, slipping through its grasp with an ease that made Adrian's breath catch.

Watching him, Adrian realized, was like watching the ocean itself—wild, beautiful, and impossible to hold.

Adrian was the first to wade back onto the sand, and Logan followed soon after, flopping down beside him, his face lit with a kind of elation that seemed to catch the last light of the day.

"God, I missed this!" Logan laughed, breathless, his voice carrying over the gentle crash of the waves. "Being out there for hours, feeling...alive."

Adrian felt something settle inside him as he sat beside Logan, the warmth of his presence washing over him like sunlight after a storm. Logan gazed at him, his grin effortless and luminous, radiating a glow that made Adrian's heart flutter. With each glimpse of that beautiful smile, Adrian found himself smiling back, feeling a little piece of his heart melt.

"It's the best feeling," he agreed, looking out at the water still rolling, restless, against the shore. "I could stay out there forever."

"Yeah," Logan nodded, voice softer now, almost a murmur. "Out there, everything feels clearer. Like I can actually hear myself think. The water, the rush..." he stopped, wiping some water from his face. "It's like all the noise just fades."

Adrian's gaze lingered on the horizon, feeling the words settle deep within him. "It's heaven," he said, a quiet reverence in his tone.

They sat like that for a while, letting the silence pool between them, comfortable, natural.

Adrian inhaled deeply, sensing the rush of his pulse in his neck as he pondered his next move. He wished for the day to stretch endlessly, craving the precious moments spent in Logan's magnetic orbit, paired with a flutter of anxiety. They had shared the entire day together, and yet a worry lingered—had Logan had his fill?

Just then, their eyes locked as Adrian turned toward him, and in that instant, Adrian felt a surprising conviction that Logan shared his unsaid thoughts. Words tumbled from his lips before he could rein them in, unguarded and raw, like a melody begging to be sung. "You hungry? You want to grab dinner?" He asked, his voice laced with quiet hope, desperate not to let the moment slip through his fingers like sand. Eager and painfully aching to steal more time, to stretch the breaths they shared into something endless. To hold onto the man beside him for just a little longer, to carve out a space where the world didn't reach them, where time could bend and soften around their touch. Where leaving didn't exist, and neither did goodbye.

Logan's eyes lit up, and his lips parted into a smile so exquisite, so radiant, Adrian felt that smile enflaming him. It surged through his veins and settled in his bones, causing his knees to tremble and his chest to jolt with a sudden warmth. "Starving," he said.

Adrian pushed himself up, reaching out instinctively to offer Logan a hand. Logan took it, his grip warm and steady, and Adrian felt a spark run up his spine, subtle yet electrifying. Logan rose, grabbed his board and hoodie, and they started walking back along the shore, shoulder to shoulder, the soft hush of the ocean following them.

"What do you have in mind?" Logan asked, glancing sideways at him. For a moment, Adrian wanted to reach out, brush back the loose strand of hair falling across Logan's forehead, and wipe away some of the sand clinging to his neck.

Adrian shrugged, trying to ignore the heat in his chest. "Not sure. Meet you outside your cabin in an hour?"

Logan nodded, smiling. Adrian caught him looking back, his gaze lingering, something unreadable and bright in his eyes. Logan took a deep breath, and Adrian could feel that same flicker, that unspoken current, winding through him, like a wave gathering strength just before it broke.

Chapter 3

The Altar Meant for Someone Else

Waves crashed, one after another, like the heartbeat of the sea itself, steady and unyielding. Each one rose, towering over the rippling expanse, a graceful yet merciless dance. One, two, three... they kept coming, unstoppable and hypnotic, their rhythm as ancient as time. The ocean moved with a beauty so raw, it was almost dangerous, a siren's call, luring any soul who dared to get too close. The water curled and swayed, an endless pulse, each wave sculpted with deadly allure, pulling hearts toward its depths with promises whispered in salt and foam.

I sat there for hours, or maybe it was only minutes, or maybe it was lifetimes, watching the tide pull at the edges of the world. But if I'm honest, I don't know if I truly saw any of it. My eyes were open, but my soul had already drifted far, far away past the edge of this ocean, past this continent, past this version of myself that pretends to breathe without you.

Somewhere else, on another shore only I can see, you are laughing. Your voice is the breaking of a wave in my memory, bright and wild and alive. I feel your hands on my skin still, your breath against my throat, the sacred weight of your body pressed against mine, a thousand phantom touches stitched into the fabric of my being, refusing to fade.

Your smile, that rarest of miracles, lives behind my closed eyes. The way you looked at me, like I was something holy, something worth saving, haunts the marrow of my bones.

There are whole worlds built inside the little moments we shared, moments I inhabited more fully than any life I pretend to live now.

And so, with the remnants of my pride scattered like ash at my feet, because it means nothing in the absence of you, I bought a ticket. Shoved everything I was into a shaking fist. And I left behind everything I ever knew in search of the only thing that ever truly knew me.

You.

Always you.

December 13, 2018—Seattle, Washington—Five Months Later

LOGAN GRIPPED THE WHEEL as if holding on to the last remnants of himself, though he felt like a shadow, an empty vessel going through the motions. The Thursday traffic crawled along, red taillights blinking in sync with the ache pulsing in his chest. His father sat beside him, absorbed in a phone call, oblivious to Logan's turmoil, his voice a faint hum against the chaos Logan carried inside.

Four days ago, he had proposed to Sandy. Four days, but it already felt like a lifetime, a weight pressing on his spirit, suffocating him. He remembered the night with a detached clarity, as if watching it all from a distance. There was no ceremony, no momentous kneeling, no grand declaration. Just a small box, containing a ring of his father's choosing, was placed on a restaurant table in a room where the colors had already faded to dull grays. The world around him had blurred; faces lost definition, voices melted into static. All he could hear was the beat of his own heart, trembling with dread, with regret he couldn't name but felt in every bone.

When Sandy said yes, he forced a smile that fit his face like a mask, rigid and unnatural. Her joy should have been infectious, a spark to ignite his own, but instead, it smothered every unspoken hope he'd harbored, slamming shut a door he had never been brave enough to walk through.

He dropped her off with practiced ease, exchanging a soft, hollow "goodnight" as she lingered by the car, her invitation hanging in the air. "Come inside," she had said, her voice warm, hopeful. But he deflected with a careful lie—something about wanting to take things slow—words that felt foreign in his mouth.

He drove home in suffocating silence, the hum of the engine his only company. His face remained still, betraying nothing to the world outside, but inside, he was crumbling, breaking piece by piece. The weight of his own duplicity pressed down on him, and he wondered how long he could keep pretending, how long before the mask cracked and the truth he had buried so deeply finally came spilling out.

Once alone in his room, Logan let the mask slip, feeling it fall like shattered glass around him. He sank to the floor, and a flood broke free, unstoppable, a relentless tide of sorrow he'd tried so hard to hold back. It was a grief without edges, boundless, like an endless sea, and it rolled through him in waves that left him breathless, aching. His hand trembled as he reached for his phone, the familiar ritual too strong to resist. Adrian's Facebook page glowed faintly in the darkness, a pale lighthouse guiding him toward a shore he could never reach.

It had become a ritual now, this quiet haunting. Each day, he found himself drifting back to Adrian's page, drawn there like a sailor to the rocks, knowing the hurt it would bring but helpless to stay away. His fingers moved slowly, tracing through photos like he was sifting through sand, holding each memory up to the light. There were no new posts, no updates, only the same familiar fragments: Adrian laughing beside him on a beach or in the water, eyes bright with that spark that seemed to catch every ray of sun. Logan's heart clenched painfully, his chest tightening as he scrolled, his screen a window into a world that had slipped through his hands.

He opened his laptop and clicked on the secret folder, watching as the screen filled with images from their trip. Each one hit like a wave. There was Adrian, a flash of sun in his eyes, a smile that seemed made of open skies and salt air. Logan clicked on a video, and suddenly the silence of the room was filled with the sound of Adrian's laughter—clear, bright, like sunlight spilling over the water. It filled the room, filled his empty and aching heart, until it became too much, and he slammed the laptop shut, the sound echoing in the emptiness.

The darkness returned, pressing in, deep and endless. He lay back on his bed, fingers fumbling for the old, worn lifesaver bracelet Adrian had given him, the fibers rough yet comforting in his hand. He clutched it as though it could tether him, as though it could keep him from drifting further into the depths. He held it close, feeling the texture press into his palm, like holding onto a sliver of the past, a piece of something he could never let go. Closing his eyes, he imagined himself submerging in the seawater, letting it soak him, cover him, shallow breath and cold water, and the haunting memory of Adrian.

And now, here he was, in front of a high-end suit store with his father, who had already stepped out, more excited than Logan had seen him in years.

Inside, his father took charge, speaking eagerly with the sales staff, barely sparing Logan a glance. "It's going to be a small wedding," his father explained, rolling his eyes, "but we still need something that makes a statement."

Logan looked around at the walls lined with suits, endless rows of dark fabric under harsh fluorescent lights. The whole place smelled of starch and polished leather, like a theater of empty pretense. When the tailor asked what he wanted, Logan's voice came out low and flat.

"That one," he said, pointing to a mannequin in the far left corner.

"Sir, we have thousands of options, if you'd like to look around," the tailor replied.

"No," Logan said, barely looking at the suit. He could feel his father's hand on his shoulder, his proud smile, the way his eyes gleamed with the illusion that this was a rite of passage, that his son was taking his place among men. But Logan felt hollow, his mind lost at sea, adrift on a current pulling him somewhere he did not want to go.

They took his measurements, lifting his arms, adjusting him here and there, and he complied mechanically, like a mannequin himself. His father chuckled with a proud gleam in his eye, murmuring about how it was "a man's choice" to pick the first suit, never knowing the truth. Logan didn't care about the suit. He didn't care if it fit or if it looked good or even if he showed up at the altar in it. All he could think of was how much he wished this were different, how much he wished he were anywhere else, with anyone else.

With *him*.

He could almost feel Adrian beside him as they finished up, could almost hear the echo of Adrian's easy laughter in the cold, sterile light of the dressing room.

For a fleeting moment—a mere second, a fraction of time—he dared to envision, to ponder, to wish... what it might be like if he were present now, selecting a tailored suit for a wedding ceremony alongside Adrian.

The tug in his chest sharpened, a twisting pain that seemed to tear something loose inside him, something he barely had the strength to hold onto anymore. That feeling swallowed him whole, vast and merciless, like staring into the bottomless pit of the ocean itself. It was like sinking past the last fingers of light, past the reach of the living world.

Like opening his eyes underwater and seeing nothing but black—no ground, no sky, only the crushing weight of salt and sorrow pressing in on all sides.

No breath.

No direction.

Just endless darkness, and the cold, and the slow, terrible knowing that he was too deep to ever find his way back.

In the enveloping darkness, he could still sense Adrian's hand reaching out to him. He could almost hear his voice, so faint it teetered on the edge of imagination, beckoning him home, whispering his name, uttering words Logan dared not revisit, for fear they would shatter the fragile remnants of his wrecked spirit.

"Shoes?" his father's voice cut through, bright and oblivious, slicing Logan back into the room like a knife through cloth.

Logan blinked, the world slamming back into place around him; the bright, soulless lights, the polite murmur of the tailor, the heavy pressure of the suit against his skin. His lungs felt raw, as if he had been holding his breath without realizing it. Like he hadn't breathed for far too long.

"Whatever's on the mannequin," he mumbled, voice thick, unfamiliar.

He forced a smile, the kind of smile that left a metallic taste on his tongue, sharp and wrong, and nodded toward the man waiting with a tape measure and patient hands.

As he stepped back outside, the world around him seemed vast, empty, and unsteady, as if he were adrift on an endless sea with no land in sight.

The sky above was pale and dull, and the buildings around him felt foreign, like towering rocks rising from a dark, turbulent ocean. He wanted to run, to escape to some distant shore where he could breathe again, where the weight pressing on him would dissolve into mist. But all he had was this suit, this role, this cage that felt tighter with each passing moment.

He knew now that he could keep moving forward, keep pressing through this hollow existence, even as his heart remained stranded, lost, unmoored, and forever tangled somewhere beyond the edges of this world, adrift in the waves and tethered to the only soul who had ever made him feel truly alive.

January 2, 2019—Seattle, Washington—Three Weeks Later

Between the waves, across the riptide, I have lost you. Drifted apart by streams of strong water pulling and taking away, one drifted to shore, the other sank and drowned under the pace of the ocean.

LOGAN LAY IN HIS childhood bed, feeling the silence close in around him, tightening around his neck and pressing on his chest ribs. Tomorrow was the day. He closed his eyes, but sleep wouldn't come; instead, it was as if he were suspended, drifting somewhere between waking and drowning. The night before his wedding, and all he could feel was the weight of a life that didn't feel like his own.

For weeks, he had moved through his days like a ghost, smiling on cue. He asked the right questions. He laughed at jokes that didn't land inside him.

He held Sandy's hand in a daze or draped an awkward arm around her waist.

They'd visited families on the holidays and weekends, toasted at gatherings, nodded through dinners, and let the days blur together like waves he no longer bothered to chase.

Logan made decisions for a life he didn't even recognize.

He had drowned himself in the monotony of office hours, leaving Sandy to plan the wedding without him. He couldn't even recall his wedding rehearsal. She had hired a wedding planner, taking every decision into her own hands while Logan offered nothing but a single, stubborn request: keep it small. Logan also lied his way out of the honeymoon, saying something about work and about having traveled enough. He had a vague recollection of those conversations with his father and Sandy. While his father was pleased, after all, Robert Vaughn loved work and people who worked, Sandy was mad about the lack of a honeymoon.

But Logan couldn't feel the edges of the world anymore.

He moved like he was walking underwater—each step slow, muffled, detached. Conversations passed through him like wind through mesh. He saw mouths move, heads tilt, hands gesturing, but none of it landed. Emotion had become a distant frequency—something happening *around* him, never *to* him. A faint murmur behind glass. Life continued at a safe remove, as though he were watching himself from the wrong side of a mirror.

Inside, he lived elsewhere.

There, beneath all the days and dinner tables and white linen, was a quiet shoreline. Adrian stood there, just beyond reach. That life, their life, still clung to him like salt in his skin. It was dim now, blurred by time, but it hadn't left. It waited in the folds of memory, in the tremble between blinks, in the silence just after someone said his name.

He didn't miss Adrian as one misses a person.

He missed him the way lungs miss air.

The way fish miss water.

Then came the house hunting. Logan had felt like a shadow of himself, watching as Sandy held his hand and picked out a place they would call home. His parents approved, of course, thrilled by the proximity to Logan's work, pleased that it would keep them close. The Vaughns had always lived close, never straying too far from one another. But Logan wanted to run, to escape, to leave it all behind. Instead, he had smiled, a mask of forced joy, and let Sandy hug him when he agreed to one of the houses she loved. Tomorrow, as the wedding unfolded, the decorators his father hired would finish their work on their new house. Most of Logan's things were already there. Everything was already moving forward, even as Logan remained anchored in place, adrift in an ocean of apathy.

His younger sister, Ann, had come home, filled with excitement for the wedding, her wide-eyed enthusiasm a stark contrast to Logan's numb resignation. Jane, however, had seen through him. She knew something was wrong, had known it from the first moment she saw him when he got back to the States after his trip. But Logan couldn't bring himself to explain. He couldn't bring himself to speak the truth.

Logan rolled onto his back and stared at the ceiling, feeling as if he were trapped beneath the surface of some dark sea. He reached for his laptop, feeling the ritual of it call to him like a lifeline. With his earphones in, he clicked on the familiar secret folder, and there was Adrian's face, beaming from the screen, tanned and sunlit, eyes bright with laughter that now felt like a balm and a wound all at once. He watched as the waves rolled gently behind Adrian, saw his hair, wet and tousled, saltwater glistening on his skin.

A sob tore free from Logan's chest, ragged and helpless. He pressed a trembling hand to his mouth, as if he could somehow damn the flood, as if he could swallow down the ache threatening to drown him. But the past was cruel. The video played on, unyielding, Adrian's voice curling through the room—warm, sun-drenched, touched with that sand-smooth accent that had once felt like home.

He watched as Adrian laughed, that wild, unrestrained joy spilling from him, a sound that had once filled Logan with something weightless, something unbreakable. And then... there he was, in the glow of the screen, grinning as he reached for the camera, his hands sure, his eyes alight with mischief. "*You want to film something good?*" he had said, teasing, effortless. "*I'll give you something good.*"

And then Adrian was gone, leaping from the bow of the yacht, cutting through the air like he belonged to the ocean itself. The water swallowed him whole, endless and blue.

Logan clenched his jaw, but the joy—*their* joy—felt like a mirage now, slipping through his fingers, dissolving before he could hold onto it. It was a ghost of something beautiful, something that no longer existed.

With a sharp, shaking breath, he slammed the laptop shut. The screen went black. The room swallowed him in silence, thick and suffocating, pressing against his ribs like a weight he could never lift.

Logan lay in the dark, pulling the blanket tight around him, as if it could shield him from the ache clawing inside. He could still see Adrian's face, the memory vivid even with his eyes closed: the way the light had glinted off the water, the unfiltered happiness in Adrian's gaze. Adrian had looked at him then with a joy so pure it was like sunlight breaking through fog, but now, all Logan felt was the hollow ache of absence, the bitter salt of what he'd lost.

In the early dawn, after barely an hour of fitful sleep, Logan dragged himself through his morning routine. He stared at the reflection in the mirror, at the dark circles under his eyes, the hollow lines of his face. The person staring back was a stranger, someone who barely ate, who barely slept. He was just the shell of someone who had once felt alive.

When he made it to the kitchen, his family was there, bustling with excitement. Ann called out, "Good morning, groom!" with a teasing smile, while Jane gave him a concerned look, muttering about how tired he looked. His mother offered breakfast, but he just shook his head, reaching for the coffee Jane handed him. Food was tasteless now; even coffee felt empty, dull, like drinking shadows.

As his mother and sisters bustled out the door for last-minute preparations, his father's voice boomed down the hall, announcing that Cole, his best man and Jane's husband, would be arriving soon. Logan forced a nod, but the words barely registered. The only voice he wanted to hear, the only person who filled his mind, was as unreachable as the ocean on a distant shore.

Logan turned back to his room, each step heavy, every inch of him weighed down by the knowledge that , he'd step into a life without the one person who had ever made him feel alive.

A few short hours later, Logan stood in the sterile silence of the hotel suite, the air thick with the scent of polished wood and lavender. Everything was ready for the day: gleaming surfaces, the soft buzz of unseen preparations outside the room, and the eager whispers of a future unfolding. Yet Logan couldn't shake the heaviness pressing on his chest, a weight too familiar, too unyielding.

From the large window, the green grass of the garden stretched out, punctuated by the gentle drift of white tulle. Photos hung around the venue, frozen moments in time. Some were taken before Logan had left for his trip, capturing smiles he now realized were half-truths. Others were from the past few days, Sandy glowing with excitement, her arm wrapped around him as they posed for the camera in picturesque locations nearby. But all Logan could see in the images was the absence, the gap where something, someone, used to fit.

Guests were starting to trickle in. Their voices hummed through the walls, distant but invasive. He turned away from the window, his eyes briefly catching sight of his father and Cole standing across the room. His father, dressed to perfection, looked the part of the proud father, while Cole's furrowed brow spoke of something else, something Logan couldn't articulate.

"You ready, son?" his father asked, his voice warm with a routine kind of joy.

Dressed, yes.

Shoes polished, yes.

Hair styled, yes.

But ready? No. Never.

Logan turned slowly, nodding despite the tumult inside him.

"I'm off to see that everything is set," his father said, his tone light and dismissive. "You need to meet your bride soon." He added, chuckling.

As his father left, Cole lingered. "Man, are you okay?" His words held a hesitant concern, but Logan barely caught them. He felt a tremor in his hands as he glanced at his friend. Cole's eyes widened slightly as they settled on his pale face.

"I'm fine," Logan murmured, but the words hung hollow, strange, like they'd wandered off someone else's lips and taken refuge on his.

How many times had he uttered this phrase, a quiet anthem to the lie he'd grown used to carrying? It rolled from his tongue smoothly now, practiced, too easy, like he wasn't crumbling, like his soul wasn't splintering under the weight of everything left unsaid. In truth, he was anything but fine. Each "I'm fine" was a stitch in the fabric he used to wrap himself, a disguise woven to keep the ache hidden. It was a thin shield against the urge to reach for his phone in the dead hours of the night, scrolling through Adrian's photos as if they were a lifeline, trying to touch the ghost of a time when he was whole.

How many times had he lingered there, tracing the images of sunlit beaches and stolen glances, holding his breath as though he might somehow step back into those moments? He could still hear Adrian's laugh—low, unguarded, echoing over the waves as they'd run together, salt-stung and breathless, in that wild and endless summer. He could still feel Adrian's presence beside him, a constant reassurance of safety and love, the warmth of another soul, one that felt impossibly, unmistakably his, right there next to him. He'd close his eyes, pretending he was back there, in that fleeting eternity where nothing else mattered. And each time he whispered "I'm fine," it felt like erasing that memory all over again, betraying the one part of him that still longed for Adrian's warmth, his smile, his voice.

Yes, sure. He "was fine."

He turned back to the window, where voices drifted, murmurs from another world—one filled with Sandy's laughter, his father's sternness, colors bleeding into the edges of the worst day of his life. He stared out at the garden as though it were an altar, his eyes lifting to the vast blue sky, a silent prayer clawing at his chest. For the sun, for the waves, for anything that had ever held him gently. For the pieces of himself he'd left buried in that July ocean, beneath salt-stained memories and the ache of everything he could never say.

And then his eyes froze.

A lone figure, unmistakable and haunting, wove through the distant crowd, a flicker of shadow against the daylight. Logan's breath stopped, trapped somewhere between fear and longing.

Adrian.

It was as if the sky, the sun, the tides themselves had heard his silent plea and answered—not with comfort, but with a sharp reminder of what he'd lost. Adrian, the one who had once dived into the depths after him, pulling him from the clutches of the waves when he had allowed himself to sink below the surface. Adrian, who understood the labyrinth of Logan's soul better than anyone ever could. Adrian, who had shared not just his bed and his body but the very essence of his being for the past months. Adrian, to whom he had surrendered his heart completely. Adrian, who cherished Logan as though he were the greatest treasure of time, more precious than the sky, the sun, and the tide itself.

Was it a trick of the glass? A shadow, a shape cast wrong by light? Was this a dream? A cruel trick of his breaking mind?

And time... it just fractured.

Adrian moved like something sacred through the crowd, a quiet figure slipping past clusters of strangers. His hair, still sun-kissed and wild, spilled softly over his shoulders, just as it had when they were tangled together in summer light, that endless summer. And now, here he was in a tailored, elegant suit, an impossible vision of a life Logan could never touch. The sight of him felt like a blow, a piece of earth splitting open, shifting under Logan's feet, leaving him unsteady.

Logan's breath caught mid-inhale, sharp and dry, as if the air had turned to salt. A sudden heat climbed up his spine, collided with a cold that bloomed under his skin. Every nerve fired at once, then collapsed. His fingers trembled, blood draining from his hands as though fleeing the moment. He pressed them to the windowsill, but it felt miles away. *Everything* did—except Adrian.

Adrian stood at the far corner of the garden, eyes scanning the sea of faces, but Logan knew—he knew—that Adrian's gaze was meant only for him. He could see the quiet grace in Adrian's stance, the way he held himself like a storm barely restrained, a force of nature dressed in mourning clothes. Logan's breath stilled, and in that instant, he was back in July, back in the surf, when the world had been as simple as the pull of the tide and the warmth of a hand pulling him to shore.

Jane approached Adrian, her smile wide and effortless, the kind of smile that always seemed to light up a room. But to Logan, it was like a blade sinking deep into his chest. His body was locked in place, unable to move, unable to breathe. His eyes were trapped on Adrian's face, where the pain was too raw, too exposed. It hit him—sharp, sudden, and violent—and he could feel the burn of it deep inside, an ache that spread through him like wildfire. He wanted to look away, but he couldn't. His gaze clung to Adrian, drawn to the subtle sorrow etched there, to the quiet weight of everything that happened between them. Jane reached out, offering a greeting, her hand extending toward Adrian, probably welcoming him and creating a conversation effortlessly with someone she might have presumed was just another guest, not the water and tied and the force that kept Logan's heart beating.

His knees weakened. Not from fear, not entirely; but from the unbearable, impossible joy that clutched at his chest like a vice. His heart didn't beat. It *thrashed*.

Adrian.

Here.

Now.

A single drop of sweat traced his temple. The suit clung to him like wet paper. And still he couldn't move, just stared, shaking, as the world folded in on itself.

It was as if someone had torn open the sky and let both heaven and hell spill through. The two halves of his life suddenly stood on the same soil. Logan felt something break inside, something brittle and long-ignored, like a rib that had mended wrong and finally given out.

All his wishes, all his silent, aching prayers—answered. And yet, in the same breath, he wanted to run. To scream. To weep.

Because Adrian was not supposed to be here.

Adrian's lips moved, and Logan wanted nothing more than to hear the sound, to catch even a whisper, something to anchor him in the present, to remind him of the reality he had buried beneath layers of sand.

He only knew he needed to hear them.

He needed to hear him. He needed to hear Adrian's voice more than he needed to breathe right now.

And then Jane smiled at Adrian, gesturing toward the hotel, and Logan's world shifted. The space between him and Adrian felt like an impossible distance, like everything that had happened—everything he had tried to bury—was pressing in on him all at once. His heart hammered in his chest, the rhythm offbeat and erratic. He couldn't stay here, couldn't let this moment slip away. With a burst of urgency, he left the room, his carefully constructed mask cracking and falling, slipping like sand through his fingers.

When he reached the entrance, the tide of time seemed to pull back, and there Adrian stood—solid, real, like a wave crashing against the shoreline after all these months. It had been an eternity, an eternity since that fateful night when their bodies collided with the soft sand, intertwined and lost in the moment as they surrendered to the rhythm of desire.

The photos, the videos, the memories, none of them had prepared him.

No image could contain the velocity of this moment, the violence of recognition. None of it came close to the rupture that split him open the instant his eyes met Adrian's.

Every molecule in Logan's body surged toward him. His chest seized, as if his ribs were trying to hold back a wave too vast to bear. His vision tunneled. The ground tilted. Something inside him buckled—sharp, bright, and almost holy.

Adrian was still everything to him. The air between them hummed with a tension that swelled like the sea, a magnetic force drawing him in, drowning him in the raw power of Adrian's presence.

His name rang through Logan's body without ever being spoken. It wasn't memory. It wasn't nostalgia. It was a gravitational collapse, a star imploding in real time.

But before he could take another step, Jane's voice broke through the fragile moment between them.

"Logan!" Her tone was sharp, a reminder that the world was still turning. "You have a guest who traveled all the way from Israel for your wedding, and you didn't tell anyone he's coming?" She turned to Adrian, her voice soft but polite. "I'll go to the front desk and arrange a room for you for a few days. Do you have any luggage?"

"No!" Logan's voice came out too fast, too panicked. *No, Adrian couldn't be staying here. Not like this.* His mouth was dry, a knot tightening in his throat. "I mean..." His words faltered, trailing off like smoke. "I... I forgot," he whispered, the lie tasting bitter on his tongue, too harsh, too real. He couldn't look away from Adrian's gaze, dark and heavy, a silent storm swirling just beneath the surface.

Looking at him puzzlingly, Jane murmured something about checking with the front desk and talking to the wedding planner before excusing herself.

The truth was there, just out of reach, but Logan couldn't say it. The weight of it would break everything—everything he had spent so long trying to build, trying to bury. The lie hung in the air between them, thick and suffocating.

"What are you doing here?" Logan finally managed to ask, his voice cracking. It wasn't just a question; it was an accusation, a plea, all tangled up in one. His words trembled in the space between them, carrying the weight of everything he had failed to say, everything he had tried to outrun.

Adrian's expression softened, just a fraction, but it was enough to make Logan's heart twist. The sorrow in his eyes was like the pull of the tide, the undercurrent he couldn't escape. Adrian's mouth tightened, a faint line of restraint threading through his jaw, but the sorrow was there, raw and exposed, pulling Logan under. "Facebook," Adrian said, his voice a low current, simple but deep. "Your future wife posted the invitation everywhere." Adrian's voice trembled, the ache and pain with each syllable palpable like the sun over the turquoise waters.

The words landed between them like a stone, heavy and unyielding. Logan felt the ground shift beneath him, as if the world was unsteady, out of sync. Adrian's presence, so clear and undeniable, threatened to pull him under, and Logan wasn't sure if he could breathe through the weight of it all. The silence that followed felt like a canyon between them, filled with thousands of memories that neither could erase. Adrian didn't need to say anything more; his presence struck Logan's soul with the force of the ocean's loudest cry, louder than the icequake that once thundered across the sea.

Before Logan could find his voice, Jane returned, murmuring something about talking to the planner and securing a room for Adrian. But Logan, standing like a vessel tossed in a storm, couldn't hear her. The suit felt too tight around his chest, suffocating him like the heat of midday sun. His tie felt like a rope around his throat, pulling him into deeper and deeper waters. He was drowning, suffocating, and no one could see it.

"So, Adrian," Jane's voice broke through, a sudden wave crashing over him, "we couldn't have met before, but you look awfully familiar. How do you know Logan?"

Logan's heart pounded, the blood rushing like surf pounding against rocks, and he answered quickly, his words a shield he raised between himself and everything he was trying to avoid. "From my trip," he blurted, his voice jagged, but steady on the surface. Yet Adrian's eyes—deep pools of unsaid things, the finest whisky on the planet—cut through him.

"The mystery trip," Jane mused with a knowing smile as if the puzzle was now solved. Logan wanted to swallow his words, to find a cliff and jump off, letting the current take him away. "That's right," she continued, oblivious to the crashing storm inside him. "I saw you on Logan's phone—the Facebook page. You must talk a lot on Messenger. He's always on your profile."

Logan's pulse hammered in his ears, the pressure rising inside him until his skin burned with the heat of it. His cheeks flushed a bright red. The weight of the moment—the weight of everything—pushed down on him until he could hardly stand it.

Then, to make the tense moment worse, his father approached. His presence felt like a final wave, cresting over Logan, washing away what little peace he'd tried to hold onto. "The ceremony's about to start. What are you all doing here?" Robert's eyes found Adrian, and for a moment, everything hung in the balance as he examined the unfamiliar guest at the wedding he knew better than the groom. "Hello, thanks for coming to the wedding. You are...?"

"Adrian," came the simple reply, quiet and cold, as if Adrian had swallowed the whole ocean and was now drowning in silence. "A friend of Logan's." His voice was strained, barely audible, and Logan felt his world shift, felt the pull of the tide beneath his feet.

"Robert Vaughn," his father said, shaking Adrian's hand with the firmness of a well-rounded businessman. "Logan's father." Everything about the moment felt out of place, like a shadow cast over sunlight. The air hung heavy and silent between them, a charged silence filled with implicit words. Logan, on the brink of it all, felt an impending swallow into the depths of the unknown.

The walls were closing in, the air too hot, too heavy. Logan's breath caught in his throat as he tried to steady himself. His lungs forgot how to breathe. His throat clenched. Sweat broke like a fever across his skin. His hands went numb. His spine locked. He was both burning and frozen, hollowed out and overfilled. A tremor took hold in his knees and moved upward, unstoppable.

"The ceremony's about to start," he repeated, his voice tighter, more strangled. The words came out as if they were meant to anchor him, but they only served to pull him further into the storm. He turned quickly, his steps clumsy and hurried, a man fleeing from the ocean, the storm of his own making.

But Adrian didn't leave. Logan could hear the soft, steady rhythm of his footsteps behind him, and even though every muscle in his body screamed for him to run—to escape—he didn't. He knew it was Adrian. He knew. By running from Adrian, he thought he was escaping the storm, but only now, with Adrian behind him, did he realize the truth. The storm had never been the danger. The chaos had been his own doing, the panic, the drowning, the desperate thrashing to keep a life he no longer wanted. Adrian wasn't the storm. Adrian was the eye. The calm. The place where the world finally held still. The shore he hadn't believed existed.

He stepped into the suite, the door clicking shut behind him with the finality of a wave crashing against the shore. The sound was like the end of a storm, the last breath before the flood. Logan's eyes scanned the room, half expecting Cole to be there, waiting, but even in the privacy of the suite, it was as if there was no escape. Adrian was here, stepping into the room like a sailor lured by a siren, drifting helplessly toward Logan's aura, as though it were the song of the sea itself.

Logan stood there, shaking.

He could feel Adrian's presence, thick in the air around him, pulling at his heart, a current he couldn't outrun, no matter how desperately he swam. His breath hitched, but he refused to let the tears rise, just as the sea pulls back before a wave breaks, he tried to retreat from what he knew was coming. But there was no escaping it.

Adrian's voice cut through the quiet. "A fucking text message? Really? After everything?" His words slapped Logan awake, dredging up the pain of the past, pulling him under again, just as it always had. "I'm fine. At the airport. Going back home. Goodbye," Adrian recited, the final message Logan had sent, a cold and distant thing, like the ebbing tide after a storm. But the voice, Logan remembered that voice. It had once been his anchor, the lullaby that sang him to sleep each night, the saltwater of Adrian's words mingling with his own sorrow.

For a moment, Logan was back on that beach again, the sun setting low, the waves licking at their feet as they stood in silence, but it felt like a lifetime ago, and he was drowning in it.

"What are you doing here?" Logan's voice cracked; a broken thing caught in the waves of his chest. He didn't want to look at Adrian, didn't want to feel the pull of him, but his eyes betrayed him, clinging to Adrian as though the man himself was the last breath of air in an ocean that threatened to steal away every one of his remaining sunrises.

Adrian didn't back down. He stood tall, a mountain of raw emotion. "Blocking me? I couldn't believe it, Logan. You're acting like a fucking child." The words hit Logan right in the chest.

"I'm sorry." Logan's voice was a whisper, softer than the sand underfoot, his gaze dropped, the weight of guilt pressing on him. "I didn't want you to convince me to come back." The truthful words tasted bitter.

Adrian stepped forward, but not too close. There was a distance between them now, one that could never be bridged. But his words, soft and desperate, reached Logan's heart, reached every hollow part of him that yearned to bask in Adrian's presence.

"Don't marry her," Adrian whispered, and there was a tremor in his voice, a crack like thunder in the distance. "Logan, please..." His voice cracked, the sound of it breaking Logan's heart all over again, the memory of what was lost rising.

Logan stood there, frozen, staring at the man who had once been everything, who was still everything. The man who kissed him as if his very purpose was to make Logan feel treasured, who held him as though the world had no greater task. The man who went further than anyone had ever gone, who smiled at Logan as if he were the sun rising, and loved him without tether or term, without boundary or pretense. Who had not only pulled him from the depths of water but from the deeper abyss within, saving his body, then cradling his soul. "This is what you came for?" His voice was a shell, a broken echo of the person he used to be. He ran a hand through his hair, fingers trembling, trying to hold himself together. "To tell me this?"

"Yes," Adrian replied, stepping closer. After a heartbeat, he took another step. Logan remained still, yet inside, he felt a turmoil, waves of doubt crashing against all of him.

"Please," Adrian whispered, pleading tenderly. "Don't marry her, Logan. It's a lie, and we both know it."

Logan's heart felt like it was breaking apart, like the earth beneath him was crumbling into the sea. The pain was a rip tide, pulling him under, dragging him down to depths he couldn't escape from. He wanted to fight it, to swim against it, but all he could do was stand there, helpless.

"It's not a lie," he managed, but even as the words left his mouth, they felt muffled, empty. "I don't know what you're talking about. We've been together for a long time. It's the right choice." The words sounded like a lie even to him. Was he trying to convince Adrian—or himself?

"Logan..." Adrian's voice was soft, like a wave receding, leaving Logan with nothing but the sand beneath his feet and the cold emptiness of the shore.

"If this is why you came all the way from Israel, then it's a waste of time," Logan's words came out dry. "You can go back to whatever hole you crawled out of." He felt his heart breaking as he spoke, each word cutting deeper. He needed Adrian to be angry, to walk away, to leave him in the silence he knew too well. But the truth, the truth was pulling at him.

Adrian didn't flinch. He stepped closer, close enough that Logan could see the grief etched deep into every line of his face.

"I know you lash out when you feel vulnerable," Adrian said, voice low, rough, now only a breath away. "I know you're reckless sometimes," he added, a hollow laugh escaping him—a laugh heavy with memories of every wild, beautiful, reckless moment they had ever shared. His eyes flickered, bright with something breaking. "I know you're trying to run," he said. "And I know... on some level, you're drowning." His voice cracked, barely holding. "I see it. I see you struggling. I see you, Logan. Even when you think no one else does... I do." Adrian's hand twitched at his side, like he was fighting the urge to reach out, to anchor Logan somehow, to pull him back before he drifted too far. "But I can't save you if you won't let me," he whispered, raw, almost pleading. "And I won't get the chance to try again." He swallowed hard, every word a knife. "Please... don't marry her."

Logan's breath came in shallow gasps, each inhale burning in his chest as if the very air had turned into saltwater, thick and suffocating. His body trembled, a wave caught mid-break, unable to crash or retreat, wedged in the pull of a tide that had risen too high, too fast, like the lone leaf that stayed on the tree at the break of winter a second before it descended to the frozen ground below.

The ground beneath Logan felt like sand washing away, and all he could do was cling to the fragile thread of his own will. The ocean inside him was surging, rising higher with every moment, and there was no escape, no turning back from what had always been inevitable. Not from Adrian. Not from the truth. He was already neck-deep in it.

Adrian's hand reached for him, a lifeline in the swelling storm. His fingers wrapped around Logan's palm, warm and urgent, grounding him, pulling him closer. Tears streamed down Adrian's face like rain chasing a storm, each drop an echo of the pain he carried. "Logan, look at me," he whispered, his voice reminded Logan the sound of waves braking on the shore. With a tenderness that sent a shiver through Logan's spine, Adrian brought Logan's palm up and kissed it, his lips pressing softly against the skin. The gesture was a quiet prayer, a plea for something that felt impossibly out of reach. "Ahuv sheli," *my loved one*, Adrian uttered.

Letting the only words he had left pour out of him, Adrian reached for the language of his mother—the only language that could hold the weight of what he felt. It was how he chose to say *I love you* to the man standing in front of him. The man who had once held his heart and then walked away, leaving behind nothing but ruin and wreckage.

What remained were scattered pieces: memories tucked into corners, forgotten belongings littered like debris, the faint scent of Logan still clinging to the sheets, and the echo of their last kiss, its heat barely faded from the air.

"Ahuv sheli," Adrian breathed again, his voice a thread unraveling from the center of his chest.

It was the only truth he had left. The only shape his love could still take. The only measure of hope he dared to offer—fragile, desperate, holy.

He used the words of a different language not to hide, but to shield what was left of his heart. A final barrier. A quiet act of faith. Because even after everything, it still beat only for Logan.

Logan's eyes—wide, open, vulnerable—looked back at him, and what they held was deeper than the ocean's abyss. The weight of it crushed him, the pain heavier than the deepest tides, each beat of his heart sending ripples through him he couldn't outrun. It was there, floating in the space between them, everything Logan could never say, everything Adrian had always known but never asked for. And Logan was helpless to stop it, helpless to hold back the flood.

The language of love need not be translated. Logan understood the words, though they were spoken in a tongue not his own. He didn't need to reach for a dictionary, didn't need a definition. He understood them in Adrian's voice, in the way it cracked open when he said them. In the way his eyes always lit with something akin to admiration and vulnerability when those words escaped his lips. He understood because Adrian had always whispered them in quiet, sacred moments, like a secret offering, too precious to speak aloud, too heavy to hold in.

"Ahuv sheli."

Logan understood, because he and Adrian had always spoken the same language. The language that lived beneath words. A language of glances, of touches, of breath held between kisses. A language that required no translation.

So Adrian's attempt to build a final wall, to hide behind a language not born of their shared world, was futile. It crumbled at Logan's feet like everything Adrian was: soft, breaking, and still somehow trying to protect the last flicker of his soul.

"You're everything to me, Logan," Adrian's voice cracked, and Logan felt it in his own soul. "I think about you all the time. Every second. Every moment..." His words broke like waves shattering on a jagged reef. "I think... of the last night..." His voice trembled, raw and exposed, as tears streamed from his whisky-colored eyes and Logan felt every piece of him unravel in response. "I think of our last days together... it was like a dream."

A single tear slipped down Logan's cheek, tracing a path of salt that mingled with the heat coming from Adrian's body, and the rawness of the moment tore through him like an undertow. Adrian's hand cupped his face with a tenderness that felt like the gentlest wave lapping at the shore, his thumb brushing away the tear, as if to steal away the pain that had no words. Logan leaned into it, into Adrian's touch, closing his eyes as if he could lose himself there, just in the heat of his skin.

Adrian's other hand drifted to Logan's wrist, his fingers brushing against the bracelet, the only tether to a past Logan had tried to forget but never could. Adrian's breath caught, and Logan felt the shudder in his body as he ran his fingers over the material. "You still have it," Adrian's voice carried a note of awe, of reverence, of hope.

Then, without warning, Adrian pulled him in—his lips brushing against Logan's, soft and tentative at first, like the gentle swell of the tide, rising, hesitant, yet utterly irresistible.

Logan's breath caught in his throat, and then it was as if the ocean had reclaimed him, he was back under the current and was being pulled to air, to shore again.

Being rescued, again.

His hands moved, almost of their own accord, circling Adrian's waist, pulling him closer. And when their lips met, it was a storm, a violent, beautiful collision. Adrian moaned into the kiss, his body pressing against Logan's with a force that stole his breath. The world around them disappeared, drowned out by the crashing waves of their bodies, the salt of their skin, the heat that burned between them like the sun scorching the horizon at sunset.

Logan tilted his head, his tongue finding the seam of Adrian's lips, and when Adrian opened to him, he dove in, sliding his tongue into the warmth of Adrian's mouth, tasting the salt of his tears that still streamed down, drowning in him. One of Logan's hands slid down Adrian's side, fingers tracing the curve of his body, and he melted under the touch, lost in the sensation.

Adrian's hands were everywhere—one holding Logan's face with a fierce tenderness, the other traveling to the back of his neck, threading through his hair, feeling the pulse of his skin.

Logan took control of the kiss, his body pressing Adrian against the side table with a force that sent a vase crashing to the floor, its shattering sound drowned out by the urgency between them. The hunger was raw, too strong to hold back, a tidal wave crashing over them both. The kiss was frantic now, desperate—a chaotic dance of lips and hands, each trying to chase the other, to hold on to something they knew might slip away. It was no longer about gentleness, but about needing, about feeling, about chasing the fire that burned between them.

It was about reclaiming the fragments of himself that Logan had abandoned in that tiny cabin on the edge of the world. Pieces left behind like whispers in the wood, echoes in the dust. The feeling he had tried to bury beneath dunes of time, pressing it deeper with each shifting grain, hoping the wind might scatter it forever. But the air—the air he had been starved of for months—was calling him back, stirring through his ribs like a forgotten song, pulling him toward something he could no longer escape.

It was the most alive Logan had felt in months, as if the very air between them sparked. He'd almost forgotten what it was like—how Adrian's warmth wrapped around him, how his attention was making him feel invincible, how cherished he felt in Adrian's presence. In that moment, nothing else existed. It was the best feeling in the world, like surf crashing against his chest, pulling him deeper into the current, and he couldn't breathe without it.

Logan felt the groan slip from his lips, raw and unbidden, like something torn from deep within. Fire crackled over his skin, an electric current of memory igniting every nerve. The taste of Adrian lingered on his tongue, searing and intoxicating, dragging him under. And suddenly, he was flying, weightless, untethered, back to their last moments together. Back to the edge of the world, where nothing else mattered. Where he was free.

He could feel it all as if no time had passed. The quiet mornings wrapped in Adrian's arms, his breath warm against his skin. The hand on his face, now and then, holding him close, anchoring him. Laughter tangled in sheets, soft and breathless, Adrian's fingers trailing down his spine, his grip tightening on his hip, pulling him impossibly close, kissing him like a starving man.

The lazy afternoons stretched across the deck of a yacht, the Australian sky endless above them, the sun painting their skin in gold. The salt-heavy air, the distant hum of the waves, the world slowing to the rhythm of their breathing.

Adrian's desperate moan against his lips. The heat between them, unrelenting, insatiable.

And the ocean... pulling him under, releasing him, the cool air filling his lungs as he surfaced. His gaze searching for Adrian, finding him. His surfboard bobbing at the edge of his vision, the sunlight catching in his hair. And in that moment, Logan had known—the world was good. The world was theirs. They were the tide and the shore, two forces destined to meet and part, drawn together by something older than time, crashing into one another again and again, until nothing remained but the rhythm of their hearts echoing in tandem, the pulse of the ocean threading through their veins, and the quiet thunder of a love too vast to outrun, too wild to cage.

Logan let himself drown in Adrian, just for a moment longer.

He let the sunlight and the sky and the scent of saltwater linger on his body, let the echo of all the days they had lived under the same sun take hold of him like something he'd been waiting for without knowing it. He let the memory of Adrian become everything, let it flood every corner of his soul.

The way Adrian held him, like something sacred, like something he had fought for. The way his neck strained from bending down to meet Adrian's sweet lips. The way he smelled, salt, the shampoo he'd always used, and something that always made Logan feel safe. The way his touch made Logan feel seen. Loved. Known. He memorized the shape of Adrian's body against his, the heat of his palms, the way his hands and body moved, slow and frantic all at once, like he was both savoring and starving for this. Adrian was gentle and impatient, desperate and soft, all at the same time.

Logan kissed him like it was the last time, because in some way, he knew it was. He kissed Adrian with everything he had left—every broken shard of his soul, every piece he had hidden, every apology he couldn't say, every ounce of love that had lived like a ghost beneath his skin. He poured it all into that kiss. And he took everything from it too—every breath, every taste, every tremble—because the last time they had kissed, he hadn't known it would be the last. But now the sky and the sun and the ocean had granted him this one final moment, and he wasn't going to waste it. He wanted to carry it with him. Forever.

And then the weight returned. The unbearable weight of what had to come next.

His chest seized with it, thick with grief and guilt and all the pieces of the life he'd broken. His hands trembled as they rose, and then—

Logan pushed Adrian away.

The movement was soft, but final. Like tearing a limb from his own body. He watched, powerless, as the hurt flooded Adrian's whiskey-colored eyes, that sudden flinch like a wound ripped open. And still—Logan didn't relent. He couldn't. Not now. Not when every part of him was unraveling.

"Go," he rasped, the word catching like glass in his throat. "Just... go."

Adrian's voice was barely a whisper. "Logan, don't marry her. I get it, you don't want to be with me. But don't do this to yourself... or to her. She does not deserve it!"

How could Adrian think that? How could he believe Logan didn't want him? Wanting him had been the only truth he dared to speak, the only dream he'd ever whispered into the dark. *I want you.*

But all he could say was, "Adrian! Get the fuck out of here. I don't want you here!" The words tore from him like shards of glass, bitter and merciless, a lie sharpened to wound. He lied to Adrian, wounding him with intention, even as the aftertaste of him still clung to his tongue, even as his lips still tingled from the softness of Adrian's stubble. He pushed him away while the burn of his touch still seared his skin, while the ghost of his warmth still pulsed through him. His heart drummed with the echo of that kiss, yet he forced himself to bury it, to bury *him*. Logan could not breathe; his chest tightened, seized, his lungs collapsing beneath the weight of denial.

Adrian's voice trembled as he tried again, "It's 2019. You can be yourself. You can love who you love, you can be openly gay—"

"I'm not gay! I'm not!" Logan shouted the words in a frantic attempt to hold himself together, to keep the world from slipping into the deep, dark ocean that threatened him.

Adrian's eyes were shattered, his lips trembling. "Who are you trying to convince? Me or yourself?"

"Leave now!" Logan screamed, the rawness of it ruining him. "Go back to wherever the hell you came from!"

Please, don't go... the voice in his mind screamed, but he couldn't say it. He couldn't let Adrian see him crack.

The silence between them was thick, suffocating, as Adrian stood frozen, like the world itself had stopped turning. And then the sadness in Adrian's eyes—God, it was unbearable. The way his face crumbled, the shoulders that slumped with defeat.

"I love you, Logan." Adrian's voice was a whisper, desperate and broken, as if he had bled the words from somewhere deep inside himself. His gaze fell, unable to meet Logan's, like the significance of what he was saying was too much to bear.

"You're in a mess right now, Logan," Adrian continued, his voice thick with anguish. "A mess of your own making. You're running from yourself again. Just like you did back in July. But despite everything, I need you to know..." His voice faltered, a sob escaping, raw and jagged, unraveling the last of his strength. "...you are everything to me." *The air I breathe, the sun on my face, the water of the ocean, the tides, the currents, all of it—Logan, you are everything.* Adrian's heart and soul were tethered to Logan, tied to the very atoms of his being, and it was a bond that could never be broken, no matter how far apart they were.

How much courage had it taken for Adrian to say those words? To speak his soul out loud, knowing it would tear him apart? Logan couldn't bear it. He couldn't even find the strength to meet his eyes. Instead, he turned away, tears welling up, blurring everything. The room felt heavy, and Logan could not carry that load.

And in that silence, Logan's heart shattered into a thousand pieces, each one a reminder of a love he couldn't have. The words Adrian had spoken would haunt him, the depth of them too much to hold, too much to bear.

Adrian smiled. It was a smile so wrong, so heavy with pain, that Logan could feel it tear through him like a blade. It would haunt him for the rest of his life.

"I won't tell anyone," Adrian whispered, his voice breaking, and then he turned. "Goodbye, Logan."

And as Adrian was about to disappear from his life, Logan's heart cracked open, bleeding in ways he didn't even know were possible.

"You shouldn't have saved me," Logan murmured, his words barely a whisper, slipping from the darkest corners of his soul. Was it a plea? A final attempt to hold onto Adrian just a few seconds longer? He couldn't be sure, but the pain in those words felt like it had been carved into him for years.

Adrian froze, his hand on the door handle, and Logan saw him shrink, as if each word had ripped through him like a bullet. Adrian's body trembled, and for a moment, the space between them seemed vast and empty.

"No," Adrian's voice cracked, splintering beneath the weight of emotion. "I should've saved you. I should've been there." His breath hitched, his hands trembling at his sides. "Because, on some level, I swear, fate put me on that beach for you. To make sure you made it. To pull you back when the tide tried to take you. A world without you is a world I could never live in, and I will never wish it. Not for a second. Not even when it broke me."

His voice wavered, caught between anger and grief, between love and regret. He swallowed hard, forcing the next words past the lump in his throat. "But I should've walked away. I should've left after that."

The silence that followed was deafening. A chasm stretched between them, filled with all the things they never said, all the things they could never take back. Adrian exhaled sharply, his chest rising and falling as if the ocean itself had carved his sorrow into his bones.

"I should've let you go." The lie burned on Adrian's tongue because even now, after everything, he knew—he never could.

The words hung in the air.

Adrian turned the doorknob, his hand shaking as if the weight of the moment might shatter him. For a heartbeat, he closed his eyes, pulling the last remnants of himself together, trying to steady the storm raging inside. He looked around the room aimlessly, but it was all too much, too empty. Everything he had laid at Logan's feet, every ounce of love, now felt like it had been swallowed whole, leaving only a hollow ache behind.

"I wish I'd never let you buy me that beer, I wish I walked away from you..." He whispered, almost to the walls, to the air, to himself. The words broke loose like chains wrenched from bone, cruel in their release. The regret, the longing, the ache of it all pressed against him, but there was no time left to say anything more. No more words, no more chances.

Adrian turned and walked away, each step a slow death, each movement a piece of him pulled away. With every footstep, Logan's chest cracked open, bleeding out everything he had left. He stood there, frozen, unable to move, unable to breathe, watching the man he loved walk away forever.

Adrian was walking away, leaving him to drown in the wreckage of his own choices. And even though everything in Logan screamed for him to reach out, to grasp the lifeline Adrian was offering, he couldn't. He let him go. He let his love slip away. As Adrian disappeared from view, Logan's heart followed. The last flicker of hope, the last breath of light he had held onto, slipped away. His tears fell, endless, like a tide that wouldn't recede.

I love you so much, Adrian. I'm so sorry. The words stayed locked in his throat, unspoken, unsent, a prayer that never reached its recipient, dissolving into the silence. He did not move, did not reach for him. And when the door clicked shut behind Adrian, the sound was final, merciless, like the sealing of a tomb. Logan collapsed to the floor, undone, the weight of everything he had destroyed bearing down on him. A thousand unsaid confessions tore through his chest, spilling into the silence, heavy and suffocating. He sat there shattered, his body wracked with sobs, broken open by the absence of the only one he could not hold.

Logan stood at the altar, a shell of a man, his body trembling like a leaf caught in a storm. He watched Sandy approach, radiant, her smile wide and glowing, so unaware of the war waging within him. She was beautiful, yes, in that way that made the sun seem dull beside her, but all he could feel was the cold grip of the ocean, pulling him deeper, dragging him away from everything he had ever known.

Her father gave her to him with a kiss, a gesture of love and pride that made Logan feel like an impostor. Sandy's smile was a light he didn't deserve, a beacon in a storm that he couldn't trust. His voice was steady as he told her, "You look beautiful," but the words felt like ash in his mouth. They were a mask, a thin veil over the storm that raged inside him, a storm made of regret, of love, of a soul slowly being drowned in its own sorrow.

When the priest began his sermon, Logan's gaze drifted over the gathered crowd, his breath steady, his expression composed. The words washed past him. All he could hear were Adrian's soft whimpers ghosting against his mouth, echoing through the spaces he had tried so hard to seal. He stood at the altar like a trespasser in the life he was pretending to claim. And then, cutting through the room like a lone light breaking open a dark sea, he saw him. Adrian.

His heart stumbled in his chest, as if the very sight of him had the power to break him all over again. Adrian sat motionless, a storm wrapped in silence, his eyes catching the light like polished stone beneath water, unblinking, unreadable, unbearable. There was no anger in his face, only devastation, a quiet, dignified sorrow that shimmered at the edges of his lashes, as if tears were not falling but waiting, reverent and restrained, adorning his eyes. His pain was not loud, but it was vast. His heartbreak needed no words; it was etched into his features like a tragedy too devastating to turn away from, too heavy to bear. It echoed in the set of his jaw, in the way he held himself upright like a monument to all they had lost. And in that moment, Logan felt it, like a blade buried in his ribs, like breath pulled from his lungs. He saw what he had done. What he was doing. He saw how time had done nothing to dull the wound. It had only gilded it, polished it into something unbearable, something neither of them had ever truly learned to live without.

The vows came from his mouth like borrowed language, words spoken by a stranger. They were soft, precise, and meaningless. Promises carved from ash. *To have and to hold.* He could barely breathe. *For better, for worse.* Each phrase scraped against something raw inside him. *To love and to cherish.* His voice faltered, his vision blurred, but he forced the next words through gritted teeth. *Till death do us part.* And with them, something inside him died.

He looked at Adrian again, just as the final vow slipped from his lips—empty words tied to a future he didn't believe in. Adrian's eyes met his like the strike of a match in a darkened room, sharp and sudden, illuminating everything Logan had tried to bury. The pain in them was quiet but merciless, a wound without sound, and yet it tore through him more violently than any scream could have. That gaze—steady, unflinching—was a reckoning. It held no accusation, only the unbearable truth of love abandoned. And still, Adrian said nothing. He didn't need to. His silence was a language only Logan could understand, a kind of farewell that didn't beg or break, only bled. It was the last crash of the tide, the final pull beneath the surface, and Logan felt himself go under.

And then the moment came. The minister's voice echoed, "You may kiss the bride," and it was as though the world had tilted on its axis. Logan leaned forward to kiss Sandy, his lips meeting hers in a kiss that felt like betrayal, a cruel lie that he could hardly bear. Just minutes earlier, Adrian had kissed him passionately, reminding him of everything they meant to one another. Now, that kiss was brief and cold, just a feeble gesture to finalize their agreement, yet in Logan's mind, it felt like a thousand knives piercing his heart. He could still feel Adrian's eyes on him, watching, waiting, breaking the last remaining fragments.

The applause erupted around him, but it was muffled, distant. He couldn't hear the cheers, couldn't see the smiles, because all he could see was Adrian, walking away, the love of his life slipping away from him like water through his fingers.

Logan's heart was destroyed by now, it was a thousand pieces falling to the floor with the weight of a love lost, of a choice made, of a soul that could never be whole again. His chest felt hollow, empty, a cavern where Adrian's presence had once been. The world spun around him, and he knew—he knew with a devastating certainty—that he had made the wrong choice. That in his attempt to save others, he had demolished himself.

Sandy, beautiful and kind, stood beside him, her hand warm around his, but Logan's eyes stayed fixed on the path—on the space where Adrian had stood just moments before. The place where he had turned and walked away, quiet and composed, like someone retreating from the edge of a cliff. No slammed doors, no words, just the fading imprint of his presence in the sunlight. Logan watched that emptiness, as if staring hard enough might bring him back, as if love could reverse itself like the wind.

Tears spilled down Logan's face, but the world didn't notice. No one saw the agony written across his soul. They saw the smile he forced, the smile he showed to a world that would never understand the pain of loving the wrong person. They hugged him, congratulated him, told him how beautiful the day was, how emotional he was. But all Logan could feel was the ache, the emptiness, the cruel, unyielding truth of what he had just done.

Adrian had walked away, and Logan let him. He let him slip through his fingers like sand, unable to stop him, unable to reach for him. He never said the words he needed to say. He never called out to Adrian to come back, to take him away from this.

"You're my everything too," Logan whispered to the empty space Adrian had once filled, but it was too late. The words were swallowed by the void between them.

There was no sound to a heart breaking, only the suffocating quiet that surrounded it, thick with the weight of things left unsaid. But if it had a sound, it would have been the low, almost imperceptible moan that slipped from Logan's throat, a sound the ocean might have recognized. He watched Adrian vanish into the crowd while his bride clung to his arm, innocent of the storm in his chest. His tears were not for joy. They were for a grief he could not name.

If a heart breaking had a shape, it would have been etched into Logan's longing gaze, reaching for the love of his life as Adrian walked farther away. Each step Adrian took felt like a crack in the world, splitting the ground beneath Logan's feet.

Love had a shape, and it was Adrian; the way he moved, the way he *was*, carved into Logan's soul like a tide that could never be undone.

Love had a sound, and it was Adrian's laugh, bright and wild, like the breaking surf, full of life and everything Logan had once imagined for himself.

Love had a color, and it was the molten whisky of Adrian's eyes, a depth that Logan could drown in, a warmth that burned too brightly, too fiercely to hold in this lifetime. But it was already slipping away, the flame flickering in the shadow of duty, of promises he made that felt more like chains than vows.

And there was no more love—only the wreckage it left behind. Only the heartbreak that lingered in its wake, sharp as glass, endless as the tide. Only the memories, glowing ember-red, enough to sear him from the inside out.

Just the longing.

Just the wind, carrying whispers of what once was. Just the sun, casting its golden gaze upon the place where their love had flourished. Just the sky, vast and indifferent, stretching above them as it always had. Just the stream of water, winding through time, a quiet witness to the way they had once fit together, to the way they had unraveled.

They remembered them; they had witnessed the crushing of Logan and Adrian, even if the world had moved on. Even if Logan was expected to do the same.

And so, Logan stood there, a man with a beautiful wife he could never love, in a world he no longer wanted to be a part of. His soul had already walked away with Adrian, and the body that remained was nothing more than a hollow shell, a ghost of the man he could never be.

And just like that, Logan Vaughn's journey through hell had begun.

January 3, 2020—Seattle, Washington—One Year Later

*Moments, fleeting, always slipping through my grasp—chasing them like
shadows stretching in the dying light. Late nights swallowed whole by work,
by routine, by the quiet suffocation of days bleeding into one another. The
weight of indifference coiled around me, thick as smoke, a cloak of darkness
draped over my skin.*

*My aura—dimmed, dulled—once radiant, now colorless. A life drained of
vibrance, stripped of warmth, not even the faintest ember of light left to hold
onto. Just the hollow echo of something lost, something stolen by time and
choice and the cruel, unrelenting truth—I had let go of the only thing that
ever made me feel alive.*

*So I stayed buried beneath layers of fake smiles, wearing them as if they were
real. I feel my happiness eroding beneath them, as if somewhere along the
way, I have forgotten how to smile sincerely, the art of laughter stolen by my
own demons. I play pretend, burying my secrets deep within, sensing you in
the quiet spaces. The fake smiles keep the world at bay, cloaking me in a veneer
of normalcy, an illusion that became a reality.*

"HAPPY FUCKING-VERSARY." LOGAN MUTTERED, his voice rough, as he
stepped into the dim-lit bar, the familiar sting of the alcohol already pulling
at him. One year. One year trapped in the suffocating echo of a choice
that never should've been made. He had just finished work, as usual, and
once again found himself drawn here, to this quiet bar where no one cared,
where no one asked him to be anything other than the broken man he was.

The first few weeks of marriage had been hell. Sandy, with all
her well-intentioned effort, had tried to be the wife she thought she
should be—organizing dinner parties, booking restaurant reservations,

scheduling family visits, filling their calendar with noise and movement. She talked, she planned, she reached for him again and again, hoping to mend something in Logan she couldn't name. But the empty, soundless void between them had a shape, and it bore Adrian's name. Logan, on the other hand, tried to wear the smile of a good husband, though it was a mask that cracked more with each passing day. They were strangers in their own home, living side by side but oceans apart.

It had been easier, he told himself, to disappear here. To let the dim lights and the bitter burn of whisky silence the ache in his chest. Here, he didn't have to pretend. Here, he could just *be*.

"My usual," he said dryly, sinking into his seat at the bar, staring blankly at the polished wood as if it might offer him some solace. He pulled his phone from his pocket, fingers numb as he typed a quick message to Sandy:

> I'll be late.

He didn't even need to look at it as he pressed send. It was not the first time he'd sent that exact message.

A new bartender, young and eager, glanced up, pulling Logan from his thoughts. "And what would that be?"

Logan blinked up at him, slightly startled. The question was odd. He'd been coming here for nearly a year now, ordering the same damn drink every time. But then again, the bartender was new. "You're new," Logan said, his voice carrying more weariness than curiosity. "What happened to the last one?"

"Left," the bartender said simply, pouring drinks and sliding them across the bar with a casual grace.

Logan nodded absently, running a hand through his hair. "Whisky neat."

The drink slid to him, but Logan didn't feel the immediate comfort he once did. Instead, he stared at it, watching the liquid swirl inside the glass. It reminded him of something, of a place he couldn't go back to, a life he couldn't unlive. He could feel Adrian's presence behind his eyelids, even though Adrian had long since stopped calling, stopped texting, stopped being a part of his life.

He took his phone out again, finding himself refreshing Adrian's Facebook page again, even though he knew there would be nothing new. Not a word. Not a photo. Just silence, like a door slammed shut between them. His fingers hovered over the screen, then he closed it, shoving the phone into his pocket, his chest tightening with that familiar pang of longing.

God, he missed him.

His breath hitched as he swirled the whisky in his glass. He drained it in one go, the warmth of it spreading through him, though it couldn't warm the coldest parts of him, but maybe he could numb that ache that seemed to live just beneath his skin.

His phone beeped. A message from Sandy:

> Okay. I'm waiting for you. Thanks for the flowers, by the way. Got them a few hours ago.

Logan cursed under his breath. Of course. The assistant had taken care of it, sending her the flowers and chocolates, booking the weekend getaway Logan had pretended to plan. She was too kind, too hopeful, and Logan had allowed her to keep believing in something that he had long since stopped believing in himself.

He scrolled back through the gallery on his phone. Adrian's smiling face, caught in a moment that felt like a lifetime ago. He stopped on a photo of Adrian, playing the guitar, unaware that Logan was even watching him. Adrian had been so carefree, so alive, so full of everything Logan wasn't. He found himself staring at it, that ghost of a smile pulling at his lips, as though it could ever be enough to fill the emptiness in his chest.

But it wasn't.

Not for the first time, Logan silently thanked his relentless need to capture moments, to cling to time in frames and fragments. His love for filming had always been an obsession, a quiet compulsion, but now, it felt like salvation.

During their trip, with his beloved GoPro—the one he, too, had left behind—he had captured Adrian in ways the world never could. He had filmed laughter woven with sunlight, hands reaching, bodies falling into each other like gravity itself had conspired to keep them close. He had recorded fleeting seconds of love so raw, so unguarded, they now felt like relics from another life.

These memories, etched in light and inked in happiness, *should* be enough to last him a lifetime.

They must be.

They must.

And yet, as he sat in the silence of the present, drowning in the ghosts of their past, he knew they never would be.

Logan couldn't live in that memory forever. He couldn't stay trapped in a ghost of a life he had let slip away, so he stood, leaving money on the bar, his stomach turning with each step he took away from the only thing that was able to numb him.

The drive home was silent, the weight of it pressing down on him harder than any hangover. One drink hadn't been enough. He needed more to escape the reality that had been clawing at him, that had been pulling him further and further from himself.

When he arrived home, Sandy was waiting for him, standing in the doorway with that smile, the smile that he had to learn to hate. She was wearing a robe, her black tights accentuating her legs, and Logan's stomach churned as the thought hit him with brutal clarity: he was going to have to have sex with her again.

The only person who suffered in that marriage more than Logan was Sandy—trapped in a union just like him, with a man who wore a smile like armor, but whose heart was never really hers to begin with.

"I'm sorry," he murmured as he kissed her, the hollow kiss of a man who had long since given up on being a husband. She smelled of lavender and warmth, and he wished it didn't feel so wrong. But it did.

They had sex before, sure. But he managed to be away from home as much as possible, mostly by coming home when she was asleep. On weekends, he would usually tell her he went surfing even though he hadn't set foot in the ocean since he got back home. So, he limited the possibilities for sex as much as possible. Plus, he always bought her some special gifts like plane tickets to some fancy country, hotels, or spa—anything that would get her away from him, with the hope that he could buy the happiness he would never give her.

He cared for Sandy but never loved her.

Inside, the house was quiet, candles flickering on the table, casting soft shadows against the walls. Logan's throat closed as the scent of dinner filled the air.

"You work so hard, Logan," Sandy said softly, her voice a tender echo in the quiet room.

"Yeah," he replied, the words hollow as they slipped from his lips. "You know how my dad is... and I don't want people to think I'm just there because of him... I need to prove myself." It wasn't a lie, exactly. He did work hard, but it was more than that. He worked to avoid the weight of his own soul, to escape the ghost of Adrian that clung to every corner of his mind. His work was a prison, a way to drown out the agony of coming home, of pretending that the life he built was enough. Three lies wrapped in one act of relentless motion.

Sandy had arranged everything. The table for two and the aroma of warm food filled the air, but the comfort was empty; he did not deserve any of it.

"Something smells wonderful," Logan remarked, his voice tense, battling the ache in his chest.

Sandy's face lit up, her smile like a flickering candle in the dark. "Thank you," she said, the words too innocent, too unaware of the chasm between them.

Logan reached into his pocket, the red envelope crinkling in his hand like a small, desperate apology. "It's for you," he said, handing it over, his fingers brushing hers for a moment. Sandy took it with a smile, so eager, so full of hope.

"It's a weekend at a hotel," he continued, his voice a little quieter now. "Spas, pools, massages... all that stuff."

Sandy's eyes widened with excitement, a spark of joy lighting her face. "Oh my god! We're going to a spa?!"

Logan's heart sank. "Oh, no. I can't. I have to work." His words were sharp, too quick, but he couldn't help it. "It's an open ticket. You can take one of your girlfriends or something."

"What? You're not coming with me again?" Her voice wavered, the hurt slipping through, but Logan cut her off before she could argue.

"I'm sorry. I can't," he said, his voice cracking ever so slightly. He stepped closer, cupping her face in his hands, feeling the warmth of her skin, but it did nothing to thaw the coldness inside him. His thumb traced the curve of her cheek, a gesture so familiar yet so foreign. "But I want you to go. You deserve it. You've been alone so much... Go and enjoy. We have a lifetime to be together."

His lips brushed hers, soft as remembrance, yet heavy with the taste of treachery he had long since learned to bear. The kiss carried no warmth, only the ghost of what love had once been, trembling like a dying ember in the hollow of habit. It tasted of sorrow, of rusted promises and quiet rot, of a tenderness that had forgotten its name.

He kissed her the way a man confesses; not out of devotion, but out of duty to the life he built upon his own undoing. Each touch was an echo of pretending, an act of survival disguised as affection. Her mouth was familiar, yet foreign, a landscape he wandered without belonging.

And beneath it all, he felt the tremor of another truth. The one he could not speak, the one that burned behind his ribs. A longing for the man whose name he never dared whisper in the dark. That kiss was not love, but a requiem for it: a ritual of guilt and yearning, of trying and never arriving, of reaching for a dream that dissolved at the edge of his own shame.

"You told me last week you were ready to launch your clothing line, but you needed to finalize some last details. Use this time for that. Take some time off to get everything in order and finish the things you need before it all happens."

Sandy nodded, her eyes soft with understanding, but there was something else—something too sad to name. She lay her head against his chest, her arms wrapping around him, and for a moment, Logan wished he could feel something.

Anything.

"Missed you, Logan," she murmured, her words breaking something inside him. "So, so much."

"Me too," he lied, his own voice like a whisper in the dark.

"I'm so lucky to have such an amazing husband," she whispered, her voice so soft, so full of love.

But Logan knew, deep down, he wasn't the husband she thought he was. He wasn't the man who could love her the way she deserved.

She let go of him and walked toward the kitchen, placing the envelope on the counter. And not for the first time, Logan stood there, feeling like a stranger in his own life.

"It smells like you've made something special."

"Oh, you don't know. I'm just getting started," she looked back at him, her eyes seductive, as she pulled her robe up, exposing a tiny lace thong, and a suspender belt. Biting her lips. "I think you will like the other things I planned for us tonight."

Logan swallowed hard and hated himself, knowing that move should have made him throbbing in his pants, going over to her and tearing that robe. But he could not feel anything other than panic to have to go through it again. Even before meeting Adrian, he wasn't a very sexual person; sex had been tolerable, and he had it with women, Sandy among them, but it was never the fuss people made it to be.

The only thing that had ever unraveled him, that had shattered his carefully built control, was *Adrian.* Only Adrian had ever made him reckless, made him storm through a room without a second thought, driven by nothing but raw need. Only Adrian had ever made his blood burn, his breath hitch, his body *demand*—every nerve alight, every inch of him aching, throbbing with something deeper than desire. With Adrian, restraint had never stood a chance. He was fire in Logan's veins, a pull too strong to resist, a gravity that had always drawn him in.

No, he should go to her, kiss her like a man, claim what was his, and then lead her to the bedroom.

And that's exactly what he did. In a single motion, reckless and void of thought, he crossed the space between them. He spun her around, his lips crashing against hers with the force of a lie, a kiss that tasted like regret.

It felt wrong—so wrong—and yet he clung to her, his arms tight around her, suffocating himself in the bitter taste of self-loathing. The more he pressed into her, the more he drowned in the hollow space between his body and his soul.

"Let's eat later," he said and started walking her to the bedroom. Once they reached the stairs, he put his hands around her hips, and she jumped up, clinging to him. With one hand on Sandy, and the other holding the railing, Logan climbed up the stairs, kissing his beautiful wife.

Once they reached the bedroom, Sandy took a step away from him and slowly started undoing her robe, taking it off as her eyes picked up beneath her lashes and her white teeth biting her lips. The satin robe fell to the floor, leaving her in just a tiny lace black bra that revealed more than it covered, and a thong that tantalized with the view of her pussy through the sheer fabric.

She moved her hand on the suspended belt, the move slow and her fingers seductively touching her skin and the belt. Her hand drifted lower until her thin fingers rubbed on her pussy through the fabric.

Logan mentally prepared himself for what was about to happen; he had done it before, and he could do it again. He took off his suit jacket, then his shoes, his pants, and by the time he was opening the buttons of his shirt, Sandy was in front of him, her hands on the front of his boxers' briefs. Her hands grazed his soft member.

Then she lowered herself to her knees and pushed the boxers down. Logan shrugged off his wrinkled white shirt, letting it fall to the floor. Across from him was the vanity mirror and the stranger that looked at him took his breath away: hollowed cheeks, ribs jutting sharply under his skin, the once-toned lines of his abs faded into shadows. Every ounce of joy he'd ever known had vanished with Adrian, leaving behind only the hollow ache, a silhouette of the man he once was.

He shut his eyes, letting his brain rest and trying desperately to focus clearly on the warmth his dick was enveloped in, the moving hand on his base, and the soft moans Sandy made.

Nope. Nothing.

He gazed down at Sandy as she took his soft cock to her mouth, and he wailed his body to start responding. His body remembered—achingly, vividly—the time before the hollow ache, when every touch felt electric, setting his skin on fire. Once, he was alive under another's hands, a breathless mess of want, where even the graze of fingers on his arm would send sparks spiraling through him. The air around them had pulsed with something thick, charged, so that each breath felt like too much and not enough. He remembered the weight, the warmth pressed against him, the slow burn that built with each passing second. His body knew, even now, what it was to be cherished, and it mourned for that lost spark. He thought of whisky-colored eyes locked on him as he deep-throated him, and then his cock stirred in Sandy's mouth.

He cracked open the hidden box within him, releasing memories he had buried so deep he'd nearly forgotten the weight of them. These were memories tinged with salt and sun, wrapped in the scent of ocean air and held close by the rhythm of waves crashing endlessly against the shore. In those memories, there was only him and another, the silent sea their only witness. They moved together, timeless and unbound, every moment searing, every laugh stolen against a backdrop of fading light. In that place, he'd felt endless, weightless, filled with a kind of joy he barely dared to remember.

He recalled the moment vividly: his fingers had gripped Adrian's long hair tightly, the silky strands slipping through his fingers like water, and the intensity of the memory held him captive. As he stood there, his hand instinctively moved toward Sandy's hair. He felt the soft waves brush against his skin, and he tangled his fingers in different strands. Though his mind was aware of the distinction between the two, in that moment, he sought comfort and connection, embracing whatever familiarity he could grasp amidst the confusion.

He remembered Adrian's fingers grazing his skin and the buzz that followed, the way he kissed down his stomach and licked him, how he kneed his ass while admiring his cock. *"You are so damn sexy, Lo,"* he heard the fantom of Adrian's voice as he lavished attention on his dick like a desperate man.

His eyes were closed as he let the memory engulf him. Logan's dick finally came to life, showing interest in the memory of the man of his dreams. *"You take my finger so well,"* he heard Adrian's voice, the husky way he'd said it, the way his breath ghosted over Logan's skin. *"I want to eat you out,"* Logan audibly groaned as those words played in the depths of his mind.

Then Sandy let him go and pulled him to the bed as she lay on her front, spreading her legs and inviting him in.

Logan reached for a condom from the nightstand, even though he knew Sandy was on the pill, Logan wasn't willing to take any chances with pregnancy.

He got himself ready and stroked himself a bit as he felt his passion cooling down. His hands tugged the little thong, pulling it down from Sandy's body. Almost mechanically, he positioned himself against her entrance and filled her with one push, making her moan. Dissociating himself from this scenario, from the moment, from the life he was trapped in, he drove in and out of her. At this point, Logan did not know if it was actually related to Sandy or to the deep melancholy that suffocated him, taking his air, and drowning him.

Sandy reached between her thighs and started rubbing her pussy as Logan continued fucking in and out of her. Her moans and whimpers fill the room, and she screamed as her orgasm ripped through her body, shaking and quivering around Logan, who was far behind her.

He moved within her with the rhythm of someone keeping time, each thrust a heartbeat closer to silence. His body obeyed its duty, but his mind drifted elsewhere, to the man whose touch still haunted the edges of his skin. He counted the moments, not in pleasure, but in escape, each breath a quiet plea for it to end.

She bit her lip beneath him, her body trembling with life, while his remained elsewhere, hollowed by absence. The room pulsed with her sounds, with the illusion of closeness, yet he felt nothing but the slow suffocation of repetition. It was not desire, but endurance, not love, but the dull choreography of need and guilt.

He closed his eyes as she came, not to savor it, but to vanish, to slip back into the dream of another body, another truth, one he could never name aloud.

Eventually, the sounds in his head swelled into noise, drowning her soft breaths. He withdrew, half-hard, half-ghost, the weight of her body fading beneath his hands. What lingered was not release, but the hollow ache of unfinished desire, the taste of someone else's name on his tongue, swallowed before it could escape.

"I... can't come." He said silently.

She was panting and turned around to him. "Keep going," she urged, her hand softly touching his thigh.

Logan wiped the sweat from his forehead and shook his head. "It's... just not. I, hum... guess I'm just tired from work, and... there is that someone... thing. Something with work... that I... have to do—" he started mumbling, trying to find excuses as to why his sexy-as-hell wife wasn't enough to get him off.

Sandy took her thong completely off herself, then her bra, leaving her wearing only the suspender belt and the chiffon-laced thighs.

"What do you want me to do, Logan?" she asked softly, palming one of her breasts.

Shame engulfed him as he watched her loving eyes gazing at him. She was probably willing to fulfill every bedroom wish he had, no matter what came to mind. And he knew she wouldn't drop the subject if he asked her to just leave it alone, that he was too tired to come right now.

He sat in silence for several minutes, trying to find something to say to her. He couldn't understand what was different about today. When they had had sex previously, Logan managed to get himself off, at least to calm his body's needs.

He gazed at the lifesaver bracelet on his wrist, its charm shimmering like the first day he received it. It still carried the essence of salty ocean air, cool water, and soft sand.

Even now, as he stood firmly on solid ground and breathed freely without struggle, it continued to protect him in its own quiet way. Each day, it offered a gentle reminder that the memories he held were not merely figments of his imagination but tangible pieces of his Adrian.

"Porn maybe...?" she suddenly offered and rose to her feet.

"Wha...?" He blurted out. "Yeah, okay." He managed to say.

"Your laptop is here?" she asked.

No way was he going to let her touch his laptop. He would never let any living soul look at this device for even a second. His laptop contained a world he wasn't ready to share, a place where secrets and personal reflections were safely tucked away from prying eyes.

He shook his head, and she went for a second, then came back to the room carrying her own. Sandy typed on the keys and the screen.

"What do you want?" she asked silently, sitting on the bed with the laptop next to her.

"I... hum." He started and felt himself blushing in embarrassment as he watched the little pictures that represented videos and categories.

"Don't be shy with me, Logan. When you watch porn, what do you like?" she asked, her little soft smile easing his embarrassment a bit.

When he watched porn... it was always the same type. Always men who looked like *him*—tanned skin, muscular build, long hair that had some blond sun-kissed strands in it, a perfect mix of soldier and surfer. That rare, impossible blend that only Adrian had ever truly embodied.

There weren't many videos that fit the mold. Not enough to satisfy the ghost of what he craved. But it never really mattered. Because in the end, when he got himself off—on the rare occasions he even felt the need—his mind never needed substitutes. It was always Adrian.

It was Adrian's hands he felt, Adrian's voice in his ear, Adrian's body pressing into him, claiming him, undoing him. The memories were sharper than any fantasy, burned into his skin, etched into his bones.

"Just, whatever you want..." he said, too flustered by the situation to think clearly. "Just... ahh, pick something."

And she shook her head with a little smile on her face and clicked a few times on the screen, and then moans and exaggerated sex noises filled the room as the video played in which a young, muscled, tattooed guy was getting his dick sucked by a woman. Logan was hyper-focused on the guy; he watched as his ass flexed when he shoved his dick down the girl's throat. He watched intently as his thighs tightened with each movement, the powerful muscles rippling beneath the surface, evidence of countless hours spent training. However, it was his arms that truly captivated him. They were not just strong; they were impressively massive, with bulging biceps that seemed to swell with every motion. The defined veins just beneath the skin hinted at the hard work he had put into sculpting them. Each time he raised his arms, his shoulder blades shifted gracefully, emphasizing the sheer power within him and creating a striking silhouette that radiated confidence and vigor. And it worked, his cock jerked to life, and he felt the pressure in his balls.

"So, you have a thing for blonds?" Sandy pointed, giggling lightly.

"Huh?" Logan said, and only then did he notice the woman.

Right. The woman was blonde.

He chuckled uncomfortably and nodded to his wife.

He pushed her back on the mattress and covered her body with his. As he kissed her, he made sure to keep his eyes glued to the screen, where the guy was now fucking the girl from behind. He flipped Sandy to her back and pushed into her with one movement, imagining it was the gorgeous guy he wanted to be with.

The moans from the computer and from Sandy and himself filled the silent house as Logan finally found his release. His cock jerked into the condom as he thrust in and out of Sandy's body, holding her hips with one hand. As his orgasm eased, he still lay on top of his wife, and reached with one hand to close the laptop's lid, and the room went completely silent, just the sound of his and Sandy's breathing broke the soundlessness.

"Thank you," he mumbled and kissed her shoulder. Her skin was soft and smooth.

"I love you, Logan," she whispered and turned her head to search for his lips. He kissed her mouth briefly before he pulled away.

"Me too."

It wasn't a lie. He did love her, just... not like he knew he should have.

Chapter 4
The Shape of What I Felt

July 10, 2018—North Shore, Oahu, Hawaii—One Year and Six Months Earlier

LOGAN STUDIED HIMSELF IN the cracked mirror hanging in his tiny beach cabin, lit only by the amber slant of the sun dipping into the horizon. The ocean whispered just outside his window, beckoning as it always did, filling his mind with the ceaseless rhythms of tides and waves. He and Adrian had been riding those same waves together for five days now, and somehow, it felt like lifetimes. Days of salt-washed mornings, golden afternoons, and nights that pulsed with laughter had stretched between them like the unbroken line of a wave—intense, boundless, and yet always threatening to crash.

He felt that Adrian was a part of him now, mornings and evenings together, full days side by side, and he could not fathom the idea of being out there alone.

Every thought of Adrian stirred something deep in him. His grin faltered as the memory surfaced: sooner or later, Adrian would have to leave, just like the tides always pull away, just like waves eventually fold back into the sea. The very idea of it tightened his chest, a slow, creeping chill that felt all wrong here in the warm cradle of sand and surf. Adrian hadn't mentioned when he'd be leaving, hadn't said anything concrete, but Logan could feel the clock ticking, the slow pull of an undertow. And yet, every time he thought of asking Adrian to stay, fear gnawed at him—fear of seeming too needy, fear that Adrian might say yes just to spare his feelings, an answer that would feel like driftwood between them, floating but hollow.

A soft knock broke through his reverie, scattering the tangled thoughts like foam on the shore. Logan opened the door, and there he was—Adrian, leaning casually with that easy, sunlit grin that made Logan's pulse trip over itself. His stomach tightened, a rush of heat rising before he could will it down. He rolled his eyes, fumbling for composure like it was something he'd left on the floor.

"I told you, you can just come in," he muttered, turning away to wrestle with his shoes, hoping the motion would hide the flush creeping up his neck.

Adrian's laugh was soft, and Logan's heart skipped a beat when he caught it. "Feels wrong somehow," he murmured, stepping in and shutting the door with a quiet click. Logan felt Adrian's presence like a familiar swell at his back; constant, gentle, carrying a subtle power that steadied him even as it made him come undone.

Finishing with his shoes, Logan stood up, "Let's go?" he asked, glancing at Adrian while combing his fingers through his hair.

Adrian's eyes were transfixed on him, something passing through his gaze as he looked at Logan adoringly. "Yeah." He finally answered.

They walked together through the dusky twilight toward the crowded beach club, a sprawling jumble of bodies and light and music. Logan glanced over at Adrian, catching glimpses of him in the dim, flickering light. Adrian wore a faded black shirt, its buttons mostly undone, revealing a chest shaped by the ocean's endless rhythm, each muscle sculpted. The thought rose in him, soft yet undeniable, like a tide he couldn't resist: Adrian was beautiful, breathtaking as the sea itself, fierce and endless and achingly alive. Logan quickly pushed that thought back down, letting it dissolve in the ebb of the moment.

The party spilled out across a half-open deck, stretching to the edge of the beach where waves rolled close, whispering against the sand, mingling with the bass that throbbed through the night. Bodies swayed and collided, barely clothed, painted in smudges of neon and glitter that caught the flickering lights, casting a surreal, electric glow over the crowd. The air was thick with heat and movement, people shifting in waves, blurring in and out of Logan's vision.

Logan's heart drummed against his ribs, a steady rhythm that felt offbeat in the chaos around him. He let Adrian pull him toward the bar, warm, firm fingers wrapping around his wrist in an easy movement. A touch so casual it shouldn't have meant anything, but it left something unsteady in its wake. When Adrian let go, Logan felt it like a drop in pressure, a sudden absence that settled in his chest. He took the shot Adrian handed him with more eagerness than he wanted to admit, hoping the burn would dull the strange pull tightening under his skin. He welcomed the fire in his throat, willing it to dissolve the awkward tension that clung to him, to loosen the ache he couldn't name. He wanted to dissolve into the current, to belong in this wild sea of strangers who moved; colliding, parting, endlessly free.

Adrian slipped easily into that current, as if he belonged to it—his body loose, moving to the beat like he was one with the music, his face open and relaxed. Logan watched from the edge, rooted to his spot by the bar, painfully aware of his own stiffness, his own self-consciousness that only deepened as he watched Adrian lose himself in the music. Here, with Adrian, he felt raw and exposed, out of his element, unsure of how to fit into this vast, untethered space. He felt small, like he might disappear in the shadows.

And then Adrian noticed, slipping back through the crowd, his face lighting up as he came close, his eyes soft and full of something Logan couldn't name. Adrian leaned in, his breath warm against Logan's ear as he spoke over the music, the brush of his cheek a fleeting touch that sent an electric shiver down Logan's spine.

"Come dance!" Logan could hear the grin in Adrian's voice, felt it in the way he said the words, in the curl of laughter lingering.

Logan shook his head, resisting, feeling a hot flush rise to his cheeks. "No," he mumbled, barely trusting his own voice. The feel of Adrian's stubble brushing his skin almost made him gasp, the softness and warmth so unexpected it left him dizzy.

"Come on!" Adrian's hand slid to Logan's hip, gentle but insistent, pulling him toward the dance floor. His hand was steady, sure, and something in his touch made Logan want to let go, want to trust. "It's fun."

"No, but you go. I'm fine," he lied, the words coming out awkwardly, almost stilted, his heart pounding so hard it drowned out the music.

Adrian stepped back, his face falling into an exaggerated pout, looking at Logan with mock disappointment. Logan couldn't help it, he laughed, the tension easing just enough for him to let out a shaky breath. And then he caved, letting Adrian guide him onto the dance floor, his face breaking into a smug smile that left Logan feeling both flustered and strangely light.

Logan let the music wash over him, letting the alcohol dull his edges just enough to move, enough to sway along with Adrian's easy rhythm. The crowd closed in around them, the heat and press of bodies blurring the edges of the world until it felt like it was just the two of them, moving together in the dim, flashing light. Girls drifted toward them, their faces painted, their eyes bright, but Logan didn't feel the need to look. Adrian didn't either—his gaze stayed close, focused, the warmth in his eyes a silent pull that made Logan's chest sing.

When Logan grew tired, he broke away, slipping back to the bar, feeling his pulse slow as he watched Adrian from a distance, his silhouette moving freely, beautifully, lost in the music and the night. Logan didn't know how long he sat there, lost in the sight of him, his breath catching at every easy movement, every flash of his smile. Adrian was untamed, boundless, steady, ans so powerful it was hard to look away.

After a while, Adrian found his way back to him, leaning close again, his hand steadying himself on Logan's thigh as he leaned in to talk over the roar of music. The touch was casual, yet it lingered, sending a rush of heat through Logan's veins. "You disappeared again," Adrian said, half-accusing, half-teasing. His hand rested just above Logan's knee. The touch sent a ripple through Logan's entire body, a quiet undoing he tried to hide. Adrian probably didn't even notice. It was just a hand. Just skin. Just warmth. To Logan, however, it felt like a fault line splitting open.

Then Adrian's gaze dropped, fixating on the place where his hand lay. His teasing smile faded, replaced by something else—something heavier. When he looked back at Logan, there was hunger in his eyes, soft and unmistakable. He didn't move his hand. If anything, his fingers shifted, tracing a slow, tender line along Logan's thigh, an unspoken yearning wrapped in a casual gesture. Like he wasn't even thinking. Like he just needed to feel connected.

Logan stopped breathing.

"I'll come in a few. You're having fun. Go," Logan managed, his voice barely steady, but the words felt hollow as soon as he said them, as if something in him was already regretting letting Adrian go.

At once, Adrian pulled his hand back, but not before his eyes lingered—full of something warm and unguarded, a gaze that held Logan for a breath too long. Then he nodded with that soft, crooked smile and turned back toward the dance floor, leaving Logan behind, aching, the distance between them suddenly vast despite the nearness.

But just as Logan began to watch him disappear, Adrian turned.

And then—he ran back.

Not with urgency, but with a boyish, earnest energy that made Logan's chest ache. Adrian leaned in close, breathless and grinning, his face lit by something pure and unfiltered.

"Promise you'll come?" he asked, voice low yet hopeful, eyes wide with something bright and real.

Logan smiled—helplessly, quietly—nodding before he could even think. Adrian was already turning back toward the dance floor. He looked lighter now, like just asking had been enough.

And Logan, still seated, felt his heartbeat rise with a force he didn't recognize, a quiet storm of emotion tightening in his chest. He didn't understand it, wasn't ready to name it, but he didn't want it to stop.

The music pounded, filling the room with an electric, thrumming energy that only seemed to magnify the flickering lights and the crush of bodies moving in the dark. Logan's gaze repeatedly wandered to Adrian, drifting back to him time and again, as if magnetized by this beautiful man. Adrian was laughing, his hair falling loose from its tie, his eyes shining as he lost himself in the music, his body moving with a freedom that seemed as natural as breathing. He looked beautiful, unbound, and Logan's chest ached with a feeling he couldn't place, something deep and sharp that seemed to expand with every passing beat. Adrian was the one who was always open, always inviting, connecting with people as if he were meant to belong everywhere.

And then Logan saw him. Another guy had drawn close, his hand slipping easily onto Adrian's shoulder, leaning in to speak, their laughter rising over the pulse of the music. Adrian didn't pull away; he leaned in, his expression warm, listening with that easy, open smile, the one that seemed to welcome anyone and everyone.

Logan's pulse surged, a wildfire spreading beneath his skin, hot and consuming. His breath hitched, his body tensing with the sharp, electric edge of something primal, something too tangled to name. He stepped forward, muscles coiled tight, a single, urgent thought hammering through his skull: *Get your hand off him.*

How dare that bastard touch Adrian like that?

The world narrowed, his focus pinning to the scene before him—the guy's fingers still resting on Adrian's shoulder, casual, claiming. A smirk curled at the edge of the stranger's lips as he angled his phone toward Adrian, the screen flickering with images that seemed almost too perfect: dreamlike landscapes drenched in golden light, wild and boundless.

Logan's stomach twisted, the weight of something unspoken pressing heavy against his ribs as he watched Adrian lean in, closer, laughing—soft, familiar, like a sound spun from warmth and memory. A laugh meant only for *him*. And yet, here he was, sharing it with someone else. Someone whose touch lingered just a second too long.

"You have to come!" The guy's voice carried just enough over the music, loud enough to reach Logan. "We're leaving in a couple of days, it's one of the sickest places ever!"

"Sounds cool," Adrian replied, his voice light, noncommittal, but Logan caught a flicker of intrigue in his eyes, something that dug deep into Logan's chest.

"You must come! The waves are amazing, and the beaches are to die for!" the man's hand was now around Adrian's hips. "We'll have the best time!"

Logan felt himself moving forward, an instinct he couldn't stop, his feet dragging him closer as if he could dissolve whatever connection was forming between Adrian and this stranger. But then they were drifting off, walking toward a dim corner of the room, leaving him in the open, stranded and aching in a way that was sharper than anything he'd ever felt. Logan's throat tightened as he watched them disappear, something raw and desperate gnawing at him, a jealousy so fierce it was like a wave crashing over him, pulling him under.

Images flashed like lightning behind Logan's eyes—fragments he couldn't bear to see, yet couldn't stop imagining as they came like a flood sweeping through Logan's mind and drowning him in something he didn't have the words for.

That guy—*him*—standing in the spaces that used to belong to Logan. Sitting across from Adrian at one of the restaurants and cafés they loved to frequent, bickering lovingly over what to get. Surfing beside him, their laughter echoing over the waves, effortless and easy. Walking shoulder to shoulder down sun-drenched streets, brushing close in ways that Logan had never let himself think about too hard. He could almost *see* it—see Adrian looking at him, *not him*, like he was the person Logan used to be in Adrian's life.

Every stolen moment, every inside joke, every piece of Adrian that Logan had quietly gathered over the few days they had together, it was all slipping, being handed off to someone else. And what shattered him the most was that Adrian didn't even seem to notice. Didn't see that Logan was *right here*, unraveling.

A hot, suffocating ache clawed at Logan's chest, twisting into something almost unbearable. *Why did this hurt?* Why did the thought of Adrian with someone else feel like waves holding him beneath the surface, like he could not breathe, like the ground beneath him was shifting, making it impossible to stand?

He didn't understand. He *couldn't* understand.

All he knew was that it felt wrong, like he was losing something, like something vital was being stolen from him, even if it had never really been his to begin with.

Without thinking, he turned away, weaving his way through the crowd, past the thrum of bodies and music, the press of heat, the flickering light. His breath came fast, jagged, as he pushed toward the exit, fighting the swell of anger and pain that surged with each step. By the time he stepped into the cool night air, he was trembling, a pulse of something unfamiliar pulsing through him—something fierce and stinging, something he didn't want to acknowledge.

Logan practically sprinted through the night, the sand and path blurring beneath him, his chest burning with something hot and fierce, something he didn't even know he could feel. It was as if a fist had seized his heart and squeezed, punching the air from his lungs the second he'd seen that stranger talking with Adrian, leaning in with a familiarity that made Logan's blood boil. Adrian, laughing easily with someone else, like he hadn't just spent the past few days filling Logan's world. *It shouldn't matter*, he told himself. Adrian probably had dozens of *friends* scattered across the world, friends who saw the easy charm, the open warmth he carried like the sun glancing off the waves.

But that didn't stop the burning ache clawing at Logan's chest. It didn't stop the jealous rage that seethed through him, even if he couldn't understand it, couldn't name the reason for it. All he knew was that the feeling was there, thick and wild. He stumbled into his small cabin, yanking off his shoes and slumping down on the bed. He tried to distract himself, glancing at his phone, flipping through notifications without really seeing them, his mind still replaying that stranger's hand on Adrian's shoulder and Adrian going with that man away to some deserted corner. The image flared like a bruise, and he tossed his phone aside, getting up to get a drink from the minibar.

But then, his own mind betrayed him.

A vicious, vivid image flickered behind his eyes, unbidden and merciless. Adrian, lips brushing against his—that guy's. Adrian's hands sliding over him, pulling him closer, pressing against him in ways that Logan had never let himself imagine. Adrian letting himself be touched, melting into it, into him.

A piercing, agonizing twist coiled within Logan's gut, echoing the turmoil of his thoughts.

Stop! His mind screamed, his breath coming fast, unsteady. *Stop it. Stop thinking about it.* But the more he fought it, the deeper the image sank in, like poison seeping into his veins. He squeezed his eyes shut, trying to block it out, trying to force himself to feel nothing.

Then came the knock, it was a sharp, pounding sound that rattled through the floor and up into Logan's bones. He didn't move. Didn't need to. He already knew who it was.

Still, he made no rush to answer. Let the door stay shut. Let *him* be the one to open it.

A beat later, the unlocked door swung wide, and Adrian stormed in like a force of nature. His breath was ragged, chest rising and falling with the remnants of his run, his skin still damp, slick with sweat. His hair clung to his forehead in dark, damp strands, and his cheeks were flushed, not just from exertion.

Logan's pulse thudded, too fast, too loud.

For a moment, neither of them spoke.

The air between them crackled, charged with something Logan didn't dare name. Adrian's eyes were wild, intense, locked onto him like he was searching for something, *demanding* something.

Logan swallowed hard, but the lump in his throat stayed lodged there. He forced himself to hold Adrian's gaze, even as everything inside him screamed to look away.

"Is everything okay?" Adrian's voice was taut with worry. "Where've you been? I looked everywhere for you! I have been running around looking for you!"

Logan leaned back against the table, his posture deliberately casual, refusing to let his face betray him. "Didn't feel like partying anymore."

Adrian's eyes narrowed, his anger shifting to frustration. "You could've told me! I looked for you! I thought that maybe something had happened."

"Didn't want to disturb you," Logan muttered, gripping his bottle a little tighter. "You were busy with that guy, right?" The memory of that stranger, with his hand on Adrian and his voice in Adrian's ear, standing close, laughing with him before backing away. Walking away to a corner.

Had he finished his business with that guy before he came looking for me? Had Adrian kissed him first? Touched him? Enjoyed that guy's touch before deciding, oh, maybe I should go see Logan now? Had he come? The thought sliced through him, cold and bitter.

At that, something flickered in Adrian's gaze, a softness that broke through the frustration. He stepped closer, his voice gentler. "He is another surfer I met here shortly after I landed. He's from Australia and has many friends here. I surfed with them for a few days, and he wanted me to come say hey." Adrian didn't have to explain himself, but he desperately wanted to.

Logan nodded; no voice came to him. *Did you hook up with that guy before? Are you even gay or bi? Or maybe you're straight?*

No. Logan *did not* care, and he would not be going to those thoughts.

"When I couldn't find you, I got worried and searched for you," Adrian added.

"Why?" Logan's voice came out sharper than he intended, his fingers shredding the label on his bottle. "In a few days, we'll probably never see each other again. It doesn't matter." The words tasted bitter, hollow, but he forced them out, steeling himself against whatever was building in his chest.

Adrian took a deep breath, his gaze never wavering as he leaned against the counter, shoulders relaxing, his expression almost vulnerable. "I didn't mean to leave you tonight, just went to say hey.... And I never... I never meant to leave Hawaii without..." he murmured, the words soft as a confession. "I was actually trying to... well, ask if you'd want to keep traveling with me."

Logan stared, his heart a wild, uneven rhythm in his chest, his mind trying to catch up. "What?" he whispered, the word barely audible.

Adrian glanced down, rubbing the back of his neck. His voice trembled slightly as his other hand moved absentmindedly over the counter, fingers fidgeting. "Yeah... I've been thinking about it for days, but I wasn't sure you'd even want to. I thought maybe... maybe we could go somewhere together. The Philippines, maybe, then Australia... but I'd stay here too, if that's what you wanted." He hesitated, then met Logan's gaze, his eyes earnest, a quiet vulnerability Logan had never seen before. "I like being with you, Logan. Didn't know how to say it."

The ache in Logan's chest was raw, an emotion he couldn't name. The jealousy, the uncertainty, the self-doubt, they all faded, replaced by something warmer, a quiet thrill that made him feel dizzy and grounded all at once.

"I thought you traveled alone," Logan said, his voice catching slightly, sounding almost broken.

"I was," Adrian replied softly, taking a step closer, his hand brushing lightly against Logan's. "But... I'd much rather be with you."

Logan's heart hammered, each beat a rush of adrenaline, hope, and something that felt dangerously close to happiness. "I... yeah, I want to go," he said, breathless. "When?"

Adrian smiled, and Logan felt his own lips curve in response, his pulse steadying, his thoughts quieting as he felt that, maybe, this was exactly where he was meant to be.

"Whenever we want?" Adrian asked, chuckling, his laughter light, like foam catching the last rays of a setting sun.

"Works for me," Logan replied, his voice soft with a new ease, a tide of relief he couldn't hide. He paused, eyes flickering back to the glow of the party on the distant shore through the window. "Hey... I'm sorry I left. You want to go back? It's still early."

But Adrian shook his head. It was enough, this quiet space between them. Logan smiled, stepping over to the fridge to grab a beer, pressing the cold bottle into Adrian's hand, the simple gesture feeling oddly intimate, as if he were handing over some small, precious secret, a simple offering of peace and "I am sorry for being a jerk."

"Thanks," Adrian murmured, fingers brushing over Logan's. He looked down, then back up, a playful spark in his eye. "So, now that I ran all this way to find you... can I actually have your number?" He gave a little laugh, tinged with something honest, almost raw. "Didn't realize until just now that I couldn't even call you." Adrian pulled his phone from his pocket.

Logan felt a shy grin spread across his face, and the flicker of something—hope, maybe—ignited low in his chest. He took Adrian's phone, typing his number in carefully, letting his fingers linger over the screen just a bit longer than necessary. After he finished, he pressed 'dial', and his own phone rang from the bed for a second. He handed the device back to Adrian, the moment feeling raw, and big somehow.

There was a beat of silence, and then Adrian glanced around. "Well," he began slowly, setting his half-finished beer on the counter. "Guess I should get going—"

"Stay?" The word escaped Logan's mouth almost before he'd fully decided to say it, soft but bold, and his gaze lifted to meet Adrian's. "We'll look at flights, maybe figure out some plans? There is much more to do in Hawaii before we leave here."

Adrian's expression softened, as though Logan had opened a window to something he hadn't quite believed could be real. "You... you really want us to do it together?" His voice was quiet, barely above a whisper, touched with a disbelief that made Logan's heart ache. It was as if Adrian feared this moment might dissolve if he spoke it too boldly.

Logan's nod felt like a promise, one he didn't fully understand yet, but that he wanted to give all the same. He couldn't say why, but he did want this—this adventure, this time, this inexplicable bond growing between them. He felt the anticipation wash over him, a feeling as constant as the ocean itself, carrying him somewhere new, somewhere right.

"All right," Adrian murmured, smiling with a soft intensity that sent a ripple of warmth through Logan. He took a step closer as Logan pulled his laptop from his bag, a mischievous grin spreading over Adrian's face. "But you're doing all the reading," he announced, dragging a hand through his already messy hair. "I can't with that English anymore..." he grumbled, and Logan laughed, the sound bright and free. "It hurts my brain!"

"Oh, shut up," Adrian called as Logan was just laughing harder and sat on the bed.

"Do you want me to correct your grammar if it's wrong?" Logan asked, barely containing his grin, especially when Adrian turned to him with that pissed-off, cocky, thoroughly amused look—the one that always made Logan's pulse stutter. "If you want, we can also work on your vocabulary, and your accent could use some work—"

"That's it!" Adrian declared, snatching the nearest pillow and launching it straight at Logan's face with mock annoyance, his smile wide, eyes glinting with humor. Logan caught the pillow mid-air, his laughter spilling out, feeling somehow as vast and open as the sea beyond the walls of the tiny cabin. He tossed the pillow back at Adrian, who took it, propping it under his head with a smirk as he settled on the bed.

They slipped into an easy rhythm, Logan clicking through flight options as Adrian lounged on the bed beside him, close enough that Logan could feel the gentle warmth radiating off him. He pointed out places they could go, barely able to believe that they'd actually be traveling together, as if the universe had decided to nudge him toward this unfamiliar, wonderful current, pulling him toward a journey he hadn't planned but wanted desperately now.

They booked a flight for a week and a half later, their fingers brushing occasionally as they pointed to destinations and plans on the screen. The hours slipped by, the two of them falling into laughter and quiet, murmured ideas about all they wanted to see—the wild waters in the Philippines, the warmth of the sunbaked beaches. Logan felt his heart swell with each new image that flickered across the screen, each plan that formed was new and exciting, they moved from places in Hawaii to the Philippines, moving the conversation along and confusing places altogether.

Adrian stretched, arms reaching above his head, muscles shifting beneath sun-kissed skin. His head tilted back, exposing the long line of his throat, and then, slowly, he let his eyes flutter shut, telling himself he would just rest them for a bit. His breathing evened out, slipping into that steady, peaceful rhythm Logan recognized all too well—the same rhythm from the days they spent chasing waves, carving through the ocean until exhaustion weighed their limbs, until they collapsed onto the sand, warm and salt-streaked. Sometimes, Adrian would nap right there on the beach, the tide rolling in and out like a lullaby, their bodies moving in quiet harmony with the pull of the water.

Now, in the dim hush of the room, Logan glanced over and found him lost in sleep again. His long hair spilled across the pillow, tangled and messy and beautiful. The sharp edges of his face had softened, lost to the quiet of dreams, the usual fire in him dimmed to something gentle, something unguarded.

Careful not to disturb him, Logan closed his laptop, set it on the nightstand, and turned back, unable to resist looking at Adrian for a moment longer. He knelt beside the bed and gently slipped off Adrian's shoes, noticing the way his shoulders rose and fell with each soft breath. His heart ached, sharp and sweet, watching him like this, vulnerable and so close.

He covered Adrian with the thin blanket, letting his hand linger just a moment over his shoulder, tracing the warmth there. In this quiet moment, he felt something settle between them, something that seemed to reach deep within him and hold him, like the gentle tug of an undertow, pulling him in, deeper than he could have expected. He slipped into bed beside him, leaving a small distance yet feeling closer than he had to anyone in years. There was a growing bond forming between them, and it felt deeper than ever before, more important than anything he'd shared with other people. He could almost feel an infinite, imperceptible thread weaving their souls together.

In the dim light, with Adrian's steady breath a quiet rhythm beside him, Logan closed his eyes and let himself drift. And for the first time in what felt like forever, he wasn't just *falling* into sleep, he was *sinking* into something vaster, something deeper, something that felt like the beginning of everything.

It wrapped around him, warm and electric, like the stream pulling him into an ocean he was never meant to escape. Something endless. Something raw. Something so powerful it made his chest ache, made his fingers tremble with the weight of it.

It felt like holding onto a moment too big for words, like catching a glimpse of forever.

Like he would never be the same again.

When Adrian stirred, the morning light spilled gently through the half-open curtain, golden and soft. For a moment, the world felt suspended. He blinked into the quiet hush and realized two things: he didn't remember falling asleep, and Logan was curled beside him in the hush of dawn.

Logan lay on his side, his skin kissed red by the sun, one strong arm folded beneath his cheek, his lips parted slightly in sleep. His brow, usually furrowed with thought or laughter, had smoothed into something pure, something unguarded, almost boyish. The shared blanket tangled around them, and Adrian felt the slow, steady warmth of Logan's body radiating through the cotton.

And in that stillness, something inside Adrian ached—not with pain, but with wonder.

He had never felt this way about anyone—certainly not in so few days. Could it really have been less than a week since Logan first came crashing into his life like a wave too vast to see coming? It felt impossible. Adrian couldn't remember a time before him. It was as if Logan had always been there, threaded into the fabric of his memory, hidden in the silences between breaths, waiting.

He'd had crushes before, fleeting and harmless, like sparks flickering out before they could catch. But this, this was different. This was gravity. This was being pulled without resistance, drawn not just to Logan's laugh, or his body, or his smile in the sun, but to the very atoms that made him. He was already lost to him, entirely and without defense. And the strangest part was, it didn't scare him.

It felt like surrender.

It felt comforting, like finally being home after spending years searching for it.

He didn't move. He didn't want to break this moment, this feeling of suspended time, so he just listened to Logan's slow and steady breaths. Sunlight glinted through the blinds, catching on Logan's sandy-colored hair, falling messily across his forehead and cheeks. Adrian's fingers itched to reach over, to brush those strands back, but he stayed still, watching instead, committing this picture to memory.

Eventually, Adrian sat up carefully, trying not to disturb Logan. He glanced down, noticing his shoes neatly placed beside the bed—shoes he didn't even remember removing. He felt a quiet gratitude fill him. Logan, it seemed, had taken care of the small details, even as he himself drifted off.

After splashing his face with cold water in the tiny bathroom, Adrian slipped out of the cabin, heading back to his own to take a quick shower and change into something more comfortable. He needed to be ready; there were still things he wanted to do before they left Hawaii.

After finishing at his cabin, he made a brief stop to rent a motorbike before heading to the local grocery store. With the engine humming beneath him and the island wind tousling his hair, he rode down the gently curving road along the coastline, catching glimpses of the vibrant blue ocean through the palm trees. He paused at a small market and selected a modest bag of groceries: fresh eggs and butter, sweet bread, some bacon, a handful of mangoes, avocados, and a pineapple. As he moved through the space, a quiet excitement stirred inside him, an almost giddy kind of tenderness.

Without a second thought, he halted at a roadside cart and ordered two coffees. Adrian quickly learned that Logan required caffeine to function upon waking, and that was non-negotiable. When he finished ordering, he handed the barista the reusable glass travel cups that Logan had bought them a few days back. It had been just their third day together. Adrian remembered it with impossible clarity: the morning sun still sharp over their shoulders as they stood waiting for their drinks, Logan rolling his eyes at the barista reaching for paper cups and plastic lids. Without hesitation, he grabbed two large glass travel cups from a display near the counter and told the barista to use them as if it were nothing. Like it was obvious. As if they were going to continue doing mornings together.

"Single-use is bullshit. I can't stand it anymore," Logan had muttered, waving off Adrian's raised eyebrow. "Microplastics, landfills, all that crap ends up in the ocean. And the ocean's home. You don't trash your home."

Adrian had laughed. Logan might've thought it was at the reusable cups, or his impromptu environmentalist speech. But it wasn't. It was the helpless kind of laugh that comes when something hits you too hard and too fast, because in that moment, it only confirmed what Adrian had already begun to suspect.

Logan was perfect.

And the idea of having a cup to share morning coffee with him made Adrian's chest crack open, sharp and sweet. It wasn't about the object. It was about what it meant: that on day three, Logan had already pictured mornings. He'd already imagined *more*.

That small gesture wrecked him.

It terrified him.

It gave him hope he wasn't ready for.

And still, they used the cups, kept them in Logan's cabin since they always met there anyway. Or maybe Logan kept them there so Adrian would have a reason to come back.

Maybe that was just wishful thinking now.

They had eaten out for nearly every meal since arriving. Today, he wanted to make something, however simple. The cabin's kitchenette was barely functional, more of a suggestion than a space to cook, but that didn't matter. He could still throw something together.

Inside the cabin, Logan was still sound asleep, sprawled across the bed in a relaxed, tangled position across the bed. Adrian chuckled softly to himself, setting the bag down in the compact kitchen. He rummaged through the supplies he had gathered, laying them all on the counter. As he turned to find a pan, he sifted through the cabinets until he uncovered a weathered skillet that he had washed before using.

Adrian cracked the eggs into the buttered skillet. He scrambled a few with a wooden spoon, then fried the rest until the edges crisped just slightly. It wasn't the prettiest meal, he'd never been much of a cook, but when he stole a small piece and let it melt on his tongue, he smiled. It tasted right.

He laid the eggs onto mismatched plates, then set the skillet back on the burner and dropped in the bacon, which he knew Logan would like. Next, he sliced the pineapple, avocados, and mangos, laying the pieces carefully beside the bread he'd warmed on the pan's edge.

The cabin filled with the hum of breakfast coming to life, eggs, fruit, coffee, and crisping bacon. Adrian paused for a moment and looked toward the bed.

Logan hadn't stirred.

Still sprawled in the tangled sheets, one arm slung above his head, face turned toward the window, breathing deep and even. The clink of utensils, the low hiss of the skillet—none of it reached him. Adrian's gaze softened as he approached the bed, hesitating a moment before he reached out to Logan. "Lo," he murmured, voice soft as the morning light. "Morning."

Logan stirred, his eyes fluttering open. He squinted, his lips curving into a faint smile as he focused on Adrian's face, as though still drifting between dream and waking. "Really?" he whispered, barely awake, a spark of warmth in his eyes.

"Yup." Adrian nodded, his gaze lingering on Logan, tracing the unruly strands of hair falling across his forehead. It took all his restraint not to reach out, to let his fingers trail through that sunlit mess.

Logan was a force of nature, a storm in human form. He was the ocean's pulse, the wild tides that rise and crash with unyielding urgency. Every movement, every glance, was a wave, a tide pulling relentlessly forward, unpredictable, raw. There was a fire in his eyes, an intensity that burned like the sun at noon, scorching and bright. He was the sun on the horizon, an endless surge of energy that could neither be tamed nor ignored. His spontaneity was like the wind—wild, untamed, impossible to predict. Every spark he ignited blazed across the sky, and Adrian couldn't help but be pulled into its orbit, helpless to resist. In contrast, Adrian was the anchor, the quiet depths of the sea, the part of the ocean that stays still while the world above swells and churns. He was grounded, with his feet planted firmly in the sand, the steady ebb and flow of tides beneath him. Where Logan was fire, Adrian was water, calm but vast, holding everything in gentle sway. They were opposites, like the pull of the moon on the sea—Logan, the tempest that never stayed still, and Adrian, the unshakable calm that always held him, no matter how wild the storm.

But Adrian was mesmerized. How could he not be? Logan burned with a fire that could never be contained, a fire that made the air around him crackle with energy. Adrian stood in awe of it, the heat of it seeping into his bones. He couldn't help but be drawn in by the tide, the irresistible force of Logan's spirit, a force that swept through him like the ocean's waves, crashing over him with a power that left him breathless, unable to look away.

"I smell food," Logan mumbled, eyes drifting closed again, his voice hoarse and edged with sleep.

"Eggs, fruits, bread." Adrian's voice was soft but proud. "And bacon."

"Oh god, I love eggs and bacon," Logan replied, his voice a sleepy murmur, but his grin broke through, broad and genuine. He opened his eyes fully, glancing over at the small table set with breakfast.

Adrian's laugh echoed softly, a warm sound that curled around the room like the first rays of sunlight creeping over the ocean. He dropped his gaze for a moment, the quiet between them thick with an unspoken pull, before looking back up at Logan. "Come on," he teased, his voice carrying a playful lilt, "it's getting cold."

Logan groaned, sluggish but unwilling to stay still, his body dragging itself into a sitting position. He rubbed his eyes, fingers running through his hair, pushing it back from his face. "Two minutes," he said, flashing Adrian a grin that could light up the room.

True to his word, he emerged from the bathroom moments later, his smile wide and uncontainable.

Adrian watched him, heart skipping at the sight—Logan was a whirlwind of energy, and Adrian couldn't help but admire him. Logan's gaze wandered over the table, his silver eyes wide with something like wonder, and Adrian could feel the warmth of that look in his chest. "Wow, thanks," Logan said, grabbing a few slices of mango and pineapple, savoring them with a childlike joy. "You got avocado too!" he declared, reaching for the plate with the sliced avocados.

"Yeah, of course," Adrian grinned, feeling a rush of warmth sweep over him just from watching Logan's joy. Adrian filled his plate, trying to stifle the butterflies in his belly.

"That's good," Logan mumbled through a mouthful, his words punctuated by soft laughter. "Did you just make this while I was passed out?"

Adrian nodded, his smile widening as he took a deep breath. "I have to confess," he began, his voice lowering with teasing seriousness. "It was just breaking eggs in a pan; I didn't do anything but break them in the pan."

Logan burst into laughter, shaking his head in disbelief. "I should have known," he said, cutting into his eggs with a fork, "But it's good. And you did cook it while I was basically passed out."

They ate in a comfortable silence. The soft light of morning wrapped them in a quiet embrace, and for a while, it felt like nothing existed outside this small moment. Logan sipped his coffee and looked at Adrian.

"You know, I can cook okay, but my mom makes much better omelets. She adds onions, herbs, and mushrooms, and it's incredible. I didn't even try to replicate that." Adrian remarked.

Logan looked up, his gaze softening. "Your mom?" His voice quieted, becoming thick. He remembered the brief mention Adrian had made of his mother, how she had passed when he was young.

"Oh," Adrian's voice dropped slightly, the air around him shifting. "Yeah. My dad remarried. My mom died when I was around six. My dad remarried when I was nine. I call her 'mom' too."

Logan nodded. "I uh—" he started, uncertain. "I didn't know. It's not... You know what, never mind, it's none of my business."

Adrian met his gaze and gave a small, reassuring smile. "It's okay." His tone was steady, the walls he'd built around that part of his past still standing strong. "It's thanks to her that I know how to surf so well."

Logan raised an eyebrow, intrigued. "How so?" he asked, taking another sip of his coffee.

Adrian's laugh was light, almost playful. "She started taking me to the beach whenever she could. Even when I sucked at it—believe me, I sucked. I fell off the board so many times, smashed into the water, all bruised. And she was always there cheering me on, saying, 'You did so well, Adrian!'"

Logan was mesmerized, swept into the warmth of Adrian's words like a wave pulling him deeper. "That's amazing," he said, his voice hushed, as though touched by something sacred.

Adrian paused, watching him for a moment, before asking, "What about you?"

Logan's smile faltered just for a second, a shadow crossing his face. "I... you know, the usual. Mom and dad, nothing special."

But Adrian caught the slight shift in Logan's gaze, the way his voice lost its edge. Adrian didn't press, but the silence that followed felt thick with something that didn't need to be said for Adrian to understand it was there, lingering, like a storm on the horizon.

Logan's voice broke the quiet. "My dad... he's a hard one," he said, the weight of his confession lingered in the air.

Adrian's eyes were steady, the ocean in them a calm, silent place where Logan could almost drown, lost in the stillness. He leaned in, but Logan was already sinking into the depth of his own thoughts. "He makes the calls," Logan continued, his fingers tracing the rim of his coffee cup, the motion almost like the restless lapping of the waves against the shore. "Thinks he knows what's best for all of us... had my life mapped out before I even took my first breath. It's one of the reasons I ran."

Adrian's gaze never wavered. "What are the other reasons?"

Logan's eyes narrowed, as though something inside him was pulling back, hesitant to speak. It was the first time he ever dared to share it with another soul.

When he finally answered, his voice seemed to shift, ebbing like the tide pulling out, leaving nothing but raw honesty. "Everything. I ran from it all. The pressure, the weight of it—it crushed me until I couldn't breathe anymore. When I was going through this, it was fine, I didn't really notice it, but over time, it got worse. So, I had to get away, you know? I had to find air that wasn't suffocating me. I didn't even know what I was running toward. I just had to go. To find air that wasn't filled with someone else's expectations." His hands shook, just enough for Adrian to see the tremor, like the ripple of a distant wave ready to break. "I felt like I was wearing someone else's skin. I could make it through college, I had some freedom there, but after that? The path was already set, *my* life already planned out... but it wasn't mine. It wasn't what I wanted. I needed air, clean and empty, not this suffocating weight."

Logan's eyes drifted past Adrian, toward the ocean, where the waves kissed the shore with a tenderness that seemed foreign to him. "I don't think I even know who I am anymore. Not without him... without him telling me every move. For twenty-four years, I was a machine, a thing with a set program. And now... now I'm just... lost." His voice cracked then, like a wave breaking too soon, sending foam and salt into the air, leaving only silence behind. There was a stillness in him that filled the space between them, a deep ache that pulsed like the heart of the sea itself.

He looked at Adrian then, his silver eyes shining with something fragile. "Haven't spoken to them since I left," he admitted, his words falling like stones into the stillness between them. "Not a word. Not a call."

Adrian raised an eyebrow. "Really? They must be worried sick about you."

Logan's mouth twisted into a tight smile. "They are. My phone rings nonstop. Mom. Sisters. It's like they're drowning in worry, trying to reach me." He let out a hollow laugh, his fingers pushing at the crumbs on his plate, avoiding Adrian's gaze. "They keep asking when I'm coming back, if I'm okay. Physically? Yeah, I'm fine. But I don't know if I'm really okay, you know?"

Logan's eyes dropped to his plate, then slowly, painfully, met Adrian's. "And then there's him. My dad. He'll talk to me, but I know that I'll hear the disappointment in his voice, like I've let him down, like I've drifted too far to be pulled back in."

Adrian's lips parted to speak, but Logan stopped him, shaking his head slowly. "Just drop it," Logan muttered, picking up his fork again, but not really eating. The silence between them hung heavy, a rhythm all its own, like the lull between two waves before the next rush.

Adrian leaned forward. "You're not a disappointment, Logan. Not because you chose your own way. And even if you end up being one... at least it'll be because *you* decided. Not him. Not anyone else."

Logan nodded, his fork twirling the piece of untouched food on his plate. But there was something in his gaze that softened, as though Adrian had thrown him a lifeline and he hadn't known he needed it until now.

Adrian grinned then, a spark of mischief in his eyes. "Tell you what," he said, leaning back in his chair. "I've got something planned. But when we get back, you're calling your family. And I'm calling mine. Deal?"

Logan's lips quirked at the corners. "What did you plan?"

"Deal first," Adrian pressed, his smirk deepening.

Logan chuckled softly. "Fine. Deal." Then, after a moment, "But I'm texting them. Not talking."

Adrian's eyes twinkled with amusement. "Fine."

Logan's heart kicked in his chest, but he stood, stretching his arms above his head, his back arching like a wave cresting. The warm sun hit him, and for a moment, he forgot everything—his father, the distance between him and his past, the guilt that lingered like a shadow.

Adrian started to collect the plates, but Logan shook his head, playful but firm. "No way. You cooked, I'll clean."

"Let's just do it together," Adrian offered. "We'll be quicker that way."

They moved in tandem, elbows brushing now and then as they cleared plates. It only took them a few minutes, but each moment felt suspended, filled with the quiet hum of the morning and the brewing tension between them.

Logan went to his still-open suitcase, rummaging through it, hunting for fresh board shorts.

"Yeah, I really need to do laundry soon," he said absent-mindedly.

"We'll take care of it this evening," Adrian replied.

Logan, barely thinking, tugged off his sleep clothes and pulled on his shorts and a loose T-shirt, catching Adrian's glance darting away, the faintest blush creeping over his cheeks. It was a small thing, but Logan felt it—a quiet thrill sparking under his skin as he turned back, casually dropping his phone in the nightstand drawer before they left.

Outside, Adrian tossed him a helmet with a small, satisfied grin. "I'm driving," he announced, already slipping his own helmet on.

Logan shot him a skeptical look, half-joking. "Please tell me you've got a license for this thing."

Adrian laughed, a warm, confident sound. "Yup. And don't worry, you're driving back."

Logan climbed onto the bike, hesitating a beat before he settled in behind Adrian. He'd ridden with friends before, but this felt different, more intimate somehow, each inch of space charged between them. The engine rumbled to life, and they surged forward, the wind catching against Logan's arms and legs, the warmth of the sun pressing close.

They wove through streets dotted with relaxed locals and other travelers, passing the faint strains of music spilling from packed bars and food stands. Over everything he could hear the muffling sounds of the waves and feel the salty air all around. It was easy to get lost in the world here, where time seemed to stretch, and each turn of the road opened into something new.

At a red light, Logan leaned forward, his voice low but clear above the idle hum of the engine. "Do you know where we are?"

Adrian's chuckle was soft, and Logan felt it through his chest, vibrating back into him. "Yeah, I checked the map earlier. Trust me."

And Logan did trust him, with a depth and certainty that felt as easy as breath. Every inch of him trusted Adrian fully, every fiber in his being believed in him. After all, Adrian had once dove headlong into the stormy waters of the North Shore, plunging into waves wild and unforgiving, just to reach him. Adrian had risked himself, dove deep to alter fate's cruel turn, battling the relentless surf to bring him back to life. In that moment back then, with nothing but ocean and sky and a dwindling hope, Adrian had pressed his mouth to Logan's and breathed life into him.

Now, with quiet care, Adrians reached down and took Logan's hands, lifting them from where they rested loosely at his waist, guiding them with gentle insistence to circle his torso. The movement was both casual and intentional, and in it, Logan felt something sacred, something that echoed far beyond words. "We're in for a few rough turns up ahead," Adrian murmured, his thumb lingering just a moment on Logan's wrist, brushing the small charm of the lifesaver bracelet he'd given Logan, a token of safety, of belonging.

It was his mother's bracelet, a small piece of her love given to Adrian to keep him safe, now passed along to Logan. As his thumb traced the charm, a silent prayer moved through him—a plea to his mother, wherever she was, to guard this life he held so carefully, this fragile thing that had become more precious than anything. For a beat, he lingered there, pouring all he couldn't say into that simple touch.

Logan felt his heart crack open, the edges raw and vulnerable, as he tightened his hold around Adrian's waist. He could feel the solid strength of Adrian's body under his hands, the steady rhythm of his breathing, the warmth that radiated from his chest, and it was all he could do to hold on, trying not to break under the weight of the moment. In that closeness, every unspoken feeling he carried swelled like a rising wave, crashing into his heart with a ferocity he hadn't known was possible.

The world blurred around them, but Logan was anchored there, to this man who had held his life in his hands and breathed him back to shore, who now carried him forward with every turn of the road, like a promise that went beyond words, beyond time.

Logan felt an ache rise within him, deep and consuming—a need to be closer to this man, to press himself against Adrian as though proximity could somehow fuse their souls. Without thinking, he leaned forward, resting his cheek against the warm curve of Adrian's neck, breathing him in like he needed Adrian's scent to steady his own heartbeat. It was the kind of thing he might do, something instinctual and real, nothing his father would ever approve of. But these past days had stripped away layers of restraint, leaving him raw, freer than he had ever been. His heart hammered, reckless and alive, threatening to burst from his chest.

Eyes closed, he clung to Adrian, the roar of the road and wind fading into the silent pulse between them. Here, he was someone else—a man unafraid of closeness, of vulnerability, of needing someone like this. And in that instant, there was no past, no family expectation, no judgment, only this new self, pressed against Adrian on a foreign road, feeling whole.

They rode on, each turn drawing them closer, each rise and fall of the road blurring the world around them until there was nothing but the steady, unspoken rhythm of their bodies, an intimacy woven from silence, from touch, from everything words could never say. He felt his dick starting to push against the comfort of his board shorts. A surge of awareness so sudden it jolted him, a blush of mortification prickling beneath his skin. Instinctively, he shifted his waist, desperate to loosen the closeness he'd been savoring just moments before. *Oh God, not now*, he thought, embarrassed by his own response, feeling absurd, hoping Adrian hadn't noticed his change in posture.

But then the bike slowed, the low hum fading as they came to a stop on the cliff. It was only as Adrian's hand grazed his own—a light, drawn-out touch—that Logan realized he hadn't let go. He released Adrian's waist, fingers tingling from the brief touch, and slipped off the bike, still feeling the warmth of Adrian's body as he breathed in the wild, fresh air around them. Adrian followed, unfastening his helmet and then extending his hand for Logan's, taking it gently as he stowed the helmets away. For a fleeting moment, their fingers brushed again, sending a quiet, unspoken current between them.

Needing a moment to collect himself, Logan moved toward the edge of the cliff, looking out over the landscape. Beneath them, a jade-green lake lay in a fold of forest, mirroring the sky's endless blue. Sunlight glinted off the water's surface, casting a shifting web of light across the green leaves around them, and the scent of damp earth and foliage drifted up, mingling with the crisp scent of the lake below. It was as if the world held its breath, waiting, this place suspended in time, just for them.

"Wow," Logan murmured, wonder unfurling in his chest. The lake's surface was so clear he could see the stones glinting on the bottom, each one catching the light like a small, secret treasure. The hills rose around them, lush and alive, and it felt like he was looking down at paradise itself.

"Right?" Adrian's voice came softly behind him, and Logan caught the smile on his face, warm and unguarded.

"I want to dive in," he declared, voice buzzing with untamed energy. "Right now."

Adrian huffed a breath of amusement, shaking his head as he rolled the bike forward. "Yeah, me too. I just wanted us to see the view before riding down—"

"No need." Logan was already stripping off his shirt, a sheen of sweat glistening on his skin, the humid air pressing close, heavy and damp against him.

"Lo—" Adrian's eyes widened, shifting from mild confusion to full-fledged horror. "What are you doing?"

Logan flashed him a wicked grin, his fingers making quick work of his shoes and socks. "What does it look like I'm doing?" His storm-dark eyes burned, alight with the kind of mischief that meant trouble.

"No way. That's way too high—"

But Logan was already backing up, feet digging into the dirt, every muscle coiled tight with anticipation. He lifted his wrist, letting the silver bracelet catch the sunlight, a smug smirk curling at his lips. "I've got my lifesaver," he teased.

Adrian stared at him, his eyes flickering between the bracelet and the steep drop beneath. "If you believe a stupid bracelet will prevent your head from getting crushed on the rocks, you've got some serious problems—"

But before Adrian could finish, Logan launched himself forward, feet pounding against the earth before the world beneath him disappeared.

And for a single, breathtaking moment, he was weightless.

The sky, the trees, the lake, everything blurred into a dizzying rush of wind and light as he soared, his heart thundering in his chest, adrenaline roaring in his veins. Then, with a triumphant whoop, he crashed into the water, the cool embrace surging around him, exploding into a thousand glittering shards.

He surfaced with a sharp gasp, tossing his wet hair out of his face, laughter bubbling up from somewhere deep and untamed.

"Come on!" he shouted, treading water, his grin stretched wide and reckless. "It's amazing!"

Adrian groaned, dragging a hand down his face, but he was already peeling off his shirt, already kicking off his shoes. "You're insane," he called down.

But Logan could see it. The spark in Adrian's eyes, the way his body shifted forward, the way his hesitation cracked, giving way to something just as wild, just as restless.

"Come on!" Logan yelled, voice carefree and joyous, the adrenaline rush vivid in his tone. "I'll catch you!"

"Fuck you!" Adrian called back, laughing. "You almost gave me a heart attack!"

"Are we going to have an entire conversation shouting, or are you jumping in? You could also climb down like an old man, I'll wait!" Logan teased, his voice bright with laughter, daring him.

With a muttered curse, Adrian took a few steps back, bracing himself before he sprinted forward, his heart thudding as he launched himself off the cliff. Time seemed to slow, the world going silent as he flew, and then the lake welcomed him with a cold rush.

He surfaced, gasping, and Logan's laughter filled the air as Adrian found himself pulled close, Logan's hands reaching for him, steadying him, grounding him. Their eyes met, and for a suspended moment, the water held them, shimmering around them like a world that belonged only to the two of them. And in that closeness, in the laughter and breathless wonder, Logan's grip was sure, his eyes alive with something deeper than words, joy as boundless as the sky, wild and unbroken as the waves.

"Told you I'd catch you. Wasn't so scary, right?" Logan smirked, water dripping from his hair, his grin sharp and triumphant.

Adrian let out a breathy laugh, shaking his head, his chest still heaving from the adrenaline. "You are going to get me killed, Logan Vaughn."

Logan scoffed, flicking water in Adrian's direction. "You're overreacting." The lake lapped at his chest, cool and steady, the rush of the jump still humming through his veins.

Adrian arched a brow, amusement tugging at the corners of his lips. "Am I? Because I've known you for less than a week, and I've already been this close—" he held up his thumb and forefinger, leaving only a sliver of space between them "—to death twice now."

Logan only grinned wider, tilting his head like he was considering it. "Then maybe you should stop following me."

That was not going to happen, and Adrian knew it. He would follow that man everywhere he went and be thankful for the opportunity to be there by his side.

But Adrian didn't move, didn't step back. Instead, he gazed at Logan with something softer, something weightless and unguarded, like he was caught in the quiet pull of something neither of them fully understood.

Logan was still riding the high of the fall, his heart thundering, his breath light and easy, until suddenly, it wasn't.

His pulse stuttered, because that look—the way Adrian was watching him, eyes dark and blissful, his lips slightly parted, his skin still slick with the lake's shimmer—did something strange to Logan's chest. Made it feel tight, stretched thin, alive in a way that had nothing to do with adrenaline.

Before he could think, before he could stop himself, his hand lifted—hesitant, shaking just slightly—as he reached forward.

A single strand of hair clung to Adrian's cheek, damp and curling from the water. Logan swept it away with the barest brush of his fingers, his skin grazing Adrian's with a touch so light it was almost unreal.

Adrian didn't move. Didn't speak.

And Logan, God help him, couldn't look away.

The air between them thickened, heavy with something unspoken, something weightier than the fall, than the water around them.

Logan swallowed, but it did nothing to steady the wild, uncharted thing clawing at his ribs.

What the hell was this?

His throat felt tight, a deep ache as he swallowed, feeling the steady pound of his heart echo in his chest. Every nerve seemed to wake under Adrian's gaze, his presence filling the air between them, charged like the sun-slicked surface of the ocean before a storm. The slight brush of his fingers against Adrian's cheek felt electric, sending a low hum through him, a tether he couldn't pull away from.

Logan's hand lingered on Adrian's face, fingers skimming slowly over his skin, his palm warm against Adrian's cheek. But then he heard himself whisper, almost as though the words surfaced from a depth he hadn't known was there. "Who was he?"

Adrian's breath hitched, his hand lifting to cover Logan's gently, like the delicate brushing of sea foam on sand. "Who?" His voice was so soft, filling the air between them, gentle, and yet steady as a returning tide. His fingers traced the back of Logan's hand, soothing, tender.

"The guy you talked to yesterday," Logan managed, his voice barely holding. His hand trembled lightly, and he didn't know why he asked, why he couldn't shake the thought of Adrian speaking with that man. The ease of their laughter, the way he touched Adrian, and how he looked at him. Logan's chest tightened as he remembered the way they'd seemed, the way Adrian's face had softened in that man's presence. He didn't know why it mattered so much. But it did... some ancient ache, quiet but immovable, lodged beneath his ribs, clinging to him, refusing to release its hold.

But Logan reminded himself that while Adrian talked with that other guy, Adrian's eyes scanned the crowd for him, and when Adrian could not find him, he left everything behind—that man included—to search for Logan. How Adrian had run back to him, like the wave chasing the shore, Adrian bolted back to him and spent the night with him, and cooked for him, and now they were here together.

Adrian found himself confused by this question; after all, he had already told Logan that this guy was another surfer he had met before. "I told you, I met him around here before—"

Logan shook his head softly. "No," he insisted, one word that carried so much more weight, begging Adrian to understand. "Who is he... to *you*?" Logan was trembling now, maybe it was anger at that guy, maybe it was the expectation for the answer, or just the chill waters.

Adrian stilled, and suddenly everything fell into place. The way Logan had disappeared last night, the look in his eyes now, the tension thrumming between them like the pull of the tide—

Logan was jealous.

Adrian felt a spark of something warm and fragile ignite in his chest, like a flame he'd only dared to imagine.

"He is no one to me, just barely a friend." He reassured Logan, grabbing his hand tightly now, his head just scarcely pressing back against Logan's soft palm. Adrian's voice barely above a breath, the words catching on the air, the hum of the live nature around them buzzing.

Adrian longed to articulate his thoughts, his heart brimming with sentiments yearning for expression. He wished to convey the depth of his feelings while tenderly preserving the delicate bond they were nurturing. Logan was clearly bothered by this guy. The last thing Adrian wanted was to sow seeds of doubt in Logan's mind or jeopardize the beautiful connection they were forging for some guy he didn't even care about.

"When we met, he tried... but he isn't what I want." His gaze held Logan's, burning steady as he added, "He tried last night too. But I don't want him. I want..."

He didn't finish the sentence, but Logan felt it, felt the unspoken words hum between them like an unbreakable thread. His hand, still resting against Adrian's cheek, drifted down along his jaw, feeling the faint scrape of stubble, feeling Adrian tremble beneath his touch. Logan's fingers moved almost unconsciously, brushing along Adrian's neck, and he felt the quiet shudder that coursed through Adrian's body, the way his eyes closed for a single, quivering moment.

Adrian's hand never left Logan's, clenching his wrist, not with force but with a quiet urgency, as though release would unmake something fragile and invisible. Around them, the world seemed to contract, folding in upon itself until there was nothing left but the hush between their breaths. The silence was taut, shimmering, full of words that trembled yet refused to be born. They lingered there, tethered by a touch as delicate as salt spray on skin, yet freighted with the gravity of all that remained unsaid.

Logan's voice finally broke through, hushed and thick. "Let's... let's get out. The water's freezing."

Adrian nodded, unable to trust his own voice, his mind hazy as he let Logan's hand drop. They moved toward the shore in silence, each step carrying the ache of something beautiful and unknown, something that ebbed and flowed between them like the endless, pulling tide.

Chapter 5

I Am Here Waiting to Save You

I could almost hear them—the faint whispers in the dark, curling around the edges of my consciousness like ghosts. I could almost feel them on my skin, a breath that never quite touched me, a presence that never fully arrived.

Night after night, I found myself chasing the color of your whiskey eyes at the bottom of a bottle, tilting it back, hoping—aching—for the amber burn to match. But it never did. The liquid swirled, rich and golden, but it was flat, lifeless. Nothing like the way your eyes used to catch the light, flickering with something untamed, something alive.

Something that used to make me feel alive. Something that used to be mine.

But that feeling is gone now.

All that I have left is a heap of indelible memories and a whiskey bottle that fails to mirror your eyes, and neither quenches my thirst.

March 9, 2020—Seattle, Washington—One year and Eight Months Later

LOGAN SLAMMED THE GLASS against the bar with a force that rippled down his arm, the sharp crack against the wood cutting through the dim hum of voices and clinking glasses. It was his fourth drink, and the night was young. He'd tethered himself here, to this dark and cheap bar, where the sting of whiskey ebbed through him, tugging him under, drowning out the voices that filled his head.

As he lifted his phone, he noted the time: eleven. Sandy would still be awake, her light still on in their quiet, picture-perfect house. He'd be sure to come home only when her breathing had settled into deep, unbroken waves, when she was miles away in dreams that he wasn't part of. The clock marked time, but his mind was somewhere else—somewhere where the air was warm and salty, where Adrian's laughter had lifted like spray off a breaking wave, bursting against the walls he'd kept so carefully guarded.

But that was over a year ago, wasn't it? His life now felt like the empty shore left behind when the tide pulled too far out, leaving nothing but sand and the bitter residue of salt. He'd married Sandy like a man clinging to a rock in rough water, convincing himself he could build something solid if he tried hard enough. But every night, he felt the pull of memory, dragging him back to Adrian, to those wild and shimmering days. Now, even with Sandy, intimacy had withered, cracked like dried seaweed on sun-bleached rocks. Without something artificial to drown out the ache, without the blaring images he forced between them, he felt his desire slipping further into the deep.

Sandy had noticed, of course. Her husband was doing everything in his power to get away from her touch. Maybe she also saw the shadows deepening under his eyes, the way his laughter—once rare but real—had vanished like sunlight swallowed by storm clouds. It had come up, more than once, that maybe he needed help, that maybe some invisible weight was draining him. Her words curled around him like ripples on a still lake: perhaps they should seek some medical help together, maybe even therapy, or that his job—the unyielding hours, the constant demands—was grinding him down and needed to be set aside, if only for a while, so he could find himself again. He remembered how hopeful she was, how much her eyes pleaded with him. After all, he imprisoned her as well in that marriage and she had given everything within her to make it work.

He'd laughed it off, stormed out of the house, leaving her words to crash against him as he fled. And now he was here, clutching the bottle like a lifeline, craving the sweet, numbing flood of the next drink, the only thing that dulled the undertow of memories.

He drank to drown in the sunlight of Adrian's gaze, to chase away the melody of his voice that once wove through Logan's soul, smoothing even the jagged edges like gentle waves caressing ancient stones. The warmth of the alcohol was a soft tide, subtly silencing the dawn's scent of Adrian—his skin's tender glow, the whisper of his favorite soap, and a raw, pure essence that sent shivers whispering along Logan's spine. It was a delicate fog, blurring the vivid memories until they shimmered like muted dreams, fading, yet lingering. Just enough to forget, or perhaps to pretend, how Adrian's stubble, rough and warm, left a trail of fire upon his skin when they kissed, a whisper of heat that echoed long after the moment was gone.

Just enough to erase the feeling of those slow, deliberate touches, the way Adrian's mouth moved over him, the scrape of stubble against his chest, his stomach, over his cock and between his cheeks, kisses that felt like a reunion with the other lost half of his soul.

But each glass brought him back to it, the bitter taste morphing into salt on his tongue, a persistent reminder that some loves, once felt, linger forever—crashing like relentless waves, regardless of how far he'd drifted.

He scrolled down Adrian's Facebook page once more, eyes tracing each familiar line and picture, knowing well there would be nothing new, not even a shadow of a post. The absence didn't surprise him, but still, he lingered, drawn by a need to connect, to cling to this fragment—the last remaining trace of Adrian, a digital ghost of his existence, proof that once, somewhere, he had been real.

Sometimes, in those late, dragging hours, a green dot would appear beside Adrian's name, like a faint light over dark water, a signal that somewhere—maybe only a heartbeat away—they were both afloat in the same night sea, each of them gazing out at the vastness of what they'd lost. He yearned for it, that fragile thread binding two souls across the divide, a whisper of presence at opposite ends of the earth.

Logan slid from the Facebook app to his gallery, his fingers brushing over the hidden folder where he had buried the photos—each one a breath of air he could still hold onto. He had learned that drowning in them was the only way to feel anything at all.

One year and five months since he'd run, the distance between him and Adrian stretching like an endless shore. One year and three months since he last saw Adrian, since he last kissed him—those moments now slipping through his grasp like water in a hand.

One year and three months of marriage to Sandy.

Logan murmured the melody, the words barely escaping, heavy with the weight of all that had been lost. The pain stirred within him, growing, until it became a pulse he could not ignore. And in that ache, his mind came alive again, sharp and clear.

"Hey, you." Logan raised his empty glass, his voice a low drawl. "Another."

The young bartender, caught in the moment with the guy he had been flirting with, gave him a quick, apologetic smile—a fleeting touch on the hand before he turned to Logan.

"I think you've had enough. Go home," the bartender said, taking the empty glass from his hand. Without waiting for a reply, he turned to the other end of the bar, where a few ladies beckoned him with eager eyes. Logan watched as he flashed them a flirty smile, effortlessly slipping into the role of charm.

God. He has no limits. Logan thought, bitterly, as the bartender's laughter blended with the hum of the bar, a world he no longer felt part of. Every time Logan came in, which was most nights now, the bartender was either slipping out of the place or heading to the restroom, always accompanied by someone. The man was a magnet for desire, drawing people to him; he was the flame, and they were the moths. It wasn't just the way he looked, though that certainly didn't hurt. No, it was something more—a palpable energy, a raw current of sexuality that seemed to pulse from him, effortless and intoxicating. He wore it like a second skin, and Logan couldn't help but see how much he reveled in it, the way it flowed from him, unabashed and alive.

"Hey, fucker, when I tell you to pour me a drink, you pour me a drink." Logan's voice cut through the murmur of the bar as he shoved his phone back into his pocket.

The bartender turned, his eyes locking with Logan's. "Are you talking to me right now?"

"Yeah. Can you see another fucker here?" Logan muttered absently; his eyes half-lidded as he leaned against the bar. "You do two things—fucking and pouring drinks. Since you're not busy with the first, pour me a drink."

The words landed, and the bartender paused, his expression shifting. He walked over, his gaze sharp and almost intrigued. "Your wife's waiting for you," he said, glancing at the thin gold band around Logan's finger. "Go the fuck home."

Logan didn't flinch, didn't even look down at the ring. His voice was cold, direct. "Drink." Tension hung in the air. "Then you can go back and find your chip fuck for tonight. I wonder... what would that be this time, huh? The hot dick over there," and he nudged his head toward the guy the bartender had just chatted with, now leaning in and laughing with his friends, "or some fine pussy?"

"And I wonder why a rich motherfucker like you," the bartender said, leaning over the bar with a smirk, "someone who wears a suit that costs at least five thousand dollars, comes to this cheap-ass bar, night after night, drinking himself into oblivion, wasting away until he can barely stand, instead of going home to your little wife?"

Logan's chest tightened. He hated the way the bartender's cocky grin stretched across his face, the daring glint in his eyes. It was too much, like a needle driving straight into his pride. "I just saw someone throwing up in the restroom," Logan shot back, trying to deflect. "Shouldn't you go clean that up?"

The bartender chuckled, shaking his head. "You're so pathetic... Not only do you spend every miserable night of your life here, in this rotten bar, alone, but you're also jacking off on someone's Facebook page."

The words hit like a slap. Logan froze, as if time itself had stopped. His face went blank, his body went still. He'd heard the insult, but the sting of it pierced deeper than anything he had expected. The weight of his own shame crashed down on him, and the ache that had never fully left him surged back, raw and real. He was drunk, but not drunk enough to miss the venom in those words.

For a long moment, all he could do was sit there, the bartender's daring gaze boring into him, waiting for some kind of response. But Logan couldn't speak. The words tangled in his throat, and instead, he stood up, pushed his chair back with a sharp scrape. Without a word, he grabbed his wallet and tossed a few bills onto the counter.

The bartender's expression shifted, a flicker of disappointment crossing his face as he realized Logan wasn't about to say anything else. But there was nothing more for Logan to say. As he left, the sound of his footsteps echoed in his mind, the weight of the night too much to carry.

Outside, he climbed into the first cab he could find, muttering the address to the driver as he tried to shake off the moment. The sting of the bartender's words followed him like a shadow, clinging to him with each passing second.

When Logan finally arrived home, he paid the driver and added a generous tip, an apology without the words, though he couldn't quite explain why.

The house was dark and still, a hollow thing breathing around him. He let himself in, and the silence rose to meet him, thick and tender as fog. It pressed against his skin, against his ribs, until it almost felt like comfort. These were the only moments that belonged to him, small mercies of quiet, fragments of peace. He had learned to crave them the way some men crave touch. They were sacred.

He stood in the hallway, the air heavy with sleep and dust, the taste of whiskey bitter on his tongue. The world seemed to pause, holding its breath with him. There was no sound but the faint hum of the refrigerator, no witness but the dark. He felt that strange, aching joy that comes from being unseen, unneeded, forgotten.

Sometimes, when the night was this soft, he let himself slip into the lie. He would close his eyes and summon the vision: Adrian waiting upstairs, wrapped in lamplight, sheets warm with life. He could almost hear the rustle of his breath, the hush of skin against cotton. He could almost believe he had come home to a love he was capable of returning, to the right heart. As if he could imagine that his body still remembered how to want what it was given, that the warmth waiting upstairs was meant for him and not wasted on a man already half gone. As if love could rise again from bone and soul, instead of the dull habit it had withered into, stripped of all its merit, emptied of grace.

The dream pulsed in him like blood. He saw himself climbing the stairs, steady, sober, the air bright with early evening light. Adrian turning, smiling that small, knowing smile that undid him. No guilt. No whiskey. Just the quiet gravity of love, unbroken and real.

He let it swell, let it fill every hollow in his chest until it hurt. Then, as always, he opened his eyes. The house stood indifferent, the dark swallowing his breath.

Upstairs, Sandy was already asleep, the soft rise and fall of her breath a stark contrast to the turbulence swirling in his chest. He kicked off his shoes, shrugged out of his jacket, and collapsed onto the bed. The softness of the sheets felt foreign now, a stark reminder of the life he had chosen, the life he could never fully inhabit.

His eyes grew heavy with exhaustion, the need for sleep overwhelming him. As he turned on his side, he heard Sandy's voice, barely a whisper in the darkness.

"You stink of alcohol and cigarettes," she murmured, not even bothering to look at him.

Logan paused, allowing a moment of silence to envelop him as he took a deep breath, steeling his thoughts. "We closed a deal," he finally voiced the lie. With a deliberate motion, he turned to face the wall, hiding from the world. "The guys wanted to go celebrate."

"Yeah... again?" she said, her voice flat, already resigned to his silence. She didn't expect him to answer, and when he didn't, it didn't surprise her. The weight of the night hung between them, but neither of them knew how to lift it.

The next morning, Logan woke early, as he always did. The same feelings of pounding head and dry mouth, a constant in his life now, accompanied him this morning as well. He showered and shaved, trying to scrub the night off his skin, and donned a suit that cost more than some people made in a month. He left the house while Sandy slept, her steady breath the only sign of life in the still house. Outside, the world appeared too bright and too pristine. He then called a cab to return to the bar.

The parking lot was nearly empty, silent except for the buzz of a flickering streetlight. His car stood alone, dew gathering on the windshield, an accusation in plain sight. In daylight, the place looked stripped of its excuses. He remembered the noise, the laughter that wasn't his, the burn of whiskey that had dulled nothing.

By midmorning, he was in the office; by noon, two meetings done, two weeks of overseas work already scheduled. The hours slid past, indistinct, one bleeding into the next. Something inside shifted, barely, but enough. For the first time in months, he left early. He drove past the bar and kept going, straight home. He couldn't bring himself back there after what had happened the night before.

When he arrived, it was a quiet relief to find Sandy wasn't home yet, and he was thankful that the staff only arrived during the mornings a couple of days a week. A detail he heard in passing from Sandy.

She'd recently opened her own clothing store, pouring herself into it like it was the only thing that made sense anymore. He couldn't remember the last time he'd been present in her life, the last time they'd really seen each other.

He shed his suit, letting it slip from his shoulders like another life. The fabric, once sharp and tailored, now hung too loose at the chest, too long in the sleeves. It had been only a few months since the last resizing, and already it felt like wearing someone else's skin.

He stepped into the shower, letting the water cascade over him like a gentle embrace, before enveloping himself in more comfortable attire. Yet, as he gazed into the mirror, a profound disconnection washed over him; the figure reflected back was a stranger. His face, once robust, had collapsed inward; the flesh drawn tight over bone, the eyes shadowed and sleepless. He looked like a man who had strangled his own life and was forced to watch it leak away, thick and slow, through his hands. What seeped from him was not light but blood, not grace but rot—a quiet, unending hemorrhage that no prayer could stop. Within the cloister's stone silence, he carried the stench of something dying, something that had once been love and now clung to him like ash. His body had withered, bones jutting out like fragile twigs, and he struggled to recall the last time he had a truly nourishing meal. The suits were the only ones keeping count. Every few months, he took them all in—hemming, trimming, adjusting the fabric to match the body that kept shrinking, the life that kept folding in on itself.

As he poured himself a drink in the kitchen, the sound of the door opening echoed through the house, followed by Sandy's heels clicking against the floor. Logan walked toward the living room just in time to see her setting down her handbag, a picture of her busy day etched in her tired posture. The photo gallery above the desk caught his eye, wedding pictures, smiling faces and him with his forced fake smile that somehow fooled everyone.

Had they really not seen through the mask, the fake smile that never quite reached his eyes, or had they simply been careless, too wrapped up in their own worlds to notice the cracks forming around him?

"Oh my God, Logan!" She gasped when she noticed him standing there. "You scared me. What are you doing home so early?" She put a hand over her chest, breathing in.

Logan glanced at the clock. Barely four-thirty. *Is she always home this early?* The question hung in the air, unfamiliar, like a forgotten thought. He'd never asked. And now, watching her stunned expression, he felt the weight of that silence between them. She hadn't expected him to be here.

They were a married couple, two college sweethearts who somehow ended up in this perfect, empty house. *Isn't it sad?* He thought. *That she was startled, absolutely panicked, to find her husband home in the middle of the day?* Another small proof of the mess they'd made of this life together.

"Got off early today," he said, his voice flat.

She smiled, walking over in her heels with the same lightness she always had. "Why didn't you say something?" She asked, kissing him softly on the lips.

Logan wrapped an arm around her. "Last-minute call," he murmured, his mind far from the present moment.

Sandy, ever the optimist, beamed at him. "Wow, I missed you! We never have time together anymore. Let's go out for dinner, just the two of us." She was all light and warmth, but the crack in her smile was too familiar.

Logan hesitated, his gaze drifting past her. "Maybe we stay in? Order takeout? Just... you and me?" The words felt hollow, even to him.

She blinked, disappointment flashing in her eyes, but she nodded. "Okay, I'll take a shower while you order."

As she disappeared upstairs, Logan sighed.

He scrolled through the delivery app. For the life of him, he couldn't remember what his wife liked to eat. There had been a place she dragged him to once, when he'd made the mistake of staying home for a weekend. He remembered chewing something. That was all. Chewy. She talked through the whole meal, but he wasn't really there to listen.

Now the screen blurred in front of him. He tried to think of food and thought only of Adrian. Adrian who liked fish, and meat if it wasn't mixed with dairy. Adrian who tried to keep kosher. Adrian, who ate slowly, who laughed when he liked something, who always wanted to share bites. Logan had known every detail, down to how Adrian salted his fries, fries that Logan usually ordered for him because he tried to eat healthy.

But his wife—nothing. Just the sound of her talking about meals he couldn't taste.

He clicked on the Italian category. Picked the place with the most reviews. Ordered at random: something vegan, something with cream, something spicy. He didn't care.

An hour later, the food arrived. They sat next to each other in the living room. He chewed. It could have been anything.

"How was your day?" Logan asked, breaking the quiet.

"Fine..." she said, pausing as if considering whether to say more. There was something between them, an invisible wall, neither of them had the words to tear down.

Logan smiled faintly, setting his food aside, reaching for the glass of wine she'd suggested. He let the silence stretch, listening to the clink of her fork against her bowl. Then she spoke again, her voice soft but edged with something deeper.

"What about us, Logan?" she whispered.

His heart skipped. "What do you mean?"

She met his gaze, her eyes sincere. "What about kids? I want to have children, Logan."

Logan knew this moment would come eventually, but he wasn't ready for it now. He didn't want to be a father, not now, not when his heart was in pieces.

"I do too," he said, voice distant with the lie it carried, "but we're not ready for that."

Her frustration flared. "We've been married for over a year now! My friends are having kids, my best friend is expecting, and my mom won't stop asking. What are we waiting for?"

Logan got up, his fingers tightening into fists. "We're not ready, Sandy. It's too soon." He couldn't breathe, he couldn't think, he was drowning all over again.

"But we have everything," she argued, standing as well. "We have a house, jobs, money, what's stopping us?"

Logan's chest tightened. "Who's going to raise them, Sandy? We're both gone all day. I don't even get home until midnight. How will I ever see them?"

"Well, we'll get a nanny," she said matter-of-factly. "And you'll work less, come home early a few nights a week. I'm sure you can talk to your father and he will help you find a way, I know he is also waiting for a grandkid—"

"No!" he uttered, the words low but firm. "Don't bring my father into this! This is my job and I don't want him trying to help me so—"

"But—" she tried to cut in, their tones starting to rise in the empty house, echoing across the walls.

Logan's stomach sank. He couldn't imagine it, couldn't picture himself, drained and broken, trying to be a father. "I'm not ready for this." He said in finality.

Sandy's expression faltered, and the tension between them grew. He could feel her anger bubbling beneath the surface.

"You've got to see a doctor," she said suddenly, her voice sharp, adopting a new tactic. "You can't even keep an erection anymore."

Logan's breath caught, his hands shaking. "What did you say?" This wasn't the first time this topic arose for debate, but it was the first occasion that Sandy was so direct about it.

"You heard me," she snapped. "You've got issues, Logan. You need to see someone about it. We've been over it before, and I tried to be understanding, but you just won't do anything about it! So yes, I'm saying it plainly now. You need help!"

The words landed like a lash, but he recoiled from them, unwilling to face their truth. He feared the rage swelling inside him, the crushing weight of expectations pressing down on his chest, an unyielding force he could never escape. He was trapped in this unspoken performance, a game he hadn't signed up for, suffocating in his own skin, drowning in the hollow ache of it all.

His soul ached for release—for the quiet gaze of eyes like amber whiskey, for strong arms to wrap around him, a sun-kissed chest to hold him close, to look at him as though he were the universe itself, worthy of every sacrifice, every breath.

Breathless and shaking, he was about to leave the room, a storm of emotions crashing over him, carrying him away.

He wasn't broken in the way she thought.

He was just... elsewhere.

Some part of him—*the* part—was still thousands of miles away. On a cliff. In a river. In amber eyes and strong hands. In the memory of being held like he mattered.

His breath caught, heat rising to his face, shame and anger coiling in his throat like smoke. He moved, barely aware of his own movement, ready to walk out, to escape this house, this lie of a life.

But then Sandy's voice, softer now, stopped him. "What about your urologist appointment?" she demanded. "You said you'd look into it!"

Logan felt his whole body freeze. "I'm fine, Sandy. I don't need a doctor."

"Logan, don't be stupid. You can barely get it up! You need to fix this. Maybe it is dangerous!" she pleaded. "It could be something serious. You... you don't look good, Logan." She added silently. "You... have lost a lot of weight... you barely sleep, and you drink too much!"

Her words stung, raw and painful. Logan turned away, gripping the back of the couch as his anger and shame churned within him.

"So now I've got even more problems?" he snapped, voice rising. "Go on, Sandy. What else is wrong with me?" He stepped away from the couch, hands clenched at his sides. "I work too much? You mean the job that pays for our lives? The one that helped you open your stores and pays for basically everything here?" His laugh was bitter, joyless. "Right. That's a flaw now." He turned, eyes flashing with something between fury and fatigue. "I've got stress at work, and suddenly I need a urologist? I don't sleep enough, again, working, and I have a drink from time to time, so I must be an alcoholic? I've lost weight, so now I'm falling apart?" His chest rose and fell, breath ragged, like he was trying to hold something back and failing. "Go ahead. Keep going. Let's make a list. All the ways I'm not enough for you."

"That's not what I said, and you know it," she snapped, stepping toward him, her voice steady despite the heat rising in the room. "Don't twist this into some story where you're the victim and I'm the villain." Her eyes didn't waver. "I'm not some naïve little girl who's going to back down just because you raise your voice." She took another step, hands clenched at her sides. "You're not okay. You haven't been okay in a long time." Her voice lowered, firmer now—not angry, but unshakable. "You don't want to hear it? Fine. But I'm not going to lie to make you comfortable."

He turned away, shoulders taut. "I'm fine," he muttered through clenched teeth. "You're making a big deal out of nothing. Let it go."

But she didn't.

She stood her ground, arms crossed—not defensive, but bracing herself. "If you're so fine, then why do you look like a ghost in your own house? Why can't you even touch me?" Her voice cracked, but her spine stayed straight. "Tell me the truth, Logan. Is it me?"

He froze, chest tightening like a fist inside him. His throat worked, but no words came.

"I didn't marry you to become a stranger to you," she said. "I deserve to know what I'm even trying to hold onto."

Logan squeezed his eyes shut. The ache in his chest wasn't just pain, it was pressure, memory, grief, desire, guilt, all crashing down at once.

"It's not you," he finally said, barely above a whisper. "I swear, it's not you."

He could feel the bracelet against his skin—Adrian's bracelet. His fingers found it without thinking, rubbing the worn threads like a prayer.

He wanted to explain. To pour everything out and watch her understand.

The saddest part was that he knew, deep down, if he ever told Sandy the truth... she would understand. She would cry, maybe. Shout, maybe. But she wouldn't hate him. She'd listen. She'd be kind. She would have been his friend.

But he never told her.

Not once.

Instead, he dragged her into this; into a marriage that was always half-alive. Into a home that never felt like home to him. Into a life built on the hope that if he constructed the right pieces—house, wife, job, routine—it might quiet the thing inside him. The ache.

He thought if he just acted like the man he was supposed to be, maybe he would become him.

But he didn't.

He couldn't.

Because a part of him was still back there, in saltwater and sun, in a voice that called him by name like it meant something. In arms that made him feel whole.

And Sandy... she didn't ruin anything. She just stood where he put her—loving a man who was never really *here* to begin with.

And that, Logan realized, might be the worst thing of all.

Sandy turned her back on him, quietly gathering the dishes. She didn't speak, but her shoulders trembled. She didn't want him to see her cry, but he did. He just didn't know what to do with it.

"I'll make the appointment," he said, his voice hoarse and barely above a whisper. "I'm sorry."

For the appointment he'd never make. For the silence he couldn't fill. For all of it.

She nodded. "Logan, you didn't eat," she said softly, holding up his untouched food. "You want to finish?" her eyes were glassy as she tried to change the subject.

"No," he whispered, "I'm not hungry. I had a big lunch at the office." He lied, the thought of food making him nauseated.

Later, as Sandy went to bed, Logan stayed behind. He grabbed his phone, pressing play on the one song that had become his lifeline, the familiar strings wrapping around him like an old memory.

And as the words drifted into the quiet, Logan closed his eyes, finally finding a moment of peace in the chaos.

The next night, Logan walked into the bar later than usual, moving with the kind of deliberate slowness that came from too many thoughts and too little patience for them. He scanned the room, bypassing the barstools, ignoring the glances of a few regulars, and choosing a table in the farthest, most uninviting corner. It was the kind of seat most people avoided—dimly lit, half-forgotten, tucked into the shadows where no one bothered to look twice. Tonight, that suited him just fine.

The place wasn't much. It never had been. The neon sign outside sputtered weakly against the night, its glow barely cutting through the grime-streaked windows. Inside, the air carried the familiar mix of stale beer, cigarette smoke that had long since seeped into the walls, and something faintly metallic, like old coins left too long in a pocket. It wasn't classy. It wasn't even comfortable. But it was close to his office, and more importantly, it was familiar. A place with no expectations, no forced conversations, no one who cared enough to ask questions. His colleagues wouldn't be caught dead here. That was the best part.

He scowled at the cornered table, resentment twisting his mouth as he dropped into the chair. Damn that bartender. Logan had claimed this bar long before he had, and now, thanks to their last encounter, he was exiled to the edges like some unwelcome stranger.

The waitress appeared, jotting down his usual order. Logan barely acknowledged her, already sinking into his own thoughts, pulling at the collar of his shirt like it was suffocating him. Then, his phone buzzed. Again. A useless habit—checking it, expecting something, waiting for a call that would never come. Like the ocean itself would decide to return something it had already taken.

And then, a voice.

"Hey."

Logan looked up.

The bartender stood there, two glasses of whiskey in hand, his expression unreadable. For a moment, the hum of the bar faded, the world narrowing down to just the two of them. There was something in the way he looked at Logan.

Logan ignored him, his eyes returning to the phone in his hand. He scrolled absentmindedly, trying to silence the pulse of awareness thrumming in his chest. His thumb tapped across the screen until it landed on his favorite video. The video was old, a memory he couldn't let go of. Adrian, effortlessly paddling through the ocean off the coast of Australia, his figure cutting through the waves with ease. Logan watched as Adrian balanced on his board, the sun casting a golden glow over his tanned skin. And then, in a flash, the board slipped from beneath him, and he tumbled into the water, swallowed whole by the swell of the wave. But what hit Logan hardest wasn't the fall. It was the laughter that followed. Adrian's carefree laughter, light and free, as if the world couldn't touch him. Couldn't touch *them*.

The sound of a chair scraping the floor as it was drawn back cut Logan's memory, the one where he heard Adrian's laughter in his mind and not through the speakers. The bartender sat down across from him without waiting for an invitation.

Logan locked his phone screen and gazed at him.

"Look, I'm sorry," he said, his voice softer than Logan expected, then slid the drink to Logan, who caught it but merely for a second before letting go. "I waited for you last night throughout my shift." Logan hadn't replied. "I'm so glad you're here," the young man continued. "I waited for you last night." He said again. "Even stayed two hours after my shift. When you didn't show... I was very upset."

Logan didn't respond, his gaze staying fixed on the bartender's face. He sighed, clearly trying to fill the silence, but Logan wasn't ready to say anything back yet.

"I'm really sorry about the other night." He continued.

Logan nodded to him.

"I'm glad you're here," the bartender continued like he needed to fix whatever crack had formed between them. "So... are you coming back to the bar? This table doesn't really suit you. You're more of a barstool kind of guy."

Logan smirked, raising the glass the bartender had slid toward him. "I'm guessing this one's on the house?"

The bartender grinned, his eyes flickering with something that Logan couldn't ignore. "Nope. This one's on Zack," he said. "I'm Zack, by the way."

Logan gave a single nod. "Logan."

The silence that followed felt different this time, like something unsaid was hanging between them. Zack's attention flickered to the bar, but it didn't last long. Logan noticed the way Zack's hair was slicked back, shiny and dark, and the sharp lines of his jaw, a little stubble lining his face. He looked good. Too good.

"So," Zack's voice lowered, a little huskier now. "What do you say, Logan? Are you joining me at the bar?" Voice suggestive.

Logan felt a sudden spark of excitement flicker in his chest as his eyes tracked Zack's movements. The black button-down shirt Zack wore clung to his body in all the right ways, accentuating the lines of muscle beneath. The top buttons were undone just enough to show a hint of his chest, the sleeves rolled up casually, exposing forearms thick with strength. Logan's gaze followed the way Zack's Adam's apple bobbed as he spoke, a subtle, rhythmic motion that drew his focus. His eyes then drifted to the cross necklace hanging loosely around Zack's neck, the metal catching the light in the low-lit bar.

Logan couldn't look away.

"Tell you what," Logan circled his finger around the rim of his glass, a soft chuckle escaping his lips. "For now, I'm good here. But tomorrow... maybe I'll sit at the bar. You won't have to wait to see me then."

Zack's grin widened, and Logan finished his drink. "Another. Please."

Zack took the empty glass and stood up, his height and broad shoulders filling the space around him. As he walked away, Logan's eyes followed, taking in the way Zack moved, the way his jeans clung to his hips, the confident swagger in every step.

Logan couldn't help but watch as Zack ignored the rest of the bar and the long lines of patrons that had piled up during the moments that they'd talked, as he poured the drink with deliberate ease.

As their eyes met across the room, Zack gave him a slow, teasing wink. Logan felt a jolt of heat shoot through him, his body reacting instinctively, tightening in his pants. Everything about Zack screamed "Bad Boy"—the raw confidence, the daring smirk, the mystery. There was a wildness in his presence, an allure that was both dangerous and magnetic. Logan could feel the pull, the rush, the undeniable drawing toward something unfamiliar, something thrilling. Zack exuded sex in every movement, and it was impossible for Logan to look away.

It was a subtle thing, but it was enough to make Logan's pulse quicken. Something was happening, something neither of them had fully acknowledged yet. But Logan could feel it—something had shifted.

June 27, 2020—Seattle, Washington—Three Months Later

The world had dimmed, as if someone had turned down the contrast, bleeding everything into dull shades of gray. I moved through my days like a man watching his own life from behind a pane of glass—close enough to touch, but never quite able to. I breathed, but it never reached my lungs. I spoke, but the words felt borrowed. I existed, but I wasn't there.

There was a house, warm and filled with things that should've felt like home. A woman who loved me, whose laughter should have been enough. But I never stayed long enough to feel it. I was always somewhere else, lost in the spaces between memories and regrets, slipping further from myself with each passing night.

Maybe I had drowned that fateful July back in Hawaii. Maybe the ocean had taken me, pulled me under, swallowed me whole. Maybe the waves had claimed me, the currents wrapping around my limbs like silent hands, dragging me down, down, down—until there was nothing left of me but a ghost in the water.

Maybe I had never been saved.

Maybe Adrian had never dived in after me, never reached for me through the tide, never pulled me unbreathing back to the surface, never breathed life back into me. Maybe that moment had never happened. Maybe it had only been a cruel trick of the mind, a dream spun from desperation, a false memory to make me believe I had ever truly been found.

Because wasn't I still drowning?

LOGAN SAT AT THE table, the clinking of silverware and the low hum of conversation drifting in and out of his awareness like the soft tide of a distant ocean. His body was anchored to the chair, but his soul had drifted far, carried by currents he couldn't see, couldn't control. The world moved on, its laughter like the rolling surf, but he was stranded, stuck in the sand of a life he never wanted. His eyes stayed fixed on his plate, the food untouched, a reflection of the emptiness that had grown inside him. His appetite had abandoned him long ago, along with everything else he used to care about. The laughter around him—light, genuine, carefree—seemed to ripple over a surface he could no longer feel. It wasn't real; none of it was real.

He used to be part of that world, once. He used to surf until his muscles burned with the ocean's rhythm, smile without effort, laugh with ease. He was a man, whole, the kind of person who didn't have to think about the world to make it his. Now he was like the food on his plate—left behind, discarded. He pushed the meat around with his fork, wishing it were something more. Something he wanted.

The chatter about Jane's baby was loud enough to feel the weight of it in his chest, but he didn't care. He hadn't cared since... well, since Adrian. His fingers clenched tighter around the fork, the wood of the chair creaking beneath him.

The laughter around him was like the sound of waves crashing, but it only made him feel smaller. More alone. The air was thick with warmth, but all he could feel was the cold ache of something long lost, a tide that had pulled away and never returned. *Adrian*, the name swam in his mind, a current too strong to resist, too powerful to escape. He closed his eyes for a moment, remembering the rhythm of those days, the way Adrian had been the sun in his sky, the one who lit up everything, who made him whole. Before he had let him go, as if love were a thing that could be cast into the sea and disappear.

Logan blinked, pulled from his reverie by Jane's voice—sharp like a sea breeze cutting through the haze. She stood behind him, hands warm on his arm, urging him to leave the table and follow her to the safety of his old room.

"Logan," Jane said, her voice trembling. "What's going on? You've—" She paused, searching for the words. "You've disappeared. You're fading, Lo."

Logan's gaze fell to his hands, his fingers white-knuckled around the edge of a chair, only now realizing he had grabbed it—perhaps unconsciously, as a last resort to keep himself from slipping away entirely. The truth was there, rising inside him like the swell of an unseen wave. But he couldn't let it break. Not now. Not here.

"I'm just tired," he whispered. "Work, stress... It's nothing." He let go of the chair and sat on the made bed.

Jane wasn't fooled. She never was.

"Lo, don't lie to me," she said, sitting beside him, her eyes searching his face, trying to decipher the language of his heartbreak, of his whining, trying to give meaning to his wavering frame and eye bags, to this thinning frame and lost mind. "You're not eating. You're not sleeping. And you're not... you're not *you* anymore."

Logan flinched, as though the words had splashed against him, too cold to ignore. The wave of guilt crashed hard, pulling him under for a moment, but he fought it back. He couldn't drown here. Not yet.

"I'm fine," he said again, the lie tasting bitter in his mouth as he rubbed his hands together. "I'm just... I'm normal, Jane. I'm fine."

But the lie shattered beneath the intensity of her gaze, and for a fleeting instant, Logan sensed the whirlpool of his own suffering, drawing him in, ready to drag him under. He could no longer sit still; too restless to hold back, he rose abruptly, taking several steps away, seeking to create space between himself and her.

"Logan," she whispered, standing too. "You look like you've been drowning for months. You're *not* fine. This isn't you. You're just... empty."

Her hands reached for him, cupping his face gently as though trying to steady him against the tide of whatever storm raged inside him. The warmth of her touch was a lifeline, but Logan knew it wouldn't save him. Nothing could save him now.

"I'm happy," he said, though the words were hollow, swallowed by the vastness of the ocean inside him. It had been five hundred and ninety-three days since Logan Vaughn was happy.

Jane's tears fell then, like raindrops on the surface of a storm-tossed sea. Logan felt them, each drop a sharp sting against the ache in his chest. Her pain wrapped around him, and for the briefest moment, he wanted to let himself be carried away. To let himself drown in her care, in the promise that he could be whole again.

But he couldn't. He wasn't sure who he was anymore, or if he could ever return to the shore.

He grabbed her hands, pulling them away from his face, taking a step back. "I'm really happy for you, Jane," he said, his voice heavy, as if each word carried the weight of a thousand unspoken things. "You're living the time of your life. You have a beautiful baby girl, and a husband who loves you." His fingers pressed against his forehead, trying to rub away the ache that was building there. He took a breath, quiet and shallow. "I'm happy in my own way," the words slipping from his mouth like a drowning man gasping for air. "Even if I'm not going all over the place showing it."

But Jane didn't let him off the hook. She stepped forward, her tears still falling, each one a quiet plea for him to speak the truth, to admit what they both already knew.

"Logan," her voice cracked as she cupped his face in her hands. "That's not you. This isn't you." She searched his eyes, as though trying to find the man he once was, the man she remembered. "I don't know what you're going through, but you can't keep lying to yourself. It isn't about Sandy, it's about you. You hear me, Logan? *You.*"

He closed his eyes, squeezing the words back down, trying to drown the rising surge of everything he wanted to say but couldn't. He wanted to reach for the truth, but it was too vast, too deep to pull from the ocean of silence he had surrounded himself with.

"Jane—"

"No!" Her voice rose, raw and desperate, her hands trembling as she wiped her tears away. "You listen to me, Logan! Hate me as much as you want, but I won't let it go. You look like you've been sinking for months now. I'm not going to wake up when it's too late."

Logan's chest tightened, his breath shallow, and for a moment, he thought the ocean inside him might finally consume him whole. "Please," he whispered, his voice breaking in a way he had never let it before.

"I will help you, Logan. I swear to god, just talk to me!" Her voice was thick with urgency. "Please, I'll do anything! Just tell me what's wrong. Please..."

He could feel the tide rising inside him, the pull of everything he had buried crashing over him, but he couldn't let it break through. He couldn't.

"You're overreacting, Jane," he said, but the words felt like sand slipping between his fingers. "I'm fine."

Her head shook in defeat, a slow motion that felt like the final breaking of a wave against the shore. She knew him too well. She could see the cracks, the storm that he was trying to bury. But even if he told her the truth, what good would it do? Adrian was gone, and the life he had chosen was a cage made of steel, lacking sand. What could he say? That he had traded his soul for a promise that was never his? That he was a ghost of the man he once was?

Maybe his father was right. Maybe, if he just waited long enough, time would smooth away the jagged edges of this life, and he would learn to love Sandy the way he was supposed to.

But deep down, he knew the truth. He would never love her. Not the way she deserved. Not the way he had loved Adrian. He would remain here, drifting, a shadow of himself, waiting for something to change, knowing nothing ever would.

On the drive back home, the silence between him and Sandy felt like the calm before a storm. Sandy had spoken again about babies, about the future. Her words were soft, but they burned with the heat of something he could never feel. "No," he had said, his voice distant, like the far-off roar of thunder.

She cried. She yelled. But Logan said nothing. He only stared out ahead, watching the world move by, the familiar landscape blurring into a haze of colors. As soon as they reached home, Sandy opened the passenger door and stormed off, and as Logan quietly followed her into the house, he could hear the door of the master bedroom being slammed shut, the sound echoing in the silence of the house.

The message was clear.

Logan sat in the dim light of the living room, the weight of the silence pressing down on him like the deep sea pulling a drowning man beneath the surface. The temptation clawed at him, gnawing at the edges of his mind. He tried to ignore it, tried to convince himself that tonight would be different. But it was useless. His feet moved on their own, leading him into the kitchen, where the liquor cabinet stood like a familiar old friend, waiting for him with an open embrace. He opened it, pulled out the bottle, and filled his glass, each pour a whisper of solace he could no longer resist. The amber liquid caught the light for just a moment, like a tiny flame flickering in the dark.

He carried the bottle back into the living room, his fingers tightening around the cool glass as though it could steady him, even as it pulled him further into the storm inside. He grabbed his laptop as well, thinking he could get some work done while he was up.

The cold glass sat on the table in front of him still untouched, as he clicked through his emails with mechanical precision. The minutes slipped one after another as he scrolled through messages, his eyes skimming the words but not truly seeing them. When he finished, he reached for the glass again, intent on numbing himself to the ache that was gnawing at his insides.

But then, something stopped him.

His thumb hovered over the glass, his hand still for a moment longer than it should have been, before he grabbed his phone instead. It wasn't even a conscious decision. It was instinct, like the tides pulling him in a direction he knew all too well, though he never wanted to go.

He opened Facebook, his eyes scanning the blur of stories of strangers' children, dinners plated like paintings, lives that seemed to move forward while his own remained stalled. But then, his pulse quickened, his breath catching in his throat as his gaze locked onto the very first post at the top of the page, like it had been waiting for him.

It was *Adrian*.

The algorithm knew. It always knew. At that point, Logan didn't even need to type Adrian's name; it appeared immediately as the first result. The algorithm had memorized the ache of his search, those countless nights spent typing Adrian's name only to delete it again and again, before ultimately giving up and clicking search. It held onto what Logan's heart refused to forget.

And now here he was, suddenly alive before him, not a memory but a *presence*. Logan's pulse hammered against his ribs. His chest tightened, as though a wave had crashed over him and left him gasping for air.

Logan's fingers froze, trembling ever so slightly as he stared at the screen. Adrian's face, so alive, so real, yet impossibly distant. The sight struck him like a sudden fracture through glass, splintering him back into a time when the world had felt whole, before it had collapsed under the weight of regret. His heart thudded painfully, a relentless pulse in his chest, and for a moment, he wondered if he could ever breathe again without the weight of that name in his lungs.

Logan stared at the time of the post, the digits blinking at him, each one a cruel reminder of how much time had passed since that moment. Seven hours. Seven hours since Adrian had shared something that, despite everything, still seemed to call to him like a beacon in the dark.

It wasn't even Adrian himself who had posted it. No. It was a friend, some distant face that Logan knew to be Adrian's best friend, Dean, who was the one to pass this link along, a video. A video that, from the thumbnail, he could already tell was Adrian, sitting there on a stool. On a stage.

His heart skipped a beat.

Logan's hands moved like they were on autopilot, fumbling through his bag, searching for his earbuds. He nearly knocked his glass off the table, but he didn't care. He couldn't care. He needed to hear Adrian's voice, needed to see him again, even if it was through a screen, even if it hurt. His fingers trembled as he finally pulled them from the case, almost breaking the lead in his haste. He put them in, the cold plastic now the only tether to something real.

"Come on..." he whispered hoarsely, his voice raw, a whisper of desperation in the silence of the room. He pressed play on the video, and his body tensed, waiting for the few seconds it took to load, though it felt like hours.

His fingers drummed on his thigh in rhythm with the beat of his racing heart. Every second stretched longer, thicker, like the pull of an undertow that wouldn't let go. Finally, the video started to play.

Ten thousand views already. Two days since it was uploaded. Ten thousand other people had seen this, had heard his voice, had witnessed the same thing Logan was about to. It made him sick with jealousy, and yet he couldn't stop himself.

The video opened with a dark room, shadows dancing across the walls like forgotten memories. It looked like a club—dim lights, small stage, a crowd he couldn't see but could almost feel in the thick air. And there, in the center of it all, was Adrian. Logan's breath caught in his throat.

Adrian sat there, his long hair pulled back, wearing a simple white t-shirt and ripped jeans, looking impossibly at ease. His guitar hung in one hand, casually held, as though it had always been an extension of himself. He leaned into the microphone, speaking to the crowd, his voice smooth and warm, but Logan couldn't understand a word. The language was foreign, a barrier between them that made him feel small, foolish. He wished—God, how he wished—that he had learned it, that he had done more.

Frustration crept up his spine as he watched Adrian's lips move, but the words were just beyond his reach.

The crowd cheered softly, and then Logan's heart lurched as Adrian's fingers moved over the guitar strings. The sound that filled his ears was unfamiliar, a haunting melody that Logan didn't recognize. It wasn't the music of the world he knew, the familiar songs he'd listened to countless times. No, this was something else. Something pure, something deep.

Then, Adrian's voice.

Logan's chest tightened as the voice that had once filled his days and nights broke through, raw and untamed, the sound rich with emotion. It wasn't a cover. It wasn't something anyone had heard before. This was *his* song.

Adrian's song.

The melody wrapped around Logan like an ocean current, pulling him deeper into the memory of what once was. The song, the way Adrian sang it, spoke more than words ever could. It was *him*. The very essence of him. The part of Adrian that Logan had left behind.

And in that moment, as the music washed over him, Logan realized that he hadn't just lost Adrian, he had lost everything. The rhythm of his heart, the sound of his laughter, the quiet hum of his voice in the mornings—they were all gone. And nothing, not even a thousand videos, would ever bring them back.

The glow of the screen cast a faint light in the darkened living room. Adrian's voice slipped through the buds straight to Logan's ears, achingly pure, carrying a tone Logan had almost forgotten but never stopped craving. His first note was a balm and a blade, angelic and unearthly, piercing the cold silence that had become Logan's life. As the song poured forth, each word laced with a quiet intimacy, Logan's tears surfaced, unbidden, like they'd been lying in wait for this very moment.

I think of you when the sun climbs high,
I reach for you when I breach the tide,
I search for you whenever I rise from the depths,
I dream of you beneath the moon's soft embrace,
I'll take a breath just to give you mine,
Do you long for me as I ache for you through these endless days?

Adrian's eyes were downcast in the video, almost shy, as if he were singing only for himself—yet Logan felt every word as if it were meant for him alone. He watched Adrian, enraptured, as he let his whole body surrender to the song, hands hovering over his guitar as if coaxing the notes from some hidden place deep inside him. Logan's breath hitched. It was the sound of a man broken, of a man drowning by the same storm that Logan had created.

When you left, you took the best of me with you,
Was it hard for you to rise and leave?
Does your heart bleed as mine does still,
All I wanted were the things we'll never build,
I craved the pieces of you that I can't fill.

As Adrian began the chorus, the melody darkened, rising with a raw intensity, his fingers weaving through the chords like he was conjuring something sacred and unbreakable. Logan's breath caught, seized by the realization that every word, every note, was a message meant for him. The lyrics spoke his name in unspoken syllables, unraveling memories and emotions he had buried so deep they'd nearly disappeared.

His chest tightened, an ache blooming and radiating through his body, paralyzing him with longing and guilt. Tremors spread from his fingertips to his spine, anchoring him to the spot as Adrian's voice climbed higher, unwavering, his gaze distant yet piercing. Logan felt exposed, like Adrian could see him right there, falling apart in the shadows of a life he never wanted.

And I called your name, but the winds stole it away,
Can you hear my silent cries, drifting through the waves?
Be my lifesaver, and I'll be yours,
We'll weather the storms that crash on distant shores.
We'll find safe harbors where the winds are still,
And wait till the waves are gone, till our hearts can heal.
Be my lifesaver, and I'll be yours,

Together we'll stand through the tempest's roar,

We'll find the shore where the storms can't find,

I'll keep you safe, through the tides unwind.

We'll trace our path from the heart of the deepest blue.

He couldn't look away, couldn't move, trapped in the bittersweet agony of the song's embrace, feeling every word echo the love he had lost, and the man he still was somewhere underneath it all.

Your eyes burned through me, lighting up the dark,

They still haunt the quietest nights I've ever known,

In your smile, the world was whole and true,

You stole the dark, but when you left, it's all that lingered.

I spent hours beneath the ocean's grace,

Dove to the depths in search of you,

Sank into the ocean's heart but couldn't find you.

In the abyss, my heart yearns for you,

In every crowd, I long to see your face,

And the sound of your voice still echoes the same,

It haunts my soul and will do it until my last breath.

Logan wiped his eyes, though it was hopeless; the tears kept spilling over, blurring the screen as Adrian's voice filled his head and existence. Every word felt like it was meant for him alone—a confession, a plea, a memory spun into song, and a swell of anger rose in him that this private moment was shared with strangers online. Adrian was singing to him, his voice reaching through the distance and the silence that had grown between them.

When Adrian reached the chorus again, the words changed and his voice was gentler, rawer, as if he, too, was struggling to keep his voice steady.

The words struck Logan harder now, and his resolve shattered. His hands shook as he set the phone down on his lap, burying his face in his hands, his shoulders wracked with sobs that had been waiting, so long, to be released. He cried like a child, undone, as Adrian's voice wrapped around him, pouring every lost promise and unspoken regret back into his heart.

I draw each breath only to offer it to you,
Be my lifesaver, and I'll be yours,
We'll weather the storms that crash on distant shores.
We'll find safe harbors where the winds are still,
And wait till the waves are gone, till our hearts can heal.
Be my lifesaver, and I'll be yours,
Together we'll stand through the tempest's roar,
We'll find the shore where the storms can't find,
I'll keep you safe, through the tides unwind.
We'll trace our path from the heart of the deepest blue.
I'll be your lifesaver,
Even if you don't wish to be mine.
I'll guide you to safe shores,
And keep you alive until your true love arrives.

Logan picked up his phone again, clutching it tightly, his other hand pressed to his chest as though he could soothe the ache that had lodged there for five hundred and ninety-three days. Memories of Adrian flooded back, unbidden—moments of laughter, stolen glances, the quiet warmth they'd shared. As Adrian reached the fifth verse, Logan felt his control slipping, his pulse pounding with the urge to close the video, to fling the phone across the room, anything to escape the torment.

But he didn't. He couldn't. He sat there, rooted to the spot, transfixed by the familiar voice he loved more than anything in the world. On the screen, Adrian sang with such raw honesty, each word a confession of heartbreak and loss. Logan watched, helpless, as the love of his life bared his soul, singing a song of ruin—one that told the story of how he, Logan, had shattered everything they once had.

When I close my eyes, silver waves will seek me,
They pull me down, with you always out of reach.
I'll dive deeper than the ocean's floor,
Needing you to save me once more,
I called your name, but I couldn't see you,
I begged for you but you turned away,
I truly thought you'd come, I thought you'd save me too.
I draw each breath only to offer it to you,
Be my lifesaver, and I'll be yours,
We'll weather the storms that crash on distant shores.
We'll find safe harbors where the winds are still,
And wait till the waves are gone, till our hearts can heal.
Be my lifesaver, and I'll be yours,
Together we'll stand through the tempest's roar,
We'll find the shore where the storms can't find,
I'll keep you safe, through the tides unwind.
I'll be your lifesaver,
Even if you don't want to be mine.
I'll guide you to safe shores,
And keep you alive until your real love arrives.

When Adrian sang the chorus again, Logan felt a surge of life stirring within him, a bittersweet spark in the darkness that had swallowed his world. This time, the chorus carried a depth that hadn't been there before—Adrian sang with an intensity that was both passion and agony intertwined. Logan could feel every ounce of emotion poured into those words; he felt Adrian's hurt bleeding through, raw and exposed.

But Logan didn't need to *feel* it to understand. He lived that pain daily, carrying it like a wound that never healed, an ache that gnawed at him every second. He knew with chilling certainty that it was Adrian's shattered heart woven into each lyric, his sorrow crafting every line, his pain binding the melody together. When Adrian sang the chorus one last time, his voice rose in a shout that echoed across the ocean, bridging the distance between them, electrifying the air.

Logan's breath hitched as Adrian's voice poured through his earbuds, haunting and beautiful, every word heavy with truth. His skin prickled, hairs standing on end as Adrian's smooth, deep voice resonated with fierce intensity, singing each word as though it were his last confession. Logan knew, in that moment, that Adrian meant every syllable, that his heart had been poured into this song—a love letter written in heartbreak, echoing across the miles that had torn them apart.

Then the music softened, dropping to a hushed, haunting tone, and Adrian's voice trembled as he sang the final verse.

I saw the parts you keep hidden from the light,
I loved you in your darkest, most fragile fight.
I always wonder if you ever think of me,
Does my memory soothe you like the sea?
If you're broken now, I can't fix you,

Nothing of my soul survived the final dive.
But if you're damaged, maybe you need me as much as I need you?
I am fractured, but if you are whole, then I'll find my peace in your joy,
I believe my fate was to cross paths with you,
To be the one who saves you,

Logan's shattered heart broke further, splintering into pieces as he watched Adrian struggle to continue. His voice wavered, barely holding the melody, his breath catching on each word, until a single tear slipped down his cheek, landing softly on the guitar. Logan's hands gripped the edge of his seat, helpless, as he saw Adrian lift his head, his face streaked with raw anguish, his eyes reflecting a depth of sorrow that was almost unbearable to witness. A choked cry escaped Logan as he took in the full weight of Adrian's pain—so familiar, yet somehow deeper than he'd ever known.

That last sentence was a whispered confession, a tender farewell, the last thing he would hear from Adrian:

So when the end draws near, and life leaves you,
I'll be here, waiting to save you.

Tears streamed down Adrian's face as he abruptly rose and left the stage. The screen went dark, and the video ended, leaving a suffocating silence in its wake. Logan cast his phone to the other side of the couch, yanking his earbuds out and letting them fall onto the pristine carpet and couch, his body finally surrendering to the torrent of emotions he had kept buried. He let himself cry, truly cry, as hot tears poured from his gray eyes, carrying the weight of all the pain and self-hatred he'd suppressed for so long. The ache in his chest was like a living creature clawing through him, devouring him from the inside, a torture he knew he deserved.

He sat there, lost to time, sobbing until he was breathless, his words breaking through the silence as he whispered, "I'm sorry," and screamed, "I love you," as if Adrian could somehow hear him across the miles. It felt as though he were drowning in his grief, the weight pressing harder and harder, an agony that didn't subside but only grew, each tear a testament to how deeply broken, how utterly in love he still was. He'd made the choice he thought was right, yet his heart bled openly, calling to Adrian with a desperation that felt like it would consume him whole.

Eventually, Logan reached for his phone, fingers trembling as he pulled up Adrian's Facebook page, his thumb hovering over the message button. He needed to reach out, to say something, to cross the distance. The image of Adrian's face, etched in grief, filled his mind, and fresh waves of self-loathing washed over him. But still, all he wanted was to hold him, to pull him close and tell him... tell him what?

The tiny green dot glowed like a pulse—steady, unrelenting—next to Adrian's name. A beacon. A wound. Proof that he was there, somewhere, existing in the same digital ether, breathing in the same time, though a world apart. Logan's fingers trembled above the keyboard, the weight of unsent words pressing against his chest like stones in a riverbed. It would take only a moment. Just one flicker of courage, one keystroke, and he could cross the distance.

But could Adrian see him? Was he watching that same small dot, tracing Logan's presence like a ghost?

The song still rang in his ears—Adrian's voice, raw and golden, weaving the shape of them into melody. A song for him. A song about them. A song that held him captive, wrapped in the echo of a love that never learned how to end. And still, he was silent.

In the quiet aftermath of his breakdown, Logan couldn't help but long for those stolen moments: sitting with Adrian on a beach, watching the waves, listening to him play their songs. He wanted to kiss him, to run his fingers through his hair, to drown in the warmth of his whiskey-colored eyes.

A shudder ran through his body, and he wiped the fresh tears from his phone screen, his heart beating painfully with each thought of Adrian, each memory that refused to fade. He wanted nothing more than to bridge the chasm he had created, to be near him again, no matter what it cost.

Logan shoved the phone back into his pocket, his fingers shaking as he did. He couldn't send the message; he wasn't able to. The words were trapped in his throat, suffocating him. And what good would it do, anyway? Nothing. He'd missed his chance, hadn't he? He'd let time slip through his fingers, let the distance grow too wide between them, until all that was left was regret.

The reality of it settled in, a heavy weight in his chest, as if the decision had already been made for him, long before he even realized it. And now, all that remained was this unbearable silence, the endless ache of knowing he could never undo the past, never go back to when Adrian's heart had still been his.

I draw each breath only to offer it to you,
Be my lifesaver, and I'll be yours,
We'll weather the storms that crash on distant shores.
We'll find safe harbors where the winds are still,
And wait till the waves are gone, till our hearts can heal.
Be my lifesaver, and I'll be yours,
Together we'll stand through the tempest's roar,

We'll find the shore where the storms can't find,

I'll keep you safe, through the tides unwind.

We'll trace our path from the heart of the deepest blue.

As Logan closed his eyes, Adrian's words echoed in his mind, sharp and haunting. More tears spilled from his eyes, each one a reminder of the devastation he had caused. The thought of Adrian, sitting somewhere, believing that Logan didn't love him—that he wouldn't be his lifesaver—cut through him like a blade. He couldn't bear the weight of that belief.

But, of course, how could Adrian know the truth? With everything Logan had done—ditching him that day, blocking his number, pushing him away when he needed him most, and *marrying someone else* in front of him. Logan's heart twisted at the memory, the image of Adrian's face, betrayed and broken, flashing before him like a constant, living, bleeding wound.

Logan rose to his feet, his body moving on autopilot, numb from the inside out. The walls of his home closed in on him, the weight of it unbearable. He needed to escape—needed to breathe. The thought of staying in that house, surrounded by everything that reminded him of his mistakes, felt like a prison. He needed air. Without thinking, he grabbed his keys and left the house, the air thick with suffocating regret. He strode toward his Mercedes, barely feeling his steps, and slammed the door behind him before driving away.

He wanted to scream. To let everything out in one soul-shaking, throat-tearing cry. But what was the point? Screaming wouldn't change anything. It wouldn't make Adrian hear him. No matter how loud he shouted, the one person he needed to reach was gone. He could yell into the emptiness, and still, Adrian wouldn't come.

Tears streamed down his face as he drove, each one a silent testament to the loss, to the choice he couldn't take back. Every few seconds, he had to look away from the road, wiping them away, trying to erase the evidence of his broken heart.

At one red light, Logan couldn't stand it anymore. He pulled out his phone, hands trembling, and clicked play on the video again. He tossed it onto the passenger seat, letting Adrian's voice fill the car. The melody wrapped around him like a warm, cruel embrace. The song—so painfully beautiful, so filled with sorrow—was a confession, a truth Logan had been too afraid to face until now. Each note was a reminder of what he'd lost. Every word felt like a cut, but he couldn't stop listening. He let Adrian's voice wash over him, the most heartbreaking song he had ever heard, the kind that tore apart everything inside him and left him gasping for air.

"When you left, you took the best of me with you,

Was it hard for you to rise and leave?" Adrian's voice echoed throughout the car, permeating it and bleeding through the fragile fabric of Logan's being.

Logan's fist slammed against the steering wheel, the impact reverberating through him like the crash of a wave against jagged rocks. The tide of his frustration, guilt, and regret surged up all at once, an overwhelming swell he could no longer hold back. Each strike against the wheel was like a breaking wave—violent, uncontrollable, and desperate.

His breath hitched as a scream tore from his chest, raw and fractured, echoing through the empty car like a distant storm crashing against the shore. The sound of it was like the roar of the ocean in his ears, but it couldn't drown out the silence of his own brokenness. He pounded the wheel with the force of a tidal wave, his body trembling as the weight of his self-loathing pulled him deeper into the undertow. "Yes! Yes! Yes! Goddamit, yes!" he cried out, his voice ragged, barely recognizable, as though it had been pulled from the depths of a storm. "The hardest thing I've ever done!"

"*I always wonder if you ever think of me,*"

"Yes! All the fucking time, Adrian! Of course, I think of you!"

"*If you're broken now, I can't fix you,*

Nothing of my soul survived the final dive.

But if you're damaged, maybe you need me as much as I need you?

I am fractured, but if you are whole, then I'll find my peace in your joy,

I believe my fate was to cross paths with you,

To be the one who saves you,"

"I am! I do! I'm so fucking broken, you can't fix this! It's too late! I need you so much! I'm sorry! I'm sorry!" he yelled into the suffocating silence of the car, his voice crashing through the night like a rogue wave, desperate and uncontrolled. His foot slammed harder onto the accelerator, the car surging forward as if trying to outrun the hurricane of emotions that had taken hold of him.

"You can't fix this! You can't! It's been too long!" The words ripped from his throat, the echoes shaking the car's walls as though the very air around him was being torn apart.

Logan's body trembled violently, his hands no longer steady enough to hold the wheel, as if the weight of his guilt and grief was too heavy, pulling him under. His tears fell, blurring his vision, the salty sting in his eyes another reminder of the wreckage inside him. Every sob was a wave crashing over him, and no matter how hard he tried to stay afloat, he felt himself sinking deeper into the cold, merciless depths.

"So when the end draws near, and life leaves you,

I'll be here, waiting to save you."

"I don't deserve you waiting for me, Adrian! I don't!"

Memories surged within him, crashing over Logan, pulling him under, dragging him back to some secret places he'd buried deep beneath the surface. He could still feel the heat of the final kiss he shared with Adrian, moments before he stepped into the prison of his own making. It was the kiss of a man who knew he was about to lose everything—raw, desperate, filled with the kind of longing that could drown a person. Adrian's lips had tasted like candy and sorrow, like a storm about to break. The memory of Adrian's touch, the warmth of his skin against his own, lingered in Logan's every cell, as if he could still feel it. Adrian's scent, the way his presence filled every empty space, the soft strength of his heart that Logan had never fully understood until it was too late.

And now, that heart was gone, drifting far away, leaving Logan's own fragile core barely beating, barely alive. The pain was an ocean, vast and deep, swallowing him whole. Every breath felt like he was drowning, the weight of his own self-destruction suffocating him. He thought the pain could kill him, and part of him waited for the final wave to crash down and put an end to it.

When Logan reached the bar, he tried to steady himself, wiping his tears away as though they were nothing but the remnants of a storm that had already passed. He put on the mask of normalcy, pretending that nothing had shattered him, pretending that the last piece of his heart wasn't still caught in the undertow of Adrian's absence.

"Whiskey," he said, his voice a whisper that barely rose above the hum of the bar. "A glass, and a bottle."

Logan stared down at the bracelet Adrian had given him, the metal cool against his wrist, a cruel reminder of the love he had thrown away. The memories flooded him again, pounding at his fragile resolve, the weight of them threatening to crush him. He missed Adrian with an ache that felt like it was tearing him apart, piece by piece.

"Wow, what happened to you?" Zack asked, his voice cutting through the haze, but it was too late. Logan had already disappeared into the sea of his thoughts.

"Not now, Zack," Logan murmured, his voice heavy with a weight that was too much to bear. He let his head fall into his hands, elbows braced on the counter. "Whiskey. A lot of it."

Zack set a bottle and a glass down beside him, and Logan was grateful when Zack filled the cup without a word. He needed the burn of whiskey, the fire in his throat to numb the ache in his chest. The warmth of it spread through him briefly washing over the pain, but it wouldn't last. Nothing could drown this. Nothing could wash away the wreckage he'd made of his life. Still, he drank, hoping the ocean of whiskey would carry him far enough away from the storm raging inside.

Chapter 6

My Best... Everything

August 14, 2018—Siargao Island, Philippines—One Year and 10 Months Earlier

THEY'D BEEN HERE, SWALLOWED whole by the warmth and the wild beauty of the Philippines, for what felt like a lifetime or maybe just a breath. About three weeks had passed, but the days here were ever-rolling, never-ending. Each one bled into the next, seamless and fluid. Every sunrise brought a new shore, a new stretch of sand beneath their feet, a new horizon to chase. Together, they surfed the Pacific's embrace—riding her swells, carving her curls—like travelers who had forgotten the art of standing still. The islands were a labyrinth of saltwater and sun, and yet, despite the endless beauty of it all, it was the presence of Adrian that had become the most intoxicating part of it.

This was the third hotel they'd shared since landing in this paradise. There was no logic, no need to take two rooms, a room was just a place to breathe, to rest, and to hold their belongings, most of them scattered carelessly around, mainly Logan's fault and Adrian's inability to keep picking up after him, like pieces of a life half-lived, a life that wasn't quite real.

Logan finished his shower with the careful precision of someone trying to avoid thinking. The hot water had been a balm on his sun-kissed skin, which still carried the memory of the ocean's salt on it. His face was flushed, cheeks a warm shade of bronze from the sun. His sandy blond hair, a shade or so lighter than when he first got to Hawaii, clung to his scalp in wet, unruly strands.

He stood for a moment in front of the mirror, eyes tracing the stubble along his jawline, the whisper of a beard starting to grow in. There was a silence, thick and pressing, but it was his own voice in his head that thundered the loudest.

What are you doing? His eyes flicked to the small lifesaver bracelet still wrapped around his wrist, silver catching the light from the bathroom window. It gleamed like a distant star, always present, always pulling him toward something he couldn't quite reach.

With deliberate movements, he picked up the razor, his fingers brushing against the worn handle. The metal felt cold against his skin as he traced the blade along his jaw. Each stroke felt like an effort, like something he needed to do, something that gave him control over the chaos of his thoughts.

When the last of the stubble was gone, he tugged on boxer briefs and sweatpants, the fabric soft against his skin. He wanted to hurry, wanted to escape the quiet that hummed in his chest, but he couldn't. Not yet.

As he stepped into the room, he saw Adrian, sprawled lazily on one of the chairs by the window, his body a sculpted work of sun and muscle, tanned skin glowing in the soft light that spilled through the curtains. He was talking on the phone, his voice carrying that strange, foreign cadence—words and sounds Logan couldn't quite grasp, but that filled the space with a rhythm all their own. It was that rhythm, that lilting tone, that unsettled Logan in a way he couldn't explain.

Just Adrian, he told himself. But it wasn't just Adrian, was it? Nothing here was just anything. The air between them felt thick with something that buzzed, something that hummed, something that grew in the silent spaces between their breaths.

Logan tried to ignore the pull of it—the way Adrian's broad shoulders moved and rippled with each movement, the way his muscles moved beneath his skin like currents in the deep sea. But the more he tried, the more it seeped in. Every little thing about Adrian, his quiet strength, the way his eyes caught the light, his kind smile, tugged at Logan's resolve.

Shaking himself, Logan grabbed his phone, needing to ground himself in something familiar. It was a habit now, to check in with his mom every few days, to send a text and remind her that he was okay, that he was still out there in the world, doing the thing he loved. He typed her a quick message, then added one for Ann, his younger sister, the words light with affection, a smile creeping onto his face. His mom replied almost instantly, as if she were holding the phone, constantly waiting for the moment Logan would reach out.

> I miss you so much. Are you really spending all this time by yourself? Please stay safe. I love you, and we're waiting for you back home. Dad misses you too.

He doubted that his dad missed him. Waiting for him? That's for sure, but his dad didn't miss him. His mom's message hit him with a sharper shame than guilt, a reminder of how little he'd told either of them about this trip. He hadn't told them about the journey they were on, hadn't shared the mornings when the sun rose like fire over the waves, or the nights when the ocean whispered lullabies. He hadn't shared how Adrian's presence, quiet and constant, had begun to settle in the spaces between his thoughts, like the moon pulling the tide.

Logan swallowed, his fingers hovering over the keyboard as he fought the wave of emotions rising inside him.

> I miss you too. I'm doing okay. Don't worry, I'm being safe. I love you.

Logan swiped over to his chat with Jane, watching the stream of her messages pass by, each one more disconnected than the last, a patchwork of half-truths, vague updates, and empty words. They spoke often enough, but it never felt like they were really talking.

He wanted—no, *needed*—to say something real, to spill the storm that was brewing inside of him onto the screen, to find a way to speak the feelings that tangled in his chest. His hands flew over the screen, starting to type.

He wanted to tell her about Adrian—the way his presence had seeped into everything, the way his laugh echoed in Logan's mind like the pulse of the ocean, the way Adrian's smile could make the world feel both too big and too small at the same time. He wanted to say that, maybe, just maybe, there was something between them that went beyond the usual rhythms of friendship, something deeper, something that terrified and exhilarated him all at once.

This was not the time. This was not something he could share.

Not even with Jane.

He deleted the message, his thumb lingering over the empty space where he might have poured out his heart. Instead, he typed something else, something simpler, easier to say.

> How are you sis? Miss you lots. I'm having the time of my life. It's the best. Love you. Talked to mom. Sent a text to Ann. Call you later this week.

He snapped a quick selfie—grinning, a flash of bright white teeth—and attached it to the message, the image of his face a moment captured, a life suspended.

And yet, despite the message, despite the distance he put between himself and the ache in his chest, the room still hummed with the quiet tension between them. The weight of Adrian's presence felt like the pulse of the ocean itself, constant, inevitable, and far too much for Logan to ignore.

As Logan hit *send* on his message, a subtle shift in the room caught his attention. He glanced up from his phone and found Adrian's eyes on him, steady, unwavering.

"Looks good," Adrian said, his voice casual, but there was a hint of something behind it—a silent appreciation glistened in his eyes, paired with a lingering, wonder-filled gaze etched onto Logan.

Logan pressed his hand against his freshly-shaved jaw, feeling the smooth skin beneath his fingertips. "Thanks," he muttered, the word slipping out almost absentmindedly. He didn't trust his voice right now, too many thoughts, too many things left unsaid. He cleared his throat and asked, trying to fill the silence with something familiar, something safe. "Talked to your mom?"

"Yeah, earlier," Adrian replied, his voice flowing like a gentle ocean breeze. "It was some friends of mine." He approached the bed and picked up a towel from the stack of clean linens. Logan couldn't take his eyes off him, yearning to see and hear Adrian. "By the way, my mom says hi." The words lingered in the air, and Logan, for reasons he couldn't quite understand, felt the heat of a blush rise to his cheeks. He nodded, trying to mask the flutter in his chest, that uninvited wave of warmth that threatened to pull him under.

Over the weeks they'd spent together, Adrian had told his parents about their travels, about the days spent riding the endless waves. His mom had even called a few times, checking in on them both, a tangle of care threading through the static of their video calls. Logan remembered one call vividly, the way Adrian had half-laughed, half-grinned at the camera, his voice carrying that familiar affection as he said, "This is Logan, the one I've been telling you about!" Logan had barely managed a weak hello, his voice shaky in the face of Adrian's pride, his heart drumming wildly in his chest as Adrian's parents—both of them—smiled warmly at him through the screen, their English accented and broken but full of kindness. It felt like too much, too fast, but still, Logan had smiled back, had nodded, had breathed through the moment.

But that moment had passed, and the room was now filled with a different tension—one Logan didn't know how to navigate.

"My friends are here... they landed yesterday," Adrian began, rubbing the back of his neck in that way that always seemed to stir something in Logan.

It makes sense, it's a prime spot, always packed with surfers, Logan thought. "They're heading out to Pacifico Beach tomorrow, it's about twenty or thirty minutes away. They've got a ride set up. It's supposed to be great."

"Oh," Logan said, the word barely escaping his lips, more a breath than a sound. *Here it comes*—that familiar, sharp edge of uncertainty. The question hung between them, unanswered, like the space between two waves just before they crashed. Was Adrian going to leave? Would he vanish into the crowd of his friends, the way people did, drifting away like foam caught on the tide?

Was this the end of the road for them?

A gnawing panic clawed at Logan's chest. Should he help Adrian pack? Should he say goodbye with some weak hug, a parting phrase that meant nothing and everything? The thought of it made his skin crawl, made him wish for the comfort of the ocean's roar to drown out the churn of his thoughts.

But before he could settle on any of that, Adrian's voice broke through his spiraling thoughts. "So... um..." Adrian hesitated, as if unsure of his own words, his soft accent melting into a deeper, more familiar lilt with each day they spent together. "You coming? You coming with us? The waves are killer there!" he added with a smile, and there was something in his eyes—a flicker of hope—that made Logan's breath catch in his throat. It was an invitation, simple and hesitant, and yet it felt like a lifeline.

Adrian's heart hammered in his chest as he watched Logan, his eyes tracing every movement, every fleeting expression. He wanted Logan to come with him and his friends so badly it ached, but the uncertainty gnawed at him. *Would he?* He wasn't sure. The thing about Logan was that he wasn't like anyone Adrian had ever met. He was... unpredictable. While Adrian thrived in the energy of groups, reveling in the chaotic hum of voices and the rush of new experiences, Logan wasn't so easily swayed by the currents of others.

Logan was keen on being with Adrian—yes, absolutely—but Adrian could feel it, that resistance in him when it came to anyone outside their small, tight-knit bubble. Logan didn't open up easily. There were walls built around him, sturdy and thick, shaped by a solitude Adrian could only guess at. Over the past month, they had spent hours together, traveling between islands, surfing the same waves, sharing the same silence, laughter, and air. In all that time, Logan had barely mentioned his family. Not once had he spoken of friends, and when Adrian tried to ask, the conversations were always short, clipped. The way Logan retreated when the topic shifted to home made Adrian wonder if he truly was a loner, if perhaps the ocean was the only place he could breathe freely.

But despite all of that, Adrian knew.

They clicked.

It was something beyond logic, beyond explanation. It wasn't just the way Logan's sharp wit could leave him in fits of laughter, or how Adrian found himself endlessly captivated by the small shifts in Logan's moods. It was everything, the way Logan's quiet intensity steadied Adrian's wandering mind, the way Logan's spontaneity coaxed him out of his caution and into the world at its fullest. Their silences were never empty; they had the familiarity of people who could communicate wordlessly. Logan was a tangle of contradictions, open yet distant, impulsive yet guarded, and somehow, in all those fractures, Adrian found perfection.

"Yeah. Sure," Logan murmured, the words slipping out without thought, the decision already made in his chest even if his mind couldn't fully grasp it. Adrian's face broke into a grin, bright and effortless, the kind of smile that could light up the darkest corners of the sea.

"Great!" he exclaimed, his voice full of that warmth that made Logan's chest tighten. "I'll go take a shower; you've been in there forever." He turned, his broad shoulders shifting as he made his way toward the bathroom.

Logan watched as Adrian moved, the sway of his body a slow, liquid dance. His muscles rippled beneath his sun-bronzed skin, a rhythm that seemed to pulse with the heartbeat of the earth itself. Something stirred deep inside Logan—an undercurrent, subtle and powerful, rising like the morning sun, building with the force of something he couldn't name, but could feel with every fiber of his being. He was changing, or was it just that the world was shifting beneath him? It was as if he were standing on the edge of something vast, his soul stretching out like a surfer poised on the crest of a wave, ready to ride.

His chest clenched as his heart leapt, a scorching wave crashing through him. The air around him thickened, heavy with unspoken tension, a hum that vibrated through his veins. His body, taut and alive, thrummed with an insatiable hunger. He yearned to move, to follow Adrian into that bathroom, to bridge the gap with a fierce, reckless abandon reminiscent of the water's embrace. He longed to feel the gentle pulse of Adrian's skin beneath his fingertips, to taste the salt of him on his lips, to drown in the rhythm of his breath, to inhabit that fleeting moment of surrender. Deep within, Logan knew—without doubt—that Adrian would return his longing, answer his call, and hold him close, caressing his soul as if it were the rarest gem, shimmering with eternal light.

But his feet were rooted to the floor. Breathless, Logan stood still, his lips tingling, his mind thrashing, caught between the urge to act and the weight of fear pulling him back. *What if...* The thought unfurled in him, quiet at first, then impossible to contain. What if he stepped forward, crossed that invisible line, and kissed Adrian—finally felt the scrape of his stubble, the pulse of his hands against his skin? What if?

But the door clicked softly shut behind Adrian, and Logan exhaled a breath that trembled in the stillness. The ache in his chest didn't subside; it only deepened, swelling like the current as it pulled him farther, deeper, into the vastness of what he wasn't ready to face. It was heat gathering under his skin, rising until surrender felt like the only choice.

Logan turned and walked over to the sole bed in the room, falling into what had become his side of the bed, scooting to the farthest side. Moments later, Adrian emerged from the shower, his damp hair falling in darker strands around his shoulders, his body a quiet composition of sinew and muscle draped in nothing but black boxers. The sight hit Logan like a surge—unexpected, inevitable—and he quickly pulled the blanket over his body, hiding the heat he couldn't seem to control, hiding the evidence of how much he craved this man.

On the first night they had shared a room, Adrian took the small sofa there. Logan had tossed and turned through the hours, tangled in thoughts and the weight of proximity. By midnight, the restlessness had been too much to bear. He sat up, feeling the tension coil around him, and, in a moment of impulse, ordered Adrian to get his damn ass into bed. Adrian looked at him, bleary-eyed, his confusion more endearing than annoying. But Logan was firm. It was ridiculous. They'd been traveling together for weeks, shared the same breath in the ocean, the same space in the world. Why not the bed?

Logan felt the mattress shift as Adrian slid into the far side of the bed, a silent agreement between them—an invisible line drawn across the sheets, each leaving space as if it could separate the storm in their chests. Logan closed his eyes, but sleep wouldn't come. Not like this.

"Lo?" Adrian's voice broke the quiet, soft and knowing, as if he could feel the struggle inside him.

"Yeah?" Logan whispered back, not sure what he was answering, just needing to acknowledge the sound of Adrian's voice, the steady presence of him.

There was no reply, no more words. Instead, Adrian reached across the divide, his fingers brushing Logan's arm in a gesture that was simple and yet impossibly intimate, a silent promise. *I'm here.*

And in that moment, something inside Logan shifted. His heart seemed to stumble, then race. He crossed the line of the bed without thinking, without hesitation, pressing his body closer to Adrian's side. He laid his head on the same pillow, his breath mingling with Adrian's in the dim light, sharing the same air. The world outside was distant now, irrelevant.

Adrian, without a word, pulled the light blanket over them, the soft rustle of fabric the only sound. Then, Adrian's arms found Logan—strong, warm, and reassuring—pulling him closer, drawing him into a space where there were no boundaries, no walls. Just them, tangled in the quiet, the rhythm of their breathing matching the pull of the ocean, soft and inevitable.

The morning light filtered softly through the window, casting a muted glow over the room, but Logan's mind was still wrapped in the fog of sleep. He awoke to the weight of Adrian's body pressed against his, the firm hold of his arms wrapped around him like a tether to something solid. Adrian spooned him, his body fitting perfectly against Logan's, as if they were two halves of a whole. It was a strange kind of intimacy—unspoken, raw, but undeniable. A hold that was urgent, like a lifeline clutched in the hands of someone stranded at sea.

Logan stayed still, surrendering to the last hazy moments of sleep, trying to ignore the way his body was reacting to Adrian's touch. Every inch of Adrian's body seemed to press into him, and Logan was keenly aware of the heat between them, the hardness of Adrian's morning arousal, the thin cotton of their clothes offering no barrier to the electricity sparking between them. A low, involuntary moan escaped Logan's lips, a sound he couldn't control. He brushed his hand over Adrian's arm, still holding him close, as if the simple gesture could break the tension coiling within him.

But Adrian didn't pull away. He didn't even stir, just nestled closer, his head pressing gently against Logan's neck, as though seeking more closeness, more connection. The current between them shifted subtly, almost imperceptibly, but Logan knew—he felt it, deep in his chest—that the direction they were heading had been inevitable from the very beginning. Every moment, every shared glance, every brush of skin had led them here. And yet, in the stillness of the morning, it felt new, like the first wave breaking on an uncharted shore.

Then, Adrian stirred, and Logan felt his body shift, drawing him in tighter. Adrian drew in a slow, gentle breath, his face nestling into the soft curve of Logan's neck. He inhaled deeply, absorbing the rich fragrance of his skin, the mingling essence of salt, sun-warmed sand, and the warmth that entwined itself within their very being, becoming an integral part of him. It was an intimacy that stretched beyond friendship, beyond the brotherly bond they had once called it. But Logan didn't care. His chest tightened in something deeper, something raw, as he let Adrian hold him a little longer, not questioning the tenderness of the moment, just allowing it to happen.

The world outside still felt distant, but reality came knocking when Adrian finally broke the quiet with a soft, murmured, "Ready?"

Logan nodded, slow and reluctant, as if peeling himself away from something sacred. Adrian's warmth still clung to his skin, the echo of his body curved around him like an afterglow. Their silence was thick, not heavy, but full, like the resonance of a chord that still vibrates after the strings have stilled. They moved around each other as if guided by a wordless dance, two souls who had already found their rhythm long before the first time their eyes locked.

Adrian slipped quietly into the bathroom, his shadow disappearing behind the door. Logan, heart thudding in his chest like it was trying to speak, darted out. The morning air was crisp, biting at his cheeks as he walked briskly to the corner café, returning with two hot coffees in their glass travel cups and a pair of breakfast sandwiches wrapped in crinkled paper.

When he returned, Adrian had just stepped out of the steam, towel slung low on his hips, hair damp. Logan gestured silently to the small table by the window, where their breakfast and coffee sat. Adrian's eyes ensnared his, and the air itself seemed to still, trembling on the cusp of silence. That gaze—amber made liquid, light caught and trembling within—seeped into him like honey into flame. Gratitude glimmered there, fragile and infinite, a quiet devotion suspended in gold. The lashes that framed it were shadow-thick, dusk spilled upon dawn, the very border of dreaming. In that look lived something sacred, too delicate for mortal touch, too exquisite for sound. As Logan's breath faltered, the ache unfurled within him, tender as first light, cruel as beauty itself. His heart fluttered like a trapped bird, desperate yet unwilling to escape. To stop breathing would be no loss at all; it would be a worthy sacrifice indeed, he thought, if eternity could be spent drowning in that molten amber, where time itself bent to wonder.

He had to dig his fingers into the edge of the counter, ground himself. Every cell in his body begged to close the short space between them, to press against Adrian's chest again, to tuck his face into the curve of that neck and breathe him in. Just a hug. Or maybe more. His body remembered last night too well—the warmth of Adrian's arms wrapped around him, the way they fit like puzzle pieces carved by the same hand.

He looked away.

Logan took his turn in the bathroom, letting the water scald his skin, as if heat could cauterize longing.

After drinking their coffee and finishing breakfast, when they were both dressed and had boards in hand, they padded barefoot through the sand, the grains cold beneath their soles. Shoulder to shoulder but never touching, they walked toward the pickup for Pacifico Beach. The morning sun climbed slowly and golden, spreading soft light across Adrian's face.

Logan glanced sideways. Adrian's jaw was sharp in profile, his brow soft, eyes already squinting toward the horizon.

The sun's warmth caressed their skin, yet a different glow shimmered between them, a silent, humming tension, electric and alive. It lived in the spaces between breaths, in the accidental brush of fingers, in the way neither dared to speak too loudly, as if afraid of shattering something fragile and unfinished.

"Adrian!" A voice split the quiet like a gull's cry, reaching over the beach and striking a chord. The voice shaped Adrian's name differently than Logan ever had. Where Logan's tongue stretched it into *AY-dree-uhn*, soft at the edges, this voice cut cleaner—*ah-dree-AHN*—the vowels firm, the ending sharp, each syllable struck like a note. It was the same name, yet it carried a foreign weight, familiar and estranged all at once.

Logan watched as Adrian's face broke into a radiant grin, warmth surfacing like the sun spilling over a wave. He crossed the sand to embrace the stranger who'd called out to him, drawing him close, murmuring something soft and fluid in a language Logan couldn't understand. The cadence of it, though, felt intimate, like an old melody that should've been dissonant but wasn't.

"Logan, this is Dean, my best friend, we even served together in the Navy." Adrian gestured toward Logan, eyes bright but searching, as though gauging his reaction. "Dean, this is Logan." Logan's name hung there, alone and naked in the salt air, no embellishment or warmth to cushion it. Just "Logan." Was he disappointed that it was only his name and nothing more? The thought rose and swirled in him, unbidden, unsettling.

"I just told him you're the guy I've been telling him about," Adrian added quickly, filling in the gaps Logan could only guess at.

Dean's eyes landed on him with a mischievous glint, and he grinned, half-amused, half-possessive. "So you're the famous Logan," he said, gripping Logan's hand with a playful strength that bordered on challenging. "You've gone and stolen my best friend, huh?" He laughed, but something flickered there, something just beneath his words.

Logan held his gaze and managed a small smile. "I guess I have," he replied, barely a ripple of humor in his voice. As they were shaking hands, Dean gazed locked on Logan's wrist, where Adrian's lifesaver was, ever since the first day they'd met.

Suddenly, Dean's hand darted out, catching Logan's wrist like a fish hook sinking deep. His eyes fixed on the bracelet—the one Logan had worn without question, without thought—the same bracelet Adrian had worn every day since his mother had given it to him. Dean's gaze shifted from the bracelet to Logan, a flash of recognition rippling across his face, shifting from wonder to something sharper, angrier, as if he were seeing a storm swell on a clear day. Then Dean's head turned, eyes darkened, and spoke in Hebrew, his words rolling over Logan in a language he couldn't swim in, crashing syllables that seemed to rise and fall, building and breaking, leaving him stranded on the edge.

Logan's chest tightened, a pang echoing there, frustration prickling like salt in a wound. He'd never imagined wanting to understand Hebrew, had never needed it until now, but here he was, caught between them, suspended like driftwood in the current, unable to steer himself to shore.

Adrian's mind raced, his heart stammering with an unease he hadn't let himself feel in years. *Shit*, he thought, the word cutting through his fog. He hadn't anticipated this, hadn't even paused to think what might happen if Dean saw the bracelet, let alone read between the lines so quickly, tracing the invisible lines of tension from him to Logan like paths carved into the sand. Having his mother's bracelet on Logan's wrist had become so normal to Adrian, felt so right, and seemed such a natural thing that he never anticipated the moment his friends would notice it. He hadn't prepared for their understanding of the deep meaning it held—for what it revealed about him, about the quiet truth that he had given a piece of himself to Logan.

"Speak English, you idiot. He can't understand you." Adrian's tone was sharp, a spark of irritation flickering in his voice, but the faint blush creeping up his neck betrayed something softer beneath, something exposed and vulnerable. Dean only smirked, his defiance unbroken, the Hebrew words left hanging, untranslated, like a secret they shared alone—a language as intimate as an old scar, one that Logan couldn't trace.

Logan felt his throat tighten as Dean sauntered off toward the bus, leaving a silence that felt like the receding pull of a wave, tugging him back to shore yet keeping him stranded with Adrian. Adrian's eyes followed his friend for a moment, then flicked back to Logan. Leaning in, voice hushed like a confession, he murmured, "He just said it... looks like I care about you. Something like that." His cheeks deepened in color, gaze dropping to the sand beneath their feet, as if embarrassed by the weight of those words. He looked restless, uncertain, like he'd been handed something fragile, something too real, and wasn't sure whether to cradle it or cast it away.

Translating Dean's words felt like an exposure, a risk; but leaving them veiled in another language felt like building a wall between them. Caught between distance and closeness, Adrian stood, suspended, as if he'd let something slip that could never be taken back. But Adrian felt like a jerk because he hadn't translated it fully; he'd left a part out, too afraid to let it all out there.

The introductions flowed seamlessly together—Tom, Ben, Sergi, Shoam. They were friends of Adrian, each face radiant with sunshine, adorned with easy smiles and sun-kissed shoulders. Logan nodded and smiled, quickly forgetting their names as they arrived.

There were more. Others gathering with boards slung under arms and towels draped over sunburnt shoulders—two guys and three girls from Australia, a tall surfer from New Zealand with a deep laugh, three bronzed men from California, another from Hawaii, all wind-swept and sun-creased.

Logan stood just outside the circle, half-listening, half-floating. Laughter swelled and broke like waves, the scent of salt and coconut oil drifting on the breeze. Adrian was deep in conversation with—Shoam, maybe? Logan wasn't sure. Their closeness stirred something in his chest he didn't have a name for.

"Hey," a voice said beside him, low and easy.

Logan turned. One of the California guys, though he couldn't place a name. Tall, maybe an inch shorter than him, golden-tan like he belonged to the sun, with wavy blond hair and ocean-blue eyes that lingered when they looked at you.

"Hey," Logan replied, shifting his weight slightly, one hand brushing the back of his neck.

"Jack," the guy said, reading the pause in Logan's face. He flashed a dazzling smile—casual, but practiced. "You're Logan, right?"

"Yeah," Logan said, returning the smile, though not quite as effortlessly. "How's it going, man?"

"All good," Jack replied, voice smooth and relaxed. "Where're you from?"

"Seattle."

"Ah, cool." Jack nodded slowly, eyes scanning Logan just a moment too long. "Long way from home."

"Yeah." Logan chuckled softly, rubbing a thumb along the edge of his surfboard. "What about you? How do you know them?"

"Barely do," Jack said, with a lazy shrug that made the muscles in his shoulders ripple slightly. "Most of us met yesterday. I think Justin and Cody—those are the Aussie guys—knew the Israelis from before." He stretched slightly, arms behind his head, the movement slow and deliberate. "But someone suggested a group surf, and... here we are. No complaints so far."

Logan nodded, trying not to overthink the way Jack's eyes flicked to his mouth when he smiled. The tension was light, almost playful, but unmistakable.

Logan had the sense Jack was about to say something else, something bold, maybe reckless, when another surfer, name forgotten, hooked an arm around his shoulder and pulled him into a different conversation. Jack threw Logan a parting grin, something teasing in it, before he disappeared into the swell of voices.

Logan let out a breath, shifting his board in his grip. He was just about to slip away—find a quiet corner, maybe trail back to Adrian—when someone else approached.

"Hey," another voice called out, this time with a thick accent. Logan turned to see Tom, one of Adrian's friends. Stockier build, quiet eyes.

"Just saw Dean being a dick before and wanted to say," Tom murmured, stepping in close enough for privacy, "don't mind Dean. He's strange about Adrian. They've known each other and were inseparable since first grade, joined the Navy together, went through wars together. Dean's protective, you could say. Maybe jealous now that Adrian's stepping away."

Logan's mouth went dry, an unnamed question catching in his throat like salt from the sea. *Was there something between them, something deeper than friendship?*

Tom's gaze softened, as if sensing the rawness in Logan's silence. "Not like that, not romantic," he hurried to explain, though his words washed over Logan like a sigh, a tide both soothing and stirring. "But yeah, Dean's possessive. Adrian's been his anchor through it all, and I think maybe he's not ready to see him drift, you know? Ad said he wanted to do some, soul searching, you might say, in English, but seeing him traveling with you was not easy on him."

Logan nodded, trying to ignore the pull of his own thoughts, the churning questions lodged deep beneath the surface. As he watched Adrian laugh, saw Dean's lingering glances from across the beach, Logan felt himself caught in a riptide, something powerful and undeniable pulling him further into waters he was only just beginning to understand.

Logan nodded, already liking Tom. "Thanks."

Tom offered Logan a brief smile and a reassuring pat on the shoulder before leaving him to his turbulent thoughts, which now resembled sharp rocks protruding from a tumultuous shoreline. Their group had gathered by the edge of the sand, boards stacked on the battered old bus, the ocean glinting in the morning sun. Logan tried to focus on the water, on the thought of catching the day's first wave, anything to steady his nerves—when a figure sprinted toward them, calling Adrian's name with a familiarity that detonated inside Logan, like glass shattering through a hundred floors of silence, every shard finding its way into his heart.

The newcomer barely paused before crashing into Adrian, wrapping him in an embrace that felt too tight, too long, too *close*. Logan felt the flicker of a simmering, inexplicable rage take hold. This stranger didn't hold Adrian like a friend would. The man hugged him fiercely, head bent, face hidden against Adrian's shoulder. Logan watched, fists clenching, as this stranger's hand drifted over Adrian's back, possessive, caressing.

Logan's voice was tight, edged with something raw. "So... he knows Adrian, then," he muttered to Tom, forcing nonchalance even as his pulse pounded in his ears.

"Yeah, you could say that," Tom replied with a sigh. "That's Itay."

Itay. He hated that name. The sound of it punched through him, jagged and merciless, as if it had been carved to wound. His chest tightened, something hot and volatile flooding his ribs, rising fast, unbearable. Each beat of his heart struck like stone splitting under pressure, ready to crack wide open. Itay, bronzed skin, sun-washed curls, long, lean muscles flexing as he held onto Adrian like he owned him, like Adrian wasn't Logan's world but *his*. Itay finally pulled back, and Logan watched with a growing sense of helplessness as he gazed at Adrian with undisguised admiration, his blue eyes smoldering with something that stirred every instinct in Logan to step between them. Itay leaned in, murmuring something to Adrian in Hebrew, his hand lingering just a little too long on Adrian's arm, as if staking a claim. Every fiber in Logan screamed to shove that hand away, to tear Itay from him, to make clear that Adrian was *his*—if only he could admit it out loud.

Adrian's eyes found Logan's across the sand, an uncertain softness in them, almost like an apology. He stepped away from Itay's grip, and Logan felt a flash of relief, a hope that maybe Adrian was pulling back, that this was all just a moment of awkward reunion. Adrian moved toward him, his focus fixed on Logan with an intensity that was both grounding and fragile, as if whatever was between them was written only in the way Adrian's gaze sought his, unspoken but real.

"Itay, this is Logan," Adrian said, eyes still on Logan as if Itay were an afterthought. "Logan, this is... Itay."

But Adrian didn't add a single word to explain. He didn't say *who* Itay was, or why the sight of him had twisted Logan's heart into a vice. And before Logan could gather himself enough to respond, Tom jumped in, filling the silence.

"I thought you weren't supposed to be here," Tom said to Itay, an edge of tension in his voice. "Didn't you say you were off with Aaron, Dmitri and Luke today?"

Itay's expression turned from feigned indifference to sharp irritation, his eyes flicking between Tom and Logan before landing back on Adrian. "Yeah, well... someone forgot to mention that Adrian would be here." He spoke in Hebrew, and Tom, already on Logan's side, translated right away.

The words hit Logan with an ache he didn't want to acknowledge, and then Itay, without hesitation, slung his arm around Adrian's back and shoulders, pulling him close, like he'd done it a thousand times before. The sight of it cut through Logan, each beat of his heart a painful reminder that

Adrian had belonged to someone else once, someone who still looked at him with open longing.

Logan's fists clenched until his nails dug into his palms, his throat tight as he fought to keep his expression calm. But the sight of Itay's arm around Adrian, the way his hand settled so comfortably on Adrian's back, made his vision pulse with anger. He forced himself to breathe, jaw tight, every muscle twisted to the breaking point as he glared at the place where Itay's hand lingered, resting on Adrian like a brand Logan wanted to rip away.

Adrian, noticing the tension, casually slipped from Itay's grip, stepping out of his hold, but Itay didn't flinch, didn't seem fazed at all. He looked at Logan then, eyes narrowing in a way that felt like a challenge, and muttered something else in Hebrew, his gaze flicking up and down, assessing, dismissive.

"Speak English," Adrian muttered, barely hiding his irritation.

Itay frowned, giving Logan a look full of quiet disdain. "Speak English, Logan doesn't understand you," Adrian insisted, voice clipped.

The indifference in Itay's eyes dissolved into annoyance as he stared at Logan with the same dagger-sharp look, as if Logan were an interloper, a stranger trespassing into something sacred. Logan could feel his hands curling again, an instinct to retaliate thrumming under his skin, but he held himself back, watching with a barely contained fury as Itay's expression turned smug.

Itay's gaze roamed over Logan with a sharp, calculating intensity, as if measuring him, weighing the impact of his presence, gauging the intrusion he might represent. Then his eyes dropped, settling on Logan's wrist—and in a heartbeat, his hand shot out, gripping Logan's wrist with a force that was almost desperate. His face contorted as he stared at the bracelet, horror flickering across his features before he turned to Adrian, his expression unraveling into something far more wounded, raw, a depth of pain Logan had yet to see.

Itay's gaze lingered on Adrian, fractured, as though each look cost him something. His eyes glistened, catching the light, unshed tears brimming but refusing to fall, as though he were holding back a tide of words and memories too heavy to voice. In that moment, a silent exchange passed between them, a conversation spoken only in the fragile language of old hurt and shared history. Logan felt the power of it, felt himself pushed to the margins of a story he couldn't understand, yet couldn't escape.

"Yalla!" Dean called from the bus, snapping the tension. "C'mon, all of you. Boards are loaded, and we're burning daylight!" Dean called in English.

Itay dropped Logan's hand and walked away, the silence he'd left behind roaring.

The group started moving toward the bus, but Logan stayed back, grabbing Tom by the arm, hoping the thread of trust they'd begun to form would hold. "Wait," he said, his voice low, rough. He couldn't tear his gaze from Adrian and Itay, couldn't shake the searing image of Itay's hands on Adrian. "Are Itay and Adrian...?" He couldn't finish the question; words faltered before the tumult of fear and anger simmering within him. Yet, the way Itay's touch brushed Adrian's skin, the gaze they exchanged, it whispered of depths unfathomable, a silent symphony of intimacy. The hurt shimmering in Itay's eyes revealed a grief too profound for words, echoing the silent grief of a man mourning a lost loved one.

Tom hesitated, glancing at Adrian, who was busy talking to Dean. "Look, Logan, maybe you should talk to Adrian. It's not my place," he said softly, but Logan's expression was relentless, silently demanding an answer.

With a resigned sigh, Tom looked back at him. "Itay... and Adrian. They were... Itay... he shouldn't have come. They were..." Tom trailed off, his voice quiet, as if sharing a confession. But Logan barely heard him. His pulse drummed against his ribs, too loud, too uneven, as if his body had turned traitor. Heat gathered in his chest, not the clean burn of sun on skin, but something sourer, something that clenched his jaw tight.

Tom placed a hand on Logan's shoulder, trying to steady him. "But whatever they had, it's over," he added, trying to calm the wildfire Logan could feel swelling in his chest.

Logan stalked toward the bus, each step heavy, anger and jealousy thrumming under his skin. He shoved his board into the bus's trunk without looking, as if the motion could burn off the heat rising under his skin. His thoughts snagged on last night: the way Adrian had held him, touched him in the dark with a tenderness that felt unrepeatable, as if it belonged only to them. This morning, Adrian had been wrapped around him, breathing him in, tangled so closely that doubt had no room to breathe. But now he felt that connection slipping, tainted by the presence of someone who had once owned Adrian's heart and, as it seemed, had no intention of letting him go.

Adrian caught Logan's eye as he stepped onto the bus, something unspoken flickering there, half-question, half-concern. Logan held the look, his own gaze sharp, words of so many questions pressing at his throat like broken glass. He forced them down, lowered himself into the seat next to Adrian, the motion stiff, deliberate. Logan sat rigid, caught between the memory of Adrian's hand on him last night and the echo of another man's touch that morning, both clashing inside him until he could hardly breathe.

"Thanks," he muttered, not trusting his voice to hold steady.

"Of course," Adrian said softly. "You're sitting with me."

There was no playfulness in his tone, only quiet certainty. Logan felt a rush rise within him, as the warmth of Adrian's shoulder brushing his, the closeness that sparked something deep in his chest, equal parts comfort and ache.

Itay and Dean had slipped into the row across from them, Itay making sure to snatch the aisle seat to be closer to Adrian. Logan noticed how Itay leaned over to speak, just loud enough to draw Adrian's attention, their exchanges marked by an easy familiarity that unsettled Logan.

Itay spoke something in Hebrew, which Adrian completely ignored until he repeated it in English. "Did you sleep well last night?"

Adrian responded with a tight-lipped smile. "Yeah," the dryness in his tone unmistakable. He then turned to Logan, offering a warm smile that conveyed the shared memory of their night together.

"Where are you staying, Adrian?" Itay inquired again.

"We," Adrian emphasized, "are staying not far from here." His words were short and noncommittal. Logan couldn't deny that it made his chest swell with a hint of pride that Adrian wasn't trying to engage in conversation with his ex.

Then came Jack. Jack sauntered in full of confidence and a big Californian smile that seemed to light the entire bus. He slid into the seat behind Logan and Adrian, stretching long legs with a theatrical sigh of satisfaction.

"Well, damn," Jack said, voice dipped in playful honey. "I was kinda hoping to sit next to you, Logan."

Logan blinked, caught off guard, but only for a breath. He turned slightly on his seat, shoulders squaring, lips curving with dry amusement. "Already taken, I'm afraid."

Next to him, Adrian went still. Not the easy kind of stillness, but the kind that coils under the skin—shoulders taut, jaw tight, his entire body drawing inward like a pulled bowstring. Logan felt it more than he saw it. When Adrian looked at Jack, the warmth he usually wore like sunlight was gone, replaced by something sharp and glinting, cold fire behind calm eyes.

Jack leaned casually against the seatback, unbothered. "Just sayin'," he went on, eyes locked on Logan, "I've got plenty of room right here." He patted his thigh, smirking. "We could enjoy the ride, stretch out a little."

It was more teasing than serious, Logan could tell that. A flirt, maybe half-hearted, maybe not. But the tension it stirred in Adrian was anything but playful.

Adrian's hands clenched into fists at his sides, fingers twitching like he was holding back something with teeth.

Logan turned back to Jack, a slow grin playing at his lips. "I don't think a ride with you would be all that impressive."

The bus erupted in laughter—snorts, whistles, someone slapping the seat.

Jack clutched his chest in mock agony. "Damn, man, breaking hearts before we've even left the parking lot."

Then, with a wink, he tugged at the hem of his shirt and leaned forward again. "In case you get cold... or tired of the view... I'm just a row away. Maybe we can meet up later, just the two of us?"

Logan laughed, shook his head, not unkindly, but next to him, Adrian was granite. Stone-faced. Furious. Maybe it was ridiculous, but Logan felt a thrill crawl up his spine. He loved seeing Adrian like that, possessive, fierce, unfiltered.

Adrian turned, shoulders squared, his voice low enough to cut but not rise. "Back off."

Jack lifted his palms in mock surrender, a grin tugging at his mouth. "Relax, big guy. Just giving Logan some options." His tone was light, but the words hung heavy, a spark tossed into dry brush.

Before Adrian could fire again, Logan's hand found his shoulder. The touch was firm, coaxing him away from Jack's smirk. "I'm not interested," Logan said, steady, meeting Jack's eyes without a blink.

"Suit yourself." Jack's grin slipped, but he slouched back into his seat as if nothing mattered.

The bus lurched forward, the windows rattling, the road unspooling along the coast.

Logan sank down beside Adrian, their shoulders brushing in the narrow space. He leaned close enough for his words to be meant for Adrian alone. "Hey," he murmured, voice gentler now, "he's just being an idiot." His shoulder pressed deliberately against Adrian's, a quiet tether, a promise disguised as something casual.

Adrian didn't speak right away. But, after a deep breath, he relaxed enough and let his head rest on Logan's shoulder, their height difference making it nearly unnoticeable.

The bus filled with stories and laughter, the boards in the trunk thudding softly whenever the road curved. The scent of sea salt and sunscreen mingled with the faint tang of gasoline. Everyone was friendly enough, legs tangled, water bottles rolling on the floor, voices rising and falling with the road's rhythm. Tales of wild adventures and mishaps spilled into the air—missed flights, stolen flip-flops, jellyfish stings. Adrian's friends added their stories from cities where no one spoke their language, miming out misunderstandings to howls of laughter. They spoke mostly in English, and when someone tripped over an unfamiliar word, Adrian would lean toward Logan, his voice warm with laughter, translating with a grin.

Logan found himself laughing so hard at one story that his ribs ached—a story of Adrian mistaking a friend's girlfriend for his mother.

"She looked old enough!" Adrian defended himself, red-faced with laughter. "She called him sweetie!"

"You told them that is so nice that he took his mom out on Friday night! That she must love her son!"

"But she was 42 years old. I was not wrong!" Adrian kept on insisting that his mistake was justified.

"They broke up after that!"

"That's nothing," said the guy sitting next to Jack, Leo. "You don't know what I've been through with this idiot. The other night, he was so drunk he couldn't even stand. We were at this party, and he swore up and down he'd crash at the hotel."

Jack groaned. "You're exaggerating—"

"Shut up, I'm telling it," Leo grinned. "So he leaves the party, completely shit-faced, like wobbling, eyes in two different time zones. I figured he made it back okay."

Everyone leaned in.

Leo continued, "Next thing I know, I get a call at four in the morning. Jack's panicking, yelling something about screams and police and that I need to bring towels."

Jack slapped a hand over his face, already laughing. "It's not what it sounds like—"

"It's exactly what it sounds like," Leo cut in. "He went into the wrong hotel. Walked straight into the honeymoon suite. Got butt naked, climbed into bed, passed out."

Laughter erupted up and down the bus.

Jack was doubled over now, tears in his eyes. "I woke up to *screaming*, man! Like, *murder-movie* screaming. The wife's freaking out, the husband starts chasing me—"

"—and he ran naked down the street," Leo said triumphantly.

"I never got those clothes back," Jack muttered, laughing helplessly.

Logan had to wipe his eyes, his chest shaking. Even Adrian was howling now, head thrown back against the seat.

"You're lucky you didn't end up on some island watchlist," Dean chimed in, snorting.

"That man had a machete by the bed!" Jack cried. "A fucking *machete!* Who the hell sleeps next to a machete?"

"Oh, I think I've got a better one," said Amelia, one of the Australian surfers, grinning as she turned in her seat. She jabbed a finger behind her. "Brad," she called out, pointing to the wiry New Zealander lounging in the row behind her. "Lost a bet in Spain."

"Please don't," Brad groaned, already sinking lower in his seat.

"Shut it," she laughed. "He had to surf for a week in this *tiny* pink Speedo. No boardshorts. No shame. I swear, it looked like a piece of bubblegum trying to hang on for dear life."

The bus burst into laughter.

"He'd strut down the beach like he was on a damn catwalk," she went on, "and that thing barely covered his, well, let's just say, the entire beach was *very* aware of Brad that week."

"I have nothing to hide," he bragged, clearly deciding to own it.

"You got kicked off the beach by day two!" she added, wiping tears from her eyes.

Brad grinned, sitting up with a wink. "Yeah, but not before I got more phone numbers than a nightclub bouncer. Those Speedos did their job. My dignity didn't survive, but my dick thrived."

"Your junk almost fell off."

"Were you looking closely?" Bred leaned forward, locking eyes with Amelia. "I've got nothing to hide. I'll wear them right now if you're interested. Might just sweeten your vacation."

Amelia laughed, tossing a rolled-up towel at him. "Save it for the next lost bet, Romeo."

"I say wear them!" Jack called from the back. "Somebody bet Bred already so he can lose!"

"I'd pay not to see that," Dean muttered dryly.

"That's okay, baby," Bred fired back. "Just send a pic to your mama, she'd *love* it."

The bus erupted again, laughter bouncing off the windows as someone fake-gagged and someone else called Bred a national hazard. Even the driver cracked a grin in the rearview mirror.

But the laughter didn't drown out the sidelong glances Itay shot Logan's way. His eyes were like shadows at the edge of his vision—curious, maybe a little wary. Logan felt Itay judging him, questioning his presence here, intruding in the world Adrian had shared with them long before Logan entered the picture. He noticed the way Itay sought Adrian's attention, leaning too close, his gaze intent and glassy, as though he could still lay some claim to Adrian's loyalty.

Gradually, the bus quieted, voices drifting to murmurs and the soft clicks of scrolling phones. Logan's eyelids grew heavy, his head tipping against the cool glass of the window. As he turned slightly, he caught Adrian's eyes on him, that familiar, steady gaze watching him, calm as a quiet sea. Adrian leaned close, his voice a barely-there whisper in Logan's ear.

"I'm sorry," he murmured, his breath brushing against Logan's skin, warm and intimate as he spoke directly to his ear. "I didn't know Itay would be here today. If I'd known... we wouldn't have come."

Logan nodded, his heart tightening with questions that lodged in his throat, thoughts he couldn't bring himself to voice. Was Adrian remembering this morning, when they'd lingered in the haze of dawn? Did he wonder, as Logan did, what it would be like to spend a lazy morning wrapped in each other's warmth, to let their moments stretch?

"Dean's the best," Adrian continued softly. "But he's... he has a hard time with new people. And I told him I wanted to travel alone, so I think he's... surprised."

Logan didn't miss the way Adrian's voice dropped to that quiet, vulnerable tone. He felt Adrian's breath warm against his skin, seeping into him, twisting him up inside. The soft edge to Adrian's voice, the subtle heat of his body close beside him—it all felt like a choice, a silent confirmation that Logan wasn't just a passenger on this journey. Logan felt his insides getting warm and tingling at the thought of Adrian choosing him, of him occupying more space in Adrian's life, more of his time, his essence.

"So... why me?" Logan blurted out before he could catch himself.

They'd spent countless hours together, side by side on beaches and in crowded markets, in the unspoken camaraderie of the waves. They laughed at the same things, moved with an ease that felt as if they'd known each other for years. But this—this was something else. This was a space where the air hung heavy with unsaid things, where even silence seemed to hint at more.

Adrian didn't answer. Instead, he just looked at Logan, his eyes soft, glinting like sunlight over the water. There was something shy in his smile, a faint color rising to his cheeks, and Logan felt his heart lurch, as though it were reaching toward something deep and elusive. That look held the answer—an answer so fragile, so close, that he could almost feel it, like the sea's hush just before the wave breaks.

The rumble of the bus lulled Logan into a state where thoughts softened and exhaustion crept in, blurring the edges of reality. His hand lay inches from Adrian's, the memory of Itay's touch still fresh and bitter as salt on his mind. Itay, with his lingering hand on Adrian's hip, his gaze that knew too much, the weight of a history Logan could only guess at.

In a small, reckless moment, Logan bridged the distance. His fingers slipped into Adrian's, hesitant yet resolute, like a swimmer diving into deep water, unsure of what might be waiting below the surface. And then it was done; their fingers laced together, a simple, miraculous knot. Logan felt Adrian's hand jolt in surprise, his breath hitching.

For a second, Logan feared Adrian would pull away, but instead, Adrian's fingers tightened around his, firm and warm, an anchor in the restless current of Logan's feelings. Logan felt the ground beneath him steady, felt something profound settle in his chest, filling the space where doubt had been. Boldness sparked through him, and he allowed himself to drift closer, leaning his head against Adrian's shoulder. His eyes closed as he let his face rest in the crook of Adrian's neck, breathing in the scent of ocean and sunbaked skin.

Here, leaning into Adrian, he was weightless, as if every insecurity, every unknown, had been swept out by the tide. And beneath the pulse of Adrian's breath, he could hear the sea inside him, a vastness he was no longer afraid of, a feeling as deep and powerful as the ocean's pull.

He opened his eyes, taking in the sight of their tangled fingers. It felt like a revelation, the kind that's known in the body long before it reaches the mind. This connection, simple yet anchoring, was a wordless answer to all his silent questions. And Adrian was watching him, his lips softening into a smile that felt like sunrise over still water, warm and open, unfurling something in Logan's chest that had been knotted tight for too long.

"It's okay," Adrian murmured, his voice low, brushing over Logan. His thumb traced a small, reassuring arc over Logan's knuckles, and Logan felt his own heart answer, settling into an easy rhythm that felt like home.

They shifted together, trying to get comfortable in the cramped seats, laughing softly as they did, the sound filling the small space between them, echoing with something both unspoken and understood.

"You are too damn tall!" Adrian said lovingly, his hand holding Logan's tight.

"Just saying that I got room back here," Jack interfered from behind them. "I will kick Leo away in a heartbeat for you, Logan."

"Thanks, man," Leo said dryly. "Can't believe you're my best friend."

"So, Logan, what would it be?" Jack pressed.

"Shut up," Logan called.

Logan smiled at Adrian fondly, feeling as if he were high as his hand was laced with Adrian's, like a tangled shoreline where land and sea can't quite let go of each other. The feeling rushed over him, electric and endless, like the thrill of riding a wave he thought might break too soon.

When the bus finally stopped, Logan stepped out, his legs shaky with the sudden release of everything he'd been holding inside. The beach sprawled out before him, waves cresting and breaking against the shore with a power that felt almost alive. The salt air filled his lungs, sharp and cleansing, and he stood there, awestruck, not caring about the crowd around him. It was as if the sea itself had welcomed him, as if he'd come home.

Adrian appeared beside him, handing him his bag and board, a small, ordinary gesture, but one that left Logan speechless. It was the little things that Adrian did, the quiet attentions, that spoke loudest to Logan, and he felt his heart beat just a little faster.

The sea called to them both, and as Logan looked at Adrian, he could see his own yearning mirrored back at him. Here, with the ocean stretching vast before them and the warmth of Adrian's hand still imprinted on his own, Logan felt like he'd found something he didn't even know he'd been searching for.

"You brought your camera, right?" Adrian's voice was easy, playful, and Logan grinned widely in answer, the excitement rising sharp and bright beneath his skin as he pulled his shirt off. The thrill of capturing these moments—the waves, the way sunlight glanced off the water, the way Adrian looked at him sometimes like he was trying to solve a mystery—was all part of the day's promise.

Before he could say more, they heard Dean call from down the beach. Adrian answered with a casual "Coming!" as he peeled off his shirt, revealing sun-kissed skin, his muscles shifting beneath. Logan didn't miss how Itay lingered close to them, how his eyes were glued to Adrian's half-naked body.

Logan tried to keep his expression still, tried to mask the slow, gnawing thing inside him, but jealousy was an unruly beast, and it stirred deep in his chest, restless, hungry.

Itay's gaze was a weight, heavy with knowing, with something possessive, something Logan couldn't compete with. He wasn't even subtle about it—his eyes tracing Adrian like a map he already knew by heart, like a song he had memorized long before Logan had even heard the first note. There was history there, woven into glances, stitched into the space between them, and Logan hated it.

It was the knowing in Itay's eyes that ruined him. The certainty. The ease.

Itay moved toward them, cutting through the salt-laced air with the kind of confidence that made Logan's pulse tighten. "Adrian, can we talk for a moment?" His voice was smooth, deliberate—and in English. Logan clenched his jaw. It wasn't lost on him. Itay could've spoken in Hebrew, could've made it a moment just between them, but he didn't. He wanted Logan to understand. He wanted Logan to hear.

Adrian hesitated, a flicker of apology in his gaze as he looked at Logan, something uncertain settling in the space between them. But then he nodded and followed Itay, and Logan had to watch as Itay stepped closer, as their bodies fell into an old rhythm—muscle memory, familiarity. Logan could see it in the way Adrian's shoulders tensed, in the way his hands fisted momentarily at his sides before relaxing. A battle fought and lost in the space of a breath.

Logan didn't move, didn't speak, but his eyes tracked every motion, every shift, the way Itay ignored his presence entirely, like he was nothing more than an afterthought, a shadow at the edge of their story. Itay moved with a slow, deliberate grace, a storm rolling in without hurry, knowing the damage it would leave behind.

And then—

Itay reached for Adrian's hand.

The touch was soft, almost absentminded, but Logan saw the intent behind it. He saw it in the way Itay's fingers traced along Adrian's wrist, in the way his lips dipped close, brushing against the shell of Adrian's ear, words murmured too low for Logan to hear but loud enough to shake something loose inside him. Adrian's expression faltered—just a flicker, a shadow of something Logan couldn't name. Regret? Longing? The remnants of something that refused to die?

The ocean was a roar in Logan's ears, but his heart was quiet.

He watched, unmoving, as Itay's hand drifted lower, skimming over Adrian's waist, fingers just barely catching on the waistband of his board shorts—a touch so casual it might have been meaningless to anyone else.

But Logan wasn't anyone else. He saw it for what it was. A quiet claim. A reminder.

And then—it was there. A nudge of the head, a subtle gesture toward the trees behind them.

Logan felt it like a punch to the ribs.

Logan was aware of everything—the way Itay's fingers lingered, tracing an intimate path over Adrian's side, moving slowly, whispery toward the front of Adrian's shorts, as though trying to remind him of something, trying to repeat history, trying to evoke the emotion, awake the memories that lingered in the past. The way their eyes met, a silent conversation that left Logan feeling like an outsider, on the shore, watching the tide come in but never able to be part of it.

Logan's hand tightened into a fist, his body thrumming with the urge to step forward, to rip Itay's hand away, to break that gaze with the force of his own. He knew the weight of that look, the dangerous undertow of it, and the silent invitation Itay was making. But he was powerless, caught between his rage and the helplessness of being an outsider to their history.

Logan was standing there, his heart a roiling sea of fear and desire, the pulse of it crashing against his ribs. He could feel the weight of the moment pressing down on him—each breath like a tide pulling him further from the shore of his sanity, dragging him toward something he wasn't sure he could face. His gaze was fixed on Adrian, on the way his body moved with effortless beauty, how the sunlight caught in his hair, how he exuded something elemental, something that Logan both longed for and feared.

He begged the ocean. *Please,* he thought, the word a prayer lost in the wind. He begged the sky, a silent cry, fingers gripping the salty air like a lifeline. He begged the wind, that ancient force, to tear the current of the moment apart, to push Adrian away, to keep him from following. Because if Adrian stepped forward, if those familiar eyes caught *his*, if those hands reached out to *him*, Logan would crumble.

He would break like a wave that crashes on the rocks, splintering into nothing but foam, retreating into the depths, unseen, unheard, swallowed whole by the ocean. He would *fade.* He would vanish like the spray of water that dissipates before it can touch the shore, like the last whisper of the wind before it is gone, leaving nothing but an aching emptiness in its wake.

Please, he begged again. *Please, don't go with him.*

The words exchanged between them were fast, fluid, a dance of whispers in Hebrew that Logan couldn't grasp but felt like the crash of waves he could never ride. And the tone—God, the tone—shifting from arrogant to something else, something far more painful. Regret? Longing? Logan couldn't tell, but he felt the shift in the pit of his stomach. He wanted to understand, to break the silence, but he knew it wasn't his place.

Then Itay's other hand cupped Adrian's face, tilting it toward him with the possessiveness of someone who had once owned every part of him. His lips were close now, Logan could see them, feel the tension hanging in the air. Itay was close, close enough to kiss him, to pull him back into that history that Logan had no place in.

Logan felt himself starting to dissolve like the foam on the shore, fading into nothingness, retreating into the vast, cold ocean, where no one could touch him. He would cease to exist. He would vanish. He would become the water, a ghost of the wave, always ebbing and never quite reaching the shore.

But Adrian pulled away.

The air seemed to catch its breath, the world holding still for a moment as Adrian brushed Itay off, the movement practiced, almost rehearsed. It was gentle, but firm—final. Logan could see it in Adrian's eyes before the words even came. He could see the resolve, the unshakable certainty that this was the end of something.

"Ani matzati et ha'ehed shely," Adrian said, his voice steady, but soft. *I have found my one person.* Logan, standing nearby, caught the sound but not the meaning. And perhaps it was better this way, better that he couldn't grasp the weight of those words. It was too much, too soon, a truth Adrian wasn't ready to fully claim, let alone share. But Itay needed to hear it. He needed to understand. "Just one more time," Itay had murmured in his ear, his voice slick with practiced ease. "Fast, hot. Like before. One more time." He brushed against Adrian, fingers trailing in a way that spoke of rehearsed seduction. "We could have that again, you know. You and me, just us. Let me remind you how hot we are together, how good it was." So Adrian had been firm, telling him no, that he had found his one true person.

Logan's heart skipped a beat. He saw the weight of the words in Adrian's gaze, saw how he looked away from Itay to settle his focus on Logan. It was a simple truth, but it was as final as the crash of the waves on the shore.

Logan's chest cinched tight, every breath snagging as if his ribs were iron bands. The air thickened, stretched until it was almost unbearable, a silence so sharp it seemed to cut. And then it struck him—sudden, brutal—the truth crashing through him like glass shattering inward. There was no stopping it, no turning back; the moment had already chosen him. It ripped through his body with the inevitability of fire racing dry grass, devouring, unstoppable. He felt himself tipping, helpless, into something vast and consuming, and he knew, in a place deeper than thought, that he would not come out the same.

Adrian had made his choice.

And Logan? He could either stand there, adrift, or dive into the depths of it all. There would be no turning back.

When Adrian turned and caught Logan standing there—still as stone, eyes anchored to the space he had just vacated—the world seemed to shift, the air thickening.

Behind him, Itay had already melted into the sea, paddling effortlessly into the waves. Adrian's gaze found Logan again, and for a breath, the world quieted.

Something flickered in the space between them, something raw, unformed, trembling on the edge of being named. He wanted to explain, wanted to reach across the silence, to tell Logan that history was not the same as love, that familiarity was not the same as longing, that whatever Itay had been to him, it was over, it had been over long before this moment.

But the timing was all wrong.

So he said nothing.

Instead, his body moved on its own, his feet carrying him toward Logan as if tethered by something unseen. But it wasn't unseen at all, it was the pull of Logan's gaze, the quiet weight of his thoughts, the curve of his mouth, the unguarded kindness that lived in him. Logan was a force, magnetic and undeniable, and Adrian followed, not because he chose to, but because resistance had never been possible. He stood in front of him, close enough to see the way Logan's chest rose and fell, each breath measured, controlled, but betraying the storm brewing just beneath the surface. Close enough to see the hurt and confusion reflected in his storm-cloud irises, dark and restless, a sea on the verge of breaking.

Close enough to feel it—the quiet tempest in Logan's breath, the tension coiled beneath his skin like a held-back wave, like something waiting to crash.

Adrian didn't move. Didn't speak.

The space between them felt impossibly fragile, stretched thin with things unsaid, with questions neither of them had dared to ask. And yet, despite the weight of it, despite the uncertainty thrumming between them, Adrian had never felt surer of anything than this; standing here, caught in Logan's gravity, tethered to something they hadn't named but had already become everything.

And it struck Adrian then, with a force that left him breathless.

There was nowhere else he wanted to be.

Over the past month—through mornings wrapped in salt air, through evenings bathed in dying light, through the pull and crash of waves and the quiet moments in between—he had found something in Logan. Something steady, something familiar, something that felt like home.

And standing here, close enough to feel the electricity between them, close enough to breathe the same air, he realized—nothing compared to this.

"Lo," Adrian called, the nickname slipping from his lips like it was the only word his heart could let out. It wasn't just a name—it was a tether, a pull, a current that made Logan's pulse skip, made the heat under his skin rise in a way that had nothing to do with the sun.

Logan blinked, trying to shake the sting of bitterness that lingered in his throat, the anger that still clung like sand to wet feet. "Yeah?" His voice, though rough, couldn't hide the softness that Adrian's voice always seemed to draw out of him.

Adrian, seeing the tension in Logan's stance, nudged him with a playful elbow. The simple touch—the lightheartedness of it—was enough to coax Logan back, to pull him from the deeper waters of his own emotions. Logan's gaze softened as Adrian's grin brightened the space between them.

"I'm sorry about that. If I hadn't heard him out, he would have kept going, so I just wanted to get it over with." He reached out and took Logan's hand again. "There is nothing between me and Itay," Adrian said, his voice steady, but with a sincerity that washed over Logan like a calm wave, smoothing the jagged edges of his thoughts. "I swear."

"I know. I believe you." Logan replied. "But there *was* something, right?" Logan's voice was barely a whisper, a question that danced on the edges of doubt and curiosity. He needed to understand, even if the answer was a painful echo from the past.

Adrian's shoulders sagged slightly, his eyes dropping to the sand as if the weight of it all were too much for the moment. He nodded sluggishly. "But it is in the past."

"Maybe..." Logan licked his lips. "Maybe we'll talk about it later?" He wasn't sure what it meant, or what they would find when they ventured into those uncharted waters. The thought of it was both terrifying and necessary, a promise hovering between them, waiting to be claimed

"Yeah," Adrian nodded. "For now, let's go show them how to properly ride those babes there?" he joked, head over the rising swells of the ocean.

They grabbed their boards and were on the verge of the water as Dean sidled up, that teasing edge to his voice. "Aren't you two lovebirds inseparable? How do you even get along so well?" There was a challenge in Dean's tone.

Adrian just laughed, casual and unbothered. "Maybe Logan's just a better roommate than you, Dean." He shot Logan a playful look, letting the words hang in the air, and Logan could feel himself smiling despite everything.

"Fuck you, man," Dean laughed, letting it go, and Logan let his laughter mingle with Adrian's, the lightness settling over him again, pushing the jealousy and questions back beneath the surface.

They stood shoulder to shoulder at the water's edge, boards tucked under their arms, staring into the heave of the sea. The wind salted Logan's lips, stung his eyes, pressed the ocean's weight into his chest as if to remind him of where he belonged. He could feel Adrian beside him—close, steady, a presence that pulled at him in ways he silently recognized. The ocean called, but so did Adrian. And on some level both callings were indistinguishable.

They plunged forward together, boards slapping against the surface, arms slicing through cold water. Logan's body remembered this rhythm like a prayer—each paddle, each burn in his shoulders, the wax under his feet when he climbed onto the board. He felt the hum of the water under him, alive, relentless, as if it carried more than just his body; it carried the part of him he could never give up, no matter how he tried.

Adrian paddled nearby, cocky grin plastered on his face, throwing water at Logan as though he could own not just the wave, but the whole damn ocean. Logan laughed, the sound torn out of him, surprised and real, his head tipping back to the vastness of sky. For a moment, the world was stripped bare: just salt, sun, sea, and Adrian.

A swell rose, and instinct took over. Logan's pulse spiked, his muscles strained as he caught the wave, body aligning with its force. He sprang to his feet, balance sliding into him as if he had been born to it. Spray kissed his face, cool and sharp, while the wave curled around him, building into a perfect barrel. He leaned low, hand grazing the wall of water, cold and electric, like touching the skin of some immense living thing.

Inside the tube, sound collapsed into a roar, the outside world erased. There was only the rush in his chest, the blur of motion, the wild grace of being held and tested all at once. For a breathless instant, he was weightless, carried and defiant, part of something vast that would never be tamed.

He shot out of the barrel clean, cutting across the face, his body snapping sharp with effortless control before slowing to a graceful stop. His lungs heaved, heart hammering, every nerve lit with exhilaration. He glanced toward Adrian, who was watching, still grinning, still his anchor, still watching over him.

Logan dragged his hand across the board, water dripping from his fingertips. The ocean still thundered around him, but inside he was quiet, still, undone. He did not know it then, but it was a truth that would find him in time: the sea was only the second greatest love of his life. And soon, he would lose them both. He would be left dry upon a land that had forgotten its colors, standing beneath a sunless sky, a wanderer in a desert of his own making. He would be surrounded by concrete and silence—silence heavy with words almost understood, syllables that brushed against meaning only to slip away, elusive as shadows in the dark.

The night had already settled in by the time they made it back to their little cabin. It looked the same; the air still carried the scent of sea and sunscreen. Their clothes were draped over a random chair, and there was another stack of clean clothes from when they had taken them to the laundry.

They dropped their bags by the door and leaned their boards against the window, still wet and streaked with salt, facing the ocean. It had been a long day. Not exactly easy, Logan had spent it among people he didn't know, catching fragments of stories that weren't his, and watching Adrian's ex hover nearby, always angling for his attention.

But even with that, it was a good day. The waves at Pacifico had been incredible. They'd surfed until sunset and ate with the small crowd of surfers they met. Things progressed smoothly despite just having met that morning, with shared laughter and beers circulating. Numbers were exchanged, and casual plans were set.

Logan stepped into the cramped kitchenette, grabbed a cold beer from the fridge, and took a long swig. "Want one?" he asked Adrian.

"No, thanks," Adrian replied absently, hunched over his phone, shoulders drawn tight as if to brace against some invisible current. Logan's mind still reeled from the afternoon's undertow of unease—those moments when Itay's hands skimmed over Adrian as lightly as foam over a breaking wave. Now, Logan found himself with an odd, irrational fantasy: that Adrian might wash himself in scalding water until every trace of another man's touch was carried away. The memory clung to him like seaweed tangled around an ankle, impossible to shake loose.

Outside, the ocean breathed gently against the shore, its rhythm soft and steady like the heartbeat of the island. But inside Logan, a storm was beginning to gather. The quiet between them was fragile, hanging by a thread, until Adrian lifted his head and spoke. His voice was soft, almost hesitant. "They're going to some party tonight. Supposed to be a decent club, good music."

The casual mention of 'they' twisted something in Logan's gut. He didn't need to ask who, it was probably the same group as today. He saw Adrian in that imagined darkness, moving to the music, sweat and strobe lights catching the curve of his neck and Itay right there next to him, his hands on Adrian's body, trying to reclaim him. He imagined the shared laughter echoing under the hum of low lights and bass. The thought alone dimmed everything around him; the colors in the room seemed to fade, as if dusk had fallen too early, and the world had dulled to a grayscale hum.

Logan sat still, muscles tight beneath sunburned skin. The day had been too much—too many people, too many voices, too many eyes on him that didn't quite welcome. While he'd smiled and made small talk, a part of him had remained just out of reach, floating somewhere beyond the circle. He had planned to unwind tonight, to lie in the hush of evening beside Adrian and find peace in stillness, to go over their plans for tomorrow and the upcoming days, to get a nice dinner from a local place, and maybe walk around. But now, the idea of another night surrounded by the same people made something inside him recoil.

The air felt heavier now. The pulse in Logan's temples beat slow and deliberate, a steady thrum of frustration and ache.

"Will Itay be there?" Logan asked, trying to keep his voice level, though the syllables tasted of bitterness. Adrian lowered his gaze.

"I think he might."

"So... you're planning to spend the evening with your ex, basically?" Logan's words were as hard as rocks near a break line.

"It's not like that—" Adrian began, his tone gentle, uncertain.

"Don't," Logan said, stepping back, increasing the space in their tiny cabin as if he could carve out a cove of safety for himself. "He was all over you today, clinging like a lost puppy, pleading for every drop of your attention." Logan's voice trembled with the strain of holding back something deeper—something he didn't dare name. He felt raw as an open wound and exposed as shoreline at low tide.

"You said," Logan began, forcing himself to meet Adrian's eyes. "You said you'd explain about him."

"I did. But... I don't have much time and I... I don't want to leave it hanging." Adrian drew closer, trying to close the space that now felt wider than any ocean. "Let's just say for now, that we broke up for a reason, and I do not want him." Adrian's words were firm, each one spoken with intention, hoping Logan would understand what he hadn't fully voiced.

"Of course you're going," Logan said, a hollow smile on his face. "I am not going. Have fun."

"Please come, we'll have fun, I promise. I will talk to Dean—" Adrian's voice trembled slightly, as if he could sense quiet tension seeping into the spaces he'd begun to associate with safety and happiness, the ones that, now, could be referred to in short as "Logan." "He's just upset because, to him, I abandoned him for someone new. And... I have been through so much with him, so he is hurt, he is hurt because I decided I would rather be alone than with him, and suddenly... here you are."

"Sounds too co-dependent for just friendships," Logan muttered.

"Logan... I am 25 years old and I have been to no less than 4 wars..." Adrian paused, as if tasting old memories. "And Dean and Tom have been with me through all of it. That is why we are close. And I have known Dean since I was a boy. To him, I abandon him for you."

Adrian let the words settle. He knew Logan was stubborn, that once he made up his mind, it was as solid as a reef holding its ground against the tide.

Without another word, Adrian headed for the shower. When he finished, he returned to find Logan sitting in the same spot, staring into the darkness outside, the distant hush of waves coloring the silence.

"What will you be doing tonight?" Adrian asked softly, tugging jeans shorts from his duffel bag.

"Donno," Logan murmured, voice distant.

Adrian sensed Logan's anger like a tension in the air, but he didn't push it. He understood he couldn't just ignore his old friends after such a long separation. Meeting them here, so close, was a rare chance. As he pulled on a black shirt, he caught Logan's eyes flick toward him, reflecting confusion and something else Adrian couldn't name.

"Lo, I must go," Adrian said, his voice low, almost pleading. "I really have to go."

"Got it," Logan said, voice tight. He rose and slipped into the bathroom, turning on the water. The sound of it running over tile and porcelain filled the cabin, washing over the silence Adrian left behind.

Adrian laced up his shoes and tied back his long hair. Stepping outside, he closed the cabin's door gently, feeling the weight in his chest like heavy water pressing against his lungs. Beyond the door, the night and the shoreline waited, unchanged, as he walked away with the surf's quiet rhythm trailing behind him.

Logan pushed out of the cabin into the humid Philippine evening, fresh from the shower, sweat already beading again as he went looking for food and quiet. He'd become accustomed to Adrian's constant presence over the past month—waking up to his face every morning, sharing every meal, feeling the gentle warmth of his company at all times. Now that Adrian was off somewhere else, with his ex of all people, Logan felt the absence like a hollow space that did not sit right with him.

After dinner, he found himself drawn to the shoreline. The sky above was nearly colorless in the darkness, and the ocean moved steadily before him, its surface reflecting distant lights. Logan sat at the edge of the water, cool foam washing over his toes, and tried to sort through the tangled feelings twisting inside his chest. Tried to sort through the feelings he had spent too long pretending not to understand. For weeks, he had told himself this was friendship. He had convinced himself that what he felt for Adrian was just the product of proximity, of long days and nights spent chasing waves and sharing quiet moments beneath the sun.

But he knew better now.

It had taken root in him, deeper than he had ever intended—reshaping him, changing the way he moved through the world. Adrian was not just someone he cared about. He was the gravity that anchored Logan, the presence he sought out in every moment, the breath he counted without even realizing. It was terrifying how much he had come to need him.

And yet, Adrian had left him tonight.

Somewhere, in this very moment, Adrian was sitting in a dimly lit club, laughter spilling between drinks, voices low beneath the hum of music.

Somewhere, Adrian was with Itay.

Itay.

The name rose like bile in Logan's throat, sharp and bitter, weaving itself into every thought, every doubt. Logan hadn't asked Adrian not to go. He hadn't had the right. But still, it gnawed at him, the way Adrian had made the choice so easily, the way he had walked away, leaving Logan to sit alone at a table meant for two, to finish a meal that had turned cold in his mouth.

It felt like abandonment. Like a quiet kind of rejection.

And maybe that was unfair. Maybe it was selfish.

But as Logan sat there, watching the skyline blur into the sea, he couldn't shake the feeling that Adrian had made a choice tonight.

And it wasn't him.

A decision began to form like a closed fist in his mind. He needed to leave, to go before he sank any deeper into the uncertain depths of whatever they had become. He rose and walked back toward the cabin, glancing at the time on his phone. Adrian had been gone just barely an hour, plenty of time for Logan to gather his things and find another place to stay before heading to the airport in the morning. They needed to break this current that pulled them together; he needed to be on his own.

Back inside, Logan worked quietly, digging through drawstring fabric sacks, shoving his clothes into his duffel without bothering to fold them. He grabbed his toiletries from the bathroom and stuffed them in, too. Within minutes, nearly everything he owned was packed up, including his still-damp board shorts, which he shoved into the laundry sacks, not caring if they grew musty.

The door opened, and Adrian stepped inside, his hair damp as if he'd walked through a sudden burst of rain. The wet season could do that here, drenching a traveler without warning.

"Hey," Adrian said.

Logan didn't respond. He ducked back into the bathroom, making sure he'd left nothing behind. Adrian continued, as if oblivious to the tension. "What have you been doing tonight?" he asked lightly, noticing Logan unplugging his charger.

Logan ignored him again, slipping the charger into his duffel, followed by his laptop. He could feel Adrian's eyes on him, searching for an explanation.

"Are you going somewhere?" Adrian asked. There was an unmistakable tremor in his voice, a note of panic that made Logan's heart pound a little harder.

"Yeah," Logan said simply, like it was a minor decision, like it hadn't been boiling inside him for the past hour. He moved to the chair where he'd been casually tossing clothes since they arrived, now just a makeshift pile of shirts and shorts. He scooped them into a reusable cotton bag and shoved it into the duffel, not caring how crumpled they got.

"Where?" Adrian asked, his voice quavering as he came closer. Logan could almost sense him reaching out, though he didn't touch him.

Logan zipped his duffel up, then scanned the room one last time before putting it on. "I don't know yet." Logan's voice was flat. Controlled. Too controlled. The lie tasted bitter as it left his mouth. "I just thought about it and... maybe it was a mistake. Us traveling together. I mean... we barely know each other." The words took on an angry tone now, it was a failed attempt to use anger to mask the hurt he felt. "It was nice," he added, a final stab dressed as politeness. "But I think it's time we part ways."

He wouldn't admit how much he'd miss Adrian or how hard it was to leave. Instead, he turned toward the door, determined to find his own path and break free from the uncertain bond tugging at him from behind.

But Adrian was faster.

In an instant, he was in front of him, planting himself between Logan and the exit like a wall made of heat and heartbreak. His body blocked the doorway, but it was his eyes that stopped Logan cold—wide, wounded, carrying the shape of something cracking open.

"Are you kidding me?" Adrian's voice landed like a slap, sharp and bright as shattered coral beneath a calm wave. "You're just leaving? Why? Because I went with my friends?"

He stood too close, close enough for Logan to feel the warmth radiating off him, close enough to catch the scent of alcohol on his breath and the cologne still clinging to his skin. The ghost of laughter followed him in, echoes of the night he chose to share with others.

And suddenly, Logan couldn't breathe. He imagined Itay's arm slung casually around Adrian's shoulders, imagined Adrian smiling in that easy, familiar way he hadn't smiled at Logan in hours.

It was unbearable.

He felt it again—that bite. Sharp. Merciless. The thought of Adrian choosing that tide over him, floating back into old currents as if Logan had never existed.

And here Adrian was now, blocking the door, eyes wide and voice cracking, asking *why*.

But Logan didn't know how to answer. Because the real answer wasn't about the party. It was about the pain of wanting someone who might still belong somewhere else.

Adrian chose *him*.

The thought of Adrian caught in Itay's pull, orbiting someone else's gravity, sent a hot surge through Logan's chest, as if something had torn him out of place.

Logan tried to shoulder past him, but Adrian caught him, strong hands gripping tight, refusing to let go. Beneath Logan's skin, an undercurrent of frustration and hurt churned, dangerous and unseen. He twisted free for a second, but Adrian held fast, determined, like a reef catching a stray line and refusing to give it back.

"How dare you?" Logan spat, voice rough. "You're my only friend here, and you fucking ditched me! You left me alone to go and spend the night with your ex!"

"What are you talking about?" Adrian's voice cracked, a sudden fault line. "I was gone for, what, an hour?" he pleaded. "Logan—"

"Let me go!" Logan snapped, eyes bright and ferocious. He flung Adrian's hold off again, as if trying to scatter the memories of Itay's lingering presence. "Go back to your fucking friends and their damn party! Go back to fucking Itay."

Adrian's eyes widened, caught between shock and something else—something deeper, a wound deemed to remain open for all the days to come, denied any chance to heal, left only to burn and ooze. Logan lunged to open the door, but Adrian slammed it shut, blocking the exit with his body, like a wall of muscle and breath that refused to give way.

"Move!" Logan ordered, voice cutting through the humid air. Outside, the rain-whispered night waited, heavy and warm, holding its breath. Inside, Logan's cheeks burned, not just with anger, but something more complex, something too large to name. His eyes, shining in the lamplight, revealed not fury but a raw ache beneath the turbulent surface. "Move!" Logan demanded again, voice just as harsh, just as unyielding.

"No!" Adrian replied, voice stern but not yelling, he was not going to move from that door. "You're not going like that!"

"Like hell, I'm asking you what to do!"

"Logan—" Adrian started.

"Have you fucked him?" Logan spat.

Adrian saw it then; the ache that lived beneath Logan's fury, the way every tender truth was buried beneath a blade of words. He had seen it before, each time Logan's guard slammed shut: fear igniting into violence, vulnerability breaking into a roar, and shame—worst of all—flaring into a fire that consumed everything within reach, even the things he loved. Adrian felt something break inside his chest at the sight, like a longboard cracking in a massive wave, leaving him off-balance in the current.

"Logan," Adrian said softly, voice trembling over the sound of distant surf. "Could it be you're jealous? 'Cause it sure as hell looks like it!"

For a moment, Logan froze, and the air between them thickened with unspoken desires and resentments, a salty humidity that pressed in from all sides. Then Logan's bag fell from his shoulder and hit the floor with a dull thud. His hands came up to Adrian's chest, pushing him hard against the wooden door. Adrian's body met the impact, breath hitching, heart pounding, but he did not yield.

"Go to hell, Adrian!" Logan shouted, each syllable tasting like bitterness. "What could I possibly be jealous about?" He gripped Adrian's shirt, shaking it as if trying to rid himself of the unwanted images flooding his mind—Adrian's words in some dark corner with Itay, flashing him that beautiful smile with his molten whisky eyes, memories Logan could not compete with, Itay's hand traveling over Adrian's chiseled body, Adrian softly whimpering and moaning under Itay's familiar touch.

He could have thrown Adrian harder. He could have hurled him off like a breaking wave smashes a swimmer against the reef. But he didn't. He held back. It was there in the trembling tension of his muscles, in the way his fury broke against Adrian's steady gaze. The storm inside Logan was fierce, but not merciless. He would not truly hurt Adrian. He wanted him too badly, even if he couldn't yet understand what that want truly meant.

His breathing was ragged, drawn too fast, like he was gulping air after being tossed beneath a breaking wave.

"Is there something going on between us that I don't know about?" Adrian asked.

Adrian stood there, trembling, caught between terror and a strange thrill. Logan's fury—so raw, so bare—proved that this wasn't some quiet misunderstanding. There was a current tugging them together beneath all the half-spoken words and guarded silences. Adrian's heart twisted, half terrified, half exhilarated. He wanted this longing to have meaning, to be something real, something that cut deeper than any surface friendship.

"What?! No!" Logan insisted, his voice cracking, his eyes darting away like a startled fish fleeing a sudden net. His hands fell from Adrian's chest. He stepped back, his shoulders tense, and the anger seemed to drain from him, as if drawn out by the unspoken between them. Adrian saw confusion flood into its place. Logan's gaze roamed the room, as if searching for a safe harbor, but found only the quiet hush of what they had never dared to name.

"Logan…" Adrian breathed, his voice hitching like a line caught on a reef. "Do you want me to say it?" He felt tears gathering at the corners of his eyes, hot and burning. "Do you want me to put it all out there?" Adrian's voice was broken, choked with tears, and the fear that hung over him with Logan's sudden desire to depart.

Logan nodded, and in that small gesture, Adrian felt his chest tighten. Adrian tried to speak, his lips parting and closing, words tangled, squeezing him from within as he attempted to form them. Finally, the truth spilled out, each word echoing like a confession whispered under starlight.

"I want you," Adrian said, voice breaking on the words, letting them tumble forth like pearls freed from a broken string. "I've wanted you since the beginning. Itay means nothing, nothing compared to this… pull I feel toward you. He doesn't stir anything in me the way you do. Dean and the others… they knew as soon as they saw my m—bracelet on your wrist what *you* mean to me. I would have never given that piece of my past to anyone."

His tears finally spilled over, each drop carrying a secret he had guarded too long. "And when I left tonight, every moment was hollow. The music, the laughter… I stood there feeling like I was holding my breath underwater, waiting—just waiting—for some sign of you, I kept checking my phone and left as soon as I could. This thing between us… it's real, and it's so much more than I've dared admit. I know you're not ready, and I get that. I'll take whatever you can give, even if it is friendship, I don't want to lose our friendship. But don't pretend it's nothing. Don't pretend you don't feel it, too."

He stopped, swallowing hard. The silence in the room was thick, a humid hush broken only by the tremor in their breathing. Adrian's cheeks burned with truth, tears carving salty trails down his face. He had bared himself as if stripped by a rogue wave, every defense was a scattered driftwood on the shore. And in the wake of that confession, Logan moved.

Logan's hands rose, steady and deliberate, his touch carrying the heat of the sun-baked sand yet trembling with the urgency of an incoming tide. His palms cupped Adrian's face, as though cradling something fragile—something that could slip through his fingers like seafoam dissolving under the weight of the next wave, thumbs brushing over cheekbones with a reverence that felt like both worship and desperation as he tilted Adrian's head back and bent a bit to capture Adrian's lips with his own. When their lips met, it wasn't gentle; it was the clash of oceans meeting cliffs, a fierce and unrelenting collision that reverberated through Adrian's core. The kiss was raw, desperate—a storm rolling in from the horizon, thunder and salt pounding against the shoreline of their unspoken truths.

That kiss, the moment Logan's lips met Adrian's for the first time, carried months of stolen glances and held-back words, of fingertips brushing too long against sun-warmed skin, of nights spent closer than friends should be, wrapped in something hushed but undeniable. It was Logan's attempt to brand himself into Adrian's bones, to carve his name into the spaces Itay had once filled, to erase every doubt, every hesitation, every moment Adrian had spent not knowing where he belonged.

And Adrian—Adrian had never been kissed like this.

Never been kissed like he was something someone couldn't bear to lose. Like he was the eye of the storm and the storm itself, chaos and calm entwined.

It was everything and nothing, too much and not enough, and yet, in this moment, in the wild crash of lips and breath and longing—there was only this. Only them.

Adrian froze for a heartbeat, caught in the riptide of disbelief, unable to fathom that the ache he'd carried quietly for weeks had finally found its release. It was as if the sea itself had whispered its blessings, delivering this impossible moment like a treasure washed ashore. He had told himself again and again that friendship with Logan was enough, that to have him in any measure was better than a life without him. But now, the tide had shifted, and the pull was irresistible.

Adrian's hesitation dissolved as the rhythm of Logan's kiss steadied him, the same way the first paddle out steadies a surfer against the churning waves. He slid a hand to the small of Logan's back, the muscles beneath his fingers taut and the skin smooth, dry, and warm. His other hand tangled in Logan's hair, anchoring himself against the swell of sensation. When he kissed back, it was everything—a surge of passion, unrelenting and pure, like the sea claiming its shore. Every fiber of his being burned, not with fire, but with the salt-laden electricity that was all Logan.

Logan's fingers curled tighter against Adrian's skin, pulling him in, anchoring him in the gravity of this moment, of this undeniable thing between them. His lips parted, and Adrian barely had time to breathe before Logan deepened the kiss, his tongue sweeping against Adrian's, a slow, devastating slide of heat and want that sent a shudder through his spine.

Logan's scent, a mix of soap and ocean and something uniquely his, filled Adrian's senses, drowning out the world beyond. The taste of him, sharp and intoxicating, was like diving headfirst into deep water, the kind that swallows you whole and leaves you gasping. Their movements ebbed and flowed, a rhythm born of the sea that had shaped them both, and in that moment, they were no longer just Logan and Adrian—they were the tide and the moon, inseparable, drawn together by forces they couldn't name but could no longer resist.

A moment later, they broke the kiss, but the gravity between them remained unbroken. Logan's forehead rested against Adrian's, their shared breath the only sound in the stillness that surrounded them. Adrian felt the tremor in Logan's body—a quake beneath the surface, threatening to drown them both. The room seemed to hold its breath, knowing the significance of this moment. It was a delicate balance, a fragile wave teetering on the edge of breaking, poised to either build something unshakable or scatter them in its wake. Adrian knew this truth as surely as he knew the rhythm of the sea.

Out of the corner of his eye, Adrian caught sight of Logan's duffel bag, hastily packed and thrown on the floor. The ache in his chest returned, sharp as a rock hidden beneath a wave, but he shoved it aside. This wasn't about him—it was about Logan. He needed to steady them, to be the shore Logan could hold onto, unyielding and constant.

"Logan, hey," Adrian murmured, his voice soft. "Look at me."

Logan did, his storm-gray eyes meeting Adrian's with a raw vulnerability that made Adrian's heart twist. They were turbulent waters, full of questions and confusion, but Adrian wouldn't let him face them alone. He closed the space between them once more, his lips brushing Logan's in a kiss so gentle it felt like a breeze over the water at dawn. It carried a quiet reverence, a promise woven from a hundred sunsets, the crest of the perfect wave, and the endless horizon of Logan himself.

"Lo," Adrian whispered as they parted, the name a prayer on his lips. "It's just me and you, okay? It's us."

Logan's breath, warm and uneven, fanned across Adrian's face. Adrian raised a hand, his fingers tracing the curve of Logan's cheek, the line of his neck, grounding himself in the solidity of this moment. The storm inside him calmed, anchored by the presence of the man in front of him.

"Let's go to bed," Adrian said, his voice wavering with emotion. "It's been such a long day, and I'm exhausted. All I want right now…" His voice broke, and he paused, letting himself drown for a moment in the deep, shifting gray of Logan's gaze. It was the color of storm clouds rolling over the sea, of a sky moments before dawn. "All I want is to hold you close and fall asleep with you."

Logan's reply was quiet but sure. "I want that too."

Logan's hand gently rose, his fingers gliding through the delicate strands of hair that had escaped from Adrian's ponytail. With a soft tug, he freed the tie, allowing Adrian's hair to tumble down in graceful waves, cascading over his shoulders like a shimmering waterfall spilling from a secret source. There was something achingly tender in the gesture, a silent acknowledgment of the moment they were sharing.

"Let's go to sleep," Logan said, his voice carrying the weight of trust.

And together, they moved. The nightly routine was familiar—shedding clothes, tossing shoes aside, brushing teeth—but tonight, the air between them felt different, charged. Stripping down to their underwear, they caught each other's glances in the mirror. It was playful, a dance of shy smiles and lingering stares, until Adrian, with his usual ease, broke the tension. He gave a playful nudge, bumping his hip against Logan's, a ripple of lightheartedness breaking through Logan's lingering unease.

Adrian had always embodied a carefree spirit; his physique, a masterpiece forged by sun-soaked days and relentless dedication to his body. Logan's eyes couldn't help but wander—over the sharp definition of Adrian's abs, the powerful curve of his biceps, the gentle sprinkling of hair across his chest. It wasn't new; they'd spent weeks together like this, surfing in nothing but their trunks, existing in an easy, intimate rhythm. But now, it felt different. Logan's gaze lingered, caught on the contours of Adrian's body, and heat rose to his cheeks when Adrian's eyes met his. Adrian was watching him, not just looking but *seeing*—hungry, reverent, unguarded in a way that made Logan's breath catch.

By the time they slipped into bed, the room had gone dark, but the awareness between them burned brighter than ever. Adrian lay back, waiting, giving Logan the space he needed. When Logan finally shifted closer, pressing into Adrian's arms, it felt like taking a breath after being submerged for far too long. Adrian's voice was a low murmur in the darkness, gentle and grounding. "Lo, nothing has to happen tonight. Nothing you don't want. Just kissing you... it's more than I ever dreamed of having. I don't want you to feel pressured."

Logan's fingers sought Adrian's in the dark, their hands locking together like the seamless weave of a rope. "Thank you," he whispered, his voice heavy with emotion. And then he found Adrian's lips again, soft and searching, a quiet declaration that he wanted to stay.

After a while, Adrian's voice broke the stillness, tentative but earnest. "I do want you to understand. Why I had to go tonight. I think it's important."

Logan nodded, the motion barely more than a breath, as if speaking would shatter whatever fragile thread had just been tied between them. Then his hands rose—slow, reverent—and found Adrian's face, cupping it like something precious he was afraid to lose again. Their eyes met, a beat suspended in time, and then Logan leaned in, closing the space with a kiss that tasted so sweet, Adrian just let the taste consume him.

He kissed him deeply—hungrily—his mouth pressing hard against Adrian's, devouring the silence between them. His body hovered just above, trembling slightly, the tension in his limbs slowly melting into Adrian's warmth. Logan moaned softly into the kiss, the sound caught between need and relief, as if this was the only way he could breathe again.

His fingers tangled in Adrian's hair, pulling gently, anchoring himself in the only thing that felt real. Their chests aligned, skin to skin, breath syncing in quiet rhythm. Adrian's arms wrapped around him, strong and certain, pulling him closer with that quiet, masculine gravity that had drawn Logan to him from the beginning.

"I can't stop kissing you," Logan whispered, his breath warm against the curve of Adrian's neck. "Now that I *can* kiss you, I can't stop."

He said it again, softer this time, like a confession falling from somewhere deeper. He pressed his lips to Adrian's cheek, then lower, brushing his ear before trailing down the strong line of his neck. Adrian melted beneath his touch, body arching subtly, as if his skin had been waiting for this, remembering the shape of Logan's mouth and aching for it even in absence.

After a quiet beat, Logan hovered over him, one elbow tucked beneath his weight, the other hand splayed gently across Adrian's chest. He gazed down at him, eyes filled with something that bordered on awe, as though he were still convincing himself this was real.

Then, in a whisper that seemed to tremble in the space between them, he asked, "Was... was he there?"

He turned his face away as the words landed, eyes drifting toward the wall, unable to meet Adrian's gaze. The dim light washed over them in soft gold, enough to see Adrian's eyes, but Logan silently hoped it might blur the expression he couldn't quite hide.

Adrian reached up, tenderly, lovingly, cupping Logan's jaw in his palm. He pulled him back, brought their lips together in a kiss that was gentle and full of understanding.

"He was," Adrian murmured against his mouth. "We're over. We've been over for almost two years."

His thumb brushed Logan's cheek, grounding him, calming the storm behind his eyes.

"Remember today, when Jack was doing everything in his power to get your attention?"

Logan snorted. "He was just a clown—"

A quick kiss silenced him.

"You found it ridiculous," Adrian said with a soft smile. "That's exactly how I felt about Itay. Even tonight, he could've..." He paused, searching for the most absurd image, lips quirking. "Started stripping and rubbing oil on himself—"

Logan groaned and smacked him playfully on the chest. "Really? Now you're picturing him like that?"

"And I still wouldn't have cared!" Adrian laughed, arms wrapping around Logan as he pulled him down into a warm, anchoring embrace, holding him against his chest.

"I'll call Jack!" Logan declared teasingly.

"Don't you dare!" Adrian laughed, holding him tighter. "I just told you," he whispered, his tone shifting, quieter now, earnest and fragile and fierce all at once. All traces of laughter faded into something else. "I want you, Logan. That's it."

Logan's smile bloomed slowly and unguarded, and something inside him—tightly wound for so long—finally, finally gave way. Something broke free. And in that moment, as he lay over Adrian's heart and listened to it pounding wild beneath his ear, he knew. It wasn't nerves. It wasn't adrenaline. Adrian's heart was racing because *they were here, together*. Because of *him*.

The idea was dizzying. Exhilarating.

They had spent so many nights side by side, breathing in rhythm and never crossing that fragile line. But tonight was different. Not because they had changed, but because the space between them had. That delicate undercurrent, the one they'd been skating around for weeks, had finally surged upward—irresistible, undeniable.

Logan lifted himself again, leaning on one elbow. His eyes searched Adrian's face with something luminous shimmering behind them—adoration, want, reverence. He leaned in and stole another kiss, slower this time, lingering.

He ached for more of this closeness—the kind they had been both craving and fearing. He moved without hesitation now, sliding one leg over Adrian's waist until he was fully straddling him, draped over him like a second skin. Adrian's breath caught, stuttered out in a quiet laugh that trembled in his throat. His hands moved instinctively—one to Logan's neck, the other anchoring at his hip.

They kissed again, and this time there was no holding back. Adrian chased Logan's mouth with breathless need, lips parting between gasps and moans. Logan pressed down, arms wrapping around Adrian's shoulders, hands pulling him impossibly closer, desperate to collapse the inches that still separated them.

Their bodies moved together, breath hitching as heat bloomed in the space between fabric and skin. Logan's hips rocked gently, slowly, instinctively. Their height difference made Logan's arousal brushing against Adrian's upper thigh, while Adrian's cock pressed firm and hot against the hard abs of Logan's lower belly. The friction was maddening and perfect. Nothing hurried, nothing forced—just pressure, just pulse, just the implicit language of: *I missed you, I want you, I'm here.*

Logan's hand moved slowly from Adrian's chest, dragging gently down his side, the curve of his fingers following the ridges of bone and muscle beneath the cotton. His fingertips hovered at the edge of Adrian's hipbone, pausing just above the waistband of his boxers. He could feel the heat radiating through the thin fabric, the rise and fall of Adrian's breath shifting beneath his palm.

"Is that okay?" Logan whispered, his voice trembling with both need and hesitation. He rested his forehead against Adrian's, their sweat-slicked brows pressed together, breath mingling in the hush between them.

Adrian's hands slid to his waist, gripping him firmly—steadying them both, like an anchor cast in stormy waters.

"Yes," he breathed, the word more exhaled than sounded. "Yes. Please don't stop."

Logan's hand moved lower, his knuckles brushing the hard length beneath Adrian's boxers. He swallowed, heart hammering in his throat, and then let his palm settle there—over Adrian, over *him*. He began to stroke gently, feeling the shape of him through the fabric, the way Adrian arched slightly into the touch, a soft moan spilling from his lips and dissolving into the air like sea mist.

Each sound Adrian made went straight to Logan's chest, to his gut. He had never touched another man like this, but this didn't feel strange. It didn't feel foreign. It felt *inevitable*.

It was Adrian. And with Adrian, it made sense.

"Ad..." Logan moaned, the name dragging out of him, half prayer, half surrender. His hand continued its rhythm, slow and steady, coaxing soft gasps from Adrian's mouth. "I've never been with a man before," he whispered, almost ashamed of how new this all felt. "Is that... okay?"

Adrian's response was immediate. "Perfect," he said, voice thick, reverent. "You're perfect."

Then Adrian shifted beneath him, one smooth movement bringing their hips into alignment. Their cocks pressed together, separated only by cotton, and the jolt of contact sent a shiver through both of them.

"Come here," Adrian said, voice shaking. "Kiss me. I need you."

Logan surged forward, gladly. It was a bit awkward with their height difference, bodies pressed together, noses brushing, but he didn't care. He found Adrian's mouth, kissed him with a hunger he hadn't known he possessed. Their lips slid together, soft and wet, breath catching between them.

As they kissed, Logan began to move his hips—slowly at first, just testing the rhythm, his cock grinding against Adrian's through the fabric. He groaned, the sensation almost too much—the friction, the pressure, the heat between them.

"Fuck," he gasped into Adrian's mouth. "You feel so good..."

Adrian's legs wrapped loosely around his waist, heels pressing into the small of Logan's back, urging him on. Their cocks rubbed together, the damp fabric clinging to them, creating a friction that made Logan's spine arch and Adrian's hands dig into his skin.

The pace stayed slow, tentative, reverent. Logan buried his face in Adrian's neck, his lips brushing his skin with every breath, every moan. Adrian held him tightly, one hand sliding over Logan's back, palm gliding over the sweat-slicked skin of his back, fingers splayed over trembling muscles.

"You're doing so good," Adrian whispered, his voice rough and broken. "Just like that..."

Logan's hips rocked harder now, more instinct than thought, grinding them together with growing urgency. The air between them was hot and heavy, every inch of their bodies straining to be closer, to disappear into one another.

Adrian was panting, his moans sharp and rhythmic, his hands everywhere—waist, back, shoulders, hair—as if he couldn't decide where to hold Logan, so he held *all of him* at once.

Logan's voice cracked. "I'm gonna come—I can't—"

"Me too," Adrian moaned, wrapping both arms around Logan's shoulders, crushing him close. "Harder, Lo. Please."

Logan rocked into him one last time, their cocks pressing together just right, and then he came with a shuddering cry, his whole body locking against Adrian's as the wave of release crashed over him. Adrian followed seconds later, his breath catching in his throat, his back arching, his voice breaking open in a low, desperate groan.

And then, stillness.

The sound of the waves returned slowly, soft and distant, as if the world had held its breath for them and was only now exhaling.

Logan collapsed over Adrian's chest, boneless and trembling, face buried in the crook of his neck. Adrian's arms wrapped around him again, gently this time, stroking the back of his head, fingers tracing through damp curls.

Neither of them spoke.

They didn't need to.

They just held each other, breathing in sync, hearts pounding in time—closer now than they had ever been.

"Fuck. I didn't know it could feel like that," he whispered eventually, his voice muffled against Adrian's chest.

Adrian smiled. "That was amazing."

Logan grinned, lips brushing against Adrian's skin. "Worth the laundry? Because I only wore those boxers for, what, an hour? And now I need a new pair."

Adrian chuckled, fingers tracing lazy lines along Logan's spine. "I'd wait through forty loads of laundry if it meant more time like that with you."

"Oh, stop with the sappy stuff," Logan groaned, though the way he kissed Adrian's chest betrayed how much he liked hearing it.

He slowly peeled himself off the bed, wobbly on his feet, and padded toward the bathroom. A moment later, he returned with a damp face towel and two pairs of clean boxers. He wiped himself down with quick, sleepy swipes, then mumbled, "I can't do a shower now. I'm about to fall asleep standing."

Boxers changed, he turned to Adrian, still sprawled on the bed in the hazy aftermath. Logan knelt beside him, gently pressing the warm towel into Adrian's hand, then set the clean boxers beside him like an offering.

Adrian raised a brow at the towel now discarded on the floor. "Seriously?"

"Clean tomorrow," Logan said with a half-smile, already sliding under the covers. He pulled Adrian in without hesitation, wrapped around him like it was the most natural thing in the world.

"Let's sleep," he murmured, voice already dissolving into the edges of sleep.

Within seconds, his breathing slowed, deepened, a soft snore curling into the silence as he held Adrian to his chest.

Adrian didn't move for a long time. He just lay there, listening to Logan's heartbeat, one arm draped over his waist, lips barely grazing the edge of his collarbone. There, in the stillness, Adrian closed his eyes and let himself enjoy.

He fucking kissed Logan Vaughn today.

He fucking made out with Logan Vaughn today.

He had Logan Vaughn touching him today, until they both unraveled.

Life had never felt this bright.

The light creeping in through the wooden blinds was pale and diffused, soft enough to not wake them harshly. The smell of the sea slipped in with it, faint but familiar. Logan stirred first, groaning into Adrian's shoulder, then blinking up at the ceiling like he wasn't entirely sure where he was, until he looked down and saw Adrian, already watching him.

"Hey," Adrian said softly, brushing a thumb beneath Logan's eye.

Logan yawned. "Hey."

For a while, they just lay there, limbs tangled, the silence easy now, like it had finally stopped needing to be filled.

Adrian reached up to smooth his hand through Logan's tousled hair, a faint smile on his lips. "You snore," he commented.

"Shut up," Logan replied, though a grin spread across his face as he closed his eyes again, filled with warmth for Adrian.

"Are... are you okay?" Adrian felt it necessary to check in after last night.

Logan opened one eye, still smiling at Adrian, looking satisfied, and nestled close to him. "I'm perfect," he sighed, running a hand along Adrian's side, causing goosebumps where his skin was touched.

"I have something on my heart," Adrian confessed after several minutes. "I have been ready to tell you that yesterday and... well, we got a little distracted last night." His voice was tender and careful.

Logan was alert in an instant, pulling up slightly from Adrian's chest, alarm flickering in his eyes. "Is something wrong?"

"No, no," Adrian said quickly, sitting up against the headboard. He reached out and cupped Logan's face in both hands. "We're okay. I promise. I didn't mean to worry you. I just need to say a few things. I need to get it off my chest, and it's... about last night, too. Why I left."

Logan searched his face for a beat, then nodded. "Okay," he said quietly. "Bathroom. Two minutes."

When Logan came back, Adrian rose wordlessly and padded into the bathroom. By the time he returned, the room was flooded with morning light—bright enough to sting their eyes, so he closed the blinds a bit, letting it be dimmed with just a few rays of the morning sun.

Adrian stood by the bed, "Can I hold you while I tell it?" Adrian asked, his voice quieter now.

"You're scaring me," Logan replied, he was beneath the covers, turning toward Adrian without hesitation. He opened his arms like a quiet invitation, and Adrian slipped in beside him, their bodies meeting again in the middle of the bed like magnets remembering how to touch.

Logan reached up, rested his hand on Adrian's cheek, light but steady. "It's okay," he whispered. "I'm here."

Adrian hesitated, his voice heavy with something raw and unspoken. "They've been with me through so much," he began, the words slow and deliberate, each one heavy with the weight of years. "Dean, Tom, and I... we shared everything. Missions, training, even the little moments in between. For years, we lived in each other's shadows. They became my family, more than my own in some ways. We've been through wars, operations... things I can't even begin to explain. I spent almost every moment, awake or asleep, with them."

Logan stayed silent, his fingers brushing lightly over Adrian's cheek, encouraging him to keep talking.

"They stood by me," Adrian continued, his voice fracturing, the pain unmistakable. "Even when... when everything fell apart, and I couldn't even stand under my own weight, they stayed. You can't just... put that aside, you know? I owe them. I owe them so much."

Adrian's voice faltered, and Logan, his heart twisting, pressed gently, "When what? Adrian, when what?"

Adrian's body seemed to shrink in the dark, curling in on itself. "It's a long story," he murmured, and Logan heard the fear in his words, the fear of losing something fragile, something new.

"You don't have to," Logan said softly, his hand never leaving Adrian's face, his thumb brushing a reassuring line along his jaw. "But I want to hear it. I want to know. I'm here, Adrian."

Adrian closed his eyes, the pull of Logan's unwavering presence anchoring him. There was a storm inside him still, but in Logan's arms, it felt possible—if only for this moment—to ride the wave to its end. And maybe, just maybe, he wouldn't be left alone on the other side.

Adrian's voice was low, steady at first, but every word carried the weight of something unrelenting. "I was a commander, *Seren rank.* It's like a lieutenant in the Navy. I think. I led an elite commando unit in the special forces. Tom was at the same rank as me, and Dean was my second. We worked together like a well-oiled machine. Years of training, missions, and trust. On this particular day, it was just another drill. Routine, really. We were running an operation, coordinating with the air force, attacking from the sea. Everything had to be seamless."

He paused, his breath hitching, his eyes scanning the room as if searching for a lifeline. Logan remained silent, watching Adrian's hands tremble as though the memory was something tangible, clawing its way back.

"We got down from the ship," Adrian continued, his voice quieter now. "Into the water. Weapons in hand, moving silently, the way we always did.

They call us the *people of silence,* you know? It's a name you earn. But that day…" His voice faltered, and Logan saw it—the moment Adrian's walls cracked, the pain bleeding through.

"What happened?" Logan asked gently, his own voice barely above a whisper.

Adrian flinched, the words clearly dragging themselves out of him. "I had a negligent discharge." The words were fragile, spoken like they might shatter him. "The bullet… it hit one of my soldiers." His voice broke completely, and his hands covered his face. "He died that second. A nineteen-year-old. I killed a nineteen-year-old kid."

Logan's heart clenched, his instinct to reach out battling the sense that Adrian needed space to unravel at his own pace. "Adrian—" he started, but Adrian shook his head sharply, Logan felt his tears on his chest, so he just hugged him harder.

"They took my ranks. A few months before my service was supposed to end, they stripped everything. I spent seven months in military prison." Adrian's breath hitched, his voice a mix of anger and sorrow. "I deserved more, Logan. So much more. And Dean—" He choked on the name, his body trembling. "Dean was there. He testified for me, fought for me, and helped me with the lawyer. I didn't have anything left, and he never gave up. He visited me, kept me sane. He was more than a brother to me. I never realized how strong that bond was until everything else was gone."

Hot tears streamed down Adrian's face. Logan could only watch, his chest aching at the sight of Adrian unraveling, every word peeling back a layer of the man he thought he knew. Adrian wiped his face roughly with the back of his hand, his breath unsteady.

"When I got out, I knew I had to leave for a while... Dean, Tom, and the others were planning this trip. They set the dates to match my release, and assumed I'd come. They wanted to bring me back into their lives, their world. But I... I couldn't. I wanted to be alone. I needed to get away from everything."

He shook his head, his voice quivering with emotion. "I worked for months, saved everything I could. Took what I had from the army, my savings, and just... left. No explanations, no goodbyes. I had to."

Logan nodded, though his throat was tight, his words stuck somewhere between his heart and mouth. He wanted to comfort Adrian, to tell him he was still here, but it felt like anything he said would pale against the weight of Adrian's story.

Adrian turned his head slightly, his eyes shining with unshed tears. "That day I saw you drowning, Lo... I felt like I was back there. Back in that moment. I didn't go into the ocean because I'm some kind of hero." His voice cracked, his words rough as if they'd scraped against him on their way out. "I did it because I'm selfish. Because I couldn't bear another..."

He broke off, inhaling sharply, as though the very thought threatened to consume him. After a moment, he continued, softer now, his voice barely more than a breath. "I took a life, Logan. But I saved another. Because... if it weren't for everything that had happened, I would not have been there in Hawaii that day, I would have still been serving probably."

The silence that followed was heavy, filled only with the sound of their breathing. Logan, his heart aching, cupped Adrian's face, his thumb brushing away the new tears that Adrian didn't seem to notice. "Adrian, you did not take a life!" he insisted, his voice firm but gentle. "You carry so much, and I can't pretend to know what that feels like. But it was an accident."

"No... It's not true. That kid was under my responsibility." Adrian said, leaning toward Logan's touch. "I was his commander. I needed to keep him safe, guide him, to die myself before letting something happen to him. Not kill him."

Logan shook his head slowly, his thumb brushing away the tears from Adrian's eyes, catching them before they could fall, as if refusing to let them touch the ground. Adrian's voice, broken and quiet, rose between them like the whisper of the sea on a still night.

"I was so lost, Logan... so sad," Adrian began, his voice trembling. "After it happened... after I pulled the trigger by mistake and one of my men never came home, I carried that death inside me. It pressed against my chest like a stone, heavy, immovable. I couldn't breathe under it. Things I used to love, like playing music or even surfing, seemed pointless all of a sudden. I thought of ending it more times than I can admit. His face never left me; I haven't closed my eyes once without meeting him again." His hand rose to Logan's cheek, rough thumb trembling as it brushed away tears neither of them had noticed. "You think I saved you. But the truth is, you're the only reason I'm still here."

Logan's breath broke, a sound more fragile than words. "No..." he whispered, his voice frayed, chest caving as fresh tears blurred his eyes.

"When I pulled you out of the waves, it felt like the sea had handed me back a reason to live. Like I was allowed to exist only because I had saved someone," Adrian went on, truths he never intended to reveal spilling out from his lips. "And then there was you. Not just someone. You became the center of it all—my compass, my breath, my best... everything. Pulling you from the waves didn't just give me purpose. It gave me you. And you... you set fire to the places in me I thought were already ash."

Logan couldn't hold back anymore. He pulled Adrian further into his arms; their embrace was an inferno, two fires fusing until neither could be told apart. He held him tightly, his hands firm against Adrian's back, offering comfort that words couldn't carry. Adrian's tears soaked into the crook of Logan's neck, and Logan tightened his grip as though holding him could keep him from falling apart. His own tears spilled over, staining Adrian's skin as he buried his face into his shoulder.

"You may not believe this, Adrian, but it's not your fault," Logan murmured, his voice steady despite the storm inside him. "Accidents happen. You're human. You couldn't have prevented it."

Adrian's body trembled at Logan's words, and for a moment, neither spoke; the silence was filled only by the sound of their breath and the soft rustle of the blanket as they clung to each other.

Logan pulled back just enough to look at him, his hands moving instinctively to Adrian's face. His thumbs wiped away the tracks of hot tears left behind, his touch as gentle as the first kiss of sunlight on the horizon. "We're each other's lifesavers," he whispered, his gray eyes locking with Adrian's, their depths holding everything Adrian needed to hear.

Adrian's heart ached at the words, his chest tightening with emotions he never knew his heart can contain. Logan was still here, still holding him, still *with* him. He reached out, cupping Logan's face as though he might vanish if he let go, and wiped the tears from his cheeks. Somehow, even crying, Logan was breathtaking. The vulnerability made him even more beautiful, his every feature illuminated by the rawness of the moment.

Adrian pressed against Logan, chest to chest, his arms wrapped tightly around him, trying to fuse them together. Logan's hand slid over Adrian's head, their faces so close that Adrian could feel the light scruff on Logan's jaw against his skin. His breath hitched as Logan let out a soft, contented sigh, his hand roaming Adrian's back, tracing the hard muscles beneath soft skin. Their legs tangled beneath the blanket, a hidden intimacy that felt so natural.

Adrian's breath tickled Logan's neck, and Logan found himself waiting for each one, reveling in the warm air washing over him. He felt the steady rhythm of Adrian's heartbeat against his own, a grounding cadence that calmed the chaos within him.

"You said something about playing music?" Logan asked softly, breaking the silence with a quiet curiosity, wanting to keep that moment alive. He fought the urge to press a kiss to Adrian's cheek, the proximity and the intimacy of the moment overwhelming him.

"Hmm, yeah," Adrian replied, his voice barely above a whisper, reluctant to move from the comfort of Logan's arms. "Just guitar. Not much."

"Really?" Logan murmured, his admiration evident. "Surfing, playing music... Is there anything you *can't* do?"

Adrian chuckled softly, the vibration brushing against Logan's neck. "No, no wow," he said modestly. "I'm just an amateur, really. I like to try new things, so I picked up playing here and there, but surfing's my first love, really. Music is just... something else I enjoy. But I'm not great at it."

"I didn't see you bring a guitar," Logan remarked, his voice still gentle, his fingers tracing soft patterns on Adrian's back.

"Easier to travel without it," Adrian replied, his hand still resting on Logan's back, the contact grounding them both.

Logan let the moment stretch between them, the quiet weight of their closeness speaking louder than words ever could. They were a storm and the calm that followed, tangled together in the stillness of the morning, each finding solace in the other's presence.

"You know, Adrian," Logan whispered into the silence after a while, his voice hesitant. "It seemed like I had the perfect life. Even during college, everybody always said it, how easy it was for me. But it wasn't." He stopped for a moment, his words faltering.

Adrian remained silent, yet he shifted slightly, no longer positioned directly atop Logan. Instead, he lay carefully beside him, one arm draped warmly and steadily over Logan's torso, gently exploring his skin in a soft and soothing caress. It was all the strength Logan needed to keep going. Adrian never asked much about Logan's family, but Logan always felt that Adrian just understood. As if Adrian read the unwritten words, gathered the loose evidence, and compiled them into a whole puzzle that told the story of Logan without bothering Logan to share the details. "I do come from a wealthy family. I attended the best schools, no matter what. Never had a financial struggle. But it wasn't easy." He paused again, and this time he couldn't stop the sigh that escaped his lips. "I always had to prove myself, to be worthy of my name, to make my dad satisfied. I always did what he wanted. He didn't even have to tell me, most of the time I just knew. If I wanted him to pay for school, I had to study what he chose. And I did it, not because I was lazy or didn't want to work, but because I wanted him to approve of me. I wanted him to look at me with pride. But it rarely worked. He always made sure to tell me how I could do things better. Be better."

Logan's voice grew softer, and Adrian could hear the undertones of a pain that had gone unspoken for too long. When Logan stopped speaking, Adrian's gentle response came. "So, you left."

"Yeah." Logan nodded against Adrian, his body moving closer, as if clinging to a lifeline in open water. "One of the few choices I made for myself. It felt good, you know?" His arms tightened around Adrian as he continued. "To not give a damn about what he would think, or say, or how he'd ignore me the next day. God, I hated it when he ignored me. Pretended I didn't even exist."

Logan's voice broke slightly, and the morning light spilled across the room, soft yet unyielding, leaving him nowhere to hide. Vulnerability felt sharper in daylight, every truth laid bare, but the gentleness of the hour made it almost forgiving. Adrian was beside him, steady and patient, listening without a word. Logan knew he wouldn't judge. He could open himself completely, and if he asked Adrian to carry it into silence forever, he knew he would.

"It started when I was like ten or eleven. Him ignoring me, I mean." Logan swallowed hard, feeling his throat tighten. "I was surfing by that time. He didn't know about it. My mom got me a board when we got back home from the vacation where I started, and I spent a lot of time training. I loved it. And when I was finally getting better, I told him." Logan's voice wavered, and he tightened his grip on Adrian as if the memory was dragging him under.

"He didn't like it. Said it was primitive. Not a hobby for me. A waste of time. Something like that, he wanted me to take on a real sport, like football, baseball, basketball... He didn't speak to me for a month after that day." Logan's voice cracked, and he let the silence fill the space for a moment, gathering himself. "I almost quit, but my older sister wouldn't let me."

The words hung between them, weighted with years of unspoken pain and defiance. Adrian's hand moved slowly over Logan's back, his touch a steadying force, like the rhythm of the waves that had always called to Logan.

"She told me I was good at it," Logan said, his voice softer now, tinged with a faint warmth. "Told me I couldn't let him take away what I loved. So I didn't. Surfing became... it became my escape. My way to breathe. My freedom."

Adrian shifted slightly, his body leaning back just enough to meet Logan's gaze. The room dimmed, bathed in soft rays of sunshine filtering in, illuminating the space as delicate motes of dust danced gracefully in the light. Adrian sought Logan's eyes, as if even the briefest connection could tether them both in this fragile, vulnerable moment. His voice pierced the silence, tender and laden with anguish. "I'm so sorry, Lo."

Logan shook his head, his hair brushing against the pillow. "It's okay," he murmured, though the words carried the weight of a thousand unshed tears. "No matter how much I hated him, I loved him. I wanted him to care about me." He paused, his voice trembling as if carried by a gust of wind.

Adrian's hand slid away from Logan's back, and he cupped his face instead, his touch gentle but firm, like a lifeguard pulling someone from the undertow. He wanted to absorb all of Logan's pain, to pull it from him and carry it away like the tide.

"And since then," Logan continued, his voice quieter now, almost lost to the night, "he's always ignored me whenever I did something he didn't like. He'd come home, talk to my sisters, spend time with them, buy them gifts... but he ignored me. Like I never existed."

Logan's voice cracked, and Adrian felt it like a physical wound. He stayed silent, letting Logan empty his heart.

"My mom tried," Logan whispered, his voice thick with memories. "She'd spend time with me, buy me things, talk to me. But it wasn't enough. It wasn't her I wanted. It was him. And the way he ignored me... it was like I wasn't even a person. If I was in the same room, I might as well have been a chair, or a picture on the wall." Logan's breath hitched, and Adrian tightened his grip on him, steadying him like a rock in the storm. "Once," Logan continued, his voice fraying at the edges, "he picked my sisters up from school on a Friday and just... didn't come home with them. The whole weekend, I thought maybe they'd gone somewhere boring, maybe I wasn't missing much. But when they came back, their faces were glowing. They told me about the carnival, the circus, the zoo—cotton candy, elephants, rides that made them scream until they laughed. They got all of him. And I was left behind, like I didn't even exist."

"Lo," Adrian whispered, his voice cracking with emotion. "I'm so sorry. You didn't deserve any of it." He pulled Logan into a fierce embrace, his arms wrapping around him like a shield. "You didn't deserve any of it."

Logan nodded but said nothing. His silence was heavy, but Adrian didn't push. Instead, he leaned closer, his voice a soft promise.

"Lo, you're perfect," Adrian murmured, his words a balm against Logan's raw edges.

Logan closed his eyes and sighed deeply, those words sinking into him, a sunlight breaking through storm clouds. Adrian brushed his lips over Logan's, a tender, ghost-like touch that seemed to say *I see you, I feel you, I'm here.* Logan inhaled sharply, as if Adrian's breath was filling his own lungs, and in that moment, he felt lighter, freer.

"I never told anyone about this," Logan muttered, his words brushing against Adrian's lips like a secret carried on the wind.

"Thank you for trusting me," Adrian whispered back, his voice trembling with gratitude.

Logan leaned forward and kissed him again, their lips meeting in a quiet, unhurried dance. The kiss deepened, their bodies pressing closer together, their shared warmth chasing away the chill of painful memories. Logan's hands gripped Adrian tightly, afraid to let go, and Adrian melted into him, their hearts beating in sync.

Logan felt heat bloom through his body, his need rising. Adrian's body against his stirred him, and he could feel Adrian's thick cock pressing against his, the lightest of touches as Adrian softly, almost instinctively, rubbed his shaft against Logan's, chasing friction. His heart ached for more, his body craved it, but Adrian didn't push. True to his nature, Adrian simply held him, his touch reverent, his focus entirely on Logan's lips and the moment they shared, their bodies wanted, but the light and soft touches were enough for now.

When the kiss finally broke, Logan was left breathless, his chest rising and falling. He closed his eyes and listened, focusing on the rapid thrum of Adrian's heartbeat, the way Adrian's body enveloped his own like a cocoon.

"My dad cut my wings so much," Logan whispered brokenly, his voice cracking like fragile glass, "that I'm sure I'll never be able to fly again." His hand settled on Adrian's hip, a quiet plea for reassurance.

Adrian's voice came immediately, steady and unwavering. "That's not true," he stated, his hand finding the curve of Logan's neck and massaging it gently, soothing him with the touch of someone who wanted to heal. "You ran away. You escaped. You're already spreading your wings."

Adrian's fingers brushed Logan's hair, his voice soft but full of conviction. "And from where I'm standing, Lo, they're marvelous."

Logan let out a shaky breath, Adrian's words sinking into him like the tide retreating, leaving a calmer, smoother shore behind.

September 18, 2018—Palawan, Philippines—A Month Later

THE HUMID AIR CLUNG to Logan like a second skin, his shirt plastered to his chest and his breath coming in shallow pants. The Philippine forest surrounded them in a lush, green embrace, its towering trees and the distant call of birds weaving a tapestry of natural beauty. Logan wiped the sweat from his brow, his GoPro strapped to his chest capturing glimpses of the trail they'd been hiking all morning. Adrian was at his side, his presence as constant and comforting as the rhythm of Logan's own heartbeat.

It had been a month since their first kiss—a month of discovery, of stolen moments and quiet tenderness. Awkwardness had come and gone, but what lingered was the sweetness of shared mornings, of kisses that tasted like promises, and of a bond that grew stronger with every passing day. Logan glanced at Adrian, his gaze lingering. The way Adrian's damp shirt clung to his frame, the way his messy hair fell into his eyes—it was enough to make Logan's heart stutter.

The trail wound deeper into the forest, and Logan couldn't help but marvel at the vibrant life around them. They'd decided on a two-day trek to fully immerse themselves in the beauty of the land, leaving their boards back at the cabin they'd rented. Logan's camera caught snippets of it all—the sway of the trees, the play of sunlight through the canopy, and Adrian's easy grin as they hiked together.

Out of nowhere, Logan felt himself shoved backward, his body hitting the rough bark of a tree with a muted thud. Before he could register what was happening, Adrian was on him, their bodies flushed, their sweat-slicked skin melding in the humid air. Logan let out a breathless laugh, the sheer audacity of Adrian's sudden boldness catching him off guard.

"Ad—" he started, but Adrian silenced him with a kiss, fierce and consuming.

Logan melted into it, his fingers tangling in Adrian's unruly hair while his other hand gripped the back of Adrian's neck. The heat between them was intense, both from the tropical air and the raw passion igniting between their bodies. Adrian tasted like salt and heat and something wholly his own, and Logan couldn't get enough.

Adrian's hands grew bolder, sliding up beneath Logan's damp shirt. His touch was electric, every brush of his fingers setting Logan's nerves alight. "You're driving me crazy," Adrian growled against Logan's lips, his voice low and rough, sending shivers down Logan's spine.

Logan's fingers curled around the straps of Adrian's backpack, unfastening the weight from Adrian's shoulders before letting it slip to the jungle floor. The impact was soft, muffled by the damp, loamy earth, but the moment between them was anything but gentle. With a swift motion, Logan reversed their positions, pressing Adrian against the moss-covered trunk of an ancient tree, his breath warm against Adrian's jaw.

Adrian gasped—a sharp inhale that turned into a chuckle, low and breathless. He barely had a moment to react before Logan's hands gripped the back of his strong thighs, lifting him as though he weighed nothing. Instinct took over. Adrian's arms wrapped around Logan's shoulders, fingers digging into the sinewy muscles beneath his damp shirt, his legs tightening around Logan's waist.

"You're heavier than you look," Logan murmured, his voice laced with amusement, but his grip never faltered.

Adrian smirked, his lips ghosting over Logan's ear, teasing. "You can handle it." Adrian gently detached Logan's GoPro from its snug position on his chest, muttering something about it being in the way. He lifted the camera, capturing their moments together with a sense of spontaneity, the lens now filming them in that quite untamed moment in the wilderness in the middle of nowhere.

Their laughter mingled with the rustling leaves, carried away by the breeze that swept through the jungle, thick with the scent of orchids and rain-washed stone.

Then, Logan kissed him, deep and unrelenting, as if he could carve his feelings into Adrian's very bones. It was a kiss of discovery and promise, of... everything. Adrian answered in kind, his fingers curling into Logan's damp strands, tugging him closer. The world around them melted; there was no jungle, no distant call of birds, no past nor future. Only now.

Adrian's pulse thundered against Logan's chest, their breaths tangled, their bodies pressed together in the wild heart of Palawan. The jungle watched, silent and knowing, as if it had seen love bloom like this before, urgent, hungry, electric with the thrill of something new, something vast and unknown.

"God, Adrian," Logan whispered against his lips, his voice hoarse with emotion.

Adrian's laughter was easy and full of happiness, the kind that could barely be contained and controlled, one hand holding the camera, the other threading through Logan's damp hair as he rested his forehead against Logan's. "What?"

"Everything," Logan murmured, his voice stripped bare, the raw honesty of the word hanging in the humid air between them. He caught Adrian's lips again, claiming them with a fervor that had been building for weeks. The shift in their height—Adrian perched at eye level, Logan not needing to bend anymore—was a novelty that thrilled him. For a moment, it felt like everything aligned, their bodies, their breaths, the rhythm of their shared longing.

But beneath the kiss, something deeper churned in Logan's mind. *More.* The word pulsed like a heartbeat, a quiet plea echoing through him. More touches. More of the electric connection humming between them. More of this thing bubbling beneath the surface that neither of them dared to name. He had never been this insatiable, never spent so many nights tangled in his own sheets, breathless and aching, his mind filled with Adrian. Never had he spent long moments in the bathroom jacking off as he thought of the man on the other side of the door. By now, he was certain Adrian felt it too, the length of Adrian's long showers was enough of a clue.

Every kiss left Logan hard and panting, teetering on the edge of something unknown and overwhelming. He wanted, but he feared the wanting. He needed, but he didn't yet dare. He could feel Adrian holding back, too, respecting the words he had told Logan on the first night they kissed. And though he was grateful for Adrian's patience, some secret part of him hoped Adrian would take that step for him, bridge the gap between longing and action.

It wasn't that Logan was inexperienced. He wasn't a virgin. But with Adrian, everything was heightened—sharper, deeper, more vulnerable. The intensity scared him. The emotion scared him. Adrian wasn't just a passing connection; he was everything Logan didn't yet know how to handle.

"Hey," Adrian croaked, breaking through Logan's thoughts. He lowered the camera, quickly fastening it again on Logan's chest. Then his hands cupped Logan's face, the calluses on his fingers grounding Logan like the rough bark of the tree against the back of his palm. Adrian rested his forehead against Logan's, their breaths mingling in the heavy, tropical air. "Where did you go just now?"

Logan opened his eyes and was met with Adrian's gaze, dark and molten, brimming with concern and something deeper—desire, restraint, love. Adrian's accent thickened, each word rolling off his tongue with the richness that only came when he was breathless, or caught in the throes of excitement, or, like now, utterly consumed by lust. Logan adored it. The way Adrian's voice seemed to draw him closer, like a wave pulling him into the ocean.

"I was just thinking," Logan said, his voice softer now, tinged with laughter and embarrassment, "about how I'm supposed to finish this trail with... you know." He glanced down, biting his lip as his laughter bubbled up, as the outline of his visibly hard dick was palpable between them.

Adrian followed his gaze and let out a breathless laugh of his own, his problem mirroring Logan's. "Yeah," Adrian agreed, his voice rough with humor and heat, "I don't think we planned for this kind of... obstacle."

Logan leaned back slightly, his laughter fading as he looked at Adrian again, his heart squeezing at the sight of him. Adrian's hair was a mess, his face damp with sweat, his chest rising and falling in quick, shallow breaths. There was nothing composed or polished about him in that moment, and Logan was floored by it.

But beneath the humor, beneath the teasing, Logan felt the ache of wanting—an unspoken hunger that curled deep in his chest, aching with a need he hadn't yet learned how to name. It was the pull of something bigger than desire, something deeper than the thrill of the moment.

Adrian must have sensed it, because his teasing smile softened, his fingers brushing over Logan's cheek, tracing the line of his jaw with a gentleness that unraveled him. That small, absent touch sent shivers skimming down Logan's spine, tightening low in his stomach, a silent plea wrapped in sensation.

And then Adrian kissed him—not just with passion, but with something weightier, something like necessity. As if he couldn't breathe without it. As if Logan had already become air, water, something vital. Logan opened to him, parting his lips, and Adrian met him there, their tongues tangling, tasting, learning.

Logan groaned into Adrian's mouth, gripping him tighter, as if letting go wasn't an option. Slowly, deliberately, he thrust his hips forward, pressing himself against Adrian, grinding into him with a deliberate rhythm. A low, desperate whimper slipped from Adrian's lips, swallowed by the kiss, lost in the space between them.

"Fuck—" Logan groaned when they finally broke apart, his breath ragged, his body humming with a hunger he had no idea how to contain. His cock ached in his shorts, the friction unbearable, but even that frustration was lost in the haze of Adrian—his taste, his scent, the way his fingers had fisted in Logan's hair like he never wanted to let go.

Then, like a splash of cold water, a burst of laughter rang through the jungle, a pair of passing travelers, oblivious to the fire they had interrupted.

Logan stiffened instinctively, but when he turned to look at Adrian, he found his face flushed, lips pink and swollen from their kiss. Adrian's eyes flicked toward the giggling voices before he let out a chuckle of his own, shaking his head.

Logan couldn't help it; he laughed too, a breathless sound, and let his forehead fall against Adrian's shoulder, inhaling the warmth of his skin, the steady rhythm of his breath, loving the feeling of Adrian's weight on his arms. Adrian's arms were wrapped around him, his fingers squeezing Logan's shoulders before he murmured, "Let's keep going." His voice was soft but certain, tinged with the accent Logan adored, the one that sent warmth curling through his chest every time he heard it. "Or we'll never make it before sunset."

Logan sighed dramatically, lifting his head just enough to press a kiss to Adrian's jaw before releasing Adrian, letting him stand back on his feet. "Fine. But you owe me another kiss at the next stop."

The trail stretched out before them, dappled with sunlight filtering through the leaves. And though the tension between them still simmered, Logan felt a little steadier, a little braver, knowing Adrian was walking this path beside him.

Each step was heavy with unsaid things, a current tugging beneath the surface. Their connection had grown like the roots of the jungle trees around them—twisting, deepening, impossible to disentangle now. Logan felt it every time Adrian's voice broke the silence, every time Adrian's hand brushed his arm, steadying him when he stumbled. There was an anchor there, though Logan wasn't ready to call it by name.

The path wound through the forest, dappled with sunlight that broke through the canopy in slanting beams, warm and fleeting. They passed by small villages where children laughed and waved, their voices carrying like the wind skimming over waves. Logan, grinning like he owned the world, spotted a coconut tree and took off toward it.

"Bet I can climb faster than you!" Logan called, already halfway up the trunk, his body moving like it had always belonged to the wild. His arms and legs worked in perfect rhythm, muscles flexing with effortless power, gripping bark and branch like second nature.

It never ceased to amaze Adrian—the sheer physicality of him. The way Logan's body seemed built for movement, for flight, for conquering anything in his path. Adrian had his own strength, honed by military discipline, by training, and endurance. But Logan? *Logan* was something else entirely. He moved like he was part of the earth itself—fluid, instinctive, fearless.

And seeing him like this, so free, so alive, took Adrian's breath away.

"Logan, get down before you kill yourself!" Adrian shouted, but there was laughter behind his words, a buoyancy he couldn't suppress. Logan reached the top, grabbed a coconut, and promptly slid back down, his momentum too fast. Adrian caught him in a tangle of limbs before he hit the ground.

"See? No death today!" Logan said breathlessly, his grin brighter than the sun, holding his coconut proudly. "I brought us a snack."

Then Logan stopped, his sharp eyes catching something just off the trail—a rusted trail marker, half-hidden by creeping vines. He pointed, excitement sparking like fire in his gaze.

"Ad, let's go that way," he said, already pulling out the map, his mind whirring. "That path looks far more interesting."

Adrian sighed. "Logan—"

Logan barely heard him. He unfolded the map with practiced ease, ever the perfect planner beneath all that wildness, scanning the terrain with the precision of someone who knew exactly how to balance recklessness with control.

"It actually leads to the river we want," he announced triumphantly, looking up with that wild, untouchable joy that made Adrian's heart stutter. "Let's go!"

Adrian wanted to argue, wanted to say that leaving the trail was a terrible idea, that every survival instinct in his body screamed against it.

But then he looked at Logan.

At the way his whole body hummed with the thrill of discovery, at the sharp intelligence lurking beneath all that carefree energy. Adrian had learned something about Logan in their time together—he wasn't just reckless, he was calculated. His wildness was never blind. He took risks, yes, but always ones he had measured, ones he had already decided were worth taking.

Adrian let out a slow breath, shaking his head.

With anyone else, he'd say no.

But with Logan?

He'd follow him anywhere.

"Lead the way," he said adoringly.

So, putting the coconut in Logan's bag, they stepped off the marked trail, walking side by side on the narrow path, arms brushing as their conversation flowed effortlessly. Vines draped over the narrow path like fingers reaching, the humid air humming with the pulse of unseen life. It smelled of damp earth and rain-soaked wood, of something ancient and alive. Then, they reached it—a narrow wooden bridge spanning a dizzying ravine, its weathered planks warped and blackened by time, the ropes sagging under the weight of decay. Below, the chasm yawned wide, a sheer drop into the dense, tangled jungle.

Adrian stopped short, his jaw tightening.

"We're not crossing that," Adrian said firmly.

"Relax, Ad." Logan pointed to a tree nearby, its gnarled branches stretched over the ravine. From its highest point hung a tangle of jungle vines, swaying gently in the breeze. Logan's eyes lit up, mischief sparking like sunlight on water.

"No," Adrian said, already knowing where this was headed. "Whatever you're thinking, don't. This is the kind of thing that ends with us needing a rescue helicopter."

Logan's laughter burst forth, a wild, unrestrained melody that danced through the dense foliage of the jungle. "Come on! We swing across like Tarzan! It's absolutely perfect!" he exclaimed, his excitement palpable. With anticipation sparkling in his eyes, Logan meticulously inspected the GoPro fastened securely to his chest. His fingers deftly adjusted the angle, ensuring that it would not merely capture the exhilarating leap, but also encompass the vast expanse of the sky, the terrifying rush of his body soaring through the air, and the vibrant green tapestry of the jungle blurring beneath him in a breathtaking kaleidoscope of motion.

Adrian groaned, dragging a hand through his hair, but Logan was already moving—already part of the moment before it even happened.

Then, he ran.

Power coiled in his body, every muscle primed, every motion fluid, effortless. He wasn't just running—he was cutting through the air, feet barely skimming the earth before he kicked off, leaping like he belonged to the sky.

"Logan—" Adrian's voice cracked, sharp with panic, but it was too late.

Logan seized the vine midair, his grip instinctive, unshakable, like he had always been meant to fly.

And then—he swung.

A whoop tore from his throat, wild and electric, a sound that belonged to the ocean and the wind and everything unchained. It echoed between the cliffs, carried by the jungle, swallowed by the vastness of the world around them.

For a fleeting moment, he was a feather, weightless and floating in limbo between the vast expanse of earth and the boundless sky, akin to the ocean caught in the throes of a magnificent mid-wave. Adrian held his breath, his heart a wild drum racing in his chest, as he beheld Logan, who descended with an elegant flourish onto the other side, releasing a triumphant echoing laugh, the sweetest melody to Adrian's ears.

"Lifesaver bracelet for the win!" Logan hollered, his voice reverberating like wind tearing through a forest. He stood tall, arms spread wide, bathed in the golden light of the sun. Surrounding him, vibrant hues of green framed his figure, transforming him into a reckless yet beautiful deity of nature. "Your turn!" His grin was impossibly wide, a beacon against the shadowed cliffs.

Adrian stood rooted to the ground, the vine heavy in his hands, his chest tight with a strange, aching pull. Logan was maddening—chaotic and unrelenting—but he was also magnetic. Impossible to resist. He was the crash and the calm, the storm and the stillness that followed. Adrian cursed under his breath, shaking his head, even as his lips curled into an inevitable smile.

"You're going to be the death of me, you know that?" Adrian called, his voice steadier than he felt.

"Yeah," Logan said, softer this time, the teasing edge in his tone giving way to something quieter, deeper. "But what a way to go."

Adrian swallowed hard, feeling the weight of those words settle in his chest. And by now, resistance was futile. Logan was everything—power, life, and thrill condensed into one impossible person. If following him meant throwing himself off cliffs or swinging into the unknown, Adrian didn't care. He'd already surrendered, his heart tethered to Logan like a boat to its anchor, helpless against the pull of the sea.

"Come on, grandma!" Logan's voice shattered the moment, playful and warm. "We're losing daylight, and I want to get to the river before dark!" He stood there, hands on his hips, grinning like the world bent to his whim.

Adrian huffed a breath, shaking off the lingering hesitation. The Navy hadn't trained him to be outdone by a college kid with more charm than sense. Testing the vine's strength one last time, he stepped back, bracing himself.

"I'm coming, you lunatic!" he shouted, his voice echoing through the air, as he sprinted forward, the ground blurring beneath his feet. He arrived at the precipice, and with a fierce determination, he propelled himself into the open sky, the vine stretching taut like a bowstring as gravity clutched at him. A sharp, shrill cry may have escaped his lips as his feet abandoned the solid earth and soared into the boundless blue. For a fleeting moment, time seemed to freeze. The world hung suspended in a delicate balance, cradled within the palpable silence that accompanied the rush of adrenaline, his heartbeat a thunderous symphony reverberating in his ears.

He landed with a thud on the far side, not nearly as graceful as Logan's elegant descent, but at least he had touched the ground. His knees buckled slightly beneath him, a testament to the impact, and before he could regain his balance, Logan was there—his laughter ringing out like music in the air. With a hearty slap on the back, Logan beamed, "Not bad for an old man!" A glimmer of mischief danced in his bright eyes, while his breath came in quick, excited bursts, adding to the lively atmosphere of the moment.

Adrian looked at him, shaking his head but smiling despite himself. "You're insane." He snorted. "And we are practically the same age!"

"I know," Logan replied, his grin softening, his voice quieter now, like the lapping of waves on a tranquil shore. "But you have an older soul." And for a moment, Adrian forgot the jungle, the ravine, the world beyond this moment. All he could see was Logan.

"That's just because you have the soul of a four-year-old on a sugar rush!" he shot back, his voice dripping with mock exasperation.

He didn't say it out loud, but Adrian knew: he'd follow Logan anywhere. Into the ocean, into the jungle, into the unknown. He didn't care if it meant risking everything. Logan was worth the fall.

Logan's laughter erupted, loud and unrestrained, echoing through the jungle. "You say that like it's a bad thing!" he teased, nudging Adrian's arm with his shoulder.

Adrian smirked, rolling his eyes, but the corners of his mouth betrayed him, lifting into a reluctant grin. "It's exhausting," he muttered, though his voice was tinged with fondness.

"It's exhilarating," Logan countered, his tone light but his gaze unwavering, piercing in its intensity. "I'm putting some life in your old bones. Think about it, without me, you'd be comparing vitamin supplements, and yelling at kids to get off your lawn, even though you don't have a lawn."

"I fucking been surfing in Hawaii before I met you!" Adrian defended himself. "I've been to—"

"Yeah, yeah," Logan said absentmindedly, his grin breaking the tension like sunlight piercing through clouds. "Now come on, old man," he said, bounding ahead toward the faint sound of rushing water. "The river's not going to find itself!"

Adrian sighed, following with a shake of his head, the edges of his heart softening with every step. Logan might've been chaos personified, but he was also freedom, a wild, untamed force that Adrian couldn't help but be swept up in. And for once, Adrian wasn't afraid of the current.

A few hours later, they reached the river, its crystalline waters winding through the dense jungle like a secret vein of life. The sound of it was intoxicating—gentle ripples punctuated by the occasional cascade over rocks. The air was thick with the scent of earth and greenery, alive with the hum of insects and the distant calls of birds settling into the dusk.

Logan dropped his backpack onto the ground with a satisfying thud, already toeing off his sneakers, his eyes locked on the glimmering water.

His body ached and tingled, craving to feel the cool relief after hours of trekking. "Coming?" he called over his shoulder, his grin daring.

Adrian let out a groan as he shrugged off his heavy pack, the weight lifting off his shoulders. "Right behind you," he called out. His movements were slow and fluid; he quickly peeled off his shirt, tossing it aside with a careless flick, then kicked off his sneakers before sliding out of his shorts.

Logan wasn't ready. His breath caught as he turned, his gaze snapping to Adrian. Even though they'd been sharing space—surfboards, rooms, waves—for two months, he still wasn't prepared for the sight of Adrian like this, almost naked with just the tightest boxer brief covering his lower half. The sweat from the hike glistened on his skin, highlighting every muscle, every line of effort and strength. The boxer briefs had slipped just low enough to expose the sexiest tan line imaginable, a slash of contrast that fed straight into that devastating V, which seized the gaze and dragged it downward, an inevitable pull toward the thick, commanding bulge straining against the front of his briefs.

Adrian noticed the lingering look and laughed softly, rubbing the back of his neck. There was a faint bashfulness in his expression, rare but disarming. "I just thought I'd freshen up," he said, almost apologetically. "And, well... I really don't want to put those disgusting shorts back on after sweating in them."

Logan snapped his attention back, willing himself to keep his voice steady. "Yeah, sure," he said, trying for nonchalance but landing somewhere closer to breathless.

He stripped off his own shirt, shoes, and shorts, leaving only his boxers, fully aware of what this did to Adrian. The air was thick with unspoken things, the kind of tension that coiled tighter with every shared glance.

When Logan finally turned toward the river, Adrian's audible groan broke the stillness, and Logan couldn't stop the grin that tugged at his lips.

"Something wrong?" Logan called over his shoulder, feigning innocence as he stepped closer to the water.

Adrian exhaled sharply, shaking his head. "Just you being... you."

The river was cool and inviting as Logan waded in. The water shimmered with the last golden rays of daylight, rippling softly around them as they swam. The coolness of the river washed away the day's grit and exhaustion, leaving behind only the unspoken tension between them. Adrian stayed close, his eyes tracing Logan's every movement, captivated as though he might miss something extraordinary if he looked away for even a second.

"How are you feeling?" Adrian asked, his voice low, testing the boundary between casual and intimate as he moved closer. Today had shifted something between them—a spark had grown into a flame. His newfound confidence urged him to take another step, to close the distance, to let himself feel everything he'd been holding back.

Logan turned to him, a half-smile tugging at his lips. "Tired," he admitted with a playful shrug. "Wouldn't say no to a hot shower right about now." He looped an arm around Adrian's neck, pulling him closer, their wet skin brushing. "How about you?"

Adrian's heart swelled, his voice steady but thick with meaning. "Never been better." And he meant it.

How could he not? They were in the heart of the most beautiful place he'd ever seen, alive with the symphony of the jungle, the rustling leaves, the chirping birds, the cool, clean water cradling them. But none of it compared to the man beside him. Logan, with his wild hair, his radiant energy, and the quiet, tender way he cared for the world around him, was the most beautiful thing Adrian had ever known. Logan carried Adrian's mother's bracelet like a badge of honor, as though it were the most precious thing in the world. And to Adrian, Logan was.

"I bet you got some amazing shots today," Adrian said softly, his lips quirking into a smile as he edged closer, their faces nearly touching now.

"I did," Logan replied, his voice low, his gray eyes locking onto Adrian's. "I filmed almost everything, including that wild jump." His smirk was pure mischief.

"You mean the death jump?" Adrian laughed, his hand lifting almost instinctively to Logan's jaw. His fingertips brushed against the strands of Logan's blond hair, damp and curling slightly at the ends.

"You're still standing here, aren't you?" Logan teased, but his voice had softened, his bravado giving way to something more tender.

"I am," Adrian breathed. His gaze held Logan's, searching those stormy gray eyes. Logan's hands slid down Adrian's back, firm and steady, pulling him closer until their bodies pressed together in the cool embrace of the river. The water lapped gently around them, but Adrian hardly noticed; every sense was consumed by Logan.

"Every day, it's like a dream with you," Logan murmured, his voice a quiet confession, raw and unguarded.

Adrian's heart surged, his breath hitching at the words. These moments, when Logan let the walls around his heart fall away, were everything. Adrian ached to hold onto them, to preserve the vulnerability that felt like a gift. "For me too," he replied, his voice equally soft, carrying the truth of a thousand unspoken words.

The space between them dissolved as Logan leaned in, their lips brushing in a kiss so gentle it felt like a ripple across still water. It was soft at first, exploratory, the barest touch of connection. But the pull between them was too strong to resist, and the kiss deepened, growing bolder and more urgent. Logan's hands gripped Adrian's back, their bodies melding together as though the river itself had drawn them into its flow.

Adrian's fingers tangled in Logan's hair, and their mouths moved in perfect sync, tongues meeting with a desperation that spoke of weeks of unacknowledged longing. The water rippled and splashed around them, but neither cared. They were immersed in each other, consumed by the raw, unfiltered emotion of the moment. It was wild and feral, an unstoppable force of nature they could not hope to contain.

And neither of them wanted to.

The tension between them erupted, primal and electric, as Logan's hips ground against Adrian's. Every nerve in his body felt alight, every movement sending shockwaves that made him gasp into Adrian's mouth. He couldn't control the sounds spilling from him—whimpers, moans, desperate gasps—as his hands roamed, finding Adrian's ass and squeezing with a hunger that bordered on frantic. The friction, even through the soaked fabric separating them, was maddening. It was chaos, it was fire, it was too much, and not nearly enough.

"Lo," Adrian growled, breaking the kiss for a fraction of a second, his forehead pressing against Logan's as his hips kept moving, grinding hard. His breath came in sharp bursts, his voice rough and almost pleading. "I'm about to come."

"Me too," Logan rasped, his voice shaky, caught somewhere between a moan and a whimper. His lips found Adrian's again, like letting them part was akin to losing air, and he poured everything into the kiss—the pent-up longing, the firestorm of lust, the undeniable pull that had been building for weeks, months.

Adrian tried to speak again, "I—" but Logan silenced him, his hands sliding down with a boldness he didn't know he possessed. His fingers brushed over Adrian's length through the wet fabric, and that was all it took. Adrian's breath hitched, and his body tensed, a guttural groan ripping from his chest as the heat and friction overwhelmed him. He came hard, shuddering against Logan, his head falling to Logan's shoulder, lost in the sheer intensity of it.

The euphoria was contagious. Logan followed seconds later, his body trembling as the wave overtook him, his release leaving him breathless, clutching Adrian like he was the only thing tethering him to the earth. Their foreheads pressed together, lips brushing but not quite kissing anymore, as they shared shaky, uneven breaths.

The world around them fell away—the river, the jungle, everything fading into insignificance as they stayed locked in that moment. Logan didn't care about anything else. Not about the soaked boxers clinging to their skin, not about the way his body ached from the day's exertion. All that mattered was Adrian—his weight against him, the heat of his breath, the steady thrum of life between them.

Logan let out a shaky laugh, his voice hoarse. "Well... that escalated quickly."

Adrian chuckled weakly, lifting his head to look at Logan, his face flushed, his expression somewhere between awe and disbelief. "I wanted..." he murmured, his voice soft, the edges of his lips curling into a smile. "I wanted..." He started again, voice trembling, cheeks rosy. "I wanted that the next time we'd do something would be... more romantic." He confessed. "Not like two teenagers. And maybe not coming within ten seconds would have been nice, too."

Logan smirked, leaning in to brush his nose against Adrian's. "It was absolutely perfect," he promised. "And... I think we both really needed it."

Adrian sighed, his arms tightening around Logan as if to hold him closer, as if to keep him there forever. "Yeah," he confessed.

All the little kisses and make-out sessions across the passing month have been building for this moment, for the moments when they would have to let it all go, to not stop at the last second. And yet. It was still not enough. Logan's skin was buzzing, every nerve ending alive with the wait of more, with the expectation of a night spent with Adrian again.

After a moment or two, they found it in themselves to leave the waters, the chill of the jungle night beginning to creep in. Logan stumbled onto the riverbank, his hair dripping and plastered against his forehead, his skin alive with the lingering warmth of Adrian's presence. They shared breathless, flushed grins, their laughter bubbling up uncontrollably, as if it had been eager to break free all day.

Logan fumbled with the tent poles, the pieces slipping through his fingers. "Okay, I think it's safe to say I'm better in the water than on land," he admitted with a sheepish grin, his hair still damp and clinging to his forehead. Adrian chuckled, his voice low and warm, stepping in to take over with practiced ease.

"You're lucky you're cute," Adrian teased, his hands deftly assembling the tent. Logan watched him, leaning back against a nearby tree, his eyes tracing the curve of Adrian's back, the confident way he moved. There was something hypnotic about it—how Adrian's calm grounded him, how his presence filled every space.

By the time the tent was up, the last traces of twilight had given way to darkness. Fireflies flickered like tiny, wandering stars, and the jungle's symphony grew louder. They changed out of their soaked boxers, trading them for dry clothes, the cool fabric a relief against their sun-kissed skin. Dinner was simple—some pre-prepared meals and a handful of fruit—but it was shared in a way that felt easy, intimate. They sat close, their knees touching, scrolling through Logan's camera roll and planning their path for the next day.

Every now and then, their laughter would dissolve into something quieter—small kisses exchanged like secret promises, glances held just a second too long, touches that lingered, whispering of what might come later. The air between them felt charged, as if the jungle itself held its breath, waiting.

When the temperature dropped and the cool air began to creep in, they retreated to the tent, ducking inside one after the other. The space was snug, the walls of the tent brushing their shoulders as they lay down. A single sleeping bag was all they had, not wanting to carry too much for such a short trip, and it forced them to press close, their bodies aligning in a way that felt both inevitable and necessary. The faint glow of the lamp cast soft shadows across their faces.

They lay on their sides, gazing into each other's eyes. Logan's palm caressed Adrian's cheek, his touch as delicate as a whispering breeze, reminiscent of a wave softly kissing the shore, his thumb gliding over the subtle stubble. His fingers moved as if tracing Adrian's features, not for the first time but still breathtaking like it was, memorizing every line, every contour. His eyes were dark pools, fathomless and searching, holding a storm that threatened to spill over. Adrian could feel it, the weight of something unspoken, as palpable as the humidity in the air.

Over the months, Adrian had learned to read Logan like the tides—every shift, every flicker of his eyes, a telltale sign of what he was feeling. Tonight, the waters were restless, swirling with a depth Adrian couldn't ignore.

"What is it?" Adrian whispered, his voice soft as a breeze threading through the canopy above them. He slid an arm around Logan's waist, pulling him closer, until their bodies aligned. He pressed a kiss to Logan's lips, a tender, exploratory gesture.

Logan sighed against Adrian's mouth, his breath trembling like the ripple of water disturbed by the wind, and he felt the strength he was able to gather by Adrian's kiss. "Adrian..." His voice broke, the sound fragile but resolute, as he kissed him again, deeper this time. Their hips shifted, their bodies pressing flush, the contact sparking a warmth that cut through the cool night air. "I know you... said... that we don't have to rush—"

Adrian nodded, his heart a steady drumbeat in his chest, grounding him. He understood without needing to ask. This wasn't just about tonight; it was about every kiss, every touch, every moment that had led them here.

"Back in the river..." Logan's words faltered, but his fingers didn't. They slid into Adrian's hair, threading through the strands with quiet desperation, tugging gently, grounding himself in the sensation. "That was the first time I—" His voice caught, and Adrian felt the tremor in his hand. "This was the first time you didn't stop us since our first time." Logan finally let it out. Over the course of the months they had shared, Adrian had been the one to voice what lingered in the spaces between them. His easy-going nature, the way he wore his heart on his sleeve like a badge of courage, made him bold. It wasn't that Logan didn't feel, far from it. His emotions were a deep current, swirling beneath the surface, hidden and powerful. But he struggled to bring them to light, to shape them into words that matched the intensity of what was in his chest. Adrian had spent time navigating his own depths, finding clarity and calm like someone who had learned to read the rhythm of the sea. Logan, meanwhile, held his emotions like a tightly wound knot, uncertain how to untangle them. Still, he wanted to say it. God knew he'd felt it rising inside him for weeks now, unspoken and raw. "I want you to lose control, Ad."

Adrian's breath hitched, his brow furrowing as he searched Logan's face. There was something raw in Logan's eyes, a vulnerability that cut through him. "Lose control?" he repeated, the words foreign and heavy on his tongue. He needed Logan to clarify because that was not something he could do with half words and half statements. He needed Logan's clear instructions.

Logan nodded, his fingers tightening in Adrian's hair, just enough to send a shiver down his spine. "When we're together," he began, his voice low but steady, "I can feel you holding back. The way you kiss me, the way you stop when things get too heated. Like you're afraid."

The dim glow of the lamp caught the blush that crept across Adrian's cheeks, turning his skin the color of a setting sun. He looked away for a moment, his lips parting as if to speak, but no words came. Finally, he said, "I just... I wanted to give you time. I know this is new for you, I know you've never been with a man, and I didn't want to push."

"I know," Logan said, his tone softening. "And I needed that time. I needed it to move slowly at first." His other hand moved to rest against Adrian's chest, right over his heart, feeling its frantic rhythm. "But now, I need you to stop holding back. I need you to let go."

The words were a ripple that became a wave, crashing over Adrian with an intensity that left him breathless. He stared at Logan, the space between them charged, electric. Slowly, he cupped Logan's face, his thumb brushing over his cheekbone. The kiss he gave him this time was different—not gentle, not hesitant, but deep and consuming.

"Are you sure?" His eyes searched Logan's, needing the answer, needing certainty.

"Yes," Logan said, and when he smiled, it was like sunlight breaking through the dense canopy above, a light that banished every shadow.

Adrian nodded but hesitated for a moment. "I need to say something," he murmured, breaking the silence. His voice was steady, but his fingers twitched slightly where they rested on Logan's hip.

"Oh no," Logan teased lightly, though his voice was soft. "That sounds serious."

Adrian huffed a quiet laugh, rubbing the back of his neck. "It's not—it's just..." He sighed, shaking his head at himself. "I need an unsexy moment before we... before this."

Logan propped himself up on one elbow, watching Adrian with a lazy, lopsided smile. "An unsexy moment?" he repeated. "Okay." Logan's voice was all mock seriousness.

Adrian groaned, pressing his palm over his face, his laughter muffled. "I hate you."

"No, you don't," Logan said smugly, lying back down, one arm draped over Adrian. "Go on. Let's get this unsexy moment over with, so we can move on to the sexy part of the night."

Adrian sighed but smiled despite himself. "It's been a while for me," he admitted. "Like... a... you know.... A long while. Before this trip, I got checked, you know, since I had to get a bunch of shots anyway, so... I guess they have checked other stuff too... and I just—I wanted you to know that." He exhaled, his fingers toying with the hem of his shirt. "And I wanted to ask if... if you're comfortable..."

Logan's laughter came, and he squished Adrian's arm warmly.

"What?" Adrian asked, brows furrowing.

"You," Logan said, his voice full of something fond, something devastatingly gentle. "The way you get all flustered over something so simple."

Adrian groaned again, covering his face with his hand, but Logan reached out and caught his wrist, pulling his hand away. Their eyes met, and suddenly, all of Adrian's self-consciousness dissolved into the background, overshadowed by the quiet intensity in Logan's gaze.

"For the record," Logan said, thumb brushing against Adrian's wrist, tracing slow circles against his skin, "same for me. I'm all checked out, and it's been a while." His voice carried the faintest hint of embarrassment, but his eyes never wavered. "Almost a year."

Something in Adrian's chest softened, uncoiling like a knot undone. He swallowed, nodding, before clearing his throat. "So..."

Logan smirked. "So...?"

Adrian narrowed his eyes at him. "We could..." he trailed off.

Logan grinned, all playful mischief. "We could what?" he prompted, knowing full well what Adrian meant.

Adrian groaned, but he was smiling. "Logan," he warned, voice full of mock exasperation.

Logan tilted his head, looking at him with that insufferable, infuriatingly charming glint in his eye. "I just wanna be sure I understand," he said, the picture of innocence, as he softly kissed Adrian's knuckles.

Adrian let out a breathless laugh, shaking his head. "You're impossible."

Logan's smile softened, the teasing melting into something quieter as he threaded their fingers together, his grip warm, steady. He lifted their joined hands and pressed a kiss to Adrian's knuckles again, lingering.

"You're beautiful," he murmured, so quietly Adrian barely heard it over the distant sound of the forest.

Adrian's breath caught, his pulse stuttering. He didn't know what to say, didn't know how to take a compliment like that without deflecting.

Logan's lips hovered over Adrian's knuckles, his breath warm against his skin, and Adrian felt something in him settle. Not the wild thrill of desire, not the pulse of anticipation, but something deeper, something that felt like belonging.

Because somehow, despite the universe's chaos, despite the relentless shifting of tides and time, he had found himself here. Adrian Leon—who had spent most of his life feeling like an outsider looking in, who had learned early how to want without expecting—had ended up with Logan Vaughn. This untamed, sun-kissed force of nature, this storm in human form, all laughter and saltwater and fire, had chosen him. And not just in a fleeting way, not just in the way people chase a thrill or a beautiful sunset.

Logan was here. Staying. Holding Adrian's hand like a quiet promise, looking at him like he was something worth getting lost in.

Adrian swallowed, exhaling slowly, letting the weight of it settle inside him before he found the courage to say it. "So we can go bare."

His own voice sounded distant, hushed, yet resolute. He half-expected Logan to tease him once more, to prolong this precious moment with that effortless, infuriating grin, one Adrian pretended to find exhausting but secretly adored and longed for. Yet, when Adrian finally met his gaze, Logan's expression transformed into something entirely different, softening in a way that took Adrian by surprise.

A quiet kind of awe.

"Yeah," Logan murmured, nodding, his grip on Adrian's hand tightening just slightly.

No hesitation. No doubt. Just trust. Just them.

Adrian exhaled, a slow, trembling breath, as Logan leaned in, closing the last of the space between them. Their lips met in a kiss that felt like Adrian's deepest desire. Logan kissed him like he wanted to leave his name etched into Adrian's skin, like he wanted to drown in him, like this wasn't just tonight, wasn't just a moment, but something that had already begun to rewrite the landscape of his life.

Adrian groaned softly, and in a heartbeat, he was on Logan again. His lips found Logan's, pouring all the words he didn't know how to say into the kiss. Their tongues tangled, their breaths mingling as the jungle outside pulsed with life. If Logan wanted Adrian to lose control, he was ready to surrender to the storm and take Logan with him.

Logan arched against Adrian, their bodies fitting together as if they'd been carved from the same wave. His soft moans were filling the space between them as Adrian's hands roamed his waist, fingers tugging at the fabric of his shirt. They broke apart for a moment, long enough for Adrian to pull Logan's shirt free and toss it aside. Logan, eager and trembling, returned the favor, ridding Adrian of his own.

Adrian dove back in, his mouth tracing a path down Logan's neck as their bare skin pressed together, heat radiating between them like a flame. The too-small tent shifted and swayed with their movements, and Logan let out a breathless laugh.

"You better not knock this tent over," he warned, his voice teasing but laced with desire. "I am *not* ending up naked on the ground."

Adrian couldn't help but laugh, the sound bubbling up even as his lips found Logan's again. "Being reckless? That's all you. I'm too practical for that."

"Then up your game," Logan shot back, his voice low and urgent, his hands moving down Adrian's back, tracing the hard lines of muscle. "Because I told you to lose control."

Adrian growled softly, the challenge igniting something wild in him. His hands slid lower, making quick work of Logan's board shorts, casting them aside without hesitation. Logan gasped, pulling Adrian back into another kiss, their bodies entwined as the jungle sang around them, bearing witness to their unrestrained, earth-shattering storm.

The air inside the tent was thick with heat and want, the jungle outside humming like a living heartbeat, matching the rhythm of their shared breaths. Adrian's lips moved with purpose, a tidal force against Logan's skin. He lingered at Logan's neck, kissing and nipping until Logan was gasping beneath him, his hands clutching at Adrian as though he were the only anchor in a storm-tossed sea.

Adrian's mouth traveled lower, the heat of his kisses igniting a trail of fire down Logan's chest. When his lips found a nipple, he teased it with his tongue, then nipped lightly, drawing a sharp, desperate gasp from Logan. He alternated, lavishing attention on each, his hands caressing Logan's sides, tracing the curve of his ribs like he was sculpting him from memory. Beneath him, Logan writhed, his hips arching in search of relief, moans spilling from his lips.

"Fuck, Adrian!" Logan groaned, his voice cracked and raw, his hand tightening in Adrian's hair. The tie holding Adrian's sun-kissed strands came loose as Logan tugged on it, and his hair spilled over his face like a golden waterfall, brushing against Logan's belly and sending shivers cascading through his body.

Adrian's lips curved into a grin against Logan's skin as he kissed down further, pausing at his belly to nuzzle into his happy trail, the coarse hairs tickling his nose. "Do not dare come, Lo," Adrian warned, his voice rough and teasing as he placed a firm hand on Logan's hips, stilling his frantic movements.

"I—" Logan's protest dissolved into another moan as Adrian mouthed his cock through the fabric of his boxer briefs, the friction unbearable and perfect all at once, as his saliva slowly coated the front of the fabric. "Fuck, fuck!" Logan breathed, his head tossing back, his body arching.

Adrian felt drunk at the sight of Logan unraveling beneath him. It was like watching a wave crest and break, powerful and beautiful, every inch of Logan surrendering to the pull of his touch. The cramped space of the tent, the awkward angle of his body, all of it faded into insignificance as he slid Logan's boxers down, leaving him bare and radiant.

Logan's body, golden and glistening in the dim, flickering light, was nothing short of a masterpiece. Adrian froze, his breath hitching in his throat as he let his eyes wander over the vision before him. Logan's skin gleamed like polished amber, every lean, toned muscle perfectly defined, a testament to his strength and grace. The faint shadow of his happy trail drew Adrian's gaze downward, a tantalizing path that begged to be explored, to be tasted.

His blond hair was a tousled mess, wild and untamed, framing his face like a halo of sunlight. And there, between his thighs, was the source of Adrian's unraveling: Logan's long, thick, uncut, and veined cock, a sight that stole the air from the tent and left Adrian reeling. It wasn't just the physical perfection that held Adrian captive; it was the sheer *intimacy* of it, the trust, the surrender, the way Logan lay before him, unguarded and utterly his.

Adrian's heart thudded like the pounding surf, a rhythm that matched the tidal pull of desire coursing through his veins. He wanted to worship Logan, to lose himself in every inch of him, to explore the golden expanse of his body until he knew it better than his own. This wasn't just lust—it was awe, reverence, a deep and quiet contentment that settled over him like the calm after a storm. To see Logan laid out before him totally naked and bare, to hear his desperate breaths and feel the tremor of his hands, was a privilege Adrian didn't take lightly.

He dipped his head, letting his tongue glide along the length of Logan's uncut cock, tasting him, savoring him. "You have such a pretty cock," he almost purred as he let himself look and feel the weight of the shaft in his hand. Logan's moans grew louder, his voice breaking with every ragged breath. Adrian buried his face in Logan's groin, breathing him in, grounding himself in the scent and heat of him.

"God, Logan, you moan so well for me," Adrian murmured, his voice rough with desire. He dragged the stubble of his chin along Logan's shaft, eliciting a strangled cry from him. "I love hearing you lose yourself," he whispered, his breath hot and teasing as it fanned over Logan's sensitive skin. "I can't wait to taste you."

With every praise that fell from Adrian's lips, Logan's passion flared hotter, each breath feeding the blaze until it roared. The words weren't just sounds—they struck through him like arrows, piercing deeper, making his body answer with a fervor he couldn't contain. His breaths came ragged and uneven, each one sharper than the last, his voice breaking loose in raw cries that shook through him, unstoppable.

Logan's gasps were frantic now, his body bucking as Adrian took him into his mouth, slow and deliberate. Adrian felt every tremor, every hitch of breath, as he moved with care, savoring each sound Logan made. He let himself get lost in the moment, in the heat of Logan's body, in the symphony of moans that filled the air, as though the jungle itself held its breath, enraptured by the raw, unfiltered passion unfolding within the tent.

Adrian's lips were sliding over Logan's shaft with a fervor that felt almost sacred. It had been a long time since Adrian had been with anyone, and his muscles remembered slowly, trembling with the effort of taking Logan deep. The bulbous head of Logan's cock brushed the back of Adrian's throat, again and again, each time drawing a gagged gasp from him, but he didn't stop. He couldn't stop.

Adrian felt drunk, utterly intoxicated by the taste of Logan's salt-tinged pre-cum, the heat of his skin, and the rich, musky scent that filled the tent. It was overwhelming, a sensory storm that left him lightheaded and ravenous. Saliva pooled and spilled from his lips, coating Logan's shaft as Adrian sucked with a hunger that made the world narrow to just this moment. The walls of the tent seemed to ripple with their movements, the humid air growing heavier as Logan's gasps and cries wove themselves into the night's symphony.

"Yes! Adrian—fuuuuuck!" Logan's voice cracked, raw and desperate, as Adrian's hands joined in their worship. One hand stroked him in perfect rhythm with his mouth, the other tugging at his balls, sending shudders rippling through Logan's body.

Logan's hand reached down, his fingers tangling in Adrian's sun-kissed hair. The loose waves slipped through his grasp like silk, but he held tight, grounding himself as his hips began to move, thrusting gently at first, then more urgently, into the heat of Adrian's mouth. "Ad... fuck, yes—" His voice was hoarse, frayed with pleasure, and when his eyes dropped to meet Adrian's, the sight stole the breath from his lungs.

Adrian's whiskey-brown eyes burned into Logan, a fire that consumed and laid bare. His lips, plush and swollen, stretched taut around Logan's cock, his face glistening with saliva as he worked Logan over and over, refusing to let him pull away. Adrian's body, all sinew and strength, moved with a grace that was both feral and precise, each motion a testament to his control and surrender.

"I'm 'bout to—fuck—come!" Logan choked out, his chest heaving as he tried to pull Adrian back, his fingers loosening their grip on Adrian's hair. But Adrian wasn't finished. He reached back, grabbing Logan's wrist and guiding his hand back to the nape of his neck, silently urging him to hold tight, to let go, to lose himself completely.

Logan's restraint snapped. His hand tightened in Adrian's hair, pulling just enough to angle him closer as his hips thrust deeper, harder, his cock sliding into the velvet heat of Adrian's throat. Adrian took it all, his eyes locked on Logan's, unwavering as he surrendered himself to the rhythm.

The sensation was too much, too perfect, and Logan came with a cry that echoed through the tent. His body arched, his muscles seizing as his release burned through him. White-hot pleasure ripped through his body, and for a moment, he thought he'd blacked out, the edges of his vision going hazy as spots danced behind his closed eyelids.

When it was over, Logan collapsed back onto the sleeping bag, utterly spent, his chest rising and falling. Adrian pulled back slowly, his lips glistening, his face flushed, his whiskey eyes softening as they gazed at Logan. Logan had never felt calmer, more alive, or more unreservedly undone in his entire life.

A moment stretched between them, taut and trembling like the surface of a wave just before it breaks. Logan's breath came in ragged gasps, his chest heaving as he struggled to find words that felt sufficient. "Ad—that was—damn." The sentence faltered, unfinished, as if he had been rendered incapable of speech by the sheer force of what had just happened.

Adrian, still catching his own breath, sat back on his knees. A sly smile tugged at his swollen lips. "Glad I've found a new way to shut you up," he teased, though his voice was rough, his body visibly vibrating with tension.

Logan's smirk faltered as he opened his eyes and truly saw Adrian—his hair a wild halo around his flushed face, his lips plump and red from taking Logan so deeply, from swallowing him whole. The realization gutted Logan, leaving him raw. His gaze dropped lower, to where Adrian's boxer briefs clung to him, his arousal impossible to ignore. The sight of it, straining against the fabric, was magnetic, pulling Logan's gaze to it with the inevitability of gravity.

Logan's tongue darted out to wet his lips. "I—" he began, but Adrian cut him off quickly, almost too quickly, the words tumbling out in a rush.

"You don't have to do anything," Adrian said, his voice tinged with something like panic, a vulnerability that made Logan's chest ache. "I'll take care of it. I can even just step outside and—"

"Why would you go outside?" Logan asked, his brow furrowing, his voice steady but curious. The afterglow of his orgasm softened his edges, but something in Adrian's frantic suggestion didn't sit right.

Adrian hesitated, his shoulders tensing. "I know it was your first time, and I... I don't want you to feel overwhelmed or freak out," he admitted, his words quiet, almost as if he was bracing himself.

Logan stared at him, the pieces clicking into place, and his heart squeezed at the thought of Adrian holding himself back, of thinking he had to. "I'll only freak out if you go outside," Logan said, his voice firm and laced with tenderness. He pushed himself up to his knees, closing the distance between them until they were face to face. "And let me remind you that it was definitely not our first time."

Adrian groaned softly and covered his face with his hands, as if he could press the feeling back inside. "It's always cool," he muttered, half-laughing, half-aching, "until someone touches your cock... or until you're the one touching a dick."

Logan reached out and removed Adrian's hands from his face. "I'm not going to freak out because you touched my dick, Adrian." Logan cupped his face, his hands steady as he pulled him into a kiss. It wasn't rushed or frantic; it was deep, deliberate, a connection that spoke louder than words. The taste of himself lingered on Adrian's tongue, salty and intimate, and the realization that Adrian had swallowed him entirely made Logan moan into the kiss, his body surging closer.

"I'm not some blushing virgin," Logan whispered against his lips, his voice filled with a quiet intensity. "I wanted every moment of this, and now... I want you to come undone. Because I'm not a selfish lover, and I—" He hesitated, his confidence faltering for just a moment. "I've been thinking about it. A lot. Lately. So—"

Before Adrian could respond, Logan grabbed him, his movements bold and unrelenting. With one swift motion, he pressed Adrian down onto his back, the sudden shift causing the small tent to groan under the pressure. Logan moved over him, his body lithe and commanding, and for a moment, Adrian could do nothing but stare, breathless and captivated.

The jungle outside seemed to fade into silence, as though even the wild night had paused to watch them. Logan's golden skin glowed in the dim light, his eyes dark and steady as they bore into Adrian's. "Let me," Logan murmured, his voice soft but full of determination. "I want to give you what you gave me. I want to watch you fall apart."

The smile Adrian gave him could have melted a thousand glaciers and caused a world disaster, as it brought civilization to its knees with that beautiful smile. So radiant, disarming, and utterly unguarded, it wasn't just a smile, it was a promise, a beacon that illuminated every dark corner of Logan's heart. It was the kind of smile that could make a man leave everything behind without a second thought, to cross oceans and continents just to be near it. It was a smile that whispered of a future filled with reckless abandon and quiet, simple joys, the kind of future that might include white picket fences and a thousand small, beautiful moments that made life worth living.

Logan felt the weight of it, the pull of it, a gravitational force that anchored him and set him adrift all at once. That smile was chaos and home, all wrapped up in one, and he knew he would do anything—*anything*—to keep it.

Logan started with a kiss, as though Adrian's taste was the very air he needed to breathe. A moment without it felt unbearable now that he knew the sweetness of it, the addictive depth that left him dizzy and yearning.

"Logan, I'm going to come in five seconds," Adrian warned, his voice ragged and desperate. "Giving you that blowjob was so hot I almost came with you in my mouth."

The words alone sent a shiver through Logan, making his cock twitch in response. "Damn it," he cursed under his breath, desire spiking as Adrian bucked against him, their bodies colliding like waves in a storm.

Logan moved downward, the pull of Adrian too alluring to resist. Some part of his mind acknowledged what he was about to do—that he was about to touch, taste, and worship another man's cock, a boundary he'd never even considered crossing before. But this wasn't just any man. This was Adrian. Adrian, who had saved him, seen him, and become everything he hadn't realized he needed.

His fingers trembled slightly as they brushed the thick shaft through the fabric of Adrian's boxers, and he felt Adrian shudder beneath his touch. The power of that moment, the ability to elicit such a visceral reaction, filled Logan with a giddy kind of wonder. Smirking, he slowly dragged the boxers down, unveiling Adrian inch by inch, like uncovering a treasure buried beneath golden sands.

Adrian's cock was thick and cut, the soft curves of the shaft catching the dim light like the ridges of a smooth, glistening rock pulled from the ocean's depths. "Jewish indeed," Logan teased, the words slipping out as a joke, but the sight of Adrian's flushed skin and the way he covered his face with a laugh sent a warm bloom of affection through him.

Even in this moment of intense vulnerability, they could laugh. They could banter and tease and weave their friendship into their intimacy, the threads of their connection unbreakable. Their intimacy was no mere conflagration of passion and lust, but a quiet symphony of laughter, layered histories, and the rare grace of being wholly known and unmasked.

"I can honestly say that no one had ever brought up my religion in bed," Adrian quipped, his voice still light with humor.

Logan felt the faint sting of jealousy, the thought of someone else ever touching Adrian an unwelcome shadow at the edge of his mind. For a moment it pressed on him, heavy and suffocating, but he refused to let it take root. Instead, his mind clung to the memory of their first kiss—the way Adrian's eyes had locked on him, steady and unflinching, when he said:

I want you. Nothing compares to this... pull I feel toward you.

I never gave that piece of my past to anyone

His gaze dropped to his own wrist, where the bracelet Adrian had gifted him still rested, worn and treasured. Relief flooded Logan, washing away the shadows of doubt. Adrian had given him his most cherished possession without hesitation, a piece of himself no one else had held. That knowledge steadied him, not like sand that shifts with every wave, but like bedrock beneath the sea, something unmovable, something meant to endure.

Logan leaned forward, his lips grazing the length of Adrian's shaft once more, savoring the warmth and salt of his skin, the taste of a moment he wanted to etch into his memory forever. Adrian's soft moan filled the tent, low and resonant, like the murmur of distant waves calling Logan deeper into the tide. Logan smiled against him, feeling the weight of Adrian's trust, and let his touch become exploratory, reverent, and eager.

He wrapped his hand slowly around Adrian's cock, fingers curling experimentally as he tugged gently at the smooth skin. It felt different from his own—the absence of foreskin giving the shaft a new texture, a new shape to learn. Logan's movements were tentative at first, deliberate as he became accustomed to the unique feel of Adrian. He caught glimpses of Adrian watching him, his chest rising and falling rapidly, his head tipping back with a moan as Logan's fingers worked over him.

Logan's thoughts flickered, unbidden, to the shadowy ghosts of Adrian's past lovers. How many hands had traced these lines of muscle? How many mouths had kissed Adrian where Logan now ventured, daring to claim uncharted territory? The questions curled in his mind like stray wisps of smoke, but he banished them quickly, pulling his focus back to the present, to the visceral reality of Adrian beneath him. Adrian's breathless surrender, the tremble in his limbs, the moans spilling from his lips—these were Logan's now, and he burned with the need to ensure they stayed that way.

He wanted to eclipse the memories of anyone who had come before, to leave a mark so indelible that Adrian could think of no one but him. The blowjob Adrian had given him earlier had shattered Logan in ways he hadn't known were possible. It was beyond anything he'd dreamed, a perfect storm of pleasure that left him dazed and unmoored. In its aftermath, Logan feared he was irrevocably ruined and nothing could compare. But as he gazed down at Adrian, flushed and trembling, his chest rising and falling with shallow breaths, Logan knew he wanted to give

Adrian the same. Selfishly, desperately, he wanted to wreck Adrian, to turn his world upside down, to make him feel as undone as Logan had been.

It wasn't just lust. It was a need, raw and all-consuming, to be the only one Adrian remembered in this way.

Bending down, Logan let the head of Adrian's cock brush against his lips, hesitating for only a moment before taking it into his mouth. The taste was electric, salty and musky, filling Logan's senses as he swirled his tongue experimentally around the tip. Adrian shuddered, his body trembling beneath Logan, the sounds of his pleasure vibrating in the tight space of the tent. Logan couldn't tease the way Adrian had, but the urgency in Adrian's flushed skin and throbbing cock told him they didn't have time for that. Adrian was already teetering on the edge, and the realization sent a thrill through Logan.

The salty slickness of Adrian's pre-cum coated Logan's tongue as he swallowed reflexively, the sensation drawing a louder moan from Adrian. Gaining confidence, Logan took Adrian deeper, his throat tightening slightly as he adjusted to the stretch. He couldn't take Adrian all the way, not like Adrian had done for him, but he compensated with his hand, stroking what his mouth couldn't reach. Logan's head bobbed rhythmically, the weight of Adrian's cock against his tongue and lips intoxicating. The taste, the texture, the sheer act of pleasuring Adrian consumed him, a heady mix of arousal and pride.

Feeling Adrian's body tense beneath him, Logan pulled back suddenly, wanting to prolong the moment. He moved lower, his tongue tracing the curve of Adrian's heavy balls, his lips pressing soft kisses against the sensitive skin. The deep musk of Adrian's scent filled Logan's lungs, primal and inebriating, as he licked and sucked gently, drawing deep groans and guttural sounds from Adrian. He heard snatches of Hebrew spill from Adrian's lips, words Logan didn't fully understand but felt all the same, raw and unfiltered in their passion.

When Logan finally returned to Adrian's cock, taking him back into his mouth, the desperation in Adrian's voice grew. "Logan," Adrian gasped, his accent thick, words tumbling out as if he couldn't hold them back. "Ani—I—fuck—Logan, I'm coming." A mix of Hebrew and English that flew from his lips as his brain fought to keep up with the languages.

Logan braced himself, his hand steadying the base of Adrian's shaft as the first hot spurt hit the back of his throat. He swallowed eagerly, wanting to take everything Adrian gave him, but some escaped, dripping down his chin as Adrian groaned, his body arching, trembling, utterly undone. The sound of Adrian's release, the raw vulnerability of his pleasure, was a melody Logan wanted to play on repeat.

When it was over, Logan wiped his chin with the back of his hand, his chest still heaving. Adrian reached for him, pulling him up with surprising strength. Their lips met in a deep, consuming kiss, Adrian tasting himself on Logan's tongue, his hands roaming over Logan's body in a silent thank you. Logan melted into Adrian's touch, their breaths mingling, the intimacy of the moment overwhelming. Adrian's fingers brushed through Logan's hair, over his back, grounding him in the afterglow of their shared storm. In that moment, the world outside didn't exist—there was only them, adrift in the uncharted sea they had created together.

After a while, they lay intertwined, their breaths tangling with heat and hush, as their bodies quivered from the lingering intensity of their shared experience. The tent was a cocoon, holding them close, sheltering them from the world beyond. Logan's fingers lazily traced patterns on Adrian's chest, his touch soft and almost absentminded, as if grounding himself in the reality of this moment.

Adrian turned his head, his whiskey-brown eyes locking onto Logan's. There was something unspoken there, a vulnerability that made Logan's chest tighten. "You okay?" Logan asked softly, his voice rough from exertion but filled with genuine concern.

Adrian's lips curved into a slow, tender smile that reached his eyes. "More than okay," he said, his voice steady but quiet, as if speaking louder might shatter the fragile magic of the moment. He reached out, brushing a strand of Logan's blond hair away from his forehead. "What about you? Any regrets?"

Logan chuckled, the sound low and warm, shaking his head. "None. Zero. Not even close." He pressed a kiss to Adrian's shoulder, lingering as if to prove his point. "But..."

Adrian raised an eyebrow, his grin falling, replaced by concern. "But what?"

"But," Logan continued, his fingers brushing along Adrian's jawline, "I think I'm going to need you to teach me how to do what you did earlier. That... that should be illegal."

Adrian's laugh filled the tent, a sound that was equal parts amusement and affection. "I don't think you need much help. You're a natural." He pulled Logan closer, their bodies aligning perfectly. "But if you're asking for more practice, I think I can arrange that."

The playful banter gave way to a softer moment, the quiet stretch of intimacy that felt like the aftermath of a storm, the sea calm and glistening under a moonlit sky. Logan's gaze dropped to the bracelet

Adrian had given him, still snug around his wrist. He ran his thumb over it thoughtfully, his smile softening.

Adrian caught Logan's hand, his fingers brushing the bracelet he'd given him, and kissed it softly, his lips lingering for a moment before turning the gesture into a kiss on Logan's palm. It was a small, tender act that spoke volumes, a grounding touch that made Logan's heart throb in his chest.

"What do you think about trying to sleep?" Adrian murmured, his voice low and soothing. "We've got a long way to go tomorrow."

Logan nodded but hesitated, reluctant to let the moment slip away. "Don't think I could fall asleep now," he admitted, shifting slightly to rummage through their bags in the corner of the tent. The tight space forced his movements to be deliberate, but he didn't mind—it gave him a chance to look at Adrian again, who lay back on the sleeping bag with a drowsy, almost blissful smile on his face.

Completely naked.

Logan grabbed a bottle of water, took a sip, and then passed it to Adrian. He reached for his phone and saw the time—1 a.m. "It's late," he said softly, almost to himself.

"Maybe plug in our phones if you're there?" Adrian suggested, his voice tinged with sleep but still carrying that easy warmth. "I think the power bank's in my bag."

"Sure," Logan replied, his hands already rifling through Adrian's belongings. The zipper of Adrian's bag gave way easily, revealing its contents. Logan found the power bank and Adrian's phone tucked into a hidden compartment, alongside his wallet and passport. On a whim, Logan opened the passport, his thumb brushing over the slightly awkward photo inside. He smiled fondly at the man in the picture, his gaze lingering for a moment on the details: Adrian's name, his birthplace, his date of birth.

He carefully placed the passport back and plugged in their phones, tucking the power bank into the corner.

On impulse, Logan reached for his favorite playlist. Scrolling through the songs, his finger hovered before pressing play. The soft, familiar chords of *Everything* by Lifehouse filled the small space, weaving through the air like a thread connecting them to the present and something eternal. Without looking, Logan knew Adrian was smiling, that gentle, knowing smile that made Logan feel like the luckiest man alive.

The melody wrapped around them as Logan lay back down, his body curling instinctively into Adrian's. The song, once a constant in his life, suddenly felt different—richer, more profound, as though Adrian's presence had rewritten its meaning. Each lyric felt etched with the weight of the night, their intimacy, and the electric connection that bound them. Logan closed his eyes, letting the music blend with the sound of Adrian's breathing, the rise and fall of his chest a rhythm he found himself syncing to.

Adrian pulled Logan closer, his arms a protective circle around him. He kissed Logan deeply, slowly, as though trying to memorize the taste of this moment. When their lips parted, Adrian whispered the words of a song that is yet to be written softly into Logan's ear, his voice raspy and full of emotion.

"I believe my fate was to cross paths with you," he murmured, words that were not from the familiar lyrics, but they made Logan's heart beat differently, beat for that perfect man next to him, his voice barely above a whisper as he turned off the lamp, plunging them into darkness.

The world beyond the tent faded into nothingness, leaving only the echo of the music, the warmth of their bodies, and the infinite possibilities that awaited them in the morning. For now, they floated together in this perfect, unbroken moment, etched forever into the melody of their lives.

The next morning unfolded like a dream blurred at the edges, a kaleidoscope of sensations and stolen moments. Logan awoke to the velvet heat of Adrian's mouth wrapped around his cock, the soft rustle of the jungle mingling with his own ragged breaths. Adrian's movements were practiced yet full of reverence, as though he was savoring every second. Logan's moans filled the tent, a symphony to the dawn, as Adrian brought him to the brink and beyond.

When Logan reached down to stop Adrian from stroking himself, his voice was firm but laced with longing. "No," he said, breathless. "I want you in my mouth again." Adrian grinned, the kind of smile that could break a man apart and put him back together. Their morning stretched long, their bodies moving like waves cresting and breaking against the shore, leaving them utterly spent but glowing in the aftermath.

By the time they stumbled out of the tent, the jungle greeted them with its verdant embrace. The air was cool and alive, the river glinting like liquid silver in the morning light. Without hesitation, they dove in, the water a refreshing contrast to the heat of their skin. They swam lazily, splashing each other and stealing kisses between breaths. Logan, who had once scoffed at couples who seemed drunk on each other's presence, now found himself utterly disarmed by the giddiness swelling in his chest. Adrian's laugh was a melody, his joy infectious, and Logan was powerless to resist it.

Breakfast was quick—rehydrated noodles that Logan eyed with disdain. "This can't even be called food," he muttered, poking at the limp strands with his fork.

"I promise to get you pizza when we're back," Adrian said, planting a kiss on Logan's head as he stood.

"Don't say pizza now," Logan groaned, leaning back dramatically. "Now I'm even hungrier."

Adrian laughed, his eyes crinkling with amusement as he grabbed their packs. "Whiny suits you."

They set off on the trail, their steps falling into an easy rhythm. The jungle around them was a cathedral of green, the sunlight breaking in golden shards, illuminating their path. They paused often, sometimes to admire a view—a waterfall cascading like liquid diamonds into a pool below, or a cluster of wild orchids bursting with color—and sometimes just to kiss. Adrian's lips were addictive, leaving Logan dazed and grinning like a fool every time they parted.

On a wooden bridge spanning a narrow, whispering stream, Adrian caught Logan's wrist and pulled him close, their bodies colliding with the force of something inevitable. The world blurred, the emerald canopy above, the river murmuring below, the distant hum of birdsong fading into nothing.

And then Adrian kissed him.

A kiss so deep, so consuming, that Logan forgot how to stand. His knees buckled, his fingers tightening in Adrian's shirt, holding on like he was the only thing tethering him to the earth. It wasn't just a kiss—it was a *claim*, a declaration, a fire set ablaze between them. Adrian kissed him with the kind of certainty that made Logan dizzy, like he had known from the beginning that this was where they would end up.

And then, Logan felt something shift between them. A small, mischievous movement.

Adrian pulled back just enough to smirk against his lips, one hand still tangled in Logan's waves, the other clutching Logan's GoPro.

"You—" Logan gasped, half-laughing, half-breathless.

Adrian simply grinned, holding up the camera, the little red light blinking. "For the memories," he murmured, his voice thick with amusement.

And there, on the bridge, with the river running wild beneath them and the jungle breathing around them, they were captured forever, the moment suspended in time, a kiss immortalized in pixels, in light, in a stolen heartbeat that neither of them knew would one day be all that was left.

Adrian's happiness radiated from him, appearing divine and luminous, sparkling and bubbling, flowing out and touching everything around making the sunlight seem dull in comparison. Logan could see it in the way Adrian's eyes sparkled, in the lazy grin that seemed permanently etched on his face. It was contagious, and Logan found himself smiling so much his cheeks hurt.

As they continued, they encountered other travelers along the way. Adrian, ever the extrovert, struck up conversations with anyone willing to chat, his charm drawing people in effortlessly. Logan, usually content to stay on the sidelines, found himself watching Adrian with quiet admiration. The way Adrian's laugh carried through the trees, the way he seemed to connect with everyone, made Logan's chest tighten with affection.

Whenever the trail allowed, their hands found each other's, fingers intertwining as naturally as the vines that clung to the jungle trees. The afterglow of their morning lingered in their steps, in the shared glances that needed no words.

Each moment felt like a treasure, each kiss an anchor in a world that had become infinitely brighter, as though the jungle itself conspired to reflect the joy that shimmered between them. And as they walked, Logan couldn't help but marvel at the simplicity and enormity of it all—Adrian, the jungle, the trail, the giddy pull in his chest.

This, he realized, was happiness.

By the time they returned to the cabin, Logan felt as though his legs were about to give out. The scent of pizza wafted upward from the boxes in Adrian's hands, a smell so heavenly that Logan swore it might have been the only thing keeping him upright. The day had been grueling; endless trails, tired feet, and not a single proper meal to redeem it. But now, at last, there was pizza.

"Wow, I am so happy to be here," Logan announced, tossing his duffel bag to the side with no regard for where it landed. He let out a long sigh of relief and stretched his arms, hearing a satisfying crack in his back.

Adrian, who usually would've made some quip about tidiness, was too tired to care. He set the pizza boxes on the table and threw his bag beside Logan's. "I second that. We made it. Barely, but we made it."

"Next time we hike, better food," Logan declared, walking toward the table with a single-minded focus. "I'm talking sandwiches. Gourmet. None of this dried noodle crap."

Adrian chuckled as he flipped open the lids of the boxes. "Deal. But let me remind you that it was your idea to pack light."

"Yeah, well, I regret everything," Logan groaned. He stared at the pizza with an expression that was almost reverent, then wavered. "I can't decide if I want to take a shower first or eat."

Adrian smirked. "If you stare at the pizza any longer, I might start to get jealous," he teased, stepping aside to let Logan get his fix.

Logan shoved him lightly. "Shut up," he mumbled, already grabbing two slices of pepperoni pizza and stacking them together like a sandwich. The first bite had him groaning in pure bliss. "Oh my God," he said between mouthfuls. "I've missed you so much," he mumbled to the pizza.

Adrian laughed, sitting down and grabbing a slice of mushroom pizza for himself. "You're impossible," he said, shaking his head.

"I'm a growing boy," Logan shrugged, shoving another bite into his mouth. "My mom says I've been hungry since birth. I gained pounds like crazy as a baby, but I was a tall one, even then." Logan finished his slice and took another one. "When we were growing up, my grandma was a church-on-Sundays type. So whenever we visited, she insisted that the whole family go. When I was little, we used to go to these big Christmas services."

Adrian tilted his head, chewing quietly.

"One year, I was maybe eight, they brought out these giant, gooey cinnamon buns after the service. I was starving, so I just grabbed two and started eating right in the middle of grace. One in each hand. Glaze all over my shirt, and of course, I was in my Sunday best. My baby sister Ann saw me and joined in." He grinned at the memory. "The pastor paused mid-prayer, probably trying not to laugh, while Mom and Grandma gave me the kind of look that said I'd broken some sacred law."

Adrian chuckled. "So... was Christmas ruined?"

"Hell no," Logan said, laughing. "Mom can't stay mad at me for more than ten minutes. I'm her boy. Got cool gifts that year, too."

Adrian laughed harder, shaking his head at Logan's ability to weave his appetite into any conversation. "I love that even when you're exhausted, you can still monologue about food."

"Food is sacred," Logan declared dramatically, finishing off his second makeshift sandwich and reaching for another slice. "But this? This is holy. We should've had pizza after every hike."

"Well, next time, I'll make sure we include it on the supply list," Adrian said, taking another bite of his own slice. "And for the record, *I* wasn't the one whining about rehydrated noodles all day."

"I wasn't whining," Logan countered, his tone defensive but playful. "I was *stating facts*."

Adrian snorted. "Right. Facts." He leaned back in his chair, taking in the sight of Logan devouring the pizza with the kind of enthusiasm that bordered on theatrical. It was infectious. Watching Logan like this, carefree and utterly himself, brought Adrian a quiet happiness that resonated deep within him, flowing through his bones and veins, allowing that exhilarating feeling to become part of who he was.

After demolishing both pizzas—a feat neither of them thought possible after the day they'd had—they headed for the shower. The warm water was a relief, washing away the grime and aches of the day. The small space forced their movements to be close, deliberate, but neither minded. Adrian's hands roamed over Logan's body with the same ease and familiarity they'd cultivated over their journey together.

"Your turn to whine about something," Logan teased, leaning into Adrian's touch.

"I'll pass," Adrian murmured, his lips brushing Logan's ear as he wrapped his hand around both of them, stroking in rhythm. Logan moaned softly, his body melting into Adrian's as the water cascaded around them.

Their mouths found each other in a kiss that was nothing short of elemental. It was not the tentative exploration of new lovers, but something deeper, more ancient—a collision of forces that had always known how to fit together. Logan pressed in like he'd been waiting his whole life to remember the shape of Adrian's mouth. The taste of him was heat and warmth and something that tasted like home—tender, addictive, impossible to get enough of. Logan parted his lips wider, tongue plunging deeper, desperate to gather every drop of him, every trace of that flavor that made his blood surge.

His tastebuds sang with it. His whole body trembled, shivering under the weight of sensation. Adrian's lips against his were a revelation. It was as though Adrian had unlocked something within him, and Logan, usually so controlled, so wary of surrendering, found himself pliant and eager under Adrian's guidance. Every touch, every stroke was like strings drawn tight and played without pause, each movement a note in their unbroken song, leaving Logan gasping as Adrian worked them together, their bodies moving in perfect rhythm. Logan could only cling to him, lost in the storm of sensation, his voice breaking on Adrian's name as he reached his crescendo, the world tilting and then stilling around him.

Adrian followed him over the edge, his breath catching, his body trembling against Logan's. For a long moment, the water was the only sound between them, cascading over their entwined forms as though the earth itself was celebrating their union.

By the time they stumbled into bed, their skin clean but their hearts raw, exhaustion clung to them like a second skin. Logan pressed himself against Adrian's side, his damp hair sticking to Adrian's chest as he breathed him in, a heady mixture of soap and something uniquely Adrian.

"Goodnight," Logan murmured sleepily, his voice soft and content.

Adrian pressed a kiss to Logan's damp hair, his hand trailing absently along Logan's back. "Goodnight, Lo."

The morning unfolded like so many others before it: the rhythmic cadence of their feet hitting the sand as they ran side by side, the sun barely cresting the horizon. The sea beckoned them after, their boards cutting through the water as they explored untamed beaches and waves that seemed to stretch into infinity. They lost themselves in the current, their bodies moving with the tide, yet the air between them carried something new, an unspoken weight, heavy but not unwelcome.

Adrian felt it like the shift in the wind before a storm, subtle but undeniable. Logan was quiet in a way that wasn't entirely natural. His gaze seemed fixed inward, as though he were charting unknown waters within himself. Adrian wanted to ask, to reach out, but fear tethered him. He was afraid to pry, afraid to shatter whatever fragile realization Logan might be grappling with. So he let it be, biting back his questions and hoping the ocean would coax out the words that he could not.

And it did, if only for fleeting moments. When Logan caught a wave, his hesitation melted away, leaving behind someone freer, lighter. The boyish grin on his face as he stumbled from the water, drenched and breathless, was the Logan Adrian knew best. It was in one of those moments, as they stood dripping on the sand, that Logan kissed him. It was an unshackled kiss, the first breath after drowning, the sudden blaze that scatters darkness to ash. It broke open the ribs of silence and set language trembling, each heartbeat a spark against the void. Worlds bent toward its gravity, names fell away, and in the hush between pulses Adrian's heart spoke a word his mind refused to hear.

By late lunch, Logan nudged Adrian toward the shower. "You've got seaweed in your hair," he teased, his voice light but his eyes still distant. "Go clean up. I'll grab us some food."

Adrian hesitated, tempted to argue, but Logan's disarming smile dissolved his resistance. He relented, though not without a hint of mischief. "You better not take forever," he called out as he stepped into the shower. It felt wrong to shower alone now, after discovering the warmth of Logan's presence there, the way water seemed to draw them closer. The memory brought a smile to Adrian's face as he rinsed the salt and sand from his skin.

When he emerged, the scent of their favorite meal filled the small cabin. The table held familiar containers from the roadside restaurant they had discovered during one of their first days here: crispy chicken, steamed rice, and a side of vegetables because Adrian, ever disciplined, insisted on keeping them both healthy. But Logan was nowhere to be found.

Frowning, Adrian scanned the cabin, his unease growing with every empty corner. His phone buzzed faintly where he had left it, and he snatched it up to find a message from Logan:

> Went out to get some supplies and a new leash for my board. Be back later.

Adrian's brow furrowed as he read it. *Supplies? What supplies?* They didn't need anything, and if they did, it was always a task they tackled together. Something about the message felt off.

"What the hell?" Adrian muttered aloud, his voice filling the quiet cabin. The words were vague, strange, almost dismissive in their tone. He stared at the containers of food on the table, his appetite dissolving into the growing knot in his stomach.

Logan had been distant all day, but this, this felt like something more. Unease washed over Adrian like a wave breaking too hard against the shore, leaving him soaked and unsteady. The cabin, usually so warm and alive with Logan's presence, felt cold and empty.

He sat down but didn't touch the food, his eyes flicking to the door, willing Logan to appear out of thin air. The silence pressed down on him, heavy as the humid air outside, and he couldn't shake the feeling that something had shifted—something beyond his reach, like a wave slipping back into the sea before he could catch it.

Adrian leaned back in his chair, the unease settling deep into his bones. Whatever was happening, it was a storm building on the horizon, and he wasn't sure if he was ready for it. But for Logan, he would face it. For Logan, he'd weather anything.

Still with a towel slung low around his hips, Adrian felt as though the ground beneath him might give way. His chest was tight, his pulse erratic, and the humid air of the cabin felt stifling. Logan was probably freaking out; he could almost see it in the cryptic message, the curt detachment of the words. The realization crashed into him: *I knew it was too fast! I knew!*

He pressed the heels of his palms into his eyes, as if to block out the rising tide of guilt and self-recrimination. He had been reckless, he knew that now. He should have let Logan take his time, let things unfold naturally, instead of letting the heat of the moment sweep them both away. But no, he had pushed, not just Logan but himself, diving into intimacy when he should have stepped back and taken care of his own needs alone.

Adrian stared at Logan's message, still glowing on his screen, the words unread yet burned into his mind. He left it there, unanswered, his thumb hovering over the keyboard before he let the phone fall to his side. He didn't know what to say. He wasn't even sure if Logan wanted him to say anything.

Feeling like he might drown in his own thoughts, Adrian pulled on some clothes hastily, leaving his hair damp and wild as he stepped out into the pre-evening air. The humidity threaded through his clothes and hair, seeping into every pore, but the open space was a relief compared to the walls of the cabin that now felt far too small. With his phone in hand, he made his way toward the beach, drawn instinctively to the rhythm of the waves.

The sea stretched out before him, endless and vast, the kind of constant he needed right now. He dismissed a flurry of notifications from his friends—group chats buzzing with irrelevant jokes and updates that felt a world away. Instead, he fired off a quick text to his mom and dad, a simple assurance that he was fine, before hovering over Dean's name. His finger hesitated only for a second before he tapped the call button.

Dean answered after barely two rings, his usual teasing drawl already on full display. "Hello to you, b—"

"I think he's avoiding me," Adrian interrupted, his voice sharp, shaky. The words tumbled out before he could stop them, and with them came the full weight of his fears. Logan's distance over the day, the coldness in his message, the knot of unease Adrian had carried all afternoon, they were suffocating him, pressing down harder than he'd realized.

Dean, to his credit, dropped the playful tone immediately. Adrian could hear shuffling on the other end of the line, the sound of him sitting up straighter. "What happened?" he asked, his voice serious now.

"We..." Adrian faltered, glancing at the waves, as if they might give him clarity. How much could he say? How much *should* he say? "Promise me you won't tell anyone."

"You insult me," Dean replied indignantly. "I've kept worse secrets than your little love story with Princess."

Adrian's laugh was bitter, humorless. "You know how much he means to me," he said softly, the vulnerability in his voice catching even himself off guard.

"I do," Dean said, his tone gentler now. "And I'm sorry, again, for being a dick to him. Tell me what's going on."

Adrian hesitated, the words catching in his throat. Finally, he exhaled and started, his voice low and halting. "After we spent that day with you guys, we kissed. And... we've been getting closer, you know, really close. Then two days ago... we took it further... You know, sexually." He swallowed hard, his cheeks heating despite the empty beach around him. "It was the best thing I've ever experienced, Dean. I mean that. But now... now he's distant. He's been distant all day, and then he left. Made some excuse about supplies."

There was silence on the other end, save for the faint sound of Dean breathing. Adrian wiped at his eyes, pretending the dampness there was from the ocean breeze. "We've gotten so close this past month. And these past two days? They were... perfect. Like a dream. But now he's pulled away, and I don't know what to do."

"Adrian," Dean said softly, his voice grounding. "Logan's never been with a man before, right?"

Adrian sniffed, his voice barely audible. "No. Never."

"Then I'll skip my usual speech about not messing with straight dudes," Dean said dryly, though his tone carried no judgment, only care. "Listen, he's probably just trying to wrap his head around everything. You two spend, like, every waking moment together, yeah? Maybe he just needs some time to figure out his own thoughts. That doesn't mean he's pulling away for good."

Adrian clenched his jaw, his fingers digging into the sand as he lowered himself to sit by the shoreline. "It feels like he's slipping away, Dean. Like I pushed him too far, too fast."

"Stop that," Dean cut in firmly. "You didn't push him into anything. If he wasn't ready, he wouldn't have done it. He's just processing. And believe me, the way that guy looks at you? He feels it too. You've got to trust that."

Adrian let out a hollow laugh, shaking his head. "I can't believe I'm sitting here crying because he left for a few hours. I feel so dumb."

"You're not dumb, you're just human," Dean replied. "You've been pining for this guy for *months*, Ad. Now it's happening, and of course you're emotional. That's normal. And trust me, Logan's got it bad for you. You should've seen the way he looked at Itay, it was pure death glare material. If looks could kill..."

Dean's words resonated with Adrian in a way that only someone who had known him since they were six years old could manage. Dean had been there for every breakup, every high and low, every version of Adrian he'd grown into over the years. Adrian's little brother, Alon, might have been his blood, but Dean had always been his brother in spirit, a constant presence, a grounding force.

Adrian laughed through his tears, a genuine sound this time. "It's mutual. I'm crazy about him."

"I know," Dean said warmly. "And for what it's worth, I'm sorry for how I treated him when I first met him. I thought you bailed on us for a fling, but I get it now. He's important to you, and that's what matters."

Adrian nodded, though Dean couldn't see him. "You'll make it up to him?"

"Absolutely," Dean promised. "But listen to me: give him space. Let him work through his thoughts. He'll come back. And when he does, you'll know it's because he's ready, not because he felt pressured. Be patient, it's your strong suit after all."

They stayed on the phone for a while longer, Dean's voice soothing as he shared stories and jokes to distract Adrian from the gnawing ache of Logan's absence. When they finally hung up, Adrian slipped his phone into his pocket and turned his gaze to the horizon, watching the waves swell and crash. The ocean carried his anxiety away with each tide, leaving behind something quieter, more resolute.

Logan might need space, and Adrian will wait. The waves always returned to the shore, and so would Logan.

Adrian couldn't say how long he had been sitting at the water's edge, the waves curling around his feet like whispers of comfort that never quite reached his heart. The horizon stretched endlessly before him, a hazy meeting of sky and sea, but it brought him no solace. He felt raw, vulnerable, and achingly foolish, his chest tight with the weight of his emotions. He suddenly understood why Logan had been so angry a month ago when Adrian had gone off with his friends without him. Being alone in a foreign place, after growing so accustomed to each other's constant presence, was a kind of emptiness he hadn't prepared for.

And if Adrian had even thought—*even for a second*—that right now, at this very moment, Logan was with an ex, he would have been wild with it. Wild with anger, wild with fear, wild with something even deeper, something primal, unrelenting, unbearable.

The thought alone was a knife, twisting sharp and cruel in his ribs, splitting him open in a way he could barely contain. It was the kind of ache that left a man restless, pacing, his hands clenched into fists, his mind spiraling into every dark possibility.

Because he understood now.

He got it.

He didn't want to go back to the cabin. The thought of the silent, shared space made his chest ache. He felt too restless, too tangled in his own thoughts to be confined by four walls. So, he stayed where he was, staring into the distance and letting the waves lap at his toes, their rhythm soothing but not enough to quiet the storm inside him.

The weight of someone settling beside him broke through his haze, and Adrian turned, startled. Logan was there, smiling softly, though the expression quickly shifted into concern as he took in Adrian's face. Without a word, Logan dropped to his knees in front of him, his hands cupping Adrian's face with such tenderness it almost broke him. His thumbs brushed away the evidence of tears, the warmth of his touch grounding Adrian in the present.

"What happened?" Logan asked, his voice low and intent, his entire focus on Adrian's tear-streaked cheeks and the puffiness around his eyes.

"Nothing," Adrian said quickly, his voice thick as he tried to brush away the tears himself. "It's just the salt, the sand... I got sand in—"

"You're not lying to me now," Logan interrupted, his voice firm but gentle. His movements were deliberate as he shifted forward, straddling Adrian's thighs. His knees sank into the sand on either side, and before Adrian could protest, Logan's arms were wrapped around him, holding him close. His warmth, his presence, his steady breath; it was everything Adrian had been missing in those few hours apart.

Adrian let himself melt into the embrace, his arms circling Logan as he buried his face against Logan's chest. "It's stupid," he murmured, his voice muffled by Logan's skin. "Where were you?"

Logan exhaled, his hand moving in slow, soothing strokes along Adrian's back. "Just... needed a moment. I've been to the cabin and saw you weren't there. You didn't touch the food."

"Waited for you," Adrian admitted, his voice soft as one hand slid up to thread through Logan's hair. He breathed him in, the scent of salt and the faint musk of the ocean clinging to him. Logan's presence was intoxicating, calming the storm that had been raging in Adrian's chest all afternoon.

Adrian's mind repeated the same mantra: *Logan is here.*

Logan is here.

Logan is here.

Logan kan.

Logan kan.

The tension that had gripped him all day melted away, replaced by a soothing warmth that seeped into his bones. He felt utterly ridiculous for how overwhelmed he'd been by Logan's absence, but that didn't matter now. Logan was here, and the world felt right again.

"Tell me what's wrong," Logan insisted, his voice soft but resolute as he gazed into Adrian's eyes.

Adrian had never been good at hiding his emotions, and now was no exception. He let out a shaky breath, the words tumbling out of him before he could stop them. "It's nothing, it's just... you've been kind of distant today, and I got all in my head about it. I was afraid that you'd been overthinking what happened between us, that maybe you regret it. If you do, it's fine, but I wondered if I should have stopped us and waited a little longer—" He broke off, realizing how foolish he sounded. "God, I'm so dumb. You were gone for a few hours, and I got so anxious..."

Fresh tears spilled down his cheeks, though this time they carried relief as much as anything else. Logan's hands cupped his face gently, thumbs brushing away the wet streaks. One hand tucked a stray strand of Adrian's sun-kissed hair behind his ear, and Logan smiled at him, fond and unshakeable.

"If you remember," Logan teased lightly, "I was ready to leave altogether when you left me alone that first time."

Adrian let out a wet laugh, the sound bubbling up unbidden. Logan grinned, his eyes twinkling with humor. "So, all things considered, you're handling this way better than I did."

The laughter melted into something quieter, something warmer, as Logan leaned in, his lips brushing Adrian's in a kiss so gentle it felt like the ocean's caress. It deepened, Logan's teeth grazing Adrian's lower lip before their tongues met in a slow, tender rhythm. The kiss was not hurried, not frenzied, it was a reassurance, a quiet promise. When Logan pulled back, his hand slipped to the nape of Adrian's neck, his fingers threading through the long hairs there.

"I'm sorry," Logan said, his voice a mix of tenderness and regret. "I should've been more candid with you. I was a bit distracted today, but I regret *nothing*. Adrian, get this through your thick skull—" Logan tapped his hand gently, lovingly on Adrian's forehead for emphasis. "I wanted you, I still want you, and what happened between us? That was the best thing that's ever happened to me."

Adrian blinked, the words settling into his chest like sunlight breaking through the clouds. He nodded slowly, his voice steady as he said, "I'll remember this."

He let his head rest against Logan's chest, listening to the steady beat of his heart. Logan's arms circled him, holding him close, and they sat in silence for a moment, the world around them reduced to the sound of the waves and their breathing.

"Don't you want to ask me where I've been?" Logan said after a while, breaking the quiet.

Adrian shook his head. "No. If you needed time alone, I understand. You can go whenever you need to, it's totally fine."

Logan laughed, the sound rumbling in his chest, and suddenly he leaned forward, reaching behind Adrian to grab something he had dropped in the sand earlier. Adrian sat up, his brow furrowed in confusion. "What—?"

Logan straightened, holding something in triumph: a guitar, brand new, its wood glowing faintly in the soft evening light. "Happy birthday, Adrian!" Logan announced, his grin wide and unrestrained.

Adrian's mouth fell open as he stared at the guitar, utterly dumbfounded. "What? Logan—" he stammered, his words tripping over themselves.

Logan shifted nervously, the guitar resting awkwardly in his lap as he watched Adrian's face for any hint of a reaction. The silence was unbearable, stretching out between them like the ocean at low tide.

"I saw your passport the other night," Logan began, his voice quick and uncertain, "when I was looking for the power bank, remember? And I saw the date. I *cannot* believe you weren't going to tell me it's your birthday." His words came in a rush, as if filling the void would ease his nerves. "So, I wracked my brain trying to figure out what to get you. When we were trekking back yesterday, the idea hit me. I called a music shop last night after you fell asleep and started asking questions. Believe me, it was not easy."

Adrian's eyes softened, but he still didn't speak, letting Logan continue.

Logan scooted back slightly, positioning the guitar between them, and pointed to an engraving at the bottom of the instrument. "Look," he said, his voice quieter now, more hesitant.

Adrian leaned forward, his breath catching as he read the words etched into the wood:

To my life-saver.

Logan smiled sheepishly. "It was a pain in the ass to find a place that engraves, but I asked around, Googled a bunch, and eventually found someone. Then there was the issue of you being left-handed. I wasn't sure if you used a left-handed guitar or had adapted to a regular one. But I couldn't ask you outright, because that would've ruined the surprise."

Adrian's lips parted, but no sound came out. His gaze flickered between Logan and the guitar, his eyes glistening.

"So," Logan continued, clearly trying to fill the silence, "I went to Facebook and found some pictures and a video of you with a guitar. The salesperson and I analyzed them like we were some detectives, which wasn't easy since his English wasn't the best, and we eventually figured out that you play upside down on a regular guitar. So, I got this one, and I got it engraved."

Logan hesitated, watching Adrian's expression closely. "Shit. Have I done something wrong? You don't want it? Please don't tell me you play a left-handed guitar! Oh God, Adrian, you *really* need to say something right now!"

But Adrian didn't say a word. Instead, he carefully took the guitar from Logan's hands, laying it gently on the sand beside them. Then, with a sudden surge of motion, he pushed Logan back against the sand, pressing him down with a kiss that spoke every word he couldn't yet say. The wind dried Adrian's tears as they fell, leaving glistening tracks on Logan's cheeks where their faces brushed.

The kiss deepened, Adrian pouring every ounce of gratitude, relief, and affection into it. When they finally broke apart, breathless, Adrian buried his face in the crook of Logan's neck, his tears mingling with the salty air.

"Thank you," he said at last, his voice thick with feeling. He pulled back just enough to see Logan's face, his own expression reverent, almost fragile. In Adrian's eyes flickered a tenderness that hadn't needed a name to be real, something that grew sharper, stronger, every time they drew close; something that lived in the space between words, waiting. "I spent all this time afraid you had second thoughts, and instead you were out getting me the most thoughtful gift I've ever received. I... I don't even have the words."

"Did I get it right? You play a right-handed guitar and flip it?" Logan asked, his voice laced with a rare uncertainty. He shifted his weight, hoping—*really hoping*—he hadn't screwed this up. He wanted this moment to be perfect.

Adrian blinked, his gaze dropping to Logan's lips. For a moment, he said nothing. Then, a slow smile spread across his face, something gentle, something that made Logan's stomach flip.

"Yeah," Adrian murmured, nodding. "You got it right."

Logan exhaled, tension melting from his shoulders.

Adrian ran his fingers over Logan's lips, soft and plump, his touch almost reverent. "Learned to play on some old guitar a neighbor lent me," he said, voice quiet, thoughtful. "Didn't know there was such a thing as a left-handed guitar until I was, like, eighteen. By then, I was already too used to playing this way." He smirked, shrugging. "Guess I never really did things the right way."

Adrian traced the line of Logan's jaw with his fingers, his touch tender. "You didn't have to get me anything, really. Having you here with me is the best gift I could ever ask for. Sleeping beside you, waking up next to you, kissing you, touching you—that's more than I ever dared to wish for in my entire life." He paused, his voice trembling with sincerity. "But I love it. I love this guitar, Logan. Thank you."

Logan's lips parted in response, but before he could speak, Adrian leaned in again, brushing their noses together in a playful, intimate gesture. The guitar rested beside them, forgotten for now, as the waves crashed tenderly in the background

Logan sighed, an easy smile tugging at his lips as he kissed Adrian lightly, his voice teasing but laced with sincerity. "You really can't go around saying things like that," he murmured, pressing his forehead against Adrian's for a brief moment before pulling back. "Besides, you said you didn't bring your guitar because you didn't want to travel with it. So, good thing you've got another man with you, I can share the load."

Adrian smirked, eyes glinting with mischief as he leaned back, lifting himself off Logan and shifting onto his knees. For a fleeting second, Logan felt the absence of his warmth, the cool air rushing in where Adrian's body had been pressed against his. But then, Adrian turned his gaze outward, looking past the edges of their world, out toward the horizon.

The sunset caught him, casting him in gold, in fire, in the kind of light that made men believe in things they shouldn't. His features softened in the glow, shadows dancing along his jawline, the light tracing over the curve of his shoulders, the slope of his back.

And then, without a word, he reached for the guitar.

Logan watched as Adrian adjusted, shifting his weight, cradling the instrument against his body like it was another limb, something natural, something instinctual. His fingers found the tuning pegs, twisting them with absentminded precision, listening for the right pitch, for the right tension.

"I want to play you something," Adrian said, his voice light, casual, like this wasn't everything.

His fingers ghosted over the strings, testing them, finding their rhythm.

"You mind?" he added, but there was something in his voice, something unspoken. Like he already knew Logan wouldn't say no. Like he already knew that, in this moment, Logan would take anything Adrian was willing to give.

"I was counting on it, actually," Logan replied, settling himself cross-legged in front of Adrian. The last rays of the setting sun illuminated him, casting a warm glow over his face that made Adrian's chest ache.

Adrian strummed a few chords, testing the strings, before the unmistakable melody of *Everything* by Lifehouse began to spill from the guitar. Logan froze, his breath hitching as recognition bloomed. It was his favorite song—a piece of music he thought no one knew he cherished as much as he did. And then Adrian started singing.

His voice, soft and slightly raspy, carried the lyrics with a clarity that sent a shiver through Logan's entire body. Adrian's eyes never left his, grounding him in a way that felt both overwhelming and comforting. As Adrian played, Logan was transfixed—by the fluidity of his fingers on the strings, by the way his voice carried every note with raw passion, and by the man himself, sitting there like he belonged to this moment and this moment alone.

When Adrian's voice swelled for the chorus, rising in strength and emotion, something deep within Logan cracked open. Adrian wasn't just playing or singing; he was baring his soul, pouring everything he had into the music. The words struck Logan with a force he hadn't expected, echoing truths he hadn't allowed himself to name.

The world around them blurred, fading to nothing as Adrian's silvery voice wrapped around Logan's heart, squeezing tight. He didn't notice the small crowd that had gathered, drawn by the melody floating over the beach. He didn't care. His focus was entirely on Adrian—his lips, his hands, his voice, the raw emotion he was laying bare with every note.

By the time Adrian reached the final chorus, singing the words with a kind of intensity that sent shivers racing down Logan's spine, Logan's eyes were glassy with unshed tears. He didn't think it was possible for anyone to outshine the original version of the song, but Adrian had. And the realization that Adrian had done this for him—the learning, the singing, the playing—made something deep inside Logan ache with gratitude and longing.

Adrian finished, his voice lingering in the air like the fading rays of the sun. The small crowd clapped, their scattered cheers punctuating the quiet, but Adrian's attention was on Logan. His gaze was steady, searching, as though Logan's reaction was the only one that mattered.

Logan didn't speak right away, his throat too tight with emotion. Adrian tilted his head, a faint crease forming between his brows as he said, "The original's with an electric guitar, not acoustic—"

Logan shook his head, cutting him off. "It was amazing," he whispered, his voice unsteady but full of conviction. "Absolutely amazing. I didn't think you'd know the song. It's old and... I just didn't think you'd know how to play it."

Adrian's lips quirked into a smile, his voice soft but amused. "I may have looked up the chords online," he admitted. "With how much you love that song, and how often you listen to it, I figured it'd be good to know it."

Logan didn't even think—he surged forward, wrapping his arms around Adrian, pulling him close despite the guitar pressing awkwardly between them. "You're aware I'm going to have you play it nonstop now, right?" he murmured against Adrian's ear, a teasing lilt to his voice.

Adrian chuckled, his hands coming up to stroke Logan's back. "I should have seen it coming," he said lightly, though Logan knew he'd play until his fingers bled just to see Logan smile again like he did now. "Hey, by the way, when's your birthday?" Adrian asked, suddenly realizing he did not know that.

"November 12th," Logan answered, stretching his arms behind his head, his voice easy, unguarded.

Adrian hummed, rolling the date over in his mind. It was just a number, just a day, just another thing to tuck away with all the other little details about Logan that he was quietly collecting, like seashells along the shore.

And yet—

Here, on this beautiful beach in the Philippines, Adrian had no way of knowing what that date would come to mean.

Had no way of knowing what November 12th would bring.

Had no way of knowing that it would unravel everything.

That it would wreck him.

That it would carve itself into his bones as the day his world fell apart.

That, for years to come, he would look back at this date and wonder—if things could have been different.

But for now, there was only this—the quiet rhythm of the waves, the heat of Logan's sun-kissed skin beside him, the illusion of forever stretching out before them, endless and untouchable.

Adrian nodded, then stood, brushing the sand from his shorts and offering Logan a hand to help him up. "Let's go back inside," he suggested, his voice dipping lower. "I'm dying to show you how much I appreciate my gift."

Logan's eyes darkened, his gaze locking onto Adrian's with an intensity that made his cock grow hard in his pants. He could already feel the night stretching before them, filled with music, laughter, and sweat drenched bodies as they rode their pleasure, and moments that would linger like the melody of the song Adrian had just played.

Adrian will play to him all night long, but... after.

Chapter 7
Almost Is Never Enough

There is an ache inside me, deep and boundless, like the hush before a storm, like the tide that pulls and pulls but never returns what it has taken. Something is missing. A piece of me is lost in the vastness, in the space where you used to be. I feel it in the hollow of my ribs, in the silence between heartbeats, in the way my hands reach for something they will never hold again.

I have spent a lifetime at the water's edge—though perhaps it has only been months, or days, or mere moments stretched thin beneath the weight of remembering. The ocean knows my name now. The wind hums lullabies through the bones of the cliffs, and the waves, tireless and unyielding, lap at the shore as if trying to soothe something raw inside me.

I sit here, watching the horizon blur into nothing, and I let myself rewind. Again and again. You, turning toward me in golden light. You, laughing like it was something sacred. You, eyes full of words you never said. I pick apart each glance, each breath, as if I could find some hidden meaning, some secret thread that might have changed the ending. But there is no changing it. The past is a tide that does not return.

And still, beneath the sorrow, beneath the wreckage of what was and what had been and what could have been, I find something else—something almost like gratitude. Because for a brief and beautiful moment, I was yours.

For a breath in time, I lived in the warmth of your orbit, and that is more than most ever get.

But even the brightest stars burn out. Even the strongest waves must break. I am tired now, in a way that sleep cannot cure, in a way that is deeper than the body. I have been carrying the weight of something too heavy, something that lingers in my blood and in my bones, something I no longer wish to fight. It is not fear, this surrender—it is relief. It is the quiet acceptance of an ending long written in the spaces between words.

I do not want the struggle, the slow unraveling. I have seen it before. I have seen it hollow out those who fought with everything they had, only to lose anyway. I will not let that be my story. I will not let it strip me down, steal from me piece by piece.

I will go on my own terms, like the last ember fading into the night. I will slip into the wind, into the water, into the hush of things left unspoken.

And maybe, in the place where endings fold into beginnings, where time is soft and love is not something to be lost—maybe there, I will find you again.

June 27, 2020—Seattle, Washington—One Year and Nine Months Later

THE HAMMERING IN LOGAN's head was relentless, a rhythmic pounding that felt like someone was driving nails into his skull. He forced his eyelids open, squinting against the dim light filtering through a sheer curtain covering a large window. The room was unfamiliar, a stranger's world of mismatched colors and thrift-store charm.

His eyes drifted to the floor, an ugly shade of brown that clashed with a round, threadbare carpet. Nothing about this place jogged his memory. He jolted upright, his heart racing, only to cry out as the pain in his head intensified, shards of glass stabbing behind his eyes.

Where the hell am I?

Logan scanned the room, the layout slowly coming into focus. It was a loft apartment, open and spacious, with a small kitchen and a cozy living room visible from the bed. The furniture didn't match, but the space had a certain warmth, an odd, homey charm. Tangled white-and-blue sheets clung to him, and the athletic pants and T-shirt he wore weren't his.

Oh fuck.

The realization hit him like a wave crashing onshore: these weren't his clothes, nor the ones he'd been wearing last night. And he couldn't remember anything past a blur of alcohol and pain. He tried to piece it together, the pounding in his head growing louder with every failed attempt. He pushed harder, trying to claw his way back to the moments before the oblivion, and then—

Adrian.

The name sliced through the fog. The video. The song. Adrian, sitting under the dim lights of an open bar, his voice trembling with raw emotion as he sang about Logan. About *them*. About love and heartbreak and longing. Adrian's tears, the way his voice cracked with every note, the way his words laid Logan bare. It was too much to process, and last night, the only way Logan had known how to deal with it was to drink. And drink. And drink.

Now, the memory of Adrian's face in the video made the ever-present ache in Logan's chest burn with fresh intensity. His breath caught, the weight of everything—the lies, the choices, the years—pressing down on him until he thought he might suffocate. He wanted to curl into himself, to disappear into nothingness. And yet, a small, desperate part of him wanted to find Adrian and hold him. Just once.

"You finally awake," a voice cut through the haze, casual and amused. "Morning, sunshine."

Logan turned toward the voice and saw Zack stepping out of what must have been the bathroom, a small black towel slung low on his hips. Water droplets clung to his chest and shoulders, catching the light as he moved with an effortless confidence.

"Zack?" Logan croaked, his throat dry and raw. "Where am I?"

"My place," Zack replied easily, crossing to a nearby closet. He began rummaging through it for clothes, as if this were the most natural thing in the world.

Logan's head throbbed with every beat of his heart, and Zack's words only made the situation more surreal. He felt trapped in a nightmare he couldn't wake from, a concoction of shame, regret, and the bitter aftertaste of too much whiskey.

"What am I doing at your place? And why am I wearing different clothes?" Logan snapped, his voice laced with anger as he leapt to his feet, swaying slightly as dizziness washed over him.

"Take it easy, big boy," Zack said, pulling a plain T-shirt over his head.

"Would you *tell* me already what the fuck I'm doing here, and why?" Logan barked, his tone sharpening as he gestured to the unfamiliar surroundings.

Zack's expression darkened, and his own irritation bubbled to the surface. "Hey! Relax!" he shouted back, his voice cutting through Logan's anger. "Believe me, I *wanted* to send you home last night, but you were drunk out of your mind and *clingy* as hell. You cried like a baby when I tried to put you in a cab and begged me not to send you back. You kept saying you couldn't handle it anymore."

Zack's voice softened, a flicker of guilt crossing his face as he remembered. "You were a mess, Logan. You wouldn't stop crying. And then you started calling for someone—Adrian, I think? You kept saying you needed him, that he'd make everything better."

Logan froze, his face flushing with equal parts humiliation and pain. Adrian. Always Adrian. The name was a ghost in the air, a reminder of everything he'd buried under layers of lies and self-denial.

Zack continued, his tone less biting now. "I couldn't just send you home like that. You looked so miserable, man. Like, not just the usual 'drown your sorrows in whiskey' kind of miserable. It was another level."

Logan dropped back onto the bed, burying his face in his hands. "I made a complete fool of myself," he muttered, the words muffled by his palms.

Zack perched on the other end of the bed, shrugging with a wry smirk. "Not the first time someone's made a fool of themselves in front of me.

But no, we didn't... do anything," he said, his voice dripping with sarcasm. "As much as you're a catch," he added, rolling his eyes, "I like my partners to be a bit more... responsive. And, you know, not covered in puke."

Logan groaned, mortified. "I threw up?"

"All over yourself. And my floor," Zack confirmed, his tone tinged with irritation. "So, yeah, I showered you and put clean clothes on you. You're welcome, by the way."

"You showered me?" Logan repeated, his voice cracking as he ran a hand through his hair.

"Yeah, well, I wasn't letting my sheets get wrecked by your fancy-suit-puke combo. Speaking of which, I threw the suit away. It reeked."

Logan stood again, swaying slightly as the pounding in his head reached a crescendo. "Where's my stuff?" he asked, scanning the room. "My phone, wallet, keys?"

Zack gestured toward the kitchen. "On the counter."

Logan found his way to the kitchen, his steps unsteady. His phone, wallet, and keys were exactly where Zack said they'd be, and his eyes darted around for his shoes.

"Did you toss my shoes, too?" Logan asked, his voice quieter now.

"No. They're by the door," Zack replied from the sofa, where he flopped down with a pillow and blanket. Logan realized then that Zack had given up his bed for him and taken the couch instead. The pang of guilt in his chest deepened.

Scrolling through his phone, Logan's stomach sank as he saw dozens of missed calls and messages from Sandy. He swore under his breath, gripping the edge of the counter to steady himself.

"Zack—" he started, turning to face him.

But Zack waved a dismissive hand without looking up. "Just leave, Logan. You ungrateful son of a bitch."

Logan couldn't help the small smile that tugged at his lips. "I'll bring the clothes back tomorrow," he said as he headed toward the door.

He paused, realizing something, and turned back. "Zack, my underwear—?"

"Just keep the damn clothes and *leave*!" Zack barked, throwing a pillow in Logan's general direction.

Logan chuckled under his breath, shaking his head as he slipped on his shoes. As he stepped out into the blinding light of the day, the weight of last night—and everything it meant—settled heavily on his shoulders. He went straight to his car, knowing that he maybe should not be driving now, but not really caring. Anyway, it seemed that he vomited the majority of the alcohol he had consumed.

Logan gripped the steering wheel tightly, his knuckles pale against the worn leather as he navigated the quiet streets. Zack's words echoed in his mind, fragments of last night piecing together. He felt the weight of them pressing down on his chest, but he drove anyway, the hum of the engine filling the silence. The morning sun cast long shadows, the light too sharp for the heaviness clinging to him.

When he pulled into the driveway, Sandy burst out of the house like a storm, her face streaked with tears. She reached him before he could fully step out of the car, throwing her arms around him in a crushing embrace. He froze for a moment, caught off guard by the wetness of her tears soaking into the borrowed shirt.

"Oh, God, Logan!" she cried, her voice breaking. "I was so worried! I called you all night! Are you—are you okay?" She pulled back just enough to cup his face in her hands, her eyes wide and searching. "I didn't know what to do. I thought... I was so scared something terrible had happened. I wanted to call the police or your dad—"

Logan stiffened, his jaw tightening. "Did you call my dad?" he snapped, his voice sharper than he intended.

Sandy blinked, her lips parting in shock. "Wha—?"

"Sandy, did you call my dad?" he demanded, his tone rising. "You can't do that. I'm not a teenager. I have responsibilities. I don't need him meddling—"

"I didn't!" she interrupted, her voice cracking. "I didn't call anyone!"

The words hung between them for a moment before Logan exhaled slowly, his shoulders slumping. "I'm sorry," he muttered, his voice quieter now. "I'm sorry, I shouldn't have talked to you like that." He pulled her back into a hug, his movements stiff and automatic. "I'm fine. I just slept at a friend's place."

"A friend?" she asked, her voice uncertain.

"Yeah," Logan said, stepping back and forcing a small smile. "I had some drinks, didn't feel great, so I crashed on his couch."

Sandy's eyes brimmed with fresh tears, her lips trembling as she tried to speak. "Logan—"

"Everything's fine," he cut in quickly, his words clipped. "I'm fine, Sandy. Sorry for scaring you. I'm just late for work." Without waiting for her response, he turned and jogged into the house.

Inside, Logan moved on autopilot, his body going through the motions even as his mind felt detached. He stripped off Zack's borrowed clothes, tossing them into a reusable cotton bag, and stepped into the shower. The water was too hot, scalding his skin, but he didn't adjust it. He scrubbed himself clean, as though he could wash away the heaviness that clung to him, but it lingered, persistent and immovable.

He donned one of his tailored suits, which had somehow become too loose; its crisp lines and polished appearance served as a perfect façade for the chaos hidden underneath. He tied his tie with precision, glanced at his reflection in the mirror, and avoided his own eyes. Picking up the bag of Zack's clothes, he left the house, calling out a perfunctory "goodbye" to Sandy as he went.

The world outside moved on, indifferent and unyielding. Logan slipped into the current of his life, playing along with a script he had written for himself long ago, one where every line felt hollow and every scene dragged endlessly. As he pulled out of the driveway, the ache in his chest remained, a quiet companion he didn't know how to part with.

It was one of the busiest days Logan had endured in weeks. His head swam with every step, the pounding hangover from the night before a persistent reminder of his own self-destruction. He had downed so many pills throughout the day that he wondered if it was only a matter of time before his body gave out altogether.

Ada Mae, his efficient and ever-cheerful personal assistant, stepped into his office with her tablet in hand, rattling off updates and schedules. Her voice was light, professional, as though she couldn't see the exhaustion etched into Logan's face. She reminded him of upcoming meetings and the flights he'd need to catch next month for a series of business trips with his father across the States.

"Great. Could you email me the flights details?" Logan asked absently, his fingers rubbing his temple.

"Already done, Mr. Vaughn," she replied with a smile.

"You're the best, and again, just call me Logan," he muttered, standing and grabbing his phone. "Oh, can you send some flowers to Sandy? And book her a vacation, something relaxing."

"Sure. Where this time, Mr. Vaughn?" Ada Mae asked, typing quickly into her tablet.

"Where would you want to go?" Logan asked, not really thinking.

"Hawaii," she said dreamily, and Logan paled visibly.

"No. No Hawaii," he said too quickly, the words tumbling out before he could stop them. "Book something in California. Some fancy hotel. Make it for three or four people, she'll probably want to bring friends."

Ada Mae hesitated, glancing at him with a mix of pity and professionalism. "She was in California just a few months ago for her birthday," she reminded him.

Logan faltered for a moment, the weight of his hollow gestures pressing down on him. "Right," he said, sighing. "You know what? Just book whatever you think she'd like. A week, maybe more."

Ada Mae nodded, her sympathetic gaze lingering for just a second longer than Logan could stand before she left. By four o'clock, she'd informed him the flowers had been sent and asked if she could leave early. Logan waved her off with a reminder to enjoy her evening and made a mental note to show his appreciation for her loyalty more often, though he knew he probably wouldn't.

The day bled on, its minutes a blur of meetings and emails. Logan hadn't eaten breakfast or lunch, but he forced himself to prepare for a late lunch—or early dinner, depending on how you looked at it—with one of his clients. He hated these dinners, despised the charade of pleasantries and small talk. But at least the man he was meeting was neat, punctual, and efficient. The deal would roll smoothly, and Logan could get through it all with minimal effort.

Sitting in one of the city's most exclusive restaurants, Logan played his role to perfection. He was the heir to Vaughn Global Lines, expected to expand the empire his father had built, to swallow smaller firms and carve new routes across the seas. Tonight was just another piece of that inheritance. He discussed numbers, bargained, analyzed every angle with a practiced ease that would have impressed anyone watching. And yet, with every word he spoke, he felt the acid in his chest growing, the sensation of suffocation creeping closer. He smiled, nodded, and signed off on plans as though his life weren't crumbling with every breath he took.

When the deal was closed, the client shook his hand, finished his meal, and hurried off to catch a flight. Logan texted the details to Ada Mae, instructing her to contact the firm's legal team to draft the contracts. As he stepped out into the cool evening air, the noise of the city hit him—cars honking, people laughing, the hum of a world moving on without him.

Logan's fingers grazed the bracelet on his wrist—the one Adrian had given him so long ago, when life had felt expansive and untamed. It was Adrian's mother's bracelet, a sacred piece of her memory. Logan had always known its weight, not just the physical coolness of the charm against his skin, but the gravity of what it meant to Adrian. It had been one of the few things Adrian carried from his mother, who had passed when he was just a boy. And yet, Logan kept it.

A hypocrite, he thought. *Ungrateful*. He'd turned over the idea in his mind a hundred times—of reaching out to Adrian, offering to return it, asking if he wanted it back. Maybe Adrian had tried to contact him. Maybe he had. Logan wouldn't know; he'd blocked the number, slammed the door so decisively shut on that part of his life that even the brilliance of Adrian's smile couldn't force its way through the smallest imagined fracture. And still, he wore the bracelet like a thief carrying a stolen relic, an unbearable reminder of the life he had destroyed with his own hands.

He stopped abruptly on the sidewalk, his breath hitching, his eyes squeezing shut as though the sheer force of his will could keep the tears at bay. The texture of the bracelet against his wrist burned, an ache not meant for anyone's eyes but left for his wounded soul to carry. It was a quiet, concealed pain, one he had lived with for so long that it almost felt natural. But here, on this unfamiliar street, with people moving around him in shapes he barely registered and voices fading into a low murmur, he felt it sharper than ever. It was the pain of memories too beautiful and too clear to shut out, the ache of longing that refused to die. And yes, it was just a bracelet. But it was here. He could peel it off, god knew how much he yearned for it some moments, he could peel it off and end the torment, but he stayed tethered to it because he refused to let go of the last proof that Adrian had ever been his.

Run. The voice in his head was a whisper, a pulse, an echo of something both familiar and foreign. *Run. Disappear. Leave everything behind.*

It was the same voice that had driven him to the airport the day after graduation, when the world had felt too tight, too scripted, too certain. A time that now felt like it belonged to someone else, some other version of him that had never really learned how to stay.

It was the same voice that had carried him across the sky, over restless oceans, and straight into the arms of a man who smelled like salt and sun and something dangerously close to home.

It was the same voice that had led him to Adrian.

So maybe—just maybe—it hadn't been wrong after all.

He opened his eyes, sharp and unseeing, and forced himself to move forward, his steps mechanical. Running wouldn't save him. He knew that now. It hadn't saved him when he left Adrian; it hadn't saved him when he married Sandy; it wouldn't save him now. But still, he walked, not toward anything, just away.

Sliding into the smooth leather of his black Mercedes, he tossed his phone onto the passenger seat with a force that betrayed his calm façade. He couldn't let himself hear Adrian's voice again, not after last night. But God, he *wanted* to. He wanted to replay the song, to soak in the ache of Adrian's words, to let himself crumble under the weight of his longing.

Somehow, he ended up at the beach. He had no memory of the drive—no recollection of streets or turns or lights. One moment, he was in his car; the next, he was standing in the sand, the ocean sprawling before him, dark and infinite. The air was heavy with salt and possibility, but Logan's mind was a storm, raging with memories he couldn't escape.

Adrian's hand in his, pulling him to the cool sand. Adrian's lips, warm and urgent, pressing against his with a fervor that felt like coming home. *"You're the best gift of all,"* Adrian had whispered, his voice filled with unguarded sincerity. Logan could still feel the echo of those words in his bones.

No.

No.

NO!

The thoughts screamed through his mind, threatening to tear him apart. Last night had been the final straw. Seeing Adrian's face, hearing his voice—it had cracked Logan open, and now he was bleeding out. He couldn't pull himself together, couldn't piece himself back into the man the world needed him to be. He wasn't strong enough for that.

So, instead, he wandered into a waterfront bar and took a secluded table at the edge, where he could see the ocean but still feel invisible. His favorite bar, the one Zack tended, was off-limits now. He couldn't face the aftermath of his humiliation, couldn't stomach the pity he'd see in Zack's eyes.

He ordered a beer, light, easy, something that wouldn't spiral him further down after last night. The waiter eyed him curiously, probably wondering what a man in a tailored suit was doing in a beach bar on a cool evening alone. Logan ignored the look and stared out at the water. It was dark now, the waves barely visible under the faint glow of the moon.

But Logan didn't see the waves. In his mind, he was back in the Philippines—or maybe it was Australia. He couldn't tell anymore. It didn't matter. All he could see was Adrian, sitting on the sand with a guitar in his lap, his fingers moving with practiced ease, his voice filling the night with something so raw and beautiful it made Logan's chest ache.

Logan leaned back in his chair, letting his head fall against the wood. His eyes fluttered shut, and Adrian was there again, smiling at him with that boyish grin that always seemed to melt the world away. He was laughing, his eyes alight with joy, his voice carrying through Logan's mind like a melody that refused to fade. Other memories surfaced—Adrian in the ocean, his body alive with the rhythm of the waves, the unbridled freedom of surfing mirrored in his movements.

Logan's lips parted in a silent gasp as the memories tightened around him. He was drowning in them, and for once, he didn't fight it. He let the weight pull him under, let the tide carry him to a place where Adrian still existed, where he could still feel his warmth, hear his voice, and see the spark in his eyes.

Because in the dark reality of his present, Adrian was all he had left. Even if it was only in his mind.

Logan's body had not felt the ocean's embrace since that last time with Adrian. The waves he once trusted to cleanse his soul now seemed like an unspoken accusation, a reminder of what he had abandoned. He missed it, missed the salt and the rhythm, but more than that, he missed Adrian, missed the way they had been part of the sea together, wild and unbreakable. Now the shore felt like a boundary he couldn't cross, a wall between what was and what would never be again.

A single tear traced its way down Logan's cheek, catching the dim light, a shard of broken glass dancing in his heartbreak, echoing the love he bore for Adrian and the sorrow he could not set down. The moisture marked a fleeting path along his skin, drawn from the eyes that had once held Adrian as reality, not wish. He didn't wipe it away. He let it fall, unacknowledged, as he thanked the waiter who placed a beer in front of him. His hands trembled slightly as he pulled out his phone. He shouldn't do this. He wasn't strong enough to hear the song again, but the pull was irresistible.

He wanted—no, *needed*—to hear Adrian's voice more than he needed air in his lungs.

He scrolled through his YouTube history, his chest tightening when he saw the thumbnail: Adrian, illuminated by dim bar lights, the familiar guitar cradled in his hands. Logan's thumb hovered over the screen, his breath catching as he saw the title, the name of that song. *Lifesaver.* Of course, that's what Adrian had called it. How could it have been anything else?

He pressed play, and the first notes ignited him from the inside out, his heart a furnace, molten and uncontainable, dissolving within his chest as he fought to draw breath into lungs that no longer knew how to breathe air unshared with Adrian. Adrian's voice followed, trembling and raw, filling every hollow space, fueling the roaring flames inside Logan, giving name to his pain and intensifying it. It wasn't just music; it was a haunting, a calling, a tether to a world Logan had abandoned but could never escape. Adrian's voice was like the sea itself, vast and unforgiving, yet capable of holding him in its depths.

As the camera panned over Adrian, Logan saw the guitar, and his breath caught in his throat. It was *that* guitar—the one Logan had given him in the Philippines. The sight of it was a blow he hadn't expected. He let out a laugh, but it was jagged and bitter, carrying more agony than joy. That guitar was a piece of wood, an afterthought, a frantic decision made on a whim. Yet here it was, still in Adrian's hands, still carrying their story in its strings.

The engraving was still there: *To my lifesaver.* He remembered the hours spent trekking through unfamiliar streets, the frantic search for a shop that could carve those words before the night ended. He hadn't even known if it was a good guitar, but Adrian had loved it. He had played for hours, his fingers coaxing life from the strings, his voice weaving melodies that became the soundtrack to their love.

Logan smiled through his tears, his heart twisting painfully. That guitar had been a gift, but Adrian had turned it into something sacred. It was the same instrument Adrian now used to pour his heartbreak into the world. And Logan, sitting alone in a beach bar with a beer and a phone pressed to his ear, was the reason for that heartbreak.

Adrian's voice climbed as the chorus swelled: "I draw each breath only to offer it to you, be my lifesaver, and I'll be yours…"

The words cut deep, carving through Logan's defenses like a tide reclaiming the shore. He closed his eyes, letting the sound surround him, letting the fire consume him. Adrian's voice was everywhere—in the air, in his blood, in the ache that lived in his chest. Logan wanted to reach through the screen, to touch him, to hold him, to tell him all the things he hadn't said.

The song ended, and Logan pressed play again. And again. Each repetition was a fresh wound, but he couldn't stop. It wasn't just a song—it was a lifeline, a reminder of everything he had lost and everything he still carried.

The beer sat untouched on the table. Logan didn't notice. His eyes were fixed on the ocean, but he didn't see the waves. In his mind, he was somewhere else: Adrian sitting on a sandy shore, laughing, playing foolish games just to make Logan smile. Adrian's voice wasn't just music; it was an invocation, pulling Logan back to a time when the world had made sense.

He whispered the lyrics under his breath, his voice trembling with emotion: "When you left, you took the best of me with you, was it hard for you to rise and leave?"

"Adrian," Logan whispered into the emptiness, his voice cracking. "You don't understand. Leaving was hard, but living without you? That's harder. That's impossible."

He pressed play once more, the melody cascading over him, enveloping him completely, transforming him into something other than himself. He was a man unraveling, a soul fragmented by the notes of the one who had ever stitched him together. And he would listen endlessly, for it was the sole pathway to sensing Adrian's essence, even if it shattered him from within.

The phone trembled in his hands as he whispered the final lines with Adrian, his voice a prayer, a confession, a plea: *"I'll be your lifesaver, even if you don't wish to be mine..."*

Logan lowered the phone, his heart heavy as the weight of the words settled over him. The ocean stretched out before him, dark and endless, a mirror of his own despair. He thought of Adrian, somewhere out there, playing that guitar, singing that song, carrying a pain that matched his own.

And for the first time in so long, Logan let himself weep openly, the tears falling like rain into the sea of his grief.

Logan's mind wandered back to his wedding day, a day shrouded in the dull haze of regret and misplaced duty. He could still see Adrian, standing amidst the crowd, a storm of emotion in his eyes as he tried to reach Logan. Adrian's voice had been raw, pleading, as he begged Logan to remember—to remember their love, their shared moments, the way they had held each other as though the world couldn't touch them.

And then Adrian had kissed him. God, that kiss, it had been everything. Adrian's lips tasted like his sweetest memories, soft and firm, a claim and a plea all at once. Logan had felt owned in that moment, utterly undone, as Adrian reminded him of what it meant to be kissed senseless, to be wanted, to be *alive*. That kiss had lingered in Logan's soul long after the ceremony ended, haunting him with its certainty, its truth.

Now, sitting in the dim glow of the bar, Logan's chest tightened with a desperation he couldn't contain. He pulled out his phone, his fingers trembling as he opened the Facebook app. He didn't know what he was looking for; he only knew he needed to see Adrian, to find a glimpse of him, a digital echo of the man who had once been his entire world.

His breath caught with the need to search for that small glowing green dot, to see it next to Adrian's name. It was foolish, meaningless, and yet—if he saw it, it would mean Adrian was alive, breathing, existing in the same moment, even if an ocean stretched between them. Even if Logan's night sky was silvered by the moon while Adrian's world burned golden beneath the sun.

Somewhere, they were both looking at the sky. Somewhere, they were both breathing the same air. Somewhere, they existed in the same gravity.

Maybe Adrian was sitting by the water, watching the horizon, just as Logan was now. Maybe, against all reason, they were both whispering the same silent prayer.

He went to the search bar, but strangely, Adrian's name, the first result for so long, was no longer there. Uneasy, he typed the first three letters of Adrian's name, expecting the app to do the rest. It should have been effortless; his fingers had traced this same path a thousand times before, his restless mind returning to it like a tide pulled to shore.

After all, he had spent night after night searching, staring at the screen, hoping for some trace of him. By this point, the algorithm was the only one that truly knew Logan.

But tonight, for the first time, his name didn't appear.

Nothing. Panic bubbled in his chest as he typed Adrian's full name, his breath hitching. Still, nothing. *What?* He typed it again, his heart hammering as he pressed the search button. No results.

Had Adrian blocked him?

The thought hit Logan like a punch to the gut, and the panic spilled over, rising like a tidal wave. His chest ached with a suffocating pressure, and he struggled to breathe. He knew—he *knew*—he had no right to feel this way. He had been the one to block Adrian's number, to shut him out, to walk away. But the thought of Adrian severing the last tenuous thread between them was unbearable.

Without thinking, Logan stood abruptly, his chair scraping against the floor. He moved to the closest table, where a couple was sharing a quiet dinner, their conversation interrupted by his looming presence. "Excuse me," Logan said, his voice unsteady, barely more than a whisper. "I'm so sorry to interrupt, but could I borrow one of your phones? Just for a second. Mine's dead."

The man hesitated but eventually handed over his phone, unlocking it with a swipe. Logan's hands shook as he opened the Facebook app, his fingers fumbling to type Adrian's full name into the search bar. He pressed the search button, holding his breath, but the result was the same. Nothing. No account. No trace. Adrian was gone.

He stared at the screen for a long moment, his vision blurring. Then, slowly, he deleted the search and handed the phone back to the man. "Thank you," Logan murmured, his voice hollow. "I'm sorry for disturbing you. Enjoy your evening."

The couple exchanged polite smiles and returned to their conversation as if nothing had happened. Logan stumbled back to his table, threw down enough cash to cover his untouched beer, and walked out into the night, his legs unsteady beneath him.

He sat in his car for a moment, gripping the steering wheel so tightly his knuckles turned white. Adrian had deleted his Facebook account. It shouldn't have mattered; they hadn't spoken in years, and the account itself had been dormant since Logan left. But it had mattered. It had been a lifeline, a fragile connection he had selfishly clung to, a flicker of hope that maybe, one day, he could reach back across the divide.

And now it was gone.

The realization tore through him, ripping open wounds he had spent years trying to ignore. Adrian was truly gone. The last tether to him had snapped, leaving Logan adrift in a sea of his own making.

The scream erupted from him before he could stop it, raw and guttural, echoing through the empty car. It carried everything he couldn't say—the regret, the longing, the unbearable weight of losing the one person who had ever made him feel whole. It was the sound of a man breaking, his pain spilling out into the silence of the night. And when it ended, Logan was left with nothing but the hollow ache of his own breath and the knowledge that Adrian was lost to him forever.

Logan lost track of time as he navigated the winding, shadowy streets, the darkness blanketing him in a way that seemed intentional, easing him farther and farther away, letting the abyss consume him, the fog settling once and for all in his mind, with only the faintest hints of Adrian's smile clearing the edges, traces Logan would chase for the rest of his days.

The hum of the engine was the only sound in the stillness of the night, and the headlights pierced through the blackness, illuminating fleeting glimpses of the world outside. When he finally parked his car outside the bar, the clock on the dashboard blinked ominously—four a.m. The bar's neon sign flickered in the distance, casting an eerie glow that contrasted with the quiet of the hour, hinting at the long night still lingering in the air.

Zack's bar.

The bar was silent when Logan walked in, the heavy click of the door locking behind him punctuating the emptiness like a gunshot. The lights were still on, casting a warm glow over the wood and glass, but the usual hum of life and laughter was gone. Zack stood behind the bar, a towel slung over his shoulder, his head tilted in weary acknowledgment.

"We're closed," Zack called without looking up, his voice flat and indifferent.

Logan ignored him, his footsteps deliberate as he crossed the room. His suit was rumpled from hours of driving, but he straightened it instinctively, a hollow attempt at composure. He didn't need alcohol. Not tonight. He needed something else, something raw, something that could drown out the ache clawing at his insides.

"Oh, it's you..." Zack muttered, glancing up. "A bit late for you, isn't it?"

Logan didn't answer. His silence was heavy, loaded with intent. He moved behind the bar, stepping into Zack's space, his presence electric and unyielding.

"Look, man," Zack began, raising a hand as if to ward him off. "If you need a drink—"

The words died in Zack's throat as Logan grabbed the front of his shirt, his fists twisting in the fabric, and crushed their mouths together. The kiss was brutal, desperate, a collision of need and anguish that left no room for gentleness. Logan's lips moved over Zack's with abandon, his body pressing Zack back against the counter.

Zack froze, breath catching, before his hands found Logan's face, gripping him with a desperation that mirrored his own, fingers pressing into skin as if trying to carve meaning into something meaningless. Logan kissed him harder, forcing himself deeper into the moment, into the illusion, chasing a warmth that no longer belonged to him.

When his tongue flicked at the seam of Zack's lips, Zack yielded, parting for him, letting their mouths tangle in a fevered, clumsy dance. Logan felt the slick heat of it, the way their bodies moved in sync, but it was all wrong.

The taste—wrong.

The shape of the lips against his—wrong.

The breath, the weight, the rhythm—hollow.

It wasn't Adrian.

When he kissed Adrian, it always pulled at his neck, a gentle strain as he bent down to meet him. A quiet ache, a necessary surrender. And somehow, he had loved it, the way Adrian's lips tilted up toward his, the way he had to reach for him, the way it felt like gravity had shifted, and Adrian had become its center.

Zack was taller.

There was no need to bend, no need to reach. Their mouths met too easily, without effort, without struggle, without the ache that had once made kissing feel like a giving of oneself.

No matter how fiercely Zack held him, no matter how deep he drowned in this moment, it was still an empty ocean, a shipwreck of a kiss.

And yet, Logan let himself sink.

Because emptiness was better than nothing.

Because if he closed his eyes, if he let his edged mind and the darkness blur the edges of reality, he could pretend. Pretend it was Adrian's mouth against his, Adrian's warmth sinking into his skin, Adrian's breath tangled in his own.

Pretend he hadn't ruined everything.

For a fleeting second, he let himself believe... but the lie shattered the moment it touched him, sharp and cold against his skin.

It wasn't Adrian.

It would never be Adrian.

Logan moaned into the kiss, a guttural sound, as his hands roamed over Zack's body, anchoring himself in the heat of him.

Their bodies moved together, a frantic rhythm of friction and longing. Logan felt Zack's hands slide down his back, gripping him tightly as their hips aligned. The hard press of Zack's cock against his own sent a bolt of pleasure through him, and he gasped, his hands fumbling with the buttons of Zack's shirt.

Logan felt himself unraveling, the fragile thread he'd been clinging to fraying with each passing moment. It wasn't sudden, it never was. It was a slow, merciless descent, like the tide receding inch by inch, leaving him exposed and empty on the cold, barren shore. His thoughts drifted, slippery as seawater, too scattered to hold, too heavy to release. He had come here tonight not to find anything, but to lose himself; to drown in the chaos, to sink beneath the weight of it all, to numb the aching hollow where Adrian used to be.

His lips moved, but the sensation felt borrowed, like it belonged to someone else. Heat pressed against him, skin on skin, Zack's breath ragged in his ear, the crush of mouths clashing, seeking, taking.

Logan floated above it.

Adrian's face burned behind his eyelids—sharp at first, so vivid it ached, then blurring at the edges, dissolving into smoke no matter how hard he clung to it. He tried to chase it, tried to hold him in place, but each frantic kiss, each hollow motion, stripped another layer away.

Zack's hand gripped his hip. Logan didn't feel it.

Somewhere inside him, a voice screamed Adrian's name, begged him to turn around, to come back, to hear him. He wanted to tell him everything, to confess, to explain, to say the words he had swallowed for years: *I love you, I love you, I love you.*

But Adrian kept slipping further, his face dimming, until Logan was left touching someone else's body while mourning his own.

He closed his eyes tighter, pressed harder, as if he could force the ghost back into the room, but all he found was silence, and a body he didn't want beneath his hands.

Logan's breath hitched as he sank to his knees. His hands were moving, tugging, pulling, but it wasn't the rough denim he felt; it was the cool air of a beach at dawn, the memory of Adrian's laughter in the waves. He pressed forward, his mouth opening, but it wasn't Zack he tasted—it was salt, the sea, the remnants of a love he had drowned in.

He wanted to forget, he wanted to run, but somehow he ended up back there again.

He let his hands roam, fingers digging into flesh, but they found no purchase. Every touch felt hollow, a ghost of something he couldn't hold onto. His body moved out of rhythm, jerky and frantic, as though trying to outrun itself. His chest ached, not from the exertion but from the weight of everything he couldn't say, couldn't feel, couldn't face.

When Zack turned, when their bodies came together again, Logan felt a flicker of sensation—a heat, a pull—but it wasn't enough to ground him. His hands trembled as Zack pressed a condom into his palm, the small packet slick and foreign. He opened it mechanically, like a man following instructions in a language he barely understood.

The lube came next, another packet handed to him with a smirk that Logan could hardly process. His fingers moved as if detached from his body, slicking the liquid onto himself, then dipping down to Zack's opening. He felt the give of flesh, the heat of another person's vulnerability, and pushed his fingers inside, slow and deliberate. Zack gasped, his voice rising in broken moans, but to Logan, it sounded distant, as if it were echoing through water. Dim. Barely there.

He heard Zack speaking to him, words carried on shallow breaths, but they didn't land. He understood them, and yet he didn't, like trying to hold onto the words of a dream slipping away upon waking.

When Logan positioned himself against Zack, pressing forward, the sensation hit him like a wave—not the soft, rolling kind but the kind that knocked the air from your lungs, tumbling you helplessly beneath the surface. It was too much, and it was not enough. A paradox that twisted inside him, pulling him apart. His body responded—his hips moved, his muscles clenched—but his mind was elsewhere, sinking into an ocean of memory, guilt, and longing.

As he moved, the tears began to burn behind his eyes, hot and insistent, threatening to spill over. But he bit them back, swallowing the lump in his throat. He couldn't cry. Not here. Not now. Yet the feeling surged anyway—a rising undertow of grief and self-loathing that left him gasping for air he couldn't find. He felt like he was underwater again, drowning in a sea that didn't care whether he lived or died.

His fingers threaded through Zack's hair, roaming aimlessly, desperately. The strands beneath his touch were too stiff, too neat, slicked back with pomade that felt foreign against his skin.

He tried to trick his mind, to let memory overwrite reality. Tried to believe.

Tried to imagine that the hair beneath his fingertips was longer, softer, sun-kissed and salt-streaked, wavy from the ocean, wild from the wind. That if he just closed his eyes, just breathed deep enough, he would find traces of the sea, of Adrian.

But the illusion slipped through his fingers, dissolving like foam against the shore. No matter how hard he tried, the waves would not come back.

He thought of Adrian—not in the quiet, deliberate way of remembering but in the desperate, reflexive way of a drowning man reaching for the surface. He thought of Adrian's arms pulling him from the waves, the sound of his voice, clear and sure, calling him back to life. He thought about the way Adrian unraveled beneath him, how his body trembled, how his breath hitched and broke into something raw, something real. He thought about how, in those last moments before he came, Adrian always retreated into his native tongue, words slipping from his lips in whispered Hebrew, syllables tangled with gasps, lost somewhere between prayer and surrender. And afterward—that look. That hazy, dream-drunk expression, eyes glazed like sea glass softened by the tide, lips still parted, skin flushed with the afterglow of something that felt too big for either of them to hold.

It was the kind of beauty that branded itself into the bones, the kind of memory that no amount of time, no amount of distance, could ever wash away.

He thought of how Adrian had steadied him when he couldn't steady himself, had been his lifeline, his lighthouse.

His lifesaver.

But Adrian wasn't here.

Logan's movements faltered, his breath hitching. The room blurred around him, the edges fading like the horizon on a foggy day. He felt Zack's hands on his back, Zack's voice urging him on, but it only deepened the ache. He wanted to feel something—*anything*—but all he could feel was the weight of the ocean pressing down on him, cold and relentless.

Adrian's name caught in his throat, unspoken but heavy, as he moved. His hands gripped Zack's hips, but in his mind, it wasn't Zack at all. It was Adrian, turning to him with that half-smile, that look of pure devotion that Logan had never deserved. He squeezed his eyes shut, trying to block it out, trying to lose himself in the physicality, but Adrian was everywhere. In the tilt of a head, the shift of a body, the heat of skin.

Logan's movements grew erratic, his breaths ragged. He chased something he couldn't hold until his body shuddered and stilled. But even then, the emptiness remained, vast and unyielding, a void that no amount of heat or friction could fill.

When it was over, when the quiet settled back in, Logan pulled away. The air felt too cold now, his skin damp and clammy. He avoided Zack's gaze, his own eyes fixed on the floor as he tied the condom, threw it out and buttoned his pants, his hands trembling. He felt hollow, a shell of a man, and Adrian's name echoed in his mind like a song he couldn't forget.

He had tried to run from himself, to drown in someone else, but it hadn't worked. It never worked. Adrian was still there, lingering in the spaces between, in the silence that stretched after every desperate gasp.

Zack turned, unabashed by his half-nakedness, his body catching the faint glow of the rising sun filtering through the grimy blinds. His abs and pecs gleamed like carved stone, a satisfied, sleepy smile playing at the edges of his lips. He looked at Logan, head tilted, his gaze half-curious, half-knowing.

"Something you like?" Zack's voice was low, teasing, each word dripping with lazy seduction. He took his time tucking himself in, his fingers lingering as if daring Logan to keep watching.

Logan did. For a moment too long, his eyes roamed over the lines of Zack's body, the sharp edges of his muscles. But then he shook his head, trying to clear it, trying to push that feeling down where it couldn't reach him. Ducking low, he grabbed their discarded clothes, tossing Zack's shirt toward him. The fabric unfurled in the air, landing neatly against Zack's chest.

"So," Logan began, trying for casual, trying for cool, "is this the second suit you're ruining for me, huh, Zack?"

Zack grinned, his eyes sparkling with mischief. "Can't wait for the third," he said with a wink, his voice playful and shameless.

Logan forced a smile, but it didn't quite reach his eyes. He made a mental note to tell Ada Mae he'd need new suits again. His shirt had survived the night, somehow, but his jacket—soaked in liquor, its fabric torn and embedded with shards of glass—was a lost cause.

"You know you're helping me clean this up, right?" Zack said as he tied his shirt around his waist with a practiced flick, his tone light but insistent.

Logan let out a weary laugh, though it sounded hollow to his own ears. "Don't you have someone whose job it is to clean this mess up?"

"Yeah," Zack replied, grabbing an empty crate to collect the glass shards. "Me. And I'm guessing explaining the broken bottles is not in the job description."

Logan smirked faintly and knelt to the floor, picking up the larger pieces of shattered glass. "Tell them it was a very... productive night," he said, his voice tinged with mock amusement. Zack's laughter was genuine, full-bodied, and for a brief second, it lightened the oppressive weight pressing down on Logan's chest.

But as he worked, his hands slowed. Among the fragments, the light caught on something that made his stomach churn. His wedding ring, glinting like a cruel reminder. And just below it, Adrian's bracelet, worn with the years it spent first around Adrian's wrist and then his, resting in the usual spot, always there to remind him what he had and what he had lost. The sight of the two together struck him like a blow, shame spreading through his body like ice water.

How had he managed to betray *both* of them?

His fingers tightened around the glass, and for a moment, he thought of Sandy, probably at home now, wondering where he was. Worrying, maybe.

She hadn't called this time, but the texts were there when he pulled out his phone. Brief, restrained messages, each one heavy with the weight of their strained silence.

> Are you coming home tonight?

> It's late.

> I'll assume you're working again, even though it is 1 AM.

> You didn't say you'd be out.

> It's almost morning, where are you?

He typed a quick response, his fingers moving like he was erasing a crime scene.

> I'm okay

He shoved the phone back into his pocket, as if putting it out of sight would make it disappear.

"Hey," Zack's voice interrupted his thoughts. He was standing over him, broom in hand, his brow furrowed. "Are you okay?"

Logan nodded too quickly, brushing the question away. "Yeah, yeah," he said, rising to his feet, avoiding Zack's gaze. "Let's just clean this up."

Zack shrugged, taking his cue to let it go. "Fine. But hurry up. I actually want to sleep this morning," he said, flashing a lazy smirk. Zack's phone buzzed in his pocket, and he glanced at it, grinning as he typed. Logan didn't need to ask who it was; another text, another hookup waiting for him.

By the time Logan slid into his car, the sky had begun to lighten, streaks of soft pink and orange breaking through the horizon. His hands gripped the steering wheel, heavy with the weight of the ring on his finger, the bracelet brushing against his skin. Shame twisted in his chest, tangling with something darker.

How could he look Sandy in the eyes now?

How could he look at himself?

The worst part wasn't the act itself, but the fleeting moment afterward—a breath suspended in time when his body remembered how life could feel again. It wasn't pure joy, but a reflex, a tremor, a glitch in the machine of his senses. A mere second when his flesh recalled the touch of a man. It wasn't the blessing he shared with Adrian; that had been genuine, raw, a blaze of love that both burned and mended. No, this time with Zack was different—a salve, temporary and hollow. He used Zack's body like a buoy amid stormy seas, clutching at something to silence the chaos, a borrowed vessel to quiet the noise. But it only sank him deeper into emptiness, the same void he desperately sought to escape.

Zack had always been fire, heat without hesitation, something that burned because it could. Zack was ephemera, blazing flames that quieted, leaving ash in their wake, but Adrian... he was perdurability, the eternal song of the ocean, the crushing waves.

And Logan had never been built for fire. What he craved, what he returned to again and again, were the streams of water that had already carved their mark into him. He yearned for the quiet strength of the current, the promise of waves that held memory, the pull of a tide that spoke in truths rather than sparks.

How could he choose flame when water had already shaped him, when a love written in the waves and echoed in the tide had remade him entirely, sculpting him with every rise, every fall, every returning stream?

As he drove home, the memories swirled—Adrian's laughter, the warmth of his touch, the life he had walked away from. And the sound of glass breaking, the ache of betrayal.

He loved Adrian. He used Zack. And Sandy... Sandy deserved better than the vestige of the man she married.

Logan lost Adrian.

And this time, it was truly final.

When he arrived home, the world was still bathed in the muted gray light of early morning. The house was quiet, but as he stepped inside, Logan saw Sandy sitting on the couch. Her posture was rigid, her legs curled beneath her, her lap filled with design sketches and charts for her shop. She looked like she'd been waiting for him.

"Where have you been?" she asked, her voice cold, the warmth it once carried now a distant memory.

"Went surfing after work," Logan lied, his words heavy on his tongue. "Then spent some time with friends. Crushed at their place."

"Yeah, right," she said with a bitter laugh, shaking her head as if she had heard this story before.

Logan didn't linger. He jogged up the stairs, avoiding her gaze, and disappeared into the guest bathroom, skipping their shared bedroom altogether. He told himself it was better this way. The lie tasted bitter, but the truth would destroy them both.

As the shower hissed to life, Logan stepped under the stream, letting the scalding water hit his skin. It wasn't cleansing him. It wasn't washing away the shame or the ache lodged deep in his chest, but it was warm. It was the only comfort he had left in this cold, unrelenting world he had built for himself.

If Logan closed his eyes hard enough, if he focused on the rhythmic sound of water streaming and hitting the tiles, he could almost feel Adrian beside him. The heat of another body, the faint press of skin against skin. He could almost see the way Adrian would stand close, their bodies brushing as the steam rose around them, blurring the edges of the world.

He could hear Adrian's laughter, low and teasing, as he tilted Logan's face down to meet his. *"You're too tall for your own good,"* Adrian would say with that mischievous grin, his hands firm yet gentle. Logan could feel it—the press of Adrian's palms on his cheeks, the way his thumbs brushed his jawline, the warmth of his lips as they kissed him, soft at first and then deeper, more urgent. The kind of kiss that made Logan forget the world existed.

Adrian's touch would follow, tracing the lines of Logan's body with deliberate care, every movement a soundless declaration of love. Fingers sliding over his chest, down his arms, like he was memorizing him. Like Logan was something to be cherished, not just held. The water would stream down between them, tracing paths over their skin, but none of it mattered. There had only ever been Adrian, solid and real, grounding Logan in a way nothing else could.

Logan's eyes flew open, the mirage collapsing into a thousand silent splinters as the dream dissolved in hush and shadow, brittle beauty undone in a breath, and though no sound escaped, the rupture rang through his bones. The tiles gleamed under the spray, cold and sterile, the room empty except for him. The air felt hollow, the warmth of the water a poor substitute for the heat he craved. Adrian was gone, just a memory now, and no matter how hard Logan tried to summon him, to hold onto that fleeting sensation, it remained only water always slipping through his fingers.

The ache in his chest deepened, a sharp pull that left him breathless. The ghost of Adrian's touch lingered on his skin, cruel and bittersweet. Logan turned his face into the stream of water, letting it wash over him, hoping—praying—it could drown the pain.

The water cascaded over his face, his hair, his shoulders, but it couldn't touch the filth beneath his skin. He braced himself against the tile, his breath hitching as he tried not to let the weight crush him. He couldn't touch Sandy again. He knew it now, as surely as he knew the sun would rise. Porn wouldn't help this time. Pretending wouldn't help.

He wanted Zack again. Even now, even in the suffocating fog of self-loathing, the thought of Zack's body—his touch, his warmth—sent a shiver through him. It was wrong. It was disgusting, the betrayal, the cheating, the mess he'd made of his own life. But it was also true.

Logan tilted his head back, the water streaming down his face, and mumbled lyrics from a song that had become his everything all of a sudden. Adrian's song. *Logan's* song. The song that was born from the depth of pain Logan inflicted on Adrian.

"I am fractured, but if you are whole, then I'll find my peace in your joy... I believe my fate was to cross paths with you, to be the one who saves you."

The words felt like a cruel joke now. He was fractured, yes, but Adrian hadn't been able to save him, not now, not again. And Logan—Logan had never been able to save himself.

When he finally stepped out of the shower, wrapping a towel loosely around his hips, he didn't look in the mirror. He couldn't bear to see his reflection, the hollow man staring back at him. He grabbed clothes from the bedroom he shared with Sandy, her perfume lingering faintly in the air, and retreated to one of the guest rooms.

He texted Ada Mae, telling her to cancel his appointments. Sick day. That's what he called it. Sandy passed by the door, pausing when she saw him lying in the bed meant for guests.

"I think I'm coming down with something, I don't want to get you sick," he said softly, his voice a fragile excuse. He saw the hurt in her eyes, the way she swallowed her questions, her pain, but she didn't press him.

Logan flipped off the light and sank into the mattress. The soft pillow cradled his head, and for the first time in so long, he let himself collapse into the darkness. The blanket felt like a cocoon, wrapping him in an illusion of safety, shielding him from the storm he would face tomorrow.

Tomorrow, he would put on the mask again. He would be the devoted husband, the successful businessman, the dutiful son. Tomorrow, he would drink until the pain dulled, until the memories of Zack's hands, Adrian's laughter, and Sandy's wounded eyes blurred into a haze.

But tonight, in this borrowed bed, Logan let himself sleep.

And in the early morning hours, within the ethereal realm of dreams, his essence discovered a sanctuary—a safe shore. There, amidst the chaos swirling in the subconscious depths of his mind, he found Adrian. Beneath the layers of hurt, he surrendered to the embrace of the man he loved, cocooned in a tender fantasy. And even if the moment bloomed only in the garden of dream, conjured by ache and woven from want, it cradled him with the tender gravity of truth undeclared, a bittersweet benediction soft enough to soothe, a lullaby of almost-s, strong enough to shatter.

Chapter 8
The Air I Breathe Underwater

October 29, 2018—Rottnest Island, Western Australia—One Year and Nine Months Earlier

AUSTRALIA WAS SOMETHING ELSE—WILD, untamed, and full of life. They had been here for just over three weeks, moving from place to place every week or so. This time was long enough for Logan to fall in love with the endless skies, the way the ocean kissed the shore in shades of turquoise and white foam. But nothing in this vast, beautiful country compared to the man beside him.

He remembered their flight from the Philippines to Australia vividly. Adrian had insisted Logan take the window seat, and Logan spent most of the flight gazing at the world below—a sea of clouds breaking apart to reveal glimmers of earth and water. But it wasn't the view that made his heart race; it was the way Adrian's eyes lingered on him. The way he smiled at Logan, his eyes shimmering, sparkling, as if he alone was the only thing worth looking at.

Adrian had rested his head on Logan's shoulder somewhere over the ocean, his sun kissed hair brushing against Logan's neck. He had fallen asleep, his breathing steady and soft, and Logan had tried not to move, afraid of disturbing this perfect moment. When Adrian woke, they shared a quick, sleepy kiss, a gesture so small yet filled with a quiet tenderness that Logan could feel in his bones. In that moment, nothing else mattered; not the cramped airplane seats, not the turbulence. Just them, lost in their own little world.

The need to touch Adrian had become something almost primal for Logan, a pull he couldn't ignore. Holding Adrian's hand was second nature now; their fingers fit together as if they had always belonged. Kissing Adrian was like breathing; waking up with their bodies tangled together felt like the most natural thing in the world. Logan craved that connection, the way Adrian's rough palm felt against his, the way his thumb would idly trace circles on the back of Logan's hand, grounding him in a way he couldn't explain.

Adrian played for him often, his guitar a constant companion on this journey. Whether they were alone in their small cabin or sitting on the beach with dinner balanced on their laps, Adrian's voice would fill the air, raw and beautiful, each note cutting through Logan like the first rays of dawn. And when Adrian's eyes would meet his, filled with something soft and unspoken, Logan felt like he was melting from the inside out. He would ask for another song, and Adrian would always oblige, as if Logan's slightest whim was reason enough.

Something was happening between them, something Logan wasn't ready to name. He didn't need to. All he wanted was to breathe in the man beside him, to revel in the way Adrian looked at him, touched him, made him feel like he was something more than just a wandering soul chasing waves.

"Lo, are you coming?" Adrian's voice pulled Logan from his thoughts.

"Not the way I wanted to..." Logan uttered under his breath. "But, yeah."

Adrian chuckled softly, eyes bright and a broad grin stretching across his face. "You'll get what you want," he promised suggestively.

Logan smirked in reply as he finished tying his running shoes, then followed Adrian out the door into the cool morning air.

The beach stretched before them, the sky painted with the first streaks of dawn. Logan hated running—he really did—but somehow, Adrian had convinced him to join his morning runs. Not every time, but often enough that it was becoming a habit. Well, sometimes Logan managed to persuade Adrian to stay in bed instead, usually by kissing him senselessly and trailing his mouth over Adrian's skin until running was the last thing on his mind. But not today. Today, Adrian had won.

"You know," Logan grumbled as he jogged alongside Adrian, "it's basically a crime to make me run this early without coffee first. I'm pretty sure there are laws about that."

Adrian laughed, his smile radiant against the backdrop of the waking world. "You'll survive. Besides, the beach is empty, the air's fresh, and you're with me. What more do you need?"

Logan shot him a sidelong look. "Coffee. And a surfboard. If we're going to surf later, why are we running now? It's redundant."

Adrian just laughed again, his joy infectious, his pace steady and sure. Logan hated that he found it charming. Well, no. He loved it. He loved the way Adrian looked so alive, his long hair catching the breeze, his skin glowing in the golden light of the rising sun.

Logan huffed, his fake annoyance melting into a grin. He loved him, though he couldn't say the words—not yet. But it didn't matter, not really.

It was there in every laugh, every stolen kiss, every moment they spent side by side in the vast, beautiful world they were exploring together.

And Logan thought, as Adrian glanced at him with that dazzling, carefree smile, that maybe he didn't need coffee after all.

"Next time, I'm going alone. You're too slow," Adrian teased, his voice laced with mock seriousness. It was the same threat he always made, and it worked every single time. And yet, they both knew the truth: Logan was anything but slow. With his long legs and effortless stride, he could outrun Adrian on most days, his body built for speed, for motion, for the kind of reckless energy that turned every sprint into flight. Adrian never actually left him behind; he wouldn't dare.

Logan glared at him. "Fuck you. You're like five inches tall! You know what? See that rock over there?" He pointed to a jagged boulder sitting at the edge of the beach, half-shrouded in the golden morning light. "I'll race you there."

Adrian smirked, his eyes glinting with mischief. "And what do I get when I win?"

"Hah! If *you* win, I'll run with you every morning for a week—no excuses, no trying to drag you back to bed," Logan smirked, a teasing glint in his eyes, though the heat beneath it was unmistakable. "But if *I* win? A whole week of *no* running at those ungodly hours. You stay in bed where you belong."

"It's on," Adrian declared, and without waiting, they both took off toward the rock.

Logan might have complained endlessly about running, but his long legs and athletic frame didn't betray him. He sprinted hard, sand flying behind him with each powerful step. Adrian, however, slowed slightly, letting Logan gain the lead. Watching Logan push himself like that, his hair messy and wild in the wind, his determined expression, made Adrian smile.

When Logan reached the rock first, he braced himself against it, panting hard but grinning wide. "Who's slow now?" he bragged, his chest heaving with effort.

Adrian arrived seconds later, grinning as he slowed to a stop. "Yup... you beat me," he said, out of breath.

Logan flashed a cocky smile, reveling in his victory. "I can sleep in most mornings and still beat your ass."

Adrian raised a brow, his grin growing sly. "Uh, Lo? I let you win."

The smugness vanished from Logan's face, replaced by disbelief. "Huh? Nah. That's loser talk." He waved a dismissive hand, shaking his head.

Adrian chuckled, unable to resist teasing him further. "Yeah... I was really just letting you win."

Logan's jaw dropped, his whole expression falling like a sandcastle hit by a wave. Adrian tried to feel bad for him but failed miserably. It was too funny. Still, he couldn't stop himself from closing the distance between them, his laughter giving way to a softer, more genuine smile.

"Rematch!" Logan demanded, his voice almost a growl.

Adrian's grin widened, playful but with a touch of sincerity. "Okay, but if I win, remember you have to come running with me every morning. No skipping. No excuses."

"You said I'm slow," Logan countered, folding his arms over his chest.

"Yeah, but it's way more fun with you than alone," Adrian said, his voice dropping into something warmer, quieter. He stepped closer, wrapping his arms around Logan, as if nothing about Logan—messy hair, tired breath, sweat- and sand-coated skin—could ever deter him. "I'll take any excuse to spend more time with you," Adrian murmured, the humor fading into something deeper.

Logan's resolve softened at those words, the sincerity in Adrian's voice cutting through his playful bravado. "Deal," Logan declared, his smile returning.

Adrian's cocky grin reappeared, his tongue flicking out to wet his bottom lip as his eyes locked on Logan with a daring, mischievous glint. "Good," he said, just before he turned on his heel and sprinted back down the beach.

This time, Adrian gave it everything he had.

Logan's eyes traced the sheer force of will that radiated from Adrian's every movement. His arms pumped with precision, his legs slicing through the sand in a rhythm that spoke of discipline, control, and the kind of strength that wasn't just built, but earned. He watched him with such focused clarity, caught somewhere between admiration and amusement, completely enchanted and utterly drawn to every movement of his body that he forgot to start on time.

Adrian had spent his adult life training his body for war—for endurance, for command, for survival. He had led men, won battles, and carried weight that no human should ever have to bear. And yet, here he was, running like a kid racing to the water, all fire and freedom, all raw, electric life.

Logan pushed himself harder, sand kicking up behind him, but Adrian was already a streak of sunlit motion ahead, a force of nature, unstoppable.

When Adrian reached makeshift finish line, he turned to face Logan, his chest heaving, his grin victorious and radiant in the morning light. "So,"

Adrian said between heavy breaths, his voice still teasing but with that unmistakable affection lingering beneath it, "tomorrow at five a.m.? Or should we make it four?"

By the time they were back in the cabin, Logan was slick with sweat, a salty sheen clinging to his skin. The moment the door closed, Adrian was on him, their bodies colliding. Logan didn't hesitate, pulling Adrian into his arms, tearing his tank top away, their heat fusing together as he pushed him against the nearest wall. The friction between them was electric, the kind of raw energy that could reshape shorelines.

"You're so fucking hot when you're like this," Adrian panted, his breath warm against Logan's ear, his voice like the whisper of the wind before a storm. "I was running with a hard-on."

Logan pressed his lips to Adrian's neck, tasting the salt of his skin, drawing a deep, broken moan from Adrian's throat. "I get it," Logan murmured, his voice rough like the scrape of sandpaper, before their mouths collided again, desperate, searching, unrelenting.

"Bed—" Adrian managed to gasp as his fingers found the hem of Logan's soaked T-shirt and tore it away. The fabric fell to the floor, forgotten, as Logan wrapped his arms around Adrian and lifted him effortlessly. Adrian laughed, a sound that ran through Logan like a spark along a fuse, as he hooked his legs around Logan's waist.

"I'm too heavy for this," Adrian chuckled, his head tipping back as Logan stumbled toward the bed.

"Not a chance," Logan grunted, though his labored breaths and near fall betrayed him. He barely made it to the mattress before tossing Adrian down, following him with a grin and a hungry kiss, his body covering

Adrian's. "You've got to stop with those morning runs," Logan muttered as his lips traveled downward, worshipping every inch of Adrian's body.

Adrian's chest, slick and defined, was a canvas of strength and beauty. Logan's tongue traced the curve of his abs, the salty tang of sweat igniting his senses. "Damn," Logan moaned, his voice thick with reverence as he licked and kissed his way back up, drunk on the scent of musk and man. Adrian's hands explored the sticky expanse of Logan's back, his touch as soothing as the lull of the waves after a storm.

"And miss this?" Adrian teased, his voice ragged but playful. "Miss seeing you sweaty, out of breath, and knowing every single person who looks at you wishes they could have what's mine? Not in your dreams."

Logan paused, lifting his head to smirk at Adrian, his hands already tugging at Adrian's shorts. "Everybody looking? Adrian, no one's even awake at those god-awful hours."

"You're so oblivious," Adrian laughed, raising his hips to help Logan peel the damp fabric away. "Everywhere you go, Lo, people—men, women—look at you like you're a goddamn snack. They trip over themselves trying to get your attention. Fuck—yes." Adrian's words broke into a moan as Logan's hand wrapped around him, stroking him with a steady, deliberate rhythm. Logan couldn't help but chuckle, his lips ghosting over Adrian's stomach as he worked him.

"Snack, huh? You've got it backward. It's you they're all staring at, Adrian."

But right now, Logan didn't care about anyone else. He didn't care about the world beyond this room, beyond the bed where Adrian lay beneath him, radiant and breathtaking. All he cared about was this moment: the way Adrian's body felt against his, the way his laughter melted into gasps, the way his hands gripped Logan's shoulders as if to keep himself from drifting away.

Adrian was everything: the storm, the calm, the endless expanse of possibility. And Logan was lost in him, willingly adrift in a sea that he never wanted to leave.

The morning light painted the sea in hues of gold and sapphire, the waves rippling like molten silk under the rented yacht's steady glide.

It had been Adrian's idea. They'd been sitting on the beach the day before, beers in hand, when Adrian spotted a flyer for private charters at a small marina just down the coast.

"What if we rented one?" Adrian had suggested, his eyes lighting up with that mischievous spark Logan had come to love. "Just us, the sea, and a couple of days to ourselves."

Logan had laughed, brushing some sand off his legs. "A yacht? Seriously? You think we're that kind of fancy?"

Adrian had grinned, his sun-dappled face practically glowing. "Doesn't have to be fancy. Just the two of us exploring the reefs, diving, surfing, whatever. Come on, you know you want to. You are usually the one with the crazy ideas, not me."

And, of course, Logan had wanted to. They'd booked the charter within the hour—a two-day escape with a skipper to navigate and no one else to share it with. A splurge, sure, but neither of them cared. Their time together felt fleeting, and the ocean always had a way of making life feel infinite.

Now, as the yacht skimmed over the endless expanse of ocean, Logan and Adrian sat in the cockpit, wearing nothing but board shorts, sun-kissed skin, and wide, unrestrained smiles. The horizon stretched out like a promise, where sky and water fused into a soft, shimmering haze. This wasn't just an adventure; it was a pause, a moment suspended in time, where nothing mattered but the waves beneath them and the salty breeze tangling in their hair.

At the bow, the forward edge of their little vessel, their temporary slice of freedom, they stood side by side. Logan threw his arms wide, his laughter tumbling out, raw and full of joy, carried away by the wind. The bow sliced cleanly through the waves, sending up sprays of saltwater that misted their faces. Logan, ever the storyteller, had his GoPro in hand, capturing the rhythm of the yacht as it danced across the swells, the sunlight splintering into diamonds on the surface.

Without warning, Adrian snatched the camera, spinning it until the lens was pointed at himself.

"Hey!" Logan's protest was half-hearted, tinged with laughter.

Adrian grinned, his eyes glinting like sunlight off the sea. "You want to film something good? I'll *give* you something good."

And with that, Adrian leapt from the bow, his body arching gracefully before plunging into the ocean's embrace. The camera, held tightly in his hand, captured the exhilarating chaos of his jump, the spray of water, the rush of sky, the rippling world beneath the surface.

Logan's laughter turned into stunned disbelief. A few months ago, he'd have been the first in the water, shouting for Adrian to follow. Now, Adrian had leapt before him.

At the edge of his vision, he noticed Lia, the skipper, rushing toward the bow with her alarmed voice. Lia, a woman in her late forties with the straightforward attitude of a seasoned sailor, seemed as if her heart might jump out of her chest. "What was he thinking? That's dangerous!" She shouted, the words piercing through the gust.

Logan raised his hands, laughing apologetically, yet secretly proud of Adrian. "I promise, he's fine. Adrian's... well, he's Adrian."

It wasn't like Adrian to do something so impulsive. He was usually the measured one, the planner, the one who thought through every possibility before acting. But maybe, just maybe, some of Logan's carefree attitude was rubbing off on him. Or perhaps it was something deeper; his Navy background, the way he had always understood boats, deep water, and the relentless pull of the ocean. The sea had a way of calling to him, whispering promises of freedom and adventure he couldn't ignore.

And then there was Logan.

The relationship they had nurtured, the way it had blossomed so naturally, had begun to change Adrian in ways he hadn't anticipated. Being with Logan made him feel lighter, braver, like he could jump without second-guessing whether there would be something to catch him. Logan had that effect, stripping away Adrian's careful armor and replacing it with a raw, exhilarating sense of trust.

Sure enough, Adrian surfaced a moment later, grinning triumphantly, the camera held high above the water as if he were Neptune himself, victorious. Without pause, he dived again, cutting through the waves like a dolphin.

Lia huffed, muttering something about reckless young men, and returned to the cockpit. But Logan, unable to resist the siren call of the sea, or Adrian, shrugged, took a running leap, and dove in after him.

The water was shockingly cool, wrapping around Logan like a thousand welcoming hands. He broke the surface just in time to see Adrian's mischievous grin before a wave of saltwater splashed into his face. They swam together, bodies cutting through the blue-green depths, the yacht drifting lazily beside them like a guardian keeping watch.

For a time, they were just two souls suspended in the endless ocean, the world reduced to nothing but the push and pull of water, the sunlight streaking through its surface, and the sound of their shared laughter echoing across the waves.

When they finally climbed back aboard, water streaming from their bodies and pooling on the deck, Adrian reached for Logan's hand. His fingers were warm, steady, even as they trembled slightly from the exertion. Without a word, Adrian leaned in and kissed him, brief but full of meaning, like a secret shared between them and the sea.

Then, with that same irrepressible grin, Adrian handed Logan the camera and pulled him toward the bow again. The challenge in his eyes was as clear as the sky's reflection on the ocean's surface.

Logan didn't need to be told twice. Gripping the camera tightly, he stood at the edge, heart pounding in his chest. The sea called to him, vast and wild, promising danger and exhilaration. He smiled back at Adrian, whose gaze shimmered with a quiet wonder, as if he had missed countless dawns before and, for the first time, was witnessing one. Then, Logan jumped.

The wind screamed in his ears, the world blurring into a rush of salt and sun and spray. When he hit the water, it was like breaking through a barrier into another world—silent, weightless, infinite.

It was dangerous. It was reckless. And it was glorious.

In the moments that followed, as they swam together in the ocean's embrace, their laughter mingling with the rhythmic lull of the waves, Logan realized there was nothing else he needed. Not the camera, not the yacht, not even the shore. Just Adrian, the sea, and the unspoken understanding that together, they could dive into any unknown and come up laughing.

As the yacht continued to glide over the shimmering expanse of blue, they grew tired of chasing its stern through the water. Logan and Adrian climbed back aboard, water dripping from their sun-kissed bodies, and found their place side by side on the deck. Lia gave them an exasperated lecture on safety, her voice stern yet tinged with amusement, and they promised—half-laughing and half-genuine—that they wouldn't jump again.

The yacht rocked gently beneath them, the rhythm of the waves soothing, the air fragrant with salt and sun. Logan leaned back, closing his eyes, surrendering himself to the symphony around him.

Adrian's hand rested on Logan's thigh, casual but grounding, a silent tether that kept him present. The weight of it wasn't heavy; it was steady, reassuring, like the gentle tug of an anchor in shallow waters.

When Adrian spoke his name, Logan opened his eyes, and the sight of Adrian—hair wild from the sea breeze, eyes shining with mischief and warmth—brought an unbidden smile to his lips. Without hesitation, Logan took Adrian's hand in his, loving how naturally their fingers intertwined, how effortlessly they fit together.

Adrian drew him closer, a grin dancing on his lips as he kissed Logan, playful and proud, merriment flowing between them. The kiss was endless, stripped of the ordinary laws of beginning and end. It pulsed, alive, looping through itself, a rhythm that refused to die. Logan felt it under his skin, an electric hum spreading outward, trembling through the fine edges of his nerves. It unfolded inside him like fire that forgets its purpose when it finds oxygen, too full of itself to burn, yet too fierce to fade.

The taste of Adrian, familiar by now, still startled his tongue into song—something once holy that had learned how to sin. And maybe Logan knew the end was near, because he tried to name the moment, to archive it inside the labyrinth of his own fractures, to preserve the tremor before it was gone. But words—freedom, hunger, ruin, love—collapsed before they could take shape. Language was too small, too human. What lived between them was not a kiss, but an unmaking, a quiet detonation beneath the ribs.

Together, they rose and walked to the bow, Logan grabbing a towel as they went, and shaking it loose before spreading it over the sun-warmed deck. They stretched out side by side, shoulders brushing, their breaths syncing to the rhythm of the sea. The sun blazed above, hot and unrelenting, and the heat mingled with the sweat that slicked their skin.

They talked, as they always did, about everything and nothing. Their voices were light, the kind of easy conversation that flowed effortlessly. Their hands stayed entwined, a quiet, constant connection, and every so often, one of them would lean in for a lazy kiss, lips soft and warm, their shared laughter carried away by the breeze.

At one point, Logan turned onto his stomach, and he felt the faint hesitation in Adrian's grip as their hands parted. He glanced back just in time to see Adrian's reluctant expression, as if even the brief separation was too much. But the moment Logan settled, Adrian's fingers found his again, linking them with quiet insistence, as if he couldn't bear the distance for even a second longer.

"You're burning," Adrian said, his voice soft but tinged with worry. "Want me to put sunscreen on your back?"

"Nah, I'm good," Logan replied, his tone breezy and unconcerned.

Adrian snorted, shaking his head. "Yeah, right. You tough guy." His voice dipped into affection as he added, "You'll be all sore and miserable later if I don't. So, I'm putting some on you anyway."

A moment later, Adrian returned with the sunscreen, the bottle cool and gleaming in his hand. Without a word, he straddled Logan's back, his weight settling just enough to make Logan exhale a soft, shivering breath. Adrian's crotch pressed against the curve of Logan's ass, a deliberate, tantalizing closeness that sent a rush of heat through them both.

Logan felt the first touch of Adrian's hands as he smeared the lotion over his palms, then onto Logan's sun-warmed skin. It started simple, practical—but as Adrian's hands moved over Logan's back, smoothing the sunscreen into his shoulders, the practicality melted into something else. Adrian's touch was slow, reverent, tracing the curve of Logan's muscles, pressing into the tension that had built up from hours of paddling through the waves.

"You're going to kill me," Logan murmured, his voice low and heavy with need. The words slipped out before he could stop them, a quiet confession to the way Adrian's hands undid him.

Adrian smiled softly, though Logan couldn't see it. He let his palms roam higher, massaging the ache from Logan's shoulders, his thumbs working into the tender spots until Logan let out a broken moan, unable to hide how much he loved it.

Adrian shifted slightly, his body moving with a slow, careful rhythm that made Logan's breath hitch. His hands explored further, sliding down the length of Logan's spine, feeling the subtle flex of muscle beneath his fingertips. Adrian's breath caught in his throat as his palms skimmed over the dip of Logan's lower back, stopping just at the edge of his board shorts. From his vantage point, Adrian couldn't ignore the perfect curve of Logan's ass, the way his body seemed to invite every touch, every caress.

His body reacted instinctively, heat pooling low in his stomach as he pressed against Logan, his hard cock straining against the thin fabric of his shorts. Logan opened his legs slightly in response, a silent invitation that made Adrian's head spin. The soft sigh Logan let out as Adrian pressed into his hips was nearly enough to undo him.

Adrian's hands moved, sliding down the length of Logan's arms, tracing the sinews and veins beneath his skin. He didn't stop until he reached Logan's palms, intertwining their fingers, grounding them both in this intimate, unspoken moment.

Logan felt everything—Adrian's touch, his weight, the unmistakable press of his arousal against him. The air felt thick, heavy with heat and salt and longing, the kind of charged stillness that came before the ocean erupted into a wave. He closed his eyes, exhaling a soft breath, hoping the skipper was far enough away not to hear the quiet, electric hum of tension between them.

Adrian leaned down, his breath ghosting over Logan's ear, his voice a whisper carried on the breeze. "You have no idea what you do to me."

Logan didn't reply. He didn't need to. His body answered for him, arching ever so slightly into Adrian's touch.

"God, Adrian, I'm so turned on right now," Logan whispered, his voice trembling as Adrian's lips brushed the back of his neck. Adrian moved his hips deliberately, his arousal pressing against Logan's ass through the thin fabric of their board shorts, creating a friction that sent sparks shooting through Logan's body.

"Damn, me too," Adrian murmured, his breath warm and ragged against Logan's ear. "I want to make you come right now. I want to taste you." His voice was thick with desire, his hands firm as he rubbed slow, languid circles along Logan's sides. His calf nudged Logan's, urging him to spread his legs further, the motion possessive and teasing.

"You're insatiable," Logan teased, his words laced with a grin despite the flush spreading across his skin. "You tasted me this morning, the night before, and practically twice a day ever since we started."

Adrian chuckled lowly, the sound reverberating through both of them. His movements weren't frantic; they were lingering and conscious, each press of his hips a promise, a challenge, a confession. "I *am* insatiable when it comes to you, and shall I remind you of the day of deep throating you twice more in addition to the usual two?" he admitted, his voice heavy with emotion and lust. Then, with a slyness that was unmistakable, he added, "But I wasn't talking about your beautiful cock."

The smirk was audible in Adrian's tone, and Logan felt his entire body melt beneath him. He was reduced to a trembling mess under Adrian's touch, his mind swirling in a haze of want and heat.

In the month since they had begun exploring this new side of their relationship, they'd taken their time, learning each other's bodies with a care that made Logan's chest ache. They hadn't yet ventured beyond hand jobs, blow jobs, and the intoxicating friction of their bodies pressing together, but Logan's curiosity burned brighter every day. Adrian, ever patient, had once traced a finger along the edge of Logan's hole, and the memory of that touch, the way it had sent him over the edge instantly, haunted Logan in the best way.

Adrian was careful, too careful. No matter how much Logan begged him to lose control, Adrian's gentle soul held them within their unspoken boundaries. But now, feeling Adrian's weight above him, his body frantic and unrestrained, Logan wanted more, needed more.

"Fuck," Logan moaned, his voice barely above a whisper. Adrian laughed softly, nipping at his shoulder in playful retaliation. "You think the skipper is watching us?" Logan asked, half-teasing, half-wary, as his body arched slightly under Adrian's ministrations.

Adrian paused, shifting above him to glance around, his movements sending a shiver down Logan's spine. "We're barely visible from here," Adrian said, his voice sinful, dripping with intent. "And there aren't any boats around. But..." He leaned down, his lips brushing against Logan's ear. "No one will see what I'm about to do to you."

The promise in his voice was undeniable, and Logan's body responded instantly, his pulse thrumming. Whatever Adrian had planned, Logan was more than ready to surrender to the tide, to let it take him wherever it willed.

Logan's heart pounded like the crash of waves against jagged cliffs, wild and untamed. He was pinned beneath Adrian's weight, the heat of his body pressing him into the smooth surface of the yacht's deck. Every nerve in his body was alive, electric, as he felt Adrian's breath against his neck, the stubble of his jaw grazing his skin.

"Do you want it?" Adrian's voice was quiet, a low whisper that carried the weight of the moment.

"Yes, please," Logan moaned.

Adrian pressed a kiss to Logan's neck, his lips soft but deliberate, followed by a flick of his tongue that sent a jolt down Logan's spine. He released Logan's hand, though his presence remained an invisible tether that kept Logan grounded.

"I really want to taste you right now," Adrian murmured, his lips brushing against Logan's ear, "but this... this will have to do for now." He slid a finger into his mouth, wetting it thoroughly, his eyes locked on Logan's as he reached down and pulled Logan's shorts just far enough to expose the smooth, golden globes of his ass.

"Lo," Adrian murmured, his cheek pressed against Logan's, voice steady, grounding. Logan could feel the faint scratch of Adrian's stubble, the warmth of his breath ghosting over his skin. The world around them had faded; it was just the two of them, the ocean stretching endlessly beneath the hull of the yacht, the wind curling through their hair, and the sun crowned the sky, flooding the earth with white fire.

Adrian's lips brushed against Logan's temple, his breath slow and sure. "Tell me to stop if you want. If it's too much, if you don't like it, whatever the reason. Just tell me, and I'll stop."

Logan nodded, his throat too tight, his chest too full.

Adrian wasn't finished. "Lo." A little firmer now, his voice laced with quiet insistence. "I mean it."

Logan swallowed and finally found his voice, soft but certain. "I know. I will. Adrian, *it's us.*"

Adrian exhaled against his skin, his lips curving faintly as he whispered back, "It's us."

And that was everything.

Adrian's hands roamed over Logan's back, fingertips tracing the lines of his body, memorizing him like scripture. He shifted above him, balancing himself on one arm while his other hand slid lower, cupping Logan's ass with a reverence that sent a shiver through Logan's spine.

"I love this ass," Adrian muttered, squeezing gently, his fingers pressing into firm muscle, the skin silky beneath his roughened hands. He groaned, low and guttural, leaning in to bite at the curve of Logan's neck. "Dammit, Lo, I want to taste you."

His mouth was hot, insistent, a slow burn against Logan's skin. He sucked at the sensitive spot beneath Logan's ear, his teeth grazing just enough to make Logan gasp, his body arching instinctively beneath him. Adrian was patient, teasing, giving him just enough to feel the heat, before pulling back, leaving him wanting.

The yacht hummed beneath them, the gentle rumble of the engine blending with the rhythm of the waves. The wind curled around them, warm and salty, the scent of the ocean mixing with the musk of sun-warmed skin. Logan closed his eyes, letting himself sink into it, into this moment, this touch, this man.

Then Adrian pulled back slightly, bringing his fingers to his lips, wetting them slowly, thoroughly.

Logan swallowed, his body taut with anticipation, every nerve alive as Adrian's fingertips ghosted over his skin, tracing the curve of his lower back before sliding lower, lower—

Adrian's breath caught.

He moved with care, with intention, his wet fingers grazing the rim of Logan's entrance, teasing, just a whisper of sensation before retreating, before returning.

Logan trembled beneath him, his breath hitching, a soft sound spilling from his lips. Not just from the touch, but from the way Adrian touched him, like he mattered, like this mattered.

Because it did.

"How's that?" Adrian asked after a moment, his voice low, his focus entirely on Logan. Those whimpers were music to Adrian's ears, a melody he could never tire of, the most beautiful soundtrack to his life.

"It's... weird," Logan admitted, his voice trembling, "but good."

Adrian smiled against Logan's shoulder, sliding his finger just barely inside, testing, coaxing. When he withdrew, he brought the finger to his lips again, wetting it with his tongue. Logan's body tensed beneath him, on the brink of coming undone at the sight. Adrian hovered above him, one hand glistening with a mix of his own saliva and Logan's essence, the other intertwined with Logan's, grounding him in the moment. Adrian's focus was absolute, his entire being concentrated on making Logan feel good.

"I want to make you come like this," Adrian said, his voice reverent, as if confessing a secret to be taken by the wind. He leaned down and captured Logan's lips in a kiss, the angle awkward but perfect in its imperfection.

Adrian slowly slid his finger back into Logan's body, swallowing the moans and whimpers that spilled from Logan's mouth. The wind and waves seemed to swell around them, a private symphony that muffled their sounds and wrapped them in its embrace.

"Shit, Ad—" Logan panted, his body arching beneath Adrian's touch. "Keep going. Please—fuck, fuck..." Logan moaned as Adrian's finger moved slowly inside of him, feeling the pressure in his opening, the fullness of just one finger inside.

Adrian moved his finger with a steady rhythm, in and out, each motion sending Logan spiraling further into a state of bliss. He kissed Logan's collar, nuzzling the nape of his neck, his breath hot against Logan's skin. "You take my finger so well," Adrian rasped into Logan's ear, his voice dripping with praise.

Logan shuddered violently, a soft cry escaping his lips. Adrian had discovered, over their many nights together, that Logan craved praise; it unmade him, left him pliant and eager beneath Adrian's hands.

"I want to eat you out," Adrian murmured. "You taste so fucking good, Lo. I almost came in my shorts just from the small taste I got." His words spilled into Logan's ear, sending shivers cascading through Logan's body, his mind lost in the sensation, in Adrian's voice, in the pull of the tides within him. Adrian exhaled slowly, his breath warm against Logan's shoulder, his fingers moving with the same measured reverence as a man tracing the edges of something sacred. He didn't rush, didn't demand. He just explored, letting Logan feel every soft press, every teasing graze, every moment of giving before taking away. "I want to open you out with my tongue, to lick you, and then gag on your thick dick."

Logan's body trembled, his skin slick with sweat and sun, as Adrian continued to guide him through waves of pleasure, each one building toward something vast, something infinite, something utterly consuming. "You're incredible," he whispered, his voice heavy with awe, with hunger, with something deeper than either of them could name. "You are perfect, every inch of you is perfect. Do you have any idea what you do to me?" Adrian's voice was hushed. His lips traced Logan's spine, slow and deliberate, as his finger was plunged deep in Logan's ass. "You drive me crazy, Lo. You're so damn beautiful, you don't even realize it."

Logan let out a shaky breath, his body melting into Adrian's touch, into his words.

"Say it again," Logan murmured, his voice barely above a whisper, as if he was afraid to ask for too much, his body vibrating with need and lust.

Adrian smiled against his skin. "You're perfect," Adrian repeated, just as tenderly, raspy voice dripping with longing. Adrian was more than happy to praise Logan all day long, knowing that he would do it for the rest of his life if needed. "You drive me wild. I am horny twenty-four seven because of you."

Adrian's pace quickened, his finger moving with purpose as he explored Logan's body, searching for that elusive, magical spot. The moment he found it, Logan's entire body tensed, his breath hitching sharply. Adrian was relentless, pressing and rubbing against that spot with precision, his movements filled with both care and hunger. "Yes, moan, whimper for me. I want to hear you. You look so hot right now, taking my finger and enjoying it. You are so fucking hot, Logan. I cannot wait to eat you, to fuck you with my tongue. Fuck, I want you in a bed right now."

Logan's fingers tightened around Adrian's, their grip a silent cry of pleasure and surrender. Adrian leaned down, capturing Logan's mouth in a kiss that swallowed the moans spilling from his lips. The sounds were visceral, uncontrolled, all pulse and need and breath trembling against skin, as Logan's body bucked beneath him, the heat radiating between them like the sun on the open sea.

Adrian felt Logan shatter, his climax ripping through him with a force that left him trembling. The sight, the sound, the sheer *feel* of Logan's release was enough to send Adrian over the edge as well. Rubbing himself against Logan's sweat-slick body, he groaned low and deep, his own release crashing into him like a rogue wave, all-consuming and inevitable.

"Wow," Logan breathed after a moment, his voice a mix of awe and exhaustion. "That's never happened before. Coming without touching my dick. That was so hot."

Adrian felt ten feet tall, smug and impossibly proud, a grin spreading across his face as he slowly withdrew his finger from Logan's body. He moved carefully, pulling Logan's shorts back into place with a gentleness that made Logan's heart miss a frantic beat. But Adrian didn't move away. He stayed where he was, his body draped over Logan like a blanket, pressing soft kisses to Logan's shoulder.

"It was amazing," Adrian murmured, his voice soft but filled with satisfaction.

"You came?" Logan asked, glancing back at him.

"Of course," Adrian said with a low chuckle, his lips brushing against Logan's skin. "It was the hottest thing ever, feeling you around me like that." His dick twitched just at the thought, his body still alive with the memory. "Seeing you like this? Fuck, Logan. You turn me on by existing, but this? I am just a man."

A moment later, Logan shifted slightly, nudging Adrian to move off him. They both turned onto their backs, Logan pulling Adrian into his arms. The intimacy of the moment lingered, even as the discomfort of their damp shorts made them grimace. Without a word, they grabbed the towel and used it to clean themselves as discreetly as they could, laughing softly at the absurdity of it all.

When they settled again, Logan wrapped an arm around Adrian's shoulders, and Adrian rested his head against Logan's chest, their bodies fitting together like two pieces of the same puzzle. The sun warmed their skin as they drifted into a light snooze, lulled by the gentle sway of the yacht and the rhythmic lap of the waves against the hull.

Half an hour later, the yacht's engine rumbled to a stop, waking them both with a gentle jolt. They sat up to see Lia, the skipper, walking toward them with diving gear in her arms. She handed them sleek masks, small air cylinders, and fins, her expression stern but faintly amused, as if she could sense the lingering heat between them but had chosen not to comment.

"Time to dive," Lia announced, her voice breaking the quiet.

Logan and Adrian exchanged a glance, their cheeks flushed but their smiles wide. The ocean called to them again.

No wetsuits were necessary; the sun had warmed the water to a perfect, inviting temperature. Their goal was simple: to see the reef, to explore the underwater world that thrived just down below.

Logan and Adrian stood at the edge of the yacht, listening to Lia's safety instructions. Logan's eyes occasionally flicked to Adrian, who stood calm and attentive, though Logan knew he was already familiar with every word. Adrian had spent years in the navy, mastering the art of navigating the depths. Still, he let Lia finish, his respect for her clear in the way he listened, a faint smile on his lips.

Then, with an excited whoop, Logan leapt into the water, the cool embrace of the ocean rushing up to meet him. Adrian followed closely, his dive graceful and controlled, like a creature returning home.

As soon as Logan opened his eyes underwater, he was struck by the kaleidoscope of colors and life that greeted him. Coral stretched out like underwater cities, vibrant and intricate, teeming with fish darting in and out of their hidden crevices. The sunlight pierced through the water, illuminating the reef in golden beams that danced with the currents. Logan felt as though he had entered another world, one untouched by the chaos above.

But as the regulator settled between his teeth, something felt profoundly wrong. The air, though there, was stripped of warmth, dry, metallic, and alien. It filled his lungs but offered no comfort, as if the act of breathing had become a performance rather than a lifeline. The water pressed in from all sides, heavy and ancient, and every inhale felt like dragging breath through silk soaked in shadow.

Logan's chest cinched as if the sea itself had coiled around his ribs. The mask pressed close, the regulator filled his mouth, yet every breath felt thin, stolen, not enough. The hiss of air scraped his ears, sharp and uneven, followed by the frantic rattle of bubbles fleeing upward. His pulse drummed faster than the current.

The reef before him, alive only moments ago, bled into a blur of wavering color. Coral became a smear, fish dissolved into streaks of silver.

All that remained was the cage of his breath and the echo of fear beating in his skull.

And then the sea shifted. He was no longer here, not in this place, not in this body. He was back in that July water, the moment that had carved itself into his bones without him even realizing it. The waves had folded over him, dragging him down, flipping him like driftwood. Salt burned his throat, and each gasp came too late, oxygen slipping away like something stolen. Light fractured above him, just out of reach, while his lungs screamed against the silence.

Then, through the swirl of rising dread, something broke the loop: a hand, strong and steady, closed around his arm. Solid. Present.

Adrian.

Adrian pulled him up with ease, his strength and calm presence cutting through Logan's fear. As soon as their heads broke the surface, Logan tore the mask from his face and spat out the regulator, gasping as the open air filled his lungs.

Beside him, Adrian lifted his own mask, slipped the regulator free. "Everything's okay," he said, his voice even, though his eyes betrayed the worry burning behind them. He held Logan close, repeating it as if the words themselves could keep him afloat.

"I'm... sorry," Logan rasped.

"Don't you dare," Adrian said firmly, brushing wet strands of hair from Logan's forehead with a gentleness that disarmed him. "No apologies."

Logan's chest still heaved, but his breaths were lengthening. "I don't know what happened," he managed, voice raw.

Adrian studied him, brows furrowed. "You were breathing too much... and then you weren't." His gaze didn't leave Logan's face, as if searching for something deeper than the words.

"The air—" Logan's throat caught. He swallowed, his voice trembling. "It felt wrong. Like I was pulling it in, but it wasn't reaching me. And then—" His eyes flicked away, ashamed of the quake in his voice. "Then I was back there. That day. The fall. I never remembered it until now. Just flashes, waves crashing... waking up on the beach. With you."

Adrian's jaw tightened, but his tone remained calm. "Maybe we should go back to the boat."

Logan shook his head, quick and determined. "No. Now that I know... I can face it."

Adrian hesitated, the shadow of worry in his eyes softened by love. "You're sure?"

"Yes."

He exhaled slowly, nodding. "Alright. It's strange at first," Adrian said, slipping into the quiet authority of someone who had guided men through storms darker than this. "The air tastes dry, too sharp. The hiss is kind of odd. But it steadies after a while. Trust me. You'll find the rhythm."

Logan nodded, swallowing hard, clinging to Adrian's words. The pressure in his chest eased as Adrian's hand remained, warm and firm, on his arm, an anchor against the undertow of panic.

"It felt like drowning," Logan whispered, hating the fragility in his voice. "Like I was drowning again."

Adrian's thumb brushed lightly over his skin. "Never. Not as long as I'm here."

Logan had spent his life surfing, mastering the rhythm of waves, learning how to hold his breath underwater. Surfers had to be comfortable with the ocean's unpredictability, with the moments when air was a luxury and not a given. And yet, here he was, struggling with something as basic as breathing from a tank.

The weight of Adrian's gaze made it worse. Logan didn't want Adrian to see this side of him—the fumbling, inexperienced side. He wanted Adrian to see him at his best, to see the confidence and ease he carried in the water. But with Adrian, the stakes felt different. He wanted to impress him, to be someone Adrian could admire as much as Logan admired him.

He doubted he'd feel this need for anyone else.

Adrian's voice broke through the fog of Logan's thoughts. "You feel better?" Adrian's words were calm, steady, and his smile—a soft, patient curve of his lips—was disarmingly kind.

"Yeah, let's try again," Logan said.

"Okay. Just be calm when you're down there, breathe as usual, okay? I'm with you."

The reassurance settled something in Logan, like the gentle lap of waves easing the tension in a taut rope.

"Hey! Is everything all right?" Lia's voice carried from the yacht, concern evident in her tone.

"Yes," Adrian called back, his tone light but firm. "Just talking a bit. Everything's okay."

He turned back to Logan, his hand still resting on Logan's arm, grounding him. "Let's try again. If you feel uncomfortable, just come back up. I'll be right there with you, okay?"

Logan nodded, embarrassed but determined. He slipped the mask back over his face, secured the regulator between his lips, and watched Adrian do the same.

Adrian reached for Logan's hand as they sank beneath the surface, his grip firm, certain, a silent vow that Logan was not alone.

The first breaths still felt strange, the air too dry, too sharp, each pull through the regulator unnatural. But this time the panic didn't rise. Adrian was there, close enough that Logan could see the calm in his eyes through the blur of the mask. With every brush of his thumb, with every sure beat of his presence, the chaos inside Logan stilled.

What had felt like drowning moments ago now became rhythm. Breath in, breath out. The ocean no longer pressed down on him; it carried him, and with Adrian's hand in his, the water felt almost like home.

When Adrian sensed Logan's breathing had evened out, he let go of his hand, giving Logan the space to explore. And as the initial discomfort faded, Logan began to see the underwater world in all its glory.

The reef was breathtaking. Coral towers rose in twisted spires, each crevice alive with motion. Silver schools of fish rippled past, shifting and turning as though the sea itself conducted their dance. Shafts of sunlight pierced the surface above, breaking into golden columns that swayed with the tide, setting the water alight.

Logan drifted closer, wonder widening his eyes. Blues bled into yellows, patterns more intricate than any canvas. He checked his GoPro, a fleeting gesture to be sure it captured this, but even as the red light blinked, he knew no lens could contain it.

He felt as if he wasn't just swimming in the ocean; he belonged to it. His breaths fell into the rhythm of the sea, each inhale a surrender, each exhale a hymn.

He turned. Adrian hovered just behind, steady as ever, watching him. Even through the mask, Logan could see it: the soft crinkle at the corners of his eyes, a smile carried not on lips but in the soul.

Logan felt his earlier embarrassment melt away, replaced by a quiet gratitude. Adrian's patience, his untiring support, had made this moment possible. And as Logan swam deeper into the reef, he realized he didn't need to prove anything to Adrian. Just being here, together, was enough.

When Logan spotted the little shark—a shy, harmless creature weaving hesitantly through the coral—he immediately reached for Adrian's hand. He tugged gently to get his attention and pointed toward the small shark. Adrian's eyes crinkled with delight behind his mask, and he gave Logan a thumbs-up, his excitement infectious.

For half an hour, they swam together through this otherworldly expanse, exploring the reef's vibrant tapestry. Logan felt a connection to the sea that he hadn't realized he'd been missing, but more than that, he felt Adrian's presence beside him, a constant, steady force.

Eventually, Logan noticed his breaths becoming shallow, the regulator giving less and less. He patted his hand over his mouth to signal to Adrian that his tank was empty, then started to swim toward the surface. But before he could ascend, Adrian grabbed his arm, stopping him.

Adrian pulled the regulator from his own mouth and handed it to Logan, the motion smooth, almost instinctive. Logan hesitated, the weight of the gesture sinking into his chest. When he accepted it, his whole body shuddered as he drew in a deep breath, the air filling his lungs like a second chance. He passed the regulator back, and they repeated the process, breathing together, sharing the same lifeline.

It wasn't just air. It was a connection. A trust so deep it transcended words. Logan had never felt anything like it.

In that moment, Logan knew with unwavering certainty that no one in this world cared about him like Adrian did. They had never spoken about these things, their feelings, the quiet truths that existed between them, but sometimes, silence was louder. And right now, Adrian was screaming underwater everything that mattered with every breath they shared.

When Adrian passed the regulator back again, he reached out and laced his fingers with Logan's, holding tight. Logan's chest ached, not from lack of air but from the enflamed flood of emotions crashing over him like waves. Every day, they grew closer, discovering new pieces of the world, and of each other. Logan couldn't fathom how there had ever been a time when Adrian wasn't in his life.

Adrian handed him the regulator again, waiting patiently as Logan breathed deeply. Logan passed it back, and they continued their exploration, Adrian ensuring that Logan inhaled life before taking a breath himself.

Because for Adrian, air was only worth breathing when Logan shared it.

Finally, Logan signaled for them to surface, and together they rose, breaking through the water's embrace. The sunlight hit them like a burst of warmth, the world above loud and vivid after the quiet depths.

Adrian laughed, his smile bright as he spoke about the reef, the shark, the colors, and the awe of it all. But Logan didn't wait to respond. Instead, he grabbed Adrian, using the weightlessness of the water to pull him close. Their mouths met in a kiss that was desperate and consuming, Logan wrapping his legs around Adrian's waist to anchor himself. Adrian kissed him back with the same intensity, their bodies entwined as the sea held them suspended.

And yet, the most incredible thing Logan had seen wasn't the reef, or the shark, or the vibrant underwater life. It was Adrian.

Because with every beat of Logan's heart, he realized it no longer beat for himself. It pumped blood and life for Adrian, for the man who had become his entire world.

That truth was both terrifying and astonishing. It was like diving into unknown depths—dark and endless, but also full of promise.

Logan didn't know what to do with that knowledge, with the fact that Adrian was now the center of his existence. But for now, with Adrian's arms around him, the sea cradling them both, he let it be. And it felt like the most natural thing in the world.

As they reached the yacht, both grinning like kids who had just discovered the world's greatest secret, Adrian gestured for Logan to climb the ladder first. Logan pulled himself up, water streaming from his body, and when Adrian followed, Logan tossed him a towel. They both stood on deck, drying off, their laughter carried away by the sea breeze.

The trip back was a blend of lively conversation and comfortable silence. They sat side by side, Logan's arm draped casually over Adrian's shoulder as he held him close, while Lia shared stories about her years at sea as the yacht sliced through the water. Along the way, they stopped at another reef, this one just as stunning but shallower. Donning snorkels and masks, they dove back into the water, their excitement undiminished.

As they docked at the marina near evening, the sun dipped low on the horizon, painting the sky in hues of amber and rose. They had sailed through so many waters, explored hidden corners of the ocean, their skin tanned from the sun and their bodies invigorated by the salt and waves.

Lia, ever practical, gave them a quick rundown of the yacht's amenities. They had hired it for the full day and night, and she explained where everything was—the locks for the yacht if they wanted to explore on land, the compact but well-equipped kitchen, and the phone number mounted on the fridge for ordering pizza. "Just say my name when you call," she said with a grin. "They'll charge it to me. And help yourself to anything in the fridge, it's fully stocked."

She showed them around the yacht, pointing out the three rooms: one was her personal quarters, and the other two were for guests. Logan and Adrian listened intently, though their smiles hinted at the mischief of two boys handed a world of possibilities for the night ahead.

As the tour ended and Lia departed, Logan looked out over the water, the horizon still glowing faintly with the remnants of the day. Adrian stood beside him, the wind tousling his hair, his presence as constant and vital as the waves lapping against the hull.

They took the steps down, the yacht rocked gently beneath them, as if cradling the moment in reverence. Their luggage was still hastily thrown by one of the rooms, a patchwork of surfboards, battered duffels, and Adrian's guitar, a possession Logan saw how well Adrian treasured and took care of.

Adrian playfully shoved Logan into the room, telling him to take the first shower while he got started on dinner. They usually ate out, but every so often, to save money and ensure they ate something a little healthier, they'd make a quick stop at the supermarket for essentials. Their go-to menu was dependable yet straightforward: chicken breast paired with a mountain of vegetables, or occasionally accompanied by white rice, and on special nights, a hearty steak with potatoes. Neither of them would claim to be chefs, but together, they managed to scrape by with the basics.

The tiny shower barely fit Logan's broad shoulders, the spray splashing unevenly against his skin, cold at first, then warming into a soothing cascade. He chuckled at the tight squeeze, his movements careful. The scent of saltwater still clung to him, mingling with the sharp tang of soap. Emerging freshly scrubbed, his damp hair clinging to his forehead in unruly strands, he caught the aroma of something warm and rich wafting from the galley, like a siren's call to his ravenous hunger.

His stomach growled audibly as he stepped into the main cabin, drawn by the enticing aroma wafting through the air. Adrian stood at the stove, bathed in the soft, golden glow of the cabin lights. His movements were fluid and unhurried. The sight of him, so at ease, was captivating. Adrian glanced over his shoulder, a warm smile curving his lips, his eyes alight with quiet affection.

"How was the shower?" he asked, crouching to check on something in the small oven.

"Good. What are you making?" Logan asked, leaning against the doorway, the tension of the day already melting away.

"Pasta," Adrian said, straightening up. "Chicken breast, some vegetables, nothing fancy. I was starving, so I threw together something quick."

Logan laughed, his voice rich with amusement. "How long was I in the shower? You're a miracle worker. We haven't eaten since this morning, and I'm dying over here. Need help?"

Adrian shook his head, the soft clinking of utensils against pots creating a rhythmic melody in the cozy space. "Almost done. Just waiting for the chicken to finish. The sauce is from a can, though, so don't expect too much."

"Too much?" Logan teased, his voice playful as his gaze lingered on Adrian. "This smells like heaven. I'd eat my shoe at this point, so pasta and chicken are pure luxury. Seriously, thank you."

Unable to resist, Logan stepped behind Adrian and wrapped his arms around him, pulling him close. He pressed a playful kiss to Adrian's neck, breathing in his familiar scent, a mix of sunscreen, ocean, warmth, and something distinctly Adrian.

Adrian chuckled softly, his movements steady as he divided the food between two plates. The portions were generous, the aroma filling the cabin with a comforting warmth that felt almost like home.

Once they sat down, Logan dug in immediately, his fork clinking against the ceramic as he moaned appreciatively. "This isn't just a canned sauce," he said between bites, his voice muffled by food. "You added something. Admit it."

"Maybe a dash of spices I found," Adrian confessed, his smile soft and unguarded, free and wild as he watched Logan adoringly, his looks and the small tilt of his lips like a secret whispered between the wind and the waves. "Nothing fancy."

"Fancy enough," Logan murmured, his eyes meeting Adrian's for a moment that stretched. The simplicity of the meal, the quiet comfort of the moment, it all felt like home in a way Logan couldn't quite articulate.

When the meal was done, Logan insisted on cleaning up, he was taught some manners, after all, and he ordered Adrian into the shower, his hands moving quickly over the plates. The sound of water hitting tile mingled with the faint creak of the yacht's wood, a rhythm that soothed and stirred Logan in equal measure. His thoughts drifted to the man behind the closed door, his mind reeling from the events of the day. The vibrant corals, the crystalline water, and the way Adrian's laughter had echoed over the waves all seemed like a dream he was reluctant to leave behind.

It didn't take him long to finish the dishes. Afterward, Logan made his way to one of the yacht's bedrooms, the larger of the two they'd chosen for their stay. Without a second thought, he threw himself onto the bed, the plush mattress soft beneath him. Logan lay sprawled across the bed, his limbs stretched out in lazy comfort, the cabin door left slightly ajar. The sheets smelled faintly of floral detergent, and he closed his eyes, letting the gentle rocking of the yacht lull him. Footsteps drew near, and he opened his eyes to see Adrian in the doorway, his hair damp and tied back, dressed in shorts and a loose tank top that clung to his bulging shoulders. The soft light painted him in golden hues, making him look almost otherworldly.

"You're not asleep, are you?" Adrian's voice was low, teasing, but it carried that familiar warmth, the kind that curled around Logan like a blanket pulled from the past. It wasn't just the words; it was *him*. The softness of his accent, the way certain vowels lingered longer, the subtle cadence that made even the quiet feel like a confession. Logan had grown addicted to it, to *him*, to the way Adrian would sometimes hesitate, brow furrowed, when Logan used an idiom or a phrase he didn't quite catch. Those moments felt like secrets shared between them, quiet cracks in the wall where intimacy lived.

Logan's heart pounded loud enough to drown out the quiet. He could hear it in his ears, feel it in the hollow of his throat, in the tremble of his fingers. Every nerve was awake now, every inch of him tingling with a familiar ache, not just to be with Adrian, but to *have* him again. To be close, *really* close, in a way that no words or air or silence could interrupt. Adrian was right here, not even an arm's length away, and yet the distance between them felt unbearable.

"Not even close," Logan replied, sitting up with a grin.

"Do you want to go out for a bit? Explore the area?" Adrian suggested, his voice low and easy, a gentle ripple against the quiet of the cabin. The yacht rested in a different port than the one they had sailed from earlier, its moorings swaying gently in rhythm with the tide. Tomorrow, they would return to their starting point, but for now, the night stretched before them, vast and uncharted.

"Not really," Logan replied, his gaze meeting Adrian's with quiet honesty. "I don't feel like people tonight."

Adrian smirked, the corner of his mouth curling with that familiar mischief that made Logan's chest ache in ways he couldn't explain. "The liquor cabinet is full of good stuff," Adrian offered.

Logan's lips twitched in response, his voice dropping to a murmur. "Actually," he said, drawing out the word like a wave building momentum, "I have something else in mind." His smile turned suggestive, the kind of smile that held secrets between its curves. He extended his arms toward Adrian, the motion was both an invitation and a promise. "Come here," he said, patting the space beside him, his voice a soft current, pulling Adrian closer.

Adrian's lips curved into a knowing smirk. "You're trouble, you know that? You know what you're doing to me when you look like that."

"Like what?" Logan murmured, feigning innocence with the ease of someone who knew damn well he was anything but. His voice dripped with silk and sea-salt, lazy and warm, and though his tone played at naivety, the crooked curve of his smile gave him away. He stretched out across the bed in a slow, deliberate sprawl—each movement unhurried, feline, as though he had no idea the sight of him like this could undo a man.

His hair was a sun-bleached mess, wild and sleep-mussed, a halo of golden rebellion around his face. Mischief sparked in his eyes, that teasing glint Adrian had never been able to look at without wanting to ruin and worship him all at once. The hem of his worn T-shirt had crept up as he moved, exposing a sliver of skin that caught the light as if it were something sacred. The flat plane of his stomach rose and fell with the rhythm of his breath, and just beneath it, that maddening trail of hair that led downward, disappearing beneath the waistband of loose-fitting sweats. The faint shadows of his abs curved like brushstrokes on a canvas, each one whispering promises Adrian had no power to ignore.

"Come here already," Logan said, voice low, thick with mischief and a threadbare ache he barely disguised. His grin curved slowly across his face, teasing, yes, but shadowed with a hunger that trembled just beneath the skin.

Adrian moved toward him in silence, unhurried, each step carrying a quiet certainty. Heat flickered through his body, low and insistent, spreading until it reached every nerve, every hidden place that craved to be filled.

The air trembled between them, dense with the static of unsaid things, of questions neither was ready to ask but both were already answering.

When Adrian reached the edge of the bed, he paused, eyes locked with Logan's. Then, with a softness that belied the fire in him, he climbed onto the mattress and leaned over him. Adrian was staring into those silvery eyes with the wonder of a man who had somehow stumbled into his greatest dream and could not, for the life of him, retrace the path that led him here. Their limbs aligned, muscle to muscle, breath to breath, and the room seemed to hush, holding the moment like a secret.

"I seem to recall a promise of amorous activities," Logan whispered, his voice wrapped in a crooked smile, his lips grazing Adrian's as he spoke. Adrian's fingers had already found their way beneath Logan's shirt, slow and awed, his touch mapping the heat beneath the surface, coaxing a shiver from him. Logan's eyes fluttered, his breath catching as if Adrian's fingertips were plucking at something deeper than nerve, memory, maybe. Or longing.

"Or maybe," Logan murmured again, his words brushing Adrian's mouth like the tide kissing the edge of a rock, "you're all talk and no bite—"

Adrian answered not with words, but with the quiet ferocity of a kiss. His mouth claimed Logan's in one fluid motion, fingers tightening their grip, palms sliding with purpose. There was no gentleness now, only want. His hands roamed over Logan's skin as though trying to memorize it by feel alone, tugging at it, grounding them both in the here, the now.

Their bodies moved together like a storm meeting its echo, turbulent, precise, undeniable. In that moment, the world outside ceased to exist. There was no past, no future. Just the gravity between them, and the sound of breath catching, of hearts racing.

Something in Adrian's gaze shifted, the air between them growing heavier, like the charged stillness before a storm. His voice, low and hoarse, slipped through the space between them, igniting every nerve in Logan's body. "I want to do so many things to you," he whispered, the words a confession, a promise. His eyes burned with intensity, holding Logan captive. "Tell me what you had in mind."

Logan felt the heat creeping up his neck, his cheeks flushing like the first bloom of dawn. He swallowed, his voice unsteady but playful. "Well, maybe we'll pick up from where we left off on the deck?" The memory alone sent a shiver down his spine, a wave of sensation rolling over his skin.

Adrian's lips curved into a sinful smirk, one that seemed to illuminate the sharp angles of his face while softening the warmth in his eyes that never dimmed. He bit his lip, his gaze locked on Logan, studying every flicker of emotion that crossed his face. "Did you like it?" he asked, his voice a seductive melody laced with mischief and heat.

Logan's breath hitched, the teasing edge of Adrian's question drawing him closer to the edge of control. "The way I came untouched in my pants wasn't answer enough?" he whispered, the words slipping out with a raw honesty that matched the fire building inside him. To emphasize his point, he ground his hips lightly against Adrian, unable to ignore the way his body reacted so completely in Adrian's presence. Lately, it seemed impossible not to; his constant arousal was a testament to the magnetic pull between them.

Adrian's fingers traced a casual and precise path along Logan's stomach, each touch igniting a trail of heat. His hand moved as if memorizing Logan's contours, reverent yet charged with intent. "Would you want to do that again," Adrian murmured, his voice trembling slightly despite his efforts to sound confident, "or would you want more?"

Though his words carried the bravado of experience, the faint hitch in his breath betrayed him. The question hung between them, weighty and alive, each second stretching as Adrian waited for Logan's response. His chest rose and fell unevenly, and the flicker of vulnerability in his eyes revealed the truth: he wasn't just asking about the physical. He was asking about trust, about crossing another line together, about the uncharted waters of their connection.

Logan's hand slid up to cup the side of Adrian's face, his thumb brushing over his cheek. For a moment, he simply looked at him, taking in the way Adrian's emotions played across his features: the way his body tensed with anticipation, the subtle shake in his exhale. Logan could feel the depth of what Adrian was holding back, emotions rooted deep, layer upon layer, like roots tangled beneath the soil, unseen but impossible to tear free.

"You," Logan whispered finally, his voice steady now, filled with certainty and something deeper. "I want *you*. Whatever that means, whatever we find together, I want all of it."

Adrian's breath escaped him in a rush, and the tension between them broke like a dam. His lips captured Logan's in a kiss that was not just passion, but need, a physical expression of everything he couldn't put into words. His hands, still under Logan's shirt, pulled him closer as though he could fuse them together.

And in that moment, the world around them dissolved. The yacht rocked gently beneath them, cradling their vulnerability, the ocean outside whispering its eternal song. Whatever boundaries they had once known were swept away by the tide, leaving only them, raw and bare, unafraid to face it together.

Adrian pulled back just enough to see him, their foreheads still pressed, their breaths caught in the fragile space between heartbeats. His eyes had darkened, not with shadow but with depth, like a sky heavy with constellations, vast, unspoken, infinite, and yet steady, fixed entirely on Logan.

He lifted a hand, fingers tracing the line of Logan's cheekbone with a slowness that felt like veneration, as though each touch were an act of inscription, carving the memory of him into his own skin.

"Lo..." His voice was thick, breathless. "You have no idea what you do to me."

His chest tightened, the pressure of everything unsaid rising like a tide, threatening to spill over. His words came in a rush, cracking at the edges. "Sometimes I wish I could go back... back before I knew you. Just to find some way to cross paths sooner. To change the wind, the waves, anything... just to reach you earlier."

He gave a soft, self-conscious laugh and buried his face in Logan's neck, as if the warmth there could calm the storm in him. "Ignore me. I'm saying stupid things."

He tried to breathe, to swallow the swell of emotion before it broke open.

But even as he said it, the thought bloomed, uncontainable.

Oh, how he longed to journey back—back to the moment before Logan's name graced his lips. He'd sweep through every fleeting instant, redraw every course, all to discover him sooner. He'd bend the wind, shift the tides, reshape the very essence of the ocean if it meant he could steal more moments with him. Those countless years prior? They were mere waiting rooms. Lessons learned in solitude, lonely checkpoints, each one preparing Adrian for this, for the extraordinary Logan. And now that he'd found him, it's like everything else was just the map trying to lead him here.

But Logan didn't move. Didn't speak. The silence stretched, not empty, but electric. Like the whole world had stilled around this one truth. Finally, Logan's hands rose, cradling Adrian's face. He guided him gently up until their eyes met again.

"You're not," Logan whispered. "It's us, Adrian."

Those words—words they had said to each other before, again and again, like a secret language—held new weight now. In Logan's voice, they were an anchor. A vow.

And something in Adrian cracked open.

Adrian's hands moved with precision, stripping Logan's clothes with deft ease, peeling away layers. Logan followed suit, his fingers trembling as he cast Adrian's clothes aside. And then, at last, they were bare—skin to skin, a mingling of heat, and the faintest trace of sun lingering on their bodies. Their mouths met in a frenzy, lips and tongues colliding desperately and relentlessly, an untamed rhythm they couldn't control.

It was hunger, raw and unfiltered, but it wasn't new. They had kissed, touched, shared moments stolen under the sun and moon, but tonight, it was as if the ocean inside them had breached its shores. Each caress was a current pulling them deeper, each moan an undertow dragging them into the depths. Logan could feel every brush of Adrian's body, every press of skin against skin, as though his entire being had been rewired to respond to this—*him*.

"You're my addiction," Adrian murmured, voice low and frayed, his lips brushing the crook of Logan's shoulder as he inhaled deeply, drunk on the scent of him, a mix of saltwater that was engraved into their DNA by now, soap and something undeniably Logan. His words clung to the air like the aftertaste of sea spray, intoxicating and sharp.

Logan's breath hitched, his fingers threading through Adrian's sun-kissed hair, tugging gently until the tie slipped free, and the golden-brown strands cascaded like a waterfall at sunset. "God, your hair," Logan whispered, voice thick with awe and desire. "You look like something out of a myth, some sinful god sent to ruin me." His voice cracked, his lips crashing against Adrian's once more, desperate to drown in the taste of him.

"Lo," Adrian breathed, their mouths breaking just enough for air, their foreheads pressed together, the air between them fevered with truths that had simmered too long, now spilling hot and unstoppable. He looked into Logan's storm-gray eyes, luminous and wild, brimming with a trust so deep it felt ancient. The look pierced through Adrian, leaving him raw, vulnerable, wrecked in the best possible way. "You're beautiful, you are too damn beautiful," Adrian said, voice barely above a whisper, each word carrying the weight of a thousand lifetimes. "It's so unfair... How are you even real? How do I get to have this—you?" it sounded for a moment, like Adrian was not speaking to Logan, no, he was thinking aloud.

Logan's heart clenched at the reverence in Adrian's voice, a quiet awe that bordered on disbelief. But before he could respond, Adrian's lips curled into a mischievous grin, his eyes darkening with something untamed. "I'm going to wreck you tonight," he promised, the words a vow, a tempest waiting to be unleashed.

The air between them was heavy, electric, charged with a tension that shimmered like the moonlight on the waves outside. Logan's chest rose and fell in ragged breaths, his pulse crashing in his ears like the endless surf. Adrian was a force of nature—steady and unyielding but with a tenderness that anchored him. Logan was lost in him, drawn under by the current of his gaze, but then, a flicker of fear rippled through his mind, a shadow against the light.

"Ad..." Logan's voice was quiet, vacillating, breaking the rhythm of their fevered moment as Adrian's lips ghosted lower. He swallowed hard, his throat dry, his courage a fading flame. "I don't know..." His cheeks flushed as he forced himself to continue, voice barely audible. "I don't know if I'm ready... for you to... you know... *get inside me*. Like, fully." His voice cracked, his hands twitching with the weight of his admission. Embarrassment burned like salt in an open wound, but this was Adrian—his Adrian—and with him, everything felt safe.

Adrian stilled, his eyes softening as he cupped Logan's cheek with infinite care. His thumb brushed gently against the stubble there, grounding him, tethering him. "Lo," he said, his voice a low, soothing tide. "I will never, ever pressure you. You know that, right?"

Logan nodded, but Adrian continued, his tone calm, filled with the warmth of a summer sunrise. "I'm verse," he said, his lips quirking into a small, almost sheepish smile. "I probably should've mentioned that earlier. And we should have had this conversation before now, but... here we are. I'm good either way, Logan. I mean it. I usually lean toward being more dominant, but with you? I'll love whatever we share, however it feels right. You don't have to do anything you're not ready for."

Logan's heart swelled, his chest aching as he stared into Adrian's whiskey-brown eyes, which shimmered like warm honey under the faint cabin light. Adrian's honesty was a beacon, guiding him through the sea of his uncertainties.

Adrian smiled, the corners of his mouth lifting as if he were savoring the moment, then his voice dropped, rich and husky, a low murmur that sent shivers down Logan's spine. "I wanted to surprise you tonight, you know, let things flow naturally," Adrian admitted, his hand still cradling Logan's face. "But... it was obviously the wrong decision. I think I'll just tell you. You said you wanted me to lose control, to not hold back, so this is what I had in mind." He leaned closer, his breath warm and teasing against Logan's ear. "I want to rim you into oblivion, Lo. I want to taste you, devour you, make you come undone with my tongue. I've been dreaming of eating you out, of tasting that beautiful ass of yours, like you're my favorite meal for weeks now."

Logan's breath hitched, his pupils blown wide, his lips parting in a gasp. Adrian's words washed over him, intoxicating. "And," Adrian added, his voice dropping even lower, "if you're up for it, I'd love for you to fuck me. I want to feel you, completely. But if there's anything you don't want, anything that doesn't feel right, just say the word."

Logan swallowed hard, his body trembling with a desire that felt almost too big to hold inside. Adrian's confession jolted through him, sharp and exhilarating, leaving his nerves humming, his breath uneven. Logan had never imagined that the thought of someone—of Adrian—pressing his mouth, his lips, his face against the most intimate part of him would ignite something so raw, so consuming inside him. He never even thought about it, never had it been a part of his repertoire when it came to sex. Never once had it crossed his mind that such a thing could unravel him, set his nerves alight with anticipation rather than hesitation. And yet, just the way Adrian spoke of it, the ease in his voice, the quiet certainty, sent a wildfire through Logan's veins.

It should have made him self-conscious, exposed in a way that felt too much, too bare. But instead, it did the opposite; it undid him, thread by thread, the edges of his control fraying beneath the weight of Adrian's words.

The vulnerability of it was staggering, almost unbearable, but Logan didn't pull away. Didn't try to fight it. Instead, he let it settle deep in his bones, let himself feel it, let himself want it.

His voice was hoarse, hurried, as he managed to respond. "I want it," he blurted, his words rushing out, his cock twitching, leaking a pool of precum against his stomach. "Goddamn it, Adrian, I want it more than anything."

The look in Adrian's eyes then—part lust, part reverence—was enough to undo Logan completely.

Adrian's smile was a sin wrapped in silk, a quiet promise of things unspoken but deeply felt. His eyes, dark with desire, held Logan captive as he began his descent, a slow, deliberate journey down the length of Logan's body. Adrian's hands moved, caressing the smooth expanse of Logan's skin, mapping him, claiming him.

When Adrian's mouth closed around him, taking Logan's cock to the back of his throat, the sound that tore from Logan's lips was nothing short of a storm breaking free. A raw, unrestrained cry echoed in the small room, his head falling back as pleasure surged through him. But Adrian didn't linger; his lips left Logan aching, swollen, wanting, as they continued their journey lower. His hands found Logan's ass, kneading the flesh like a sculptor shaping something holy. And then, with a slow, unyielding strength, Adrian's hands drifted down the back of Logan's thighs and pushed them toward Logan's chest, opening him completely.

Logan felt exposed in a way he never had before. His breath came in shallow bursts, his chest rising and falling as heat flushed his entire body. His hole, bared and vulnerable, was the center of Adrian's focus, and the hunger in Adrian's gaze made Logan's pulse thunder in his ears. But it was Adrian. Always Adrian. The man who had seen him—truly *seen* him—not just his surface, but every scar, every shadow, every light within him. Adrian had explored Logan's soul with the same care he gave to Logan's body now, and there wasn't a moment of doubt. If there was anyone to guide him through this first, this new frontier of intimacy, it was Adrian. No one else could have made him feel this safe, this wanted.

Adrian spread him further, Logan's breath catching as he felt the cool whisper of air against his most sensitive flesh. And then—

Adrian's mouth. His lips closed over Logan's entrance, pressing open-mouthed kisses that sent jolts of electricity through him. Logan's body tensed and then melted under Adrian's touch as his tongue teased him, brushing over the tender flesh with a skill and precision that made Logan's mind spin. Each pass was a new discovery, a spark igniting a fire he didn't know could burn so fiercely.

Logan was shaking now, his entire body vibrating with a need so profound it consumed him. The sensations Adrian evoked were like nothing he'd ever experienced before, pleasure that was sharp and overwhelming, yet somehow tender, like the ocean's pull as it carries you away. His mind emptied of everything but this; Adrian's mouth, Adrian's hands, Adrian's love.

Every flick of Adrian's tongue left Logan gasping, trembling, his body taut like a bowstring ready to snap. He felt utterly entranced, his world narrowing to this single, infinite moment. For the first time in his life, Logan felt what it truly meant to surrender; not to lose himself, but to give himself fully, completely, to someone he trusted more than he trusted the ground beneath his feet or the waves beneath his board. And it was beautiful. Adrian made it beautiful.

Logan's moans spilled from his lips; his dick was rock hard between his legs, spilling precum on his belly as it twitched from the ecstasy. Adrian remained utterly unhurried, his kisses a gentle touch, patient and calm, as though he had all the time in the world to worship Logan, to savor every inch of him. His mouth moved with the kind of devotion that spoke volumes without a single word, and Logan was helpless against the pull.

"Fuck," Logan moaned, his voice a trembling wreck of need. "Adrian—mmph—*more*," he begged, his body torn between the urge to grasp his aching cock and the desperate desire to let this exquisite torment stretch on forever.

Adrian heard him, felt him, and his tongue responded with fervor. It took on a bolder rhythm, more insistent now as it pressed and probed against Logan's entrance. His tongue alternated between sucking at the sensitive pucker and lapping at it like it was the sweetest treat on a sweltering summer's day, savoring every moment. Each pass was deliberate, Adrian letting his tongue breach the tight ring of muscle, teasing the tender inside walls with slow, agonizing strokes.

Logan's entrance was slick with saliva, glistening under the dim light, and Adrian was drunk on it; on Logan's taste, his scent, the primal symphony of his moans filling the cabin like the melody of waves against the hull. Adrian was utterly undone, consumed by Logan's essence, and he couldn't stop himself. His tongue worked faster, more frantically, stiffening to push deeper into Logan, thrusting in and out, each motion coaxing sounds from Logan that bordered on desperation. With his tongue stiff, Adrian started to fuck Logan, licking his inner walls, drunk and totally lost in sensation, before retreating and pushing his tongue back again.

The cabin was alive with sound: Logan's cries, the soft squelch of Adrian's tongue against him, and the distant, rhythmic lull of water lapping outside. Adrian was relentless, lost in Logan, lost in the intoxicating flavor and feel of him, his mouth and tongue moving as though they were made for this moment, for Logan.

Finally, Adrian drew back, sucking one finger into his mouth as his eyes flicked to Logan's face. His lips were wet, swollen, his gaze darkened with lust and a touch of mischief. He considered getting lube but decided against it, just one finger for now, as he did not want to leave that spot; he did not want to stop even for a moment. He licked Logan's entrance again, coating it generously with saliva, ensuring it was as slick as possible, before pressing his finger inside.

Logan gasped, his breath catching in his throat as the intrusion sent a bolt of pleasure through him. Adrian's finger was unhurried, gentle, moving with care until it found its destination. When he brushed against Logan's prostate, a sound tore from Logan's throat, half-moan, half-cry, his body trembling like a storm-tossed wave.

Once.

Twice.

Adrian's touch was sure, precise, the pad of his finger stroking Logan's most sensitive spot, drawing out moans that seemed to reverberate off every surface. Logan's cock jerked, precum pooling at the tip, and then, like a breaking wave, his body tensed, his hole tightening around Adrian's finger. With a choked scream, Logan came, his release spilling in thick, hot ropes over his stomach, his cries mingling with the rhythm of the sea.

"Fuck, fuck, *fuckkkkk!*" Logan's voice broke, his body shuddering, caught in the overwhelming intensity of his climax. Adrian didn't stop. He kept massaging Logan's prostate, his tongue teasing at his entrance even as Logan's body trembled in the aftermath. Adrian was savoring every moment, every sound, every tremor, as though he was committing it all to memory, engraving it onto his soul.

Logan lay still, his chest heaving as he panted, his eyes closed, his body trembling with aftershocks that rippled through him in sporadic waves. Adrian moved slowly, reverently, his touch light as he gently withdrew his fingers from the depths of Logan's body. He pressed a tender kiss to the spot where Logan's torso met his thigh, a gesture of affection as much as it was of worship. Then Adrian traveled upward, his lips and tongue tracing a path along Logan's skin.

When Adrian reached Logan's stomach, his lips brushed over the pearly remnants of Logan's release. He licked it clean, savoring the taste like it was ambrosia, as though it were his reward for the orgasm he had coaxed from Logan's very soul. Adrian felt insatiable, drunk on Logan's essence, his addiction clawing for more, always more.

Finally, Adrian settled beside him, his body close but not overwhelming. Logan stirred, his lashes fluttering open, and Adrian was greeted by the sight of him—messy, wrecked, and utterly breathtaking. Logan looked undone in the most exquisite way, his cheeks tinged pink, his lips slightly parted, his stormy gray eyes hazy with exhaustion and contentment.

"For the second time in a row," Logan murmured, his voice a little hoarse, a little awed, "you've managed to make me come without even touching my dick." A blush deepened on his cheeks as he added, "You deserve an award."

Adrian laughed, a sound rich with joy and affection, and he pulled Logan into his arms, threading his fingers through the strands of Logan's sandy-blond hair. The sensation of Logan in his arms, warm and pliant, filled him with a quiet wonder. Every inch of him marveled at the fact that he got to be here, that he got to love this extraordinary man.

"I don't need an award," Adrian teased, brushing his nose playfully against Logan's. "But if you insist, I'd gladly accept the honor of being your personal chef. You've just become my favorite breakfast, lunch, and dinner." His lips curled into a wicked grin as he continued, "Between eating you like that and blowing you, I could feast on you all day long and never get tired."

Logan huffed a breathless laugh, his blush deepening even as a playful smirk tugged at his lips. Adrian's words were bold, shameless, but the way he said them, with a lightness that wrapped around the depth of his devotion, made Logan feel cherished, adored, and utterly his.

Logan reached for Adrian's face, cradling it in his hands lovingly, and pulled him into a kiss. It was deep, slow, and filled with the taste of Logan branded over Adrian's insatiable tongue, a hunger that simmered just below the surface, a promise of what was to come.

"So," Logan murmured when their lips parted, his eyes darkening with lust as they roamed over Adrian's body, flawless and maddeningly enticing, every curve of muscle taut, his cock thick and full, resting against his sculpted stomach. "The rest of those activities you mentioned earlier... are they still on the table?" His own cock twitched at the thought, already stirring to life, his body vibrating with anticipation. He knew that in less than fifteen minutes, he'd be more than ready, but with Adrian looking like *that*—all naked and glorious—he figured it'd be much sooner.

Just the thought of being inside Adrian, of sliding into his tight heat and losing himself entirely, was enough to make his breath hitch and his skin hum. He could already picture it: Adrian arching beneath him, moaning his name, drawing him deeper until there was no part of Logan that wasn't consumed by him. The idea alone sent a sharp jolt of arousal through him.

It still surprised Logan how voracious he was with Adrian. He had never thought of himself as an overly sexual person, at least, that was what he told himself. In past relationships, his girlfriends had often taken the lead while he coasted along, playing the part expected of him without questioning why he always felt like a spectator in his own desire. He had assumed it was just how he was built, more cerebral than carnal, more in his head than in his body. Most of the time, he had been content to take matters into his own hands, quite literally, relieving himself and jerking off when the mood struck without much thought. It was simpler that way. No expectations, no confusion, no having to explain why he wasn't reaching for the person beside him in bed. With his last girlfriend, it had unraveled even further, an unspoken distance growing between them, widening like a crack in glass.

He had avoided sex for almost the last year of their relationship. He had blamed it on the pressure of his MBA, on the long hours hunched over research papers, on exhaustion and stress. He had convinced himself that the problem was time, that if he could just clear his head, if he could just get through this phase, things would settle. But they never did. And the truth was, he had started enjoying the time they spent apart more than the time they were together. He had felt more like himself when he wasn't trying to force something that wasn't there, when he wasn't pretending.

But Adrian... Adrian had rewritten every rule, turned every expectation on its head. With Adrian, Logan was always hungry, always aching, always reaching for him. They couldn't keep their hands off each other. Every touch, every kiss, every stolen glance was charged, electric, leaving them both vibrating with want.

It was as though their bodies had synced to the same rhythm, an unspoken agreement to never let a day pass without wringing every ounce of pleasure from each other. Twice a day was a minimum, but more often than not, they reached three or four, driven by an intoxicating mix of youth, passion, and the closeness of spending every waking moment together. Hands, mouths, bodies—nothing was off-limits, and everything seemed to ignite the flame between them.

Adrian grinned wickedly, his dark eyes flashing with heat. "It's so on the table," he said, his voice a low rumble that sent shivers down Logan's spine. Before Logan could respond, Adrian sprang from the bed with a kind of effortless grace and disappeared for barely a moment. When he returned, he held the lube and a box of condoms, his grin still in place. Logan smirked at the speed, knowing that even a marathon runner would have applauded Adrian's record time.

The unopened box of condoms caught Logan's attention immediately, a detail that seemed to stand out in the haze of desire. It was new, untouched, and it tugged at a quiet curiosity in the back of his mind. He hadn't seen it before, and the thought that Adrian might have bought it in secret sent a flicker of something unnamable through him. Did Adrian pick it up recently, quietly preparing for this moment? Or, selfishly, Logan wondered if Adrian had bought it long before they met—when his life had been untouched by Logan—and had never found the right moment to use it because now all thoughts of anyone else had been eclipsed by him.

The possibility sent a strange, possessive thrill through Logan, though he kept his voice steady. "Do we need it?" he asked, glancing at Adrian, his tone carrying more curiosity than hesitation.

Adrian paused, considering Logan's question with the same openness he always approached their conversations. "I don't know," he admitted. "We've already had the talk, we both got checked, and we've only been with each other since. But..." He looked at Logan with a softness in his eyes. "I thought you might want it, just as a precaution. In case it made you feel more comfortable."

Logan shook his head, his voice firm. "No," he stressed, leaning forward as he let his hand skim along Adrian's cheek. "I don't want anything between us. I want to be bare inside you," he declared, the honesty of his words echoing between them.

Adrian's eyes darkened with a mixture of heat and emotion, and he let the box of condoms fall to the side, forgotten. Logan reached for the lube, his intent clear, while Adrian climbed back onto him, their bodies aligning perfectly. Adrian's lips wandered from Logan's chest to his shoulders, laying down tenderness that would one day return to Logan like a phantom, a touch remembered more vividly for being gone. Adrian's cock, flushed an angry shade of purple, bobbed between them with every movement, a visual testament to his need.

Logan's hands found Adrian's hair, his fingers threading through the strands, tugging gently as he spoke. "Do you—" He hesitated, his voice soft, filled with a kind of shy eagerness. "Do you like to be rimmed? Do you enjoy it? Because I really... I really want to try that on you."

Adrian froze for a moment, his breath hitching as he processed Logan's words. Then, his lips curled into a slow, sinful smile. "I do," he admitted, his voice low and thick with arousal. "But hearing you say that, hearing you want it... I think I might enjoy it even more now."

Logan's pulse quickened, the thought of returning even a fraction of the pleasure Adrian had given him setting his blood on fire. His hands tightened in Adrian's hair as he whispered, "Then let me."

Adrian groaned loudly, the sound raw and guttural, as though Logan's words alone were enough to push him to the edge. His hand moved instinctively to his cock, gripping the base tightly in a desperate attempt to stave off the impending orgasm. "I do, dammit," he panted, his voice rough and trembling. "But if that pretty mouth of yours touches me, I'm going to lose it. I swear, Logan, I'll come the second you do."

Logan's lips curled into a wicked smile, his gray eyes darkening with a new confidence, a command that Adrian found utterly irresistible. "So, for now," Logan said, before he moved swiftly, flipping Adrian onto his back with a grace and strength that left them both breathless, "I'll take just a small taste of you. Then, I'll prep you."

Adrian's body tensed, his breath hitching as Logan leaned over him, the shift in their dynamic sending shivers cascading down his spine. Logan's gaze burned into him, filled with intent, and his voice dropped further, taking on a commanding tone that made Adrian's cock throb painfully. "And you're not allowed to come until I say so," Logan declared, his words leaving no room for negotiation.

Adrian's head fell back against the pillows, a strained groan escaping his lips as he fought to keep himself from unraveling right then and there. His cock twitched, leaking against his stomach, and the weight of Logan's dominance made him tremble. "Fuck," Adrian hissed, his body arching involuntarily. "You can't just say things like that... I'm.... Logan, I'm so close."

Logan smirked, leaning down to press a firm kiss to Adrian's hip, his breath warm and teasing against his skin. "You'll hold it," Logan said simply, his voice steady and firm. "Because I said so."

Adrian bit his lip, his hands clutching at the sheets as he nodded, every inch of his body stiff with anticipation and the delicious agony of restraint. Logan's touch, his words, his very presence, had Adrian on the edge of surrender, and he couldn't help but revel in it. For all the times Adrian had been the one to lead, to guide, Logan's unexpected command now felt like a storm overtaking him, wild and unstoppable, and Adrian, for once, was more than willing to let himself be swept away.

There were so many sides to Logan. He was a kaleidoscope of contradictions, a tapestry woven from countless shades and textures that Adrian could never tire of exploring. He was sunlight breaking through storm clouds, laughter dancing on the edge of melancholy, and a quiet strength that hid behind an ocean of vulnerability. Every glance, every touch, every word revealed a new facet of him, and Adrian marveled at the endless depth of his soul. There was the Logan who stood fearless on the crest of a wave, daring the sea to test him. The Logan who laughed with abandon, his joy as infectious as the golden rays of the sun. The Logan who held his silence like a fragile shell, shielding himself from the world but allowing Adrian to see inside, to glimpse the raw, unguarded beauty within. Adrian adored every part of him. The rough edges, the hidden wounds, the flashes of tenderness that stole his breath away—each piece of Logan felt like a treasure, a secret waiting to be unraveled. He was a complex song, each note rich with meaning, and Adrian could spend a lifetime learning its melody.

To love Logan was to love the ocean: vast, unpredictable, and achingly beautiful. It was to dive deep into the unknown, to surrender to the tides, to be humbled by the power of it. And Adrian had never been more willing to let himself be swept away.

Adrian's entire body trembled as Logan moved with purpose, his lips trailing quickly down Adrian's torso. The urgency in Logan's movements was palpable, and Adrian lifted his legs instinctively, granting Logan full access, exposing himself without hesitation. Logan's gaze fell to the star-shaped opening before him, framed by a soft dusting of hair, and he bit his tongue, his cock already hard and aching.

"Fuck, this is so hot," Logan murmured, his voice reverent, as though the sight of Adrian like this had completely unraveled him. He hadn't expected to find this view so intoxicating, but here he was, utterly captivated, his desire roaring.

With a breath caught between veneration and craving, Logan leaned in, his hands anchoring against Adrian's hips. He pressed a kiss there first, before his tongue flicked out, tentative and slow, dancing over Adrian's entrance. The taste of him bloomed instantly, earthy and electric, and

Logan felt it unravel across his tongue, a sensation that gripped him low and deep, as though Adrian had written himself into his body with nothing more than heat and skin.

Logan's tongue on his most intimate part sent a shockwave through Adrian, his body jolting as a deep, guttural groan escaped him. His hand gripped the base of his cock with white-knuckled restraint, the need to hold off his orgasm overwhelming him. Logan's lips twitched into a smirk at the sight; it was a heady feeling, to have this kind of power over someone as strong and composed as Adrian.

True to his promise, Logan kept it brief, though every moment felt monumental. He pressed his lips to Adrian's opening, kissing it softly, then let his tongue glide over the sensitive skin. When he pushed the tip of his tongue inside, just for a fleeting moment, Adrian gasped, his body shuddering, his thighs quivering against Logan's shoulders.

Logan pulled back reluctantly, his breath coming in shallow pants as he reached for the lube. His hands shook slightly, not from nerves but from the sheer magnitude of the moment, as he poured a generous amount onto his fingers, the cool liquid pooling in his palm. He glanced up at Adrian, his gray eyes blazing with determination and desire.

"You're incredible," Logan said softly, almost to himself, as he positioned his slick fingers, ready to take the next step. The trust and vulnerability Adrian offered him in that moment felt like a gift—a sacred, unspoken promise—and Logan vowed to treasure it.

"You can start with two fingers," Adrian said, his voice shaky but firm, his cheeks flushed. "But go easy, it's been a long while for me."

"Okay," Logan replied, his own breath coming in ragged bursts, his chest rising and falling as he fought to stay composed. His hands trembled slightly as he brought his slick fingers to Adrian's entrance, brushing softly around the sensitive ring of muscle. He ignored Adrian's suggestion to start with two, instead easing just one finger inside. He wasn't willing to take any chances; not with Adrian, not with this. The last thing he wanted was to hurt him, even unintentionally.

Adrian's response was instant, a deep moan rolling from his throat as his back arched off the bed. His head fell back, messy hair spilling across the pillows, and one hand pinched his nipple, his lips parting in a breathless gasp. The sight alone was enough to make Logan's cock throb, and the temptation to reach down and stroke himself was overwhelming. But the thought of being inside Adrian, of feeling that tight warmth and suction around his shaft, was infinitely better.

Logan moved his finger in slow, steady thrusts, marveling at the way Adrian's body seemed to pull him in, as if it had been waiting for this. Each sound Adrian made, every gasp and moan, spurred Logan on, but he kept his movements careful, patient. When he felt Adrian relax further, he added a second finger, gently scissoring them to stretch him, his other hand resting on Adrian's thigh to steady him.

Adrian's moans grew louder, his hips rocking in time with Logan's movements, and Logan couldn't resist any longer. He leaned forward, still working his fingers inside Adrian, and kissed him deeply. Their lips met in a clash of passion and desperation, the kiss primal and consuming.

"Does it feel good?" Logan asked, as he pulled back just enough to see Adrian's face. Sweat glistened on Adrian's brow, his skin flushed, his eyes hazy with lust and need.

"Yes," Adrian breathed, his voice trembling as Logan picked up the rhythm, his fingers pushing deeper, finding the spot that made Adrian's whole body jerk. "Add another one," he managed to get out, his hands gripping the sheets as if anchoring himself. "Another one, and then you can fuck me. I need you, Logan. I need to feel that amazing cock inside of me. I need to feel *you* inside of me."

Logan's heart thundered in his chest, the sound echoing in his ears as though the world had shrunk to just this: Adrian, spread beneath him, trembling with need. He pressed a soft, grounding kiss to Adrian's temple before adding more lube and carefully sliding a third finger inside. Logan moved slowly, carefully, working his fingers in a rhythm designed to coax Adrian open, to prepare him for what was coming.

When his fingers brushed against Adrian's prostate, the reaction was immediate. Adrian's body arched off the bed, his head thrown back as a silent scream escaped his lips, his cock twitching violently with the touch. Adrian's hand gripped the base of his length harder, his knuckles white, as he moaned, writhing beneath Logan like the sea in a storm.

"Get. Inside. Me. Lo. Now," Adrian demanded, his voice broken and breathless, his need palpable, his accent thicker now.

Logan obeyed, slowly withdrawing his fingers, his hands trembling as he reached for the lube. He coated his cock with a generous layer, the cool slickness doing little to temper the heat coursing through him. Positioning himself against Adrian's opening, Logan took a deep, steadying breath. The sight of Adrian flushed, panting, and waiting was enough to make his head spin.

He pushed forward, gently but firmly, feeling the tight muscles give way under the slight pressure. Adrian's body welcomed him, the resistance easing as Logan sank deeper, inch by inch, until he was fully seated inside. His eyes rolled back as he bottomed out, the heat and pressure of Adrian's body around him, along with the taste of Adrian's opening still lingering on his tongue, made him shudder. It was a feeling that consumed and wrecked him. He let out a shaky breath, his forehead falling to Adrian's shoulder as he tried to hold himself together.

"Just a moment," Adrian murmured, his voice soft as he shifted slightly, his body adjusting to the intrusion. "Fuck Logan, you're huge." He moaned and pulled Logan into a kiss, their lips crashing together in a desperate, almost primal need. It wasn't graceful or controlled; it was messy, raw, the kind of kiss born from two people struggling to breathe through the intensity of their connection. "You feel amazing inside me," Adrian breathed against Logan's lips, not stopping the kiss as he let his tongue tangle with Logan's.

When Adrian finally pulled back, his chest heaving, his eyes locked onto Logan's with a fire that sent a shiver through him. "Move," Adrian instructed.

Logan obeyed, pulling back slowly before thrusting back in. The sound that tore from Adrian's throat was loud, uninhibited, and Logan was sure anyone on the neighboring boats could hear it. He didn't care. He couldn't care. He was too consumed by the sensation of Adrian around him, the tight heat, the way his body clenched and released with every thrust.

"Fuck," Adrian breathed, his voice breaking as Logan began to set a rhythm, each movement sending shockwaves of pleasure through them both. Their bodies moved wildly, as the world around them blurred into nothingness.

In that moment, Logan felt invincible—a god among mortals, the most powerful being alive. The sight of Adrian, undone beneath him, moaning and writhing in pure ecstasy, was intoxicating. Knowing that he was the one bringing Adrian to this point, that every sound, every shudder, was because of him, filled Logan with a heady sense of purpose.

But he also knew his control was slipping, the overwhelming pleasure threatening to undo him. Determined to make every second count, Logan leaned back, grasping Adrian's legs behind the knees and lifting them over his shoulders. The shift in position arched Adrian's back off the mattress, opening him further, and Logan felt himself sink even deeper into Adrian's heat. The sensation was blinding, raw, and perfect.

Logan tightened his grip on Adrian's hips, holding him steady as he began to thrust with purpose, each movement sharp and precise, feeling the room with the smacking sound and the wet sound of the lube as he pumped himself in and out of Adrian's channel. His hips slammed against Adrian with an intensity that grew with every motion, the angle perfectly designed to strike Adrian's prostate again and again.

Adrian's moans filled the cabin, spilling from his lips in a tangle of Hebrew and English, his voice breaking with each shuddering gasp. There was something primal in it, something unrestrained, as if pleasure had stripped him down to the barest version of himself, leaving only need, only feeling.

And God, Logan wanted to give it to him, all of it. He wanted to push him past the edge, to draw out every sound, every tremor, to make Adrian remember this with every fiber of his being. He wanted to ruin him for anyone else, to mark him, to brand this moment into his skin and his soul so deeply that no touch, no kiss, no breath against his body would ever feel quite the same again.

Adrian's hands were everywhere—gripping, clawing, desperate—searching for something solid, something real, as if the ground had fallen away and only Logan could hold him above the dark. His fingers curled into flesh like lifelines, like prayers, like he was afraid of vanishing. And Logan... Logan drank it in, every shudder, every gasp, every tremor of surrender. He moved with purpose, with devotion, unraveling Adrian slowly, reverently, until there was nothing left but sensation, nothing left but Adrian's body and Logan's name on his lips, claimed without words, wholly, completely, his.

Leaning forward, Logan tilted his head to press a soft kiss to Adrian's ankle, the tender gesture a stark contrast to the relentless pace of his thrusts. He let his teeth graze the delicate skin, biting down just enough to elicit another loud moan from Adrian. The sound sent a jolt of electricity through Logan, and he groaned, his own pleasure cresting dangerously close to the edge.

"Come," Logan commanded, his voice rough and filled with authority, sweat dripping from his brow as he fought to hold himself back. The word hung in the air like an unbreakable vow, and Adrian obeyed, his body tensing as he let go completely. His release was explosive, his cries echoing through the room as he came, his body clenching tightly around Logan.

The sensation of Adrian's walls spasming around him sent Logan spiraling. With a guttural moan, he followed closely behind, his hips stuttering as he thrust deeply one last time. His release tore through him leaving him breathless and trembling.

For a fleeting, infinite second, Adrian felt his soul slip free; untethered, drifting beyond the edges of the room, of his body, of thought itself. It floated somewhere weightless, somewhere silent, before collapsing back into him in a rush of breath and trembling flesh. His release hit with the force of something divine, too vast for his body to contain, too bright to fully survive. After being held at the edge for so long, after the ache of denial and the fire of wanting, the unraveling was volcanic. Shattering. Sacred. It left him gasping, wrecked in the most exquisite way, as if pleasure had rewritten the rules of gravity and time.

His body trembled faintly in the aftermath, his breath coming in shallow pants as he clung to the remnants of his composure. For a long while, neither of them moved, their bodies tangled together, their hearts pounding in an unspoken rhythm that felt like an extension of their connection. The room was quiet, save for their breaths and the faint hum of the ocean beyond the cabin walls.

Slowly, Logan shifted, lowering Adrian's legs with care as his hands stroked down the length of Adrian's thighs. The gesture wasn't rushed; it was deliberate, tender, an unspoken testament to how much Logan cherished this moment, cherished *him*. He leaned forward, pressing a feather-light kiss to Adrian's forehead, his lips lingering as though to silently convey the depth of his awe.

Adrian let out a shaky breath, his voice barely more than a whisper as he broke the silence. "Oh my fucking god."

Logan chuckled, his voice low and warm, a sound that vibrated between them like the faint rumble of distant thunder. "Indeed," he agreed, his tone carrying a mix of satisfaction, wonder, and a playful edge. He brushed a stray strand of hair from Adrian's damp forehead, his thumb lingering for a moment before pulling back just enough to look into Adrian's eyes.

The moment between them was tender, and steeped in an intimacy that went beyond words. They lay there for a beat, their breaths gradually syncing.

"I'll be right back," Logan said softly, his voice laced with care. Reluctantly, he pulled out of Adrian, his movements gentle, mindful of the tenderness in the wake of their passion. He slipped off the bed and padded to the adjacent bathroom, his steps light but hurried. Grabbing a face towel, he ran it under warm water, wringing it out before quickly returning to Adrian's side.

Adrian had barely moved. He lay there, his body lax, utterly spent and still trembling faintly from the intensity of their shared experience. Logan couldn't help the flicker of pride that coursed through him as he took in the sight. He'd done that. He'd brought Adrian to this beautiful, wrecked state, and the thought filled him with both satisfaction and a deeper tenderness.

Sitting beside Adrian, Logan began to clean him with the utmost care. He tenderly wiped Adrian's chest and stomach, his movements unhurried, his touch reverent. He worked his way lower, softly running the warm towel over Adrian's cock and the sensitive skin around his entrance, cleaning him thoroughly. Groaning when he saw his cum spilling from Adrian's hole, he watched it, feeling his cock give a little twitch, an effort to stand again, but it was futile for now.

Adrian's breathing hitched for a moment but then settled, and Logan smiled softly to himself, finishing quickly before wiping himself down with efficiency. Once satisfied, he tossed the towel aside and climbed back into bed, straight into Adrian's arms.

Adrian sighed contentedly as he enveloped Logan, their bodies fitting together as though they'd been made for this, for each other. Reaching for the switch by the bed, Adrian flicked off the light, leaving the room in near-complete darkness save for the faint, golden glow spilling in from the galley. The atmosphere felt cocooned, safe, like the world had faded into the background.

"Logan?" Adrian murmured into the quiet night, his voice filled with sincerity.

"Mmm?" Logan replied, his embrace tightening ever so slightly.

"I'm so glad I met you," Adrian said, the weight of his words hanging in the still air between them.

The words stripped Logan bare more than touch ever could, leaving his skin prickling, his throat tight, his whole body humming with the ache of wanting to answer in kind. "Me too," he hushed, pressing a kiss to Adrian's shoulder. "Best day of my goddamn life."

The words resonated like a tender promise, yet both understood the unwritten pact that forbade them from voicing their dreams of the future. This silent understanding formed a delicate boundary, a gossamer thread neither was brave enough to sever. Their love existed in the present moment, vibrant and unvarnished, yet it was softly cloaked in the unacknowledged truth that all beautiful things must eventually come to an end.

Adrian nestled into the moment, eyes closed as his fingertips danced gently over the contours of Logan's chest. Thoughts flickered in his mind like fleeting candlelight: *When this ends, I will gather the fragments of my heart. I will endure. I always find a way.*

There would be an "after" of Logan Vaughn, and it loomed heavy with the promise of heartbreak.

Yet for tonight, all that existed was this—Logan's enveloping warmth, the rhythmic pulse of his heart, and the serene haven found in the embrace of the man Adrian had dared to love.

For now, Adrian decided, he would live in this moment. He would let Logan's gentle touch anchor him, allowing the warmth of his body to seep into every aching corner of his soul.

The weight of Logan's thigh draped over Adrian's, the slow bloom of sweat cooling between their bodies. The faint scent of salt still clung to their skin, mingled with the rich, musky warmth of sex and summer. Logan's hair tickled Adrian's shoulder, while the scratch of his stubble against Adrian's collarbone felt like an anchor, something real in a dream that was already beginning to slip through his fingers.

It was perfect. Too perfect.

He absorbed it entirely. Every nuance, every sound, every transient flicker of motion. He endeavored to weave it into the fabric of his memory, thread by delicate thread, ensuring that when it inevitably unraveled, he would possess this moment to retreat to again.

And still, beneath the euphoria and the warm ache blossoming in every limb, beneath the shimmering afterglow, there lingered a quiet ache, a truth that was both inevitable and heart-wrenching: his heart was destined to break. It was not a matter of if, but rather when.

The ache of certainty nestled deep within his chest, yet Adrian embraced it without hesitation. He was prepared to offer Logan his heart, fully aware of its impending shatter. When the moment arrived, Adrian would make it effortless for Logan to break his heart, for he would do anything—absolutely anything—for him. Logan possessed his heart wholly, each bruised and battered fragment of it, and Adrian had no desire to reclaim it. Logan was the sole reason that scarred heart continued to beat, the only reason Adrian truly felt alive.

But it couldn't last. Adrian knew that.

Adrian had always known that love like this wasn't made to last, not for him. He was made of borrowed things: borrowed time, borrowed countries, borrowed moments that never belonged to him. He didn't have the luxury of permanence. He didn't come from a place where love stayed.

He had nothing to offer someone like Logan, nothing to anchor him to this fleeting, beautiful connection they'd built. Logan came from a world of opportunity and freedom, a world Adrian had only glimpsed from the outside. Adrian's own world? It was more an echo than a reflection of this one, with no safety net and no gilded future. He hadn't come from wealth or privilege. His parents had scraped by, and as a teenager, Adrian had worked just to help them keep the lights on. When he'd joined the military, a chunk of his paycheck had gone straight back home for years, a lifeline for his family until his father had finally found a steady footing.

There wasn't some grand career waiting for him when this bubble burst. No degree. No apartment of his own. Just the stark reality of going back to that dot on the map in the Middle East, a far cry from Logan's world. Adrian's bank account was already stretched thin, and once this dreamlike adventure ended, he knew Logan would return to the States, to the life waiting for him there. And Adrian? He would go back to his.

They were too different, too far apart in every way that mattered. This was a bubble, fragile and fleeting, and Adrian could feel the tension building around its edges. It was going to pop. He knew it.

It was just a matter of *when*.

But for now, for tonight, he let it all go. Adrian closed his eyes and focused on Logan's touch, the gentle rhythm of his breaths, the weight of his body pressed close.

He sank into it, letting the warmth cradle him, letting the love wash through him like the tide pushing a lone man clinging to driftwood, carrying him toward shore instead of away. Logan's breath slowed into the rhythm of sleep, but Adrian stayed awake, gathering it all: the hush of sheets, the cadence of breath, every impossible detail, as if holding fast to driftwood of his own, unwilling to let it slip from his grasp.

When this chapter closes, as it eventually will, he will carry the weight of these memories with him. He will hold onto this night, allowing it to warm him through the impending, cold silence that follows.

And when all of it comes crashing down, he will harbor no regrets. Not even a fleeting second of remorse. Instead, he will softly express gratitude for the devastation. It was genuine, a tangible piece of his existence.

Even if it was only for a brief moment.

Chapter 9
When the Fake Smile Finally Cracked

I try to remember. I always do. I close my eyes, and I chase the moment—trace the edges of time, desperate to find the exact second I fell in love with you.

Was it the moment you gasped for air on the beach, seawater spilling from your lips, eyes wild and desperate, your chest rising in frantic, uneven heaves beneath the merciless sun? Or was it later, when you finally caught your breath, when you pushed the hair from your face, salt-streaked and trembling, and grinned at me like life was some grand, reckless adventure and you had already decided I was coming along for the ride?

Was it the moment my hands, still shaking from the weight of pulling you back from the storm, reached for my mother's bracelet, the only thing I had left of her, the only thing I swore I would never part with, and gave it to you? Was it the moment my body, my heart, my everything made a decision before my mind could catch up, that you, a stranger then, should have the one thing that had always meant safety to me?

I wonder if I should have known then, in that instant, that I was already losing myself to you. That when I let you walk away with that bracelet fastened around your wrist, I had given you more than a piece of metal.

I had given you my history. My protection.

And maybe, without realizing it, I had given you my heart.

No. That was too soon. Wasn't it?

Perhaps it was that night, the first night, when you invited me for a beer. I remember stepping into the bar and seeing you there, waiting for me, tall and broad your blond hair styled and already messy from the humidity in the most perfect way, leaning back in your chair like you belonged to the world and nothing could ever touch you. And something inside me, something deep, something ancient, whispered, that is the kind of man I want in my life. I should have known then that wanting you would be the beginning of my undoing.

But I didn't.

We talked. We laughed. You held your beer bottle lazily between your fingers, spinning it on the table, eyes never leaving mine. And I remember thinking: how is this happening? How am I sitting across from you, and how do I already feel like I've known you forever?

When we left the restaurant, when we walked side by side beneath the hush of the streetlights, I remember how badly I wanted to kiss you. The wanting was unbearable, a pulse beneath my skin, a hunger in my bones. But I held myself back. I bit the inside of my cheek, shoved my hands into my pockets, forced myself to wait. I didn't know how to touch you yet, didn't know how to reach for you without breaking something fragile and unnamed between us.

But God, I was burning.

And you—you knew. I saw it in the way you looked at me, like the whole night had been leading up to something inevitable.

That was when I knew.

Not just that I wanted you, not just that I was falling, no, falling is too gentle a word. I was crashing. I was shattering. I was being undone.

And maybe you'll call me dramatic.

Maybe they'll say I was young, and love does that to young men. But if that
was just youth, then why, after all these years, after all this wreckage, I still
close my eyes and find myself there? Tell me why my body still remembers the
exact shape of your laughter, the precise cadence of your voice when you said
my name with that thick American accent of yours?
Because the truth is, I never stopped being that man in the bar, staring at you
like the earth had tilted beneath my feet.
So if we go back to my first question, if I try to trace the moment I fell, if I try
to carve it into time, find the exact second my heart recognized yours—
It wasn't a single moment.
It was that night. It was every glance, every laugh, every breath. It was the
way my hands trembled with the weight of wanting you, the way the space
between us felt like a tether, invisible but unbreakable. It was the first time I
saw you, and the first time I had to leave you, and the first time I knew, with
something deep and primal and terrifying, that this—you—was it.
I never stopped being the man who burned for you.
And yet, here I am.
A body wasting away. A life measured in the slow, inevitable collapse of time.
And you, you are not here.
You, who promised me nothing and still managed to take everything.
You, who left without warning.
You, who put a ring on another's hand and walked away like love was a thing
that could be discarded, like it was sand slipping through your fingers.
You, who were my greatest joy and my undoing in equal measure.
I always try to remember.
And maybe that is my curse. That even now, as time stretches thin and my
body betrays me, I am still chasing the moment I lost you.

Even as my body withers, as my breath grows thinner, as time folds in on itself, I am still reaching for the shadow of you. Still tracing the shape of your name in the quiet spaces of my mind, still hoping... God, still hoping.

And if I am being honest—if I am letting it all spill out now, letting the truth slip from between my fingers like grains of sand—then here it is:

From all the things a man can wish for in his final days, from all the fleeting prayers whispered into the dark, having you is my deepest wish.

Not more time. Not mercy from what is coming. Not a reprieve from the inevitable.

Just you.

You, walking through that door, back into my life, back into my arms, like you were never gone. You, with the same reckless smile, the same impossible light in your eyes, the same hands that once held me like I was something irreplaceable.

You.

November 10, 2020—Seattle, Washington—Two Years Later

LOGAN LAY SPRAWLED ON his stomach, his body aching in that sweet, numbing way that followed a night of abandon. The sheets beneath him were cool now, sticking to his damp skin in places, and he could feel the slow thrum of his pulse in his ears as his breath evened out. He was back in Zack's bed again, the room thick with the tang of sweat, musk, and the faintest trace of Zack's cologne clinging to the air.

Being with Zack was like chasing the horizon only to find himself trapped in a painted sky. It was like yearning for the ocean's untamed embrace and being given a shallow, chlorinated pool instead. He craved the crash of waves, the unpredictable pull of the tide, the way the salt air clung to his skin like a second heartbeat, and instead, he was met with the sterile perfection of repetition. The water moved, yes, but it lacked the chaos, the breath of something alive.

He stood there, ankle-deep in a memory of what he wanted, what he needed. The pool pretended to be the ocean, but it didn't roar; it didn't shatter against the shore, singing songs older than time. There was no horizon here, no line where the sun kissed the sea in an endless promise of more. No expanse to lose himself in, no wind to tear his name from his lips and hurl it into the wild.

Instead, there was chlorine burning his nostrils, concrete cutting off the sky. The water was cold, yet lifeless; clear, yet soulless. Around him, laughter echoed like static, distant, meaningless. He saw walls instead of vastness, faces instead of freedom. The pool was a mockery, a hollow echo of the thing he truly craved.

And Zack—he was the water beneath his feet, filling the void but never quenching the thirst. He smiled, he touched Logan, and for a moment, Logan almost believed it was enough. But it wasn't. Zack didn't have the depth, the force, the storm in his eyes that made Logan ache. He wasn't Adrian. He never would be. He was the placeholder, the shadow of the thing Logan couldn't reach, and no matter how tightly he clung to him, the ocean would never come to him.

So he floated in this pool, pretending not to notice that the horizon was gone, that the waves were silent, that his soul was still stranded somewhere far, far beyond the breakwater.

For a moment, he closed his eyes, letting the haze of the night blur in his mind. The sex had been a blur; a storm of limbs, moans, and the fleeting touch of hands that knew too well where to press, where to linger. And yet, even as Zack touched him, coaxed him, and pulled him into his orbit, Logan's thoughts had drifted elsewhere. They always did. Back to the ocean. Back to Adrian. Back to the feeling of being saved, only to drown all over again.

He rolled onto his back, wincing slightly at the soreness in his muscles, and glanced over at Zack. He was lying next to him, naked and gleaming in the low light, his chest rising and falling as he caught his breath. Zack's lips curved into a smug, satisfied smile as he turned his head toward Logan.

"I've got to admit," Zack said, his voice rough and low, "at first, I wasn't thrilled about canceling my other plans for tonight when you showed up. But now..." He let out a soft chuckle, still glowing from their time together. "God, that was good."

Logan forced a smile, thin and brittle, like a mask he barely remembered how to wear. He reached for the towel they'd thrown on the bed earlier and began wiping himself clean, his movements mechanical. Zack didn't like his sheets dirty; Logan had learned that quickly. It was one of Zack's rules, as clear as the one he'd made after that wild encounter in the bar bathroom a couple of weeks after their first time together.

"That was great," Zack had said back then, still flushed and grinning after a particularly enthusiastic blow job against the stall door. "But from now on, it's bed only. I have standards, you know."

Logan had nodded then, just as he did now, falling into the rhythm Zack set with the same passivity he brought to everything lately. Over the past three months, between his busy schedule and the gnawing emptiness he refused to name, he'd shown up at Zack's doorstep every chance he got.

It wasn't the sex. Not really. Not the heat of it, not the weight of another body against his own. It wasn't even the quiet after, the stillness that people always claimed was peace. For Logan, there was no peace, only blur, those hazy stretches where his body went slack and his mind hovered just outside of him, watching, waiting.

Sometimes it came before, sometimes after, sometimes right in the middle. He could never hold onto it long enough to know. But in that split in time, that sliver where the edges softened, he could almost believe. Almost see Adrian's face instead of Zack's, almost trick his body into remembering what it once knew as love.

The illusion never lasted. It never gave him pleasure, not the kind that lingered. When it ended, it left him scraped raw, emptier than before, as if something had been burned out of him, destroying his emotions so completely that tears no longer remained to mourn what was lost.

Adrian's face flickered in his mind, unbidden. The way his eyes had lit up whenever he laughed. The way his hand had felt, pulling Logan back to shore, to safety, to life. The way he moaned and trembled beneath Logan's touch. The way Logan felt when he was making love to him. Logan squeezed his eyes shut and exhaled slowly, willing the memory away. Zack was still talking, his voice a distant hum that Logan barely registered.

He didn't deserve to think about Adrian, not after what he'd done. Not after running. Not after marrying someone he didn't love, locking himself into a life he couldn't bear. And yet, Adrian was always there, waiting in the back of his mind like a tide that wouldn't recede.

Logan turned his head toward Zack, his expression carefully neutral. "I should get going soon," he murmured, already reaching for his clothes.

Zack frowned slightly but didn't protest. "You always leave so fast," he said, his tone teasing but laced with something else, something softer, something wanting.

Logan didn't reply. He couldn't. Instead, he slipped into his jeans, pulling his shirt over his head, and stood at the edge of the bed for a moment, staring at the floor. He felt Zack watching him, but he didn't turn around. He couldn't bear to look at him and see the shadow of someone else in his gaze.

Logan moved through the world like a blade; sharp, unyielding, and devastatingly precise. The boardroom had become his arena, and he dominated it with an effortless grace that made even seasoned executives falter. Numbers flowed from his lips like they were etched into his bones, and his ability to read a room was uncanny, a predator's instinct honed over years of grooming. His father, always a hard man to please, beamed with pride as he watched Logan close deal after deal, the family legacy securely in his son's capable hands.

This was the role Logan had been born into, the life meticulously carved out for him from the moment he could walk. And he played it well—brilliantly, even. Ruthless, composed, and always in control, he was every bit the magnificent Vaughn his father had raised him to be. But beneath the polished exterior, Logan felt like a shadow of himself, hollowed out by the weight of expectations and the secrets he carried.

Zack stretched lazily, his naked form bathed in the hazy light of the apartment. He grinned as he stood, running a hand through his tousled hair. "I'm thinking about ordering a pizza," he said, his voice warm and teasing. "Are you staying?" He was already looking for his phone, rummaging through the chaos of their discarded clothes and sheets.

Logan moved through the room with deliberate slowness, gathering the pieces of his own clothing Zack had practically torn from him earlier. His hands brushed against the fabric, but his mind was elsewhere, pulled inexorably toward a distant shore. *Adrian.* The name came unbidden, a whisper at the edge of his thoughts, and with it came a flood of memories he had tried so hard to bury.

Adrian's scent—salt and sun and something indescribably his. The weight of his body against Logan's, grounding him, anchoring him. The way Adrian laughed, a sound so rich and free it felt like sunlight spilling into a dark room. And his body, lithe and golden, moving effortlessly as he surfed the waves. Logan closed his eyes for a moment, letting the ache settle in his chest, sharp and familiar.

"No, thanks," he said flatly. He forced himself to look away from Zack, away from the here and now, and glanced at his phone. Sandy. Her name sat on the screen like an accusation. She didn't know he had landed yet; he'd made sure of that. He didn't want interruptions while he was here, while he was trying to forget, trying to chase, trying to disappear.

Logan pulled his shirt over his head, his movements brisk, almost mechanical. "I've got to go home," he added, the words hollow even as he said them. He avoided Zack's gaze, not wanting to see whatever flicker of disappointment might be there. Zack didn't ask him to stay; he never did. And Logan was grateful for that small mercy.

Zack paused mid-motion, his expression shifting as if weighing whether to say what was on his mind. Finally, as he pulled on his underwear, he spoke. "So, Logan... does your wife, uh, know?"

The question hit Logan like a slap. He froze, mid-step, his heart thudding uncomfortably in his chest. "Know what?" he asked, his voice just a shade too high, betraying the panic simmering beneath his composed exterior.

"About us...?" Zack shrugged casually, though his tone held a pointed edge. "I mean, I'm not judging. Some wives are cool with the fact that their man is... gay—"

"I'm not gay!" Logan snapped, the words cutting through the air with sharp finality. Too sharp. Too quick. He could hear the desperation in his own voice, but it was too late to take it back. "I'm not into men. I'm not gay."

Zack blinked at him, his brows lifting slightly as he studied Logan's face, searching for some crack in the armor. When Logan didn't flinch or retract, Zack burst into laughter, a loud, disbelieving laugh that made Logan's jaw clench.

"What's so funny?" Logan growled, his anger rising to the surface.

"You... oh, God. You're serious!" Zack said between chuckles, a smirk still curling at the corners of his lips. "Logan, come on. You can't honestly stand there and tell me you're not attracted to men; you must be at least bi. I just fucked you, and let's not forget the part where you fucked me, so, yeah, I think that ship has sailed."

"Shut up, Zack!" Logan barked, his voice thunderous, his chest heaving with the effort to control the fury that burned through him. He couldn't remember the last time he'd felt this angry, this exposed.

Zack's amusement faded slightly, though a trace of his smile lingered. "Okay, okay. I'm sorry. I shouldn't have laughed. It's just... come on, man. The wife doesn't know, then? I didn't think you were still, you know, in the closet. I mean, with the way you—"

"Stop." Logan's voice dropped, cold now, his hands clenching at his sides. He moved with purpose, grabbing his shoes and heading for the door, the overwhelming need to escape driving him forward.

This was Logan's method, wasn't it? Run. Always running.

He ran to Hawaii. He ran from Adrian. He ran right back to the life he knew. He ran to his wife. And then he ran as far from that life as he could.

He ran to Zack when he needed. He ran from Zack when he couldn't bear it.

Run, run, run. And now?

Now, he was exhausted. The kind of tired that devoured every glimmer, darkening even the brightest light. Drained from carrying an ache as he fled from his life, he could never outrun himself. No distance could unravel this tether. No matter how far he journeyed or how swiftly he moved, Adrian lingered, forever just beyond the breakwater.

Zack followed, his expression softening as he caught up to Logan. "Lo, wait. I'm sorry," he said, his tone gentler now as he reached for Logan's arm. "I didn't mean to upset you. I just... I don't know. This whole thing with you being married... It's starting to feel a little wrong. Like, I didn't sign up to be a part of that."

Logan hesitated, his hand on the doorknob, his back to Zack. He didn't turn around, didn't let the apology sink in too deep. "I get that," he said quietly, his voice hollow, stripped of the earlier fury. "I have to go. I'll see you, okay?"

Before Zack could respond, Logan yanked his arm free, his movements jerky, uncoordinated. He didn't look back as he walked out the door, the weight of the conversation echoing around him, joining his usual shadows. As he stepped into the early morning hours, the cool air bit at his skin, but it did nothing to ease the fire still raging inside him.

Logan spent the day locked in his office, ignoring the steady stream of well-wishers who visited to congratulate him in advance on his upcoming birthday. The words grated on him, every chirped greeting a reminder of the passage of time, of everything he'd buried and couldn't seem to forget. He loathed his birthday; the forced smiles, the shallow congratulations, and the weight of another year spent living a lie.

When night finally fell, he sent a text to Sandy, claiming he'd be out with colleagues from work. He told his father that Sandy had planned something special for the two of them, a fabrication designed to keep everyone at bay. Then he slid behind the wheel of his car and drove away from the expectations, the lies, and the suffocating pretense. His destination was clear in his mind before he even started the engine: Zack's bar.

The bar was warm and dimly lit, a haven that smelled of spilled whiskey and faint citrus cleaner. Logan found a stool near the far end and settled in, watching Zack work behind the counter. Their conversation was light, effortless, and for the most part, shallow. They slipped back into their rhythm, unacknowledging last night's tension, choosing instead to drift in the easier currents of familiarity.

"You're not paying," Zack said with a teasing grin as Logan reached for his wallet, pulling out a crisp bill. "I thought you'd be used to that by now."

Logan smirked, his lips curving into something softer than his usual mask. He folded the bill and dropped it into the tip jar with deliberate slowness. "So, it's all for you, then."

"Oh, when you put it like that..." Zack's grin widened before he turned to serve another customer, his laugh carrying lightly through the air.

When the bar emptied out and the hum of conversation faded to nothing, Zack turned back to him. "You coming up?" he asked, his voice low, his smile laced with something dangerous and seductive.

"Hell, yeah, I do," Logan replied, his voice laced with more eagerness than he intended.

"Good. Let's go," Zack said with a wink, turning to usher out the last stragglers. "I'll clean up tomorrow."

Minutes later, they stumbled into Zack's apartment. The tension between them shimmered in the air, but Logan barely noticed. He moved on autopilot, letting Zack guide him, letting the night press its weight down until he couldn't feel anything except the pull of familiarity. The world blurred at the edges, sounds muffled and indistinct, like he was wading through a thick fog.

His hands traced Zack's skin, but the sensation felt distant, muted, like touching glass instead of flesh. The movements were automatic, mechanical—reaching, pressing, clutching—yet his mind was somewhere else, slipping further and further from the room with every breath. The smell of saltwater filled his nostrils, sharp and vivid, even though the sea was nowhere near. He could almost hear it, the rhythmic crash of waves, the low hum of the tide pulling away, over and over, endlessly.

Adrian.

The name hovered on the edge of his consciousness, unspoken but deafening. He wasn't here, not in this room, not in Zack's arms. Logan was adrift, caught between the heat of another body and the haunting memory of Adrian's touch. He could feel him—surely it was him—the weight of his body against Logan's, the warmth of his breath grazing his ear, the way he smelled like the ocean itself, like sunlight and salt and the impossible.

Logan's fingers stretched across Zack's back, but it wasn't Zack he felt beneath his hands. It was someone else entirely. He closed his eyes, and the room dissolved into a vision of golden light and endless blue, of Adrian chuckling, his voice untamed and alive. Logan could almost see him there, riding a wave, the sea curving around him like it was meant to carry him and no one else. The vividness of the image was uncanny, a near-perfect echo of the man he loved. It felt like a herald from hell itself, bearing only sorrow yet wearing Adrian's borrowed face, destroying him with the very thing he longed for most. It taunted him with that merciless "almost," a cruelty shaped in familiar light. He believed he stood only at the threshold of damnation, taking hesitant steps toward it, never realizing he was already burning.

And then, suddenly, hands pulled him back—Zack's hands, solid and insistent, grounding him in the now, when his mind kept slipping into the past. Logan moved, his body responding without thought, falling into the rhythm Zack set. Words tumbled from his lips, but they were fragments, incoherent and fractured, whispers from a place far away. He couldn't remember what he said, didn't know if Zack understood, and he didn't care. It wasn't for him.

Adrian's laughter echoed in his ears, louder now, almost mocking. For a moment, Logan thought he might reach out and touch him, hold him, but the image slipped away like water through his fingers.

"Adrian," Logan's lips shaped the name, but no sound escaped. It was a whisper without a voice, a ghost of a word that had haunted him for two years. He hadn't spoken it aloud, not once, not since the day he left. He'd thought about it endlessly—sometimes as a comfort, more often as a wound—he let his lips form the word with out a sound, but now, the shape of it felt foreign on his tongue, like an artifact unearthed after years buried in the dark.

His chest tightened as the name lingered in the air between thought and speech, a fragile thing threatening to shatter. *Adrian.* It wasn't just a name; it was a life, a moment, a choice he couldn't undo. And now, as his lips moved soundlessly, saying his name like a prayer as he came by the hands of another, it felt as though saying it might break him entirely.

When it was over, Logan collapsed into the mattress, his breath ragged, his mind still miles away. Zack's voice broke through, soft and teasing, but

Logan didn't hear it, didn't process the words. He was staring at the ceiling, his heart pounding, his body spent, yet he felt hollow, untethered.

They lay side by side, their bodies slick with sweat and their breathing uneven, Zack turned to him. "Logan, stay," he said softly, his eyes locked onto Logan's silver gaze.

"I can't—" Logan began, but Zack interrupted him.

"Come on. You look wrecked. You need sleep, man. I'll wake you in a couple of hours, I promise." His hand brushed against Logan's, a gesture as simple as it was firm. Without waiting for an answer, Zack reached over and flicked off the light, deciding for both of them.

Logan lay there, staring at the darkness, his mind fighting to resist the quiet that crept in. But his body betrayed him, and his eyes closed despite himself. *Just for a little while*, he told himself. *Just for now.*

When Logan opened his eyes, the faint light of dawn painted the room in muted hues of gray and gold. Zack was sitting at the edge of the bed, freshly showered, his damp hair curling slightly at the edges, dressed in a clean T-shirt and jeans. He looked at Logan with a quiet smile, his easy confidence softening as the morning light brushed against him.

Logan rubbed his eyes, his limbs heavy with the weight of interrupted sleep. He stretched, offering Zack a lopsided, groggy smile. "Morning?"

"Yup. Kind of," Zack said, checking the time on his phone. "It's 7 a.m. Just finished cleaning the bar," he added with a playful wink. "Totally worth it."

Logan huffed a small laugh and shook his head. "So, you're going to sleep while I go to work? Great."

"Like always," Zack teased, smirking. For a moment, they sat in a companionable silence, the weight of the day not yet pressing on them.

Then Zack's expression shifted, softening as his voice dipped lower. "Happy birthday, Logan."

The words struck Logan like a low, dull ache in his chest. *Right.* The twelfth. He sighed deeply, the date settling heavily over him like a shroud.

"Thanks," he murmured, his voice flat. "How'd you know?"

"When you're drunk, you get really chatty," Zack replied, grinning, clearly pleased with himself.

Logan flushed slightly, shaking his head at the thought. But his mind was already drifting elsewhere. Instinctively, his gaze fell to his wrist, searching for the familiar weight, the thin thread and charm of his lifesaver bracelet. It was an unconscious ritual, one he'd performed a thousand times, especially on days like today... days when he needed grounding, when the ache of memory throbbed louder than usual.

But it wasn't there.

Logan froze, his breath catching sharply in his throat. His wrist was bare. The discolored band of skin where the bracelet had sat for years stared back at him, stark and unforgiving. A scar of absence.

He stared at it for several long, still seconds, his mind refusing to catch up, his body going cold. Then the panic came—flooding him like a rising tide, crashing into every corner of his being. He bolted upright, nearly tripping over himself as he stumbled out of bed, his movements frantic and jerky.

"Where is it?" The words barely escaped his lips, rasping and thin as he tore through the room, grabbing at his clothes, his hands shaking so violently he couldn't focus. He flipped through pockets, tossed shirts and jeans to the floor, scattering them without thought. He ripped the blanket off the bed, shaking it loose, his breath coming in shallow gasps. The bracelet wasn't there.

Adrian.

Logan could see him, as clear as if it had just happened. Adrian, standing on the shore, his face lined with fear, his eyes wild, his hands trembling as they pulled Logan from the waves. The taste of saltwater still burned in Logan's throat, the sting of the sea clinging to his skin, but it was Adrian who breathed life into him again, who coaxed his heart to beat and his lungs to expand. Adrian's voice rang in his ears, steady yet tinged with panic, calling him back from the brink, saying words in a language Logan did not know. And then, that moment—*the moment*—when Adrian's hands trembled for an entirely different reason. When he untied the thin, weathered bracelet from his wrist, the charm dangling between his fingers. Adrian had laid the bracelet on the sand between Logan's knees, his hands shaky with nerves, his expression raw, unguarded. Logan had picked it up, clumsy fingers fumbling around the fragile thread, and looked up in confusion. But Adrian's gaze held him captive, his eyes carrying a quiet certainty that felt older than the storm that had brought them together. From the first glance, Adrian had known. The storm had called them to the depths, introducing their fates, and the ocean, merciful for once, had granted them both a second chance to see the shore.

The bracelet had been a mark of that promise; a silent vow Adrian couldn't yet put into words. It was the most sacred thing he owned, tied to the memory of a mother who had loved the sea, a mother who had passed her hope and protection onto her son. And Adrian, with the reckless generosity of someone who already loved, had given it to Logan. To guard him. To remind him of the life he had been spared.

The memory tightened around Logan's neck now, suffocating him, leaving him drowning once more, but this time, there was no hand pulling him back to shore. His wrist was bare, and the loss felt unbearable, like the flow had swept away not just the bracelet but Adrian himself—his voice, his touch, his quiet courage.

Logan stumbled, his breath hitching in his throat, his body trembling as he clutched the air where the bracelet should have been. The charm, the thread, the silent promise, it was gone. And with it, it felt like everything that had ever tethered him to who he truly was had been stripped away, leaving only an empty shell, adrift in a sea of his own making.

Logan's knees buckled slightly, but he caught himself on the edge of the bed, his hands clutching at the sheets as though they might give him answers. His chest heaved, the edges of the room blurring as tears pricked his eyes.

"Lo, Lo!" Zack's voice broke through the chaos, sharp and concerned. He was standing now, watching Logan with wide, wary eyes.

Logan snapped his gaze up to meet Zack's, and Zack recoiled slightly at the feral look in his eyes. Logan's face was pale, his expression wild, manic. His body trembled as he clutched a crumpled shirt in one hand, his knuckles white with the effort. "Where?" he demanded, his voice cracking. The word wasn't a question; it was a plea, raw and jagged. "Where is it?"

"Logan—" Zack tried, stepping forward cautiously, his hands up like he was trying to calm a wild animal.

"Where?!" Logan shouted, his voice shattering in the stillness of the morning. He looked unhinged, a man unraveling thread by thread, the desperation pouring out of him in waves. His fingers dug into the fabric in his hands, his grip so tight it seemed as if letting go might shatter him completely.

"Where?!" Logan roared, his voice splitting the fragile stillness of the early morning, a sound torn from somewhere deep within him. "Where is the bracelet, Zack? Did you take it off? Because I sure as hell didn't take it off myself!"

His movements were frantic, uncoordinated, as he rifled through his pants pockets before tossing them to the floor in frustration. He snatched his suit jacket next, his hands trembling so violently that the fabric slipped from his grip. His mind was a storm, circling one word, one name, over and over: *Adrian*. His heart ached, screamed for the man he had loved with everything he had. *Please. Please. Please.*

"I just cleaned the bar, I think I saw it when I swept the floor, but I didn't think much of it, so I threw it..." Zack's voice was hesitant, stumbling over the confession. He reached for something on the counter, fumbling for an olive branch. "I'm sorry, but hey, I got you a present." He held up a bracelet, its thread a similar style but with a charm shaped like an anchor. "I thought you'd like—"

"You threw it?!" Logan bellowed, cutting Zack off. His voice cracked under the weight of his fury and disbelief. "How dare you! It must've fallen, and I didn't notice, and you—you—you—you just threw it away?!" Logan was shaking, wheezing, his breath a distant memory as he struggled to utter words that sounded like desperate gasps from a dying man. Saliva betrayed him, spilling from his trembling lips as he tried to form the fragile sounds. Meanwhile, his heart hammered fiercely within his chest, as if on the brink of surrender to the ever-present waves crashing through his mind.

His anger transcended mere frustration; it morphed into a maelstrom of desperation, grief, and guilt, intricately woven into a tangled knot that he could no longer contain. He could sense the delicate thread of his sanity stretching ever thinner, teetering on the brink of breaking. *I lost Adrian's bracelet.* The thought echoed through his mind like a haunting mantra, intensifying with each repetition. *I lost it because I was too busy having sex with another man.*

He gasped for breath, each inhale a struggle as his chest heaved and panic gripped his lungs, clutching at him like a vice. Stumbling toward the kitchen, he sought refuge, space, air, something, anything to mend this turmoil. Reason had slipped from his grasp entirely, leaving him adrift in a sea of instinct. With every frantic grasp, he reached out for solutions, however irrational they seemed. Zack had claimed he'd tossed it away at the bar, but that detail drowned in the torrent of his racing thoughts, the cacophony of his unraveling mind echoing louder than the world around him.

His bare feet slapped against the floor as he tore into the kitchen. He yanked open the trash can, the sound of the lid slamming against the counter echoing in the apartment. His hands dug into the empty bag, the absence of anything there hitting him like a punch to the gut. The stark emptiness of the trash was a mirror to the hollow void yawning inside him.

"No, it's not there!" Zack's voice called from behind him, heavy with guilt and worry. "Logan, it's not here. I emptied the trash *at the bar* a few hours ago!"

But Logan barely registered the words. He couldn't stop. He tore through the kitchen, his mind breaking into frantic shards. His breaths came in shallow gasps, his hands shaking as they gripped countertops and cabinets. He was still naked, but the vulnerability of his body was nothing compared to the vulnerability of his soul as it cracked open and spilled out into the room.

Images of Adrian assaulted him. The day he finally had told Logan the true meaning of the bracelet. *"It was my mother's,"* Adrian had said, his gaze fixed on the thread as though it carried her spirit. *"I was six... Six years old, and she... she took it off and placed it in my hands."*

Logan recalled how Adrian's voice had momentarily faltered, a subtle crack in the otherwise steady veneer of his composure. The weight of his memories pressed into the present, a silent testament to the unforgotten history. He could still remember Adrian's gaze then, tender, unguarded, filled with an honesty that cut straight to the soul. The palimpsest of their connection remained vividly etched in his mind, translucent yet indelible, like a manuscript that had been layered over time. The fractures within his heart threatened to resurface, delicate and fracturing, as if the very fabric of his emotions was giving way once more.

Logan could still feel the weight of the charm, the way it had always been a part of him, an anchor to the only man he had ever truly loved.

And now it had vanished into the ether. The final remnant of Adrian, the last thread binding them to the life they could have shared, slipped away, all because Logan had succumbed to the ephemeral embrace of another's warmth, momentarily escaping the reality of his loss.

Logan stormed back into the main area of the loft, his steps heavy with rage and desperation. His hands trembled as he grabbed his clothes, yanking them on with frantic, jerky movements. "You're taking me there," he growled, his voice bleeding and cracking. "Wherever you put it, wherever the hell you threw it!"

"Logan—" Zack started, his voice hesitant, but Logan cut him off with a shout that seemed to come from somewhere far deeper than his chest.

"I need it!" Logan's voice broke, the words rising like a howl, not directed at Zack but at the universe itself. "I must find it! I—" He couldn't finish the thought. The ache in his throat swallowed the words before they could form. His hands clenched so tightly his knuckles turned white, his chest heaving with breaths he couldn't control.

"Lo—" Zack tried again, softer this time.

"Shut the fuck up!" Logan snapped, his voice venomous, his body vibrating with the effort of holding himself together. He jabbed a trembling finger toward Zack, his voice laced with fury and heartbreak. "You had no right to throw it away! You know what it means to me. You've seen me wear it every single day! How could you look at it and think, 'Yeah, I'll just throw away the most precious thing in Logan's entire fucking life'? Like you don't know!"

Zack's face contorted in agony, his jaw clenching at the sharpness of Logan's words. He stepped back, his eyes wide with disbelief, as hurt danced across his features like a flickering flame. Yet, Logan remained oblivious, unable to spare a glance. His universe was disintegrating around him, fragment by fragment; Zack's emotions had grown insignificant against the backdrop of chaos. Everything felt void and empty without that fragile remnant of Adrian, the delicate thread he had clung to for what seemed an eternity.

I need you. I need you. Please. The silent cry echoed in Logan's head, stabbing at the corners of his consciousness.

He blustered out of the apartment, barely registering Zack's presence as he raced down the stairs and into the freezing morning air. The cold nipped at his skin, yet Logan remained oblivious, his mind a whirlwind of thoughts, his body thoroughly numb. He hurried toward the building's garbage room, his heart pounding insistently in his chest, as if determined to keep him alive through sheer will, despite Logan feeling like he had stopped living a long time ago.

With a powerful shove, he flung the door open, the sharp sound echoing in the confined space. His breath caught in his throat, his chest constricting painfully as he surveyed the scene. The room was immaculate. Abandoned.

The trash was gone.

"No, no, no, no, no—please, no!" Logan's voice cracked, the plea tearing through the stillness like a wounded animal's cry. He stumbled forward, staring at the pristine floor as though willing the bracelet to appear. His knees gave out, and he collapsed onto the cold, hard surface, his hands hanging limply at his sides.

The weight of the emptiness around him pressed down on his chest, crushing him. He was drowning again, but this time, there was no Adrian to pull him out. His heart felt hollow, his mind spinning with despair. He clenched his wrist, his fingers digging into the bare skin where the bracelet had rested for years, the absence of it so wrong, so alien, it felt like a part of him had been amputated.

Hot tears began to spill down his cheeks, carving burning paths down his face. He didn't try to stop them. The grief was too big, too consuming. He sobbed openly, his body wracked with tremors as the weight of his loss crushed him.

The bracelet wasn't just a piece of metal and thread—it was his lifeline. The anchor that had kept him tethered to the memory of Adrian, the only man who had ever truly loved him, the only man he had ever truly loved.

It had been his solace, his comfort, the one thing that made his empty, miserable life bearable.

And now it was gone.

Logan closed his eyes, the sharp and sour smell of garbage still clinging to the air, but he didn't care. The world around him seemed to fade into nothingness as he sat there, his mind racing, his heart shattered.

Where do I go from here?

Logan drove back to the house, his hands gripping the steering wheel so tightly his knuckles turned white. The nausea churned in his stomach, a violent undercurrent that made him want to pull over and retch on the side of the road. His throat felt tight, his chest heavy. He wanted to scream, to run, to do anything to escape the crushing weight inside him. It was too much—everything was too much—and he wasn't strong enough to handle it.

Not anymore.

He found himself submerged, enveloped by the vast ocean, being drawn and pulled into an all-consuming void. Desperately, he attempted to breathe, but every effort was futile; his lungs screamed for air yet received only silence. The powerful undercurrent tugged at him, pulling him further into the abyss. He flailed his limbs, a frantic dance in an attempt to ascend to the surface, longing for that sweet breath of life. He wanted to scream, to release the terror locked within him, but from the depths, no sound escaped his lips. All the while, he sank deeper, swallowed by the water's cold embrace.

The streets blurred around him, his mind barely registering the turns, the intersections. His body was on autopilot, his thoughts consumed by the relentless pain. A part of him wished for a car to swerve into his lane, for the impact to shatter him and bring an end to the torment. Anything, anything to quiet the storm inside.

By some miracle, he made it to the driveway. He parked the car, though he didn't remember how. He stepped out of the car like a man surfacing from deep water, lungs burning, body heavy, each movement syrup-slow, as if the air itself had thickened. The house stood before him, lit from within, quiet as a lie.

He stared at the structure in front of him, his stomach twisting at the sight.

It wasn't a home. It never had been. It was a shell, a façade, an eidolon, a monument to a life he didn't want and a man he wasn't. It was a stage dressed in beige and symmetry, the illusion of warmth curated down to the last throw pillow, a museum of someone else's dream. Its windows blinked at him like blind eyes, all reflection, no depth. He stared at the front door, that silent witness to years of pretending, and something curled inside him, something old and sharp, like rusted wire twisting in his chest.

His feet dragged at the threshold, a wordless protest born from every memory this house had etched into him. There was a truth his body understood long before he allowed himself to admit it, and it was carried in his steps, in the heaviness, in the reluctance to be here, and in the familiar sensation he loathed. That... that was a home in name, but in truth, the place he hated most.

The house welcomed him with a sterile, empty silence. It was decorated in the perfect, curated style his father and Sandy had chosen; it was a life crafted for appearances, not for living. This wasn't a sanctuary; it was a prison. The walls, the furniture, the very air suffocated him. He had spent two years escaping from this place in every way he could, but now, in that very moment, there was no escape.

The sterile walls crumbled before his eyes. One by one, specks of dust fell, each like a whisper of the past, cascading to the floor, gradually transforming the structure into nothing but a pile of ashes. It was not a home, neither for him nor for Sandy.

His mind threatened to shut down under the weight of it all. He was tired. So, so tired. Tired in his marrow. In his breath. In the silence between heartbeats.

Too tired to keep carrying the unbearable pressure.

Too tired to keep pretending this was enough.

Too tired to keep pretending he was okay, to keep acting like the gaping hole Adrian left in his life wasn't swallowing him whole.

Too tired to lie beside someone whose touch made him feel even lonelier.

Too tired to keep fighting the pain that had etched itself into every fiber of his being.

Too tired to keep missing Adrian and pretending he didn't.

Too tired of pretending this life fit him.

Too tired of being a husband in name, a ghost in truth.

Too tired to keep screaming underwater just to have his screams drowned.

Too tired to live in the memory while trying to convince himself it was enough. Tired of swallowing the memory of Adrian like poison every single day.

"Logan?" Sandy's voice cut through the silence, startling him. She stood in the living room doorway, wearing sweats and holding a steaming coffee cup. Her expression was one of surprise. "I wasn't expecting you. I thought you'd go straight to the office," she said lightly, walking past him as though the sight of him unraveling wasn't obvious.

Logan's chest tightened, his breathing ragged. He stared at her, at the woman he had married, the woman he had lied to, the woman who had no idea who he really was. Something snapped inside him, a dam breaking, a cage shattering.

The crumbling walls, reduced to mere dust, adorned the house like a delicate shroud, leaving nothing to support the façade that once stood so proud.

"I'm gay!" he yelled, the words tearing from his throat like a storm breaking after years of drought. His voice rang through the hollow house, fierce and unfiltered, no longer asking permission to exist, shattering the last standing walls of the house. He slammed the door shut behind him, and the echo ricocheted through the rooms like the crack of thunder in a long-silent sky.

Sandy froze, her cup of coffee trembling slightly in her hands. Her eyes widened as the words sank in, but Logan couldn't stop now. It had to come out. It *needed* to come out. He couldn't hold it anymore, couldn't live in this lie for one more second.

"I'm gay," he repeated, quieter this time, but no less firm. His voice cracked, carrying the weight of years of denial, years of pretending, years of suffocating under the expectations that had been forced on him, and the ones he had forced on himself.

He couldn't do it anymore. He couldn't look at her, at this house, at this life, and keep lying. The truth had been caged inside him for so long, clawing at his ribs, demanding to be free. And now it was out, skinned, exposed, but it didn't matter. Nothing mattered except breaking free.

This house wasn't just his prison—it was a monument to the cage he had built for himself. Admitting who he was, unleashing the truth, was the first blow to those bars. He knew it wouldn't be the last. But for the first time in years, Logan felt something other than numbness. He felt the faintest flicker of release, the promise of a life he might still have the courage to reclaim.

She stared at him, her eyes wide, almost unseeing, as if the words had knocked something loose inside her. Her hand trembled violently, and a ribbon of cream-colored coffee spilled over the rim of her cup, splattering onto the pristine, shiny floor. The faint sound of liquid hitting tile echoed in the heavy silence between them.

Logan stood frozen, staring back at her. This was his wife—*his wife*—a stranger who had shared his name, his house, his life, but not his heart. She looked at him with eyes that trembled, eyes that had once trusted him, held warmth for him, but now held only the ruin he had made. He searched her face and realized he didn't know her anymore. Maybe he never truly had. The girl he once dated felt like someone from another life. And the woman in front of him? A stranger forged by years of distance and unspoken grief.

They hadn't slept in the same bed since the first time he'd been with Zack. The thought twisted his stomach with guilt. They hadn't touched in months. Not a brush of fingers, not a glance that lingered. He couldn't remember the last time he'd heard her laugh, or the last time he'd made her feel seen, or the last time he'd seen happiness in her eyes. There were no more soft goodnights. No more conversations that meant anything. He couldn't even recall when he'd last asked her how her day had been. There was only the mechanical passing of time, like two ghosts pacing through a shared grave.

He had failed her in every way a man could fail. Not in a moment, but in slow, silent degrees, like erosion, like a tide pulling away piece by piece until all that remained was absence.

He had dragged her into a life built on scaffolding, not foundation. A lie dressed in wedding vows. A façade polished with good intentions, meant to shield him from the truth that pulsed in his blood like a secret sickness. And in doing so, he had ruined them both.

She had handed him her heart, tender, trembling, alive. And he had shuttered it. Sealed it behind glass like something too delicate to touch, too inconvenient to hold. He had taken it in his hands and did not know what to do with it, because his own heart had never been his to give. That damned organ... it didn't beat for her. It never had. It had belonged to Adrian from the first breath he pulled into Logan's drowning lungs. From the first glance of those whisky eyes that saw him, not as a lie, not as a man pretending, but as something divine.

There was nothing left inside him for anyone else. Not even a sliver. Not even a single thread. He couldn't offer her a corner of his chest, couldn't spare a single bloody tissue from the muscle that had always, always belonged to another man. And yet, he had stood beside her. Kissed her. Married her. Asked her to make do with an empty room and call it home. Offered her nothing, and expected her to fill it with love. He hadn't just broken her heart. He had starved it.

"You fucking son of a bitch!" she snarled, her voice low and venomous, trembling with fury. Her eyes burned into him, twin pools of anguish that made him want to flinch away, to run, but he forced himself to stay rooted in place.

"I'm sorry," Logan said softly, his voice cracking under the weight of the words. They felt too small, too weak, and they couldn't even begin to bridge the chasm between them.

She glared at him, her whole body shaking, her hand gripping the coffee cup like it was the only thing keeping her upright. He saw the moment it happened, the moment the pieces clicked together in her mind. Her gaze sharpened, her expression twisting as realization dawned. He saw her relive every moment, every lie, every night he hadn't come home or had slept in another room. Her eyes filled with hurt and disbelief as she connected the dots.

"I knew you were fucking someone else," she spat, her voice breaking with emotion. "Don't think for a second you were subtle about it. Staying out late, lying to me, avoiding me at every turn, you did a lousy job hiding it. But..." She shook her head, her voice rising. "But I didn't think you were screwing a man!"

Logan dropped his gaze to the floor, his shame clawing at him, hot and relentless. He felt the weight of her words like punches to his gut, each one leaving him weaker than the last. When he looked back up, he saw her crying. Silent tears streaked down her cheeks, and yet she hadn't moved a muscle. Her hand still held the coffee cup, the liquid inside long forgotten, shaking with her every breath.

"I'm sorry," Logan repeated, his voice hoarse and breaking. "I'm so sorry. I didn't know what to do—"

"Please, don't!" she begged, her voice raw, her free hand waving him off like she couldn't bear to hear him speak. "Don't you dare try to make excuses, because there are none!" Her tears fell faster, her voice trembling with every word. "I've been sitting in this house for months thinking it was me. That I wasn't enough for you. That I wasn't what you needed. I cried every night, Logan. Every night you were here, in this house, but not in our bed. I was losing my mind trying to figure out what I did wrong!"

Logan opened his mouth to respond, but no words came. Her pain washed over him, drowning out everything else, leaving him powerless.

"I thought..." Her voice cracked, the sound choking her. "I thought it was a phase. I don't know, I thought maybe you'd get over whatever it was, this need to screw around, and you'd come back to me. I loved you so much, Logan. I've loved you through everything. I waited for you when you needed time after graduation, and I waited for you now. I thought it was just a physical thing, something you had to get out of your system, but..."

She trailed off, unable to finish. The weight of her heartbreak hung in the air, suffocating. Logan could feel his own tears welling up, hot and stinging, but he didn't let them fall. He didn't deserve that release. Not when she was breaking in front of him, her love for him twisting into a pain so deep it seemed to hollow her out.

And he couldn't argue. Couldn't tell her she was wrong. Because she wasn't. She had been everything he wasn't: committed, patient, loyal. And he had shattered her in return.

Logan wiped his tears as he watched Sandy—really watched her—for what felt like the first time in years. She was standing up to him, her voice no longer soft, no longer willing to be drowned out by his lies.

"Sandy—" he began, but she cut him off.

"All this fucking time, my husband is gay! Gay! It wasn't even me!" she screamed, her voice raw, a storm of pain and betrayal surging from her. Her hands trembled as she turned away, placing her coffee mug on the nearest table with a trembling finality before she bolted upstairs.

"Sandy, please!" Logan called, chasing after her, his voice breaking as he stumbled on the stairs.

When he reached their bedroom, his heart sank further. She was yanking a suitcase from the closet, her movements jerky and forceful as she began shoving clothes inside with no regard for order. Her face was streaked with tears, but her expression was one of pure fury.

"Go to fucking hell, Logan! You've ruined my life!" she hissed, her voice shaking with the weight of her words.

"I'm sorry, Sandy. Please don't leave, I'll go—"

"I'm not staying here another goddamn second," she snapped, her voice hoarse but firm. "And don't you dare talk to me like I'm some fragile little thing you get to rescue on your way out the door."

"I'm sorry," Logan pleaded, standing helplessly in the doorway, his arms limp at his sides. He wiped at his face again, tears blurring his vision as he tried to find words that could undo the damage. But what words could ever be enough? "Of course, it's not you. You're... you're fucking gorgeous! And smart! And so kind and caring! Any man would be lucky to have you. I know you tried, I know you won't believe me, but I tried too. I tried so hard. And I failed."

The words he poured out—apologies, excuses, confessions—scattered uselessly on the floor between them like shattered glass. She kept packing, her hands trembling but determined, moving with the kind of urgency that comes only when something inside finally breaks.

"Tried?" she said, laughing, not from amusement, but disbelief. A ragged, bitter sound that clawed its way up her throat. "You *tried*, Logan?

Really?" She yanked the zipper of her suitcase with a violent swipe. Click. Final. "Keep telling that lie to yourself. You didn't try. You ran. You used me to build the version of your life that looked good from the outside. The house. The wife. The charade. And then you disappeared from it. Left me in it. Alone."

She turned to face him now, hair a mess, face streaked with tears and fury. Her eyes didn't flicker with softness, just fire.

"*I* tried," she said, each word landing like a stone. "*I* tried." She emphasized again. "I held this house together. I held us together. I was here, Logan. I was fucking here. Running the house and building my business, letting you have all the freedom to build your career, while struggling to build mine and keep it all running. I swallowed every silence and every late night and every empty look. Loving a man who was barely even present. A man who checked out of this marriage so long ago that I should have followed him right out the door. But stupid me, I stayed. I kept hoping. Kept trying."

Her voice cracked, but she didn't stop. She was unstoppable now. "And you have the audacity to tell me 'I tried?' How? Does trying mean cheating on me? Don't you *dare* stand there crying and call that an effort. Talking to me, *that* would've been trying. Reaching out. Owning the distance between us. But you didn't. You lied. You hid. You broke your vows and your silence in the arms of someone else."

"I didn't mean to hurt you—"

"But you *did*," she roared. "I dedicated years of my life to you, Logan. Years. And this is how little I mattered to you? This is the respect I get? Do you believe that because it was a man, it makes the betrayal any less? It does not. It simply adds another layer of silence. Another secret I was unworthy of. You deceived me. You humiliated me. You used me! I was nothing more than a prop in your game! You used me to hide yourself! You stole my love, Logan," she wept. Logan was sobbing now, full-bodied, guilt-stricken grief that left him barely upright.

"You stole my love, you knew how much I loved you, and you used it against me!" Her voice was broken. "This isn't just about who you love, Logan," she said quietly, her voice ironclad. "It's about how little you loved *me*."

She took a long, deep breath and spoke quieter now, but no less cutting. "You could have come to me. We could've talked. We could've divorced. Hell, we might've stayed friends. I would've understood. I would've helped you. I would've cheered you on, Logan. I would've stood next to you when you found the love of your life and said, 'This is the man I loved once. I'm proud of who he became.' But instead, you lied. You betrayed me. You humiliated me."

"Sandy," Logan said again, his voice cracking, desperate to do something—anything—to stop this spiral. But there was no stopping it. Not now. Not anymore.

She disappeared into the bathroom, her movements quick and deliberate as she swept her cosmetics into a carrier bag, barely looking at what she grabbed. Logan moved numbly to the bed—the bed he hadn't slept in for months—and sank onto the edge. He watched as she moved around the room, collecting her belongings with a grim determination that left no room for hesitation.

When she was done, she stood in front of him. For a moment, he thought she might say something, but instead, she reached for her wedding band and engagement ring. Her fingers trembled slightly as she slid them off. She stared at the rings in her hand for a second before her eyes lifted to meet his.

"You didn't just break my heart," she whispered. "You made me feel like I was never even real to you. Have a happy birthday, Logan," she said bitterly, her voice laced with pain. Then, with a flick of her wrist, she threw the rings at him. They bounced off his chest and landed on the bed, tiny metallic echoes of their broken marriage.

Logan didn't move, didn't reach for them. He just watched her as she grabbed her suitcase and handbag and stormed out of the room without another word.

He wanted to follow her, wanted to help carry her things, but he stayed where he was. He was a terrible husband; there was no point trying to be a good man now. Sandy didn't need him; she never had. She was strong, capable, and more than deserving of the freedom she was claiming for herself. He felt a flicker of pride for her amidst the crushing sorrow. She deserved better than this. Better than him.

The sound of the front door slamming echoed through the house, followed by the distant rumble of her car pulling away. And then the silence. It was deafening.

Logan dragged himself up from the bed and shuffled toward the guest room—the room that had been his sanctuary and prison for months. His body felt heavy, each step harder than the last. When he pushed the door open, his breath caught in his throat.

There, sitting on the neatly made bed, was a small box wrapped in shiny red and white paper, topped with a perfect bow.

A birthday present.

Sandy had left it for him. She'd put it exactly where she knew he'd find it, on the bed he would go to after coming home in the middle of the night. She'd planned this for him, thought of him, cared for him, even as their marriage crumbled around them.

Logan stared at the box, his chest tightening, his throat burning. His knees gave out, and he sank to the floor, his back pressed against the wall as he stared at the gift through tear-blurred eyes. The tears he believed had dried suddenly welled up again, streaming down his face.

He could no longer endure the torment. The weight of it all—the deceptions, the guilt, the profound loss—pressed heavily upon him, stealing the breath from his lungs until each inhale felt like a struggle. His sobs resonated through the barren room, a symphony of raw, unrestrained emotion. The echoes of his actions, his decisions, his cowardice, each one returned to him, constricting his chest, suffocating him with a sense of regret.

His phone buzzed in his pocket, but he didn't reach for it. He couldn't. The absurdity of his life wrapped around him like a heavy fog, suffocating every breath he took. He felt like a desolate wanderer trapped within his own skin, a hollow echo of the person he once was. In that poignant moment, all he could do was surrender to the flood of tears that streamed down his cheeks, as the very fabric of his world was unraveling before his eyes.

Logan lay sprawled on his back on the cold, polished floor, staring up at the ceiling. The ornate chandelier above him, an extravagant centerpiece of the meticulously designed house, blurred in his vision. Everything in this house was perfect, impeccably chosen, painfully expensive, but it felt empty. Just like him.

All he wanted was to be outside. To see the sun. To feel its warmth seeping into his skin, to hear the water lapping against his body, the hum of adrenaline rushing through his veins as he rode the waves. The longing for it—for freedom, for life—was almost unbearable.

All he wanted was Adrian.

All he wanted was to share that life with Adrian.

All he wanted was to turn back the clock two years and undo the choices that led him astray, yearning for the simple innocence of a bygone era.

Slowly, so fucking slowly, Logan dragged himself back to his feet. The weight pressing on his chest made it feel impossible to move, but lying there forever wouldn't erase what he'd done. It wouldn't undo the damage. He couldn't hide from the consequences of his actions, no matter how much he wanted to.

He took the present in his hands, turning that heavy object around again and again. After some consideration, he tore open the wrapping paper, revealing another box wrapped in a glossy cardboard sleeve. Inside was a dark green leather box stamped with the Rolex crown. Lifting the lid of the polished box, he examined the watch inside as it ticked steadily, each click adding to the irony of the moment. After a moment or so, he set the open box on the bed and left the room.

He stumbled to the bathroom, his steps heavy and unsteady, and splashed cold water on his face. The sting of it did little to shake the numbness clinging to him. He stepped into the shower, hoping the warmth would soothe him, cleanse him, bring him some measure of calm. But as the water cascaded over his body, it felt meaningless. He scrubbed his skin until it was pink, as if he could somehow wash away his mistakes, but the heaviness in his chest remained.

Afterward, he dried off, pulled on a simple pair of jeans and a shirt, leaving his expensive suits untouched in the closet. They felt like part of the smokescreen he couldn't bear to wear anymore. He grabbed his coat and stepped out into the cold, leaving the house behind without a second glance.

The drive to Zack's apartment was quiet, his hands gripping the steering wheel tightly. He felt numb, but beneath that numbness was a simmering tension he couldn't escape. He'd been horrible to Zack; unfair, cruel, projecting all of his pain and denial onto someone who didn't deserve it. Zack hadn't asked for any of this, and yet Logan had made him the target of his anger and shame.

As he pulled up to Zack's building, Logan felt a flicker of doubt, but he pushed it aside. He had to do this. He parked and hurried up to the apartment, his steps quick, his movements driven by something he couldn't quite name. Reaching Zack's door, he knocked hard, his fist hitting the wood with more force than he intended. He could hear the faint rustle of movement inside.

Zack was awake. Of course he was. After everything that had happened, Logan doubted Zack had gotten any sleep at all. Logan knew the hours Zack kept, working through the nights and resting during the day, but last night's events had probably stolen any chance of peace. Logan had done that; he had shattered something, and now it was time to try to pick up the pieces.

He stood there, waiting, in the cold air of the hallway. He didn't know what he'd say, didn't know if Zack would even let him in, but he had to try. He owed Zack that much, if not more.

"What do you want?" Zack asked, his voice flat, as he opened the door. His eyes were tired, dark circles beneath them, but they still held the guarded strength of someone trying to protect himself from further hurt.

"Can we talk?" Logan asked, his voice low, almost breaking. His eyes pleaded with Zack, unguarded in a way they rarely were.

Zack stood there for a long moment, silent, his hand still on the doorknob. Logan could see the hesitation in his face, the internal debate over whether to let him in or tell him to get lost. But then, with a quiet sigh, Zack stepped aside, leaving just enough space for Logan to enter.

Logan stepped inside, the familiar scent of Zack's apartment washing over him. He heard the soft click of the door closing behind him, but Zack didn't look at him, his body still tense, his jaw tight.

"I told Sandy," Logan said after a beat, his voice tentative. "My wife... I told her I'm gay."

Zack's eyes lifted then, finally meeting Logan's. There was surprise there, subtle but undeniable, and something else, a flicker of appreciation, maybe even respect. "I'm happy for you," Zack answered simply, his tone even. He didn't elaborate, didn't let his expression betray anything more. Logan watched his movements as he sat down on the edge of the couch, leaving a distance between them that felt deliberate.

Logan buried his hands in his coat pockets. "Zack, I'm so sorry," Logan murmured, standing awkwardly near the edge of the room. "I really am. I didn't mean to... to be so disgusting. I shouldn't have burst at you like that. You didn't deserve it."

Zack nodded slowly, his face still guarded. "No, I didn't," he agreed after a pause, though his tone wasn't accusatory. It was a simple statement of fact.

"It's just... the bracelet is... very important to me," Logan said, his voice faltering as he stared at the floor. The words felt too small to hold the weight of what he wanted to say, what he needed to say. He wondered if he was ready to share Adrian with someone else, if he could bring himself to speak aloud the memories he had guarded so fiercely. But the heaviness in his chest demanded release, and Logan knew he couldn't hold it in any longer.

He took a deep, shaky breath, though it felt like there wasn't enough air in the room. His hands trembled slightly as he opened his mouth again. "I met him in Hawaii," he began, the words tumbling out hesitantly at first. "I was... drowning. Literally drowning. He saved me. Pulled me out of the water and brought me back to life."

Logan paused, his throat tightening, but Zack's quiet, steady gaze urged him to continue. "He gave me the bracelet that same day. Later, much later, he told me it was his mother's... that she had given it to him to protect him. And after he saved me, he... he wanted it to protect me too."

He swallowed hard, the memories rushing back in vivid detail. "That was the day we became friends. Best friends. We traveled together for four months. He was... God, he was everything. He was always there, no matter how much of an asshole I was, no matter how moody I got. He never left." Logan let out a shaky laugh, though it lacked any real humor. "I got jealous sometimes. Stupid, pointless jealousy when he'd laugh with someone else, or talk to someone. But he never held it against me. He just... he made me feel like I mattered."

Logan's voice broke, and he closed his eyes, letting the flood of memories overwhelm him. "And his smile... God, Zack, his smile. Every time he smiled at me, I felt like I wanted to die because I couldn't handle it. I couldn't handle how much I loved him."

Zack didn't utter a word, but his expression softened, his eyes brimming with an unplaceable emotion, perhaps empathy, or something more tender and intimate. Thus, Logan allowed the dam to break, revealing everything from the very beginning. At one point, Zack rose and made his way to the kitchen. Logan hesitated, uncertain about continuing, but when Zack returned with two steaming cups of coffee, Logan recognized that his words could no longer be stopped; they flowed uncontrollably.

Logan's voice quivered with emotion as he recounted his and Adrian's journey. He relived the nights filled with laughter, the serene silences shared on the beach, and how Adrian always seemed to intuitively understand Logan's needs, even when he himself was oblivious. Logan poured out the ache that enveloped him each time Adrian's fingers brushed against his skin, how he often lay awake for hours just to observe Adrian asleep, moonlight gracefully dancing across his features.

And then Logan began to cry. The tears came suddenly, spilling over as the memories turned darker. How he had run away in the night. How he had blocked Adrian's number before boarding the plane, cutting him off completely. The guilt of it, the weight of his choices, crushed him as the words poured out.

Zack moved from his chair to sit next to Logan, his posture tense, his eyes fixed on him as though he were bracing himself for what came next. Logan told him everything. He laid it all bare, every detail, every regret, every moment he had tried and failed to bury.

When he finished, Zack leaned back slightly, exhaling a low, drawn-out "Wow." His expression was a mixture of shock and something softer, a quiet understanding that made Logan's chest ache even more. "Hey... his name," Zack started slowly, his voice careful. "Is it Adrian?"

Logan paled, his breath catching. He nodded hesitantly, his heart pounding.

"Remember when you got really, really drunk...? You wouldn't go home. You said his name. You called for him... and cried." Zack's voice was quiet, almost hesitant, as though he were unsure how much to reveal. He withheld the truth from Logan about that fateful night, concealing the depth of his despair, the way he had crumbled as he cried out for Adrian, each utterance threading his very being together. He had pleaded with Zack, urging him to take him to Adrian, his voice breaking as he repeated that name, as though it were the linchpin of his existence.

Logan recalled it vividly, the moment he awoke at Zack's place for the first time, realizing the extent of his own foolishness in that heart-wrenching situation. He remembered Zack mentioning that he had called for Adrian.

Logan blinked, trying to clear that memory. He reached instinctively for his wrist, for the bracelet that was no longer there, the emptiness sharp and unbearable. He fumbled for his phone instead, pulling it from his pocket. His hands shook as he scrolled, searching, until he found what he was looking for.

He handed the phone to Zack, his voice barely above a whisper. "Here, this... this is his song."

Zack hesitated for a moment, then took the phone. He pressed play, and the room filled with the soft, haunting melody. Logan closed his eyes as the music washed over him, the notes carrying him back to Adrian, to the life they had shared, and the love he had lost.

Logan watched as Zack's gaze fixed on the screen, his expression shifting into something close to awe as he listened to the song. The soft melody filled the room, weaving through the silence like a ghost of a memory, carrying with it the weight of everything Logan had lost. When the video ended, Zack handed the phone back, his face still etched with amazement and something heavier, sadness, perhaps, or understanding.

"I saw it for the first time that night," Logan murmured, his fingers closing around the phone. His voice was distant, like he was speaking more to himself than to Zack. "I kind of... lost it."

"Yeah," Zack spoke softly, his voice thick with distress. "I can see why."

Logan stared at the phone in his hands, the screen now dark. His thumb traced the edges absently as he continued. "The day after it was uploaded to his Facebook page, he deleted the account," he murmured, his voice low and pained.

Zack frowned, his brows knitting together as something clicked in his mind. The day after. It hit him; the memory of Logan lurching into the bar that night, his eyes glassy, his movements frantic. The night Logan had kissed him for the first time. The night they'd had sex for the first time in the middle of the bar.

It had always been about Adrian.

The realization settled heavily on Zack's chest, tightening the air around them. The room felt impossibly quiet, save for the faint hum of vibrations from Logan's phone as another ignored message came through.

They lingered in silence, enveloped in an unspoken tension that stretched on, leaving them both at a loss for words. Zack leaned back into the plushness of the couch, his arms folded tightly, and his jaw locked in a hard line. Across from him, Logan swiped a weary hand across his face, the fatigue evident in his slumped shoulders, rendering him almost diminutive and fragile in a way that Zack had never witnessed before.

Finally, Logan broke the silence. "So when you threw the bracelet..." His voice faltered, cracking as he tried to find the words. "It was like you were throwing him away. Like you were throwing Adrian. I..." He took a shaky breath, his fingers curling into his palms. "I used that bracelet to... to hold on. I don't know how else to say it. I always felt like, as long as I had it on, I'd be okay. Like it was keeping me from falling apart. Keeping me breathing. It was my safety net."

His voice broke entirely, and he wiped at the tears that spilled over. "It wasn't just the bracelet, though," he continued, his words thick with emotion. "It was Adrian. It felt like he was there, keeping me safe, even after everything I'd done. Even after I left him. It was stupid, I know, but it felt like... like he was still watching over me. Like I hadn't completely lost him."

"It's not stupid," Zack reassured, his voice steady. Logan looked up, startled by the certainty in Zack's tone.

Their eyes met, and in that fleeting moment, Logan perceived no judgment or anger, only the embrace of understanding lingered between them. He nodded slowly, a tightness clenching his throat as the weight of sharing this piece of Adrian with another began to lift. It was as if, by vocalizing his memories, Logan could feel Adrian's essence still mingling in the air, intertwining their spirits. As words spilled forth, Adrian sprang to vibrant life within Logan's mind, each recollection a stunning flash of electricity. Articulating these memories was akin to a resurrection, drawing Adrian nearer, weaving him into the fabric of the room as if he occupied a seat beside them. In that moment, Logan felt exposed yet liberated, experiencing a humanity that had eluded him for years.

"So... do you want us to try again?" Logan asked after some time, his voice almost a whisper. "From the beginning?"

"What?" Zack burst, his voice sharp, his eyes narrowing. "What the hell are you talking about?"

Logan faltered but pressed on, his gaze steady despite Zack's tone. "The other day, you said it felt wrong because I was married. So, I told my wife. As we speak, I'm pretty sure Sandy is printing out the divorce papers." He tried to manage a half-smile, but it faltered under Zack's unrelenting stare.

"No. No, no," Zack said, shaking his head emphatically. His voice was firm, almost scolding. "God, you're such a fool, Logan. Even after everything you just told me, you still don't get it, do you?"

"Get what?" Logan asked, his brows furrowing in confusion.

Zack sighed heavily, running a hand through his hair before standing. "You're still in love with him! Two years later, and you're still in love with Adrian."

Logan opened his mouth to argue, but Zack cut him off with a sharp gesture. "No, don't. Don't even try to deny it. It's written all over you. Hell, it's in the way you talk about him. I seriously don't know how Adrian could stand you when you're so blind, so in denial. It's like you've been keeping your eyes closed on purpose."

"Zack—" Logan started, his voice defensive.

"No, Logan. Listen to me." Zack's voice softened slightly, but his intensity didn't waver. "Go find him. Please. You don't want to be with me. You want him." Zack pointed toward the door, his meaning clear, though Logan didn't move, still rooted to the couch.

Seeing Logan hesitate, Zack sighed and sat back down beside him. His tone softened further, gentler now, as though addressing a child. "Look, Logan. I know what we were doing wasn't... great. And I let it happen because, yeah, you were gay and married to a woman. I'm not proud of it, but at least I knew where we stood. But I won't be with you when it's clear as day that you're still in love with someone else. You don't need me. You need to fix this thing with him."

Logan dropped his gaze, shame flickering across his features. "He won't even look at me after what I've done," he whispered, shaking his head. "I burned that bridge the day I left."

Zack gave a short laugh, though it wasn't unkind. "Logan, if half of what you just told me is true, then Adrian loves you more than you can imagine. You're not an easy man, and the fact that he put up with you says a lot."

Logan's lips trembled as a memory surfaced. "You don't understand... At my wedding... he..."

"Yeah, I heard," Zack interrupted, his voice tinged with both irritation and understanding. "You were a complete son of a bitch to him. He came to tell you how he felt, and you tore him apart. Sounds exactly like something you'd do." Zack smirked faintly, though his tone was serious. "If I were Adrian, I'd know you were full of shit. He probably saw right through you, saw how scared you were. That's what you do, isn't it? You push people away when they get too close."

Logan shook his head, fearful of letting hope's tender embrace settle in his chest. In this hollow space, he felt Adrian's absence, where the pain was as piercing now as that first day of his departure.

"That song, Logan, come on," Zack said. "That man is waiting for you, too; he is just as in love with you as you are with him. It was his way of reaching out to you."

A faint, almost imperceptible spark flickered in Logan's chest, a fragile ember of hope. He tried to ignore it, tried to squash it down, but it crept through his bones, settling in his belly and making him feel warm for the first time in years.

"You think?" Logan asked quietly, his voice tentative, almost childlike. It wasn't the voice of a grown man; it was the voice of someone desperately hoping for a second chance.

Zack smiled at him, the corners of his lips quirking up in a way that was both amused and fond. "Yeah, I'm sure. If I had an Adrian, I'd be running to him right now. So, get the hell out of here, Logan. Go find him. Do it before it's too late."

Logan couldn't help but smile, a wide, genuine grin that made his chest feel lighter. He turned to Zack and, without thinking, pulled him into a tight hug. Zack stiffened for a moment before relaxing into it, his hand patting Logan's back awkwardly.

Logan held him there for a few minutes, letting his heart process what was happening, letting the weight of Zack's words settle. Finally, he let out a harsh laugh and pulled back, looking at Zack with something like gratitude in his eyes.

"Thank you," he uttered, his voice thick with emotion. Then, without waiting for a response, he got to his feet, his movements purposeful, his mind made up.

It was time to stop running. Time to find Adrian. Time to face the love he'd tried so hard to bury.

"Sure thing," Zack said, forcing a smile. It was pained, but genuine in its way, a mix of bittersweet emotions he couldn't entirely untangle. He watched Logan hurry out of the apartment, the door slamming shut with a finality that echoed in the quiet space. Zack stood there for a moment, staring at the closed door, his chest heavy with the weight of doing the right thing.

He let out a deep breath, running a hand through his hair as he sank back onto the couch. His head tilted back, his gaze fixed on the ceiling, but his thoughts were far away. "Damn, it sucks to be a good person sometimes," he muttered to himself with a humorless chuckle.

After a moment, Zack shifted, his hand instinctively sliding into his pocket. His fingers brushed against something small and familiar, and he pulled it out carefully. Sitting in his palm was the old, worn lifesaver bracelet that had been a part of Logan for so long. The thread was frayed in places, the charm dull with age, but it was still intact, a physical representation of everything Logan had been clinging to.

Zack's lips quirked into a lopsided smile, sadness tugging at the edges. He turned the bracelet over in his fingers, feeling its texture, its weight, as though it carried the echoes of the man who had worn it. A small part of him had wanted to throw it back at Logan, to watch his face light up with relief and gratitude. But he knew that wouldn't have been the point.

This was Logan's journey to make, his truth to reclaim. Zack's role had been to nudge him in the right direction, to help him see what he'd been running from all along.

Sliding the bracelet back into his pocket, Zack sat in the quiet of the apartment, a faint, wistful smile still lingering on his lips. His life wasn't perfect; hell, it was far from it. And the little spark that Logan had brought with him was gone now, leaving behind an ache Zack didn't want to dwell on.

On some level, I had always known.

There was a quiet recognition that lived beneath the noise of everything else, a current beneath the surface, tugging at me long before I had the courage to name it. It wasn't loud. It wasn't clear. It was a subtle ache, the kind that only becomes unbearable once you stop ignoring it.

It had lived in me for as long as I can remember, curled in the shadows of my thoughts, watching, waiting. I kept it there—hidden—because I believed that if someone looked too closely, they might see it. And if they saw it, they might say it out loud. And if they said it out loud, I would never be able to take it back.

My thoughts were my confessional, and my prison. My shame was both the lock and the key. My memories—those cruel and tender things—were the only witnesses to the truth I was too afraid to claim.

Had I known all along? Yes. And also no. I felt it like a bruise I never touched. I feared it so completely that I chose not to look. I trained myself not to notice the way my heart stuttered when a beautiful boy walked past. I told myself it meant nothing. I told myself I was just different. Or broken. Or both. I ignored the emptiness that echoed in me when girls tried to hold my heart, when they kissed me and I felt only the pressure of lips, never the warmth. I made excuses. I played along. I smiled through it, and I let them believe it was enough. But it never was. It never could be.

Because I had always wanted something else. Someone else.

I longed for different arms. For a voice that settled into my bones like the sound of waves. For a body that felt like gravity. For a soul that mirrored the ache inside me.

And when I look back now, when I gather all the pieces of my past with something that almost resembles bravery, I see it everywhere. It was always there. It was in the way the ocean seemed to whisper your name before I ever knew it. In the way my breath caught the first time I saw you, like my body had recognized something my mind hadn't yet caught up to. In the way, I couldn't meet your eyes that first day, afraid you'd see too much.

It was there in the way I memorized your laugh without meaning to. In the way my hands remembered your skin before I ever touched it. It was there in every unspoken thing between us, in every silence that said too much.

It was always there. Even when I pretended not to know. Even when I lied to myself. Even when I ran.

Even now, it's still there.

Hope surged through Logan like sunlight piercing storm clouds, washing away the despair that had clung to him for so long. It was as if someone had stepped inside his body, clearing out the heaviness and planting something fragile but unmistakable in its place: the thought that he could find Adrian. That he could see him again, hold him again, explain everything. For the first time in years, he could see the horizon, clear and vast, where the ocean met the sky in perfect stillness.

It wasn't just the sadness that had lifted; it was the storm. The chaos that had churned inside him for so long had subsided, leaving a quiet calm in its wake. But calm wasn't enough. Logan knew the mistakes he'd made ran deeper than marrying Sandy or hurting Zack. To make things right, he had to go back to the beginning, to the man he had left behind, to the love he had denied.

As he drove, Logan dialed Ada Mae. He could hear the relief in her voice as she answered, likely bracing herself for another day of cancellations and meetings. Before she could begin her usual litany of reminders, he interrupted her. "Ada Mae, I need the best private investigator you can find. Schedule a meeting. Cancel everything else for today, push it all to tomorrow."

Ada Mae paused, stunned, before murmuring her agreement. Logan ended the call without another word. His focus was singular now.

When he reached the house, he walked straight to the master bedroom. The air felt different, *emptier*, without Sandy's presence. He stepped into the closet, staring at the half-empty racks where her clothes had been, scattered remnants of her hurried departure still lying on the floor. The sight made his chest tighten, but he pushed the feeling aside. He had more pressing things to confront.

From the depths of the closet, he pulled out his wetsuit. It hung on a forgotten hanger, dusty but waiting. He ran his fingers over the elastic fabric, the texture sparking a flood of memories: the rush of the waves, the salty spray of the ocean, the thrill of being alive. He had bought this wetsuit after moving into the house, convincing himself he'd make time to surf again. He never had.

The faint scent of the neoprene tickled his nose, and a shudder ran through his body. He carried the wetsuit back to the bedroom, laying it out on the bed. Slowly, Logan began to undress, each piece of clothing falling to the floor as he prepared for something that felt monumental. As he stared at the wetsuit, he felt an unfamiliar sense of rightness, a pull toward something that had been missing for too long.

His silver eyes drifted upward to the wall, landing on the photos hanging there. Wedding photos. He'd seen them a thousand times but never really *looked* at them. Now, in the aftermath of everything, they struck him with a painful clarity. He saw himself in those photos, his forced smile, the dark circles under his eyes, the sadness he hadn't been able to hide. Even then, he had known. Known he was lying to Sandy, to himself. Known that he was fulfilling a role, doing what his father had raised him to do, chasing approval he didn't even want.

Logan inhaled deeply, grounding himself. He didn't have his lifesaver anymore, but he had something else: a chance. A chance to find Adrian, to make things right. When he zipped up the wetsuit, it felt like shedding his old skin and stepping into something truer. He walked to the storage room where his surfboard sat, unused and pristine. Dust clung to its edges, a stark reminder of the years he had abandoned this part of himself.

He picked it up, its familiar weight settling into his arms, and carried it downstairs.

Stepping outside, Logan locked the door behind him, the snap of the lock echoing in the stillness. The cold November air enveloped him like a sharp blade, its icy fingers slicing through his skin. Yet, he embraced it; the chill was a much-needed jolt, a fierce reminder that he was still alive, still capable of feeling.

Everything around him was falling apart; his marriage unraveling, his life in tatters, the intricate web of lies he had woven for self-preservation now collapsing. But amid the turmoil, a clarity emerged. For the first time in years, Logan understood his call to action. He was going to surf; it was the solitary refuge that had always resonated with his soul, the only passion that had ever made him feel complete.

The board was smooth against his palm as he walked to his car, the wetsuit tight and grounding against his skin. It had been two years since he had touched the waves, two years since he had been happy. But it was time. Time to return to the ocean, to the place where he belonged, to the place where he could think, where he could *breathe*.

The thought of the salty air filling his lungs, of the water pulling him under and closing around him, made anticipation bubble inside him. He needed to feel it again, to let the waves strip away everything else, to leave him bare and free. For the first time in what felt like forever, Logan wasn't afraid of drowning.

He was ready to find the surface. To breathe. To live.

To let the streams of water carry him.

Chapter 10
Prelude to the Drownsong Apnea

November 9, 2018—Point Lookout, Queensland, Australia—Two Years Earlier

LOGAN'S SMILE WAS LIKE sunlight breaking through the waves, a reckless, radiant thing that brightened his whole face. He sat cross-legged on the floor, mesmerized by the way Adrian's fingers danced over the guitar strings, plucking melodies like whispers from the sea. Every now and then, Adrian glanced up, catching Logan's eyes with a mischievous grin, as if daring him to look away. But Logan couldn't. His heart raced in the way it did when he caught the perfect wave—wild and unrestrained, thrumming in his chest—and though he was certain his cheeks were flushed, he didn't care.

Adrian played like the smooth and rhythmic caress of the ocean's tide, each note a wave in a mesmerizing song dedicated to Logan. This melody was their sacred ritual, the deep exhale that followed their sun-drenched days spent riding the wild waves, their laughter mingling with the crash of the surf. From the golden blush of dawn until the sky transformed into a tapestry of twilight hues, they surfed, laughed, and tumbled together in perfect harmony, much like the ocean tenderly kissing the shore. Now, as twilight descended like a soft blanket, Adrian sat on the floor, guitar cradled in his arms, pulling familiar chords from its heart. Each strum resonated with longing, while Logan listened, his mind a swirling mist of cottony thoughts, and his heart a tumultuous sea full of unspoken emotions, crashing and swirling with the rhythm of the music.

"How?" Logan finally demanded, his voice shattering the enchanting silence that followed the final chord, as he set his phone aside after endlessly scrolling through his playlist of beloved songs. "How do you know all of these songs?"

Adrian's cheeks flushed a vibrant red, reminiscent of the horizon at sunset, as his gaze danced shyly down to the strings of his guitar.

"Adrian?" Logan urged, leaning forward with a curiosity that sparkled in his eyes. "What is that look?"

"Nothing," Adrian deflected, not meeting Logan's gaze.

"Adrian!" Logan pressed.

"Nothing!" Adrian insisted.

"Adrian!" Logan said again. "Spill it, you're all red!"

That only caused the blush on Adrian's cheeks to grow deeper.

Adrian exhaled softly, the sound delicate and sweet. "You know how you adore having your music on all the time? Like, it's always there?"

Logan nodded, a frown forming on his brow, confusion mingling with intrigue. "Yeah?"

"I, uh..." Adrian's fingers fumbled with the back of his neck, his eyes darting everywhere but locking with Logan's. "I may have searched for the chords to your favorite songs."

"Ad..." Logan whispered in awe.

"It's nothing... just was curious about the chords of... uh.. the songs," Adrian said, looking away.

For a moment, Logan couldn't speak. Something inside him unraveled. Adrian—magnificent, infuriating Adrian—had memorized the songs not for himself, but for Logan. Every note, every chord, every melody was a love letter written in sound, a testament to how deeply Adrian cared. It wasn't grand gestures or big declarations that got to Logan—it was *this*. The quiet, unassuming way Adrian made him feel like the center of the universe.

Logan leaned in, carefully taking the guitar from Adrian's hands and placing it aside. Then, he positioned his legs on either side of Adrian and enveloped him in a warm embrace. He pulled Adrian close, burying his face in the crook of his neck, his voice low and thick with emotion. "You're amazing, you know that?"

Adrian shook his head, his laughter soft, a ripple against the quiet. But his body melted into Logan's embrace, as pliant and yielding as seafoam giving way to the rock it cherished. They stayed like that, their breaths syncing in the stillness, the space between them charged with an electric intensity that words couldn't touch. Their connection was an endless ocean—immense and resolute, each moment a lively dance like the cresting waves they rode side by side, fierce as the tempestuous storms they faced together, yet tender as the gentle caress of the tide as it kissed the shore, whispering secrets only the sands could understand.

In Adrian's arms, Logan felt the boundaries between them blur, dissolving into nothingness. They weren't just Logan and Adrian anymore; they were a convergence, like the horizon where the sea meets the sky, indistinguishable but infinite. Friends who teased and tested each other. Lovers who explored each other with reverence and fire. Even in their most heated moments, there was laughter, giddy, unrestrained, as if the joy they shared couldn't be contained. It was everything. Absolutely everything.

And then their lips found each other, soft at first, a hesitant brush that quickly became something deeper, hungrier. These days, it was impossible to stay apart for long. They touched constantly, as if the other were their anchor, grounding them in the endless ocean of life. It wasn't just the intimacy, or the carnal pull of bodies learning each other's rhythms. It was in the quiet moments, the unspoken gestures that spoke louder than declarations ever could.

Logan had never felt more cherished, more seen, than he did with Adrian. It was in every touch, every smile, every lingering glance. It was in the way Adrian got or brewed coffee every morning before Logan was even fully awake, knowing how much it meant to him before their shared sunrise runs. It was in the way Adrian listened—truly listened—without expectation, without pushing for more than Logan could give. Even in moments when Adrian spoke on the phone with his family, the cadence of Hebrew foreign to Logan's ears, Logan would linger in the background, feeling like a visitor in a place he couldn't fully access. But Adrian always turned to him, his voice softening like the twilight surf, and would say something like, "just told her about this morning," or "just talked to her about next week." Those gestures silently said, "You belong here, even in the places where the language is unfamiliar; you are not a stranger." It was the way Adrian's fingers brushed his when they shared food or passed a waxed board, the way his smile felt like sunlight warming the water. It was the way he taught Logan to trust, not only in the waves but in himself.

Adrian didn't just love Logan; he cherished him with a tender, unwavering devotion that enveloped Logan in a warmth he had never dared to believe he deserved. This quiet yet profound adoration undulated through the air, a gentle whisper of affection that filled the spaces between their hearts, revealing the depth of feeling that transcended mere love.

Their bond resembled the lifesaver bracelet that Logan perpetually adorned, an intricate tapestry of threads, each strand knotted and entwined, woven tightly to anchor him in reality. Adrian emerged as his steadfast thread, unwavering and vital. In an awakening of profound realization, Logan yearned to embody the same supportive force for Adrian.

Had someone approached Logan months earlier—before Adrian crashed into his life like a wave reshaping the shore—and foretold that he would reside within another's orbit for four transformative months, sharing the fabric of each waking moment and yearning for even more, he would have dismissed such a notion with laughter. If they had ventured to predict that this significant person would be a man, he would have cast aside the idea as utterly implausible, lost in disbelief.

But now?

Adrian wasn't just someone. He was Logan's horizon. His anchor. His ocean. And Logan, finally, was ready to let himself drown.

Somehow, it had happened, and it was everything, raw, consuming, and extraordinary. Logan shivered as Adrian's fingers skated over the skin of his back, tracing invisible paths with an ease that sent sparks coursing through him.

"You've turned me into an addict," Adrian murmured, not for the first time comparing Logan's touch to the allure of addictive substances. His voice, low and gravelly, broke the kiss just long enough to allow his words to linger in the air before his lips found Logan's again, claiming him as if he were oxygen itself, the essence of Adrian's existence.

Logan experienced a whirlwind of sensations that enveloped him completely. Words failed to capture the exquisite way Adrian's touch undid his very being, igniting passionate fires in unseen depths. Adrian's fingers danced like soft whispers across his skin, leaving it aflame, while his lips compelled Logan to yield to the moment, pursuing those intoxicating kisses over and over, relentless in his quest for more.

"You're driving me crazy," Adrian's voice was thick with want as he peeled Logan's shirt away, letting it drop to the floor without a second thought. Logan let out a breathless laugh, his mind hazy with desire. He wondered fleetingly why he'd even bothered putting on clothes after their shower; none of it ever lasted long before Adrian stripped him bare again.

Not that he minded.

Logan made quick work of Adrian's shirt, tugging it over his head and tossing it somewhere across the room, utterly unconcerned where it landed. Every time Logan saw Adrian shirtless—even after months of surfing together—it felt like the first time all over again. The sight of Adrian's sculpted body left him awestruck: the swell of his chest, the defined ridges of his abs, the dusting of hair along his forearms, the tantalizing curve of his pecs crowned by those dark, perky nipples. He was a masterpiece, and Logan couldn't stop staring, couldn't stop touching.

Adrian was more than his body, but in moments like this, Logan couldn't help but be wholly captivated by the physicality of him. He was hard now, achingly so, his thoughts singularly focused on having Adrian naked and tangled with him in bed.

Even a moment without Adrian's lips on him felt like a crime against nature, something that should be outlawed, condemned, erased from the possibility of existence. Logan couldn't bear it, not when Adrian's breath was still ghosting over his skin, not when his taste buds still echoed with the dulcet taste of him.

He surged forward, capturing Adrian's mouth with a desperation that bordered on worship. Their lips crashed together, fevered and hungry, mouths opening, teeth scraping, tongues meeting in a slow, intoxicating slide. Logan whimpered into the kiss, a broken, needy sound as he sucked Adrian's tongue into his mouth, deep and wanting, a move he felt like a lightning strike straight to his core.

His pulse hammered, blood surging through his veins like a tide pulled too hard by the moon. Every part of him ached: his chest, his lungs, his hands trembling where they fisted in Adrian's hair, his cock throbbing, straining, desperate for more. Adrian moaned against him, a mellifluous sound that addled Logan, stirring ferocity within him, igniting a reckless craving that burned brighter with each heartbeat.

He wanted to consume Adrian, to lose himself in him, to dissolve into the heat of their bodies until there was no longer Logan or Adrian, only *this*—this breathless, aching thing between them, this gravity that pulled them toward each other, inevitable as the sunrise.

"Let's go to bed," Logan murmured against Adrian's lips, though he made no move to pull away. Adrian's hands were on him again, searing paths along his sides, his shoulders, the small of his back, as their mouths collided once more. Logan groaned into the kiss, his head spinning as their tongues danced, as Adrian consumed him with an unrelenting hunger.

"After last night, I really don't want to fuck on the floor again," Logan added with a breathless chuckle, his hands sliding over Adrian's chest as he kissed his way to his jawline.

Adrian smirked, the wicked curve of his lips sending a thrill rippling through Logan. "Are you telling me I did a bad job?" His voice was teasing, laced with that effortless confidence that drove Logan wild. But his hands betrayed his restraint, fingers continuing their slow, deliberate exploration, grazing the waistband of Logan's pants and leaving trails of fire in their wake.

Logan pulled back just enough to meet Adrian's gaze, his chest heaving as he tried to catch his breath. His eyes, darkened with desire, held Adrian's unflinchingly. "No," he rasped, voice hoarse from want. "I'm saying I want more."

The memory of last night was still fresh in his mind, causing heat to bloom across his cheeks. Adrian had devoured him on the floor—again—dragging him into a heady spiral of pleasure. Logan had been reduced to a trembling mess as Adrian feasted on his ass, licking and probing with abandon, making him feel like the most precious thing in the world. And then, Adrian had taken him apart piece by piece: fingers pressing deeper, curling inside him as his mouth sucked Logan's cock so perfectly that Logan had screamed himself hoarse.

All, and they hadn't even made it to the bed.

Logan's face burned at the memory, and Adrian's knowing smirk told him he was replaying the same scene in his mind. "You still haven't told me what got you going so hard yesterday," Logan murmured, his voice thick with both curiosity and shyness.

Adrian laughed, the sound low and deliciously unguarded. "Oh, come on, like you don't know." His eyes glinted as he tugged Logan closer, biting at his bottom lip playfully. "You wore those white board shorts—you know, the ones that are way too short, a little too tight, and practically see-through when they're wet." Adrian's grin turned predatory. "You were lying on the sand, soaking wet, stretched out on your stomach like some goddamn offering. I could see every part of that ass, Logan. Every. Single. Part."

Logan opened his mouth to retort, but Adrian cut him off, his teeth nipping at Logan's jaw before murmuring against his skin. "And don't pretend you didn't notice the way people were looking. That other surfer was this close to coming over to talk to you. He was practically drooling."

Logan blinked, genuinely surprised. "Wait—what surfer?" He smirked, unable to hide the satisfaction bubbling in his chest. "I didn't notice anyone."

Adrian groaned dramatically. "Of course, you didn't. You only ever notice me, don't you?"

Logan chuckled softly, his confidence blossoming as he stood and then reached for Adrian's hand, intertwining their fingers and starting to lead him toward the bed. "Well, you're right about one thing. I only had eyes for you. And maybe, just maybe," he added with a sly grin, "I wore those shorts because I knew you'd look at me like that."

Adrian stopped short, pulling Logan to him with enough force to make him stumble slightly. "So, you admit it?" His voice dropped, deep and teasing, as he pressed their bodies flush together. "You were trying to drive me insane."

"Maybe," Logan whispered, his grin growing wider as he felt Adrian's hands drift lower, possessive and intent. "Was it worth it?"

Adrian's answer was a low growl as he pulled Logan down and kissed him deeply, his hands sliding to grip his hips. "You have no idea," he muttered, his voice rough and full of promise.

Logan laughed breathlessly, his earlier shyness giving way to a teasing confidence he never thought he'd have. "So... were you jealous?" he asked, his voice light but laced with mischief as he tugged Adrian toward the bed.

Adrian followed willingly, his fingers digging into Logan's skin. "Jealous? Logan, if that guy had taken one step toward you, I would've dragged him into the ocean and left him there."

Logan laughed again, the sound bubbling up between their shared kisses as they reached the bed. "Good to know," he murmured, his heart racing as Adrian pushed him back onto the mattress, leaning over him like a man who had just found his treasure, before climbing on top of him.

Logan wasted no time. With a fluid motion, he rolled Adrian over, pinning him to the mattress, his body pressing firmly against Adrian's. He grinned down at him, a spark of mischief in his eyes as he began to kiss down Adrian's chest, his lips trailing heat and reverence with every touch.

Logan loved the dynamic they shared, a constant, playful dance of power. They never fought for control in a way that felt combative; instead, they gifted it to each other, willingly, eagerly. Some nights—or mornings, or lazy afternoons—Logan craved surrender. He wanted to lie on the mattress and let Adrian take him apart piece by piece, to feel Adrian's hands, his lips, his tongue exploring every inch of him. Adrian, with his firm focus and careful attention, could drive him completely wild.

Other times, though, Logan wanted Adrian beneath him, writhing and panting, utterly lost in the sensations Logan could give him. Nights like tonight, where Adrian's moans were the sweetest sound, his body pliant and eager, all for Logan. Most times, they ended up switching back and forth, as if their mutual need was a tide, pulling and giving in equal measure.

It didn't take much to ignite the flame between them. The other day, they'd been lounging in the cabin, enjoying an afternoon nap after spending the morning surfing, the kind of lazy day filled with nothing but the sound of waves outside and a Netflix series playing quietly on Logan's laptop. Logan had rested a casual hand on Adrian's thigh, meaning nothing by it—until Adrian turned his head, smirked, and slid the computer off the bed. What followed was anything but lazy, with Adrian between Logan's legs, his mouth working him with the kind of enthusiasm that made Logan see stars, as he sucked, gagged, spit, and jerked Logan's dick.

Another time, they'd been out for dinner, wandering through Melbourne's lively streets after a day of exploring. Adrian had looked effortlessly sexy, wearing one of his loose, open button-down shirts that framed his chest and forearms perfectly. Logan had excused himself to the restroom, only to return and see a tourist standing far too close to Adrian.

From a distance, Logan watched as the man struck up a conversation under the guise of asking for directions, his body language far from innocent. Adrian, ever polite, genuinely tried to help, gesturing toward the street while the guy's hand found its way to Adrian's shoulder. Logan froze as he saw it slide down to Adrian's bicep, lingering far too long before grazing his chest. "I can see you work out," the guy said, his voice oozing confidence as he leaned closer. "You want to grab a drink?"

For a moment, Adrian just stood there, stunned and wide-eyed. That was all Logan needed. He stepped up beside him, placing himself firmly between Adrian and the guy. "No, he doesn't," Logan said, his voice calm but unmistakably firm, rising to his full 6'6 as his shoulders widened and his presence filled the space, letting sheer stature do the talking. The look he leveled ended everything. The man's voice faltered into a thin apology before he retreated from the space Logan now owned.

Adrian had looked at Logan, blinking in surprise, before Logan grabbed his hand and led him straight back to their hotel. No words were exchanged on the walk back, but the tension between them was electric. He wanted Adrian *now*—against the nearest wall, in the darkened alleyway that beckoned them like a promise, like a sin waiting to be committed. The thought made his gut clench, his blood burn, but the last fraying thread of his common sense kept him from giving in, from pressing Adrian up against the rough brick and devouring him right there. The moment they got through the door, Logan pushed Adrian against the wall, his lips crashing against Adrian's as his hands began to strip away every barrier between them.

That night, Logan had fucked Adrian senseless. He didn't hold back, pouring every ounce of possessiveness and desire into every thrust. The feel of Adrian beneath him—his sweat-slicked skin, his muscles trembling, the way his ass clenched around Logan's dick like a vice—was enough to make Logan lose himself completely. Adrian moaned his name over and over, a symphony of surrender that only fueled Logan's intensity. They collapsed together, utterly spent, their bodies tangled and shining in the dim light.

Later that evening, Logan lay wrapped around Adrian's sleepy form, skin to skin, their breath slow, syncing. The sheets were tangled, their bodies already spent and sated, but Logan couldn't stop touching him. They whispered in the dark, hushed confessions and half-dreamed thoughts, their voices thick with exhaustion, yet unwilling to let the night slip away just yet. Adrian's body was warm against his, his breath deep and even, but when Logan kissed the curve where his shoulder met his neck, when he let his teeth scrape just enough to send a shiver down Adrian's spine, he felt him stir. A soft sound escaped Adrian, a breathy sigh, and Logan couldn't help but smile against his skin. "I need you again," Logan had said and reached for the lube by the bed, slicking his fingers with practiced ease, his other arm still wrapped around Adrian's waist, anchoring them together. Logan pressed his fingers to Adrian's loose entrance, teasing, easing in, feeling the heat of him, the way his body welcomed him so easily, so perfectly. When he finally sank back into him, a deep moan tore from Adrian's throat, a shudder rippling through his body. "You feel so good, Logan," Adrian groaned, voice thick, wrecked, his fingers gripping at the sheets. Adrian let out a quiet moan, shifting, pressing back against Logan.

Logan chuckled to himself at the memory, pressing another kiss to Adrian's chest. Men really needed to stop approaching Adrian, or Logan was going to start disappearing people.

All those men... they looked at Adrian and saw the surface. They wanted him for the way he looked, for his undeniable beauty. And while Logan could hardly deny how breathtaking Adrian was—how his broad shoulders, sculpted chest, and easy grace turned heads everywhere they went—it wasn't Adrian's looks that made him irresistible.

No, it was something deeper. Something that transcended appearances.

What truly captivated Logan, what made Adrian a force in his life unlike anything he'd ever known, was his heart. It was the way Adrian gave every part of himself to Logan without hesitation, without expectation. The way he cared, not just for Logan, but for the world around him. Adrian had a way of seeing people, of listening, of showing kindness in a way that felt rare and precious.

Every day, every night, Adrian amazed him. Logan found himself caught in Adrian's orbit, entirely at his mercy. It was like everything in Adrian's world revolved around Logan—not in a way that was suffocating, but in a way that made Logan feel seen, cherished, and safe. Adrian's love was a quiet kind of devotion, steadfast and staunch, and Logan couldn't help but be drawn to it like a sailor to the siren's call.

Adrian was sweet. He was kind. He was polite, always trying to do the right thing, always wanting to make the world better in the small, significant ways that mattered most. And that, far more than the way he looked, was what made him irresistible.

Logan couldn't fathom how someone as remarkable as Adrian had chosen him, but every time he looked into Adrian's eyes, he saw it: the unshakable belief, the endless love. And it was hotter, more electrifying, than any physical trait could ever be.

Adrian wasn't just beautiful to look at. He was exquisite to know, and Logan considered himself the luckiest man alive for being the one Adrian chose to love.

The next morning, they left their boards behind for a light hike. The path led them to a cliff overlooking the ocean, where the cold breeze brushed over Logan's skin, invigorating and sharp. His eyes drifted to Adrian, standing just ahead of him, his long hair whipping in the wind like a dark ribbon. Logan smiled softly.

God, he loved that view.

On the way there, they had decided on their next destination—Sri Lanka. It had been Adrian's suggestion, and Logan knew exactly why. They'd talked about it on the first day they met, Logan casually mentioning his dream of surfing the waves there. Adrian had remembered, just like he always did. He remembered everything about Logan.

And yet, Logan couldn't deny how much he loved Australia. The beaches, the quiet beauty of its landscapes, and the way it made him feel untethered and free. He loved every second they spent here. But more than the place, he loved being with Adrian. Wherever they went, Logan knew it would always feel like home because Adrian was there.

Adrian had taken a seat on the edge of the cliff, his legs dangling carelessly over the drop as he stared out at the rolling waves. Logan hung back for a moment, watching him. He was so happy that he brought his camera as he took a few shots of Adrian sitting there. The ocean below was wild, with waves crashing against the rocks, sending sprays of foam into the air. It mirrored the storm of emotions flooding Logan's mind. Adrian looked so peaceful sitting there, completely at ease, but Logan knew better. He knew the weight Adrian carried, the way he always tried to shoulder everything with a quiet grace.

Logan felt a shift within himself, a sense of rightness settling over him like the sun's incandescence on his skin. Watching Adrian, he felt an undeniable need take root in his chest—to call him his, to claim him in a way that went beyond words. Because Adrian wasn't just his best friend. He wasn't just his lover. Adrian was his soulmate.

Moving forward, Logan carefully lowered himself to the ground, taking a seat behind Adrian. He scooted closer until his front was flush against Adrian's back, his thighs straddling Adrian's hips, their legs dangling together over the cliff.

He felt the moment Adrian's breath caught, the slight hitch in his chest as Logan's arms wrapped around him and he relaxed, leaning back into Logan's embrace. Relief flooded through Logan at the simple, perfect way Adrian melted against him, as though they'd been made to fit together like this.

The sun hung high above them, the ocean below sparkling under its light. Logan hugged Adrian closer, his arms tightening around him as he felt Adrian's heart racing against his chest, a perfect mirror of his own. Adrian was so warm, his body a perfect contrast to the chill of the breeze, and Logan reveled in the way Adrian's presence anchored him, steady and real. He pulled out his camera once more, capturing some pictures of them together and recording a video of the view with them sitting there, before putting it away once more.

"You're perfect," Logan mumbled the words into his skin, letting his lips brush over the delicate curve of Adrian's neck.

He felt the shiver before he heard the quiet, breathy exhale Adrian let out. Logan smiled against his skin, pressing a lingering kiss just behind his ear, where he knew Adrian was most sensitive. The reaction was instant, a slight tremble, a soft hitch of breath.

Logan loved this. Loved the way Adrian fluxed into him, the way his body gave away emotions his words never did. Loved that Adrian let himself be vulnerable like this, trusted him with that vulnerability. It was a gift, a privilege, one Logan never took for granted.

It wasn't the first time he'd called Adrian perfect, but still, Adrian let out a quiet laugh, shaking his head as if Logan had said something impossible.

"You know, I never felt perfect." His voice was softer now, contemplative. Logan could feel the way his heart had slowed, settling into something quieter.

Before Logan could protest, because Logan always protested, always argued when it came to Adrian doubting himself, Adrian kept going.

"I was always really self-conscious about my height," he admitted, his voice somewhere between amusement and hesitation. "I was the tiniest kid in class, and I didn't even start growing until I was fifteen. But even then... I'm still not exactly tall."

Logan frowned, pressing his lips together. "You're perfect. I love your height."

Adrian made a sound that might have been a scoff, but Logan wasn't letting him argue this. He shifted slightly, lowering his chin until it rested on Adrian's head, holding him tighter.

"You have the perfect height," he murmured, voice thick with quiet certainty. "You're the perfect height to be tucked against me." There was a teasing lilt in his voice, but his grip tightened slightly, like he wanted to prove the point not just with words, but with touch, with presence, with something undeniable.

Adrian chuckled, but Logan could hear the warmth in it, could feel the way his body softened slightly, how the tension he carried in his shoulders eased.

And then Adrian hesitated.

"Once..." he started, then stopped, as if deciding how much of himself he wanted to give away. Logan stayed quiet, just listening, waiting.

"I was meeting this guy," Adrian finally said, voice quieter now, more introspective. "Some friends set us up on a blind date, and apparently, they hyped me up too much. So when I got to the date, he took one look at me and said, 'Oh. I thought you'd be taller.'"

Logan stiffened slightly, the words settling uncomfortably in his chest.

"Then it just got awkward. I didn't know what to say. I sat across from him at the restaurant, and after a moment, he just kind of shrugged and said he wasn't into short guys, so there was no reason to continue the date."

Logan's jaw clenched. He wanted to go back in time and find this guy, to tell him exactly what he thought of people who dismissed Adrian as if he were less, as if he were somehow not enough.

Adrian sighed, as if he could sense Logan's reaction. "I was nineteen. And I was already insecure about my height. And he... well, he had the right to be into what he was into, but it was the way he said it, you know? So dismissive. The way he looked at me. The way he just walked away, like I wasn't even worth a second thought."

Logan stayed quiet, his arms tightening protectively around Adrian, holding him like he could erase the memory from his skin, from his bones.

Adrian let out a faint, humorless chuckle. "Something similar happened when I was seventeen. I had a crush on this guy, he was from a different school, someone from the neighborhood. And I knew he liked boys. I thought maybe I had a chance. But when I finally got the courage to tell him how I felt, he just looked at me and said, 'You're too short.'" The words hung between them, quiet but heavy, like a wound that had never fully healed. "It kept happening a lot…"

Logan exhaled slowly, pressing his lips against Adrian's temple. "They were idiots." His voice was calm, but there was steel underneath it, the kind of quiet, unshakable certainty that left no room for argument.

Adrian hummed, as if unconvinced.

Logan leaned in closer, letting his mouth brush against Adrian's ear, his voice dropping to a whisper. "I mean it. They were idiots. They missed out on the best fucking thing that could've happened to them."

Adrian made a small sound, something caught between a laugh and a breath.

Logan kissed the side of his head again, firmer this time, letting his lips linger. "You're perfect, Adrian. Exactly as you are."

For a moment, there was only silence, only the sound of the wind, the distant crash of waves below them.

Then, softly, like he didn't want Logan to hear it but also didn't want him to miss it, Adrian whispered, "I like how you say my name." Adrian lay his head back on Logan's chest, listening to his heartbeat. "I'm the luckiest man alive…" he said dreamily.

The moment felt endless. Timeless. Like something he could reach for years from now and still feel just as vividly as he did now.

It scared him sometimes how deeply he felt when he was with Adrian. He could stay like this forever. Adrian, in his arms, the world stretched out in front of them, nothing else existing outside of this moment. But then, beneath the peace, something stirred inside him.

A quiet curiosity. A longing to know more.

They had never spoken about love, not really. They had never dared to name the thing that lingered between them, hovering just beyond reach.

And Logan found himself wondering: had Adrian ever felt this before? Had anyone else ever *held him* like this, touched him like this, loved him like this?

The thought sent something sharp through Logan's chest, something unfamiliar, not quite jealousy, but something close, fiercer.

He exhaled slowly, pressing a kiss to Adrian's temple before whispering softly into his ear, "Ad."

Adrian turned his head, his hair brushing against Logan's face as he moved. His hands rose to trace slow, deliberate patterns on Logan's arms, which were holding him so tightly, so lovingly. The simple touch sent sparks through Logan's chest, grounding him in the moment.

"Have you ever been in love?" Logan asked, his voice low but thick with meaning. He swallowed hard, his heart pounding as the words hung in the air.

Adrian blinked, the question clearly catching him off guard. He leaned further into Logan's embrace, the weight of his body settling against Logan's chest, and shook his head. "Not really," he admitted. "I thought I was, but... I'm not so sure it was love."

Logan's throat tightened. He wasn't entirely sure what he'd hoped to hear, but the admission filled him with both relief and unease. "You know," he said, his voice quieter now, "back when we met your friends, you promised you'd tell me about Itay. But you never did."

Adrian drew in a deep breath, his body tense for a moment before relaxing again. "It didn't come up that night, and I didn't feel comfortable bringing up my ex in a random conversation," he confessed. "Especially with everything between us progressing the way it has. It felt... foolish to even think of him."

"You didn't love him?" Logan pressed gently.

Adrian tilted his head slightly, his gaze fixed on the waves below. "I did. Or at least, I thought I did. But lately, I've realized... those feelings weren't as deep as I thought they were." His words carried a weight, and the unspoken meaning of them lingered between them like the wind rushing around the cliff.

"Tell me," Logan urged, his voice laced with both curiosity and apprehension. He wanted to know everything about Adrian, every part of his story, even the parts that might hurt.

Adrian cleared his throat, his fingers still idly tracing Logan's arms as if grounding himself for what he was about to say. "We were together for two years," he began. "I met him at a party. We connected, I guess, and I asked him out. After that, we just... moved along. One thing led to another, and suddenly we were together."

The mere thought of Adrian in the company of Itay sent a storm of turbulent emotion crashing through Logan's soul. Unbridled jealousy, unleashed within him like a tempest, fierce and relentless. His jaw tightened in a silent struggle, a symbol of his effort to find calm amid the chaos, yet the very idea of another's touch on Adrian, their proximity, carved a hollow ache deep within his chest, something he had never experienced before. He had nothing to compare the feeling to; it was as if fuliginous was curling into the inner part of his soul, filling it up, and he had nothing he could do to stop it.

"What happened?" Logan asked, his voice more clipped than he intended.

Adrian took a deep breath, his voice steady but laced with quiet regret. "I was in the army at the time. I was already a lieutenant, and I spent most of my time away, on base, on missions. He got upset a lot because I was gone so much, always around other men. I don't think he was especially jealous, but it bothered him. He didn't like seeing me once every few months, and when I was home, I was exhausted. I think he knew I was faithful, but the fear was always there, the frustration of being in a relationship but being alone all the time was getting to him...and... we fought. A lot."

Logan stayed silent, letting Adrian's words sink in.

"He wanted me to leave the army," Adrian continued. "He was scared about the security situation in Israel. I'm not sure if you are aware of the situation there, but there are a lot of wars, operations, and terrorist attacks, and attempts at such attacks. It feels like an endless struggle for survival and a sense of peace. I was summoned for nearly every war and operation and participated in secret missions that I couldn't tell him. I sometimes disappeared for a few days or weeks before I could reach him again. I think being apart and worrying all the time started to wear on him. Eventually, he said, maybe we'd be better off breaking up."

"After two years, he broke up with you?" Logan asked, his voice tinged with disbelief.

Adrian nodded. "Yeah. I mean, looking back, I understand. I was spending so much time away. Sometimes, months would go by without me being home. And when I was home, it was only for a few days before I'd be gone again. I couldn't give him what he needed."

"You were living together?" Logan asked, his brow furrowing. The relationship between Itay and Adrian felt stronger now, more real.

"Kind of," Adrian said, his voice softer now. "It wasn't official, but most of the time, when I was home, I stayed at his place. It just made sense."

Logan felt himself drawing back ever so slightly, his arms loosening around Adrian. Adrian must have felt it, because he quickly turned his head, his voice urgent. "Logan, it wasn't... it wasn't like what we have. It wasn't even close."

Logan remained quiet, letting him continue.

"I packed up most of my stuff the day we broke up," Adrian said, his voice tinged with a wistful sadness. "A month later, when I had a leave again, I came back for the rest of it. That's when he said he wanted to try again. Said he was sorry, that we could make it work."

"And?" Logan asked, though he already knew the answer.

Adrian shook his head, the corner of his mouth twitching into a faint, sad smile. "I said no, and then... you know."

Logan didn't press him further, especially not about what had happened with Adrian's soldier after that. He knew the story, knew the pain it carried. Instead, he tightened his hold on Adrian again, pressing a soft kiss to the back of his neck.

"That's it? It was just him?" Logan asked, his voice quiet but laced with curiosity.

Adrian shook his head, his cheeks flushing slightly. "No. I had a few boyfriends before him, but none of it was serious." He hesitated, then offered a small smile. "I'm more of a relationship kind of guy. I've never really liked hooking up. I need the connection, the intimacy. I need the cuddle." His voice softened, a wistful note creeping in. "I love having someone in my life. Someone to spoil, to think about. Sex means so much more when there's love behind it." He shifted slightly, looking down at the waves crashing below. "So, yeah. I had relationships before Itay, but they were shorter. Nothing... nothing that was love."

Adrian tilted his head, turning just enough to see Logan's face. The sunlight caught Logan's features, and Adrian's breath hitched. He reached out, brushing his fingers over Logan's arm. "What about you, Lo?"

Logan swallowed, suddenly unsure of how to begin. "Oh, uh... There was Sandy," he started hesitantly. "We were together for a couple of years." He dropped his gaze, his voice growing quieter. "I, uh... kind of broke up with her on my way to the airport for this trip."

Adrian blinked, his brow furrowing in surprise. "Logan..." he started, but Logan cut him off with a small shake of his head.

"There were other girlfriends," Logan continued, his voice rough with emotion. "But nothing too serious. Never moving in together. Never..."

Adrian nodded in understanding, and Logan pulled him closer, holding onto him as if grounding himself.

"I'm not..." Logan hesitated, his heart pounding as the words fought their way out. "I wasn't really... attracted to any of them." The confession left him raw, exposed. He buried his face against Adrian's shoulder, inhaling deeply before continuing. "I never loved them. Not really. It just... it made sense. Dating the right girl."

Logan's voice fractured softly like a fragile branch. He inhaled deeply, anchoring himself with a steadying breath, then gazed upon the distant horizon. In that silent vista, he found the quiet strength to forge on, his spirit whispering through the vast, open sky. "I... I cared about them, as friends, you know? But it was never—" He stopped, his voice faltering.

Then he lifted his head, meeting Adrian's gaze. "It was never like this," he stressed, his breath quickening, his breath heaving with the effort of his confession.

A heavy silence followed, the sound of the waves filling the space between them.

"For me too," Adrian admitted softly, his voice breaking as he spoke. He turned his head to face Logan fully, his whisky eyes shining. "I knew after the first day we met... that this—us—would be something different. Something I never even dreamed of having."

Logan's chest tightened, tears welling in his eyes. He blinked rapidly, trying to keep them from falling, but his emotions swirled, overwhelming him. "I don't understand my feelings," he whispered, his voice trembling. "Everything is too much, too strong. It's different. And it just keeps growing, bigger and bigger. I've never felt this before. Never."

"I know," Adrian said, his voice filled with quiet pain. He closed his eyes, his jaw tightening as he tried to hold himself together.

Logan took a shaky breath, trying to find the right words, trying to give voice to the storm inside him. "I... I'm attracted to you, obviously," he began, his voice faltering. "I have feelings for you, Ad. Feelings I've never had for anyone before. Not once in my life."

Adrian's fingers, which had been tracing slow patterns on Logan's hands, froze. He nodded, his eyes still closed, as if bracing himself for what Logan would say next.

"And you're a man," Logan said softly, the words almost lost in the wind. "Most of the time, it doesn't bother me. It's just a fact. But other times..." He paused, struggling to continue, his voice breaking. "Other times, it throws me off. It confuses me. And this tiny fact, it's so small, but it's..." He trailed off, shaking his head, unable to finish. "Was I always attracted to men? Am I also attracted to women? I do not know the answers to those questions."

Logan placed a hand on his chest, his voice soaring once more, brimming with fresh, diaphanous emotion. "It's like I've known you my whole life. Like you're a part of me, tangled up in my soul in a way I can't ever undo. And it's only been a few months, but I already don't know how to exist without you. The chemistry we have, the way you make me feel, everything is explosive. And sometimes I wonder..." His voice dropped to a whisper. "I wonder if I was even alive before I met you."

Adrian turned to face him fully now, his eyes wide and brimming with emotion, his lips parting as if to speak.

"I feel you here," Logan said, pressing his palm against his chest, his voice trembling. "Physically. Like you're a part of me. And you're a man." He laughed softly, shaking his head. "It's stupid, but I wonder what it says about me."

Adrian reached up, cupping Logan's face in his hands, his touch tender and grounding. "Logan," he uttered. "It doesn't matter what it says about you. What matters is what we feel. What we have." He leaned in, pressing his forehead against Logan's, their breaths mingling. "I don't care about labels. I care about you. Just you."

Logan tightened his hold, resting his head on Adrian's shoulder. He couldn't bring himself to meet Adrian's gaze as he whispered his next words, his voice trembling. "Tell me you feel it too," he breathed. He knew the answer deep within his soul, hidden in the silent language of Adrian's gaze. Yet, a longing stirred within him, an aching desire for verbal reassurance, a desperate need to be certain that, amidst the tumultuous storm that was them, Adrian was in the same place, on the same page, throbbing for him.

Adrian nodded, his head pressing against Logan's chest. But somehow, nodding didn't feel like enough. His throat felt tight, choked with emotion, but he forced himself to speak. "I do, Logan," he murmured. "I've never felt like this either."

Logan let out a shaky breath, relief spreading through him. The weight of his overwhelming feelings lightened just enough to allow him to move. He brushed his lips against Adrian's neck, his touch hesitant but tender. He felt Adrian shudder beneath him, and the sensation sent electricity coursing through Logan's veins, setting his entire body alight.

Adrian's voice was flowing like the ocean's form, softly fading into the damp sand. "Don't fight it, Logan." His words, carried by the wind, curled around Logan's heart like a lifeline cast into deep waters. Adrian's gaze held the quiet intensity of a lighthouse cutting through the night, guiding Logan toward a truth he was only beginning to see. "What we have... It's perfect."

Logan's breath hitched, a storm brewing in the depths of his chest. "It is perfect," he admitted. "God, Adrian, you mean so much to me." The words felt heavy, like stones he'd carried for too long, now tumbling free. He leaned forward, capturing Adrian's lips in a kiss that spoke the language they were starting to share.

The angle was awkward—Adrian's head tipped back against Logan's chest, their bodies bent toward each other in a clumsy dance—yet the feeling was nothing short of eudaemonia. It surged through Logan, pulling him under, the kiss drowning out the world until there was only Adrian:

his warmth, the way his hand tangled in Logan's hair, the way the wind seemed to weave around them, a witness to their quiet tempest.

When the kiss broke, Logan didn't open his eyes. He stayed still, clinging to the moment as if it might slip away like grains of sand through his fingers. Adrian's hand remained in his hair, anchoring him, but the words he needed to say spilled out. "I'm sorry for... for souring the mood," he whispered, his voice cracking as silent tears tracked down his face. "I don't even know where that came from."

"Don't apologize." Adrian's voice was steady, soothing and sure. "We should have had this talk a long time ago." His fingers brushed Logan's cheek, a gesture so tender it could have mended cracks in the earth itself. "My wonderful Logan..." The words were barely spoken, almost a prayer to the wind. "Ahuv sheli," he added in Hebrew. *My love. My loved one.*

It wasn't the first time Adrian had spoken Hebrew. Words from his native tongue often escaped his lips, sometimes in frustration, when English failed him. He would look at Logan and say something unknowable, then wave it off. Other times, it happened in passion, when he was so far from himself, so overwhelmed, that he'd tip his head back and retreat into the language of his soul, murmuring things that Logan could only try to understand.

Over time, Logan picked up a very particular kind of vocabulary:

Ken means *yes.*

Lo means *no.*

Kadima means let's go.

Nou means come on.

Sham means there.

Hazak yoter means harder.

Ken, ken, al t'afsik means *yes, yes, don't stop.*

Elohim means *God.*

Ani gomer means *I'm coming.*

It made for an oddly sex specific dictionary.

Yet that one phrase remained shrouded in mystery. Adrian would whisper it each time, especially during intense or intimate moments. And no matter how many times Logan asked, Adrian only smiled, kissed him breathless, and refused to translate.

Adrian's love for Logan was as vast as the horizon, as deep as the ocean's hidden abysses. It filled every corner of him, an ache and an ecstasy. Logan was his North Star, his cynosure, the tide that drew him forward with each breath. And now, Logan had placed a fragile, burning hope in his hands, a spark that might birth new stars or reduce him to ash.

Adrian's chest tightened as he looked into Logan's stormy eyes, their gray depths swirling with an equal amount of fear and longing. His heart shattered and rebuilt itself in the space of a single heartbeat. He yearned deeply to delve into Logan's essence, to untangle the intricate knots of doubt and uncertainty, to reveal that their bond was not merely acceptable—it was as inevitable as breathing, as the relentless waves crashing upon the shore, as the glorious sunset, as the rhythmic beating of a heart.

Adrian's heart was a storm threatening to break, its waves crashing against the shores of his restraint as he felt the heat of Logan's body against his. Every second in Logan's arms heightened his yearning; every breath was a reminder of how deeply he wanted this man. With a quiet resolve, Adrian shifted, turning carefully until he was straddling Logan, their closeness drawing them into a cocoon of shared warmth. Logan's legs dangled over the cliff's edge, the abyss below a stark contrast to the safety they found in each other.

Adrian leaned in, his movements slow. His lips met Logan's, capturing one another in a numinous clutch of skin and yearning. These were the lips he had dreamed of since that fateful day when he gave Logan his breath, pulling him from the sea's grip. Then, they had been cold and lifeless; now, they were warm and trembling with life. The gasp that slipped from Logan's mouth sent a shiver through Adrian, a signal of surrender and fear intertwined.

Adrian wanted to shout into the open sky, to let the sea and wind bear witness to the triumph of this moment, and all the moments that came before, all the moments that he had Logan.

When the kiss ended, Logan chuckled softly, breaking the silence with a humor that lightened the weight of Adrian's pounding heart. "I don't want to ruin the moment again," he said, his voice warm and full of affection, "but this is probably not the best location to get carried away."

Adrian couldn't help but laugh, his face lighting up as the tension eased. "Logan, that's usually my line. And you call me 'old man' for trying to be responsible and keep us from dying."

"Well," Logan said with a grin, the playful glint returning to his stormy eyes, "let's just say I don't want to push my luck with my life saver."

Adrian's heart swelled at the words, and he reached for Logan's wrist, his fingers brushing over the bracelet wrapped snugly there. The small token, simple yet imbued with meaning, had been his gift to Logan, a reminder of the moment that had changed both their lives. Adrian's chest tightened with pride and affection as he saw it still there, worn daily, cherished.

"You still wear it," Adrian murmured to himself, his voice soft with wonder. He brought Logan's wrist to his lips and kissed the bracelet, letting his lips linger on the cool metal.

"Of course I do," Logan replied, his gaze steady as he looked into Adrian's eyes. Adrian's questions, or his wonderment about wearing the bracelet, felt odd. After all, Adrian had spent all of this time with him, seeing that bracelet again and again.

Adrian's fingers lingered on the bracelet, his thumb tracing its edges as he smiled. The ocean roared below them, and the sky stretched endlessly above, but in this moment, there was only Logan, the man who made Adrian feel as though he were riding the greatest wave of his life—a wave that could carry him forever.

The wind carried Adrian's words like whispers of the sea, soft and reverent, as his fingers brushed the bracelet on Logan's wrist. His eyes glistened with unshed tears, reflecting the light of the waning sun. "You know... I never told you about the bracelet," he murmured, his gaze lingering on the charm before lifting to meet Logan's storm-gray eyes. They were steady, turbulent as the ocean, and Adrian felt the weight of their connection like an anchor.

"This bracelet," Adrian started. "It was my mother's." He exhaled slowly, like he was trying to steady himself. "She was... she was the sea, Logan. Not just someone who loved it, she belonged to it. A surfer, a swimmer... she spent every second she could in the water. If she wasn't home, we knew exactly where to find her, out there, chasing waves."

He let out a quiet, almost breathless chuckle, but there was sadness woven into it.

"When she turned twelve, my grandfather gave her this. Said she needed protection for all her adventures. The charm is white gold, the band's real leather. He had it handmade just for her. And she wore it every single day after that."

Adrian ran his fingers lightly over the bracelet, his touch reverent.

"Almost until the very end."

His voice cracked, and fat tears spilled from his eyes as he continued. "She taught me to love the ocean, too. She took me with her when I was barely four. I didn't understand it then, I just knew I loved being in the water with her." He paused, swallowing hard as memories clawed their way to the surface. "But the day she was dying..." He stopped, his chest heaving with the weight of the memory. He closed his eyes, but it only brought the image back sharper, clearer: his mother lying fragile and broken in that hospital bed. Her once-strong frame reduced to frailty, the bracelet hanging loose on her bony wrist like a relic of a life slipping away. Her eyes, once vibrant with the spark of waves and wind, were dull, tired, heavy with the knowledge of her own end. "I was six," Adrian whispered, his voice breaking. The words fell like stones into the space between them. "Six years old, and she... she took it off and placed it in my hands." With cold fingers and shaking hands, Aliana Leon had placed the bracelet on Adrian's palm. "She said... she said it had protected her, saved her more times than she could count. And that maybe, just maybe, it would do the same for me."

He stopped again, the weight of it stealing his breath. The tears came freely now, fat and unchecked, sliding down his face like rain on a stormy sea. "It was too big for me then," he half-smiled. "It kept slipping from my wrist, so I used a hair tie to tie it, but I held on to it anyway. I was so proud that she had given it to me. She died the next day." Adrian's voice faltered, but his tears didn't stop. His heart ached, openly bleeding, as he looked at Logan with unguarded love. "I never took it off. Not until the day I met you. And now, seeing it on you... I feel like the luckiest person alive."

Logan's chest constricted, his heart pounding as Adrian's words sank in. The weight of the bracelet felt heavier now, the history and love behind it almost too much to bear. "No," Logan whispered, his voice thick with emotion. He shifted, pulling Adrian closer as he carefully scooted them away from the cliff's edge, needing the safety of solid ground. "Adrian, you need to take it back," he urged, his hands fumbling to undo the bracelet. "It's yours—it's your mother's. It's a part of her, a part of you. I can't... I can't keep this."

"Don't you dare," Adrian said, his voice calm but firm, his hand closing gently over Logan's wrist. "I gave it to you. It belongs to you now."

"Adrian—" Logan's voice broke, but he stopped himself. His thoughts reeled back to when Itay and Dean first noticed the bracelet on Logan's wrist, their strange reactions suddenly making sense. "That's why Itay and Dean acted so weird when they saw it on me," he muttered, realization dawning. He looked back at Adrian, desperation in his eyes. "No, Ad. You need to have it. It's your mother's. She gave it to *you*, she wanted *you* to have it!"

"And I gave it to you," Adrian replied with quiet conviction, a small, tender smile on his face.

Logan froze, his breath catching in his throat. "From the first moment?" he asked, his voice hoarse with disbelief.

Adrian nodded, his gaze steady, his smile soft. "From the first moment, ahuv sheli," he said, his tone carrying a certainty that was purely Adrian, an ataraxia, a serenity that flowed like water. "I felt something so strong, so undeniable back then. I didn't even understand it fully, but I knew I wanted you to have this. It felt like it was meant for you."

Logan's breath hitched, his chest tightening as he leaned closer, his lips brushing against Adrian's in a feather-light touch. "Thank you," he murmured, his voice thick with emotion, the words carrying the weight of a thousand unsaid feelings. "I will never take it off," he vowed, each syllable filled with quiet reverence.

He rested his forehead against Adrian's, their closeness erasing the world around them. Logan's hand cupped Adrian's face, his thumb brushing gently over his cheek as if trying to memorize the contours of the man who had saved him, in every way that mattered. His other arm circled Adrian's waist, holding him securely, as if letting go was not an option.

The ocean roared below, and the wind swept around them, but in that moment, they were an island unto themselves—a place of safety, love, and promise. Logan closed his eyes, feeling the steady rhythm of Adrian's heartbeat against his chest, as if it were a melody only the two of them could hear. And in the quiet intimacy of their embrace, Logan knew he had found something deeper than the depths of the sea: he had found home.

November 11, 2018—One Day Later

I live in the memory of us
I don't live in the world anymore.
Not really.
I live in the memory of us.
I wake in sheets that remember your weight,
breathe air that once held your laughter.
I walk through days like a ghost,
haunting the ruins of what we were.
I carry you in the quiet spaces between each breath,
in the hush right before the sky breaks.
You are the beating weight behind my ribs,
the ache in the silence when the world forgets your name.
I whisper you when the absence gets too loud.
When the echo of you claws through me
like waves against bone.
I start and end each day with your face,
Sometimes real,
Oftentimes conjured by a memory too stubborn to die.
Time has stopped passing for me, it stands still in my memories,
It loops—
a reel of golden hours
and the night you disappeared.
I carry you in the quiet between each breath,
a name I whisper when the absence of you
rips through the stillness like a wound reopening.

I live in the memories of our love,

I live in the memories that we have made,

I live in the world I thought I could have with you,

My hands still tremble for you,

still remember how your skin felt like safety.

My heart, it hasn't beat the same since you left.

But it still races when the memory of us surfaces,

sudden, sharp, holy.

Like it remembers the shape of you

better than it remembers how to survive without you.

It aches for every flash of you,

Every glimpse—real or imagined.

And maybe it doesn't matter anymore.

Maybe the only thing that's real

is the dream I can't wake from.

The hours echo.

Time, cruel and circular, repeats itself.

The blood still moves,

But my soul is stranded,

on that same beach where we began.

My existence is buried in every grain of sand that once held our love,

still salted by the ocean that carried us to each other.

I taste you in the wind,

in the surf, in the salt that once clung to your skin.

I see your eyes, clear as the first day,

when something inside me said,

That's him.

That's the man I'd give anything to.

Everything I am.

Everything I could ever be.

And even now,

with distance between us like a wound that never heals,

I reach.

Across countries, oceans, years.

I reach with shaking hands and an open heart,

trying to catch the scent of you

in the wind that still dares to touch my skin.

Because I live in the memory of us.

And sometimes,

it's the only place

I still feel alive.

The distance is here now,

wide as oceans,

and I reach for you still.

With every gust of wind against my skin,

I search for the scent of you.

And sometimes—

if I breathe deep enough—

You return.

At 5 a.m. the next day, Adrian's alarm clock chimed softly, and he instinctively reached out to silence it before it could disturb the peaceful stillness of the cabin. The room was still cloaked in the blue-gray hues of dawn, and the soft rhythm of Logan's breathing filled the space, grounding Adrian in a moment he would soon have to step away from. He turned his head, his gaze lingering on Logan's sleeping form—his sandy hair tousled, his face serene, the faintest hint of a snore escaping his parted lips. Logan had Adrian entirely at his mercy, and Adrian couldn't imagine a place he'd rather be.

Reluctantly, he untangled himself from the warmth of Logan's naked body, careful not to wake him. The absence of their shared heat sent a brief shiver through him, but the anticipation bubbling in his chest quickly replaced it. He allowed himself one last lingering glance before slipping into the bathroom, where he splashed cold water on his face and brushed his teeth, his mind already racing through the list of things he needed to do.

Throwing on a t-shirt and a pair of jeans, Adrian quietly slipped out of the cabin. The crisp morning air greeted him as he stepped onto the street, his steps light and quick, propelled by the giddy excitement that had been building for weeks. This day had been planned down to the last detail—a culmination of countless hours spent crafting, researching, and dreaming of a perfect birthday for Logan.

The first stop was the car rental office, where Adrian picked up the vehicle he had reserved weeks in advance. From there, Adrian moved on to the next stop, collecting the gift he had ordered and paid for long ago. The shopkeeper handed it to him with a warm smile, making small talk as he looked at it with giddiness after planning it for so long. He handed it back to her to finalize the wrapping and thanked her profoundly as he left.

By the time the clock struck 7 a.m., Adrian was back at the cabin. He quietly slipped inside, carrying with him their travel cups filled with steaming coffee, two almond croissants from a nearby bakery that Logan adored, and two breakfast sandwiches wrapped neatly in wax paper.

Logan remained cocooned beneath the blankets, his face a picture of peace, the faintest rise and fall of his chest marking the rhythm of his dreams. Adrian moved quietly, placing the food and coffee on the small table near the bed, their comforting scents wafting gently through the cabin. With the utmost caution and care, he placed the gift in his duffel bag and then tucked it away in the closet to keep Logan's gift hidden until the perfect moment.

Returning to the bedside, Adrian knelt down, his heart swelling as he watched Logan sleep. His hair was a wild mess, spilling across the pillow in soft waves, and Adrian couldn't resist the pull of affection that brought his hand to Logan's face. He brushed a stray lock of hair from his forehead, his touch light and reverent, as if Logan were made of something more delicate than stardust.

Adrian's lips curved into a smile as he took in the quiet beauty of this moment. "Logan," he murmured, his voice soft, barely louder than a whisper. "Time to wake up, ahuv sheli."

There was no immediate response, just a faint sigh as Logan shifted slightly, burying his face further into the pillow. Adrian chuckled under his breath, leaning closer, his voice warm with teasing affection.

"No running today," Logan mumbled groggily into the pillow. His words were muffled but laced with his usual teasing tone. "And come back to bed. It's cold."

Adrian smiled, brushing another lock of hair from Logan's forehead. "No running, but you do need to wake up," he said, pressing a soft kiss to Logan's temple. "I have a surprise for you."

"Surprise?" That word was enough to draw Logan's attention, his eyes cracking open just enough to show a glimmer of curiosity. Then, as if a switch had flipped, a wicked grin spread across his face. "Is that what we're calling a morning quickie now?" he teased, biting his lip.

Adrian threw his head back, laughing. "No, you impossible creature. Maybe later, but no." He tugged at the sheets playfully, revealing more of Logan's sun-warmed skin. "It's your birthday."

Logan groaned, stretching lazily under the covers, revealing more skin that made all of Adrian's blood run south. "My birthday is tomorrow."

"No," Adrian corrected, a shy smile tugging at his lips. "It's tonight, and we're starting the celebration early. I have reservations, so you need to get up and pack a bag."

Logan's brow arched, his curiosity piqued. "Reservations? Where?"

"Surprise," Adrian replied simply, grinning at Logan's still-sleepy expression.

Logan sniffed the air, his grin softening into something fonder. "Do I smell almond croissants?"

Adrian nodded, arms crossed as he leaned against the dresser. "Yes. And coffee. And breakfast sandwiches. So get up already before it gets cold."

Logan groaned, but the sound melted into a chuckle as he finally sat up, raking a hand through his messy hair. He rubbed his eyes, then stood, stretching lazily, muscles shifting beneath sun-warmed skin. Towering over Adrian, he grinned.

Adrian tilted his head up at him, lips twitching. "You are too damn tall..." he muttered under his breath, half in complaint, half in adoration.

Logan smirked, slipping his arms around Adrian's waist, pulling him in. "Don't be jealous, babe." His voice was still heavy with sleep, warm and teasing. "I love how compact you are."

Adrian scoffed. "Fuck yo—"

But Logan was faster, catching Adrian's lips in a kiss that swallowed the rest of his words. It was slow, deep, the kind of kiss that left no room for anything else.

When they parted, Logan exhaled against Adrian's lips, eyes still half-lidded. "Good morning."

Adrian let out a shaky breath, dazed. "Good morning."

Logan chuckled, tapping Adrian's chin before turning toward the bathroom. "And thanks for breakfast," he added, voice husky, disappearing behind the door.

Adrian stayed where he was, watching Logan's naked form retreat across the room. His gaze trailed over the strong lines of Logan's back, the curve of his ass, and his long, muscular legs.

After breakfast—where Adrian valiantly managed to concentrate on his sandwich despite the sinful sounds Logan made while devouring his almond croissant—they stepped out of the cabin into the crisp morning air. Logan's grin widened as Adrian gestured to a sleek black car parked just ahead.

"You rented a car?" Logan asked, his voice tinged with curiosity as he took in the shiny vehicle.

Adrian nodded, his lips curling into a soft smile. "Yes. We need to drive there, and I thought it would be nice to have something a little different. Plus, it'll be more comfortable for the trip."

Logan's heart swelled at the thoughtfulness behind Adrian's every decision. "Ad..." he sighed, stepping closer and pulling Adrian into a kiss. It was slow, warm, and quickly deepened as Logan's hand slid around Adrian's waist. "You sure we have to go right away?" he asked huskily between kisses, his hips pressing insistently against Adrian's.

Adrian's breath hitched, his hands gripping Logan's sides. He could still feel the lingering heat from last night, when they'd devoured each other with an intensity born of love and need, breaking only for water and a hastily ordered pizza. But Adrian forced himself to step back, his cheeks flushed, his lips slightly swollen.

"Don't tempt me," he murmured, his voice rough with restraint. Logan smirked, clearly pleased with himself, but he allowed Adrian to pull away and head toward the car.

Once inside, Adrian started the navigation on his phone and began the drive. The location wasn't far, but the journey felt longer with the easy conversation flowing between them. Adrian rested his hand on Logan's thigh, the touch grounding and intimate. They pointed out beautiful spots along the way—restaurants they wanted to try, trails they hoped to hike, places they dreamed of exploring together.

Finally, Adrian pulled into the driveway of a stunning building that seemed to blend cozy and sleek, modern design perfectly. Large windows reflected the morning sun, and a sign out front read "Bluewater Retreat & Spa." The place exuded tranquility, with lush greenery surrounding it and the faint sound of water features bubbling somewhere nearby.

Logan stared, his eyes wide with awe. "Adrian," he breathed, turning to him as the car engine shut off.

Adrian's smile bloomed like the first light on a still ocean, his excitement shining through in the delicate curve of his lips. "I booked us a room for the day and tonight," he said, his voice soft. "It has a private pool and... a couples massage." His words, though simple, rippled with quiet pride and vulnerability.

What he didn't say—what Logan could never truly know—was how much had gone into this. The resort was a treasure he couldn't truly afford, but for Logan, it was worth it. It was worth digging into his modest savings, things he had saved for years and years, funds that he planned to use to elongate this trip as much as possible. This was his way of catching the effulgent light, of holding splendor before it slipped away. Two exquisite days and one immaculate night, carved into eternity, where Logan would bask in being cherished, feeling Adrian's love echo in every tender detail.

Logan's hand found Adrian's, his fingers winding around it with the firmness of a lifeline grasped in stormy seas. "You did all this? For me?" he asked, his voice breaking with disbelief, his storm-gray eyes softening with a depth of emotion that Adrian could feel radiating between them.

"Of course, now, let's go," Adrian said, his voice tinged with excitement as they left the car behind. The energy between them was electric, a mix of giddiness and awe as they walked through the sleek, polished entrance of the resort, their small overnight bags on their shoulders. The air was filled with the faint scent of flowers and luxury, and every detail seemed perfectly curated, from the sweeping ocean views to the modern elegance of the space.

At the front desk, Adrian gave his name, his heart racing as he confirmed the reservation. Within moments, they were escorted to their suite, and as the door opened, Logan's breath caught. The room was stunning—white wood accents bathed in soft natural light gave the space an inviting, cozy feel. A large bed, perfectly made, sat at the heart of the room, and beyond it, an expansive balcony beckoned. The view was spectacular: a private pool shimmering under the sun, and beyond it a secluded stretch of beach leading to the open ocean.

Logan stepped inside, his eyes wide as he took everything in. "Wow," he whispered, his voice almost reverent. He moved slowly, letting the details sink in—the gleaming bathroom, the warmth of the wood, the sheer tranquility of the setting. Turning back to Adrian, his gaze softened. "Adrian, this is... amazing."

Adrian shook the steward's hand and quietly handed him a tip, saying, "Thank you." The young man nodded and told them their massage therapists would be ready in an hour, so they could relax in the meantime before he turned and left.

Logan crossed the room in two steps, wrapping Adrian in his arms and pulling him close. His voice was low, a mix of awe and something deeper. "Adrian, you crazy person," he murmured, cradling Adrian's face in his hands. "How much did you pay for all this?"

Adrian tried to look nonchalant, but Logan saw the faint blush creeping up his neck. "You shouldn't have," Logan continued, his thumb brushing lightly against Adrian's cheek. "I mean... thank you. This is incredible. But you shouldn't have. I could've at least shared the cost with you."

Adrian placed his hands over Logan's, holding them in place as he leaned into the touch. "Logan," he said softly, his voice steady despite the emotion behind it, "you don't share the cost of a gift. And this—" He gestured around them, to the view, the suite, the moment. "This is for you. For us. You mean the world to me, and I wanted you to have a day that feels like it."

Logan's chest tightened, his grip on Adrian's face firming as he searched his eyes. He found nothing but sincerity there, a love so pure it almost hurt to look at. "You're ridiculous," Logan said with a soft laugh, pressing his forehead to Adrian's. "But thank you. For all of this."

Adrian smiled, his heart swelling at the gratitude in Logan's voice. "You're worth it," he uttered.

They stripped their clothes with a mix of giddy laughter and shared glances, the anticipation crackling between them like the electric hum of a storm over the sea. The world around them was perfectly still, perfectly theirs, no one but the ocean, the wind, and the whisper of nature surrounding the secluded paradise.

Their bare skin glowed in the golden light, and without hesitation, they dove into the pool, the water cool and invigorating against their warm bodies. The first splash was like breaking through the surface of a new adventure, their laughter echoing off the walls of the cliffs beyond.

"Bet I can swim to the other end faster," Logan challenged, his voice teasing as he took off with a dramatic, exaggerated stroke. Adrian sputtered, laughing before diving in after him, his strokes strong but his laughter slowing him down.

The race dissolved into playful chaos. Logan reached the edge first but slipped as he turned, sending a wave over Adrian's head. Adrian retaliated by splashing him relentlessly, their shouts of mock outrage mingling with uncontrollable laughter. The pool water shimmered with their movement, catching the sunlight in ripples that seemed to dance along with them.

Not content with the confines of the pool, they climbed out, dripping and grinning, their bare feet slapping against the sun-warmed deck. "Beach?" Logan suggested, his eyes gleaming with mischief.

"Beach," Adrian agreed, already sprinting.

They raced to the nearby sand, their feet sinking into the soft, golden grains as they reached the shoreline. The ocean greeted them with open arms, its waters a dazzling turquoise, shimmering like liquid jewels under the sun. The waves were calm and inviting, rolling gently as if beckoning them closer. They plunged in, the cool embrace of the sea wrapping around them.

The water was so clear they could see their feet skimming the sandy ocean floor, each ripple casting playful shadows beneath them. Schools of tiny fish darted in and out of view, their silver scales catching the light as if they were part of the sun's laughter. Around them, the shoreline was framed by lush greenery—trees standing tall and proud, their leaves rustling in the light breeze, adding a natural symphony to the soothing rhythm of the waves.

Logan's strokes were quick and determined as he challenged Adrian to go farther, his laughter bubbling up with every surge forward. Adrian followed, his body cutting through the turquoise surface like a blade through silk, his grin never faltering. Together, they swam farther, pushing each other just a little more, daring the horizon to take them in. The water, so calm and crystalline, felt like it was made for them, a sanctuary carved out of time and nature's beauty.

When they finally waded back to shore, soaked and breathless, Logan made the first move, tackling Adrian into the sand. The two of them tumbled together, a tangle of limbs and ebullience as they wrestled playfully. Adrian managed to push Logan over, pinning him down for all of a second before Logan flipped them again, both of them laughing so hard it felt like their ribs might crack.

"Truce?" Adrian panted, grinning up at Logan.

"Never," Logan teased, before leaning down to steal a quick kiss.

The sensations of their kisses lingered on their lips as they finally pulled themselves from the embrace of the soft sand, their laughter still floating on the sea breeze. They returned to their room, moving instinctively toward the shower, seeking the indulgence of warmth and water cascading over their sun-kissed skin.

The shower became their shared haven, steam rising like a veil around them, softening the edges of reality. The water poured over them in gentle torrents, washing away the remnants of the ocean and the sand, leaving only the heat of their connection. Logan's hands traced Adrian's body with the intimacy of someone memorizing a sacred map, each curve and line a journey he never tired of exploring.

Logan, his eyes darkened with desire, sank to his knees with the reverence of a worshipper before an altar. The water spilled over his shoulders, rivulets streaming down his skin like liquid light, his hands finding Adrian's hips.

Adrian's breath hitched, his body taut, as Logan's mouth enveloped him. There was no hesitation, no restrain, only Logan's devotion, his tongue gliding over Adrian's cock. The rhythm was unremitting yet tender, as Logan swallowed him whole over and over with the precision of someone who knew every inch of him, every weakness, every place that unraveled him completely.

The sound of water mingled with Adrian's quiet, fractured moans, cascading over their bodies in waves of heat and desire. Adrian's hands found Logan's damp, sand-speckled hair, clutching as though the anchor of touch might keep him from drifting into the abyss of sensation. Logan moved with purpose, his lips and tongue pulling Adrian deeper into surrender, his own arousal mirrored in the rhythmic movements of his free hand.

Then came the knock at the door, sharp and startling against the soft intimacy of their moment.

They froze, Logan still wrapped around Adrian's cock, his breath hot and teasing. "Yes?" Adrian called, his voice trying to appear calm as his dick was still buried in Logan's mouth, tickling his throat.

"You booked a couple's massage," a voice responded from beyond the main door. "If it's not a good time, we can come back later."

Logan pulled away, the water washing away the glistening saliva, the evidence of his devotion. "No," he called out, his tone composed but edged with mischief, as he kept jerking Adrian with his hand as he spoke. "You can come in. The main door's open. We'll be out in a moment."

Adrian's eyes widened. "Logan—" he began, his voice low with warning.

"Shh." Logan pressed a finger to Adrian's lips before leaning back down, his tongue flicking against Adrian's dick with deliberate intent. "Be quiet," Logan said, his voice dark with playful command, sucking the crown of Adrian's cut dick into his mouth like a lollypop for a moment. "Make me take it like a good boy. We don't have much time."

Adrian's protest dissolved into a low groan as Logan took him again, his movements precise, reverent. From the other room, faint footsteps were heard, the massage therapists in the suite preparing their space. The tension of being overheard only heightened the intimacy, the forbidden edge electrifying every touch.

"Fuck," Adrian hissed, his hand tangling once more in Logan's hair. "You feel so good around my cock." His voice was a whisper, almost lost beneath the steady fall of water. "You're beautiful like this, on your knees for me."

Logan shuddered visibly at Adrian's words, his hand slipping back to tease Adrian's entrance, and Adrian's breath hitched. "Later," Adrian murmured, his voice rough with promise, "after the massage, I'm going to spread you open and eat you out. Make you—" His sentence dissolved into a guttural moan as Logan's mouth worked him deeper, sucked him harder, took him into his throat again and again. Adrian came without warning, his body trembling, and faintly registered Logan following him over the edge moments later.

Adrian leaned heavily against the wall, his legs weak beneath him, as Logan stood, his eyes shining with triumph. Logan kissed him deeply, their connection grounding them both. "I needed that," Logan murmured with a small grin, finishing their shower with brisk efficiency.

When they stepped into the room, now dimmed with partially closed blinds, the air was thick with relaxation. Two massage tables awaited them, the scent of essential oils drifting faintly through the space. The therapists greeted them warmly, their voices soft.

Adrian climbed onto one of the tables, bare but for a pair of boxers, and Logan caught the brief flicker of the masseur's gaze across his body. Possessiveness rose, sharp and immediate, an instinct that never learned manners. Logan shot the man a warning look and dragged the second table closer before settling onto it himself.

"You need to relax, remember?" Adrian murmured, smiling at him.

Logan meant to answer, but the masseur began working oil across Adrian's back, and a rush of heat hit him hard. The world narrowed to that single point of contact on Adrian's skin.

Adrian reached out and caught his hand, lifting Logan's fingers to his lips. "Ahuv sheli," he whispered, "relax. It's a massage."

Logan breathed, reminding himself he had just had Adrian in the shower, had him coming apart under his hands, that this man was his. The jealousy was still there, but gentling under Adrian's touch, settling rather than vanishing. The room softened around them, the warmth, the scent, the quiet rhythm of hands working sore muscles.

Slowly, the tension in Logan's body unwound. The world narrowed, not to jealousy now, but to the shared stillness between them.

From time to time, their eyes met, quiet and lingering, saying everything words didn't need to. And yes, every so often, Logan still sent a lethal glare toward the poor therapist, but Adrian would just find his hand again, grounding him, settling him. Wrapped in a cocoon of peace, they napped, bodies loose, hearts full, and the rest of the world forgotten.

A while after their massages, Adrian and Logan lay side by side on the bed, the soft mattress cradling them in its luxurious embrace. The air between them was calm and content. Logan turned his head, his expression dreamy as he sighed.

"That was amazing," Logan said, his voice loose and lazy.

Adrian snorted. "Nice to hear that, because for a moment you looked ready to murder the poor man."

"He rubbed oil on you," Logan said, dead serious.

"He was working."

"You were naked."

"I was wearing boxers."

"You were naked," Logan repeated, unimpressed. "And he was ogling you."

Adrian burst into laughter, bright and helpless, and Logan couldn't hold his own back for long.

"Sorry," Logan said once he caught his breath. "I don't mean to get like that."

"Don't be sorry, ahuv sheli," Adrian murmured, pressing his forehead to Logan's. "I know how you get. It's endearing. Completely unnecessary, but endearing."

"I never thought we'd be fancy enough for something like this, a luxury hotel and a couple's massage, but, honestly? I'm getting used to it."

Adrian smiled, his chest warming at the sight of Logan so relaxed and happy as he lay back on the bed. "You've got until tomorrow to bask in it," he said with a teasing lilt. "And we've got brunch coming shortly."

Logan grinned, propping himself up slightly. Still wrapped in their robes, they answered the soft knock at the door and greeted the staff member who wheeled in a tray laden with their meal. The spread was indulgent: freshly baked croissants and danishes, a platter of ripe strawberries and blueberries, smoked salmon with cream cheese, buttery scrambled eggs, and warm brioche toast. A bottle of champagne nestled in a bucket of ice completed the feast. The worker welcomed them to explore the resort's amenities—the bars, the poolside lounges, or even a curated tour—before leaving them to their privacy.

They ate in bed, laughing between bites, feeding each other strawberries and sipping champagne from elegant flutes. The sunlight streaming through the balcony doors bathed the room in a golden glow, making the moment feel suspended in time. After their meal, they lounged by the private pool, the warm sun embracing them as they took turns resting on deck chairs, occasionally slipping into the turquoise water or wandering down to the ocean for a swim. The day was as serene as it was vibrant, a perfect balance of play and peace.

Though the setting was ideal for a nap, neither of them could bring themselves to waste a second of this paradise.

Later, they wandered the resort, exploring the grounds. They passed communal pools shimmering in the sunlight, their surfaces rippling like liquid mirrors, and several restaurants nestled in cozy, village-like clusters. At a bar perched on a cliff overlooking both the ocean and the mountains, they decided to pause, ordering cocktails and settling into a deep-seated sofa with views that could steal anyone's breath.

"Come here," Logan said, his voice low and inviting as Adrian sat beside him. Adrian hesitated, his eyes flickering with uncertainty. "Come on,"

Logan coaxed, grinning. "This is a couple's place. Trust me, they've seen way worse."

Adrian laughed softly, his eyes sparkling as he relented, settling onto Logan's lap. The moment felt intimate yet unassuming, like they were the only two people in the world. Their lips met in quiet, tender kisses, their whispers a language only they could understand. Guests passed by, most of them couples who looked fresh from their honeymoons, their smiles warm and understanding as they glanced at Adrian and Logan. It felt like stepping into a dream, as if they had slipped through reality into a place made just for them.

By late lunchtime, they found a quiet restaurant tucked into the resort, its ambiance elegant yet unpretentious. They indulged in gourmet meals, sharing plates of grilled reef fish, tuna tartare with avocado and sesame, and handmade pasta folded with prawns and cream, which Adrian confidently claimed Logan would want to try. "There is no reason you won't have it just because I don't," he'd remarked.

"This is definitely a step up from pizza," Adrian muttered with a satisfied sigh, his fork hovering as he took in the flavors.

"Definitely," Logan agreed, tipping his champagne flute toward Adrian in a playful toast before taking another sip of the endless bubbles they'd been enjoying.

"Don't get too full," Adrian remarked absently, though there was a teasing edge to his voice. "We've got dinner reservations later."

Logan set down his glass and gave him a look, a mix of affection and incredulity. "Ad, this is too much."

"No, it's not," Adrian said firmly, his eyes meeting Logan's with quiet determination. "Not for you."

And Logan couldn't fight it—the way Adrian's love surrounded him, constant and unwavering, not demanding, not asking—just there, deep and endless, waiting for him to stop resisting the streams of water.

After their meal, they kept wandering the resort's paradise, dipping into pools of crystal clarity. Cocktails in hand, they waved to passing staff who smiled knowingly, as though they too could sense the invisible thread that bound the two of them together.

At one point, a floating tray arrived, a gift from the staff—an offering laden with fruits that gleamed like jewels and bottles of chilled alcohol beaded with drops of dew. They laughed, as Logan fed Adrian a slice of mango so ripe it dripped golden sweetness down his chin. Adrian leaned forward to wipe it away, their eyes meeting in a moment that felt like the world had stopped, as if the water cradling them knew the profound depth of what they shared.

As the sun dipped lower, painting the horizon in hues of fire and amethyst, they shed their usual clothes for something finer, something that felt like an echo of the elegance Adrian had planned for the evening. Logan, in a light button-down shirt with sleeves rolled casually, looked like he had been sculpted from marble and left accidentally for Adrian to find. Adrian's linen shirt caught the breeze, every fold and crease whispering of effortlessness. They climbed into the car, hands entwined, their conversation flowing, tingling with laughter and love.

The restaurant Adrian had chosen wasn't lavish or ostentatious, but it glowed with an intimate, cultivated charm. Its windows spilled golden light into the velvety night, accompanied by the rich, intoxicating aroma of roasted meats and heady spices. The air seemed alive with possibility. Inside, they were led to a corner table nestled beneath a soft, shining lantern. The world beyond that table melted away, leaving only the two of them cocooned in the intimacy of candlelight.

Their meal arrived, and every bite felt like a celebration. The steak was cooked to perfection, the fries were crisp and golden, and the wine swirled ruby-red in their glasses like liquid gemstones. Adrian's gaze lingered on Logan as he spoke, the candlelight catching the curve of his smile, the faint lines of exhaustion etched into his features. Yet Logan's eyes shone with a quiet happiness, a serene equanimity, as if he were savoring not just the meal but the presence of Adrian across from him.

They ended with a slice of cake, for nothing on this earth could deter Adrian from indulging Logan in the most abundant way, lovingly and extravagantly showering him with affection on his birthday. At one point, Adrian leaned forward to swipe a dollop of frosting onto Logan's nose, and Logan retaliated with a mischievous grin, smearing frosting across Adrian's cheek. Their laughter filled the small space, unrestrained and pure, a sound that felt like a memory being born.

"It's your birthday," Adrian said firmly, his voice soft but unwavering as he handed his card to the waiter. Logan tried to protest, his lips parting to form an argument, but the words faded under the weight of Adrian's gaze, a gaze filled with quiet love and the kind of certainty that could anchor even the most restless soul.

The drive back to the resort was quiet, the kind of silence that wasn't empty but full, brimming with contentment. Their hands rested together on the console between them, fingers intertwined, while the car's gentle hum carried them through the velvet night. By the time they stumbled into their suite, exhaustion wrapped around them like a heavy cloak, their limbs and body weary and unyielding after the sun-drenched day that had stretched endlessly before them.

Their movements were slow, almost dreamlike, as they showered. Their touches were unhurried, more comfort than passion, a quiet reminder that they were here, together. Barely able to keep standing, they eventually emerged, hurriedly dried themselves, and then collapsed into the huge bed in a tangle of limbs.

Adrian lay beside Logan, his gaze flickering toward the clock. Each passing second felt significant, his heart beating in rhythm with the final moments of the day. When the clock struck midnight, the room felt charged with something more—a quiet electricity as he turned toward Logan. He slid an arm around him, drawing him near as the heat beneath his skin burned brighter with each touch. Then, with deliberate tenderness, he shifted to hover above Logan, his body solid and reassuring, a quiet promise in the dark.

Adrian kissed him. At first, it was soft, a gentle brushing of lips, like the waters lapping at the shore. But it deepened, each kiss carrying more weight, more intention, until the air between them felt thick with the gravity of their emotions.

"Happy birthday," Adrian murmured against Logan's lips, his voice a low, reverent whisper, as though he were offering a prayer. His breath ghosted over Logan's skin, fiery and intimate in the stillness of the room.

Logan smiled, his eyes half-lidded and glowing in the dim light. "Thank you. This is the best birthday ever."

Adrian's face softened, a quiet radiance overtaking him. In that moment, every dollar spent on the extravagant resort felt inconsequential, meaningless compared to the joy lighting up Logan's features.

"And I don't mean the resort," Logan added, his voice tinged with that familiar playfulness Adrian adored. "Although, well, I won't pretend I didn't enjoy the pampering. That massage today? I had no idea my shoulders could feel that good."

Adrian chuckled, the sound low and fond, their usual banter sliding seamlessly into the space between them.

Logan's voice softened, his playful grin giving way to something deeper. "I mean spending it with you."

Those words lingered in the air, wrapping around Adrian like a warm current. He rested his forehead against Logan's, his breath catching in his throat as his heart swelled. Beneath the playful teasing, there was a raw honesty, a truth so profound it felt like the room itself had grown brighter. And as they drifted into sleep, their bodies entwined, Adrian silently vowed to give Logan a lifetime of moments just like this one.

How might he have anticipated that fate would deny him the opening to fulfill his vow, deeming it to be broken before his lips could even form the words?

The next day unfolded like a slow, golden tide, pulling them deeper into each other before the inevitable ebb. Adrian woke him with a kiss, murmuring, "Morning, birthday boy," before his lips traveled lower, igniting a symphony of pleasure that ended in Logan moving within him as Adrian rode him, their bodies meeting in rhythm until they unraveled together.

Time slipped through their grasp like fine sand, fleeting yet infinitely precious. They reveled in the suite's luxury, wringing every drop of joy from its opulence. A magnificent breakfast in the main restaurant set the tone, their laughter soft and easy over plates of fresh fruit and pastries. They showered together three more times , each turn under the steaming water becoming its own ritual of playful touches and lingering kisses.

The pool shimmered like liquid sapphire, their dives and splashes breaking its surface, their laughter echoing against the stillness of the morning. Back in bed, they found each other again, twice surrendering to a hunger both urgent and reverent. Their moans blended with the gentle hum of the ocean outside, the room itself seeming to hold its breath as if it, too, were a witness to their love.

By early evening, they meandered to the deserted beach, the cool sand cradling their feet as the horizon blushed with hues of orange and pink, casting a serene glow over the tranquil waters. Beneath the endless canopy of stars, Adrian sank to his knees, his lips and tongue driving Logan to the edge while the waves murmured their eternal song. Logan's fingers curled in Adrian's hair, the starlight above casting its silver blessing on their intimacy.

It felt like a honeymoon—a world removed, a moment that existed solely for them. Logan knew he would carry the memory of this day forever, its warmth etched into the deepest corners of his heart. Yet as he gazed at Adrian, luminous in the moonlight, a quiet ache stirred within him. The horizon was calling, and no matter how perfect this moment was, he would have to leave.

As they approached the front desk, ready to check out, Logan turned to Adrian with a casual smile, patting his pockets in mock frustration. "Hey, I think I left my phone in the room. Could you go back and fetch it?"

Adrian paused, his brows knitting briefly in thought before nodding. "Sure," he said, turning back toward the suite without hesitation, his stride easy and unhurried.

Logan watched him retreat, waiting until Adrian was out of sight before spinning on his heel and heading to the front desk with a brisk urgency. His heart thudded in his chest as he approached the clerk, glancing over his shoulder to make sure Adrian wasn't doubling back. "Hey," he said quickly, his voice low but insistent. "The room under Adrian Leon, I want to pay for all the extras we added to the account."

The clerk blinked, momentarily puzzled, before pulling up the reservation on her computer. "It's written here that we're charging the credit card we have on file," she said, her tone polite but uncertain.

"No." Logan shook his head, fishing his wallet from his back pocket and pulling out his own card and sliding it across the counter. "Charge this one instead."

The clerk's confusion melted into understanding as she took the card. "Okay," she said, nodding and beginning to type. She began to list the charges, her voice even as she named them: cocktails and champagne bottles, their long, leisurely lunches, the decadent brunch they'd indulged in twice, and the late checkout that added a small fortune.

"One more thing," Logan added, leaning in slightly. His voice dropped to a near whisper, the intensity in his tone unmistakable. "When Adrian gets here, tell him you've already charged the card on file. Don't let him know I paid."

The clerk's fingers paused over the keyboard, her lips curving into a small, knowing smile. "You're a very thoughtful husband, Mr.—" She glanced down at the card in her hand. "Vaughn."

The word hit Logan like a surfboard to his face, crashing into him with force. His breath caught in his throat as the weight of it settled over him. *Husband*.

For a fleeting moment, the world around him blurred. The sounds of the lobby faded, the velvety light dimmed, and all he could feel was the weight of that word echoing through his chest. It wasn't true, it wasn't their reality, but something about it felt *right*, like the universe had slipped up and revealed an irrefutable and coruscating truth, he wasn't ready to admit to himself.

He swallowed hard, his throat dry, and forced a tight smile. "Thanks," he managed to say, his voice strained, before straightening and glancing over his shoulder again. Adrian wasn't back yet, but Logan could already feel the seconds ticking away.

The clerk's smile lingered, her expression kind and unassuming as she handed him back his card. "You're all set, Mr. Vaughn. It's taken care of."

Logan nodded, pocketing the card and stepping back. His pulse raced as he turned toward the suite, a storm brewing in his chest. *Husband*. The word clung to him, heavy yet sweet, like sea salt on the skin, impossible to ignore, impossible to wash away.

Adrian appeared from the hallway, his brow furrowed as he approached Logan. "I couldn't find your phone," he said, holding up his own. "Here, let me call it."

Husband. He felt its significance in every atom of his being, in every fleeting blink of his eyes. It was etched into his soul, becoming an integral part of his very essence.

He yearned to be Adrian's husband.

In this luxurious haven, he longed to celebrate their love, their honeymoon, moments of joy.

Logan froze, a flicker of panic darting across his face as Adrian tapped the screen and Logan's phone rang immediately—from his pocket.

Adrian's eyebrows arched, his gaze sharp as it landed on Logan. Logan chuckled awkwardly, the sound thin and hollow, fumbling to retrieve the phone from his pocket. "I must not have noticed it," he said, shrugging as though it were nothing, his tone breezy but betraying the faintest tremor. His eyes refused to meet Adrian's, skittering away like driftwood caught in an uncertain current.

He couldn't tell what unsettled him more: the fact that he was lying straight to Adrian's face or the lingering weight of the word *husband*, still echoing in his mind.

Why had it rattled him so deeply? He and Adrian were practically inseparable, their lives entwined like vines growing toward the same sun. They shared meals, adventures, and intimacy that left no corner of their connection unexplored. A bed wasn't even a prerequisite anymore—walls, showers, beaches, even the floor had become their playground, their sanctuary.

They were a couple. Weren't they?

And yet, the word had hit him like a rogue wave, knocking him off balance. Perhaps it was because they never spoke of the future. This trip, this whirlwind of laughter and love, wasn't forever. It had always carried an unspoken expiration date, a horizon neither dared to approach. They avoided the topic as if naming it would make it real, as if silence could stretch their time together infinitely.

But now the word hung between them, shimmering like sea glass—beautiful, fragile, and terrifying in its clarity. Logan's chest tightened as he glanced at Adrian, who still watched him with a quiet suspicion, as if trying to piece together the puzzle of Logan's unease.

Adrian's suspicion lingered, but he let it go as they turned to face the front desk clerk. She smiled warmly, performing a flawless act as she pretended to go through the checkout process. "We'll charge the card on file," she said smoothly, glancing at Adrian.

"Right, thank you," Adrian replied, nodding, though his eyes flicked toward Logan with a trace of doubt. Something didn't add up.

Once they were back in the car, Adrian slid into the driver's seat, his expression thoughtful as he started the engine. The warm hum of the car filled the silence as Logan settled in beside him, staring out the window in what he hoped was casual indifference. But then Adrian reached across the center console, his fingers curling around Logan's hand tenderly. He brought it to his lips, pressing a soft kiss to his knuckles.

"I know what you did," Adrian said quietly, his voice steady but filled with a deep affection.

Logan turned to him, startled. "How did you—?"

Adrian smiled, cutting him off gently. "First, you looked... off. Shaken, almost. And when she told me the total and said they'd charge my card, you didn't argue. You always make a fuss about it. Always. So, I realized that's why you sent me back to the room."

Logan exhaled, his shoulders sinking as he gave Adrian a sheepish smile. "You were not supposed to know about it. I cannot let you pay for all of it, Ad. It's just a small thing."

Adrian's thumb brushed over Logan's hand. "It was thoughtful. So thoughtful. You didn't have to do it, but I appreciate it more than I can say. Thank you."

Adrian's gaze lingered on Logan—raw, unguarded, and impossibly tender. Love pulsed there, undeniable and unhidden, even if the words themselves had never been spoken. Adrian didn't need to say it; the truth of his heart was as vast and evident as the ocean they both loved, constant and infinite. And Logan felt unsteady beneath the weight of it, shaken by the depth he saw reflected in Adrian's eyes and by the single word—*"husband"*—uttered so casually by the spa receptionist. It was a word he both feared and desired, a word containing a glimpse of an oneiric reality that seemed like a possibility too vast and too near.

Logan's chest clenched from his intense emotions, but Adrian's distinctive accent-laden voice cut through the turmoil within him. Logan smirked but said nothing, leaning back in his seat as Adrian's hand slipped over his, their fingers naturally interlocking. They drove in comfortable silence for a moment before Adrian spoke again. "You're quiet."

Logan raised their joined hands to his lips, brushing a kiss against Adrian's knuckles. "It was an amazing two days. Really," he murmured, heart still heavy and anxiety in him. "Like a dream." He leaned across the console, resting his head on Adrian's shoulder, yearning for the closeness that he found utterly intoxicating. The discomfort of the position barely registered in his mind as his heart melted in his chest, longing for a connection with Adrian, much like a delicate plant reaching for the sunlight, craving the warmth and intimacy between them. "I'm just tired. It's been... a long day."

Adrian tilted his head slightly to press a kiss to Logan's hair, the simple gesture speaking volumes as the road stretched before them.

They stopped briefly to return the rented car before catching a ride back to their small cabin. Stepping inside felt achingly familiar, like slipping into the rhythm of a favorite song. It was the kind of place they always sought, cheap and humble, yet accommodating enough for two souls who craved the water more than luxury. But the truth was, with Adrian, every place felt like home.

The space bore the gentle chaos of their shared lives. A lone chair sagged under a pile of hastily discarded clothes, among them Logan's hoodie, the one Adrian kept stealing on chilly nights, wrapping himself in its warmth and scent. Their shoes rested haphazardly by the door: flip-flops and sneakers, though they mostly walked barefoot to the waves. On the counter, a small basket of fruit stood sentinel, because Adrian insisted they eat something fresh each day, even if Logan rolled his eyes at the suggestion. Sunscreen bottles dotted the tables, ready to be grabbed in the mad rush of mornings that always began with the sea.

Logan lingered in the doorway, his gaze sweeping over it all. The clutter. The ease. The life they'd built together. The air folded in on itself, taut and breathless, a feeling unfamiliar yet unbearably heavy, as if in a split of a second gravity had doubled and the strain of it was too much for his chest and shoulders to bear. Or perhaps it had always been there, lurking beneath the surface like a current he'd refused to acknowledge, until now.

Adrian's touch was featherlight as he stepped behind him, fingers grazing Logan's shoulder before planting a soft, absentminded kiss on his cheek. It wasn't an effort; it never was. With Adrian, affection was as natural as breathing. Logan turned into the touch instinctively, as if pulled by the slow rhythm of the water he loved so much

"There's still light out," Adrian said quietly, his voice threading through the stillness like a breeze over water. "Do you want to go catch a few waves? It's still your birthday. Whatever you want." His arms circled Logan's waist, the gesture as effortless as the words.

Logan smiled, soft and unbidden, the kind of smile Adrian always drew from him without trying. His mind was still replaying the golden days they'd just shared, the laughter, the closeness, the stolen moments that felt eternal. "No," Logan murmured, his lips brushing against Adrian's as he spoke. "I don't want to go anywhere."

Husband. That word again, tolling through the chambers of his mind, not gentle but thunderous, not tender but searing, a sound that refused silence. It haunted him with promise, it taunted him with ache, it dangled before him like a fruit just beyond grasp. Adrian's eyes, bright with devotion, fixed upon him as though nothing else in the world dared exist. In that gaze was adoration, surrender, a quiet vow unspoken. And yet he could not answer, could not speak. The word kept circling, inexorable, echo upon echo, louder than his own breath, heavier than his own heart. *Husband.* He reached for it in thought, reached again and again, but it slipped through like mist, vanishing before his trembling hands could hold it still.

Adrian smirked, his face so close it felt like they were sharing the same breath. They stood there, tangled in each other in the middle of the cabin, swaying slightly, as though caught in a silent dance to a song only they could hear.

The air around them thickened, burdened by an invisible weight, as if time itself inhaled deeply and refused to exhale. The moment hung in the balance, both endless and fleeting, a delicate shimmer poised on the verge of silence. Logan's chest tightened with a bittersweet ache, filled with unspoken longing and sorrow. It felt as though the world was sharing a secret he was not yet meant to know, a gentle yet unavoidable whisper of what was coming. A faint shadow of goodbye brushed against the stillness, as subtle as a ghost's touch, though neither of them could yet see its form.

Still, it lingered in the air... a moment they would both reminisce, recognizing it as too tender, too ineffable, too elysian to endure. How could they have known, though? How could they have foreseen the hiraeth that lingered just beyond the veil, biding its time, waiting for the hush before its entrance, a specter of longing poised to step into their lives?

Did the waves, the wind, and the clouds—those elements that brought them together—foreknow their impending departure? Was heartbreak etched in the waves, woven through the streams of water, in that elemental love story that began at the ocean's depths?

"Turn around, Logan, and close your eyes," Adrian whispered, his voice low. Before Logan could react, Adrian spun him gently, like a dance partner, his hands firm yet careful on Logan's shoulders. Logan obeyed, closing his eyes without hesitation.

Adrian strode to the closet, retrieving his duffel where the gift had been carefully hidden since the day before. His heart quickened as he pulled it out, the weight of the medium-sized rectangle familiar and thrilling in his hands. He thought back to the hours spent crafting it, exchanging emails with the artist who owned a small boutique dedicated to bespoke, sentimental creations. When she'd sent him a video of the finished piece, Adrian had nearly cried, thanking her so effusively she laughed and asked if it was a proposal gift. "I wish," he'd replied softly, his voice betraying more than he intended.

Now, as he held the present, thoughtfully wrapped in soft, earthy tones by the artist herself, Adrian felt his chest tighten. He took a steadying breath and turned back to Logan.

"Turn around and open your eyes," Adrian said, his voice quieter now.

Logan turned, his eyes blinking open. They immediately found Adrian's, and for a moment, the gift seemed forgotten as Logan's gaze burned into Adrian, igniting his soul and every fiber within him. Adrian felt the weight of it, the gratitude, the affection, the emotion so raw it left him breathless.

"You can't have a birthday without a present, ahuv sheli," Adrian explained, his smile soft but a little unsure, like he was baring a piece of himself along with the gift.

Logan chuckled, the sound deep and warm, though his eyes shimmered with unshed tears. He looked at Adrian as though he held the entire world in his hands, and Adrian, with his heart hammering against his ribs, found himself unable to look away. Logan's smile widened, and there was something coy, almost boyish, about the way he stepped forward and hugged Adrian tightly, burying his face against Adrian's neck.

"You shouldn't have gotten me a gift," Logan murmured, his voice muffled but thick with emotion. "Not after everything you've already done."

Adrian held him close, his hands brushing soothing circles on Logan's back. "It's nothing," he whispered, though his voice wavered slightly. Logan pulled back just enough to meet Adrian's gaze, his own expression so open and raw it made Adrian's breath hitch.

"Thank you so much," Logan said softly, his words a gentle caress.

"You haven't even seen it yet," Adrian replied, a nervous chuckle escaping him, his fingers grazing over Logan's wrist as if tethering himself to this moment.

"I know it's perfect," Logan answered, and with a final squeeze, he let Adrian go and turned his attention to the gift. His fingers traced the edges of the carefully wrapped paper before he began to tear it away slowly, and when the paper fell away, it revealed a simple, leather-bound album, the cover textured and worn like something meant to last a lifetime. Logan hesitated before opening it, his fingers brushing the grain of the leather as if feeling the pulse of the memories inside.

Adrian watched, his nerves dancing with every rip and fold.

"It's not much..." Adrian breathed, his voice tinged with hesitation, a beautiful crimson dotting his cheeks. His hands fidgeted slightly, betraying the nervous energy he was trying to suppress. "But I know how much you love filming everything, taking pictures... So, I picked your best shots and the perfect moments and had an artist craft them into a memory book."

Logan's breath hitched as his legs suddenly felt too weak to hold him. He sank into one of the worn chairs, the little cabin suddenly feeling vast and quiet. He opened the small album carefully, almost reverently, as though it might dissolve in his hands if he wasn't gentle. The pages, no more than twenty, were made from textured, recycled paper, rough under his fingertips but so full of life.

As he flipped through the pages, true amazement flickered across his face. Each photo was a fragment of them—pieces of their story that Logan had captured with the care of someone who wanted to hold onto every fleeting moment. Most were of Logan himself, his smile wide and uninhibited, frozen in time, captured for eternity. Some were frames from Logan's endless videos: him mid-jump, surfing with joy radiating from his very being, utterly unguarded.

But there were also pictures of them together. Goofy faces pressed close to the camera, their laughter practically visible in the stillness of the images. The two of them surfing side by side, their bodies moving in harmony with the waves, as if the ocean had choreographed it. Each photo seemed to carry an invisible weight, a significance that went beyond the image itself.

And then Logan saw it, the hidden thread weaving it all into one. These were not mere pictures, flat and still upon the page; they were fragments of breath, of heartbeat, of time caught trembling. They were not just moments, but *their* moments, alive and burning with the echoes of who they were. The beach in Hawaii where Adrian had fought the waves for Logan's life. The river they'd jumped into. The day they'd met Adrian's friends and the surf spot that marked the beginning of something they hadn't yet named. The hike through the jungle, where they'd swung from the vines like reckless children, Logan's leap frozen midair, his body caught between gravity and flight, wild and free, as if he had never known fear. That night, the one where Logan had told Adrian to lose control, was captured there, too, etched into the pages as if the moment itself had been waiting to be remembered.

The cave they had explored, the darkness swallowing them as they stumbled through damp tunnels, their flashlights flickering against the stone walls. It hadn't taken long for them to realize it wasn't for them—Logan's playful, eerie noises echoing in the emptiness, his laughter breaking through the silence as Adrian shoved him, rolling his eyes but unable to hide his grin.

The night they spent curled up on the beach, waiting for the first light to spill over the horizon. Adrian, tucked into Logan's hoodie, the one he had claimed with effortless ease. The salty breeze tangled their hair, the sound of the waves filling the spaces between their words, until neither of them spoke at all, simply existing in the stillness of each other.

The day they stood at the edge of a towering cliff, the world dropping away beneath their feet. The heat of the sun against their skin. The pulse of adrenaline in their veins. The quick, knowing glance before they jumped—together, into the endless blue. The camera had caught them midair, their faces frozen in that weightless second before they hit the water, before they emerged breathless, laughing, alive. The yacht they had spent two magnificent days on, Logan's fearless leaps into the sea, then them exploring the vibrant reefs side by side. Each photo was a marker, a monument to a love that had grown organically, quietly, beautifully.

Each photo was more than just a memory, it was proof. Proof of *them*. Of every stolen moment, every whispered dare, every inch of love that had grown in between.

His chest tightened as the weight of it settled over him, the sheer magnitude of what Adrian had given him. He lifted his eyes to meet Adrian's, those whiskey-brown depths burning into him, setting his heart ablaze. Logan's mind was blank. Every word he could summon seemed too small, too inadequate, but his heart pounded furiously, alive in a way it never had been before.

Husband.

He reached the last photo and felt his breath wavering in his throat.

It was a shot of him, but not in a moment *he* had captured.

This was a moment *Adrian* had captured of him.

He was sitting on a surfboard, out in the middle of the sea, golden light pooling around him like it had chosen only him to kiss. His expression was quiet, contemplative, his fingers skimming the water's surface. The ocean stretched endlessly behind him, horizon meeting sky in a seamless embrace.

"You like it?" Adrian asked softly, his voice so quiet it was almost lost in the silence. There was a raw, almost desperate edge to it, as though he feared Logan might not understand what this meant, what *he* meant.

Logan placed the memory book gently on the small table beside him, his movements deliberate. He rose slowly, his eyes never leaving Adrian's, and crossed the short space between them. He needed to say something, anything, but the words that came screamed only one truth: *I love you.*

But Logan couldn't say that.

Instead, he let his hand rest against Adrian's cheek, his thumb tracing a tender arc across warm skin. He tilted Adrian's head, just slightly, enough to drink him in, enough to bare himself in return. In his gaze, he emptied everything he carried, everything words refused: devotion, surrender, the plea of a soul that had found its anchor. *I love this. I love you. I am yours. Marry me. Be my husband, my eternity. Walk with me through every breath, every breaking dawn. You are the hand that pulled me from the dark, the heartbeat that steadies mine, my life-saver, and I can't take another breath without thinking of you.*

"Love it," Logan breathed at last, the whisper trembling, carrying the weight of a vow too vast for the smallness of speech.

Adrian exhaled softly, leaning into Logan's touch, and for a moment, the world outside the cabin didn't exist. There was only this: two souls bound in a fragile knot, flesh and spirit entwined, holding fast to a moment that shimmered like eternity even as it slipped toward its end. It was human and divine all at once, the ache of love pressed against the inevitability of loss.

Logan was insatiable, a man caught in a tide he couldn't resist. His lips claimed Adrian's in a kiss that was both fierce and tender, guiding them toward the bed, its rumpled sheets still carrying the intoxicating scent of their bodies. He seemed incapable of keeping his hands from Adrian, as though every touch was a lifeline, a tether to something he couldn't name but couldn't bear to lose.

Breaking the kiss just long enough to strip Adrian off his shirt, Logan flung the fabric to the floor, his hands immediately returning to roam over Adrian's body. His fingers curled around Adrian's biceps, firm and warm beneath his touch, while his mouth found its way back to Adrian's neck, trailing kisses up to his cheek and into his hair. Logan let his fingers thread through the sun-bleached strands, damp and soft like ocean silk, each lock a reminder of countless days spent beneath the sky and the sea.

They tumbled onto the bed in a tangle of limbs, kicking away shorts, shirts, and sneakers with the impatient urgency. Logan covered Adrian's naked body with his own, pressing them together as though he could fuse their souls through skin. He kissed Adrian with a hunger that bordered on desperation, like a man starved for air after being held beneath the surface too long, like a shipwreck survivor finally finding the light of the sun after endless nights adrift.

He kissed him like someone who knew the sands in the hourglass were slipping away, faster than he could hold on.

"Ad—" Logan groaned, their bodies moving in perfect, familiar rhythm. Each touch felt like muscle memory, a dance learned through endless repetition, yet it still sent shivers coursing through him, electric and new. "I want you—" he began, but Adrian cut him off with another kiss, fierce and consuming. Adrian kissed him as if it were a declaration, as if being without Logan was a concept so foreign it couldn't be entertained.

When their lips parted, their breaths came in ragged gasps, the air between them thick and charged. "Ad," Logan whispered again, his voice rough, trembling. His lips hovered just over Adrian's, his words carrying the weight of a decision made in the depths of his heart. "I want you inside me."

The words hung in the air. Logan's cheeks glowed with gentle warmth, with a soft flush spreading from his cheeks to his neck and hairline, while his eyes remained fixed on Adrian's, steady and unwavering. His heart beat wildly as though riding the crest of a wave, a thrilling drop into the unknown.

Adrian's hips twitched at the revelation, his eyes deep and brimming with a mix of worship and need. "Fuck," he muttered, his voice a rumble, too low to catch fully. He touched Logan as if to ground himself, his hands mapping the planes of his lover's body. "Are you sure?"

Logan silenced him with another kiss, slower this time, the kind that carried every ounce of certainty he felt. When their lips finally broke apart, Logan rested his forehead against Adrian's, his voice soft yet steady. "Yes," he said, "I want to feel you inside of me."

"You sure? I don't want you to feel obligated. Like, I... I don't need it, I mean, I want to, of course I want to, but only if you do. I don't need it, I am perfectly happy, as happy as a man could be, more even in fact, with what we have now, I just—" His words stumbled, caught between longing and restraint.

Logan silenced him with a kiss, pulling the air from Adrian's protest. When their mouths parted, Logan rested his forehead against his. "I'm not some blushing virgin, remember?" His smile was tender, not teasing. "I've been thinking about it for a while. I love it when you touch me... there. I want more. I want you."

Adrian searched his eyes, hesitation flickering.

"Make love to me, Adrian?" Logan whispered, the words carrying no demand, only invitation.

Adrian shuddered, his body trembling like a wave poised to crash. And as their touches grew slower but no less intense, they moved toward each other with the kind of trust that only came from knowing every inch of the other's soul.

Adrian flipped them effortlessly, his grin wicked as he hovered above Logan. "Your wish is my command," he said, his voice rich with teasing affection.

Logan rolled his eyes, laughter spilling from him as Adrian pressed warm kisses to his chest, his lips trailing downward to the soft ridges of Logan's stomach. "Oh, how generous of you, Mr. Leon," Logan bantered, his tone dripping with mockery. "To fuck me, what a tremendous sacrifice. Truly, you're a saint. It must be so hard for you."

Adrian paused, his face buried in Logan's crotch, and looked up with a mischievous gleam in his eyes. "It *is* hard," he said solemnly, "and not fuck, making love," he corrected before pressing a reverent kiss to Logan's length. "I missed you so much," he murmured, his voice low and adoring as his tongue traced a slow, measured line along Logan's shaft.

Logan's groan escaped before he could catch it, his body arching involuntarily into Adrian's touch. "Are you—are you having a conversation with my dick?" he managed, his voice breaking with a mix of disbelief and arousal.

"Yes," Adrian said without hesitation, his tone utterly serious, though his lips quirked with amusement. "We're very close by now," he added with a wink, "Aren't we, buddy?" he added shifting his gaze back to Logan's cock, hunger burning in his eyes before enveloping Logan in the wet, searing heat of his mouth. Logan's protest dissolved into a moan, his hands clutching the sheets as Adrian worked him over with languid, teasing strokes of his tongue. Logan's legs fell open, his body surrendering completely to the pleasure coursing through him.

Adrian gave him only a few torturous moments of this before pulling back and bending Logan in half with practiced ease. Logan's breath caught as Adrian turned his attention lower, pressing feather-light kisses to the sensitive skin of his inner thighs before lavishing his tongue on Logan's entrance. The sensation sent sparks flying through Logan's body, his head falling back onto the pillow with a gasp.

"Damn," Adrian moaned softly, his voice filled with reverence as he worked Logan open with his tongue, savoring every moment. He could feel the way Logan's body trembled beneath him, the way he gave himself over completely, abandoning all control. Adrian's hands gripped Logan's thighs firmly, holding him steady as his tongue explored deeper, each movement calculated to drive Logan further into bliss.

"You're still open," Adrian murmured, his voice thick with desire. The words made Logan shiver as the memory surged back, earlier at the resort, when Adrian had spent what felt like an eternity worshiping him with his fingers and tongue, finding every sensitive spot, massaging his prostate until Logan came undone in waves of ecstasy.

Logan's moans grew louder, his body responding to Adrian's touch like a wildfire chasing dry grass, fierce and fast. His fingers tangled in Adrian's hair, and his voice, hoarse and desperate, broke through the haze of pleasure. "Adrian... please..."

And Adrian, utterly devoted, gave himself to Logan, meeting every whispered plea and sigh with ironclad attention, as though this was not just an act of passion, but a prayer.

Adrian reached into the drawer, retrieving the well-used bottle of lube they always seemed to run out of far too quickly. The slick sound of it being squeezed out broke the quiet intimacy of the room, a prelude to the touch that followed. He coated his fingers in the cool, thick liquid, pausing to warm a little in his hands before spreading it gently over Logan's entrance. Logan shuddered at the contrast—the cool slickness against his overheated skin sending a ripple of sensation through his body.

Adrian's touch was careful, adoring in its tenderness. He massaged the soft ring of muscle with trembling fingers, coaxing Logan open once again. The evidence of Adrian's earlier love was still there, Logan's body relaxed and yielding beneath his fingers, his muscles loosening in anticipation.

The thought of being inside Logan, of feeling him so intimately, sent a wave of emotion crashing over Adrian. He cherished every moment they shared, every touch and kiss, every quiet laugh between them. What Adrian had told Logan months ago—that he would have been content with friendship alone—remained true. He would have taken even the smallest piece of Logan, held it close, cherished it like a relic. But this, this moment, this gift of trust and body and love, was beyond anything he had dared imagine. It felt like standing in sunlight after years of cold, like finding breath after nearly drowning. He did not question how or why such grace had found him. He only surrendered to it, and in every glance, every caress, he gave thanks.

"Put your feet on the bed," Adrian whispered, his voice soft but commanding, and Logan obeyed, bending his legs and placing his feet flat against the mattress. The position left him exposed, vulnerable in a way that made his heart race. But he didn't shy away. He trusted Adrian. He trusted this. His body hummed with anticipation as he braced himself, willing his mind to calm even as his pulse quickened.

Adrian took a moment to admire him, the sight of Logan beneath him sending a jolt of arousal and affection through his chest. Logan's vulnerability was matched by his strength, his willingness to bear himself completely, a gift Adrian vowed never to take for granted.

As Adrian's fingers began to explore, sliding inside with ease, Logan's breath hitched, his body immediately reacting to the familiar touch. Adrian moved with care, a mix of patience and precision, his fingers seeking out that spot deep within that made Logan unravel. The moment he found it, Logan gasped sharply, his body arching off the mattress, his hands gripping the sheets as though they were the only thing keeping him tethered to the earth.

"Adrian," Logan whispered, his voice cracking as pleasure rolled through him. Adrian continued, his touch skilled and unhurried, drawing sounds from Logan that were somewhere between prayer and surrender. He felt Logan's body quiver beneath him, his chest heaving, as he murmured something incoherent, his words dissolving into the space between them.

"You're fucking gorgeous," Adrian breathed, his voice thick with awe as he gazed down at Logan, sprawled across the bed like a masterpiece. Logan's flushed skin glowed faintly in the dim light, his chest rising and falling with every shuddering breath. Adrian had never seen anything, *anyone,* more beautiful. It left him shaken, his heart cracking open in a way that both terrified and thrilled him. How had he been so lucky? How had Logan come to trust him so completely, to give himself so freely? The weight of it made Adrian's heart miss a beat, and at that moment, he fell for Logan just a little more.

Adrian's own need pulsed through him, his cock hard and aching, but he forced himself to focus. There was nothing more important than Logan right now; his pleasure, his surrender, his voice whispering Adrian's name like a prayer.

With hands that had loved Logan for an infinite number of moments now, Adrian slid his finger deeper into Logan, feeling the warmth of his body pulling him in, taking him so perfectly it made Adrian's head spin. But he wasn't done. He leaned down, pressing his lips to the head of Logan's cock before taking him into his mouth. Logan let out a sharp, broken cry as Adrian's tongue worked over him, the sound sending a thrill down Adrian's spine.

Adrian kept his movements subtle, teasing, wanting Logan to feel every sensation he gave him. He could hear Logan's breathing grow ragged, feel the tension building in his thighs as his body writhed beneath him.

Logan's hands found their way to Adrian's head, threading through his hair as he gasped and moaned. His body was alive with sensation, every nerve alight. He felt Adrian inside him, on him, overwhelming him with pleasure so intense it bordered on too much. "Adrian," he whispered, his voice shaking. "Adrian..." He couldn't stop saying his name, couldn't hold back the sounds spilling from him.

When Adrian added a second finger, stroking deep and finding that perfect spot, Logan arched off the bed, his cries turning into desperate, needy whines. His hips began moving, fucking Adrian's mouth with a rhythm that spoke of need, of surrender. "So good," Logan whimpered, his voice trembling with the edge of tears. "So fucking good—Adrian—"

And just as Logan's orgasm began to crest, Adrian pressed deeper with his fingers, rubbing against his prostate with every stroke.

Logan's hand moved to Adrian's shoulder, a soft push, his voice barely audible through the haze of his building orgasm. "Stop," he murmured. "Or I'll come," His chest heaved as he caught his breath, his body trembling. "I want to come with you inside me," he added, his voice soft but firm, his eyes dark and full of want. "I want to come on your cock."

Adrian nodded, swallowing hard. The raw need in Logan's voice was enough to make his pulse thunder in his ears.

"Get inside me, now," Logan commanded, his tone leaving no room for argument.

Adrian's lips curved into a small, breathless smile. "One more finger," he said, his voice hoarse as his fingers pressed deeper, coaxing Logan open.

"No." Logan shook his head, his voice steady despite the tremor in his body. "I want to feel you. I want *all* of you. You've been prepping me for this for so long." His eyes burned into Adrian's, fierce and unyielding. "Get that beautiful cock inside me. I don't think I have another orgasm in me after that day, so do not make me come yet."

Adrian groaned, his restraint unraveling at Logan's words. "God, I love it when you're feisty," his tone was hushed, steeped in devotion and desire.

He climbed back up Logan's body, pressing their lips together in a kiss that was deep and consuming, stealing the air from both their lungs. When he finally pulled back, his fingers slipped free, and he reached for the lube, coating his aching cock with trembling hands.

Once again, his gaze intertwined with Logan's, a question swimming in their depths, even as the answer hummed softly between them. With a deliberate tenderness, Logan drew Adrian nearer, his voice a gentle whisper yet resolute, echoing the unspoken truth. "I'm yours," he whispered. "Take me."

Desire climbed his spine like a fever, unbalancing him with every breath. His skin prickled, nerves lit like a live wire, each touch threatening to unmoor him completely. He knew he was on the edge already, the sheer thought of being inside Logan threatening to undo him. His hands trembled slightly as he guided himself to Logan, the preparation easing the stretch as the head of his cock pressed into him. Adrian stilled as soon as the crown slipped past the tight ring of muscle, giving Logan a moment to adjust, his body taut with restraint despite the overwhelming heat and pressure enveloping him.

Logan's eyes were squeezed shut, his breath coming in sharp bursts. Adrian leaned into the curve of Logan's neck, resting his forehead in the warm juncture between shoulder and throat—a place that pulsed with quiet life. He breathed in the scent of him, lips trailing slow kisses over skin that felt impossibly soft and damp with sweet sweat, as if it had been waiting just for this.

"Breathe," he whispered, voice barely there, a hush threaded with devotion. "Ahuv sheli. Just breathe." The words settled like dust in sunlight, golden in color and feathery in weight. His lips wandered next to

Logan's chin, pressing a kiss that asked nothing and promised everything. There was no rush in him. Just patience. Just presence. Just a kind of aching care that made time feel like it was holding its breath.

Logan inhaled shakily, his chest rising as he pulled in the air Adrian had offered. When he opened his eyes, they locked onto Adrian's, and the world seemed to still. The expression on Adrian's face—so full of tenderness, of love that radiated with an intensity that felt almost sacred—was unbearable in its beauty, as if love itself had mass and he wasn't ready to hold it. His throat tightened, the perfection of the moment threatening to overwhelm him. It was like he'd spent twenty-five years in darkness, and now, for the first time, he could see color. It was like breathing after a lifetime of suffocation, air filling his lungs for the first time.

Logan's arms circled around Adrian, his hands moving over the smooth muscles of his back, his fingers tracing the curve of his hips. "God," Logan whispered, his voice thick, "this is way bigger than the fingers." His lips twitched into a small, teasing smile as his hand slid to Adrian's jawline, feeling the rough stubble that dusted his cheeks.

Adrian let out a breathless laugh, leaning in to press his forehead to Logan's. "Should've warned you," he joked, his voice low and husky. His laughter faded into a groan as Logan's hand moved to his ass, gripping firmly and urging him forward.

The message was clear. Adrian exhaled shakily, his body trembling as he began to move again. He pushed deeper into Logan, his breath catching at the heat and tightness surrounding him. Logan's body welcomed him, stretched for him, and Adrian's head tipped back, a soft moan escaping as he slid further inside. He paused again, their breaths mingling as he stilled, his hips pressed flush against Logan, his balls snug against him.

"You okay?" Adrian panted, his voice thick with concern and pleasure.

Logan's head tilted back, a deep, blissful moan spilling from his lips. "Perfect," he breathed, his hands running over Adrian's back, his nails grazing his skin. He pulled Adrian closer, his mouth finding Adrian's, their lips meeting in a kiss that was all-consuming. When their mouths parted, Logan's eyes burned with untamed need. His hand rose in instinct, tugging free Adrian's hair tie. A mix of golden and dark strands tumbled loose, spilling over his shoulders, his neck, his chest, brushing against Logan's skin like whispers of silk, moving to the rhythm of Adrian's breath. "Fuck me," Logan sighed, words spilling between gasps. "I want to feel you move."

Adrian didn't hesitate, though his voice softened, reverent, as he leaned close. "I'll make love to you, ahuv sheli."

With a shuddering breath, he began to move, pulling out slowly before thrusting back in, his rhythm building as their bodies found the perfect sync. Logan's moans filled the air, his hands clinging to Adrian as if he were the only thing anchoring him to the earth. Every thrust, every shared breath felt like a declaration—of trust, of love, of two souls finding their way to each other. And as Adrian moved, he couldn't help but marvel at the way Logan made him feel, like he'd found his home.

Adrian kissed Logan deeply, bracing himself on one arm as his hips pulled back, only to thrust forward again with a moan that seemed to echo through the room. His body trembled with restraint as he moved inside Logan, caught between the desire to lose himself in hard, frantic thrusts and the craving to draw this out, to savor every second of their connection.

The push and pull of his need kept him on edge, his body already slick with sweat as he rocked against Logan.

Logan, in turn, pulled Adrian down, pressing their bodies together until no space remained between them. Adrian cried out at the sensation, the hard length of Logan's cock trapped between them, pressing against his abdomen, growing harder with every motion. It was overwhelming—Logan's heat, his weight, his skin against Adrian's as they moved together. Adrian's rhythm faltered for a moment, his breath hitching at the intimacy, before his hips began moving again, each thrust more desperate than the last.

Adrian's hand slid to Logan's face, cradling it as he kissed him hard, their tongues tangling in a heated exchange that left them both gasping. Logan reached between their bodies, his hand wrapping around his own cock, stroking himself in time with Adrian's thrusts. Adrian's voice broke into a whimper as he felt the movement against his stomach, the sensation sending shivers down his spine.

"You feel amazing," Adrian groaned, his voice trembling. "Damn it, you feel so tight." His lips found Logan's neck, biting playfully before soothing the mark with a kiss, his tongue teasing the tender flesh. "I could stay inside you forever," he murmured against Logan's skin, the words heavy with both lust and adoration.

Logan's hands gripped Adrian's ass, his nails digging in slightly as he growled, "Faster."

Adrian let out a breathless laugh, his eyes gleaming with mischief. "Yes, sir," he teased. He hooked one of Logan's legs, pressing it up toward his chest to open him further, his thrusts growing faster, deeper, more precise.

Logan's moans became louder, unrestrained, each sound sending a rush of heat through Adrian as he chased his pleasure.

Logan's hand resumed stroking his cock, his rhythm matching Adrian's movements, but Adrian was quick to take over. He wrapped his hand around Logan's length, his strokes firm and deliberate as he leaned close to his lover's ear. His voice dropped to a husky whisper, the deep timbre rolling over Logan. "You're taking me so well," Adrian purred, his words laced with raw desire. "God, you're opening this beautiful body for me, letting me in. Feeling your tight ass around my dick is the best fucking thing in the world."

Logan groaned, his head falling back, his face a picture of ecstasy as his body writhed beneath Adrian. "Yes!" he cried, his voice hoarse, his nails raking down Adrian's back as the pleasure consumed him.

Adrian's movements became erratic, his control slipping as the tension built, coiling tighter and tighter inside him. His breathing was ragged, his voice breaking as he moaned, "Lo, I'm close." His words were a confession, a plea, his body trembling as he edged closer to the brink.

Logan's arms wrapped tighter around Adrian, pulling him impossibly close as he felt Adrian's body tremble above him. Adrian whimpered his name, over and over, the sound broken and raw as his release surged through him. Logan could feel Adrian's cock pulsing deep inside, the heat of it radiating outward, the connection between them so profound it felt almost sacred.

Adrian's lips brushed Logan's, their breaths mingling as Adrian whispered against his mouth, "Fuck, Lo, I love you so much. I'm so fucking in love with you."

They couldn't form a proper kiss, their mouths hovering just inches apart, sharing the same breath as if any distance between them would be unbearable. The closeness was exquisite, felt in the electric pull of their skin, the soft rhythm of their breaths, and the moans as they moved together. Logan felt himself tipping over the edge as Adrian's hand stroked him faster, coaxing him toward release.

With a cry that seemed to tear from his very core, Logan came, his head falling back, his body arching into Adrian's as the pleasure consumed him. He buried his face in Adrian's shoulder, his voice muffled but raw as he called out, his orgasm shattering him into pieces.

He felt his release spill between them, warm and sticky, coating their chests and stomachs as wave after wave of pleasure coursed through him. It was mind-blowing, earth-shattering, every nerve in his body alight, every part of him alive in a way he'd never known before. The sensation of Adrian still inside him as he came only deepened the intensity, their bodies moving in perfect, trembling harmony.

When the waves finally began to subside, Adrian released Logan's softening cock, his breath hitching as the last tremors of his climax echoed through him. Adrian collapsed against him, their bodies sticky and tangled, the weight of him grounding Logan in the aftermath. The evidence of their connection was smeared between them, but neither of them moved to clean it. It felt right, raw, real, and perfect.

Logan didn't know how much time had passed as they lay there, their breaths slowing, their bodies still intertwined. Adrian's head rested on his shoulder, and Logan turned his face slightly, catching the faint scent of salt and sweat on his skin. Adrian's breathing grew steady, even, as though he was memorizing the rhythm of Logan's heartbeat. For a while, they stayed like that, silent but together, the quiet intimacy cocooning them.

Adrian leaned down to kiss Logan's chest, his lips lingering over his heart. Logan could feel Adrian's heartbeat racing beneath his skin, not just strong but inexorable, as if the pulse itself carried the secret language of devotion. He marveled at the miracle of it, the intimacy of being known so completely, seen so wholly, loved so fiercely.

Was this what other people had discovered long before him? Had the world been walking around with this secret pressed to their ribs, carrying it like a hidden flame, while he stumbled blind through his days, unaware of what love could be? Had they known the way it seizes you, reshapes you, breaks and remakes you all at once?

Logan could not fathom how anyone lived their ordinary lives—crossing streets, standing in checkout lines, chatting idly—while carrying this force inside them. Didn't they feel the sky shift? Didn't they feel the ground tilt beneath their feet?

Because to him, the truth was devastating in its clarity: the thought of Adrian not beside him was unbearable. The idea of losing him was not absence but annihilation, as if death itself crouched in the corner of his heart, waiting to strike the moment Adrian slipped away.

It wasn't only love, he realized; it was something older, something carved into the marrow, a force that seized his chest and held him captive. It was the unshakable knowledge that his soul had stumbled upon its counterpart, its mirror, its long-awaited home. From this moment onward, he could not conceive of a world where he would choose to release it. To let go would not simply be loss, but erasure, the unraveling of everything he was, the unmaking of himself.

He wondered if others were brave enough to step into this place, to give themselves over so completely, so vulnerably, to another person. Did they dare? Could they stand at the precipice of their heart and take the leap, knowing they might fall endlessly into it? Or did they shrink back, terrified of the cost, of how completely it could devour them?

And would this fire ever fade, this scream lodged in his chest, this ache that burned with every thought of Adrian? Would he ever stop needing him—needing to see those eyes, to hear his name spoken as if it were holy? Could he ever exist without this craving, as vital as breath in his lungs, as relentless as the beat of his heart, as essential as the blood that kept him alive?

Logan doubted it. He doubted he could ever return to the man he had been before Adrian, before love remade him into something new, before it became both compass and anchor, charting his course and holding him steady. And he wasn't sure he would ever want to. The thought of it, of a world where this feeling did not exist, was like imagining breath without air, like standing beneath a sky stripped of its sun. It was emptiness, a silence too vast to survive. No, he would not escape it. He would cradle it, surrender to it, even if it burned through every part of him, even if it consumed him whole.

After some time, Adrian gently pulled out of Logan, his movement slow, as if he feared breaking something fragile. Logan shivered at the sudden emptiness, and a faint, involuntary tremor ran through him, a tiny aftershock of pleasure. Adrian paused, his eyes searching Logan's face with a flicker of worry.

Maybe it was because he had just told Logan he loved him for the first time, and Logan hadn't said it back. Maybe because Logan hadn't said *anything* since the confession, the silence stretching between them like a brittle thread that might snap at any moment.

Logan felt the weight of Adrian's gaze, the vulnerability in it, the quiet question hanging unspoken in the air. He wanted to say the words, to tell Adrian that he loved him more than he'd ever thought possible, more than anything in the world. He wanted to tell Adrian that he couldn't imagine a version of himself that didn't revolve around him. He wanted to get down on one knee and tell Adrian how madly and stupidly in love with him he was. But as much as those feelings were true, there was another truth Logan couldn't ignore. He didn't see a future for them; there wasn't a horizon they could walk toward together. The thought was like a riptide beneath his feet, pulling him toward an inevitable separation he wasn't ready to face.

Adrian's eyes softened, deep wells of vulnerability, as if he could glimpse the storm gathering beneath Logan's stillness. That gaze peeled back every layer, pressed against every secret Logan had tried to bury. And Logan, wordless, begged to be seen. His silence was not empty; it was a scream lodged in his chest, a warning he could not voice, an ache he could not name. He wanted Adrian to hear it, to pull it from him, to understand the terror blooming sharp and wild beneath his skin.

The air between them quivered with that unspoken truth, heavy as thunder before it breaks. Adrian's lips curved into the smallest smile—merciful, knowing, and devastating in its gentleness. He leaned close, voice hushed like something uttered in a chapel, meant only for the soul it was spoken to.

"It's okay," he whispered, steady and tender, every syllable falling like balm against fracture. "I know, ahuv sheli."

The quiet assurance knocked the air out of Logan's chest. He wanted to protest, to ask what Adrian thought he knew, but before he could say anything, Adrian stood and pulled Logan to his feet. Wrapping Logan's arms around his own body, Adrian turned so his back pressed against Logan's chest, holding their hands against his stomach. They stumbled together, laughing softly at the awkwardness of it as Adrian led them to the bathroom.

Under the spray of hot water, Adrian washed Logan with tender care, his hands smoothing over his skin as if committing every inch of him to memory. Logan kissed him every chance he got—his shoulder, his cheek, the corner of his mouth—and laughed when Adrian reached for the conditioner, knowing that two days ago Adrian had used his expensive hair mask. He only used it once or twice a week, so today it was conditioner that he was applying with meticulous care to his sun-kissed hair.

Adrian's laughter was infectious, but Logan's heart ached beneath it all. He loved Adrian. He loved him so much it felt like his heart might burst from it, like it might drown him entirely. So he kissed him again, backing him against the tiled wall, letting the water stream over them as his fingers tangled in Adrian's hair. The kiss was deep, desperate, and Adrian returned it with equal fervor, his hands cupping Logan's face, his thumbs brushing along his jaw as though to memorize its lines.

When it was Adrian's turn to be washed, Logan did it gently, reverently, letting his hands move over every part of him, tracing the shape of his body as Adrian's hands roamed Logan's in return—his face, his neck, his back. It was quiet, intimate, the kind of moment that carved itself into the soul, unshakable and permanent.

But Adrian's words haunted Logan, their weight pressing into his chest. Adrian had always been expressive in his love, in his touch, in the way he showed Logan how much he cared. But hearing those three words spoken aloud was more than Logan had ever expected. It was more than he felt he could deserve. Because deep down, Logan knew he couldn't be the man Adrian needed. Not fully. Not forever.

When they finally stepped out of the shower, Adrian grabbed two towels, wrapping one around Logan and patting him dry with a care that made Logan's throat tighten. He dried himself quickly, then led Logan by the hand back to the bed. Without a word, they slipped under the covers, Adrian pulling Logan close, his arm draped protectively over his waist as he kissed him and murmured a soft good night.

As Logan lay there in the quiet, the steady rhythm of Adrian's breathing against his chest, he couldn't help but wonder if Adrian truly did know, if he could see the cracks in the foundation of their love. And if he could, how long they had before it all came tumbling down.

Logan closed his eyes, and when he opened them again, the first light of dawn was stretching its delicate fingers into the room, painting it with hues of pale gold and soft pink. Adrian lay curled against Logan's chest, his breathing deep and even, his warmth pressed against him. Logan closed his eyes again, feeling the tears rising unbidden, hot and heavy. He didn't stop them. They slipped silently down his cheeks, each one carrying the weight of a truth he wished he didn't have to face.

Staring at the ceiling, Logan tried to steady himself, but his thoughts swirled like a restless tide. He had always believed that the thing he loved most in this world was the ocean. Surfing under the sun as it rose, its heat kissing his skin, had always been the purest form of freedom he'd ever known. The ocean was his sanctuary, the only place where his spirit felt weightless, where the wind and waves carried him beyond the reach of expectations and obligations.

The buds of saltwater clinging to his skin, the sound of the waves crashing around him, the endless horizon stretching into eternity—those were the things that had kept him sane. Surfing wasn't just a pastime; it was his truth, the only choice that had ever been his. He decided what board to ride, which beach to visit, when to skip class and chase the waves. The ocean didn't care who he was. It didn't whisper his family name, didn't see him as *a Vaughn*, didn't weigh him down with expectations. In the water, he was just Logan, stripped of everything but the raw joy of being alive.

But now, staring at the first light creeping into the room, Adrian's body still pressed against him, Logan realized that he had been wrong. He hadn't known that one day he would love something more than the ocean. He hadn't known that the rush of adrenaline from riding the perfect wave would pale in comparison to the electricity he felt when Adrian touched him, kissed him, looked at him. He hadn't known the sun, his constant companion, could ever be replaced by something warmer, brighter—Adrian's smile, Adrian's laugh, Adrian's arms.

Everything he thought he knew about himself had crumbled. Adrian had changed him. Adrian had shown him something greater, something deeper than freedom, than adrenaline, than the sea itself. Logan was in love. There was no denying it. Just the memory of the night before—the way Adrian had held him, kissed him, whispered words so full of love they shook him to his core—made his whole body feel alive in a way he had never experienced. It made him want to cry from happiness.

But even as those feelings surged through him, he was still *a Vaughn*. He was still his father's son. And no matter how much he wanted to lose himself in Adrian, to make Adrian his sun and his sea, he couldn't escape who he was. He wasn't just Logan. The world wouldn't let him be just Logan.

And so, as he lay there with Adrian still sleeping soundly against him, Logan's tears continued to fall, silent and burning, mourning the love he didn't know how to keep.

And his tears were from agony—agony born from missing something he had only just found, something he now knew he had to leave behind. The weight of it pressed into his chest, unbearable and suffocating. Logan would savor this love, he promised himself, even as it broke him. He would cherish it until the day he died. He would never forget the beautiful man with whiskey eyes that could light up his soul with a single glance. Adrian would live in his memories, as vivid as the sun and the sea.

Logan knew he would always see him, even when he wasn't there. He would see Adrian in the waves, his golden hair flipping in the wind as he surfed, the way he cut through the water with effortless grace. He would hear his voice in every quiet corner of his life, a ghost whispering his name when no one else could. He would look for him, in the ocean, in the horizon, in the fleeting moments of stillness. And when he couldn't find him, when reality crushed the hope of ever seeing him again, Logan would close his eyes and lie on warm sand beneath a cool night sky. There, in the darkness, he would see him. Always.

Slowly, Logan shifted Adrian's sleeping form, carefully moving his warm body from his own. Every touch was a fresh wound, the heat of Adrian's skin against his fingers making him cry harder, his heart cracking further with every inch of distance. He leaned down, his lips trembling as he pressed a kiss to Adrian's forehead, leaving a mark of salty tears on his tanned skin. It was an unspoken promise, a goodbye, a plea for forgiveness Adrian might never hear.

"I love you, too," he whispered, his voice a fragile murmur, as though the words took flight but found no ears to receive them, leaving his heart and words intertwined with silence.

He would remember everything. The way Adrian's chest rose and fell as he breathed, the sound of his laugh like a melody crafted just for Logan. He would remember the way Adrian's hand felt against his skin, the warmth and tenderness in every touch. He would remember the way Adrian said his name, the way it sent shudders through his body and made his heart race. And he would remember the look in Adrian's eyes as he sang and played his guitar, his voice and music carrying emotions words alone couldn't hold. He would remember the feel of sinking into Adrian's body and the euphoric look he got in his eyes as he came. He would remember having a companion by his side, another half.

Logan's soul would remember its other half.

Adrian would always be his first and only love. The love that showed him what it meant to not be alone, to truly be seen. The love that illuminated how hollow he had been before, a shell of a person who had never known he could be filled with so much joy, so much light. Adrian had shown him he was perfect just as he was, without conditions or expectations, and that he could be accepted without having to fight for approval first.

Logan's tears came harder now, silent sobs wracking his body as he stood, knowing he was leaving behind the one thing that had ever made him feel whole. The one person who had shown him he was more than his name, more than his father's shadow. The love that had made him believe, if only for a moment, that he could be just Logan.

Logan slipped out of the bed, moving as slowly and silently as he could, each movement a delicate balance between preservation and pain. Every small shift felt like a betrayal, like tearing himself away from the one place where he was whole. The weight of what he was about to do bore down on him, and it felt as though his heart was being wrenched from his chest, leaving him raw, bleeding, and exposed. He could almost imagine himself lying there on the floor, unable to rise.

He had been given a gift, one he never expected or believed he could have. To love someone and to be loved in return was more than he had ever dared to hope for. And as tragic as it all seemed, Logan knew it wasn't truly a tragedy. It wasn't a tragedy to have felt this, to have been part of something so extraordinary, even if only for a fleeting moment. Because he had Adrian, he had those memories, those pieces of time that would cling to him forever. They would tear him apart, consume him slowly, but he would hold onto them regardless. The pain was a price he was willing to pay, because the idea of letting go, of not thinking of Adrian, was far worse.

As he stepped away from the warmth of the bed, Logan felt the quiet resolve forming within him, though he didn't yet understand its full weight. It wasn't a decision he could name at the moment, but one that would define him forever.

He would leave Adrian behind, but he would never truly let him go.

He would think about him every day, every hour, every moment for the rest of his life.

But he would never tell him how much he loved him.

He would never let himself love another soul, because there was no one else who could fill the hollow space Adrian would leave behind.

He would carry Adrian with him, in the quiet corners of his mind, in the pieces of his shattered soul. He would remember him on the beaches, in the sunlight, in the salt spray of the ocean—those golden days that had given him more life than he'd ever known. But he would never set foot in the water again. The waves, the horizon, the freedom he once loved—they would be too much to bear. They would whisper of Adrian, of what he had lost, and Logan would never survive it.

He would return to his life as everyone expected, slipping back into the role of a Vaughn, the name heavy on his shoulders. He would walk the path laid out for him, play the part everyone demanded. But he wouldn't surrender, not entirely. They could have his body, his presence, his compliance. But his mind, his heart, the fractured pieces of his soul—those would remain untouched. Those would stay here, forever bound to the man he loved.

Logan moved through the room like a thief in the night, collecting the scattered clothes Adrian had peeled off him just hours ago. Each piece felt heavy in his hands, as if they carried the weight of all the moments that had led to this one. He pulled them on quickly, the familiar fabric clinging to his body like a memory he couldn't shake, then slipped his sneakers back on, the laces trembling beneath his fingers.

He walked to the nightstand, each step a battle to keep himself from falling apart. His tears wouldn't stop, carving silent rivers down his cheeks as he picked up his laptop and charger, sliding them into his half-empty bag. He grabbed his phone, his wallet, his body moving on autopilot, though his soul was rooted firmly to the man sleeping just a few feet away.

Slinging the bag over his shoulder, it felt like nothing compared to the crushing agony in his chest.

His hand lingered on the fabric of one of Adrian's shirts—the one Adrian loved most, the one he wore constantly despite its frayed edges. Logan brought it to his face, inhaling deeply, his chest heaving at the scent that was so unmistakably Adrian. It was a blessing and a curse, the smell forever etched into the fibers of the shirt, a cruel reminder of everything he was walking away from. His fingers tightened around the delicate cloth, folding it with care, longing to carry a sliver of Adrian into the solitude of sleepless nights, to have his scent whispering sweet nothings in the dark. Yet, at the final moment, he hesitated; the shirt slipped from his grip, falling softly to the floor. For though it might have offered warmth, that comfort would forever be tainted by the shadows of his aching heart.

His gaze fell on the memory book Adrian had made for his birthday. His hand hovered over it, trembling, as he bit his lip to keep from sobbing aloud. The cry that caught in his throat was raw, threatening to spill over, but he swallowed it back and wiped his face with the back of his hand. Opening the album, he stared at the beautiful images—the photos of him, of them, together, their love captured in every frame. It was too much. He closed it abruptly, his breath hitching, because he knew. If he took it with him, he would come back. He would find his way back to Adrian, and that was a weakness he couldn't afford.

Logan glanced at his wrist, the little lifesaver bracelet catching the early morning light. His fingers brushed over it, the small charm and worn thread feeling like a tether, a lifeline that kept him connected to Adrian even now. He thought about leaving it, about placing it atop the memory book as a quiet goodbye. But he couldn't. He couldn't take it off, couldn't sever that final connection. It was just days ago when Logan vowed to never part with that bracelet, to never take it off. Maybe, deep down, a part of him didn't want to let go entirely. Maybe he needed to carry this small piece of Adrian, a silent marker of the man who had saved him in every possible way. Something that whispered, *you belong to him.*

The pain in Logan's chest was unbearable as he turned back to the bed. Adrian lay there, his brown sun-kissed hair scattered over the pillow, soft strands catching the first rays of light. His tanned skin glowed, the muscles of his back rising and falling with the steady rhythm of his breathing. He looked like a dream, like everything good Logan had ever known wrapped into one perfect person. The sight was too much to bear, and Logan's tears came harder, his vision blurring as he memorized the scene: the first light painting Adrian like a masterpiece, the bed still warm with the remnants of their love.

Together, they were thalassic, carrying in their veins the same ancient tides, the same saltwater that bound them inseparably to each other—the same currents that spoiled and sanctified them in a single rhythm. And when Logan left, it was in vain; for the blood in his body would keep dragging him back toward the ocean of his existence, only now his ocean had a name: Adrian.

So, Logan turned away from the warm bed, and by doing so, he was leaving behind the man whose love for him was so deep it starved him for breath, trembling violently in his wake. He left everything behind—his surfboard, his camera, his wetsuit, most of his clothes. But more than that, he left behind the love of his life. The man of his dreams. The man he hadn't known he needed until it was too late.

Everything that he loved, everything that he cared about remained in that room.

The man who had saved him in every way a person could be saved.

He stood at the door, one hand trembling on the handle, every bone in his body shaking as if it knew the betrayal he was about to commit. Behind him, Adrian slept, the rise and fall of his chest steady, peaceful, unguarded. Logan's mind screamed for his legs to move, but his soul clung stubbornly to the room, to the bed, to the man who was still his anchor. The simplest act—pressing down, pulling open, walking away—felt impossible, as if gravity itself conspired to hold him here.

He lingered, devouring the sight of Adrian's sleeping form, clinging to it as though his gaze alone could etch it into eternity. In the silence, he prayed for interruption, begged for mercy—for Adrian to stir, to wake, to catch him in the betrayal of leaving. To rise and seize him by the wrist, to call him a fool and drag him back from the edge. To banish the storm of panic with words he could almost hear: *It's okay, ahuv sheli. Everything is okay. I love you. Just breathe, just stay, just be with me.*

A sob ripped loose. He pressed his forehead against the door, but his eyes stayed fixed on Adrian. This cabin, this room, this bed—they were the last place on earth where air existed. Beyond these walls stretched only emptiness, a world stripped of breath and light. To leave was to step into a vacuum, to walk willingly into death.

Logan Vaughn was the one who walked out of that room. But Logan remained behind. The real Logan lingered there, scattered like seafoam across the floor of the tiny cabin, fragile and untethered, a fleeting trace of his true self left behind in the place where it was safe to exist.

Logan had also left his heart in that room, shattered and bleeding, every ounce of joy he had ever felt now forever etched into Adrian's existence. Loving Adrian had been the most beautiful thing that had ever happened to him. But love, like love, had cut him deeply. Letting someone in, allowing another soul to reach places within him that he'd kept hidden for so long, had left scars. Scars that ran deep, burning and bleeding with every step Logan took away from the life he'd built with Adrian.

The thought of never seeing Adrian again, never hearing his voice, never gazing into his whiskey-colored eyes—it tore at Logan's chest like claws. Never watching Adrian break through the surface of the ocean, his golden hair glistening like the sun on water. Never feeling his kisses, or hearing the soft whimpers he made when he came. Never running his fingers through Adrian's hair as it spilled in wild, sunlit waves across his face. Never hearing his steady, grounding voice when Logan's thoughts became a jumbled mess. The weight of all he would lose crushed him, but he kept moving.

He ran down the street, his tears blurring the world around him, and flagged the first cab he saw. Sliding into the backseat, Logan told the driver to take him to the closest airport. Then he buried his face in his hands and cried. He cried harder than he ever had, his sobs ragged and filled with a pain he couldn't contain. His cries turned to soft whimpers, and then back to sobs, his grief spilling out like a storm that wouldn't end.

The driver glanced at him in the rearview mirror, concern flickering in his eyes. More than once, he asked Logan if he was all right, if there was anything he could do. But there was nothing anyone could do. Nothing could fix the ache that hollowed out Logan's chest, leaving him raw and empty.

Logan's intentions were good. At least, that's what he told himself. His heart insisted Adrian deserved better—someone who could give him the stability, the future, the love that Logan wasn't capable of providing. Adrian had already given Logan everything, and it was too much. Love was too much.

It wasn't malice or selfishness that drove Logan away; it was fear. Fear that he would ruin what they had. Fear that he would hurt Adrian by staying, by dragging him into the wreckage that Logan felt he was. So, he left. Not to escape love, but to protect Adrian from it.

The cab came to a stop, and Logan paid the driver, his hands trembling as he handed over the cash. He walked into the airport in a daze, the bright lights and bustling crowds a blur. At the ticket counter, he bought the first flight out, barely registering the clerk's words or the destination printed on his ticket. The noise of the terminal washed over him, muted and distant, drowned out by the voice in his head.

It was his heart, calling him a fool, yearning for him to turn around, to go back to where air still existed. It echoed the sound of his soul shuddering, a haunting melody. Thus began a numbing sensation, creeping in slowly, battling with an intense desire to feel, to embrace the light once more.

And then—*then*—Logan Vaughn sat at the busy airport.

THE END...FOR NOW!

Thank you for reading!
Logan and Adrian's story is not finished yet, not even close!
Want to know what happens when Logan comes back?

The next book in the duet is already out and continues right where this one left off—you're warmly invited to dive in!

If you enjoyed this story, please consider leaving a review or rating on any platform you prefer. It truly helps new authors like me find more readers.

Curious about what's next? Come say hi on Instagram, I'd love to connect:

AUTHORDRMICHALGUTER

About the Author

Dr. Michal Guter is a criminologist, victimologist, academic, and author with a deep passion for exploring masculinity, trauma, male sexual assault victimization and rape and resilience. She is also a dedicated teacher and researcher, often found at her computer working on either a book or an academic article, it really depends on the day. Addicted to coffee and in love with words, Michal has published in peer-reviewed journals and finds joy in reading dictionaries and grammar books just for fun, and occasionally turns to graphic design as another form of storytelling. But most of all, she loves to read stories, and you'll rarely find her without a novel or audiobook close at hand.

www.ingramcontent.com/pod-product-compliance
Lightning Source LLC
Chambersburg PA
CBHW030838030726
47495CB00005B/1270